In the Den of Wolves

Eden James

Copyright © 2023 Robert James Eden Young

All rights reserved.

The characters and events portrayed in this book are fictitious. Any similarity to real persons, living or dead, is coincidental and not intended by the author.

ISBN-13 979-8-3857-3515-0

No part of this book may be reproduced, or stored in a retrieval system, or transmitted in any form or by any means, electronic, mechanical, photocopying, recording, or otherwise, without express written permission of the publisher.

Cover design by: Eden James and Midjourney AI

www.edenjames.net

For my parents, who taught me everything I know, and plenty more I should have remembered.

PROLOGUE
GERMANY 1945

The end. Berlin was a city under siege.

The dust from masonry, smoke of shells and taste of defeat stung the senses of her beleaguered defenders. Reds were closing in on the Reichstag. Ammunition was rapidly running out. Radio communications had been severed. The end was being written in bullet holes across the walls. Etched into the faces of the dead, the dying and the defeated.

Below ground, a heavy steel door was pushed silently open on well-oiled hinges. Light from inside the secret bunker illuminated a concrete tunnel threshold. Buffers and rail tracks beyond. A single pair of rails disappeared into the darkness and footsteps entered the tunnel. The door closed and the sounds of war, muffled and distant, rumbled overhead. Heavy machineguns rattled. Grumbling tanks grinding the cobbles above. A dull whump of an explosion. The air was warm, a little musty, unused to being disturbed.

Taking out his little Pertrix torch, the light from the small bulb was just sufficient to illuminate his path. Moving beyond the buffers, his footsteps began slowly. One in front of the other. Carefully placed. Following the direction of the horizontal luminescent lines carefully painted on the wall. Gradually, with growing confidence, the pace increased.

A moment later, the same steel door opened a second time. Wider. Two men appeared in the aperture. The light from the interior silhouetted their features. Both were in uniform. One with a machinegun slung over his shoulder. Another shining a torch down into the tunnel. At the extremity of the searching beam, the footsteps ahead became quicker, breaking into a jog. A run. Panic.

The slide on the weapon was pulled back with a menacing, metallic clatter. Then the sound of gunfire rattled down the tunnel with terrible savagery, reverberating off the concrete walls. Distant footsteps fell silent. A body fell to the ground like a sack of potatoes. Glass smashed and the torchlight was extinguished. There was a pause. A distant rumble. Then came fire, casting an orange glow in the distance. A rush of air from the explosion barrelled down with increasing intensity as rolling flames hissed and foamed behind it. Water, pouring down from the world above, carried huge chunks of earth and concrete. Hurtling straight towards the heavy steel door.

With a curse the two soldiers from the bunker quickly returned inside, swung the door closed behind them and secured the locks. There was an ominous thud as the water and masonry crashed against it. The frame buckled but remained in place. Just. The two officers looked at one another with a deep sense of dread. At their feet, murky water began to seep slowly over the lower bulkhead, swirling around their boots in silty eddies. The tunnel beyond was filling up and pressure was building. The door groaned in response. It would not be long before the portal succumbed, and their world was flooded. The corridor had to be barricaded and sealed up completely. There was no escaping the Führerbunker by underground train. Not anymore.

CHAPTER ONE
SCOTLAND 2017

"Kids!" Emma called out. "Kids! Come and try oot yer uncle Craig's new sawsedges."

Two wee bairns came scampering across the sands. Wellington boots and padded coats. A pair of Rough Collies in tow, bounding after them. All fur and flapping tongues.

Late August was the best time to have a barbecue on the mottled black sands of Talisker Bay. Midges were low, kept away by the smoke from a driftwood fire. Autumn's bitter chill had not yet bloomed into full foreboding magnificence, and the spray of the sea tinged each chargrilled morsel with the tang of kelp and salted smoke. Ancient stumps and old branches, worn smooth and bleached by their oceanic journey, blackening now as flames consumed them. Spitting with a shower of sparks and crackling comfort. Embers glowed bright orange and yellow with each fresh breeze coming in off the Minch.

The adults were gathered around on rough, woollen blankets, wrapped up in fleeces and scarves. With the sun sinking lower towards the sea, the soft summer warmth was fading fast, and layers were added.

"Heya, Flora." Her Mum greeted, embracing the fiery haired young girl in her arms. "Try these, their well gusty." She picked up a sausage, cooling on her plate, and tore a piece off.

"Jasper! Lie doon." Craig called to the excitable collies as they nudged nearer the food and the fire. The older dog obeyed immediately. His cousin followed a little more stiffly. Arthritis slowing him down.

Emma offered a piece of sausage to the young lad standing behind his huddled sister.

"Whit d'yer thunk?" she asked, popping the remainder in her own mouth.

"It tastes funny." Flora said, screwing up her freckled nose.

"It's like Daddy's drink." The boy replied.

"And whit d'yers know aboot that?" Emma asked, looking across at her husband with mock indignation.

Iain Sutherland grinned and refilled his enamel mug with a measure of whisky. "The wee laddie's got to try the odd tipple now and again. Isn't that right, Finn?" he winked.

"Whisky and wild boar is naw a hit wi the wee bairns, then." Craig chuckled, lowering his eyes to meet Flora's shy gaze. "But yer'll be wantin' some more of the ice cream though."

She nodded her head.

"Please. Please." Finn added, jumping on the spot with hand raised.

"Awright, Finn. Simmer doon." Emma chided gently.

"I think it's good." Iain remarked. "Could be another offering in the distillery shop."

Emma nodded her agreement as she picked up a second sausage and took a generous bite.

"Aye, it's a way of increasing the product line." Craig mused as he took out the ice cream from the cool bag. "Sausages made by the sea."

There was a contented silence as Craig scooped out his homemade ice cream, a variation of rum and raisin. Waves crashed against the sea stack to the south. Running back over the skerries of volcanic basalt in white foaming eddies. The waterfall to the north, much diminished in the summer, barely made the cascade to the base of the cliffs, driven by the wind in a fine spray across the beach, scenting the air with salted peat.

Iain waited until the ice cream had been served and the container returned to the cool bag before passing the catalogue across to his brother.

"So, what do you think?" he asked, indicating the marked page.

Craig picked up the auction catalogue and thumbed through it. "For the collection?"

"Aye." Iain nodded. "Might take yer mind off the Macallans."

Craig perused the details. In the glimmer of the firelight, Iain could see his brother was interested. He topped up his measure of whisky and offered some to Emma. She shook her head but watched him pour in a wee dram anyway. She smiled and adjusted her beanie.

"Aye, it could be worth a punt." Craig nodded. "A rare Glenfiddich is always a good investment."

"Good." Iain smiled. "I've got us some tickets." He looked to Emma. "Em's okay with us going away for the weekend."

"A boy's wee holiday." She smiled.

"Can I go?" Finn chimed in, prodding his chest. "I'm a boy."

"Aye, when you're a wee bit older." Iain replied. He held up his mug, an invitation to the others.

"Slàinte Mhath." He toasted.

"Slàinte Mhath." Craig and Emma replied, clinking their mugs together.

"Slan jumma." Flora chorused, holding up her spoon.

CHAPTER TWO
ENGLAND 2017

"Never start a book with a car journey or a description of the weather." He said in reply to her question. "That's what a publisher once told me. They've heard it all before. Moody skies, monotony of traffic, a personal epiphany while getting soaked to the skin, et cetera, et cetera."

She smiled as she regarded her boss with interest from the other side of the reading table. He had an engaging manner, a soft Scottish accent, and an impressive depth of knowledge he readily bestowed. They were sat in a side room of the Motoring Archives of the National Motor Museum in Beaulieu, each working on separate research projects.

"And yet if you ask me, to drive through Glencoe on a brooding October day is about as evocative a moment as anyone can ever experience." He continued. "If you enjoy driving and have the perfect vehicle for it, there are roads up in the Highlands that will bring a tear to a grown man's eye." He paused. Reflectively. "Every car has a story. Without exception. Most of them are mundane. They get the shopping in from Tesco. Pick up the bairns from school. Take Nanna to the Post Office to collect her pension. Others might have a wee special memory or two. The first kiss. First shag. First scraped knuckles. Sometimes happening all at the same time." He smiled.

Charlie giggled. A warmth blooming behind her cheeks.

"There are some particularly rare cars though which have something a wee bit special. Stories of courage and intrigue. Of bravery and resilience. Stories of survival against the odds. These are the stories worth documenting. The ones that need preserving. You see, in the fibre of each seat, the turn of every nut and bolt, between the records of oil changes and tyres are the stories of people. And in the story of those people, is where the mystique of the car can be found."

He drained his mug of tea and packed away the papers in the box file.

"The skill is in trying to draw those stories out to the enjoyment of the average lay reader. Weaving together technical details, historical provenance, and personal narratives into a richly detailed literary tapestry. Using the kind of poetical prose that carries them on an enchanting and wondrous journey which educates, informs and entertains in equal measure. They should be left feeling fulfilled, informed and astonished. A difficult feat for subject matter which, for most people, consists of little more than scrap metal."

He smiled and pushed the bifocals back up the bridge of his nose.

"Do you have all your outfits ready for the weekend?"

"I do." Charlie replied with excitement.

"But…?" he enquired, returning the box file to the shelving unit.

"How do you know there's a 'but'?"

"It's in your voice, lass."

Charlie looked down for a moment, considering how to reply. "I sometimes feel a little self-conscious at these places. Goodwood, the Salon Privé, Hampton Court."

Graham Robertson turned back from the shelves and looked at her with an expression of fatherly warmth and encouragement.

"I remember hearing a very wise man say once: "Never let the colour of your skin stop you from pursuing your passions.""

Charlie looked at him with a puzzled expression.

"Well, obviously he didn't say them to me, but he was right. Those words are as true today as they were back then." He stepped closer, lowering his voice. "That's the wonderful thing about the Revival, Charlie. Nobody gives a monkeys about such things. Everyone is there to soak up the spectacle. The cars, the fashions, the atmosphere. If a pretty lass like yourself wants to dress up as a Land Girl or a Wren or… the Lady of the Manor, it matters not a jot. Everyone is simply there to enjoy themselves, drawn by a powerful and collective love of the automobile. That invitation extends to you too."

"Thank you." she smiled sweetly. "I needed to hear that."

"There's no racism at the Revival. You fit right in. Don't you worry." He collected up the mugs and moved into the kitchenette to wash them up. "Now." He called out. "What are you going in?"

"I thought I would take the Aston." She called back, collating her own research materials together.

"An excellent choice, as always." He smiled, ambling back into the reference library.

"And what will you be going in?"

"Need you ask?" he laughed, holding up his keys. Hanging prominently from the ring was a black leather torpedo fob with an enamelled tortoise. Gordon Keeble.

"What's that?" Charlie took the metal keyring behind the fob in her fingers. It was a rectangular shape with three interlocking rings etched onto its polished surface. "That's not a car badge I recognise. Looks almost religious."

"Mother, daughter and the holy nymph." Robertson chuckled. "It's just a wee project a couple of friends and myself set up years ago. Nothing came of it though."

"What was the project?"

"To find three of the rarest cars in the world. That's what the three rings represented. Nothing mystical or spiritual, I'm afraid. I'm not that deep a thinker."

"I wouldn't say that."

Robertson looked at the keyring and smiled. Reminiscing.

"What were the cars?"

"Ah. Now that's a secret." He winked. "But if you ever find yourself in Italy, ask for Don Pietro Borromeo."

"Why him?"

"It's his family's coat of arms. We nicked it for the keyring." He chuckled. "And he's something of a car connoisseur himself. Does excellent research for Ferrari Classiche."

"He knows what cars you were looking for?"

"He should do. We posted all our research materials over to him when we found out what we could. The trail for all of them is long cooled down now, but he has his own archive, and our work was of more value to him there than they are to us here."

Robertson moved round the table to look at what Charlie was working on.

"Ah, the Blue Streak Riley Special." He mouthed fondly. "Probably one of the most powerful pre-war Riley's ever built."

"Completed shortly before the factory was absorbed by the Nuffield Organisation." She added.

Robertson smiled. Charlie was learning fast. "Don't work too late. It's a big weekend ahead."

"Seems awfully naughty leaving work on a Wednesday."

"Ah, it's allowed for Revival weekend. Are you still okay to meet up on Friday?"

"Of course. Where are we meeting again?"

"The BMW Bar in the motorcycle paddock. Do you know the place?"

"Not far from the Earl's Court exhibition?"

"Aye, not far." He nodded, moving to the coat stand. "Sometime mid-morning. Gives us time for breakfast and a wee peek at the paddocks first."

"Okay."

IN THE DEN OF WOLVES

"See you at Goodwood." He said with a broad grin.

CHAPTER THREE
USA, 1930

Mother, daughter and holy nymph.

A Duesenberg Model SSJ Coupe: *Marie*. The holy nymph. Appearing briefly. Then like a diaphanous wraith in a windswept mist, she disappeared completely. Her appearance so transitory people would later question whether her presence had been physical, or a mere apparition. She had belonged to perhaps one of the greatest motor racing drivers of her age.

The oval speedways of Woodbridge and Langhorne were the Charybdis and Scylla of American auto racing. While the one-mile dirt track near the borough of Langhorne in Pennsylvania had such memorable monikers as 'Puke Hollow' and 'The Track That Ate the Heroes', the wooden speed bowl of Woodbridge was arguably even more lethal. Fragile wooden boards often trapped the spindly Rudge-Whitworth wire wheels. Chunks of wood became airborne. Some parts even caught fire from overheating machines. Deaths were frequent. It was the most dangerous form of an already incredibly dangerous sport.

Beneath her ivory bodywork, a new supercharged Duesenberg Model A Straight-8 engine made a terrific noise as the formidable Miller 91 race car hurtled around the circuit. Where aviation had its Elinor Smith, and powerboating had its Jo Carstairs, into the gladiatorial arena of professional automobile racing rolled Mariette Hélène Delangle. Abandoning a successful stage career for the risky and unpredictable life of a racing driver, the thirty-year old French woman, still known by her stage name Hellé Nice, was enthralling the American crowds with her amazing driving feats.

It was incredible to see such a powerful machine tamed by the delicate arms of the dance hall darling. Driving as no man ever did, without a helmet so the crowd could see her flowing locks of hair. That morning Hellé had been picked up from the Savoy Plaza on New York's Fifth Avenue. Dressed for action with beret pulled low over her cornflour blue eyes. Almost four hours later, her face was seen on promotional flags, leaflets and programmes as she paraded with a cavalcade of motorcyclists around the circuit in the car she would be racing later that day.

Her courage and natural flair were never more in greater evidence than during her American tour. Though women were not permitted to compete alongside the men, she was able to achieve similar times and frightening speeds on exhibition laps after the main events. Revelling in being the centre of attention, Hellé hoped the added publicity might just lure the attention of Ettore Bugatti again, prepared to fund her return to the Continental circuits. On returning to France, she described those experiences on the board ovals and dirt tracks as some of the most frightening of her life. Perhaps they had been good preparation for what was about to unravel in Europe a decade later.

Starting out with a Citroën, with which she had toured France, it was a Duesenberg Model J that caught her eye whilst on tour. The model was intended to compete with Rolls-Royce and Hispano-Suiza, the most luxurious and powerful cars in the world. She had upgraded to the latter already, but there was something about the stately, pronounced lines of the Model J. The timing of its launch however could not have been more unfortunate. With the stock market crash the following year, the Great Depression had begun to ravage through America.

The supercharged short-wheelbase SSJ model particularly appealed to her. Though whether she could afford the hefty $5,000 price tag was another matter. A healthy $25,000 of prize money at each of the American events ensured that despite the incredible danger, there were always a ready stream of entrants prepared to dance with the devil. As an exhibition driver however, Hellé's salaried role brought in a mere $200 before deductions.

She promised herself one day though, when she made it big with Bugatti, she would pick up one of those sleek, lightweight roadsters. Meanwhile, it was back to another racing track to impress the crowds and bank the money. Hermann Schurch's modified Miller spat flames from the exhausts as she started it up. With make-up applied and a smile on her face, she posed in the driver's seat along with her sponsors, promoters, and fellow drivers, before embarking on another duel with death.

This time though there was a tinge of sadness behind the smile. A sombreness taking some of the sparkle from the eyes. Pinned to the dashboard was a photograph of 'Wild' Bill Albertson, one of her mentors and amongst the most experienced dirt track racers in the States. A message scrawled on the front read: 'To my racing pal Hellé Nice'. He had inscribed it for her just an hour before he was killed at the Middletown Speedway she was now about to drive. In the high stakes game of auto racing, the difference between life and death was balanced with frightening delicacy.

CHAPTER FOUR
ENGLAND, 2017

Back for another year, the Goodwood Revival had returned to West Sussex in all its Tweed glory. The Kinrara Trophy was guaranteed to assemble a spectacular collection of 1950s Ferraris to battle against lightweight Jaguars and tuned Aston Martins. The Barry Sheene Memorial Trophy would bring a whole host of BMW and Norton Manx motorcycles to the grid and the Settrington Cup promised to be an exciting children's race in Austin J40 pedal cars. The annual three-day festival had been recreating the glamour of motor racing at the historic circuit since 1998 and was the only race meeting of its kind to be staged entirely in period dress.

Returning to the circuit's halcyon days between 1948 and 1966, the layout and facilities were remarkably unchanged. Despite the incredible value of some of the classic cars that competed over the course of the weekend, the racing was always hard fought and intense at every level. Formula One drivers, Touring Car champions and Le Mans legends all queued up for the chance of racing some of the most exquisite machinery ever assembled in one place. Alongside the action on track, displays of vintage aircraft, period shopping and old-fashioned funfairs ensured that the whole family were entertained, regardless of motoring enthusiasm.

It was a curious paradox though that much of the off track entertainment and many of the guests that attended each year chose to dress in World War Two costume. Motor racing was suspended for the duration of the war and the circuit itself only came into existence afterwards. When the Air Ministry relinquished use of RAF Westhampnett back to the Duke of Richmond and Gordon, he decided to use the old perimeter road as a motor racing circuit.

At a stroke another chapter of the already illustrious Goodwood estate was begun.

The innocent retrospective played out at the Revival each year was a rose-tinted trip back to a time of community, old-fashioned honest values and joie de vivre. Recreating the glory days of the circuit's post-war prime on the circuit, off-track the country was nominally at war, yet nobody died. It was a time warp to a period of history that never really existed but would have been glorious if it had.

Being woken up by the dawn chorus of Spitfires and Mustangs, wheeling away in the Sussex sky was always a magical experience. Gentlemen in slacks and braces lathered up badger hair brushes of shaving soap over a bowl outside camper vans and bell tents. Ladies perfected victory rolls and drew black lines down the back of their legs to substitute for stockings. The curious nostalgia of depravation. Kettles whistled, sausages sizzled, and Jerry Lee Lewis tinkled ivories over breakfast. The unmistakeable roar of Merlin engines would inevitably give way to a plethora of sounds from more earthbound wonders. Straight-8s and inline-fours. V12s and boxers. Four strokes and two.

Captain Deakin was on leave from The Regiment and attending with his dad as they did every year. His father, Reginald, owned a classic car dealership in the South Downs and always liked to dress suitably for the occasion. He emerged with a plate of bacon, sausages and scrambled eggs from the Bertram Hutchings four-berth Winchester caravan he had been restoring for the last decade. His father's pocket watch suspended from a double albert chain was already secured to the tweed waistcoat of his outfit. Even in civvies, he still carried the bearing of the cavalry officer he had once been.

Deakin was going for the classic fighter pilot look on Friday, complete with sheepskin flying jacket, roll neck jumper and Mae West life preserver. It was a different kind of uniform than the one he was used to wearing and the ladies seemed to adore it. A poignant addition to the ensemble was his grandfather's own service dress cap. The red thread on the Tudor crown was a little faded. Its gold wire laurels a little tarnished with age and wear, though that only added authenticity to the overall look. Hainsworth had supplied the RAF's distinctive blue-grey wool from spare stock they had in the warehouse. A very uncivil war had prevented the original order being shipped out to Russia for Tsar Nikolai's Cossack uniforms. It had become an iconic colour ever since.

Sitting outside on folding canvas chairs, father and son watched the aerial displays as they ate breakfast and discussed their plans for the day. Warm ups around the circuit would begin presently. There was a parade of over 130 Fiat 500s scheduled to commemorate the model's 60th anniversary. The beauties competing in the Kinrara Trophy would kick off the racing programme in the evening, battling on into the night. There was no finer manner to spend a September weekend in all England. No better way to see out the motorsport season in speed and style.

"So, what do you make of the note?" Deakin asked.

"I have absolutely no idea." Reginald admitted, taking a sip of tea from a tin mug. "Curious little find though, eh? I'm hoping a friend of mine from Beaulieu might be able to take a look."

"Will he be here?"

"Like us, he comes every year."

"How are we going to find him?" Deakin chuckled looking around. Already the cars were backing up down the lanes. Day visitors queuing for parking.

"I've arranged for him to meet us at the motorcycle paddocks." Reginald explained. "Perhaps grab a Weissbier and Wurst from that BMW place again."

"Sounds like an excellent idea." Deakin smiled. "As long as we stay off the pretzels this time, otherwise we'll only need another beer."

"And what, pray, is wrong with that?" Reginald laughed, toying with the ends of his moustache.

Deakin rolled his eyes and joined the mirth. He treasured these rare moments with his dad. Sharing a mutual passion for vintage racing. And beer. Reginald reliving the moments that he had witnessed first-hand as a boy. Deakin seeing them re-enacted through fresh eyes in a romanticised fantasy world of glitz, glamour and gasoline. It was heaven on earth.

The venerable old Alvis that Reginald had brought across to tow the caravan was a wonderfully unusual Speed 25 Sports Saloon with exquisite maroon coachwork by Charlesworth Bodies of Coventry. Acquired from a Scottish estate, the really unique thing about it was the engine. Derived from George Thomas Smith-Clarke's 4.3-litre naturally aspirated in-line six-cylinder, the smaller 3½-litre unit had been fitted with a Marshall supercharger sometime in the 1960s.

Ordinarily Reginald would have walked away immediately at such a monstrous modification. It certainly lacked the originality he prided himself on, but the quality of the welding to the manifold was such that he had to give it a test drive at least. Even if it was just to say he had driven a supercharged Alvis that wasn't a Works Special. Immediately, he fell in love with the smooth and spirited performance of the car and decided then and there that he simply couldn't be without it.

The original all-silent, all-synchromesh four-speed transmission worked sweetly, all-round disc brakes, though an equally unusual later addition, were a marked improvement to the original drums and streamlined wings, imposing front headlights and spacious luggage locker epitomised the standard form of the English motorcar of the 1930s. Whoever had performed the modifications had been an expert at their craft. Improving on the original vehicle without losing any of its charm and tractability.

While wanting to keep the beige leather interior as original as possible, a sympathetic restoration had revealed a handwritten note, inscribed on a page torn from a notepad. The note had been placed in the lower pocket of the driver's door and apparently forgotten about ever since. It meant absolutely nothing to Reginald Deakin, but there were few things that escaped Graham Robertson.

"Do you have the wee note?" Robertson asked, quaffing another Paulaner as they met at the agreed rendezvous.

Now in his seventieth year, Graham Angus Robertson was a senior researcher at the Motoring Archives of the National Motor Museum in Beaulieu. He had originally grown up in Fort William and was a proud Scot with an impressive breadth and depth of knowledge of all things automotive.

"Here." Reginald began, slipping an envelope out of his jacket. "I kept it inside to protect it."

"Is it delicate?"

"It's old."

Robertson took the envelope and carefully lifted the flap. Inside was the notepaper, folded up as it had been for over fifty years.

"It's in reasonable condition. Must have been a good quality notebook." He slipped the paper out and began to unfold it carefully as a young woman approached.

"Is this the mysterious note?" she asked.

Deakin regretted taking a generous bite out of a German sausage at that precise moment. Mustard running down his hand as the woman stood beside him and smiled sweetly.

"Ah, Charlie. Come and see." Robertson beckoned her up to the high table they were perched around. "Reggie, this is my assistant, Charlotte Campbell."

"Pleased to meet you." he smiled, offering his hand. "My son, Christopher." He introduced, suspecting his son might wish to further the introduction.

Hastily wiping his own hand on a paper napkin, he reached across and grasped Charlie's, endeavouring to swallow the sausage quickly without choking himself.

"Sorry. Hello." He stammered.

"Charlie is rapidly becoming my young protégé." Robertson explained. "She is helping me maintain our collections. Her infectious enthusiasm reminds me every day why I got into this." He smiled, eyes misting over.

"You like cars too?" Deakin asked, rather redundantly.

"Honestly, being surrounded by cars just makes my day." She purred. Her voice was warm, intimate, a little husky. She was well spoken. Very proper, with a smile that lit up the paddock. "This is the absolute highlight of my year." She beamed, looking around at the old motorcycles, the fashions, the hairstyles and the BMW 502 selling Bavarian beer from the boot.

"I'm impressed." He nodded appreciatively. "It's unusual…" He inwardly winced as soon as he had said it.

"Because I'm a girl, or because I'm black?" she smiled, twirling a lock of her hair around her finger.

Deakin's tanned face went very pale, then bright red. What a faux pas. How could he have been so foolish? "No, I didn't…"

"Looks like you're more coloured than I am." She laughed. "Don't worry. I'm just playing with you." she squeezed his arm playfully. Her touch was like a jolt of electricity. "You are perfectly correct though. Not many girls I know understand my peculiar fascination with cars. Especially the old classics." She looked across the table. "So, what do we have here?"

"An old note I found in my Alvis." Reginald explained, looking at his son sharply. "Complete mystery to me, but I thought if it has anything at all to do with cars, our Gray's the man."

"Hmm intriguing."

Resuming his examination, Robertson finished unfolding it and looked down. Almost at once there was a look of realisation and a frown wrinkled his brow.

"What is it?" Charlie asked, peering over the paper.

Robertson handed her the notepaper and looked up at Reginald with a serious expression on his face. "Reggie, where did you say you found it?"

"In the driver's door pocket."

"In your Alvis?"

"That's right, inside the flap pocket at the bottom, you know?"

"What model?"

"It's a Speed 25 Sports Saloon." He smiled proudly. "We used it to tow the caravan here." He watched as Robertson's expression changed, as if he was haunted by something. "It's actually parked up outside the War Rooms. Are you alright, old chap?"

"Can I see it?" he asked, fumbling to place the note back inside the envelope.

"Of course. We'll head there now. Why the interest? Does this note have anything to do with my car?"

"Not just the car. I'd be grateful if I could see it, I really would."

"Say no more, old chap. We'll head there directly."

Reginald gathered up the rubbish and pushed it across to his son while he took Robertson's arm and walked his friend out. A sly tactic to delay his son long enough to keep step with Charlie and try to make amends for his errant introduction. He was a wily old fox.

"I'm sorry. I didn't mean anything in what I said." Deakin began, offering an arm, then deciding better of it and keeping it firmly by his side awkwardly. He was quietly delighted that she had waited for him but wasn't at all sure quite how to proceed. "It's just so refreshing to find a woman that actually appreciates this kind of thing. I know more than the usual amount do around an event like the Revival, but still."

"Don't worry. I completely understand." She smiled, taking his arm. "And you're right, it is unusual. For me though, that makes it feel even more special."

"Well, I'd like to make it up to you anyway."

"There's no need, honestly." She laughed, hiding her dazzling smile behind her hand.

"How about a dance after lunch." He gestured to the Richmond Lawn marquee, trying not to come across too forward. "There's a war on, you know, and it might be my last chance." He touched the collar of his flight jacket, trying to style it out by playing the role of wartime fighter pilot.

"Oh, you're a sweetheart aren't you? Does that line usually work, flyboy?"

"I have no idea. I've never used it before."

"I see." she giggled. "Well, in that case, I'll let you know."

"So, how often do you come here?"

"Is that your next best line?"

"No, no. Not at all. Serious question. My Dad has been coming here since the start. I've tried to join as often as I can, depending on my deployment."

"Are you really in the Air Force?"

"Army. Not as glamorous, but we get the work done."

"I only started coming here when I moved down for university, about ten years ago. Never missed a meet since."

"What did you study?"

"You'll laugh."

"I'm sure I won't."

"I studied Mechanical Engineering at Sussex Uni."

"You're something of a unicorn then. Beautiful, intelligent, a lover of classic cars."

"Are you suggesting beautiful women can't be intelligent?"

"No. Not at all. It's just so unusual to find someone so passionate about such things."

"I'll let you off."

Deakin smiled. This was not going at all well. He had been out of the game too long. Ever since the divorce, which had been acrimonious to say the least, he had always been a little shaky around female company. A ridiculous situation for an officer in the Special Air Service. He felt thoroughly ashamed. As they walked down the avenue, Charlie's eyes were drawn to the Ferrari paddocks. A stable of prancing horses preparing to stretch their limbs.

"Do you have a favourite?" he asked.

"That is such an unfair question." She replied with mock indignation. "The 330GTC is incredibly under-appreciated and the gorgeous lines of the 500 Superfast are my absolute favourite, but when it comes to racing Ferraris, I lean towards the 250 Berlinettas."

"Not the GTO?"

She pressed her lips together, shaking her head. "Personally, I think the GTO is hugely overrated. You pay a massive premium for those three little letters."

"That's a controversial view." He teased gently.

"Don't get me wrong, the GTO is a stunning car, but for me the Short

Wheelbase Berlinettas have more of an emotional connection." She pointed to the rear of an all-alloy bodied Competizione, gleaming in the silver and yellow colours of the old Ecurie-Francorchamps team. "They were road cars, but also race cars too. Very good at both things and particularly good looking. The thought of driving to the venue, racing it up the hill or around a circuit at the weekend, then driving it back home again ready for the commute to the office on Monday. There's something romantic about that. You couldn't really do that in the GTO so much. They're rarer, but the SWB has something a little bit extra."

"Yeah, I can see that."

"What about you?"

"Call me predictable, but I've always been partial to an Aston Martin?"

"Oh really?" she returned. A sparkle in her eyes. "Anyone in particular?"

"Ah, for me it's the Oscar India V8 Vantage. Like the one Timothy Dalton drove in Living Daylights."

"Good choice." She nodded appreciatively.

He relaxed, pleased his preference was agreeable to her. "Did Gray seem a little concerned about the note dad found?"

"I thought it was more about the car it was found in."

"Maybe. We'll find out."

The War Rooms and Officers Club were set dressed, wood-panelled dining pavilions overlooking the start/finish line with views down to Madgwick Corner. A small collection of World War II era vehicles had been allowed to park up outside to set the scene. Amongst the Standard Flying Fourteen in drab RAF livery and an SS Jaguar 3½-litre, proudly bearing its infield pass was Reginald Deakin's stunning example of a 1937 Alvis Speed 25 Sports Saloon. Graham Robertson stopped in his tracks when he saw it, almost as if he had seen an old and much loved friend.

"This is it!" he exclaimed. "This is the car."

"What car?"

Robertson walked up to the Alvis and placed a hand lovingly on the top of the front fender.

"This is a very special car." He turned, smiling at the bemused threesome. With a gesture he beckoned them closer. "BSC 475. I'll never forget it." He continued, reciting the licence plate without even looking at it. "This car belonged to a policeman I used to know."

"What did you do?" Deakin joked.

"Well, he wasn't just any policeman." Robertson smiled. "This very car belonged to Detective Chief Superintendent James Alexander Cameron. He was the Tenth Lord Dalwhinnie and a very interesting character indeed."

"Was it repainted?" Reginald asked. "I would have thought a police car would have been painted black."

"This is the original colour. Peony Red. The car was bought as new by his dad, Alexander. Now, back in his time old Alexander Cameron had been a very impressive advocate. In later years, supposedly slowing down, he had at various times been the local sheriff, the Procurator Fiscal, even the Chief Super himself. There was such a shortage of vehicles back then, personal cars were often pressed into police service. There were no light bars and not much in the way of a siren to think about equipping them with. And if you consider how rare cars were in Britain in the 1950s, imagine how much rarer in rural Scotland, and with more territory to cover. Anyway, his son, James inherited the car when Alexander passed, along with the title and the family estate."

"Glenmore House?" Reginald posed.

"Aye, that's it."

"That's the estate I acquired it from. They said it only had two owners from new. I couldn't believe it."

"Aye, believe it. It's true. Father and son. Though I'm surprised no one had ever used it in between."

"So, who added the supercharger?"

"Ah!" Robertson smiled broadly, throwing his head back. "That was all Mr Cameron. The son, James. You see, before the war, he had actually been an engineer. Worked for Bentley. Even went to Le Mans and helped them win it. Of course, he was taken on by Rolls-Royce after the buyout and that's what sent him over to India. To work on the Raj's Rolls. Not sure how he ended up in the police when he came back, but there we are."

"What's the significance of this particular car?"

"When he came back home, late fifties as I recall, Mr Cameron wanted to give her a bit more poke, you see. He wasn't one for new cars and I don't think he rated the force's Wolseley all that much. Anyway, he asked my dad to work on it for him."

"Your Dad?"

"Oh aye. He used to run McRae & Dick's at the top of the Pier Head Brae in Fort William. Automobile engineers they were. Not fitters like they are today. They had another place up in Inverness too, but back then we were in old St Mary's Kirk. Dad got the parts, and together they welded the supercharger direct to the manifold." He looked up at Reginald, a faraway look in his eye. "Do you think you could lift up the wee bonnet?"

At once Reginald and Deakin reached down to the handles at the bottom of the louvred butterfly bonnet and lifted the left half of it up to reveal the engine. The supercharger had been welded directly onto where the induction system would have been. An original copper hammer was still strapped against the bulkhead for the knock-off wheel hubs and six spare spark plugs were screwed into a plate for easy replacement. Meticulously polished, the engine bay was in pristine concourse condition.

"There it is." Robertson gasped. "The finest piece of welding I've ever seen."

"Your father did this?" Charlie asked, moving round to take a look.

"Och no. This was all Mr Cameron's handiwork. He was a magician. My dad was amazed. You see, they'd grown up together as wee bairns, but he only ever got to know him properly as a policeman when he came home." He patted the spare wheel cover lovingly. "This was the first car I ever worked on too."

"You worked on this?"

"Oh aye, under Mr Cameron's watchful care mind you. I would only have been about twelve or thirteen. Used to fill it up whenever it came in. Shell. His dad asked for Pratt's, but the octane was all wrong and she ran rough for years. Mr Cameron sorted all that out. Are the brakes okay?"

"Sweet as a nut."

"That's a relief. My dad helped me to swap the drums over for discs. I'm just so pleased to see it. I never thought I would after so many years." Robertson smiled. A tear or two welling up in his eyes. "Do you know, I'm a wee bit emotional."

"Aww." Charlie stepped forward and gave him a hug.

"That makes this all the more interesting." He said, the emotion still evident in his voice. Slipping the paper out, he unfolded it and smoothed it carefully over the fender. "This note is for an old licence plate number. Probably torn out of Mr Cameron's police notebook."

Reginald looked puzzled. "A possible suspect, perhaps?"

"Och no. Something much more remarkable than that. 'IA-1317'." Robertson read it out loud. "Now you could be forgiven for thinking this is an old Northern Irish plate. IA was once the area code for County Antrim until 1958. They issued plates out of Ballymena." He tapped the paper. "This. This is from something even more spectacular. You see, IA was also the code issued by the State Police District for Berlin between 1906 and 1945." He held up the paper. "Which means this number plate once belonged to a car registered to the German police."

"That's interesting." Deakin remarked.

Robertson indicated that they should all sit down as he prepared to expand.

"That's not the half of it, laddie. I happen to know exactly what vehicle this licence plate came from."

CHAPTER FIVE
ENGLAND, 1937

The daughter. *Manuela*. A Horch 853 Streamline Coupe. Historically significant in its own right and perhaps the single most important car to emerge from the Second World War. If it could just be found.

Danish engineer Jørgen Skafte Rasmussen wanted to build a steam-driven car, or Dampf-Kraft-Wagen. He eventually succeeded in producing a little two-stroke engine which was fitted to a motorcycle chassis and became Das Kleine Wunder, the little wonder. Rasmussen had a thing for cleverly recycling acronyms. From the mid-twenties onwards, DKW became the world's largest motorcycle manufacturer.

In the meantime, Bernd Rosemeyer was becoming a living legend.

Already he had garnered a reputation for speed and was a firm fan favourite due to his ebullient personality. Like most would-be grand prix drivers though, Rosemeyer had started out on motorcycles, competing in various local races and hill climbs on BMWs and NSUs, before attracting the attention of the DKW factory. However, by the time Rosemeyer had peaked their interest, Rasmussen's company had already been amalgamated with Audi, Horch and Wanderer to form Auto Union.

While initially the intention had been to trial Rosemeyer out for the motorcycle team, a revolutionary new Grand Prix car was being built at the Horch factory in Zwickau under the direction of Ferdinand Porsche. Thus, with hardly any experience in racing automobiles, Rosemeyer was invited to try his hand in the Typ B Grand Prix car. It was an inspired decision.

IN THE DEN OF WOLVES

In honour of his 1936 championship, the first for Auto Union after years of Mercedes dominance, Rosemeyer had just taken delivery of a brand-new 853 from Horch, their most luxurious brand. Fresh from the Erdmann & Rossi coachbuilders in Berlin, the shortened chassis had been given Fritz Fiedler's upgraded engine and a streamlined coupé body. He had proudly driven it all the way over from Germany to attend the final race of the 1937 season accompanied by his wife, Elly Beinhorn, an accomplished and beautiful aviatrix in her own name.

Despite dominating the championship standings for much of 1930s though, neither of the German marques had so far claimed honours at the Donington Grand Prix. Both teams were keen for a maiden victory at the Leicestershire circuit. Having parked their own cars up on the front lawn of Donington Hall near the ha-ha, Rosemeyer's teammates Andrew Sutherland and Herman 'Happy' Müller jumped out, grabbed their bags and gathered near the centre of the turning circle as Rosemeyer himself arrived in his wonderful new machine. Elly was grinning away in the passenger seat.

"I have named her *Manuela*." Rosemeyer announced as he silenced the smooth, powerful engine. Stepping forward from the rear-hinged door like a knight proudly dismounting his charger.

"Your first baby?" Happy replied.

"The car."

"Not Irina?" Happy returned, pointing to the licence plate. "IA-1317."

"I suggested Isabella." Elly teased gently.

"Whit a wee beauty." Sutherland declared, gazing longingly at her sultry curves.

"He must be in love." Happy chuckled. "He's not made eyes at Elly yet."

"Am I taking second place in your affections?" Elly asked, sticking out her bottom lip theatrically.

"Whenever a car like this is involved…" He winked, stepping forward to kiss her on the cheek.

Elly was two-and-a-half years older than Rosemeyer. Her blonde hair and bright, open face always made her appear a little younger than her husband though. Perhaps the demands of aviation were not as extreme as hurtling in the oily, smoky, rubber slicked tracks of Grand Prix race cars. Either that or her radiant glow stemmed from her pregnancy. She was nearly eight months gone and really beginning to show.

Just then, some of the Mercedes boys were spilling out of Alfred Neubauer's Maybach Zeppelin. The others arrived in a Typ 320 Pullman-Cabriolet with the F-type body driven by Caracciola. This was a lumbering whale of a machine with four doors and six seats in three rows. The ERA boys arrived in their own MGs and Rileys, tiny by comparison but were all in good spirits. The Italians arrived in a blaze of gravel and were typically vociferous and gesticulating about something. Prince Bira, with his cousin and guardian Prince Chula, was reserved but happy, as befitting a Crown Prince of Siam. His ready smile and eagerness to participate in the fun ever present. Already there was a heady party atmosphere building.

On entering Donington Hall, the drivers were at once greeted by the robust figure of their host, John Gillies Shields. Paintings of the formidable Plantagenet kings from whom the Hastings family had originally descended looked down upon them from the walls, wondering what frivolity was to ensue no doubt. Rosemeyer and his little Auto Union entourage gazed appreciatively around the square entrance hall. The Gothic features reminded the German contingent of some of the architecture back home. Ancient Saxon castles and princely Bavarian estates.

Whilst receiving their welcome drinks in the antechamber, bustling staff hired for the weekend relieved the guests of their bags and whisked them away to their accommodation in the rooms above. Meanwhile the drivers, team managers and guests assembled in the Drawing Room and chatted until dinner.

"What do you think of the new hairpin?" Caracciola asked.

"It's going to be heavy on the brakes." von Brauchitsch replied. "Especially after such a steep descent. What is it? One-in-eight? One-in-nine?"

"It's the brow of the hill on the way up we'll have to worry about." Lang added. "If we can get the power down, we'll be taking off before we hit the flag."

"It'll be like Flugplatz, ja?" Rosemeyer chimed, sidling up to the Mercedes boys. "We can play Wagner and ride like Valkyries."

IN THE DEN OF WOLVES

"Don't they usually pick up the dead?" Lang replied gloomily.

"That will be the ERA boys." Müller returned, keeping the tone jolly. "Dead in our tracks."

"What do you make of them?" asked Mary, a young waitress hired for the weekend.

"Who?" Mrs Baxter enquired. The housekeeper.

"The racing drivers."

"They're all the same." She groaned, rolling her eyes. "Only after one thing. In case they get killed tomorrow and that's the end of it. Over-sexed playboys. Be careful. They'll have your bloomers off before you know it."

"That Mr Seaman seems okay." Frances remarked.

"Mr Seaman is a proper gentleman." Mrs Baxter cooed. "Why he's involved in a rogue's sport, I'll never know."

"Haud yer wheesht, now." Sutherland uttered genially, handing his bag to one of the porters and sidling up to the ladies. "There's naw anything special aboot Dickie Seaman. We were all semen once." He winked and moved on. Mary's cheeks turned bright crimson as the sound of the gong announced that dinner was about to be served.

Across the entrance hall, the guests were brought into a grand dining room. There was wine chilling in wooden tubs of ice beyond scagliola columns at the far end. Beer served straight from the keg and the smell of cigarettes mixing with the bouquet of floral table centres wafted into the air. A good fire was crackling in the hearth and laughter was fizzing around the tables.

Rosemeyer's wit and charm were both in rude health and he had the Auto Union table in raptures of mirth almost as soon as dinner had commenced. Richard Seaman came over from the Mercedes table to join them for dessert, bringing Nuvolari with him and a few of the Alfa Romeo boys. Dickie Seaman had won the 1936 Donington Grand Prix with Hans Rüesch in Sutherland's Alfa Romeo. Sutherland himself had been in Germany trying out for Auto Union at the time but didn't begrudge Seaman the victory in his old car. Dickie was an excellent driver, composed and precise. Quintessentially English and a champion in the making. Sutherland was a little more ragged and lairy. Typical Scot. Spirited and promising.

"Scottie." Rosemeyer murmured into Sutherland's ear while the rest of the table were in the midst of another fit of laughter. "Come up to us when you've finished your drinks, ja? There's something we want to ask you."

"Aye, of course." Sutherland smiled cheerily, a little curious but happy to attend upon his teammate.

He turned back to the party as Mary, the pretty serving girl, refilled his beer from the jug. He winked at her and watched her cheeks flush in response. She had promised him a tour of the old chapel attached to the east wing after dinner. Apparently, there was a particularly fine organ she wanted to inspect.

CHAPTER SIX
ENGLAND, 2017

"Bernd Rosemeyer wasn't a policeman though." Deakin observed. "Why would his car have a Berlin police licence plate."

"Ah, well." Robertson replied, a gleam in his eye as the waiter brought their afternoon tea to the trackside table. "For that explanation, we need to delve into the murky history of the Third Reich."

The waiter looked a little surprised as he presented the plates before his guests.

"This is the War Room." Deakin said, by way of an explanation to the bewildered young man.

"For propaganda purposes, German racing drivers during the 1930s were automatically enrolled in the National Socialist Motor Corps, the NSKK. They could refuse of course, but unless they were members of this organisation they were seldom permitted to compete. Certainly not on the international stage."

"Wasn't that basically the SS-carpool for the Nazis?" Reginald articulated.

"In essence, yes. Though its primary mission was to train and educate its members in the operation and maintenance of high-performance automobiles. Anything from motorcycles and racing cars to government limousines and panzers. They also served as a roadside assistance group. In that sense at least, it was not too dissimilar to the AA or the RAC."

"Apart from openly supporting an oppressive regime."

"I don't recall the AA giving us a crash course in the Challenger either." Deakin laughed.

"Any organisation that didn't support the Party didn't exist for very long." Robertson explained mildly. "Of course, that did entail supplying vehicles and drivers for the Party elite. It was also the official courier for the OT."

"What was the OT?" Charlie probed.

"Organisation Todt. They were the main contractors for bunkers, flak towers and the Siegfried Line. The NSKK was used by them to transport classified documents, construction plans and reports to and from OT headquarters. Anyway, because of their membership of the NSKK, racing drivers were given honorary ranks within the Waffen-SS, regardless of whether they were Party members or not. Some were not and chose not to wear the uniform either. It was merely a means to an end for them."

"So, Rosemeyer was SS?"

"In name only. He was accorded the rank of Hauptsturmführer by Heinrich Himmler personally. It would have been unwise to refuse. So, he was basically a Captain, though in an honorary capacity."

"Just like you." Reginald nodded to his son with a half-smile.

"My Captaincy isn't honorary, dad."

"You have to remember the whole country was under dictatorship." Robertson gestured to the pre-war monsters thundering around the circuit on their qualification run for the Brooklands Trophy. "If you're a racing driver, you just want to race. You don't give a monkeys about politics but imagine having to be registered with the AA just to be allowed to get in a car. Of course, it just so happens that the AA provides a fleet of vehicles and chauffeurs for government, all branches of the armed forces and yes, even trains you donkey wallopers to tear up Salisbury Plains in the odd tank now and again. But that's not what you're in it for. You're in the racing division." He took a sip of tea and sighed with satisfaction.

"That little diversion though brings us nicely to the number plate. You see once Hitler assumed power in 1933, all the organs of policing and state security fell under the jurisdiction of the SS. The security police, secret police, criminal police etc. etc. All the Po's as I call them."

"All the Po's?"

"The secret police, the Gestapo are arguably the most well-known. The criminal police were abbreviated to Kripo. Orpo was the uniformed division. Sipo, the security police. In summary though, the reason why Rosemeyer's car had a licence plate for the Berlin police is because it was issued by the over-arching agency, of which he was an honorary member."

"The Waffen-SS."

"Aye, you've got it."

"It's strangely unsettling to think I've had a note about an SS-issued licence plate in the door pocket all this time."

"Aye, but why?" Robertson asked, choosing a sandwich from the plate stand. "That's the question."

"That *is* the question." Deakin agreed, slicing open a scone and daubing clotted cream on the bottom half. Charlie looked at him disapprovingly. "What?"

"Are you not going to put some jam on that?" she asked.

"Jam on top."

"The Devon way?"

"The English way."

"What's the English way?"

"Whichever way I want." He winked, duly applying a dollop of jam to the top before spreading some onto the top half and topping off with a dollop of cream.

"Devon *and* Cornwall? You're a heathen." She laughed.

"I have a couple more questions." Reginald picked up. "How do you know this licence plate belongs to Rosemeyer's Horch, and why on earth was this note of it in my Alvis?"

"Ah. The first one is easy." Robertson replied, dabbing his mouth with a napkin. "There are photographs of Rosemeyer alongside his car dated to 1938. Shortly before he was killed. Possibly even taken the weekend of his death, poor bugger. The licence plate is clearly visible. IA-1317. I know I'm an old duffer but even a quick Google search will bring them up. We may even have a few copies in the Archives at Beaulieu." He took another swig of tea and paused, lacing his fingers together in his lap. "As to the second question. That might be a little more interesting to answer."

Deakin and Reginald looked across at him expectantly. "The car was lost during the war." He said simply, then added. "Apparently."

"What do you mean?"

"The story goes that after Rosemeyer died, the car was taken into storage back in Zwickau and probably destroyed during the Allied bombing that followed. Zwickau and Chemnitz nearby were churning out all manner of armoured contraptions, so were prime targets. However, I've personally been researching Rosemeyer's lost Horch for years. That's why I recognised the number. I'm not so sure it was lost in the war at all."

"Where do you think it is?"

"There are a few possibilities. None of which I'm at liberty to discuss right now." He winked, sharing a glance with Charlie. "This car and one or two others make up a sort of relic hunter's holy trinity. They could be worth millions if they were ever found. Tens of millions even. Finding that note in your Alvis though does open up new possibilities as to where one of them might be."

"You think this Horch could be in Scotland?"

"Och no, I don't see logistically how that would have been possible. I think the owner of the Horch might have come back to Scotland though. Much the same way as the owner of your Alvis did."

"But Rosemeyer was killed."

"Indeed, he was."

"And the car disappeared?"

"Did it, Christopher? Did it?" Robertson smiled. "We know all of Rosemeyer's Auto Union teammates for the 1937 season. One of them was a man named Andrew Sutherland. He came from the Isle of Skye, which incidentally used to be part of the Inverness-shire Constabulary's extensive patch when I was a wee boy. Even more interestingly though, Andrew Sutherland also happened to have shared a quint at Dollar Academy with a certain James Alexander Cameron."

"So, it comes back full circle." Charlie commented.

"He told his friend about the Horch."

"This note might suggest so. Perhaps they wanted to find it again."

"I told you he would know." Reginald said, addressing his son. "A head full of extraordinary knowledge. Definitely one to have around for the pub quiz." Then, turning to Robertson. "Would you like this for your research?" Reginald offered. "It's a fascinating chapter, but I feel it needs to be told in context and you have the context."

"In itself, the note is just a note. There is no intrinsic value in it, but I would be happy to add it to my private papers."

"Feel free. I'm just pleased we were able to have some minor involvement in the story." Reginald smiled, taking up his tea and watching the cars thunder past the picket fencing.

"That's what I love about this place." Robertson sighed, slipping the envelope into his jacket. "Every car has a story."

Charlie and Deakin shared a glance and smiled, sitting back and enjoying the spectacle that was the Goodwood Revival.

CHAPTER SEVEN
ENGLAND, 1937

Rosemeyer's room had occupied the southwest corner of Donington Hall, enjoying a double aspect towards the circuit to the south, extensive rolling landscape of the deer park to the west and the benefit of an attached dressing room. Not entirely sure what to expect, Sutherland had checked the nametag above the door, handwritten in beautiful copperplate script. He knocked politely. After a moment, the door opened, and Rosemeyer's affable face appeared.

"Come in, Scottie." he greeted, swinging the door wide to allow Sutherland inside.

He was wearing slacks held up by braces and a shirt open almost to his navel, sleeves rolled up. Relaxed. Elly emerged from the dressing room wearing the only thing that seemed to fit round everything comfortably. A beautiful silk bathrobe with Chinese dragons writhing around her shapely figure.

"You've got yerselves a right bonnie room here." Sutherland remarked with nods of approbation as he looked around. "Four-poster too. They've put me up near the kirk." He laughed, gesturing to the opposite end of the house. By marked contrast, his accommodation was a box room in the northeast corner, next to the back staircase and above the corridor that led to the adjacent chapel. Still, Mary was keeping the bed warm.

Rosemeyer joined in the mirth. His ear attuned to Sutherland's Hebridean tones. "They know you need redemption, ja?"

"Aye, well." He winked, thinking of Mary kneeling before the altar only half an hour earlier.

"We wanted to ask you something." Rosemeyer said, unusually getting straight to the point. "It is a silly thing really, but at the same time important for me."

"Aye, go on."

Rosemeyer looked at Elly and smiled, holding out a hand for her to hold. His tone was unusually sombre. "If anything happens to me, I…"

"Wir…" Elly corrected, embracing his arm.

"Ja. We would like you to take on *Manuela*. I trust no one more than you to look after her. You see it even sounds silly now. It's just a car." He chuckled, putting an arm around Elly's shoulders, and pressing a hand to her distended stomach.

"Aye, course it does." Sutherland smiled. "Nothing's gonnae happen to you, but I daresay it would be a rare pleasure picking up some lasses in that beauty, if I ever got a wee chance."

"I thought you would say that." Rosemeyer laughed. "But only one seat?" He shrugged.

"They can sit on each other's laps."

Rosemeyer and Elly shared in Sutherland's humour, grateful that the rather morbid duty of dividing one's personal possessions had still been passed off with joy. It seemed Rosemeyer never wanted to be gloomy.

"In fact, I'll do you a deal right now." Sutherland proposed. "If I win this Saturday, you can have my Wanderer for the bairn."

"A puppenwagen." Rosemeyer laughed, moving to the bedside cabinet to pour them both a measure of Schnapps. "If it's a girl we can give it to the baby for her dolls."

"Ah, you're a bastard, Bernd." Sutherland sniggered as he accepted the glass offered to him.

"To good friends." Rosemeyer toasted. "Good friends and healthy competition."

CHAPTER EIGHT
ENGLAND, 2017

Applause rippled through the busy Bonhams marquee. The hammer had finally fallen on the 7-litre behemoth of the 1963 British Saloon Car Championship. Selling for an astonishing £471,900, 'Gentleman' Jack Sears' Ford Galaxie 500 had set a new world record and more than doubled its pre-sale estimate. With the remainder of his collection selling quickly it was onto the 1935 Lagonda LG45 4½-litre.

Craig Sutherland had looked over the Monte Carlo Rally car and been sorely tempted to put in a bid. His brother had kept him on track. They were here for one lot, and one lot only. At the end of the 200-lot Automobilia section, a very rare bottling of Glenfiddich single malt whisky was going under the hammer. Hopefully not in a literal sense. On the face of it, a bottle of single malt was an unusual object to be auctioned off alongside the automotive consignments but the connection between the Goodwood estate and the Glenfiddich distillery could be traced all the way back to 1836.

When George Duncan, 5th Duke of Gordon, Governor of Edinburgh Castle, and the last of his line passed away, he left his nephew, the 5th Duke of Richmond to inherit his Glenfiddich estate in Banffshire. Prior to that, the area around the River Fiddich had been a hotbed of illicit distillation. Concerned for the moral welfare of his tenants, the duke had petitioned parliament to introduce a new licensing act which would allow for smaller distillers to legally produce the spirit.

In this context, the Grant family of Speyside established the Glenfiddich Distillery on the banks of the river. However, so popular was the production of their single malt whisky that a second distillery was built next door in Dufftown, known as the Balvenie Distillery. Then, when William Grant's eldest daughter, Isabella, married salesman Charles Gordon, whose family farmed land close to the duke's Glenfiddich estate, a family dynasty was created that had continued to run the distillery independently ever since.

The particular Glenfiddich being offered by Bonhams at the Goodwood Revival was a rare eighteen year old 1966 bottling. As such it meant that the spirit had first been placed into fresh fill American oak casks back in 1948. After four years, the whisky was transferred into European oak sherry casks. This was around about the time that the chicane was added at Goodwood after Woodcote Corner. The increasingly more powerful cars needed slowing down before the start/finish line. Thus, the maturation of the whisky was inextricably linked with the entire duration of the Goodwood Circuit's original operations.

The non-chill filtered single malt promised to be a bold flavoured spirit with great depth and warmth. On the nose, elegant layers of heather honey, soft fruits, vanilla and buttered bun toast. On the finish, a palette smooth and sweet leading to waves of gentle spice, gingerbread, grilled grapefruit and was very long, and intense. The rarity of it was what had drawn the Sutherland brothers down from the Isle of Skye to the West Sussex auction. Craig was hoping to add it to his particularly fine private collection.

However, seeing the dazzling array of classic cars on display got both brothers thinking. If Lieutenant-Commander Tomkinson's 1927 Bentley 3-litre Speed Model had managed to fetch a heady £357,660 during Saturday's auction, how much might their own relic be worth? Iain was adamant that the wreck wasn't for sale at any price. Nevertheless, the value of the cars made a compelling case for its restoration. As a shrewd investment opportunity, it would be worth making enquiries at the very least.

Friday was the day Reginald and his son toured the paddocks and the airfield. Saturday they watched the racing. Sunday was a chance to look around the shops and entertainment. Robertson had agreed to accompany Reginald as they looked around a few of the stalls specialising in spare parts. As well as selling classic cars, Reginald's small but elite team also offered servicing and repairs. Finding genuine spares amidst a sea of cheap, mass-produced imitations was something of a skill and Robertson knew his craft well.

This left Deakin to wander around at leisure for a few hours. Though he appeared to have gravitated towards the National Motor Museum tent where Charlie was presently looking after things for a while. Seeing her from the other side of the alley, he disappeared to a nearby café before approaching with two malted milkshakes.

"Thought you might like one." He smiled innocently as he approached.

"Not in uniform today?" she asked, watching him approach.

"I'm on leave." He joked, looking down to his three-piece tweed suit.

"Very dapper."

"Thank you. You're looking rather lovely yourself. I wasn't sure which you would prefer, so thought I would take a risk with strawberry."

"Perfect choice." She smiled. "Thank you." she took the milkshake offered her and sucked through the straw.

"So, you've met my dad. When do I get to meet yours?"

"You don't hold back do you?"

"Sorry. Occupational habit."

"Being forward?"

"Asking for what I want." After yesterday's follies, he opted for a more direct approach.

"Do you always get what you want?"

"Invariably." He smiled. "It's the advantage of being an officer."

"The hat you wore on Friday." She started, picking up another thread. "Looked a little old. Is it an original?"

"My grandfather's." he nodded. "He used to escort the bombers over to Germany."

"I wonder if he escorted my grandad." She beamed. Deakin cocked his head to one side. Intrigued. "You see, back in the day, he answered the call of Empire and came to England from Jamaica to defend the mother country."

"He was RAF too?"

She nodded. "Air Gunner Barkley Campbell. Bomber Command. He was part of a mixed crew. Australian pilot, navigator from Rhodesia. An Indian, some Canadians and a bomb-aimer from Liverpool."

"I imagine that was fun."

"Grandpa Bobo didn't like the British Empire much, but no one wanted a return to slavery under the Nazis either. He knew if ever they got shot down and survived the landing, the white crew might be imprisoned. Him and Mohinder though would be shot on sight, but it was still a risk they were willing to take."

"He did well to come through it then. Especially being a gunner."

"Bobo was a very religious man. Always went to church back home in Kingston. He often thanked God for keeping him safe."

Deakin regarded Charlie with heightened interest while she switched her attention to the passers-by. She answered some questions on the museum, where it was located and when it opened. Handed out a leaflet. Thanked them for coming and waved them off. Wishing them an enjoyable day.

"Where do you reckon we start?" Craig asked as they came over the bridge.

"I'll get oot the map, hang on." Iain replied. Dipping into the inside pocket of his jacket. The pair had opted for the classic Scottish Laird look. Eight-panel flat cap with button crown, Harris Tweed Norfolk jacket and plus fours. "Couple of restoration specialists doon here." He said, pointing to the map. "Might be worth a wee look."

"Where did you get your impeccable accent from?" Deakin asked.

"Not from my grandparents, that's for sure." She giggled, taking up her milkshake again. "Grandpa Bobo settled down in Buckinghamshire, near the training base he was posted to first. The villagers seemed to like him. Met my gran at church. She had come over from Trinidad to work as a nurse so there was a common history there. They never drank or swore. Never smoked. Never gambled, but they managed to bring up four children." She said with evident pride.

"They had *some* fun then."

A bit of warmth came to Charlie's cheeks as she smiled bashfully.

"I'm guessing one of those kids was your dad."

"The youngest, and the only boy." She nodded. "He was christened Edward James, but everyone calls him Eddie. His sisters became my second mothers." She laughed.

"Was it him that got you into cars?" Deakin mused.

"Both of them did really." Charlie grinned. "Granddad worked at the Cowley factory and got my dad an apprenticeship there. When he had completed it, granddad gave him the money he had been saving to become a partner in a garage near Aylesbury. Dad was the better mechanic though and ended up buying out the other partner. He used to service all the Bentleys and Daimlers that rolled through. Sometimes even the occasional Rolls-Royce. That's how he met my mother."

"Ah, was she the heiress of some magnificent estate? A punctured tyre. A damsel in distress. Cold and foreboding country lanes."

"Not quite, but close." Charlie replied. "Her dad's Jaguar took a ding at the races when a horse got loose. He asked if my dad could fix it while her ladyship, my mum, was trying not to look too interested. She was always something of a rebellious free-spirit and seemed to like the prospect of marrying the only black man in the village. The shock. The scandal. It was just what she wanted." She explained, her eyes sparkling like diamonds as she romanticised the dramatic scenes in her own mind.

Deakin drooped the corners of his mouth and nodded respectfully. Both generations had shown their talent for courage in the face of adversity.

"So, you see, I'm not even black. Technically I'm mixed race, but I've got more of my dad's colouring."

"Your mum's eyes?" he looked into her dark chocolate orbs, thinking it unlikely, but wanting to keep the conversation going.

"My mum's accent."

"When did you first get involved in cars?"

"Dad always loved racing and managed to keep a local saloon car team going.

As a child I absolutely loved helping out around the garage and prepping the cars for racing at the weekends. I could change a spark plug before I could change a tampon."

It was Deakin's turn to look a little self-conscious. Not used to a woman being so candid.

"Perhaps too much information." She giggled. "My aunties were not happy at all though. They wanted me to stop being a tomboy. Despite the colour difference they got on really well with mum and together told me to get a good education and start acting like a proper lady." She continued, breaking seamlessly into West Indian patois.

"I take it you didn't." he chuckled, finding the switch in accent rather appealing and quite unexpected.

"I like to think I come across very ladylike, darling." She said, brushing her sleek black hair over her shoulder dramatically. "I suppose I do have some of my mother's stubbornness though."

"Thank you for looking after things." Came a voice from the alley.

"Not a problem, Janice. Did you find what you were looking for?"

"Ooh yes. Lovely little outfit. I think I'll wear it when we have one of our vintage days."

"I can't wait to see it."

"Well, you're relieved now, so you can go and enjoy yourself." Janice smiled, looking knowingly from Charlie to Deakin and back again.

"We will." She smiled. "Thank you. Come on then, Captain. Next question." She took his arm and headed in the direction of the bridge that would take them back over the road to the circuit.

"Favourite crisps?" he said, flailing around for something deep and meaningful.

"Prawn cocktail."

"Red sauce or brown?"

"Red for sausages, brown for bacon."

"First kiss?"

"Xiuying." She replied without hesitation. "I had a crush on her in senior school."

"Oh?" he asked, trying to keep the surprise from his voice. Sensing his chances had been dashed before even getting off the ground.

"She was a pretty girl. Family came from Hong Kong."

"Most Asian girls are pretty." He acknowledged, a little disappointed.

"Incredible mathematician. We found out early on that the girl-on-girl thing wasn't for us though. I was lusting after her mind, rather than her body, but we remained friends and travelled around Europe and Asia during our gap year."

"I see." he replied, not sure what else to say.

"Don't worry. I still prefer boys." She laughed.

"That's good to know." He smiled, somewhat relieved. Still uncertain. "Have you had Pimm's on the top deck of a bus?"

"Can't say I have."

"Well let's see if we can do something about that."

"Excuse me." Came a distinctive Scottish brogue. "Do yer happen to know where these people are?"

Two gentlemen, smartly attired in belted shooting jacket and breeks, approached with a map of the shopping village. Slipping into helpful curator mode, Charlie looked at the intended destination and nodded.

"Just carry on down here and turn to the left after the petrol pumps. Just before you reach the Butlin's roller rink."

"Thank you."

"Do you have a car to restore?"

"Aye, a fair wee wreck."

"If you need some historical advice, we might be able to help you at the National Motor Museum." She extended her arm to where they had just come from. "Perhaps there are some photographs in our archives that could help ensure its period correct."

"Aye. That would be grand. Thank you."

Charlie watched the two well-dressed gentlemen march on, looking every inch like they were out for the grouse shoot. Turning back, she caught Deakin looking at her.

"What?"

"You like helping people, don't you?"

"You don't?"

"I follow orders."

"Then I order you to take me to the Pimm's bus."

CHAPTER NINE
GERMANY, 1938

It was a very strange and unsettling sensation becoming airborne in a racing car. A distinctive tingling in the pit of the stomach. A momentary feeling of weightlessness, then the pull of gravity and the shuddering impact of landing. There was nothing the driver could do but to ride it out and see how it all worked out. Keeping the wheels dead straight on take-off and landing would help. After that it was largely anyone's guess what would happen. The suspension could give way. The car might belly itself and rupture a fuel tank. Sparks from the bodywork igniting the heady cocktail. A tyre could explode. It was no use thinking what might happen. Just deal with it when it did in the best possible way.

With four interlocking rings emblazoned upon its nose, the furious new machine scythed down the autobahn. Bernd Rosemeyer had tunnel vision once again. Rudolf Caracciola, ever his nemesis, had described the road like a narrow white band, the bridges like tiny black holes ahead. It was simply a matter of threading the car through them.

Simply?

As the cars thundered underneath the bridges, the drivers received a terrific blow to the chest, punching a hole through the air. When the record-breaking machines hurtled under a bridge, for a split-second the engine noise disappeared completely, then returned like a thunderclap once they were through the other side.

IN THE DEN OF WOLVES

More than five hundred horsepower raged behind him as a gale-force headwind pummelled the windscreen. A kilometre had disappeared in a fraction over eight seconds. The timing line waited to be broken. Porsche's 6.5litre V16-powered Auto Union Stromlinienwagen was lightning itself. Rosemeyer's previous pass had been clocked at 269mph, just 0.02seconds faster than Caracciola in the Mercedes. One final pass would confirm the glory, and the world record.

Rosemeyer's inexperience with four wheels had always been seen as an advantage. Other drivers would have suspected there was an issue immediately and slowed down or aborted the run. He on the other hand thought cars were supposed to handle erratically at speed. During the traditional Rekordwoche in June 1937, crosswinds had twice pushed his car onto the grass at dangerous velocities. In October, he became the first man ever to exceed 250mph on a public road. The following day, an engine failure caused fumes to fill the cockpit. Rosemeyer kept the car on the road, brought it home safely, but had to be lifted unconscious from the seat. After the repaired car broke down the next day, he swapped into an open-wheeled racer and set flying-start records over 10 miles. A day after nearly being suffocated at speeds only pilots experienced, Rosemeyer had claimed three world records. His legendary status continued.

Mercedes had been scorned for its failure to overthrow Auto Union during an event of national pride. Over Christmas they reworked the aerodynamics of Caracciola's Rekordwagen, substituting drag-creating radiators for an ice tank to cool the 725bhp supercharged V12 engine. The cost of hiring the autobahn for complete closure however was prohibitive. In 1937 the road had only been closed in one direction, so Rosemeyer had conducted his high-speed run through traffic. Finally, the two marques agreed to split the cost between them and share the empty straights.

The rebuilt Auto Union wore deeper side skirts, in essence resulting in an early and wholly unintentional downforce generating ground effect. Its own ice system bought ninety seconds of running before the engine overheated. Rosemeyer was bolted in under a streamlined shroud. If the engine detonated, he would have no escape. The ice tank upset the car's centre of gravity, and the skirting made the Stromlinienwagen extremely slippery but dramatically unstable. Hasty wind-tunnel testing had showed that just a six-degree deviation from the straight-ahead was unrecoverable. There was no time for a redesign. On the 28th of January 1938, the road from Frankfurt to Darmstadt was closed for the ultimate high-speed showdown.

It was bitingly cold. Rosemeyer's mechanics didn't bother adding ice to the car's cooling tank, they just pumped in water at the ambient temperature. On his final pass, from the confines of his incredibly cramped cockpit, Rosemeyer couldn't see the buckling body panels along the vehicle's flanks, warped by the incredible suction that the vehicle was developing at such high speed. Under the intense aerodynamic stress, the bodywork was simply disintegrating. The car was destroying itself. Bolts holding down the windshield sheared off, the canopy became detached and with the ferocious headwind now buffeting against his unprotected body, Rosemeyer lost control.

Sutherland often woke in the night in a cold sweat wondering what that sensation would have felt like for his friend and teammate. Knowing there was absolutely nothing more that could be done. Knowing he was finished. He thought the snaking Eau Rouge section of Spa had been terrifying enough as they ascended like a swarm of angry hornets onto the Kemmel Straight. Becoming airborne momentarily over Flugplatz and Donington's Melbourne brow had been the closest Sutherland had come to losing it completely. None of those experiences he knew would ever compare to what happened at Darmstadt.

Snaking tyre tracks betrayed where, even at 250mph, the twenty-eight year old had been fighting to save the car. The Auto Union swerved left, then right before hitting a grass embankment and somersaulting into the air. Rosemeyer's car sliced through several trees and a stone marker post before exploding. Astonishingly, when the team physician arrived, they found his body some one-hundred feet away from the road. Completely unmarked. Arms resolutely by his side. There was even a faint pulse. Sadly, that pulse faded fast. The legend had died.

CHAPTER TEN
ENGLAND, 2017

"A Horch 853 Coupé?" The voice was West Coast American. Intrigued. Guarded.

"That's what they said." Robertson replied. He was behind his desk in the study of the Lymington bungalow he called his second home.

"It has to be *Manuela*."

"It would certainly be an unusual find, wherever it was. I just find it incredibly hard to believe that *Manuela* might have found her way all the way up to Scotland."

"Where was the last place we managed to trace it to?"

"We didn't. Not specifically. We know it spent much of the war in Berlin. There was always speculation that it was destroyed in Zwickau. Nothing else definitive after that, though there were also rumours that it went east."

"I remember now. That's why all these shortened chassis keep mysteriously turning up in Ukraine every so often."

"Aye." Robertson nodded. "Informed treasure hunters wanting to make a wee fortune."

"It sounds like you're having a hell of a lot more luck than I ever did with the

Duesenberg. That trail got cold almost as soon as it started. Should have stuck with the Delage, or even that old Cord Speedster. Have you contacted Ingolstadt? I think they had a replica of *Manuela* made a couple of years ago for their museum."

"Not yet, Bob. Thought I would contact you and André first."

"How is the guy?" Bob asked.

"Very quiet." Robertson smiled "He happens to be on this conference call."

"André?" Bob called. "How are things, man?"

"Ah well, you know." André replied. A gallic shrug almost audible in the tone of his voice.

"Still no joy on the hunt for La Voiture Noire?"

"No, it is hopeless." He sighed, exchanging 's's for 'z's and dropping the 'h' predictably.

"At Pebble Beach this year, I heard talk that collectors would be willing to pay top dollar for it, if it were ever found." Bob continued. "The ultimate barn-find, they're calling it. Upwards of a hundred million at least. That makes it the most valuable of the three for sure."

"Almost worth starting again." Robertson chuckled.

"Almost." André chirped. There was a pregnant pause. "Non! Absolutely not. I am not investing more years of my life into searching for the sacred Mother. She is gone. She is lost. Irretrievably lost."

"Where was it last recorded? Bordeaux, wasn't it?"

"Could be a good time to come over and get some wine for Thanksgiving." Bob joked.

"There is only a record that it might have been sent there. No confirmation that it ever arrived. This is precisely where the trail disappeared." André protested. "The spurious speculation of one or other Bugatti to be the one is too distracting and complex to go back through again. Even for a hundred million. I am too old now."

"Alright." Robertson acknowledged, rolling his eyes. André Langier could sometimes be a cantankerous old soul. If he was in one of his moods, there was no persuading him otherwise. "So, we leave the trail for the Bugatti. We have nothing more on the Duesenberg. This note about the Horch though might open up a fresh trail."

"Could it have really found its way up to Scotland?" Bob asked suspiciously.

"We don't know, but the two gentlemen that contacted the museum share the same surname as Rosemeyer's Scottish teammate."

"Sounds too much of a coincidence." Bob remarked. "Worth checking out."

"I agree." Robertson nodded. "I'm arranging to meet with them. See what they have. Could be its just another fake. There's a slim possibility that it is the real thing. God knows how Sutherland managed to bring *Manuela* back to Scotland if he did. I wasn't aware he even returned until a few weeks ago. Convicted in absentia. A traitor to the crown. He would have been under the radar."

"As you said, why else would a Scottish policeman have a note on a very specific German licence plate?" Bob added. "Could be this Cameron guy was looking to make an arrest. Sure, they were old buddies once, but war changes people, and if they were on different sides…" he let the thought linger. "I think I'll dig into the old Duesenberg files. See if anything has come up on our Model J. Could be time to assemble the old Auto Club again."

"We'll see about that." Robertson said cautiously. "I'll let you know what I find."

Monique: The holy Mother. The preeminent of the three. A wonder of design and performance. The perfect balance between speed, grace, functionality, and style. The 1936 Bugatti Type 57SC Coupé Aero was the most coveted classic car in the world. And the most elusive.

Mother, daughter, holy nymph.

CHAPTER ELEVEN
FRANCE, 1938

Sutherland was in sombre mood as he drove *Manuela* into Paris that October night. It was nine months since Rosemeyer's accident. Elly and their son Bernd Jr were bearing up, but the funeral had been incredibly hard on her.

Upon the orders of Heinrich Himmler, all German racing drivers were given honorary membership of the Schutzstaffel, but Rosemeyer had been let off wearing the SS uniform and even mocked high-ranking Nazis on the podiums of his Grand Prix victories. He had always been more interested in racing than politics. Though Elly herself was also a national heroine, Rosemeyer had found a kindred spirit of adventure, fearlessness, and general indifference towards the regime.

Elly had requested a simple, private burial. Her wishes were completely ignored, and Hitler turned Rosemeyer's funeral into a political rally. It was done almost as a final insult. Conferring upon him the high honour and respect they refused to give him during his life in a manner he would have never wanted upon his death.

Fashions and tastes changed quickly, yet Manuela was still seen as an exquisitely elegant and desirable car. She possessed all the illuminated dials, elegant burr walnut and luxurious leather upholstery befitting a car built to the very highest standard. She was as much a tribute to her first owner as she was an example of the Berlin coachbuilder's craft. An utter joy to drive. Sutherland's little Wanderer W25K he had been using beforehand was nothing by comparison and he was glad to drive something without that problematic Roots supercharger.

Appearing in a three-piece tweed suit with Half Norfolk back and notched lapels, it was clear that Sutherland hadn't dressed for the opera at all. Instead, his choice of attire gave the impression that he had come dressed up for stalking. He didn't care either way. The style of his jacket was traditionally English and beautifully tailored using the finest herringbone tweed from one of Edinburgh's oldest sartors. Structured using a full canvas interlining, the cut suppressed the waist and gave flare to the hem. The canvas panels conformed perfectly to Sutherland's frame, giving the jacket a trim, elegant shape and effortless hang.

There was a comforting scent of new wool that reminded him of his Hebridean home. The coarseness of the material against his skin was softened by a cotton oxford weave shirt. Its weight balanced by a maroon silk tie and playful pocket square. Ever the pragmatist, instead of patent leather evening shoes, notoriously uncomfortable and lacking traction, he wore a pair of robust Loake boots fashioned on the Pennine last with Goodyear welted soles.

The guest list that evening had been a veritable pantheon of celebrities and leading lights of the age, dripping in jewellery and adorned in their finest gowns. He was in Paris to savour the intoxicating atmosphere of the season, nothing more, yet had come dressed as a Highland rogue and attracted suitably disparaging glances.

Her Royal Highness, Princess Fawzia bint Fuad, had by stark contrast commanded the room. The eldest daughter of King Fuad of Egypt and Sudan was of Circassian, French, Turkish and Albanian descent. In physical appearance, her famed beauty and film star looks had drawn striking comparisons to Hedy Lamarr and Vivien Leigh, her illustrious and critically acclaimed Hollywood contemporaries.

Described as an Asian Venus with a perfect, heart-shaped face, she had appeared every inch the exotic, oriental Princess as she attended the reception dinner in Paris that evening. Poured into a black satin evening gown, shimmering, iridescent and infused with glamour, the striking garment epitomised elegant evening wear at its finest. She radiated style and beauty as she swept into the room.

A unique two-strand necklace with round and baguette cut diamonds in platinum mounts traced a curve around her long and elegant neck. This was matched by a pair of beautiful earrings that dripped exquisitely from her ears, glistening like stars. Her chestnut hair, a rich glossy fusion of smooth, dark chocolate and burnished copper, cascaded onto her shoulders in long luxurious waves. Her voluptuous figure swept past with effortless grace and finesse, wafting perfumed wonderment over her adoring audience with the ease of someone born to refinement.

Piercing pale blue eyes surveyed the room with rare discernment in their shimmering, immeasurable lustre. Her rich dark lips curved into a radiant smile as she recognised someone in the crowd. The long, elegant fingers of her hand playfully twirled a lock of her hair. With the turn of her head, she commanded attention. Her silhouette promised breathless intention. Every move captivation.

When they had first met in Tripoli, Sutherland had been racing for Ferrari's Alfa Romeo team. The Governor-General took great pride in introducing Enzo Ferrari and his drivers to the guests of honour. Back then she had been a precocious teenager with a better command of English than Italian, so Sutherland was encouraged by the Governor to navigate his guests through the confusing and exciting world of racing cars. King Fuad appeared mildly interested. His daughter had found it fascinating.

Now, although barely seventeen years old, her imminent marriage to the Crown Prince of Iran was making global headlines. It was seen as an incredibly significant alliance. Uniting both Sunni and Shia royal houses in a region becoming increasingly divided and intolerant, a legacy of the Great War carve up and seemingly on the very edge of religious and political turmoil. A tinderbox that waited upon the merest spark.

Her glance was but a fleeting, barely perceptible glimmer across the room, yet the sparkle in those eyes spoke volumes to Sutherland where her full, dark lips could only remain resolutely sealed. When, finally, those same, promising lips parted much later in the evening, the whispered message seductively breathed out to him in the lobby was unmistakeably clear.

"Take me away from here."

"Where?" he had asked.

"Anywhere."

Her plea was authentic and heartfelt. She didn't want the life she was destined to enter, yet even for her tender years she recognised the reality of her situation. It was an unavoidable fate. A final fling of freedom was not too much to ask though, was it?

This brief reunion in Paris, her daring barefoot escape, a laughter-filled dash through the city's streets, had led them inexorably to the impressive edifice on the Boulevard des Capucines in the 9th arrondissement of Paris. Reluctantly, yet inevitably, she had slipped her shoes back on and taken her leave of her unlikely avuncular on the steps of the Palais Garnier, lost to the crowd on the Grand Escalier, never to see him again as he stole quietly away into the night.

Returning to his car, scooping up two ladies as he did so, Sutherland noticed a distinctive Franco-Italian trio of automobiles glaring with apparent disapproval across the cobbled Place de l'Opéra. Emerging from their own sculpted coachwork, their headlights scowled at the Horch as if shocked and appalled that such sleek lines had not been crafted in Paris or Milan.

Blinking away the pareidolic perception, he opened the door for the beautiful Russian Princess to enter the interior. She was followed by her sultry Italian counterpart who deposited herself on Irina's lap. The Scottish driver of the German sportscar swept round the billowing front fenders, unbuttoned his jacket, and clambered in behind the wheel to take them all, giggling and squealing, to *Le Boeuf sur le Toit* on 41 Avenue Pierre.

It took an hour before the gendarmerie found the car. Another ten minutes to locate the driver on the rooftop cabaret bar.

"Of course, I've seen Princess Fawzia, Lieutenant." he explained. "I was at the same engagement."

"Where is she?" asked the confused officer, looking around.

"I drove her to the Opera hours ago." he replied.

"Why did you do that?" he was asked with suspicion.

"Well, she asked me too." He replied honestly. "Seems she got a wee bit detached from her entourage in the lobby. So, in the confusion she asked if I could whizz her over there."

"Why you?"

"I can only guess that she wanted the most handsome driver in all Paris." He joked. "And with the fastest car too."

"Why you?" he was asked again, more seriously, the Lieutenant pronouncing each word deliberately and accentuating it with a pointed finger.

"We've met before. She knows I'm a racing driver and she obviously trusts me." He threw up his hands at their questioning. "Look, why don't you phone the Opera House now and see if she's there?"

"We will do just that." The officer said haughtily, summoning the barman over.

The call was duly made. The suspicious gendarmes waited while the Scotsman ordered more drinks and the music played on. It was while the gendarmes were waiting for a reply that Sutherland noticed two men deep in conversation at the other end of the bar. One was clearly American. He could just tell by his behaviour and deportment. The other was German. Again, all the classic stereotypical national hallmarks were in evidence.

Le Boeuf sur le Toit was a well-known rendezvous for some of the city's more avant-garde and flamboyantly expressionist residents. Sutherland wasn't into that side of things, quite the contrary. Among the many other dance halls and revues of gay Paris though, heterosexual women often felt less intimidated and threatened at Le Boeuf sur le Toit. Their own sex was far gentler in their expressions of admiration than the lascivious louts that languished elsewhere.

These two men however seemed to be engaged in a liaison of an altogether different nature. There was cool and studied detachment on the side of the German, an appealing, almost desperate approach by the American. Sutherland could see in the ice blue eyes of the German the calculations that were taking place inside his head. The pros and cons, points and counterpoints, strengths and weaknesses. He seemed to be turning the proposal around in his mind, viewing it from every angle, weighing up what it would be worth, personally and professionally, where it could be exploited, who would benefit most. Sutherland shuddered at the unseemliness of the engagement. He couldn't understand why but just looking on from the bar, whatever deal they seemed to be negotiating, there was something unsettling about it.

There was a short wait, and then it was confirmed.

"Qui Monsieur." The barman nodded, replacing the receiver, and turning to the Lieutenant.

Princess Fawzia had arrived early for the performance, was perfectly safe and well and presently enjoying the Second Act of Puccini's Tosca. The Crown Prince of Iran was alongside her, having arrived late and somewhat agitated. Their respective entourages were bewildered and shamefaced but both guests of honour were accounted for. Everyone much relieved that Her Royal Highness had eventually been found. The Lieutenant was satisfied, though sceptical and looked at Sutherland with ill-disguised distrust as he turned to leave. Wine was imbibed, and the merriment continued. Picking up the tray, Sutherland turned his back and returned to his ladies.

After the drinks, it was home for the afterparty celebrations. L'Appartement *Chanel* was to be found on the famous Ile Saint-Louis, a quaint island in the heart of the 4th Arrondissement. The palatial three-bedroom villa overflowed with a blend of old-world charm and contemporary luxury. Residing on Quai d'Orléans in the shadow of the Notre Dame Cathedral, it occupied the entire third floor of a 17th Century house. From the impressive rotunda entrance hall, a pair of beautiful wooden doors welcomed them into the heart of the apartment. Intricately detailed parquet adorned an immense salon floor, occupying the front portion of the villa, before opening out onto private balconies overlooking the Seine.

In the late autumn morning of 1938, as they smoked cigarettes together and drank freshly brewed coffee, leaning over ornate wrought iron railings, they relived the revelries of the previous evening. Conversation with the exiled Princesses turned, inexorably as most such exchanges do, to their hopes and aspirations for the future.

"When have you been at your happiest?" Princess Orlova asked, looking into his eyes.

"I'm at ma happiest now." He said wistfully, exchanging a glance with them each in turn.

"Why?" the Italian beauty to his left enquired playfully as her fingers danced across his shoulder. "Have you never been happier before?"

"I've been happy." He nodded, before taking a long slow drag on his cigarette. "But I'm happiest now and I wannae savour it for as long as I can."

"Don't you think you will always be this happy?"

"Nah." he said with a sad smile as he turned from facing them to look across the river. He placed both elbows on the railing and after sharing the last of the cigarette with the two muses flanking him on either side, he flicked the butt down into the Seine below. "I won't ever be happy again. I know that for sure."

Standing in the very centre of a crossroad in his life, it was if he was looking up as the storm clouds of war rolled in, flashes of lightning rumbling across the sky. A decision had to be made.

"But why, my darling?" Princess Orlova persisted gently. Each girl embraced him, reaching across his broad back to tussle each other's hair as they rested their head on one of his shoulders.

"Because this time next year, ma wee beauties." He said quietly, slipping his arms around each of their slender waists, hoping his words wouldn't break the spell that had settled on the three of them that crisp and magical morning. "We'll all be killing each other again."

CHAPTER TWELVE
SCOTLAND, 2017

A Gordon Keeble GT was an interesting if eccentric choice of automobile. Just ninety-nine examples of the four-seat, British grand tourer had been built before the company predictably went into liquidation, with a final example built from spares to just make the century. Graham Robertson had acquired Chassis No.89 nearly twenty years ago. Manufactured in 1964, he had immediately taken it to Ernie Knott to receive a complete body-off restoration. From an early age he had learnt that original was not always best. This was the Cameron legacy.

Ernie's brief was to retain the look of the car from the 1960s whilst improving the performance, handling, general mechanicals and comfort. Robertson wanted the car to drive daily, ensuring equivalent standards to a 'modern' vehicle. Chassis No.89 thus benefitted from an uprated L48 Chevrolet V8 engine from a Camaro Super Sport, replacing the original 327 from the factory. Changes to the brakes, steering and transmission followed.

The original period plastic interior was replaced with burr walnut centre console and fascia panels. Connolly's burgundy leather upholstery and trim and black Wilton wool carpets completed the comfortable interior, making Chassis No.89 amongst the most luxurious and best handling Gordon Keeble motorcars in existence. For the journey up to the Isle of Skye on a bleak October day, Graham Robertson was glad of the upgrades.

A typical dreich hung over the lowlands, turning into a fine smirr, drifting drizzle, on the approach to Glasgow. If the rain became stoating, so hard it was bouncing off the road, it was likely the day would become pure drookit. He smiled as he played with these uniquely Scottish words for cold, wet, and gloomy weather in his mind. There were certainly many of them, seldom heard south of the border and definitely not in Hampshire.

Something was unsettling him about the possible rediscovery of Bernd Rosemeyer's Horch 853 Coupé. A malevolent feeling that he couldn't shake off yet couldn't explain either. In some ways it was completely irrational. A car in and of itself was an inanimate object, incapable of inducing fear into anyone. Only in the hands of a person could it become something to be feared, loathed, or loved. People breathed life into a car. Both the benign and the malevolent.

Nevertheless, like that eerie period of history between the fall of Rome and the enlightenment of the Renaissance, the cultural, economic and intellectual decline many often associated with the Dark Ages, so the extensive gap in the history of the Horch 853 Stromlinien Sports Coupé presented an obscure and troublesome scene. Yet, just as the fascinating secrets of that historical epoch were slowly being revealed with the discovery of the Staffordshire Hoard, what tumultuous events had Manuela herself witnessed? Which fiendish characters had grasped the wheel in white-knuckled hands? Just how had it escaped the ravages of wartime Germany and where had it been in subsequent years? Robertson suspected the journey of discovery would reveal a good many closeted skeletons. For the first time, he was uncertain now whether he wished to continue the search or not.

With an overnight stop in Carlisle, it was full dark when the four round, five-inch Lucas headlights finally dimmed outside *Talisker House* on Skye's wild west coast. The weather had been ragged all across the western coastline. At one point, driving through sleet in Glen Shiel, Robertson wondered whether he would be able to make the crossing from the mainland at all. It was unlikely that the buffeting winds would have actually blown him off Skye Bridge, but the Gordon Keeble didn't know that and her lightweight, Giorgetto Giugiaro designed fibreglass body certainly felt every gust.

It was with some relief though when he finally silenced the car after a two-day journey of over 600miles from the south coast. At seventy years of age, he was getting too old for this kind of excursion now. He should have brought Charlie with him to share the driving. The Gordon Keeble was most definitely a comfortable and capable workhorse. He didn't want to risk the Lagonda on such an arduous journey, not until he had fettled with the engine a little more. Robertson was too old to start making repairs at the roadside and suspected most RAC types might have never even heard of a Lagonda, let alone seen one in the steel.

He hobbled over to the front gate. Reminding his hips and knees how they should function. A stiff breeze was blowing in from the bay, unseen half a mile away, but still strong even with a screen of mature trees. Moving through the garden to the house provided shelter. There was a substantial cast iron knocker and a monastery flap in a solid wooden door that seemed to pre-date the house by several centuries. He knocked twice. Slowly. The knocker was slightly corroded and stiff to move. What it lacked in speed, it more than made up for with resonance.

He expected the flap to open and a gnarled old crow to appear. Appley cheeked. All pointed chin and hooked nose with half a tooth in gums that had receded to bone. Instead, the door opened to reveal a honey-tinged glow and a pleasing young woman of diminutive stature, freckled phizog and messy waves the colour of winter bracken piled up loosely on her crown. She had a worried look in her blue eyes, an inviting smile curled upon her lips and flour upon her breast.

"Can ah help yers?" she asked sweetly. A strong Scottish accent evident in her inflection. Glasgow perhaps or Lanarkshire.

"I hope so." He breathed. "I'm here to see Mr Sutherland. Mr Iain Sutherland?"

"Och, bring yerself in, yer wee sawsedge." She beckoned, stepping back. "It's pure Baltic oot here."

He stepped inside and immediately smelt the inviting warmth of fresh baking from the kitchen.

"I'm sorry it's so late. It took me a wee while to get up here."

"Aye, ah bet it ded." She cooed, closing the wooden door with a strength that belied her slender frame. "Get yerself by the fire. ah'll get Iain doon."

Showing him into the sitting room, the woman disappeared to fetch her husband. Robertson could hear distant childish giggles from the kitchen when she returned, followed by mock indignation over some floury shenanigans. Footsteps could be heard coming down the stairs from the drawing room above. The door opened, and Iain Sutherland appeared. He was tall, mid-thirties, casually dressed. A fisherman's beard and moustache, chunky V-neck jumper and open-neck shirt. Robertson vaguely recognised seeing someone like him at the Revival, dressed in hunting tweeds and flat cap. Though with so many people there it was impossible to say for sure.

"Mr Robertson?" He stepped forward, offering his bear like paw. "It's good of you to come up all this way. I would have happily picked you up from…"

"Ah, no need." He waved down. "It gave me an opportunity to take my old car for a proper good run. Stretch her legs for a wee while."

"I've just phoned my brother. Craig lives at the top of the island. He'll join us in about an hour. Can I offer you a drink?"

"Aye, a cup of tea would be nice, thank you."

"Is that tea, ah heard?" came the woman's pleasing patter as she entered with a tray of shortbread, fresh from the oven. "ah'll mek up a wee pot. These the bairns fust batch."

"Thank you, Emma. They smell good." Iain gave her a kiss on the cheek, clearly besotted with his wife. It was a pleasant domestic scene.

"They're still het, but help yerself, Mr Robertson. Please."

"Thank you. That's very kind of you."

"Can we make up a room for our guest, Em?" Iain asked. "The Old Inn and Taigh Ailean will be closed up now."

"Aye, no bother." She smiled, pleased to play hostess and skipping out before Robertson could protest.

"I must admit, I was a little surprised by your request." Robertson began, watching Iain juggle a shortbread between his fingers to cool it down. "I've personally been looking for this particular car for nearly thirty years."

"Oh?"

"Aye, it's a rare one." Robertson nodded, wondering just how much Iain knew. "What can you tell me about it?"

"Not a great deal, I'm afraid. "Grandad dinnae tell us much about it and as kids we dinnae think to ask."

"What was your grandad's name?"

"Andrew. Andrew Sutherland. He was well into his eighties when we were bairns."

"And your grandmother?"

"Hazel. She was from Yorkshire. She was quite a bit younger than him, but he still had lead in his pen." He laughed.

"Aye, well." Robertson smiled, reaching for a shortbread finger. "What do you know of your grandad?"

"Again, not a whole lot. He dinnae talk much. At least not to us bairns."

Robertson nodded. Now was not the time to enlighten him on his grandfather's illustrious racing pedigree, even less so his Nazi affiliations. Convicted in absentia at Nuremberg, he would not have been welcomed back to the Highlands if it had been made widely known. Indeed, given such a damning reputation preceding him, Robertson was shocked that he had come back at all.

"We only knew about it after Da died really. Never even saw it before then. He mentioned it in his will. Said it meant a great deal to him and we should keep it in the family." Iain frowned as he recollected the passage of the last will and testament that dealt with the bequest. "He also mentioned something about keeping its existence secret. No idea why. He never went into any more detail."

"That is mysterious." Robertson observed. The involuntary shudder brought to the fore his earlier misgivings. It was like someone had walked over his grave, even though he was far from dead yet. "Have you seen it?"

"Not recently." Iain shook his head. "It's a fair distance away, you see. Not exactly on our local commute. It was only visiting the Revival last month that got Craig and I thinking about it. She won't go under the hammer for any price, but we were wondering whether it would be worth some kind of restoration. At least bring her back into working condition again."

"Much would depend on what condition she is in at present."

Iain grimaced. Either he knew how bad she was or had no idea how much she might have deteriorated. This was not encouraging news.

"There's a replica at Audi's headquarters in Germany." Robertson explained reassuringly. "Might be the closest thing there is to a comparison. Being a bespoke coach built work, these things are often one-of-a-kind."

"Expensive then."

"Invariably." Robertson agreed. "All is very seldom lost though. There is much that can be salvaged and what can't is often fabricable. It all depends how much restoration you require. Everything from a running chassis to a concourse, nut and bolt rebuild. Let me see if I can visit the replica. Then I can compare it to what we have left of the original. The factory build sheets might provide some useful reference too if Audi still has them. Or we can take measurements from the replica and almost reverse engineer it back again. It will take some time though and it won't be cheap."

"Time is nae a problem. The cost could be. How much do you charge?"

"Well, we can get into that later." He smiled. "But my costs would be relatively insignificant compared to the possibilities ahead. It's the craft skills that'll eat up the budget."

Iain took a bite of the shortbread and looked out to sea, musing the possibilities in his head. The rain was falling heavily again now, turning to sleet. Leaves were rustling on the boughs, unseen in the darkness but soon to be blown off completely in the unrelenting storm. Restoration was possible, but secrecy might be another matter entirely. The more people that needed to become involved in the project the less likely discretion could be maintained. The nagging question kept returning to him though. He knew it would be playing on Craig's mind even more. Why did the existence of the car need to be kept a secret in the first place?

CHAPTER THIRTEEN
ITALIAN LIBYA, 1940

Despite the ceiling fan spinning above him, Sutherland's body was sheathed in a layer of sweat. This wasn't the sweat of anxiety that accompanied another death-defying Grand Prix race. Nor did it have anything to with the nubile maiden by his side. Her naked back glistened with a glassy shimmer, droplets of perspiration running down the crease of her spine. She had been asleep for an hour or more now. Sutherland had remained awake, watching her drift off to begin with, after their amorous athletics. Then he rolled onto his back and watched the wooden blades of the fan rotate around their cast iron motor housing.

The sweat was simply down to the heat. Even in May, Italian Libya was a sultry place to be. It had been impossible to make the trip to Australia for the New Year's Day South Australian Hundred and the São Paulo Grand Prix was being contested on the same day as the Tripoli event. Not that the Silver Arrows were officially contesting anything anymore, other than air superiority and production volumes. The Tripoli Grand Prix would be the last race where a German car would be seen. Unless he had a drive for the Targa Florio at the end of the month, it looked set to be his very last Grand Prix too.

Sutherland had ignored the Foreign Office's advice to return home. He knew they would probably think he was a collaborator now. He had to find a way of convincing them otherwise. Perhaps the sweat was also because of that. He would be looked upon as an enemy at home, regarded with suspicion in Germany. Awkward.

The Mellaha Lake racetrack in Italian Libya was an 8.1mile course situated in a salt basin between Tripoli, Suq al Jum'ah and Tajura around the Mellaha Air Base. A distinctive, brilliant white concrete tower pavilion with its impressive state-of-the-art score board soared above the home straight. The grandstand opposite could hold up to ten thousand spectators. Coupled with starting lights and a host of other amenities it made the Tripoli Grand Prix a significant rival to the best of the continental European circuits.

The participants were treated like royalty, staying in luxury at the Hotel Uaddan with its casino and dinner theatre, before being entertained by Marshal of the Air Force and Governor-General Italo Balbo at his sprawling palace. Dominated by the might of German motorsport machinery, Auto Union had claimed a single victory in 1936, with the silver stars of Mercedes-Benz winning all the rest.

Yet for what would be the final Tripoli Grand Prix event on the 12th of May 1940, Andrew Sutherland was the sole representative of the Auto Union marque. Mercedes-Benz had other priorities and with only the factory Alfa Romeo and Maserati teams along with some independents in attendance, Giuseppe Farina looked to be the favourite for victory in his beautiful Alfa Romeo 158.

Sutherland's Auto Union Typ D had been emasculated with its under-developed eight-cylinder engine and never looked competitive, even though it was considerably easier to handle than the full-blooded sixteen-cylinder Typ C. The car simply lacked the punch needed to claim one final victory for the racing department's Horch works in Zwickau and Sutherland knew it. This was a token gesture, a swansong. An early retirement.

He looked across at his latest muse. Her long dark hair clung to her glistening shoulders. Her ribs gently rising and falling with each warm breath. The curve of her back, dipping beneath the sheets and narrowing at her waist, resembled the flawless Carrara marble favoured by Michelangelo in carving the incredible Pietà inside St Peter's Basilica. Sutherland had seen it once on a visit to Rome.

Considered a masterpiece of Renaissance sculpture, the youthful face of the Madonna, cradling Jesus's corpse in her arms, was said to symbolise her incorruptible purity. According to the sculptor, chaste women remained fresh and youthful much more than those who were not. How much more so would this be in the case of the Virgin who had not experienced the most lascivious desire that might have corrupted her body.

Sutherland considered Michelangelo's description to be a curiously specious explanation. As far as he could recall, scriptural testimony documented that the Virgin Mary also became the mother of James, Joseph, Simon, and Judas, as well as at least two daughters. None of them were divinely conceived. Then again, since when had the devout ever referenced the Bible properly? Religion had never really made much sense to him. This was probably why he was always getting into trouble during services at school. In any event, whatever incorruptible purity Sutherland's present companion might once have exhibited, he was fairly sure it had been irrevocably corrupted now.

Rousing himself slowly so as not to wake her, he swung his legs down onto the cool tiled floor. Standing up, he pulled on some trousers and made his way to the balcony. The architect Florestano di Fausto had employed a Neo-Moresco style for what was the grandest hotel in Tripoli. Characterised by a long row of Moorish arches providing shade for each balcony, Sutherland's room overlooked the swimming pool below. One of fifteen magnificent works Di Fausto had commissioned for the city, given free reign by Balbo to glorify the colonial capital.

Italy hadn't yet entered the war, but just as in 1938, Sutherland could sense which way the wind would blow. On another balcony in another capital city, he considered the possibilities. Recently, in a lavish ceremony in the presence of Il Duce, the great Arch of the Philaeni near Ra's Lanuf had been inaugurated, marking the border between Tripolitania and Cyrenaica along the newly built Via Balbia. It was a classic monument to Fascist ideals. With Mussolini at the helm of Italian government, even out here Sutherland knew there would be no escaping the war.

Common sense may have perhaps recommended his return to Britain, join up and defend the Maginot Line with the rest of the British Expeditionary Force. In a shooting war though, Sutherland knew there was often a good to firm chance of being killed before accomplishing anything moderately useful. A stray bullet, grenade shrapnel, a bayonet. Maybe he would be judged a coward. In any case, Sutherland wanted to fight another way. He didn't want to be cannon fodder. Bludgeoning the beast from the outside would be a long and bloody struggle. His father had enough tales of that ilk to convince him of its futility. Even with the support of the French and Belgian armies, it would be another brutal brawl against the Hun.

After all, he had seen the industrial might of Germany himself, toured the

Zwickau factory, watched Porsche at work designing tanks and armoured cars. When the Germans put their mind to something, their determination could not be won over by a plucky warrior spirit alone. Just ask anyone who had been at Donington Park, not just in 1937, but again in 1938 too. Had the teams not been recalled from the Coppice Farm buildings on the eve of the 1939 event, it would almost certainly have been total annihilation once again.

Standing on the balcony, letting the breeze cool him off a little, Sutherland didn't know that in the early hours of that very morning the German invasion of France and the Low Countries had already commenced. The French Seventh Army had collided with the German 9th Panzer Division and the advance of the 25th Motorised Division had been stopped by German infantry and tanks. Ju-87s were dive-bombing them from the air. By noon, German glider troops would go onto capture Fort Eben-Emael and force the Belgians to retreat from Antwerp before the French First Army had time to arrive and dig in.

The XIX Panzer Corps would surprise the French Second Army with a far larger force than they had expected and while 135 audacious RAF bombers tasked with raiding northern Belgium to delay the German advance were being whittled down to just 72 planes, some 1,000 Luftwaffe aircraft were bombing the French at Sedan. On the eve of the Tripoli Grand Prix, the Phoney War had suddenly and decisively come to an end. The Battle of France had begun.

Looking down onto the swimming pool, all Andrew Sutherland knew was that he needed to find another way. There was a little Adler Sutherland had noticed in the paddock the day before. Wandering around just after lunch, he found it again. He examined the interesting little car for a moment, quietly appreciative of the elegant coachwork from Berlin's Ambi-Budd press works. He had chosen this car specifically. There was something unique about it. It might be a means of getting a message out.

The Adler Trumpf Sport Cabriolet was evidently the automotive plaything for some mid-ranking Nazi officer in Italian Libya. Presumably to woo a rather more long-limbed and glamorous plaything of Italian or North African origins. In any event, whether it would succeed now it had been curiously stripped of its distinctive badge that stretched across the grille, Sutherland would never find out. The stylised Art Deco eagle, with the name of the manufacturer inscribed vertically upon its chest, was further defaced with a single word, crudely engraved horizontally across each outstretched wing.

The badge itself found its way to the Hotel Chatham on Rue Danou in the 2nd arrondissement of Paris. Jacques Holzschuh stored the badge safely inside a nickel-plated steel champagne bucket for a few days before he was able to forward the package onto the Foreign Office in London. It was safe there. No one was drinking champagne anymore. Shortly afterwards the bucket disappeared from the shelves of the kitchen storeroom and Holzschuh and his wife left Paris forever.

A few days later, the mysterious parcel arrived at Room 47. This was not some partitioned off, squalid little hovel in the Main Building of the Palace of Whitehall on King Charles Street though. Instead, it was a rather maudlin and monstrous mansion in the county of Buckinghamshire, built in a mixture of Victorian Gothic, Tudor, and Dutch baroque styles. Here, at his desk, relocated from Room 40 on the first floor of The Admiralty's Ripley Building, to the ground floor of Bletchley Park, Commander Alexander Denniston picked up the eagle and held it up to the window to better examine the scratches.

In the June sunlight, a Gaelic word scratched onto the surface could just be made out: Èirean. Putting the two words on the badge together, Adler Èirean, a cold chill rippled down his spine. Coupled with the sharp abdominal pain he was feeling because of a bladder stone, he cried out as he fell back into the chair. One of Dilly's Fillies, on hearing the cry, came rushing in to see the Commander clutching his stomach, sweat beading from his forehead as he gasped for breath through the pain and stooped to pick up the fallen object.

"What is it, sir?" she asked, panic-stricken.

"Eagle Rising." He winced. "Eagle. Rising."

CHAPTER FOURTEEN
ENGLAND, 2018

Humming neon stretched out over the dark alley. As indifferent as the frigid February weather to the events that were unfolding in the flat above. The sharp hiss of violence began, then ended abruptly. Flashes of light bloomed in the windows.

Two assassins stared down at two bodies through the yellow lenses of their tactical face masks. The dying man breathed out a final frothy mixture of blood and saliva onto the floorboards. Near the sofa, a woman lay sprawled on the floor, her party clothes torn ragged by bullets. Head tilted back against the cabinet. Eyes closed in deathly slumber.

A phone on the cabinet at her head began to vibrate as a voice message came through. One of the hitmen stepped forward, leaning over the body of the bloody corpse. He tapped the message with the gloved finger of his hand.

"Guys, where are you?" came the voice of a young woman. "Michelle is about to get on stage. Get here quick! Do you have any idea how hard it is to get a table at The Ministry?"

They looked at each other from behind their masks, each sensing the other's thoughts. Replacing the ammunition clips on their submachine guns, they both removed the sound suppressors from the end of the barrels. For the next part, they needed to make some noise.

It was time to get paid. Time for Target Alpha.

CHAPTER FIFTEEN

Fast, rhythmic beat of the club mixed with the pounding of dancers' feet on the floor. The supporting DJ had expertly tapped into their rhythm, using the baseline to control their hips, bringing the pace up little by little. Song by song. Until he was hitting 128 beats per minute. The tempo which synergised most with a dancer's heart rate. The crowd was ready for the main event. The star act. Back from the beaches of Thailand. Lights. Lasers. Smoke.

A young woman waited at a table to the side of the dancefloor. Waiting for friends that would never come. She had left a message. Where were they? Her patience was turning to worry. Those around her passed her by. The reason for their excitement was waiting back stage.

Michelle was deep in discussion with a woman in the dark, its meaning unknown. The woman was taller, with striking auburn hair and lizard green eyes. Then, the discussion was over, she turned and walked away. Flashes of red from the soles of her heels. Was she friendly? Perhaps. Fiendish? Maybe. Michelle pondered. Regardless, the show must go on. Michelle Barratt, Micky B, a shining star was to return to the London stage where it had all begun.

Above that same stage, he waited in the lighting gantries. Like a sentinel. Watching. He was biding his time. A time that would soon arrive. Micky B approached the mixing decks, about to relive her first glory in the club that launched her star.

"Are you ready London!" she cried.

The crowd cheered wildly in response. Their heroine was here. The legend. They were ready. Ready to dance. Lose themselves in the music. The moment. Be transported to another world. Instead, there would be pain. There would be fear. There would be panic. And there would be death.

Three masked men walked calmly in. Weapon lamps obscured the guns from weekend revellers. From across the floor, the advanced aiming lasers projected a thin green beam to where she sat at the table. Hidden by the light show all around.

The sentinel had seen it. He had been waiting for it. The three intruders had finally met their match. Timed almost perfectly to the baseline, two bullets left the barrel. A movement. Two, more. A final shuffle. Two. With a gun firing wildly in the air, confusion took over as the crowd began to flee. Breaking glass and sparking metal. Flames from the barrel. Bodies hitting the floor. One. Then two. Then three.

Terrified by what she had witnessed, the young woman stumbled out alone. Shock taking over. In a daze she staggered to the doors. Jostled and bruised by the crowd, she lurched outside into the night. Then in a panic she ran. Her destination unknown. Anywhere. It didn't matter. As long as it was far away.

Then, with a crack, the heel of her shoe broke. She fell. Lying on the cold stone of London cobbles, she passed out. Only to be found by the one who watched.

CHAPTER SIXTEEN

"Hey! Greg, I'm all finished here. Wake up." Her voice brought him back round.

"So, whit's the prognosis, Jo?" he grunted, coming round from his doze. "Will ah live?"

"That's Doctor Harris to you, and you'll be fine." She placed the forceps in the kidney dish with the cotton swab and moved it to one side. "Anyway, what happened? You're not on a job are you?"

"A few wee dobbers decided tae start suhin'." He murmured. His strong Scottish accent a contrast with the doctor's precise pronunciation.

"Now, let me guess. You were touching up one of their wives?" she asked, removing the bloodied examination gloves.

"She had a certain magnetism."

"Did she now?"

"Attractive from the back, repellent from the front. Ah jist tawd the truth."

"I should have known." She rolled her eyes. Spinning on the stool, she placed the waste in the biohazard bin.

"Whit d'yer mean?" he asked innocently, sitting up on the examination table.

"Well, your type isn't known for being diplomatic."

"Whit's ma type?" he asked with a playful glimmer in his eye.

"You know what I mean."

"Yer probably right, ah s'pose." He sighed, reaching for his shirt. "At the end of the day it's a job. Still, ah get tae choose who tae protect these days."

"Who was it this time?" she asked, helping him put the injured arm through the sleeve.

"Ma last one." He smiled. "ah'm due a break. Then ah'm heading back tae the cabin for a wee while."

"Early retirement?"

He shook his head, looking down to fasten up the buttons. "Naw quite. Ah have one or two things lined up."

A half-smile tipped up the corner of her mouth. "Didn't picture you as the heroic kind."

"Depends on whit yer've heard." He looked up with a curious frown.

"I've seen your rig remember. The Christmas Day cliff rescue at Botallack last year. That was you wasn't it?"

"Possibly."

"In that case you should stop getting your arse kicked. You've got valuable skills."

"Duly noted."

"So, what did the others look like?" she handed him the dark, quarter zip sweatshirt he had worn over the top. A ragged hole torn in the arm, just below the shoulder. Scorched fibres around it.

"Well, ah wis the only one tae walk oot on ma own two feet."

"That's not answering the question." She frowned, "Victory doesn't usually come with a gunshot wound."

"It's jist a wee graze. Totally different." He replied, looking behind her to the television screen silently running in the surgery.

"Is it?" she turned to see what he was looking at. "Isn't this horrible?"

The rolling news broadcast was covering reports of a nightclub shooting nearby. Three dead, a dozen injured, mostly from broken glass and ceiling tiles.

"Aye, it's naw ideal." He sighed.

"Bloody Russian gangsters in a nightclub. They're so blasé about killing in their own country, they feel it's perfectly acceptable to do the same over here. Makes me so angry."

"They wis nae Russian." He replied quickly, then instantly regretted it.

"Wasn't Mikhail Sokolov's daughter supposed to be there?" she asked. "That's what they're saying. Some kind of botched mobster hit."

"Aye, soonds like it could have been." He said, hoping she wouldn't notice his slip up. Blame the anaesthetic.

"Why would you think they weren't Russian?" she asked swivelling back. Her curiosity hardened into a frown. Her eyes narrowed. She looked at the arm she had bandaged.

Hamilton looked at her, looked at the ceiling. At the cabinet. Zipped up his sweatshirt "D'yer have any coffee in this place?"

"I think you should probably head home." She said firmly. "You interrupted my boxset binging. And you really need to get out of that life." She pointed to the news. "Doctor's orders."

"Ah'll tek it intae consideration." He winced, scratching his stubble.

"Take it easy for a couple of days. Let that arm heal."

"Aye, ah'll try." He nodded, moving to the door.

"One more thing." Hamilton looked across at her, half outside the door, a question on his face. "Next time you need a late night patch up off the books, I'm charging double."

"Yer can charge whitever yer want, Doc. Disnae mean ah'm gonna pay yers." he smiled.

"Go home!" she cried, throwing a box of gloves at the door.

He slipped out before the box struck him, letting it strike the door and fall harmlessly to the floor instead.

Back outside, he looked at his watch. Strapped to his right wrist. Unusual for a dextromanual he was told. Made him out to be a lefty. Moderately useful information. In any case it was late. Time to get back to the apartment. Stepping outside into the chilly London night, he felt a vibration against his leg. He took out his phone. An incoming call. Number withheld. Problem?

"Hey Greg." Came a familiar voice. "What's up?"

"Yer the one calling, Micky. Yer tell me?"

He heard a heavy sigh. "Something's come up."

"It's been a wee while."

"I've been out the game for a bit."

"Yer been oot the country."

"You still know the drill?"

"Aye."

"So, get yourself to *Peppermint* and meet in our usual booth. You've got thirty minutes. Don't be late again."

The line went dead. He sighed. No taking it easy just yet. Home, change of shirt, smart trousers, shiny shoes and across to Soho. Thirty minutes would be pushing it.

CHAPTER SEVENTEEN

Typical for a weekend, the clubs were abuzz with lights, music and partying. News of the nightclub shooting was just getting round, but the mood didn't seem to have been affected. Extra police were present, some of them armed. A few roads around the scene blocked off with tape and cars with flashing lights. Otherwise, London life carried on. Despite the February chill.

Peppermint was perfect for rich posers. Being an upscale venue, it attracted exactly the kind of entitled type Gregor Hamilton disliked the most. Moving down the length of the velvet ropes on the pavement, he walked straight up to the doorman at the entrance. Ignoring the queue. Whispering in his ear, the man nodded and showed him in. This annoyed the pneumatic lipped, orange ladies teetering on needle thin heels immensely. Ideal. Dressed as they were in pink-sashed leopard print mini dresses, one of them sporting a ragged veil and an 'L' plate, it was unlikely the doormen would let them in anyway. Peppermint advertised itself as a high-end establishment. Apparently.

"Chandrika?" he cried.

Just inside the door, the woman directly in front of him smiled seductively. Her Asian complexion beheld an incredible glow. Eyes framed with kohl and glitter and tipped wings. Lips shimmering with burnt umber and promise. Long, raven hair tousled loosely over one eye. Chandrika was very high-end. Positively premium.

"Greg! I was just leaving and now *you* show up."

"Am busy the night, lass." He shrugged, already regretting his greeting.

"Ah, come on! You've got a couple of minutes for an old friend." She turned and led him inside the club. The frills of her ruffle skirt glowed with a vivid intensity matched only by the music.

"Naw the night. Am here on business."

"Mmm, he looks fun." He heard someone purr nearby as he walked past.

"Nah, babe. That's a copper for sure."

"Dis yer Mam ken yer here, Chandy?" Hamilton called after her.

"Screw that bitch! What's she gonna do? Pack me off to India again?" she turned and smiled. "And you're not gonna tell her. You hate her more than me."

Hamilton couldn't answer that. There was some truth in it. The kidnapping. An arranged marriage thwarted. Family honour at stake. All very messy.

"Come on, I'll show you the backdoor." She winked, touching the tip of her tongue to Cupid's bow.

The woman on the stage was down to her underwear but seemed to know how to work the pole with athletic aplomb. Good muscle structure. Toned, yet feminine.

"Hey! Eyes on me!" Chandrika cried.

"Whit?"

"Stop perving on the dancers!"

"Yer cannae blame me." He shrugged. He was a man after all.

"She's pretty hot!" she shouted over the music. "I'll give you that. But she's ancient."

"How auld?"

"She's like thirty. You could do better."

Hamilton frowned. He would be hitting forty-one in the autumn.

"You need something young. Fresh. Forbidden. What do you think?"

"Ah dinnae have time for this, Chandy!"

Chandrika turned around and began to dance closer to him, interlacing her fingers at the back of his neck.

"Mother would have kittens if she knew I was here. She'd have a whole litter if she knew it was with you."

"Am naw wi yer."

"You could be." She said in his ear, pressing her body against his. "Come on."

"Seriously, Chandy!" he shook his head firmly, giving her an uncompromising look as he gently removed her hands. "Ah have stuff tae do."

"Damn it!" she cried with a disappointed smile, running a finger down his stubbled jaw line. "Another time then. Go do your stuff!" she tapped the tip of his nose and was gone.

Letting her dance on ahead, becoming absorbed by the crowd, Hamilton made for the private booth to one side. Micky B was sitting alone on one of the low, button-back corner sofas. White cocktail dress and sun-kissed skin. Waiting. A woman on a nearby barstool momentarily caught his eye. Leather trousers, cropped top exposing a slender back and toned midriff, shimmering dark red hair.

"Whit's up, Micky?" he called out as he ascended the two illuminated steps. "Yer gaw me oot here on short notice in the middle o' the night. Am ah gonnae get an explanation now?"

"Just get your arse over here, Greg." She hollered back.

"We'en gaw this whole booth tae ourselves." He observed. The music was less intrusive as he took the space next to her, stretching both arms across the back of the sofa. "That could nae have been cheap. Means corporate work."

"Stop fishing, Greg. Just sit down." She looked shaken, anxious, tense. Not her usual phlegmatic form.

"Whit's occurring?" he frowned, picking up on her unsettled vibe.

"You're on time for once. Don't spoil my mood." She looked up and waved away the waitress who came to take an order.

Hamilton watched her leave and noticed the girl at the bar pressing her ear. A dead giveaway that she was on a call with someone. Everybody did that. He never understood why. It was the easiest mark to make and immediately blew their cover.

"He's here." The woman at the bar murmured. "Of course…I will keep my eyes on him, don't worry…And if he says no?... How far should I go?... Of course, Madam."

"This be'er naw be another protection detail." Hamilton cried.

"First fix in eighteen months." She shrugged, "I get what I get."

"Ah'm naw doin' another babysitting job for some princess wi daddy issues."

"Do you want to see this or not?"

"Fine."

Micky handed him a tablet. The screen showed a picture of a young woman, gave her name and date of birth. A few brief details followed. He recognised her face immediately. He had already seen it once that night.

"A runaway? Whit did ah jist say, Micky? She's a wee bairn."

"This one is personal." Micky said, looking increasingly unsettled. "Tonight, a group of hitmen tried to kill her at my concert at The Ministry." Hamilton looked at her, a frown on his face. "It was chaos. No one knows what happened. I gave my statement to the police, then got the call from the client and told to bring you in. All three hitmen were killed but the girl just disappeared."

"Who took oot the hit squad?" he probed.

"No one knows, but they were top drawer whoever they were."

"Oh aye?" he asked, quietly pleased.

"Three double-taps, in the dark, from high level. Two took them in the head. Another in the chest. No one else was killed. One of the gunmen only sprayed bullets in the air as he was going down. That's some first-class army training."

"Soonds more like special forces." He mused.

"Yeah, probably, but my guess is that's why the client wants her brought in."

"This is a Code Brown." He said, handing her back the device. "Pure fan clogger."

"Right up your alley, then."

"Up yers, more like." He looked down at the tablet. "Marya Sokolova." He read the name again. "Oligarch's daughter. How did they even get in? She should have had an army of minders wi her."

"No idea. Once the gun started firing, I was outta there. But that's my point. My guess, someone paid them off to take a break or something so they could do a number on her."

"Turf war?"

"Possibly." She nodded. "They were dressed for business, Greg."

"Ah ken." He whispered to himself. "Any IDs on 'em?" Wishful thinking.

She shook her head. "The police have nothing on them yet, but their kit all looked military grade. HKs, Tac Lasers, SRUs."

"SRU helmets are only good for six mil ball bearings coming at yer at 150metres a second." He said. They were expensive and looked impressive, especially equipped with yellow lenses, but Hamilton knew the full-face Kevlar tactical helmets were no good against 7.62mm armour-piercing rounds fired from fifty metres away with a velocity of 850m/s. That's exactly why he had chosen his loadout personally. "It's Airsoft gear. Naw the real deal."

"Even so…" she cursed as a thought crossed her mind. She covered her mouth with her hand. "Whoever took them out must have been sat right above me somewhere. In the lighting gantries."

"Cosy." He chuckled. "Ah s'pose that means they knew whit wis gonnae go doon." He reasoned. "Three guys get tae stroll in wi HV rounds and laser targeting, they've gaw the advantage. So, this guy had tae be awfy good."

"The best."

Hamilton tried not to smile.

"It wasn't you, was it?" she asked. A thought had just struck her.

"Whit meks yer think that?" he frowned.

"Never mind."

"Yer said this wis personal? Yer ken that never mixes well wi business."

"I know. I haven't seen her in years, but…" she hesitated. "Marya was a good kid."

"Back when yer were jist a humble music teacher, eh?" He smiled. The transition from a teaching post in the City of London's School for Girls to an internationally acclaimed dance festival DJ was nothing if not unusual. "Ah'm guessing Daddy's gonnae be getting the heavies over from the Motherland for this one."

"He'll be more concerned about preserving his image. This is a personal attack. Possibly an inside job. Maybe someone manoeuvring for position. Someone needs to be looking out for Marya."

Someone already is, he thought. "Anything else?" he asked.

"That's it."

"This looks fair jobbie tae me."

"What do you mean?"

"Who's paying us? Where do ah tek her once ah've found her? Why did someone wannae whack the daughter of a Russian oligarch and whit are they gonnae do tae anyone else who's after the lassie?" he shrugged. "There's a ton of unanswered questions here, Micky."

"There always is."

"Naw like this."

"You're not gonna take it?"

"No. Naw this one." He shook his head. "Too much heat and ah'm only one guy."

"That's exactly why they wanted you. You're the Carlsberg professional. You can reach places others can't."

"That's Heineken." He laughed.

"What was Carlsberg?"

"Probably the best beer in the world."

"Well, both taglines fit."

"Either way, they're gonnae need a bloody army tae take doon whoever's running this op." he shook his head. "Yers ever seen whit an antitank missile dis tae an armoured Bentley?"

She shook her head.

"Naw pretty. That's what Russians do. If they want yer dead, yer dead. These guys dinnae dick aboot."

"So, what *is* this all about?"

Hamilton thought about it for a moment. "I wid have expected someone of Sokolov's credentials tae have kidnap and ransom policies oot on members of his family."

"This was definitely a hit."

"Which meks me wonder." He frowned. "If he's hard up, he might have arranged for a kidnapping tae get the insurance money. The fact that he dinnae suggests a couple o' things. Either he loves his daughter too much tae put her through a mock kidnapping or he might have already cancelled the policy. Save a wee bit o' dosh."

"He's going through a messy divorce from Madam Sokolova."

"Aye, that wid do it."

"So, whoever these guys were might have known that?"

"Possibly. They might have ken they wis nae getting any insurance money at least. This seems more aboot sending a message. They're cutting him oot of something but winna make sure he winnae make any attempt tae exact revenge."

"Why not just take him out?"

"It disnae send the same message. Killing a family member puts yer on notice. Makes yer suffer the guilt for the rest o' yer life. Someone's clearing hoose somewhere. It's naw the Russian government. These days they prefer irradiation over good auld-fashioned liquidation."

"You're intrigued."

"Aye. Disnae mean ah'm gonna tek it on." He got up to leave. "Sorry, Micky. I'm oot. Glad tae see that you're okay though. Must have been a helluva scare."

"I'll be better when I'm back in Koh Phi Phi."

"The sun looks good on yer." he smiled, regarding the pleasing contrast between her bronzed skin and the bleached locks of her long blonde hair.

She didn't respond. Disappointed Hamilton wasn't about to help. He sighed and took his leave.

CHAPTER EIGHTEEN

Hamilton's apartment was situated in the Lion Mills Building in Bethnal Green. Set on the top floor of the former cotton mill, it overlooked Claredale Street at the rear and the courtyard garden where his faithful Land Rover, *Torridon* had been securely parked up for the weekend. Formerly the building had been used by Hamilton as his London base when he was in the Intelligence Service. Back then, it had been nothing but an empty shell slated for demolition. The council were only too happy to have it off their books and sold it for a pittance.

When developers came knocking years later they found an owner who wouldn't budge. Either they paid him off handsomely or the development was stalled. In the end they reached a compromise, allowing Hamilton to have the pick of the finished apartments in exchange for ownership of the rest of the property. He didn't need the sprawling site anyway, was being hounded by the council for lack of upkeep and sensed his time on the Albert Embankment was being wound up. It would be an investment.

Choosing a modest two-bedroom residence at the back of the complex, he rented it out as a holiday let whenever he didn't need it. The income more than covered the annual service charge and gave him another revenue stream into the bargain. His brother would have been proud. Now the London job was over, he needed to pack up, ready to head home in the morning.

Entering the L-shaped, open-plan living space, he locked the front door and crashed on the sofa, feeling his eyes close. Before making his way up the spiral staircase to the master suite on the mezzanine level in the eaves he needed to rest for a few moments at least. The last effects of the anaesthetic were just wearing off. He wanted to be asleep before they wore off completely and the body remembered what it felt like to have a 4.6mm DM11 solid steel high velocity round tear through subcutaneous tissue.

Maybe Jo was right. Perhaps he was getting too old for this. Technically that's not what she said. She had suggested he was better off plying his skills as the volunteer rescue worker he was back down in Cornwall. It was him that was feeling his age. Still, he had done a good deed tonight. Marya Sokolova was back home with her mother. Safe and well. Alive. Her instincts had been right. Maternal? Perhaps. Though she didn't seem the type.

Who was the woman watching him at Peppermint? More importantly, why? Was it to ensure he would take the job? Or to ensure he wouldn't? He was better off out of it. Whatever was going on would only end in tears. And blood. The appeal of returning to his quiet, semi-retired existence felt good once more. It didn't pay as well, but it was safer.

There was a light breeze in the room. None of the arched windows were open. A gentle weight pressed down next to him. Opening his eyes, he was conscious that there was a presence nearby.

"How did yer get in?" he asked quietly.

There was a pause. His voice seemed to have startled his guest.

"Better if yer had taken the dining chair." He looked across the living space to where the two chairs faced across the table from the bench beneath the window.

"I didn't want to come across as threatening." Her voice was smooth and soft. Molten chocolate poured in his ear.

"Naked on a bed o' petals would have achieved that objective."

"Is that what you would like?"

"Whit I wid like is tae ken whit yer doin' here."

He turned his head slowly to look at her. Sat nearest the window, her form was mostly in silhouette but a cool moonlight glow from the window opposite highlighted the orbs of her eyes. A pale glimmer in the darkness.

Strands of hair fell down the sides of her face from some kind of messy updo.

"Don't you want to know who I am first?"

"Naw particularly." He glanced at the watch on his wrist. Using the lume on the hands to read off the time. 02:37. He had slept longer than he thought. "Yer gaw a minute. Then ah'm off tae bed."

"I could join you."

"Ah'm tired."

"That's okay."

"Show yerself oot then." He muttered. His patience exhausted.

Getting up from the sofa, he moved to bathroom at the end of the hallway. Wary. Half-expecting a knife in the back. Right between the shoulder blades. There was a tingle already. After his ablutions he dried his hands and opened the door, quietly appreciating the soap. Not his usual kind. Too fragrant. Some Baylis & Harding concoction. The caretaker's choice no doubt. She was better at that sort of thing. Pleasant though. Civilised. Moisturising too.

The lights had been turned on. Looking back towards the living area, the sofa was empty. He checked the front door. It was still locked. Heading back into the living area, he looked to the right, around the wall. The mysterious woman had moved to a dining chair, turned it around to face the sofa and sat with one leg crossed over the other. She was wearing a short, pin-striped pencil skirt, black heels and a burgundy satin blouse almost the same shade as her hair.

"Whit d'yer want, lass?" he asked again, heaving a weary sigh. Ten years ago, he might have been up for a more animated discussion. Now he just wanted bed. Age. Or perhaps the effect of getting shot in the arm. Two shots actually. One rather more medicinal than the other.

"I heard some rumour that you were turning into a recluse. Pulling yourself out of the game."

"Ah'm naw oot the game. Ah'm jist picky."

"So, you're above honest work now?"

"Who are yer?"

"My name is Valentina. I'm Madam Sokolova's assistant."

"Yer a lot more than jist an assistant." He said, sinking back into the sofa. "I saw yer at Peppermint the night. Yer dinnae think a wee top and leather trews would get past me, did yer?"

"Yes, I was there."

"Why? Ah did the job she asked me tae do."

"Yes, you did. We're exceedingly grateful."

"So, whit then?"

"To see how you would react to the new job offer."

"Tae see if ah wis prepared tae play both sides, yer mean? Tonight, I save her daughter, tomorrow I hunt her doon."

"You're astute. I can see why Madam Sokolova recommended you."

"Aye well, ah dinnae play games."

"No, I see that."

"So, why are yer here again?"

"Now that we know you're not mercenary, Madam Sokolova would like to know whether you would be willing to accept a more permanent position. She believes she can trust you now."

"Ah'm naw babysitting."

"Not for Marya. For her."

"Same thing."

She slowly uncrossed her legs and leaned forward. The top two buttons of the blouse were unfastened, providing a clear view of something lacy beneath.

IN THE DEN OF WOLVES

The skirt had ridden up her thighs still further. It was an invitation to check whether the orchestra pit matched the balcony. Yes, he was a man, but right then he wasn't interested. He was tired. He focussed instead on her intense, green eyes.

"Is there some way we might be able to convince you?"

"Ah'm a professional, lass," he said, "And if them chebs are real, ah'm Mother Theresa."

"We can compensate you handsomely." She purred, slowly sliding the skirt further up her thighs. "And I can throw in some extra benefits for you as well. Would that make things more attractive?"

"Naw interested. Ah did whit ah was asked. No more. Now, as ah'm probably auld enough tae be yer Da, let an auld duffer get some kip, wid yer?" He lifted a foot onto his knee and began to unfasten his shoe. Conversation ended.

"Very well." She said, standing up. His response was unexpected. She was not accustomed to being turned down. It was confusing, but she wasn't put off yet. "Expect to hear from us again though."

"Ah doot it." He said, not bothering to look up as he removed the shoe and repeated the action with the other foot. Size eleven shoes and spiral steps didn't go together all that well.

Looking up as the sound of the door closed, to his relief Hamilton found the hallway empty again. He padded over and locked up once more before heading upstairs. The bed was directly beneath the skylight, under the pitched roof and exposed wooden trusses. A bathroom suite was at the far end behind the wall. The exposed beams were an attractive design feature during the day. Not ideal for late night bathroom visits. Sometimes the reason why he used the guest room downstairs instead, next to the toilet. Tonight, though he wanted to look at the stars. He undressed and slumped onto the bed.

The second man.

It was the second man that had grazed him. He had been lucky. The partygoers even luckier. Spraying the air with bullets as he fell. That could have ended very badly for everyone. The first man had been easy. They may have had the element of surprise over the venue. He had surprised them. Two bullets smashing through the face of his tactical mask had finished him instantly. Moving to the second man, he was the lead shooter. Time was limited.

The first bullet struck him in the chest. Left side. Enough to break his target lock and open him up to the second round, already on its way. Top of the sternum. Messier. It was as he was falling to his knees with the gun in the air that the dead man's trigger finger clamped down. The bullet that struck him was one of the last in the clip. The arc of fire lowering as he fell forward. It only winged him because he had shifted position for the third man. A clean kill. Two to the face. Then a searing hot pain to the right arm as the stray bullet ripped through his clothes. In other circumstances it might have killed him. Or missed him altogether. It wasn't his best work.

CHAPTER NINETEEN
SCOTLAND, 2018

"So, what do yer think?"

In the Drawing Room of *Talisker House*, on the Isle of Skye's west coast, Iain Sutherland was addressing his brother, sitting on the other side of the fireplace. Both men were installed in elegant wingback armchairs. Old bookcases and family ancestors adorned the handsome room, looking down on the pair as they sampled the latest creation.

A rich, amber meniscus coated the inside of the cut crystal Glencairn as the liquid was swirled around in the firelight. Shaped like a tulip bulb, the glass allowed the aromatics to circulate fluidly as volatile ethanol evaporated. Opening up an intensity of flavours. The taste of the whisky was rich, deep and exceptionally complex for such a young expression. A cask strength dram. The new bottling was the first of a Single Malt Special Release, recrafting a legend from the Carbost Distillery.

Rubbing his thumb against the tips of his fingers, he licked his lips. "It has that signature maritime smoke tae it still." Craig began. "Quite peppery, but distinctly unique." He took another sip and nodded. "It's good."

Iain seemed satisfied and sat back, swilling the whisky around and gazing at its warm, hypnotic lustre. This was high praise indeed.

"Ah'm gonnae gae tae bed now, boys." Came the warm, intimate voice of Emma Sutherland from the doorway. "Dinnae keep 'im up 'til the laverock,

Craig. He's droppin' the weans off tae school in the morrow."

"Aye, I won't be long, Em." He smiled. "I promise."

"You seid that last time, and ah found yers mekin' cheese toasties at two o'clock in th' morn." She said with mild reproof, a disapproving smile, and a hand on her hip. Softened by her feminine features, husky tones and knowing smile, her Central Scottish patter sounded suitably severe in comparison to the boys' milder Island lilt.

"We were hungert." Iain protested innocently.

"Aye, and cus o' no sleep, all that day yer were a pure crabbit get, so yer were."

"I was, it's true." Iain nodded, addressing his brother. "It'll be an earlier night the night, hen." Iain smiled, giving his wife a wink. "I'll be up in a wee moment."

Emma narrowed her eyes and gave her husband a stern look with a pout of her lips and a slow shake of her head. Iain kissed the air as Craig set the glass to one side and picked up the weekend's broadsheet, rustling in unison with the fire as he opened it to the article he had seen earlier. The corner of Emma's mouth curled upwards in a half smile before she disappeared up the stairs, satisfied her husband might be more sensible this time. She could never be mad with him for long.

"There's been another murder." Craig remarked, scanning the article again. "Mulhouse in France."

"That's not good news." Iain sighed with a frown. "Los Angeles last year. Now Mulhouse. Does that make it two?"

"Aye." Craig folded the newspaper over and nodded, retrieving his glass and taking another sip. "Why kill them?" he enquired. "They're only museum curators at the end of the day."

"If I was a cynic, I'd say they were trying to find something." Iain remarked.

"You *are* a cynic." Craig returned with a wry smile. He knew his brother well. "Yer dinnae think it's gaw anything tae do wi the old relic, do yer?"

"I cannae see how. Only you, me and Gray know she exists. If they're hitting museums I reckon they're after something in them. You know, perhaps whatever they keep in storage, not on display. Something they know actually exists and what it's worth."

"On opposite sides of the Atlantic?"

"Museum exhibits move around a bit."

"There's been no burglaries though, just the murders."

Iain shrugged. "Not yet. Perhaps they're just biding their time."

"Are yer thinking organised crime?"

"Nah. I'd say more of an avid collector. You know, like an art thief. Someone well-resourced and connected." Iain explained. "Criminal gangs tend to want to move stuff on fast. You can't offload something taken from a museum without people noticing. These guys are probably after something special, something very specific."

"The kind of specialist connoisseur that might appreciate high-end whisky."

"Oh aye, I imagine so." Iain nodded. "Could be one of our clients. Or potentially a new one."

Craig paused for a moment, shuddering. "It's just, the timing seems a wee bit convenient."

"What do you mean?"

"This only happened after we asked Graham for some advice on what tae do wi the relic."

"That was months ago. Last year in fact. October, remember?"

"Aye, and this Bob Jefferson was killed a month later in Los Angeles. Now a second museum curator has been found dead."

"I don't see that there's any connection at all."

"No? What if Gray asked them for advice? What if someone is actually after our relic?"

"Ah, yer bum is out the windae." Iain replied, claiming his brother's comment made no sense in humorously Scottish fashion. "There are far more valuable relics about than ours."

"Two murders, Iain?" The paper was finally placed on one side. Mutual fire gazing ensued for a moment or two more.

"Wi the kind of unique exhibits those kind of museums tend to have, and the figures involved for people that really want them, the collectors' black market always has the potential to lead to murder." Came Iain's straightforward reply eventually. "Craig, I'm not indifferent to it." He said in response to the disapproving look of his brother. "To be honest with you, I don't know what she'd be worth, but then neither does anyone else."

"Do yer naw think we should find oot?"

The thought was considered for a moment. Another split log was added. Whisky was sipped. Sparks from the glowing wood in the hearth intertwined with voluptuous flames like lovers, their amorous, all-consuming dance crackling with heat and passion.

"If granddad thought it was worth something, he would have told us. Dad would have told us. We're just looking after an old relic."

"For how long?"

"It's a family piece, Craig." A wry smile passed across Iain's lips. "We're not selling it for any price, yer know that." He pondered for a moment. "It might be a dusty old wreck, but it's our dusty old wreck, and if Graham thinks it's worth the effort, then we'll see about tidying it up a wee bit, that's all."

"I hope yer right."

"That's the benefit of being the older brother, mate. I'm always right."

"Damn it, man, yer were six minutes older…"

"Aye, and they made all the difference." Iain put in quickly. "When you were six minutes old, I was already twice your age remember."

Craig rolled his eyes and shook his head. "I'm jist worried."

"Think aboot it. What you're suggesting is pretty unlikely. What interest could anyone have in some forgotten old wreck locked away in a dark corner of Scotland?"

"Why does anyone ever come up tae Rosslyn Chapel?" Craig asked. Iain frowned, not understanding. "In the hopes they might just be the one tae find the Holy Grail."

The men stared at each other for a moment. Iain could see his brother was serious. His twin wasn't prone to fanciful ideas, but something in the news reports had clearly unsettled him. They fell silent again, listening to the familiar sounds of the sea and the house. Even half a mile away from the beach, the raging deep could still be heard. A distant low rumble as waves crashed against the base of the cliffs. The crackling fire was interspersed with the tick of a longcase clock out in the passage. Floorboards creaked upstairs as Emma Sutherland undressed for bed. Craig sighed and took another sip.

"This really is a good single malt." He affirmed once more.

They sat in silence, savouring their new offering while the wood crackled in the hearth and the westerly wind rattled the casements.

CHAPTER TWENTY
GERMANY, 2018

Architecturally, the collection of buildings on Audistrasse in the city of Zwickau presented a curious mix of styles. On one side, a soaring three-storey Art Nouveau mansion, warm ochre walls and terracotta tiles. On the other a concrete Cold War era modernist box, cantilevered out over its ground-floor entrance. This in turn connected to a stark, century old red brick factory complex to the rear via a modern glass and steel atrium.

Steel letters attached to the concrete projection above the pavement bore the words: AUGUST HORCH MUSUEM. August Horch had been born in Winningen in 1868 and trained as a blacksmith before receiving a technical degree in engineering. After establishing Horch & Cie in the Kingdom of Saxony, he fell out with the Board, left the company and setup a rival firm just down the road. However, unable to use his own name for the new enterprise, he opted for a Latin translation instead. The meaning of his surname approximated to the German verb 'to listen', so using the Latin translation of the verb, the new company became known as Audi.

The Museum itself had been closed for several hours, but after many letters and phone calls and months of negotiations, Graham Robertson had finally been allowed to wander around at his leisure once all the visitors had gone home. Herr Meyer, the curator, had an apartment in the top floor of the adjacent mansion. Still bearing all the period decorations and furniture of its original owner, Horch had the house constructed right next to the main entrance of his new factory.

Once he had finished his private studies, Robertson was to return to the mansion and notify Herr Meyer who would lock everything up again, ready for the morning visitors. There was one particular exhibit which Robertson was spending a great deal of time around. Located in a recreation of an Art Deco dealership, as part of a limited special exhibition, was a fish-silver Horch 853 Stromlinien Coupé. It was as faithful a copy of the legendary *Manuela* sports coupé as there was ever likely to be.

Berlin coachbuilders Erdmann & Rossi had clothed the chassis with an elegant and streamlined two-door body. Combining a gently curved, low roofline, pontoon-style fenders and grand ornamental chrome grille, the resulting creation impressed power, presence, and sporty performance.

Robertson was taking painstaking notes on every inch of the car, measuring, photographing, and jotting down scribbles for later examination. Though *Manuela* had allegedly been lost in the chaos of the Second World War, the example in the museum was every-inch a perfect reflection of her original, graceful form. If his colleagues were correct, comparing the details of the reproduction with the original might help to establish its authenticity.

As Robertson crouched down to inspect the unique wheel hub design, he caught the reflection of a figure behind him, emerging from the corner of the display. A flicker in the reflection indicated that they knew their presence had been detected and a voice emanated from it.

"Where is she?"

On his knees, Robertson remained rooted to the spot, only turning his head slowly.

"Where is the original?" The voice said. It belonged to a bear of a man, tall and broad, with swarthy skin, stubbly facial hair and dark, malevolent eyes.

"I don't know what you're talking about." Robertson replied shakily.

"Don't lie to me." The figure murmured. "You know where the original relic is. Tell me where I can find her."

"I'm telling you." Robertson stuttered, his old misgivings coming to the fore. Still kneeling by the front wheel. Feeling decidedly vulnerable. "I don't know what you're talking about."

"And yet I find you here!" the man glared at Robertson. "After closing time, studying *this* particular car." He stood perfectly still, menacingly so. "You and the others know where they all are."

Robertson felt a wave of dread wash over him. "The others?" he gasped. His eyes widened. He remembered Bob Jefferson's funeral in Los Angeles. Had they got to André too?

"The Holy Trinity, as you call it. The Mother, daughter and holy nymph. Tell me where they are hidden, and you will live." From his hand, one end of a coil of wire dropped down, weighted by a turned wooden handle.

Robertson's throat became dry as he looked at the fiendish weapon, struggling to breathe. The man took a step forward, taking up the handle in his other hand and drawing out the wire. With a sharp tug the line snapped taut.

"Wait!" Robertson said slowly. "I'll tell you what I know."

Robertson uttered his words carefully, clearly and without deviation. The lie he told had been pre-arranged over another conference call some months ago when the emergence of the relic had been made known. As much as he wanted to keep *Manuela's* existence secret, he knew word would eventually get out one way or another. Not only would there be considerable interest in her whereabouts, the three friends knew attention could be brought back to the other two vehicles they had spent years researching too. It was as if they came as a set. When he had finished, the man smiled smugly.

"This confirms exactly what the others told me. I found them both. Now, you are the only one left." He uttered coldly.

This confirmed Robertson's fears. Staggering to his feet, he concluded that Andre Langier must also have been murdered, and by the same man standing before him. His thoughts were with his slain friends when, in a single-bound, the man had looped the wire about his throat and hauled him back.

CHAPTER TWENTY-ONE

From any angle, the Kunsthalle was a stunning Neo-Renaissance structure. When it was completed, its prominent glass dome was a controversial embellishment, seen to be in competition with the dome of the Frauenkirche in Neumarkt nearby. The 'lemon squeezer' located in the Old Town district of Dresden. Overlooking Brühl's Terrace with views across the River Elbe beyond. The art gallery formed part of the Dresden State Art Collection and the University of Fine Arts. The Kunsthalle in the eastern wing of the Lipsius buildings was specifically reserved for viewing and discussing contemporary art.

Pole banners attached to the trees and lampposts on the Terrace advertised the evening lecture, to be given by the university's guest speaker for the night, Natalia Bielawska. Entitled, A PHOTOGRAPHER'S EYE: THE POWER OF STORIES, Natalia had been invited to discuss the stories behind some of her finest and most recent works. Approaching her thirties, she hardly considered herself an expert on the subject. There were a great many older, more experienced and more authoritative voices out there. However, the university was keen to encourage a younger, more diverse dynamic to enrol in their latest courses, and so they had encouraged Natalia to pay them a visit.

Natalia's grandfather had left the small town of Częstochowa in southern Poland to fight for the RAF during World War II. Settling down with an English Rose, he had survived the war and raised a family on the south coast, near where he had been stationed. Two generations later, his granddaughter Natalia had become quite an accomplished photographer. She specialised in landscape and wildlife subjects, receiving commissions from numerous tourist authorities around Europe and the British Isles, yet curiously never had occasion to return to the country of her ancestry. The evening lecture in the Saxon city of Dresden was indeed the closest she had ever come to going 'home'.

"The more clearly we can focus our attention on the wonders and realities of the world around us, the less taste we shall have for the destruction of our race." Natalia began, addressing her audience in English. "Those words, spoken by esteemed marine biologist Rachel Carson in 1952 have never had greater resonance than they do today. Photography is an art form that can help us explore the wonders and realities of our world, yet with our chosen medium there is a need, a responsibility, we might even say an obligation to cultivate humility. This humility is borne from examining the world through the prism of a camera.

"The old adage that a picture is worth a thousand words is an undeniable truth. The truth within the picture, however, is an entirely different thing altogether. The story that a photographer chooses to tell through their art may influence exactly how we choose to understand and explore the world around us."

An image of an adolescent girl with green eyes in a red headscarf appeared on the screen behind her. The subject's eyes looked intensely at the audience below.

"This particular image was captured back in 1984 by Steve McCurry. Some of you may recognise it. The photographer used Kodachrome 64 colour slide film in a Nikon FM2 camera with a Nikkor 105mm F2.5 lens." She explained with a smile as she delved into the technical details. "We all know that's not the story behind the picture. So, what is the story? What does the picture say to us?

"It may tell a story of war-torn childhood, life as a refugee, the story of the Afghan Girl. We know those stories well, but there are other stories to be told. Stories of courage, beauty, and resilience. Stories of responsibility, accountability, and honesty. These are stories we all need to be acutely aware of too."

The screen then showed a magnificent landscape scene. Glen Affric, in the Highland region of Scotland to the west of Loch Ness. It was an iconic scene; brooding clouds of lavender and grey, casting shadows across snow-capped Beinn Fhada at the head of the glen. Ambers, russet browns and smoky greens flowed through the leaves, ferns and machair below. Although miniscule, the burgundy red walls of the bothy in the foreground near the bank of the river stood out, drawing the eye deeper into the image.

With this shot, Natalia had won the prestigious Scottish Landscape Photographer of the Year award. The photograph had gone onto be used by the Scottish Tourist Board and had appeared on countless websites, brochures, and posters. It was one of her earliest, and most renowned scenes. Even in Dresden, her audience immediately recognised it.

"We see an image like this," she continued. "And it may immediately conjure up thoughts and emotions. Peace. Tranquillity. Space. What does it convey to you?" she asked, opening up to the audience with a gesture to invite comments.

"The wilderness."

"The beauty of nature."

"A spirit of adventure and freedom."

"Very good. All very interesting. All valid and correct." She nodded at the responses her question had garnered. "There are other stories behind this image though. What we see now as a beautiful landscape was once a place of fugitives, a renegade prince pursued by a determined English army. The beauty afforded this special place, the flora and fauna we see, love and admire, is a direct result of the forcible expulsion of hundreds of tenant farmers. A temperate and biodiverse rainforest utterly devastated for commercial gain and gentlemanly pursuits. What we see here, is the home of endangered golden eagles. We see history, ecology, geology," she pointed to the mountains, "Meteorology," then to the clouds, "biology and botany, all captured in a single image.

"As photographers we are the world's eye on itself. That comes with a measure of responsibility. The stories we tell can be fictional, they can be factual, we can fantasise or document, but we first need to understand ourselves what story we want to tell through our medium."

"How do we know?" asked a member of the audience.

"Good question." Natalia replied. "Sometimes we don't. Even working for a client with a particular objective, a shot list is not at all like a script or a screenplay, with a precise end-product. We are often dealing with nature and the unpredictable wonder of the natural world. Sometimes the story comes to us in the moment of capture, sometimes during post-processing. At other times a story might be imposed upon the image by others. The question though is not so much about how we know what story we want to tell, but what is the right story to tell. How can we define the words behind the images we capture? Tonight, this will be our journey."

CHAPTER TWENTY-TWO

A wonderfully graceful groin vaulted ceiling was augmented by towering arched windows and terracotta floor tiles to give the restaurant an open, monastic feeling of majesty. Despite the soaring architecture, the intimate arrangement of tables, wood panelled walls and warm yellow uplighters provided a feeling of warmth and cosiness to the space. There was a lively hubbub of conversation and laughter, a heady mixture of meaty aromas and beer, the sounds of cutlery, scraping chairs and satisfied diners.

The Weinstock restaurant had been a mainstay in the heart of Leipzig for as long as anyone could remember. Three old photographs on the wall near the entrance showed the impressive four-storey building on the northwest corner of Market Square. In the first, early motorcars were lined up outside, suggesting that the restaurant had been around since at least the 1900s. The next photograph showed it in the winter of 1945, a bombed out shell with only the front façade left standing. The last photo depicted its restored splendour in happier, more colourful times.

The man sitting on his own at the table for two in the corner had just ordered a Schwarzbier from the local Thomaskirche brewery while he awaited his fillet of heifer. Settling back in the chair, he took out his phone and made the call. In such a lively room, it would be almost impossible to overhear any one conversation. This was a perfect time to report the progress.

"Ja?" came the reply, slightly distorted. It was 'die Stimme', the Voice.

"I have it." He said.

"You have the locations?" even through the distortion, it was clear there was a trill of excitement.

"Yes. All of them gave up their information."

"You believe them?"

"The details fit together with what we know too well to be contrived."

"Where are they now?"

"They're all gone. All three."

There was a momentary pause. "Excellent. I feared these old relics may have been lost forever."

The man nodded his thanks to the waitress who brought his beer. Fulsome, frothy, with a good head.

"So, tell me what I must know." The voice continued.

"*Monique* is in Bordeaux. *Marie* is near Marseille and the key for *Manuela* is in Berlin."

"Do you know where?"

"Yes. When we find the key to *Manuela*, we will know where to find the relic itself."

He then began to relate how the curators were linked together. Graphically, the three men could be represented by three intersecting rings in the pattern of a Venn diagram, or the old logo of Krupp. He even drew it out on the napkin with his finger as he spoke. In this way, one of the men, the rings, knew how their research related to their specific vehicle and snippets of the others, but not every piece of evidence for all three. They had specialised and compartmentalised the information. Covering more ground.

"You have done great service, Jaeger." The voice commended. "First, retrieve the key for *Manuela* and bring me her location. Then look for the other two."

"Of course."

"I will ensure you are well rewarded."

At this juncture, Jaeger's beef fillet arrived, glazed with an unctuous herb butter, potato gratin and traditional Germanic Speckbohnen. Green beans with smoked, cured ham. Die Stimme explained what was to be done and the call ended. Jaeger put the phone away, leaned over the aroma of the beautifully cooked meal and breathed it in. He was a man that appreciated good, hearty cuisine.

CHAPTER TWENTY-THREE

Sometimes it was the smallest things. Muffled footsteps on carpet, glass bottles emptied into the bin lorry, someone arranging the chairs and tables out on the cobbles. For Natalia, it was the smell of the bedsheets. It was a clean smell, the scent of freshly laundered linen, but it wasn't the same smell. There was no delicate floral nose, the scent of a summer breeze, the aroma of her own bedclothes.

As Natalia stirred from under the deliciously comfortable sheets, she looked around her surroundings. Having opted for a Junior Suite, the spacious room had been individually designed and benefitted from some exquisite Biedermeier furniture in the combined living, sleeping area. Covering a yawn with her hand, she remembered where she was. The Hotel Suitess, Dresden.

Had she not already been half-awake, the noise of the telephone by her bed would have interrupted a most delightful and much-needed slumber. Preparation for the previous evening's lecture had taken considerably more out of her than she had given herself credit for. The student body were enthusiastic in their questions but at times Natalia felt like she was floundering in a whirlpool of contrasting emotions.

On the one hand it was thrilling to see how passionate many of the students were towards their craft. On the other, some of their questions were somewhat intimidating and their reaction to her replies, reflected in their body language, did little to dispel any disquieting thoughts that she had beforehand about her relative inexperience. Over drinks after the lecture, her hosts had assured her that they had very much enjoyed her insights and experience. Natalia smiled and hoped that they were not just being kind and tactful.

The phone was persistent. Finally rousing herself, she sat up in bed, wafted an arm over her head to gather up her mane of brunette hair and scoop it behind her. Then she reached out to pick up the receiver.

"Hello?"

"Good morning, Miss Bielawska." It was the concierge. "I'm sorry to disturb you, but there are some visitors here to see you."

"Who are they?" she asked.

The concierge paused a second. "They are from the police." He added in a quieter tone, protecting his guest's dignity from the other staff and fellow hotel patrons. She could imagine him placing a hand over the mouthpiece as he spoke.

"Have I done anything wrong?"

The concierge assured her that he certainly didn't think so.

"I'll be down shortly. Thank you, Hans."

Natalia replaced the handset and frowned. Absent-mindedly she wondered what standard kit would be needed to tap into the phone. Giles would know. Some of the new phones were so streamlined, it made such basic surveillance ever more challenging, but that was exactly the kind of thing GCHQ were good at. Moving to the bathroom there was a second handset on the wall by the toilet, though Natalia wondered who ever used such things. Just the hygiene of it.

After a glass of water, she looked at herself in the mirror. She had naturally prominent cheekbones, a subtle spray of pale freckles across the bridge of her nose and long, dark brown hair. With discreet applications, a little moisturiser, some subtle lipstick and eyeliner, her face glowed. The freckles disappeared, the eyebrows became a little more pronounced and the contours of her cheeks were delicately emphasised. It was her armour. She was no longer the fresh-faced, sleepy young lady she had at first appeared in the mirror. Now she was the confident woman she needed to be.

Her right eye was a warm hazel colour, intermingling shades of gold, brown and a hint of green within an intricate iris pattern. Her left, by contrast, was a cool silver-blue with only a portion blending in with the hazel of the right eye. This stunning sectoral heterochromia was incredibly rare and a completely benign trait, attributed to nothing more than genetic chimerism that gifted her with a defining, striking physical characteristic for which she was quietly very proud. Barely had she got herself ready though when the telephone rang again. It was Hans.

"I'm sorry, Miss. They wouldn't wait. They are on their way to your room now. I thought I would call ahead."

"I see." She said frowning. Whoever these people were, they seemed decidedly impatient. "In that case, could I have some breakfast delivered please? Some pastries, fruit and yoghurt. Coffee too."

"Of course, Miss. Breakfast for one?"

"I don't share my food with impatient visitors, Hans." She joked.

"Very good, Miss." He chuckled.

Almost as soon as she had replaced the handset, there was a knock on the door. It was typical of law enforcement. Robust, uncompromising, just short of punching a hole through the door itself. Keeping the door on the chain, she opened it and offered the three visitors her warmest smile.

"Good morning." She began. "How may I help you?"

A man and woman were dressed in the two-tone blue Brandenburg style uniform of the Saxony State Police. Standing closest to the door, a second man wore chinos, a jacket and open-necked shirt.

"Good morning, Miss." He said, showing her his identification. "I'm Kriminalkommissar Gerhard Müller from the BKA." He handed Natalia a postcard through the gap in the door. "Could you look at this please? My boss hopes you might be able to assist us."

Natalia took the card and examined it. It was a photograph of an old car, gleaming in some kind of showroom and surrounded by similar classics. She turned the card over and read the printing on the back. It was a souvenir postcard from the Horch Museum in Zwickau, promoting their latest exhibition. No message had been written on the reverse.

"I don't know this place." She said with a questioning look.

"There was a murder last night. The victim had a flyer for your lecture in his notebook."

"Was he planning to come here?"

"We're not sure."

"Why was he killed?"

"We were hoping you might help us."

"One moment." Natalia closed the door, unhooked the chain and opened the door wider. "Come in. I have some coffee on the way."

Müller stepped in, followed by the two police officers.

"Please, take a seat." She gestured expansively to the sofa and armchairs, choosing herself to sit on the bench at the foot of the bed. "What happened?"

"The curator of the museum found the victim late last night. He was there to study a particular car in the museum. He explained to the curator that he was working on a restoration project and wanted to compare some details."

"What was the victim's name?"

"Robertson. Graham Robertson."

Müller studied her reaction. She frowned, trying to recall anyone by that name. "I don't know anyone called Graham." She replied. "I'm not sure I know any Robertsons either."

"Would you come with us to the museum…" Müller's words were interrupted by another knock on the door.

"After breakfast." She said, moving to the door to welcome in the trolley. "Thank you, please bring it in."

The waiter wheeled the trolley in, noticed the visitors and left discreetly.

"Can I offer you some coffee?"

"Thank you." Müller agreed, eyeing up the warm pain au chocolate oozing chocolate onto the plate next to the coffee pot.

Natalia served them coffee, then helped herself to some pastries and returned to the end of the bed.

"This trip was organised by the University. Apart from a few flyers around the city and at the airport I'm not sure how widely it was known."

"It's possible he knew about you before the trip."

"How? I'm still building up my portfolio."

"That's what we would like you to help us with."

"I'll try, but I'm not sure how much use I'll be." She continued, devouring the pain au chocolate with an explosion of crumbs.

Looking at the trolley, the hotel had been exceptionally generous, despite only ordering for one. It seemed churlish not to extend the hospitality to her visitors. They were only doing their job after all, and poor Müller couldn't take his eyes off her. She suspected it might have something to do with the chocolate at the corner of her mouth.

"Please, help yourselves. There is more than enough for me, and I don't like to see waste."

"Thank you." Müller said, almost with relief.

Natalia smiled to herself as she watched him try not to be overly keen to grab a Danish raisin whirl and a classic apple filled Spandauer with sticky, sugary glaze. They ate for a moment in relative silence, drank their coffee. It was an awkward little scene.

"How was he killed?" she asked after a while.

"He was...strangled." He said hesitantly. Wanting to spare her the gruesome details.

IN THE DEN OF WOLVES

Natalia winced. It was a brutal way to despatch someone. Hands clasped around the throat. Thumbs exerting pressure on the hyoid bone protecting the larynx. Waiting for the crack. Squeezing the air out of the victim. The discolouration in the face. Panic and desperation in the eyes. Clawing fingers trying to loosen the grip. She shook the image from her mind.

"The museum is closed for today." Müller added.

"I imagine it would be." She nodded. "How far away is it?"

"About 120kilometres." Müller explained. "It should take about an hour."

"Less on the autobahn." She smiled. "You Germans are speed freaks."

Müller grinned, easing the tension. "Even the police have to follow the speed limits."

"Unless you have flashing lights." She winked. "I suppose you have a car waiting already?" she concluded, placing her coffee cup back on the trolley and dabbing her mouth with the napkin.

Müller nodded. "Back at the station. It's just down the road."

"If you'll allow me to finish getting ready, I'll be just a few minutes." She said getting up. "Please finish whatever you like. Have some more fruit, there's plenty left."

As the officers finished their coffee, Müller poured himself another and took up the last pastry while Natalia moved to the bathroom and cleaned her teeth. There was a low rumble of conversation as the officers talked about something. Natalia had studied music and photography instead of languages and so couldn't understand very much at all beyond the odd word. Distant high school memories of ordering coffee and asking for directions was shamefully about her limit.

"Okay, I'm ready." She said once her ablutions were complete.

She could see on Müller's face a slightly nervous expression. Perhaps it wasn't the chocolate he had been staring at after all. His look gratified her, but like many women, male approval wasn't the reason Natalia was attentive to her appearance. She liked to feel pretty and having bouncy hair and glossy nails did wonders for her own self-esteem. Pleasing others was a secondary consideration. Müller turned and spoke a few words to the officers. They nodded and left the room.

"I've sent them on ahead." Müller explained. "It would look better if you didn't walk out with two police officers."

"Thank you." She smiled. "That's very thoughtful."

Müller coloured a little, pleased his little gesture of concern for her public appearance was appreciated. Once the officers had left, Müller closed the door and moved closer to her, uttering in a low voice.

"I must warn you, Hauptkommissar Reinhardt can be a little…how do you say? Rough?"

"It's quite alright." She smiled. "In my line of work, I've had to deal with a lot of rough men over the years."

"How have things turned out?" he asked, genuinely interested.

"Often very badly." She sighed. "For them."

Müller started and looked at her with a worried expression. Natalia winked and picked up her purse.

"Come on, let's catch up with your friends."

Stepping out onto Rampische Strasse, they turned left and ambled to the end of the street, past cafes arranging their tables for breakfast. Dominating the entire span between Rampische and Landhaus, some 480feet, and comprising four wings and three courtyards, stood the impressive Neo-Renaissance Polizeipräsidium building. Facing onto Schiessgasse, the decorative structure had purposefully been built as the Royal Saxon Police Headquarters on the Old Town side of the Elbe and provided a more cohesive arrangement of offices and rooms than the former headquarters, shoe-horned into the baroque Coselpalais nearby.

The main portal was on Schiessgasse but Müller led Natalia through the vehicle entrance off Rampische and into the first of the three courtyards. Here the two uniformed officers were waiting by the side of a black BMW M5 limousine. Müller opened the rear door for her to get in, exchanging a few words with the two officers before climbing in behind the wheel. The female officer took the front passenger seat, while her male counterpart returned to his regular duties inside.

"Erika will join us, so you don't feel on your own." Müller explained.

Erika turned and waved shyly from the front passenger seat as she fastened up her seatbelt. Müller rolled the BMW out onto the street they had just left, then headed up towards the river.

Entering the back seat of an unmarked police car was a tense experience for anyone. Doing so in a foreign country even more so. Natalia tried to remain calm and gave the impression that she was perfectly in control of her emotions. The reality was more like the swans paddling along the Elbe. Beneath the surface her heart was quivering and her mind wondering why someone she had never met would have a flyer in a notebook for a lecture they hadn't attended.

Her increasing anxiety manifested itself in the fingers, beginning to tap away on the leather seat. Playing the piano had always been relaxing for her. The small action was like her body subconsciously telling her to calm down, remember the chords, she could get through this difficult piece. That was all well and good, but she didn't even know the tune.

CHAPTER TWENTY-FOUR

Some people derived olfactory pleasure from the emissions of all the volatile organic compounds wafting from inside the passenger compartment of a new car. The off-gassing from the adhesives and sealants used in the manufacturing process were not generally harmful and indicated that the car hadn't long been in service with the Saxon Police. No stale coffee had lingered in here. Still, with Natalia's rising apprehension, it made the predictably high-speed run down the autobahn a slightly nauseating affair.

While the blue strobes behind the kidney grille were not strictly essential, they ensured that any vehicles not equally trying to break through the sound barrier moved quickly over to allow the machine to thunder past. Even with acoustic insulation, bellowing exhausts could still be heard and only added to the stress Natalia was feeling. The open fields and scattered, picturesque villages of Saxony, still covered with a light dusting of snow in places, accomplished little by way of settling her thoughts as she replayed the last couple of days over in her mind, trying to see the connection between her lecture and the murder.

Just a little over an hour later, they arrived on what first appeared to be a non-descript East German industrial back street on the northern outskirts of Zwickau. Improvements to the road were long overdue and some substantial potholes had yet to be filled. Ironic given that it was named Audistrasse. It was like being back in Britain. Mercifully, Müller soon pulled the car up to kerb outside the main entrance to the museum. A collection of police cars and tape blocked the road and pavement around the entrance itself.

"Miss Bielawska?" the man greeted as she alighted onto the pavement.

"Yes."

"I'm Captain Erwin Reinhardt." He offered Natalia his hand. She took it and gave a firm handshake.

This was something Dame Harrington had taught her. Sadly, from her own experiences, she may only be taken as seriously as the pressure she applied. Too soft, and she may be discredited. Too hard and it could be perceived that she was trying to make a point. Firm and uncompromising, a solid clasp with just the right amount of pressure and it conveyed she meant business. She was no ball-breaker, but she wasn't a pussy cat either.

"You like old cars?" he asked.

"Sometimes." She mused.

"Then you might like this place." He said flatly.

Moving to the side door he pulled it open it for them all to enter. It was evident he wasn't a connoisseur of the automobile and found the whole setting all rather theatrical. He was tall, clean shaven and immaculately groomed, wearing a dark grey, single-breasted three-piece suit that could have easily been styled by Hugo Boss. His blonde hair, silvering a little at the temples, was swept across from a side parting and he walked with an assured, authoritative gait. Two masked up BKA officers armed with machine guns stood in the lobby by the revolving door. Two more near the entrance to the museum proper. It was clear no one was going in or out without Reinhardt's express permission.

Advancing quickly through the lobby, they filed past uniformed and plain clothed police, periodically taking the traumatised museum staff up to the conference room above. It seemed they had been summoned to work purely for the intention of interviewing them. Surrounded by a show of armed and uniformed law enforcement, it was evident that Reinhardt liked using the art of intimidation in his methods.

Crossing over a glazed bridge across the basement level, there was a glimpse of an Art Deco style showroom below where the four car brands would ordinarily be represented by one of their finest historical models. This looked like the scene in the postcard. However, carrying a little further on, greeting them in the first production hall, the museum itself began with a green Horch 12/28 PS and a yellow Audi Typ B, both from 1911, both sharing the honour of welcoming visitors to the motor museum.

The lights had been left on since the body's discovery, displaying gleaming, polished automobiles in a bright, warm atmosphere. Working his way down the old production hall, Reinhardt ventured through a recreation of the Berlin Internationale Automobil-Ausstellung. The Motor Show of the 1930s, reconstructing displays of what was then the newly merged Auto Union company as it had presented its four iconic brands to the world's media for the first time. Long wheelbase limousines and sporty little cabriolets were all represented, with and without state pennants on the fenders. Beyond this, prominently set against a warm ochre wall was an arrangement of four large interlocking white rings, now famous the world over.

Passing on into the office block at the end of the production hall, Natalia peered in and could see an old wooden desk placed at an angle with a door into an adjacent office. Both rooms were filled with plain clothed officers with laptops and radios on the desks. Ordinarily only accessible with a museum attendant, it seemed that the BKA had taken over the original offices of August Horch as their makeshift base of operations within the museum.

Hurrying to keep up, Natalia passed the preserved machining workshops, assembly hall, and workers facilities, before reaching a collection of wartime vehicles on the other side of the factory building as they doubled back. There was a chill to the area as Natalia wandered through, mixing with the smell of old oil, cold steel and musty canvas.

Eventually, they arrived in the Auto Union showroom they had seen from the glass bridge near the entrance. Natalia was sure that access might have been possible from the entrance itself through some back staircase or emergency exit and wondered whether the whistle stop tour of Factory No.1 was intended in some way to disorientate her. In which case, it had worked. She wasn't entirely sure which way was in or out.

Given over to the Horch brand, the showroom display was being used as a special temporary exhibition exclusively presenting a study of the coachbuilder's art in four different and historically important models. Occupying two-storeys and lined with mirrors between polished concrete pillars, potted plants and rosewood]furniture, Natalia felt as if she had been transported back to the Art Deco pinnacle of the 1930s. Presented at an oblique angle were two pairs of cars on either side of the space.

The front pairing comprised a formidable Horch 830 Cabriolet with an example of bodywork from Gläser-Karosserie of Dresden. Opposite was an even larger seven-seater 951A Pullman Limousine from Ernst Dietzsch. Beyond these two giants, side-by-side, was the striking Voll & Ruhrbeck Horch 853 Cabriolet and the impossibly good-looking Erdmann & Rossi Stromlinien Coupé.

The scene had been well photographed, and a clean-up crew had long ago finished up, closely supervised by the curator himself. The carpet runner that ran between the cars had been removed for analysis and would probably need replacing. It would not have been appropriate to bring a civilian in the way it was.

Herr Meyer had ensured painstaking care was taken to clean up the cars. No harsh chemicals or solvents that could risk damaging the incredibly well-presented machines. They were in his opinion, just as much works of art as any Rubens or Rembrandt. It was fortunate that none of the arterial spray had made it onto the fabric roof of the Cabriolet. The result could have been catastrophic.

"This was where it happened?" she asked, looking down at the polished marble floor.

Reinhardt stood in the space between the two cars and gestured to the spot. "Right here."

Natalia stared down at the floor between the two vehicles.

"Any recollections?"

"As I told Lieutenant Müller, I've never been here before." She frowned, gesturing to Müller who had kept pace with them throughout.

Reinhardt looked at her sceptically. "Then why did he want to see you?"

"I have no idea whether he did or not."

"Did you agree to meet him?"

"I've never heard of him before, and I don't have any real interest in cars."

She paused, pursing her lips as she pondered the scenario. "Lt Müller mentioned he was working on a restoration?"

"That's what he told the curator."

"Perhaps he wanted photographs to take back with him, as some kind of record."

"He had a camera of his own."

Natalia shrugged, feeling a little irritated that her time had been so wasted. "Then I really have no idea. Maybe he was to attend the lecture later in the evening."

Reinhardt looked at her sternly for a moment. His left arm was crossed over his waistcoat, supporting the elbow of his right arm as he rubbed his chin pensively. "Maybe."

"What sort of photographs do you take, Miss Bielawska?" Müller asked.

"Landscapes mostly. Some wildlife."

"Not still life?"

"Not even portraits."

Reinhardt considered her responses for a moment, then moving to the sofa he picked up a camera and handed it to her. She seemed reluctant to touch it.

"We have cleaned it all up. Go ahead." He nudged it towards her again. Natalia took it in her hands. It was a Canon.

Natalia herself used a Nikon, but a DSLR was similar regardless of manufacturer. Some of the controls were in slightly different places, some were more intuitive than others, but largely things were where she expected them to be.

"Tell me what you think."

The on switch rotated around the shutter release, just as on her Nikon. She spent half a moment finding the play button to display the images on the screen, then the arrows to move it along. Predictably the images showed the car they were standing by. It seemed there had been a red carpet running in between the two silver-grey cars, leading towards the sofa. Natalia subconsciously looked at the marble floor to confirm that it was missing.

The photos were good, not great, but usable. He was clearly using it on full auto, which seemed odd for a DSLR. Ordinarily a photographer would play around with the options to get exactly the kind of shot they wanted, adjusting focal length and aperture, otherwise a much cheaper compact would do the job if you were just after some snaps.

There were quite a lot of overview shots of the full car from various angles. Then he focussed in on many of the details, the radiator ornament, the Horch badge, Auto Union rings, the twin horns, Bosch running lights, even the headlight lenses bearing the Horch logo in the centre. With a tape measure he recorded the height of the wheel arches, the diameter of the hubs, the length, breadth and depth of various components. On and on. All very singular.

As she got to the last frame she froze, horrified. It took all her effort not to let the camera drop to the floor as she looked down at the scene. Graham Robertson lying there, sprawled on the carpet in a lake of his own blood. Almost the entire side of the car she was looking at had been covered in blood splatter. The grotesque angle of his head told its own story. He may have been strangled, but not with hands. Something had cut deeply into his throat.

Covering her mouth to stop from her crying out, collapsing, vomiting, all of those things, she thrust the camera back at Reinhardt. He stepped forward, relinquishing it from her shaky grasp. He looked at the screen himself, taking in the scene once more before turning the camera off and placing it on the sofa.

"I need to sit down." She stammered.

Moving forward, Müller took her arm and directed her to a nearby armchair, the complement of the sofa. Tears welled up in Natalia's eyes at the shock and horror of the scene she had witnessed. She wanted to run away, or at the very least to leave the showroom, but sensed with Reinhardt's men at the door, storming out without his permission was not an option.

"Why would the killer do that?" she sobbed, suddenly feeling very weak and unsure of her own voice. "Why would they photograph their victim?"

"Oh no, the killer didn't take that last shot. That was me." He said, almost with a grin.

"You?" she gasped.

"I had to be certain. A reaction like yours, it cannot be easily faked you see?"

"Certain of what?" she cried. "That it wasn't me? I told you!" she screamed, becoming angry and agitated. "I've never even been here before! I was in Dresden, giving my lecture."

"Between eight and nine o'clock, yes. Then you went to Augustiner for drinks and something to eat. Afterwards you visited a few bars and returned to your hotel."

"You were watching me?"

"No." he shrugged, "I made sure Lt. Müller checked a few things before your wake-up call this morning."

"You think I did this?" she looked between Reinhardt and Müller.

"Oh no, we've been looking through the camera footage already." He pointed to the security camera high above her head. "We know it wasn't you who actually killed him, but perhaps you may have known who did. This is a very personal crime. I had to be sure." He shrugged casually again.

"Just because he had my flyer in some stupid notebook?" she asked, trying to control her emotions again. This was not how Harrington had taught her to react at all. "You're sick!" she cried, remembering Müller's words to her in the hotel. Reinhardt wasn't just a little 'rough'. This was extreme. "How many other people could have picked up one of those flyers? What did they get up to last night? Is that my fault too?!"

"I have my job to do."

Reinhardt seemed devoid of emotion, even as he had looked again at the appalling aftermath. How a man could have taken it upon himself to even capture such a scene, let alone show it to some random foreign citizen beggared belief. She knew crime scene photographers had to capture some awful scenes, but this was different. This was macabre. Perverse. As she wiped her eyes and looked at him, he stood there, hands behind his back, in a most Teutonic pose.

"I want to go now." She said.

Reinhardt's disappointment was palpable, yet he remained poised as he turned to address her again.

"Do you have any more engagements in Germany."

"No, I fly out tomorrow morning. I *was* hoping to explore a little of Dresden today." She let her irritation show in the tone of her voice.

"Then we shall not detain you, but we may need to speak to you again when we find out the connection."

She nodded but decided not to say anymore and hoped he would never contact her at all.

"Very well." He gestured for her to head in the direction of the exit. "I will ask one of the officers to drive you back." He nodded to Müller to make the arrangements.

"Thank you." she breathed, trying to compose herself, taking a tissue and wiping her nose and eyes again.

"One more thing, Miss Bielawska."

"What?"

She didn't mean to sound so forceful, so defensive. It was a natural reaction to what she had just witnessed.

"Do you have a card?" she frowned. "A business card? Something with your number on, so I can contact you?"

"Of course." She sighed, inwardly cursing. She never wanted to hear from Capt. Reinhardt again. Rummaging in her purse she took out a matt black card, unusually thick, with her freelance logo subtly applied in gloss.

He pulled a face as she handed it to him. "Fancy." He remarked, turning it over. "Thank you."

Natalia watched him slip it into the pocket of his waistcoat. For some reason the action of him doing that looked sinister. It was just a small gesture, but once again she was beginning to feel increasingly uncomfortable in his presence.

"You can go back to the lobby through that door." He said, gesturing to a concealed door in the mirrors.

As she suspected, Reinhardt had led her all the way through the convoluted route of the museum to try and confuse her, get her on edge or drop her guard, before presenting her with the scene of what he supposed was her own despicable crime, interviewing her in the hopes that she might incriminate herself. It was a bizarre strategy, but one that had ultimately failed because she simply had not done it.

Taking the opportunity to put some distance between herself and the unsettling officer, Natalia walked calmly, swiftly to the door. She was half-expecting him to call after her in some final, desperate ploy. Just one more thing. There was nothing. She touched the glass and the door opened.

CHAPTER TWENTY-FIVE

Erika was tasked with driving Natalia back to Dresden. When the car rolled into the layby at the end of Tzschirnerplatz, Natalia thanked Erika and climbed out. It had been a smoother journey but just as rapid. The building immediately next to her was the Albertinum. Leaving the cool air-conditioned cabin and stepping out into the bright February sunshine brought back the nausea. Natalia wasn't sure she could make it down the street and back up to her hotel room. Entering through the east portal of the Albertinum instead, she found the nearest washroom and headed inside to empty her stomach of those delicious breakfast pastries.

Somehow she had managed to keep it together on the journey back but now Natalia felt weak and incredibly dizzy. After flushing away her breakfast she sat back down on the bowl and took in deep breaths. Her forehead beading with sweat and her neck feeling clammy. She closed her eyes but each time she did, the last frame on the camera's memory card filled her vision. That was the problem with photography, a captured scene could not be unseen.

Harrington had once told her that during the war, death by piano wire was the favoured method of execution for captured SOE operatives. Usually by hanging, but sometimes in other ways. It was a brutality particularly reserved for such prisoners as an extension of the Commando Order.

Agents, saboteurs or commandos not in uniform would be handed over to the infamous Sicherheitdienst for execution. If Allied commandos were captured in uniform, even if they surrendered, they would mercifully receive a bullet to the head, or be rattled by machineguns. Either way, it was over very quickly. At least, that was the official line. There had been stories of Commandos being stripped of their uniforms prior to being handed over to the feared SD anyway, merely to satisfy their perverse and grotesque pleasure.

If death from a gun was quick and impersonal, a knife close, personal and slower, what was the significance of a garotte? Was it more than just a means of execution? Was there a message in the method? A story behind the image?

Waiting until it was quiet, Natalia staggered out of the cubicle, splashed her face with water and swilled her mouth out to remove the tang of bile. She looked at herself in the mirror, taking a series of deep breaths to calm herself down before repairing her make-up.

Natalia knew what she was getting into when she attended the interview for the job on London's Albert Embankment. Nothing could prepare you for witnessing the gruesome reality of a murder scene though. The trainers at Fort Monckton were not about to show you image after brutal image of hideous crimes in some Clockwork Orange style method of desensitisation. Just like that first combat kill, no matter how much you trained for it, prepared yourself for it, expected it to happen, the reality still hit hard.

Eventually satisfied that she didn't look like the haggard wreck that she felt, Natalia popped in a breath mint and returned to the lobby.

The Albertinum went back to the 16th century when it had been constructed as the city's arsenal. Centuries later the Saxon state parliament decided to use the building as a sculpture museum and the building was renamed Albertinum after King Albert. On another day, Natalia might have enjoyed wandering around the exhibits.

It was a different outlet to her usual loves of photography and music. She liked to widen out her horizons, consider new art forms and be inspired by the works of others. After the horror of the morning though, her head was swimming. Making her way back towards the east portal, she noticed the black BMW still sitting there in the layby. Why? Was she under surveillance now?

Paying her twelve Euros for entrance, Natalia decided to use another exit. While she wandered through, she picked up a map of the building, took out her phone, and found a quiet place to make the call.

CHAPTER TWENTY-SIX
ENGLAND, 2018

While the village of East Dean was a usual mixture of developing architectural styles, it was predominantly made up of cosy eighteenth century flint-faced cottages clustered around the church, the village green and the Birling Manor farmhouse with its monastic ruins. A small cottage directly on the green was adorned with a blue enamel plaque. It proclaimed the building was the fictional retirement residence of Consulting Detective & Beekeeper Sherlock Holmes. The Beehive delicatessen nearby seemed to corroborate this claim. Quaint cottages roundabout could easily have been mistaken for Miss Jane Marple's St Mary Mead dwelling. A murder of crows in the churchyard. A conspiracy of sleuths on the green.

It was a cold, but sunny day, though one not without its trials in the picturesque village. It was moving day and it wasn't going well. Apart from an extensive spell in London during her Service days, both during and after the War, Dame Iris Harrington had never left the village of East Dean since the day she was born in it. She was the youngest of seven sisters, and two brothers. She had outlived all of them, had never married, and so one of her sisters' granddaughters, Claudia, was available to help her move.

Claudia had recently moved back in the village after her divorce to take over the workshop cottage at the top of the green. She had graduated from art college and after a difficult, artistically tempered marriage, finally wanted to setup her own ceramics studio. Today though, she was helping her grand old aunt move into the East Dean Grange Care Home.

Neither of them wanted it. Despite her frail body, Dame Iris's mind was as pin sharp as ever. The steep stairs in the cottage though were simply too much for her now, and after a couple of embarrassing and painful falls, Harrington finally yielded to the inevitable. This, she concluded, was the beginning of the end. There was only ever going to be one way she would move out of a care home. That would be to take up a vacant plot in the adjacent cemetery surrounding the old church.

"I feel like I'm already there." She sighed, looking out of the window while her personal belongings were being brought in around her. None too carefully by the removal contractors either.

"Oh aunty." Claudia soothed. "You're nowhere near that yet."

"Don't you believe it." She replied with a sad smile. "There was many a time I should have been there already."

There was a crash as another box of crockery was bumped on the door frame. Harrington screwed up her eyes as if she herself had made impact with the edge of the portal. Claudia looked down with a look of concern and sadness.

"Did I tell you about the time I flew into occupied Belgium?" she began, opening her eyes.

"No?!"

Claudia had genuinely never heard the story. Unlike some old people, who latched onto a distant memory and repeated the same narrative again and again, Harrington by way of total contrast had so many stories locked up inside but had never told a single soul. Some would have sounded so fanciful they might have been discredited as a work of some elaborate and implausible fiction. A great many more were still officially classified and couldn't be revealed until after her death.

"Make us both a cuppa, and I'll tell you." she smiled. "It's about time you knew a few things about your crazy aunt."

Claudia smiled and went into the kitchenette to unpack the mugs and see about making them some tea. Harrington saw the light on her mobile phone twinkle, followed by a vibrating pulse. She picked it up off the window ledge and read the name: Unknown. Her wrinkled brow creased further into a frown as a bony finger pressed the screen and made a sliding action to one side. Holding the phone to her ear she uttered one single word.

"Harrington."

"Iris, it's Natalia."

"Natalia. How are you, my dear?" she smiled, her mood lifting immeasurably.

Natalia Bielawska was a charming girl, Iris recalled. A very promising prospect. She hoped they recognised that on the Albert Embankment too. So many good operatives had been let go in the consolidations of the last few years. A leaner, more efficient Secret Intelligence Service was the aim. Harrington translated that to smaller, cheaper and more vulnerable.

"Something very strange has happened to me this morning."

"Oh dear. What is it?"

Natalia went onto relate exactly what had transpired, from the moment the call came in from the concierge to the time she was dropped back into Dresden by Erika. She was still lurking outside the gallery. Harrington listened very carefully, asking a few questions, seeking a little clarification, then she paused in thought for a moment.

"The Horch Museum, you say?"

"Yes."

"That is interesting."

"Does it mean anything to you?"

"It might." She nodded, her ancient mind working back through decades of secret service. "It might mean a very great deal indeed. Where are you now?"

"I'm back in Dresden."

"See if you can get to Milan. Text me your flight details. I'll have someone meet you there."

Ending the call, Harrington looked up and smiled as Claudia arrived with the tea tray.

"Excellent timing, Claudia."

"Who was that?"

"A young friend of mine." She replied. "You would like her. She's an artist, like you."

Leaning forward, Harrington picked up the tongs and dropped in two sugar cubes.

"You should watch your sugar intake, aunty."

"I have these past ninety-nine years." Harrington replied flatly. "It's never done me any harm yet." She added with a wink that attempted to soften her brusque reply.

Claudia shook her head and smiled. Harrington turned to the window and looked out across the car park to the churchyard beyond, her mind thinking on the call with Natalia and the shadows of the past. Could they really be looking for the relic now? After all these years? Why now?

CHAPTER TWENTY-SEVEN
ENGLAND, 1940

$\pi r^3 t(T-V)Mc^2 - pV(8.314)$

"It's a crude code." Alexander said, sitting in Denniston's visitor's chair. "Although if the contact isn't familiar with cryptography, it's probably about the best they could come up with at the time."

Conel Hugh O'Donel Alexander was an Irish born chess player and mathematician working in Hut 6. His team's mission was to try and break the Wehrmacht and Luftwaffe Enigma messages. Having represented Cambridge in chess, he went on to teach mathematics at Winchester College before finally joining Bletchley Park's cryptanalyst section in February 1940.

"What does it mean?" Denniston asked.

"I think it's more of a call sign, an introduction if you will." He pointed to the sheet showing his workings. "They have basically combined formulae together to spell out a word, possibly a name, a codename perhaps. See here?" he pointed to the number in parenthesis at the end of the code.

"Eight point three, one, four."

"That, you see, is the numerical representation of the ideal gas constant used in thermodynamics."

Commander Denniston looked a little nonplussed.

"It is represented by the letter 'R'." Alexander explained.

"Ah, I see. So, each part of the code represents a different letter?" Alexander nodded. "Clever."

"It's not bad." Alexander acknowledged. "Easily breakable."

"Evidently the contact had confidence it wouldn't be intercepted."

"Or confidence that it would, and we might be lured in."

Denniston nodded sagely. "So, what does it spell?" he asked.

"Well admittedly, the first two letters are quite clever." Alexander continued. "He's multiplied the two formulae together, running them into the third letter. This part took the longest to decipher."

"How long?" Denniston asked curiously.

Alexander pondered for a moment. "About a minute. You see, he's used the formula for the area of a circle; πr^2, and combined that with a simple distance equation, rt, rate and time; thus, the letters 'A' for area and 'D' for distance. It took me a while to figure out that the 'r's actually mean different variables in two separate equations. The multiplication is simplistic, and meaningless mathematically, but as a code I can see what he wanted to achieve."

"Perhaps our German counterparts might be confounded by that one." Denniston remarked hopefully.

"Hmm, perhaps." Alexander said unconvincingly.

"Carry on."

"Well, then he's just plucked the definition for a non-relativistic Lagrangian for a system of particles, T-V, to substitute for the letter 'L', but this is the interesting part. For the next letter, he's used Max Planck's expression for mass energy equivalence, Mc^2-pV. That gives us the letter 'E', but it also tells us something more."

"ADLER." Denniston read out the codename scrawled beneath Alexander's workings.

"German for eagle. That, and the expression for energy, tells me our contact is either German, or deep inside Germany somewhere. I suspect that is the real message here. German theoretical physicists have been tackling this relativity problem for decades."

"So, as you say, wanting to lure us in, believing we have someone in deep cover, or else…" he trailed off with the possibilities.

"He may actually be in deep cover and wants to send us a message. He could prove to be a useful ally."

Denniston opened the top drawer of his desk and took out the metal car badge he had received less than a month before. He ran his fingers over it, then passed it over to Alexander. "What do you make of this?"

Alexander took it and examined the badge. There were no other discernible ciphers, just the name on the badge itself, and the single Gaelic word scratched across the front.

"Adler." He read.

"Adler Éirean." Denniston said. "Eagle Rising." He translated. "Éirean is Scots Gaelic."

"I doubt many Germans would be familiar with the savage tongue." Alexander quipped. "Though if you add another 'n' at the end it could become Irish Eagle."

Denniston looked at him disapprovingly. "Can you set up a small team, Hugh? Just a radio operator and codebreaker. Monitor anything that comes from this *Adler*? I'm not sure what to make of them yet."

"Do we know if he's even transmitting? This all suggests he doesn't have the means to do so. Is it worth the resource?"

"I don't know yet." Denniston winced as his abdominal pain resurfaced.

Alexander nodded as he looked at the strange little eagle in his fingers, spinning the Teutonic symbol around in the light.

This was Sutherland's war, but just like being a Grand Prix driver had been before, it was going to be a frightfully dangerous way to make a living.

CHAPTER TWENTY-EIGHT
ITALY, 2018

Flying to or from Dresden was never a direct route. Though the airport itself was wonderfully modern and pleasantly compact, the list of destinations was noticeably short. This almost always necessitated a stopover at Frankfurt before onward travel. The flight to Milan Malpensa was no different. She had chosen Malpensa because the flights were cheaper, and it was the right side of Milan for the subsequent journey up to Lake Maggiore. As arranged, a driver was waiting for her at the airport with a shiny new car to take her up to her appointment in Stresa, a small resort town on the lake shore.

Alighting at the Parcheggio Baia, Giuseppe Spinola, a handsome, elderly gentleman with a shock of silvery-grey hair, stubble beard and moustache was awaiting her arrival on the jetty. Dressed casually in open-necked blue shirt and chinos, with typically Italian flair, he exuded Piedmontese warmth and friendliness. The driver, who had barely spoken to her since picking her up, opened the car for her, buttoning up his black Armani suit jacket as he did so over what Natalia was sure was a loaded shoulder holster.

"Grazie." she smiled.

"Prego." He replied, gesturing to the man while he retrieved Natalia's luggage from the boot.

"Miss Bielawska." The man cried happily, holding out his arms like a welcoming grandfather.

She submitted to the inevitable exchange of kisses, pressing her smooth complexion against his craggy features.

"What a joy!" he smiled, taking her luggage from the driver and beckoning her to the jetty. "I am Giuseppe Spinola. You may call me Gigi. Come, please. Come. We have a room and some lunch prepared. Are you hungry?"

"Famished." She admitted, rubbing her stomach.

"We thought you would be." Spinola chuckled leading her to the waiting boat.

The black Aquariva Super was a beautifully sleek and modern heir to the iconic Aquarama runabouts of the 1960s. Retaining all her forebear's timeless allure, varnished mahogany top deck, full-grain leather upholstery and chromed metalwork, she continued the Riva legend with cutting edge high-tech accoutrements and wonderfully elegant lines. Assisting her onto the boat, the driver then untied the mooring line before returning to the car and driving away. At the helm, Spinola fired up the engines, giving a deep, throaty rumble, before taking the boat out onto the lake.

"I'm afraid this is only a short trip." Spinola said, taking out a pair of chic sunglasses and placing them over his eyes.

He gestured to Isola Bella, just four-hundred metres from the lakeside town of Stresa, and the nearest of the Borromean Islands. Their journey to the Grand Pier at the other end of the island was a journey of barely 700metres and would take only a few minutes, but the beauty of the island itself was a sight to behold.

With magnificent and extensive Italianate gardens, the grand Borromeo Palace and a picturesque fishing village in between, the island resembled a floating fairy tale wonderland. Statues and architectural decorations alternated with geometric shrubbery and precious plants. The parterre of azaleas was approaching its first blossoming season and the blue sky, lush evergreens and terracotta tiles were accentuated by the turquoise waters, a mountain fresh breeze, and the haunting cry of a white peacock reverberating across the lake.

"Perhaps we can take you on a longer tour later." He smiled.

Spinola pushed forward the throttles as they left the restrictions of the yacht club and headed out into the gulf proper, spinning the wheel to take them on a journey up the length of the island from the water wheel towers to the Palazzo Borromeo. Natalia, took her own sunglasses down from the top of her head, shaking her hair out behind before putting the shades on and breathing in the refreshing, perfumed breeze. Sitting back into the horseshoe sofa in the centre of the deck, she could feel the Italian sunshine pricking at her skin while the cool wind rippled pleasantly through her hair.

Natalia was still very confused and disturbed by the whole episode with Reinhardt at Zwickau. It had meant something to Harrington, and she seemed keen for Natalia to pursue it. Her holiday was coming to an end in a few days. It didn't look like this would all be resolved before then. She wondered what her bosses in Vauxhall Cross on the Albert Embankment would make of it all. The Secret Intelligence Service seldom engaged in treasure hunts.

Spinola pulled back on the throttles as they approached the jetty on the island. The magnificent edifice of Palazzo Borromeo soared above them from the piazza where the island converged onto the Grand Pier at the northern tip. Steering the Riva deftly alongside the pier, a stevedore came over to tie up the boat while Spinola cut the engines. Having secured the vessel, Spinola helped Natalia clamber out onto the jetty and immediately invited her onto the quayside with a broad sweep of his arm.

"Isola Bella." He proclaimed proudly. "Beautiful island."

"I can see why."

Natalia was mesmerised by the stunning aspect of the palace. Built on the northwest point of the island in an Italian baroque style, it was characterised by a façade some 80metres long with a curvilinear projection in the centre and low, pitched roof. The rough-faced rusticated ashlar on the ground floor contrasted with cream rendering of the floors above. Neatly manicured box hedges adorned the front façade and well-established, ancient camphor trees provided welcome shade in the piazza from which to admire the impressive building.

"You might be interested to know." Spinola whispered, leaning in closer and gesturing to the domed roof. "That the Great Hall was actually only completed as late as 1959."

"Really? It looks so much older."

"Construction was started in 1632." Spinola explained, leading her towards the palace. "But because of a plague epidemic in the Duchy of Milan at the time, the project was suspended until the latter decades of the 17th century. It was mostly finished by then, but in a few places there was still work to be done. It's there that our story begins."

He gave her a mischievous wink and guided her up the steps to the pale blue door at the foot of the curved façade, showing her inside.

"Let me give you a brief history of the House of Borromeo." He murmured quietly, his voice echoing in the vast space of the Salone Nuovo as tourists entered through a separate door from the Sala delle Armi and the small piazza to the south.

The baroque entrance hall was an incredibly ornate wonder. Grandiose stuccoed coats of arms were surmounted by portraits of the eminent characters of the various families that Spinola introduced. The heraldic devices of the Medici, Farnese, Odescalchi and Barberini were set off against pale blue plaster walls, white columns, and gilded decorations. In the centre of an intricately coffered, vaulted ceiling was the crowned motto, humylitas, in Gothic script. It was anything but a humble display.

"This Salone we are standing in was the subject of a long design process." Spinola added, after briefly tracing the aristocratic Borromeo lineage from their humble origins as merchants of San Miniato, through the bankers of Milan, to the Archbishops, Cardinals and Counts of Arona and Peschiera.

"Now come. Look at this." He hooked his finger, beckoning her to the centre of the marble floor. "The Borromean Rings."

Three topologically linked rings alternately crossing over and under each other at the points where they intersected were set into the marble floor, each ring a different colour of stone.

"These rings have much meaning and symbolism." He continued, using his fingers to count off the lists. "According to a 13th century French manuscript, they may represent the Holy Trinity: Father, Son, and Holy Ghost. There's a possible link with the three circles mentioned in canto 33 of Dante's Paradiso. For some, each ring represents a fundamental Lacanian component of reality; real, imaginary and the symbolic."

"What do they really mean?"

"For you, something entirely different." He chuckled. "Come this way." He led her to one side of the hallway where there was a door inscribed with the same Borromean Rings. "This was the very last part of the palace to be completed. The structure was finished earlier, but what lies beyond was only added in the mid-sixties."

"What is it? Some kind of vault?"

"In a way, yes, but not the kind you're probably thinking of." Spinola laughed as he led them out into the piazza at the rear. "We come back here, but first, we lunch, yes?"

Natalia couldn't argue with that suggestion. The nausea of the previous day had given way to a raging appetite. Leading her through the passage on the other side of the piazza, he began to negotiate the narrow streets of the fishing village itself. Talking further was almost impossible through the confines of the cobbled lanes. Single-file traffic. Up steps and down alleyways, squeezing between outdoor cafes and shops in the impossibly tight thoroughfares of the ancient fishing village. Emerging finally in a small piazza down by the lake, right outside their lunchtime appointment.

A few words between Spinola and the maître d saw them taken up onto the terrace where a corner table overlooking the lake had been reserved for their lunch. More warm words, kisses and gesticulations were exchanged as two chairs were withdrawn for them to take their seats.

"I took the liberty of ordering ahead." Spinola explained as bread and wine were produced.

They were each poured a glass of water from the carafe before the waiter left them in peace.

"When I mentioned the name Horch, Harrington suggested I come to you, but what does a German car manufacturer have to do with Italian nobility?" she asked. "I'm afraid I'm still very confused."

"Of course." Spinola acknowledged with an open gesture. "This is why la Dama sent you here. For enlightenment."

"You know Dame Harrington?"

"La Dama and I go back a very long way." He smiled, pouring some more water into his glass. "But we can go into that another time."

Reaching into his pocket, he produced a photograph which he slid across the tablecloth. His gesture indicated Natalia should take it and have a look. Picking it up, the photograph was an old monochrome image of a man in overalls and a cloth flying cap, standing by the side of a vintage sportscar. Natalia was no expert on automobiles, but the vehicle looked very similar to the one in the Horch Museum at the scene of the murder. The one Graham Robertson had been making carefully detailed notes about.

"I've seen this car before." She remarked.

"You have probably seen one very similar to it." Spinola nodded. "For that exact car is believed to be lost. The one you saw in Zwickau will be the replica made for the Audi Museum."

"What is the significance of this car?"

"That is an excellent question. La Dama was right to put you onto this. Most people would have asked about the man first. He is a legend, yes, but the significance of the car is possibly far greater."

Spinola leaned forward and pressed his fingertips together like a church spire.

"The car belonged to a famous racing driver in the 1930s. His name was Bernd Rosemeyer." Spinola pointed to the man in the photograph. "The car was built especially for him by Horch after he won the championship in 1936. They presented it to him a year later, just before the Donington Grand Prix in October. Sadly, in January 1938, Rosemeyer was killed attempting to set a new speed record. After that the car, which he named *Manuela*, completely disappeared." He paused for dramatic effect. "And yet…" Spinola leaned back as their antipasti arrived. "Tavolozza del Lago." He announced, pressing his fingertips to his pursed lips in that classical Italian manner. "Deliziosa."

"Bon apettito." the waiter smiled.

"Grazie."

Spinola uncorked the Pinot Bianco and poured them each a glass.

"Saluti."

He took a sip, spread the refreshing wine around his mouth, savouring its complex and voluptuous palette.

"The car may have passed onto a teammate of Rosemeyer's." Spinola uttered at last. He was clearly not a man to rush the enjoyment of fine wine and excellent cuisine. "His name was Andrew Sutherland. He came from the Isle of Skye but was also a racing driver for Auto Union in the late 1930s."

"A rival of Rosemeyer?"

"A contemporary." Spinola nodded. "Rosemeyer was almost without equal. Caracciola was a closer rival, but he raced for Mercedes-Benz."

"Why would Graham Robertson have been killed, if all he was doing was studying a replica?"

Spinola paused, enjoying his role of storyteller.

"Why would he be studying a replica, Natalia?"

"To make another one, perhaps?"

Spinola nodded. "Or perhaps to restore the original. So, why would it be worth killing him?"

Natalia thought for a moment. "Money?"

"Naturalmente. If he knew where the original *Manuela* was hidden, that would be worth an awful lot of money to someone."

"How much money would the original be worth?"

"With a one-off classic like this, it's almost impossible to say." Spinola shrugged. "No one really knows unless they come up for auction. There were a few other coupés put together by different coachbuilders in the same period. None of them are known to survive now but a modern reproduction on an original chassis fetched half a million at the Quail Lodge auction last year. The unique and original *Manuela* could fetch many, many times more."

"Unless it was a total wreck."

"Even *if* it was a total wreck." He added, holding up a finger. "The provenance of such a car is such that in almost any condition, she would be worth an incredible fortune."

"So, this car," she pointed to the photograph. "Is that what's behind those doors?"

"No, no." Spinola laughed. "The door in the Salone is merely the gateway to finding her."

"I'm sorry, Gigi." She sighed. "I still don't understand."

Spinola took a moment to enjoy a mouthful of the deliciously prepared seafood before proceeding. Natalia took a sip of the wine and tucked in herself, trying not to devour everything in one go.

"Andrew Sutherland was an interesting man." Spinola began, taking up a new story. "He was a good racing driver, not the very best, but certainly good enough for Auto Union. He may even have won his first Grand Prix at Donington but unfortunately, as we all know, things took a turn for the worse by 1939."

CHAPTER TWENTY-NINE
BERLIN, 2018

Jaeger was the German word for hunter. In military terminology the word Jaeger originally referred to light infantry and was used to describe skirmishers, scouts and sharpshooters. During the Napoleonic era, Jaegers within the German-speaking states became the equivalent of the British Rifle Regiments or French Voltigeurs, operating in a loose formation, forming a skirmish line, screening the battalion from the enemy.

His surname was a perfect description for his present activities. Whether any of his family had served in the Hessian, Prussian or Austro-Hungarian units during the Seven Years' War to give rise to this family name, he had never endeavoured to find out. Neither was his personal family lineage of any particular interest. After all, his parents had chosen to abandon him, crossing through the Wall at the first sign of cracks, leaving him to be raised by an aunt and her stream of unsuitable boyfriends.

Germany may have been united shortly afterwards, but it was clear where the 'Ossi' had stood in the hearts and minds of most West Germans once the dust of reunification had settled. After the euphoria of reunited families and long-lost relatives, the excitement quickly subdued and the reality of co-habiting with each other crept in. Migration only seemed to go one way, from the East to West, with Easterners given free money to step across the old border or exchange their obsolete currency into new Deutschmarks.

It was the looks they used to give him. That mildly disdainful, pitying look of being brought up in a society perceived to be backwards and uneducated. A slight frown, a shake of the head, a sympathetic sigh. Even the scornful laughter when he was sent to buy Ostproduckte, to be laughingly told the shop they had always bought groceries from only stocked West German goods now and they needed real money, not those Scheissmarks. At least they could still get Spreewald gherkins. That was two pickled fingers to the imagined superiority of the West.

People in the west generally didn't like Socialism. They said it was ineffective, self-serving, the great perpetuator of misery. On the street outside the apartment block that Jaeger had shared with his aunt was a bronze bust of a man that had lived in the same building. He was an engineer. He had developed some new form of energy storage for batteries, and yet he lived in a modest one-bedroom apartment on an ordinary street just like everyone else. He was a hero. He had his face permanently installed on the street corner. What did it take for the same accolade by the so-called 'enlightened' capitalists?

Doctors, teachers, railway workers, they were all given awards and decorations for exceptional service. A ribbon with a medal suspended from it. Clasps for additional citations. An Honoured Activist could be admired for outstanding improvements in occupational safety. There were medals for water management, literary arts, postal workers. People who didn't like Socialism didn't understand it. Of course, there were flaws. Even in his youth he wasn't so naïve as to be oblivious to the deficiencies. There were faults in every system. Your family would add their name to the waiting list for a Trabant. You knew you would get one. Eventually. Just no one knew when, or how well it would run. That was almost not the point. These were merely improvements to be made but everyone had more or less the same opportunities.

Jaeger was good with his hands. He had never been an academic, but he liked to make things. The Kessler foundry in Leipzig was still producing after the Wall came down and had been a good start, learning about the metallurgy of steels, working on the casting floors, pouring ladles of molten material into moulds. It was hot, physical work. Honest work. If only Schmidt hadn't questioned his parentage. He didn't know there was still some molten steel in the ladle. It had just been a reaction, a backlash against the comments about his parents abandoning him to start a new life and new family. He knew they had had more children since. He had never met them, didn't want to. As far as he was concerned, they weren't his siblings. If Schmidt had just let it go, none of what transpired next would have happened.

Jaeger was a strong man by then. Even with thermally insulated gloves, picking up an empty ladle was no problem with one hand. It had meant to be just a warning, landing well short of him. Just something to tell him to shut up. The molten residue inside travelled a little further, splashing up onto Schmidt's chest and stomach. Of course, the burns were terrible, but Jaeger realised he didn't feel any sense of regret or remorse. Schmidt was an arschloch. Everyone knew it.

The police saw things a little differently, however. Jaeger found himself languishing in a cell for several years and his promising job was gone. Effectively his life was over. That was until they had come to take him away. Ostensibly he was to be relocated to a different prison nearer to Berlin. The one just outside Leipzig was overcrowded. In reality he was taken to a dark office building and interrogated for six hours.

The Ministry for State Security had been officially dissolved with the fall of the German Democratic Republic. The feared Staatssicherheitsdienst, or Stasi, had a file on practically everybody living in East Germany and had an incredibly complex hierarchical structure, one of Socialism's flaws. Apparently an old Stasi informant working at the foundry had mentioned him to some former colleagues. A new secret investigative division was being setup and they needed facilitators. Jaeger's lack of remorse at what happened at Kessler was disturbing but could prove useful. He would be a valuable resource for the new underground Östlicher Informationsdienst. The OID.

After the interrogation, he had been given an apartment and a mobile phone, upgraded every few years, through which he would receive instructions from a faceless voice. In exchange for what was asked of him, a healthy bank balance was maintained, including whatever expenses he incurred. He never knew what department or agency he worked for, or who his immediate bosses were. It didn't matter. He had a new life now. He had money and certain freedoms. As long as he was careful and stayed one step ahead of the police, nothing could hurt him. He still needed to be cautious. If ever he was caught that would be it for him. They made that very clear from the outset. He would be out in the cold. Again.

Jaeger had been a young teenager when the Wall came down. His prospects had looked bleak on several occasions. Now though he had a purpose. A shadow with value. Skirmishing ahead of the main body, whoever they were, using his skills to keep the enemy at bay. He was a hunter. A Jaeger. Now he had a new quarry.

IN THE DEN OF WOLVES

He was on the hunt for the Horch.

Robertson had said the key to finding *Manuela* resided in Berlin. He even ripped out a page of his notebook showing a sketch of an actual key. Robertson knew the relic had been returned to its owner and they were considering restoration. He had been solicited for help because of his knowledge of old automobiles and contacts in the restoration business. Robertson had also revealed that the original craftsmen knew the exact whereabouts of the key, and with it the actual location of the relic. With these fragments of information all brought together, Jaeger discerned that the key was her unique, handcrafted ignition key. The original designs for this key resided in Berlin, at the offices of the former coachbuilder who had drawn it up over eighty years ago.

Though Graham Robertson had been born in Fort William and lived in Scotland for many years, his affinity with classic and vintage automobiles had brought him to the attention of Beaulieu. At the National Motor Museum in the heart of the New Forest his work as a researcher for the Motoring Archives specialised in lost cars of the past. Though the early classics were a particular favourite, he had helped with the search for Elvis Presley's BMW 507, was on the hunt for the Shah of Iran's Maserati 5000GT and had even assisted in finding Hull No.278. The famous Riva Aquarama ordered by Ferruccio Lamborghini in 1968 was powered by two of Giotto Bizzarini's V12 350GTV engines and was thus a historically important vessel. Now, it was undergoing complete restoration in the Netherlands with its new owner.

The history of Erdmann & Rossi was measured, yet illustrious. After they received a royal warrant from the Grand Duchy of Mecklenburg-Strelitz, even the Kaiser himself began to order coachwork for the cars he procured as gifts. Like many businesses however, they never recovered after the Second World War. With an aerial bombing of Berlin demolishing its factory, the economy in ruins, and Berlin divided, Erdmann & Rossi finally closed its doors. Nobody wanted coach built cars in the GDR.

The Erdmann & Rossi Licensing Service business on Kurfürstendamm revived both the name and the same bespoke coachbuilding ethos desired by exclusive clients. In the modern era, the quest for something completely bespoke and one-of-a-kind had seen a similar resurgence in orders for Zagato and Touring bodied supercars. Instead of modern interpretations of the coachbuilder's traditional values however, this new business built individual reproduction vehicles based on historical models on original chassis. Almost like they were a continuation of the original production run. The complex manufacturing process even extended to the materials used, Bakelite, wood and nitro lacquers.

Katrina, the young lady consulting with Jaeger explained to him the process, showing pictures and examples of their work, that it would even be possible to reproduce a one-off vehicle that was lost to history. His interest was aroused.

"For example," she continued. "If you bring to us an original Mercedes W15 chassis, one of our contractual partners can reconstruct the Streamline coupe shown here at the 1933 Berlin IAA. The original vehicle caused quite a stir and is believed to be the first mid-range car to have such a streamlined shape. Sadly, the original is lost, but today you could have your own Erdmann & Rossi recreation."

"Do you have any other examples?" he asked.

"Of course," she smiled eagerly. "Come through to our depository."

Showing him out of the meeting room, she crossed the reception and entered an office with filing cabinets, plan chests and a large conference table in the centre.

"Although much of the archive of the 1940s was lost when Berlin was bombed, many of the earlier works were salvaged along with a treasure trove of photographs from the time." She scanned his face carefully, sensing a particular objective in mind.

"What about the materials?"

"We have some of the original materials too." She nodded. "We use them as reference samples for colour and finish." Sliding out a drawer, she withdrew a piece of wooden dashboard. Beautifully layered burr woods and inlaid pinstripes lacquered to a glossy finish. "This was a popular choice for the dashboard of a high-end Horch, for example." She continued, "Then you have the engine-turned finish from this Maybach. You see this a lot today on café tables, but the original texture here is more pronounced. We can recreate that using original tooling." She offered him the piece to run his finger over. "Of course, enamelled and leather finishes are possible too. Is there a particular project you had in mind?"

"I have a few different options." Jaeger replied. "There are two or three chassis I am in possession of which could work well." He paused. "May I be allowed to have a look at the archives?"

"Of course. I will arrange for some refreshments for us."

"I wonder." He began a little cautiously. "Would it be possible to examine these pieces alone?"

She looked at him a little warily.

"I find there is an emotional connection with old cars. They're as much about texture and smell as they are about aesthetic. I need to…" he hesitated. "I need to 'feel' the right car."

"I see." She said, unconvinced.

These recreations were exclusively a one-off and therefore incredibly expensive. Such pieces were only ever sought after by the most discerning of clients and even in her short tenure with the firm, she had observed many of their unusual and eccentric habits. The original samples were priceless, often the only one of their kind in the world remaining, but the room was secured with a code that only she and the manager knew. She could essentially lock him in with the samples.

"This is something that needs to be done before I could ever consider handing over one of my precious chassis."

"Of course." She stammered. "I'll see that you're not disturbed. The door has a button here to press for attention."

"Thank you." He smiled.

This was becoming almost too easy. "I shall press when I have the right… feeling."

She smiled uneasily but decided to leave him to it. She typed in the code on the panel, waited for the light to go green then opened the door. Glancing at him one more time, she smiled nervously and closed the door behind her, hearing the electric locks click into place. There was something disturbing about his manner, beyond his somewhat odd request. Most clients appreciated the consultation, discussing ideas, comparing samples and styles and examining period photographs to recreate one of the wonderful designs that had graced the order books of the original company.

This client wished to take a more tactile and singular approach to the design selection, and she wasn't entirely sure what to make of it. Returning to her desk, she switched on the monitor and watched him on the security feed from the high-definition cameras in the room. He seemed first of all to circle the table for a moment, pacing up and down, examining the filing cabinets. A piece of paper from his pocket was placed on the table.

Reading the labels on the plan chests he selected one of the drawers and pulled it open. Katrina knew this drawer. It contained electrical plans for the ignition systems. Not the most tactile objects of any car. Without hesitation she picked up the phone and rang her boss. After a brief conversation she patched the security camera directly through to his monitor in the office above. He watched as Jaeger went from drawing to drawing, seemingly becoming more agitated with each one. Finally, he unfolded the piece of paper he had extracted from his pocket and examined it carefully. The camera zoomed in and focussed on the paper where a fine hand drawn image had been sketched of an ignition key bearing the famous Horch logo.

To start a 1930s Horch, the throttle knob on the dashboard should be pushed fully closed, the ignition thumb lever turned to about three quarters of its travel and the air control knob pushed fully forward. Two switches to the right of the large central odometer engaged the magnetos, then the starter button was depressed at the same time as the accelerator pedal, while one foot remained on the brake. There were no ignition keys for most pre-war Horch models and certainly none that resembled the drawing that was in Jaeger's possession. Not even for the most exclusive Horch models. Not even for *Manuela*.

CHAPTER THIRTY
ITALY, 2018

"So, what lies beyond this door?" Natalia asked after they returned to the palace.

"An archive." Came a voice from behind them.

On turning around, a smartly attired gentleman approached. Lean, unusually tall, stylish spectacles and slightly thinning hair. There was something peculiarly patrician about his bearing. Spinola recognised him immediately.

"Don Pietro." He ventured forward. "Allow me to introduce Miss Natalia Bielawska."

"A pleasure." He beamed, approaching her with a smile and outstretched arms. "Our mutual friend asked if I might accommodate you in our humble abode." He continued after the obligatory greetings were concluded. Producing a key, he unlocked the door and gestured for her to go inside. "Please."

Entering the room, they found themselves inside a magnificent library. In contrast with the grand salon they had just left, the room itself appeared surprisingly small. Even humble, as he said. Although the built-in bookcases still reached all the way up to the high ceiling, requiring a mezzanine level and ladders to reach the upper shelves. The walls in between were adorned with original artworks showing all manner of automotive endeavours. Ascari, Fangio, de Portago. Past masters of a different kind.

"This is a collection my father started when he completed the palace." Don Pietro Borromeo explained, closing the door behind them. "Gigi and I have added to it since." He stood in the centre of the room and turned around. "It's not exactly the Vatican archives but for me, it represents something far more important."

Natalia looked around the shelves, expecting to find weighty tomes bound in calf leather, banded spines, and gold tooled with fanciful titles. Instead, the books looked decidedly more modern, mostly linen covered and in several different languages. There were also box files, with names, numbers and QR codes on their spines. It wasn't the kind of library she was expecting. She looked at Don Pietro a little confused, but he was already reaching for a stack of box files from the bookcase marked with the letter 'A'. Withdrawing them from the shelf, he moved to a magnificent reading table and set the file box down.

"Gigi is my chief archivist here at the Borromeo Archives." Don Pietro began. "Together we research the history and provenance of old cars. It's important to our clients that they know the cars in their museums or private collections are genuine and officially recognised. These days there is a lot of money tied up in classic automobiles, so everything needs to be in order."

"Ferrari Classiche specialises in certifying any of their cars over twenty years old, but we deal with many more manufacturers." Spinola added.

Don Pietro opened the first box file and pulled out the document on top. It was bound up with string and bore a symbol of the Borromean Rings on the front of it. "You see these three rings all over this palace." He gestured vaguely around the room. "They're an ancient symbol from the family coat of arms. I'm sure Gigi has explained their possible meanings."

Natalia nodded.

"This is an extrapolation of that idea." He said, pointing to the three intertwined rings on the cover. "Back in the early 1980s, a group of well-respected classic car experts came together. Their objective was to track down some of the most treasured lost automobiles in the world through their combined research and connections. These were cars that either had historical significance, were especially rare or even one-off examples and could therefore be incredibly valuable if they still existed.

"After nearly twenty years, they sent us the results of their combined research for safekeeping and further study. Sadly, the cars have still never been found. Just as these Borromean Rings represent many different things, they were used to signify three of the greatest lost cars in history. What they whimsically called the Holy Trinity: The Mother, Daughter and Holy Nymph. For all cars are feminine in their way."

"There are three cars?"

"Si." Don Pietro nodded. "Of course, there are many more important lost cars than just three, but these three particular cars represent something unique and have long been regarded by collectors as the pinnacle of their craft. Think Leonardo da Vinci, Michelangelo and Brunelleschi."

Natalia raised her eyebrows at the comparison.

"The Auto Club, as they used to refer to themselves, were particularly interested in three vehicles which all disappeared in the 1940s. The Horch that you are interested in is called *Manuela*. She was one of them. She was considered to be the 'daughter' of the collection. Important, but a little less so than the 'mother'." He turned the pages of the Auto Club's research papers.

"The 'mother' was *Monique*, the famous Lost Bugatti, one of only four ever built, yet with unique bodywork personally designed by Jean Bugatti shortly before his death. She has always been potentially the most valuable of the three." He turned next to the back of the papers. "The third seemed to fluctuate a little. Sometimes it was this Alfa Romeo, other times it was this Delage. A one-off and beautifully streamlined coupé as you can see. There was even an aborted effort to discover the Cord Speedster that disappeared after the 1930 Paris Motor Show, but in later years they settled on another vehicle, and given recent events, this crystalises my view of what I think it might have been."

He took up one of the other box files and placed it on top. Don Pietro then tapped away at a laptop, scanned the QR code on the front and two large screens dropped down from the ceiling.

"I often use this room in my own research." He said, gesturing to the screens. "Tracing old cars, where they are now, who they have been sold onto. It makes for a fascinating exploration."

IN THE DEN OF WOLVES

Natalia wasn't convinced, but each to their own.

Don Pietro called up an image of a young woman sitting in a monstrous automobile. She looked lost behind the wheel yet smiled into the camera with confidence and charm. "The woman is Mariette Hélène Delangle. She was better known by her stage name, Hellé Nice. Among other things she happened to be a successful racing driver."

"She was a racing driver?" Natalia gasped in astonishment, looking at the face of an incredibly attractive woman.

"Oh yes, there were many female racing drivers in the early days." Don Pietro explained. "Some might argue that there were even more opportunities for women in motorsport back then. A glamorous driver, the thrill of speed, a healthy whiff of peril. All very intoxicating stuff. They did wonders for advertising." Gesturing to the picture, Don Pietro expounded on his theory. "Ignore the car she is sitting in. I don't think this is the one the Auto Club were after. Do you see the rear of another car, just making an appearance behind it?

"I think so, it's a little blurred."

Don Pietro zoomed in and sharpened up the image a little. "Hellé Nice was more famous for driving around in a magnificent Hispano-Suiza. That's the car she is sitting in, but her other car was this Duesenberg you can just see behind. This is perhaps the only glimpse of the car ever recorded. This, I believe is *Marie*, the holy nymph."

Working away at the laptop a little more, Don Pietro pulled up an image of another vehicle.

"Do you see the similarities between these two?"

"Sort of." Natalia conceded. "Is it this car?"

"No. We know where this car is. It used to belong to another racing driver, Vladimir Rachevsky. He lived in New York but sent the car over to Switzerland in the thirties for Graber to add their own cabriolet bodywork. This picture was taken in the forties and his car never went back to Europe. For me, the car behind the Hispano-Suiza also looks like the work of Graber, though it's almost certainly not Rachevsky's car, it might be the same model though. In which case that means it must be a Duesenberg Model SSJ. The rarest of them all."

He tapped away again. "Let me explain why I think that is significant." While the images of the two cars were moved onto one screen, a news article appeared on the other. "Late last year Bob Jefferson was found dead in the basement of the Petersen Museum in Los Angeles. He was murdered. The museum he was working in is one of the largest automotive collections in the world. We have both done some research for them in the past. Interestingly though, he happened to be a preeminent authority on the history of Duesenberg. He had even written books about them."

A second article appeared.

"Just last week, there was a second murder in Mulhouse at the Schlumpf Collection. The victim was an expert on Bugatti. Indeed, the museum itself holds the largest collection of historical Bugatti vehicles in the world." The third article came from the Sächsische Zeitung and was dated that morning. "Now, just this week another murder has been reported…"

"In Zwickau." Natalia uttered. "Graham Robertson."

"You know?" he gasped.

"I heard about it." She groaned. She had just managed to push the hideous image to the back of her mind.

"Mr Robertson was researching the Horch." Don Pietro uttered quietly, pointing to each of the Borromean Rings on the cover of the Auto Club's papers. "Almost certainly André Langier would have been interested in finding the Lost Bugatti."

"And Jefferson the Duesenberg of Hellé Nice. They were the three members of the Auto Club?"

Don Pietro nodded solemnly.

"These murders are all being investigated by the police though, surely."

"In France, Germany, and the United States." Don Pietro nodded. "Three separate murders in three separate countries stretched over many months. The news of Mr Jefferson's death didn't make it far out of the US headlines. I don't think the murder of Monsieur Langier has been much publicised outside of France and as for your Mr Robertson…" he held up his palms. "How long do you think it will take for these different investigations to be connected by the police?"

"It could take months, if ever." Spinola remarked.

"Yet there are too many coincidences to be ignored now, don't you think?"

"I agree." Spinola nodded.

"I can see that." Natalia murmured. "What I don't see is why Dame Harrington feels that the British Intelligence agencies should be involved. This seems like a series of professional hits for personal profit." He looked at the pair carefully. "In fact, if they didn't find out where the cars were after twenty years of research, then there wasn't any need to kill them in the first place."

"Unless something recently came to light." Spinola added.

"In which case, wouldn't they want to keep these men alive until they've found out where these cars are?"

"Fear can be a powerful incentive to talk." Don Pietro noted.

Natalia fell silent. If the fear of death had hung over them, any reasonable person might have readily given up whatever knowledge they had. The scene at Zwickau suggested that they had not been dealing with a reasonable person in return. Once the information had been obtained, they had been killed. Eliminated one-by-one. It was the kind of hallmark typical of a criminal organisation. What threat though to national security? That was much harder to determine and so far Natalia hadn't seen anything to suggest there was.

CHAPTER THIRTY-ONE
BERLIN, 2018

It wasn't possible. It couldn't be. The Auto Club was real. Jaeger had found all three of them. They had even adopted their own symbol. Three interlocking rings. Together they had been searching for three cars, though it was suspected that they now knew where they were. The three members Jaeger had interrogated confirmed it. They were the Venn diagram, the Krupp logo, the Borromean Rings.

Jaeger had gone further. He had discovered which vehicles they were particularly hunting down; they had divulged everything they knew about *Monique, Manuela* and *Marie*. Robertson had connected everything together and he had eliminated every single one of them.

Only the secret location of the ignition key had been a lie. A ruse. An elaborate hoax.

This possibility had never entered Jaeger's head. Why would it? The Auto Club had consisted of serious people, museum curators, archivists, archaeologists. They didn't play silly games like this. And yet, as he went from drawer to drawer, there were no such designs for a key anywhere. No keys for anything more than matching luggage, not even the grand Pullman limousines Horch had produced, and which were so favoured by high officials. It was all levers and knobs and push buttons. There were no locks on the doors because the cars would often be garaged. Car theft in 1930s Germany was never a consideration. Not many people even knew how to drive anyway.

Moving to the dashboard drawings of similar 853s he could see it clearly. There was not even an ignition slot for a key to go. Nowhere.

The manager of Erdmann & Rossi was standing over Katrina now at the front desk, watching Jaeger becoming even more erratic as he realised he had been duped.

"Shall we call the police?" she asked.

"No, no. We don't want a scene." He replied, conscious of the prestige of the business and the difficulties it had taken to obtain the Erdmann & Rossi licence in the first place. He didn't want it embroiled in scandal and notoriety. "I'll see if I can calm him down."

Moving to the door, he tapped the code, turned the lever and entered.

"Can I assist in any…"

Before the words were all the way out, Jaeger had turned, hurling an old speedometer at the man. His rage broke forth. He had killed three people for nothing. It was a dead end. Now they would be hunting him.

The heavy gauge struck the manager on the forehead, throwing him back against the cabinets and knocking him unconscious. Katrina screamed and got up from the desk as Jaeger seized his moment and left the premises. Running into the archive room, Katrina crouched down and pressed a tissue to her boss's head, stemming the flow of blood from the nasty gash. The pressure seemed to bring him around with a wince has he pressed a hand to hers.

"No police." He murmured. "Lock the front door. Check to see if anything is missing."

Katrina looked sceptical and worried. She clearly didn't like the idea of not involving the police. This man was violent and unpredictable. Who knows what he might do next?

"It's okay." He said in a reassuring tone. "Sometimes people see things that upset them." He pressed a hand to her knee. "After all, some of these cars were built for the Reich. Sometimes seeing that, it can affect them more than they thought."

Katrina frowned, unconvinced, but nodded eventually and acquiesced to his request. It was true, they had clients who were shocked, dismayed, even appalled when they had seen some of the designs from the late 1930s. From the drawing offices of Zwickau, the technical boxes for the chassis blueprints passed on for Erdmann & Rossi to work with had often been stamped with the imprint of the NSKK. A Reichsadler staring back at them with its malevolent eye. Proof that the client had approved the completed drawings.

The National Socialist Motor Corps had at its disposal upwards of some 5,000 vehicles to move around men, materials and senior NSDAP and SA officials. Seeing the distinctive eagle crowning a wreathed swastika still gave pause for anyone trawling through the technical drawings. Perhaps the gentleman wasn't expecting it.

Back out on the street, Jaeger was furious. Putting distance between himself and the offices, he took out his phone and dialled the number. After a short while *die Stimme* picked it up.

"You have it?" he asked excitedly, expecting the call.

"We have been betrayed." Jaeger said, seething with anger even as he spoke.

There was a pause in which Jaeger felt he heard an intake of breath. "How?" the voice asked.

"There is no key."

"Explain."

"There is no key!" He said again, more forcefully. It was difficult to know what else to say. "There never was any key. The whole thing was a lie."

"All of it?"

"I don't know."

"Does that mean the car does not exist after all?"

"I don't know."

"Then find out!" the voice demanded angrily. "We cannot afford to be wrong."

Find out? How on earth was he supposed to do that? All the information he had ever been given had come from the Voice, now the Voice didn't know anything more. Where was he supposed to begin? Perhaps the Horch had been a deliberate deception. Perhaps the real gem was one of the other cars, yet he couldn't be sure which one. The only one thing he was certain of now was that he needed to get out of Berlin.

CHAPTER THIRTY-TWO
FRANCE, 1940

For two and a half years Neville Chamberlain had been Prime Minister of Great Britain. During his time in office the country had suffered a series of ignominious diplomatic defeats culminating in the outbreak of War. It was an unbroken record of foreign policy failures, and yet Chamberlain still retained the confidence of the majority of his countrymen. Britain did not want a second war with Germany.

The shattering realities of the first conflict were all too vivid. War wounds were still healing, and the population left reeling from the repercussions of a global upheaval the like of which no one had experienced before. From the Spanish Armada to the Boer War, Britain had waged war within and for its Empire for as long as it lay claim to one. Yet nothing like the Great War had ever affected so many people in so many ways. It wasn't just the human cost, the lost lives, the broken men, it was the social cost too. A whole way of life had changed. Values had been eroded. Internationally no one would trust anyone ever again.

The Great War hadn't just been a geopolitical family feud of epic proportions, it had torn at the very fabric of society and the country was still counting the cost. Economically Britain simply couldn't afford another war. Psychologically the British people had no appetite for one. Almost a whole generation had been wiped out, if not physically, then certainly emotionally. Militarily it could not compete with the sudden and inexorable rise of Nazi Germany. Yet morally, something needed to be done to face down the tyranny of the Third Reich.

The treaties that had been designed to prevent the rearmament of Germany had simply been ignored. It seemed unconscionable that a sovereign government could just disobey an internationally imposed agreement. Yet that was exactly what had happened. From simple subterfuge like the Deutsche Luft Hansa airline developing designs for aircraft which could innocently carry passengers and freight one day, then be easily adapted into a bomber the next, to outright contravention like the training of pilots at the Lipetsk fighter-pilot school in the Soviet Union. There were deliberate failures to meet disarmament deadlines and even the development of new weapons. Krupp bought Swedish arms manufacturer Bofors, BMW and Daimler began developing aircraft engines again and Blohm & Voss were working on designs for the new H-Class battleships that were neither in accordance with, nor even keeping to the spirit of the Treaty of Versailles.

No doubt the punitive reparations from the previous war had played a part. The global humiliation and demoralisation of an entire nation had perhaps gone too far and cut too deep. The causes and consequences would continue to be debated, but quite simply Britain was not prepared to enter a second conflict. The Great British pet massacre had resulted in almost three-quarters of a million pets being euthanised in preparation for food shortages as a result of the imminent war. Panic in the population was tangible. Pacification parties were being hosted. Trying to leverage the influence of British aristocrats and politicians that were sympathetic towards stopping Britain being dragged into another war. Parliament was divided.

Of course, there are always at least two sides to every story. While there were thousands who were understandably nervous about a repeat of the Great War, there were thousands too that were more than happy to give the Hun another bloody nose, but public opinion was balanced on a knife edge. It was impossible to say which way it would tip next. As *Adler* drove up through France, the materiel being transported west suggested that a bloody nose might be all that Britain could hope to achieve.

Just outside Le Mans, near the commune of Rouillon in the Sarthe department of Pays de la Loire, *Adler* pulled the car off down a little unmarked lane that opened out through the trees into fields. Opening the Gülde fabric sunroof, he raked the seat back almost flat against the bench behind him and lay back, looking up at a clear sky. The smell of summer blossoms and warm earth filtered through to the inside of the car, pleasant birdsong emanated from the hedgerows. It was a perfect day for a picnic.

The fiery haired mademoiselle alongside him lay on her side, reaching over the transmission tunnel to unbutton his shirt and run her fingers through the hair of his chest. He leaned over and kissed her forehead, continuing to reach across to the cubby in the dashboard in front of her. He returned with a notebook and a mechanical pencil from Rotring, an innovative new multipen which allowed a variation of four colours.

Drawing an arm around her shoulders, he pulled her in closer and continued to watch the skies above, counting the aircraft that flew overhead. He added this to the number of aviation fuel tanks he had seen at the rail depot in Le Mans itself. Only twenty so far, but with the infrastructure being rebuilt following the Battle of France, *Adler* knew there would be many more on the way. Judging by the type and number of Dorniers and Stukas flying overhead, this was mainly a short-range reconnaissance and dive-bombing force at the moment. Harrying the Channel Islands most likely and probing the South Coast.

No doubt the bigger Junkers and Heinkels would fly in and take over, escorted by squadrons of fighters joining the ranks assembling on the Atlantic seaboard. Now that France was on the brink of collapse, it seemed Germany wanted to impose air superiority over the English Channel. This would ensure Continental Europe was adequately defended from a second counter-offensive on the French and Belgian coastline. *Adler* could think of another reason why this might be necessary.

Invasion.

Using all the colours at his disposal, *Adler* began to draw maps of the nearby area, marking the units he had seen, approximate numbers and armaments, annotating the sketches in Scots Gaelic in the event they were discovered. There were better ways of spending a sultry summer afternoon. Certainly, Mademoiselle Shelly had other ideas as her fingers walked up to his chin and brushed against his lips.

"Will you still love me after the war has ended?" she asked.

Adler chuckled and kissed her fingertips. "The war has nae even started, lass." He replied. "That might all depend on any of us surviving."

"Then we must make the most of the time we have." She declared, removing her blouse.

Adler sighed and packed away the pencil. Evidently sketching time was over for the afternoon.

Stanislav Holuj had facilitated the second message out with *Adler's* mathematical code. Having raced a Bugatti in the early thirties he was acquainted with *Adler*, the pair having met briefly in Lvov. Holuj was able to pass his message on to the Biuro Szyfrów, who in turn were able to forward it through to Room 47 and supply *Adler* with proper ciphers, an encryption machine and message protocols. Thus, *Adler's* third message, through the recognised channels Denniston had set up at Bletchley Park, now began to have a ring of authenticity about it.

Whoever this *Adler* was, they knew where to find information from and now they knew how to get it out. With help from the Polish Cipher Bureau, they also knew how to properly encrypt their messages. Holuj's assistance came not a moment too soon. A few days after *Adler's* message was transmitted, the Polish racing driver found himself under arrest for participating in the underground resistance organisation. Just six days later, while Denniston was hospitalised with his bladder stone, Stanislav Holuj was taken to Krzeslawice and executed.

"What does the message say?" Denniston asked of Alexander at his bedside. Alexander handed him the decoded message and waited while Denniston's eyes scanned across it. "This has been passed on?"

Alexander nodded.

"Keep this *Adler* on the line." Denniston said.

"I don't have the manpower." Alexander complained. "I had to pull someone off something else, just to transcribe that message."

"I thought I told you to have a dedicated team on this."

"You did." Alexander nodded. "But they're also dedicated to a lot of other things as well."

"If this is true." Denniston said, holding up the paper. "Then the Prime Minister needs to be told immediately."

"He knows." Alexander nodded. "Though it seems there are those that want confirmation first."

"Confirmation?" Denniston asked angrily, sitting up, then instantly regretting it as he pulled at his stitches. "What confirmation." He waved away the nurse that approached his bedside. "If we wait for that…" his voice trailed off, unable to voice his concerns in so open a forum.

Alexander nodded but said nothing.

"Halifax!" Denniston cried. "He probably has a letter prepared for the Italian Ambassador, knowing him. Listen." Denniston beckoned Alexander closely. "If this message is true, it could mean the Channel Islands are at risk. They could be used as a staging post for invasion. They've just got to…" his voice trailed off as he looked at the ceiling, then pain in his abdomen flaring up again.

"Nurse!"

CHAPTER THIRTY-THREE
BERLIN, 2018

Reprinted in the magazine he was reading, the vintage advertisement had depicted a white Porsche 911 with a solitary, roof-mounted blue light and a dark green door with the word POLIZEI stencilled upon it. Powered by the stock version of the same flat-six engine that had taken the 935, 956 and 962 to victory at Le Mans, Daytona and Sebring respectively, the tagline read: 'In Germany there are no getaway cars.' Reinhardt could only wish that were the case. It would make his job a lot easier.

Müller was driving again. Another black BMW 5-Series, though this one belonged to the BKA itself rather than the Saxony State Police. The result was the same. Tearing through traffic on the A9 autobahn, Müller had the strobes on as they hurtled north to Berlin. Over the radio they had heard that the Berlin Police were dealing with a disturbance at the offices of Erdmann & Rossi. The assailant had fled but the police were interviewing staff.

It was suspicious that the office itself hadn't contacted the police. The business next door had observed a suspicious man leaving the premises and peered in just as Katrina was locking the front door. They asked if everything was alright. She had replied in the affirmative, but they caught a glimpse of a man staggering to his feet with a head wound and called it in.

Reinhardt felt it was no coincidence that the Horch Graham Robertson had been particularly studying was a replica of the original *Manuela* with coachwork from an earlier incarnation of the very same company. Müller agreed and the pair set off from Zwickau immediately.

Though the manager of Erdmann & Rossi was keen to impress on Reinhardt the need for discretion, he did agree to share the security camera footage with him and uploaded it to Müller's memory stick. It was clear that the stranger wasn't one of their usual clients, but word was slowly spreading around, and newer customers were beginning to realise the possibilities available to them.

Mercedes-Benz was by far the most popular choice, and a couple of vineyards had ordered recreations of the wonderfully svelte 540K Roadsters to showcase their extensive estate to their most prestigious clients. A Rolls-Royce Wraith was currently undergoing production for a private collection and a very rare Audi 920 Cabriolet was being finalised for another. The order books were modest, but highly lucrative and the original designs were first-rate works of art.

Reinhardt appreciated their enthusiasm for the work but failed to get excited by old cars as he inspected the archive room for himself once the police had released the scene.

"Have you done any work for the Audi Museum?" he asked, venturing on a particular train of thought.

"Yes, one of our first commissions in fact."

"Can we see it?"

"Of course."

After a few moments looking though the files, cross-referencing with the archives, the designs were brought up on the screen in the meeting room.

"Audi had acquired a chassis that had been found on a farm in Ukraine." The manager explained as Katrina brought in some coffee and cake, still visibly shaken by the whole episode. "They wanted to recreate the streamlined Horch coupe commissioned by Bernd Rosemeyer in 1936 and asked us, as the original coachbuilders, to assist with the design."

Müller helped himself to a cake while Katrina poured the coffee, keeping herself occupied while the presentation was called up.

"Unfortunately, none of the original technical drawings survive, but from our photographic archives we were able to make these." The presentation displayed the technical drawings for a vehicle which bore a striking resemblance to the 853 Stromlinien Coupé on display at the Horch Museum.

"Were you involved in the fabrication?"

"Partially." He nodded. "Mainly for the interior where we were able to use many of the original techniques through our network of craftsmen. Much of the mechanical work was done inhouse by Audi themselves, and our fabricators worked together with them in their press shop for the bodywork." He flicked through to the end of the presentation. "Here is the finished vehicle."

Reinhardt looked to Müller. It was unmistakeably the same vehicle.

"How many of these are around?"

"Just this one." The manager explained. "The original disappeared but Audi wanted an exact replica for their museum."

"We've come from the Horch Museum in Zwickau where there is a car exactly like that." Müller observed.

"It will be this same one." The manager nodded. "They loan it out occasionally, mainly to Horch for special exhibitions."

"Has anyone else requested such a replica?"

"No one. Not yet. The original 853 chassis are very rare and increasingly hard to come by. We don't build new ones. Most clients prefer a cabriolet. The chassis needed to be shortened for this model, as it was for the original, and many collectors are reluctant to let that happen with what is already a highly sought after and very rare work."

"Did the client this morning express interest in a particular model?"

"No." Katrina replied. "He was unusually vague. He claimed he had two or three different chassis that he was considering submitting but wanted to be left with the materials to 'feel' which car would be more suitable."

"'Feel' the car?" Reinhardt asked with morbid interest.

"He said it was an emotional connection." Katrina shrugged. "Some of our clients are…"

"Passionate." The manager spoke up. "About their projects."

Reinhardt looked to Müller finishing off his cake and rolled his eyes. Passionate was polite. As far as he could see, these people were obsessive eccentrics.

CHAPTER THIRTY-FOUR
ITALY, 2018

Though the organisational structure of the Secret Intelligence Service was protected under the provisions of the UK Official Secrets Act, Natalia had a basic understanding of who was what, where and why. Contrary to the movies, however, she had never taken an elevator up to have a friendly chat with the Chief himself in his private top-floor office. Instead, she reported to one of his subordinates, the Chief Operational Officer in charge of field agents. Arthur Allardyce had been in the Service for decades. Given the nickname AA by the junior agents, he oversaw foreign operations and was her immediate boss.

Before Natalia could agree to spend any more time on these relics, she needed to consult with her superiors. Spinola agreed to show her the extensive gardens and she found a quiet corner to make the phone call. It seemed the Chief had already received an ear bending from the venerable Dame Harrington on the subject but was still unwilling to be diverted.

"Listen, Natalia, what you choose to do in your own time is largely up to you, but C isn't going to sanction some treasure hunt for lost cars." AA explained clearly. "If they're interested, we can pass onto Interpol what we know, but unless the respective forces make an appeal to them for assistance they're not going to muscle in and get involved either. As far as anyone is concerned, these are three unrelated murders."

"I've read the reports. The MO of the killer is remarkably similar, and the victims' common standing in the classic car community makes this unusual to say the least, sir."

"I agree, but it's not our issue." He replied. "There isn't anything to suggest these recent developments require our involvement. Listen, I know the old fruit myself. She was still here when I was just starting out. She has good instincts, but whatever she's driving at now is all ancient history. It's nothing for us to worry about."

"So, we're out of it?"

"Completely." He said firmly. "Look, if you want to put a watching brief on it, that's up to you," he added with a more conciliatory tone, "But don't get yourself involved at any level, and don't get distracted by it either. You've got enough going on."

"Understood." She sighed, unsure whether she felt relieved or disappointed.

Delving into a world of old cars and lost history didn't sound particularly riveting, yet at the same time the shock that just such a thing had resulted in three murders across as many countries over several months was a disturbing revelation. AA had a point though. The SIS couldn't just jump on every international criminal investigation on the off chance the outcome threatened Britain's strategic interests. Natalia wasn't even sure whether she was all that interested in observing it from the side lines either. Though the look of expectation on Spinola's face as she concluded the call was compelling.

"Well?" he asked.

She replaced the phone, quickly running through various scenarios in her head. Whichever way she played them out, there was no way she could remain completely uninvolved even if she pursued just a passing interest into the police investigations. She either had to be all in, or totally detached.

"I'm sorry." She shook her head. "They won't sanction it."

"I understand." He nodded, though it was obvious he was crestfallen. "These days, agencies need to be more careful where and how they tread." He shrugged in typical Italian fashion. "Well, there is nothing more to be done. Except…"

"What is it, Gigi?"

"Perhaps a longer tour of the lake before dinner? It would be a shame to miss out now that you're here, and the light is perfect."

She smiled. It seemed a shame not to indulge the old man one last time. He appeared to relish his tour guide duties and there were less appealing ways to wile away a crisp, clear February afternoon than a boat ride on one of Italy's most picturesque lakes.

"Okay. Why not?"

CHAPTER THIRTY-FIVE
SCOTLAND, 2018

A blackhouse, or Tigh Dubh, was a traditional dwelling common in Ireland, the Hebrides and the Scottish Highlands. The buildings were generally built with double wall dry-stone packed with earth and were roofed with wooden rafters covered with a thatch of turf and cereal straw or reeds. Packed earth or flagstones were used for flooring and a central hearth for the fire provided heat, the smoke of which made its way through the roof, allowing the soot to blacken the interior.

Traditionally a partition divided livestock from people and a fowl hole allowed feathered residents to come home to roost in the evenings. A box bed, made from spalded sycamore and larch provided a comfortable night's sleep for humans at the other end. There were still a few of the old black houses on the Hebridean islands. Some were abandoned ruins. Others were still inhabited. A few had been turned into luxury holiday cottages.

Tigh Dubh on the Isle of Skye's Vaternish peninsula could not have been more different to the traditional Hebridean blackhouse. Vertical plates of exposed, reinforced concrete projected up and out from the cliff face to support the front of a box of black galvanised steel that formed the central hub of the building. The rear of the steel cuboid was sunk deep into the landscape behind as it naturally sloped down to the western cliff edge from the hills that threaded their way up the spine of the peninsula.

Projecting forwards from this central block, a black timber-clad rectangular protrusion cantilevered out over the sea loch. Waves crashed against the cliffs below. The fully-glazed end wall of this main living space framed spectacular views across Loch Bay to the islands of Isay, Mingay and Clett out on Loch Dunvegan, the tip of the Duirinish peninsula beyond and, on a clear day, even the hills of North Uist across the waters of the Little Minch. Reflected light from the sea provided an ever changing pattern across the minimalist white interior.

The persuasive architectural integrity of rigorous rectangular forms was continued with two additional blocks extending horizontally from the central hub. Clad in white galvanised steel sheets with frameless glass looking out to the north and south respectively, the robust, linear exterior strangely blended in perfectly with the dramatically bleak rolling landscape all around. Both made a clear statement yet neither tried to dominate or outshine the other.

A strictly limited colour palette of black and white, along with the bold, structured use of concrete, steel and wood, made for an iconic and striking dwelling when viewed from the loch, projecting out and spilling over the edge of the precipitous cliff. Yet approaching it from the road, situated roughly halfway between the tiny crofting townships of Stein and Hallin, the visitor was confronted with a plain, single-storey volume. Edged with black as the galvanised steel wrapped around the margins, a timber clad façade was unadorned but for a pair of black aluminium doors.

Iain Sutherland didn't often visit his brother. He preferred the traditional architecture and cosy home comforts of the eighteenth century family seat, *Talisker House*. The clean, modernist lines and minimalist interior aesthetic of *Tigh Dubh* were too clinical, too Scandinavian Noir for his liking. Although they were twins, they were not identical, and each had very different tastes. This was why Iain always invited his brother over to try a new batch from the distillery. If Craig liked it, then there was a good chance it would do well in the market. If he didn't then perhaps it was best as a limited release only.

At least one area they did agree on was their choice of transportation. Almost nothing could beat a Land Rover in this rugged setting. The inevitable dents and scuffs that would be accrued during their lifetime on the Isle of Skye added character. On anything newer, sleeker, and more plasticky, the vehicle would look like a wreck in very short order. Even then though they had differed.

After their grandfather's Series II had finally died and rusted into obscurity, Iain had opted for a long-wheelbase Defender 130 double cab pickup. He had a wife and two children and needed the loading bay at the back for casks, bags of malt and crates of bottles. His brother had chosen a shortened Defender 90 Hardtop Utility. He just needed space for the dogs. Iain crunched up to the shale apron in front of *Tigh Dubh*, blanched as he looked at the front façade and clambered down with a bottle in hand.

A stiff north westerly gale was blowing in icy rain down from Lewis and Harris. Iain stowed the bottle in the deep internal poacher's pocket of his waxed stockman's coat, taking up his phone from the dashboard and burying it in an outside gusseted pocket. Closing the door of the Land Rover, he felt the full force of the wind as the rain was driven sideways into his face. Dashing round the back of the pickup he jogged over the shale to the shelter afforded by the broad rectangular bulk of the entrance.

Tapping in the number on the keypad unlocked the door. The steel bar handle was icy to the touch, but the right-hand door pivoted easily on its robust German hinges. He didn't need to grab the handle on the left-hand door and make a grand entrance, he just needed to get out of the biting cold fast. The door closed behind him with a smooth yet assured solidity, almost sucked back into the frame, and at once the howling gale outside was hushed. Wiping his feet on the recessed black coir matting, he removed his coat and hung it up on the rack, fabricated from a large piece of driftwood and the tines of deer antlers. One of the few nods to rustic Scotland in the whole place.

Two sheepdogs bounded carefully up the staircase from the living room to greet him. He fussed them, feeling the warmth of their fur and the familiar smell of dog. They barked in greeting, panted, accepted his fuss, and having assured themselves that all was well, returned downstairs. Iain was always curious as to why Craig preferred minimalism, then took in two Rough Collies that needed a retirement home after working the land but shed a great deal of fur everywhere. His brother was a confusion of ideas sometimes. A personified antithesis to the architecture he enveloped himself in.

As befitting a house of this style, the entrance hall was suitably bright and airy. Polished white floor, a vast skylight illuminating the stairway and glass rails in front and to the side. Though the rain couldn't be heard hammering on the glass roof above, the storm resembled a jet wash being sprayed across its expanse. The entrance hall was in fact a floating white mezzanine projecting into the central steel box of the house, entering near the top of its vertical extent with the bulk of the structure sunk into the hillside below him. A single black steel stringer supported the floating stairs from below like a central spine as it descended to the next level where a lobby area contained full-height bookcases, access to the bedroom wings in the north and south and opened out into the main living space situated in the narrower timber-clad projection to the west.

Beyond the library, clean fluid lines of the open-plan kitchen flowed seamlessly to the dining area. A low, double-sided fire partitioned the dining area from the sprawling lounge without breaking into the view afforded by the full-height glass windows. The monochrome aesthetic was broken only by the surprising and extraordinary sight of a green and yellow Lotus 49 mounted vertically to the left-hand wall.

Constructed at the end of the 1967 season, Chassis R4 first contested the South African Grand Prix of 1968 where Jim Clark achieved pole position, recorded the fastest lap and claimed his final career victory. After its discovery, the restored chassis had been reunited with an original Ford Cosworth DFV engine, a ZF 5 DS12 gearbox and was in full working condition prior to being affixed to the wall like a bizarre hunting trophy. As a piece of automotive engineering, the Lotus formed an interesting manmade counterpoint to the natural world flooding in through the windows. Another paradox.

Access to the lower floor of the projection was through a circular cellar in the kitchen. Hinged round glass doors between the rear wall units and the central island opened like a clamshell to access a three-metre deep cylindrical wine rack entered via an internal spiral staircase. Though each deep bin could store either twenty-seven bottles of Bordeaux or fourteen Burgundy bottles, Craig Sutherland was using them to store an extensive and impressive collection of rare and highly sought after Single Malt Scotch Whiskies.

The room in this lower floor of the central projection was considerably shallower than the space above and did not extend right to the edge of the space. Instead, the glass wall at the far end opened onto a balcony sheltered by the structure above that led to the edge of the box in which it was situated. Glass railings ensured the uninterrupted views were retained while their elevation from the deck and deep guttering beneath the decking boards allowed the rain and occasional seawater sprayed up from below to cascade back down to the foreshore.

Instead of being a fully enclosed cylindrical vault, the spiral cellar was open on one side and continued into a more traditional arrangement, almost mirroring the library above, exchanging books and art pieces for whisky grouped by region, distillery, and age. A portion was reserved for some of the artistic tubes and boxes, both new and old, in which the whisky had been packaged. Arranged alphabetically by the five main whisky regions, they formed a unique collection of the distillers' craft.

A small bar area facilitated the mixing of cocktails with some of the more ordinary whiskies on offer. Though the brothers were purists when it came to savouring ancient and rare single malts, they were not adverse to mixing a few cocktail blends to enjoy the beverage in new ways.

The walls of the room were panelled with seamless, smooth boards of dark wenge hardwood from Central Africa, providing a contrasting texture to the grey, polished slate floor. Vintage explosion proof brass ceiling fixtures and bulkhead accent lights illuminated the room with a warm, cosy glow. Deep corner sofas and comfortable lounge chairs offered a relaxed seating arrangement to savour a wee dram and gaze out at the mercurial temperament of the sea lochs.

This was Craig's favourite haunt. A basement level snug suspended over the loch. The dark, cosier décor contrasted with the bright and open spaces of the rest of the house above. There was a more rustic feel to the room, almost akin to a traditional blackhouse with sheepskin rugs, wood burning fire and deep, exposed joists, yet all executed with a minimalist, contemporary twist.

"To what do I owe the pleasure?" Craig asked, not even looking up from the book he was reading.

"Thought yer might like this for the collection." Iain replied, presenting his brother with the bottle he had removed from his coat. "Just came today."

The bottle was a very rare 1967 29year old Islay single malt from the Ardbeg Distillery. Finished in an oak sherry cask, the whisky possessed a distinctive reddish hue and original label from Kingsbury's bottlers of Aberdeen. Retailing at upwards of £30,000, the expression was almost impossible to come by now and would make a fine addition to anyone's collection.

"Yer know ma weakness for sherry casks." He said, half-appreciative, half-scornful. "How can I naw have a wee tipple of this?"

"Well, that's yer choice." Iain chuckled. "Any luck with the Macallan?"

Craig patted his brother gratefully on the shoulder as he received the bottle. It was the closest either of the Sutherland boys came to any overt show of affection.

"Naw yet." He sighed, ambling over to the racks to add his latest acquisition. "After the 72year old, yer wid have thought the 55 would be easier tae come by."

"Aye, but it's the Lalique effect." Iain remarked. "That one was a highly sought after design."

The Speyside distillery had released their special edition of staggeringly old whiskies in exquisite, specially commissioned, and uniquely designed crystal decanters by Lalique Maison. A set of their Six Pillars series in a bespoke natural ebony cabinet had auctioned for nearly a million pounds in Hong Kong the previous year, selling to an undisclosed private collector.

"There's another auction coming up, but I daresay it will go tae some sheik or oligarch or someone." He sighed. "Yer just cannae compete these days."

Iain nodded in sympathy. A new wave of rare whisky collectors from Asia, Russia and the Gulf states had driven up the prices at auction almost exponentially, being willing and able to pay almost any price to acquire whatever they wanted. For many it was no more than a mere show of wealth, an investment in a commodity that would only ever go up in value, like the Bugatti Chiron on the driveway that had nothing more than delivery mileage on the clock. To serious collectors like the Sutherland's who also appreciated the subtleties of the craft but were not backed up by the financial resources of a People's Republic, an oilfield or mineral mine, it was becoming increasingly difficult to match the same level of investment.

Taking up his phone, Iain unlocked it and held it out as Craig returned from adding the bottle carefully to his collection. Craig took it and looked up.

"Three now." Iain muttered, pointing to the article. It was from the *Sächsische Zeitung*, a regional daily newspaper published in Dresden. "Gray was killed in the Horch Museum a week or so back."

Craig looked grim. "This is naw a coincidence anymore."

"I agree." Iain replied, his former reluctance evaporated with the latest revelations. "But why these three? What is it…" he paused, correcting himself with a wince, "What was it aboot these guys that someone wanted tae kill them for?"

"Perhaps it really is aboot our relic." Craig sighed, returning to the lounge chair. "That's the only thing I can think aboot now." He gestured to Iain's phone. "Finding Graham in the Horch Museum, he was obviously doing research on it. For us."

"Aye it's looking like it." Iain nodded. "We do have one thing on our side though." He observed, taking the companion chair nearby.

"What's that?"

"It now only leaves us two knowing anything about it."

"That's worse. What if Graham told his killer where tae find us, or the relic?" Craig remarked. "If he consulted these other two guys and they put him ontae the Horch Museum, maybe that's why they were killed. Either someone is trying tae silence them, or someone really wants tae find it."

"It's just an old car."

"They've now killed three people, Iain." Craig cried. "Yer said yerself, the money these things can fetch…"

"I know, I know." He nodded, his eyes staring at the accompanying footstool as he clasped his hands.

"I dinnae think it would get tae this."

"Neither of us did." Iain shook his head.

"How did word get oot that we wanted tae restore her anyway?"

"I don't know." Iain murmured. "Maybe someone Graham works with. We don't know that it has though, we're still just guessing here."

"Maybe. It just feels like someone somewhere knows how much *Manuela* is really worth and wants tae get their hands on her."

"They know more than us."

"Seanair always kept things close tae his chest."

"Aye, a little too close perhaps."

Craig got up and wandered over to the wall. Completely unadorned but for an old World War II era Jerry Can, the utilitarian object had been converted into a minibar. Dropping down the laser cut front flap revealed a partitioned interior of beautifully moulded Canadian oak plywood with a rich American walnut veneer. The can contained a Czech non-lead crystal decanter and two double-walled borosilicate tumblers from the Norlan glassworks.

"Maybe it was to protect us." Iain mused. "After all, it was him that had the relic first."

"What would he have done, do yer think?"

"Old man Sutherland?" Iain pondered for a moment. "Probably would find whoever these people are and chib the bastards."

"Aye, yer probably right." Craig sighed, setting the two tumblers on the pouring table, and reaching in for the decanter.

"What are you on now?" Iain asked, referring to the whisky his brother was pouring.

"This is a wee Royal Brackla." He explained. "Finished in Palo Cortado sherry casks. Gaw a lovely, sweet finish."

He replaced the decanter's precision machined aluminium stopper and carried the two glasses over. Gazing outside, the storm was still lashing across the balcony. The small isles barely visible through the rain, appearing nothing more than dirty smudges in an ocean of grey.

"It's not letting up, is it?" Iain commented, receiving the glass Craig offered him as he continued to cross the room to check the fire on the opposite wall.

"I have a feeling these people will nae either." Craig said gloomily, adding another couple of logs to the wide, wood-burning stove, inset flush to the wall. "Naw until they've gaw what they want."

"What is that?" Iain asked in reply.

"Honestly, I dinnae know." Craig shook his head. "Either they want what Seanair stashed away, or they want tae destroy it. But why, and why now, I cannae think."

When Craig became agitated, his accent became a little thicker and he slipped in more and more Gaelic into his speech. It was unconsciously done and an unusual trait, but it always amused Iain. He was the traditionalist and yet his brother had the stronger accent and used the ancient tongue more than he did. Seanair was the Scot's Gaelic word for grandfather.

Iain shrugged as Craig returned to the lounge chair once again. "Plan of action."

Craig looked at him with an anxious expression.

"Clearly we can no longer do nothing." Iain began calmly. "That much is obvious. Whatever we do decide, it needs to be done quickly, but quietly."

"We need help, Iain. This is too big for us now. It's already gaw out of hand."

"What would yer suggest?"

"As much as I hate tae admit it, yer the brains of this family." Craig murmured, taking a sip of the 18year old single malt.

Setting it down on the side table, Craig got up and disappeared back through the cellar. Emerging in the kitchen above, he ventured on into the library. One of the central shelving units slid sideways to reveal a metal gun safe. Unlocking it, he took out one of the 12-gauge Westley Richards side-by-side shotguns and a box of shells. Locking it back up again, he returned to the kitchen, negotiated the spiral cellar stairs and returned to the lounge chair to take another measure of whisky.

Iain mirrored his brother's action, imbibing a measure and staring at the storm battering the north coast of Skye. He watched his brother break open the breach and load in two shells. He knew they would be back out again before the end of the evening. This was just a reaction, but it made him think about his own guns back at *Talisker House*.

How much had Graham Robertson told his killer? Would it get to that? When they had ventured upon the idea of restoring their grandfather's old classic car to its former glory, they never envisaged the chain of events that it would initiate. Now they didn't know how to stop them either.

CHAPTER THIRTY-SIX
GERMANY, 1941

Adler's Horch 853 Sport Coupé gleamed with a luxurious patina as the car rolled through the streets of Munich. On the northeast corner of Brienser Strasse and Türjenstrasse, the Bosch servo-assisted brakes brought the shimmering car to a graceful stop outside the Wittelsbacher Palace.

This red brick, Neo-Gothic building was constructed by Friedrich von Gärtner and Johann Moninger between 1843 and 1848, for Crown Prince Maximilian, later King Maximilian II of Bavaria. It served as the retirement residence of King Ludwig I and became the official residence of Ludwig III from 1887 to 1918. Indeed, it was Ludwig III who addressed the population of Munich from the balcony of the palace at the beginning of August 1914, upon the outbreak of the First World War.

Adler thought about that fact as he gazed up at the impressive edifice. He had a vague memory of a more innocent time, somewhere else in the world, when the declaration came in. He was in a soapbox cart he had made with his dad, using his old pram wheels and a rope for steering while this Cameron boy over from the mainland pushed him before clambering on behind. It was a heady summer's day, rare for Talisker Bay on the west coast of Skye. Entertainments were being had all along the black sands of the beach. A perspiring manservant came running up from the house to inform his father there was an urgent telephone call. Then that was that. The world changed in a single summer's afternoon.

In 1919 the Wittelsbacher Palace became the meeting place of the

IN THE DEN OF WOLVES

Aktionskommittee of the Bavarian Soviet Republic, but by 1933 had been taken over as the Munich headquarters of the Geheime Staatspolizei. It was for this purpose that *Adler* alighted from the Horch, rounding the front of the vehicle, before assisting a young Fraulein out of the passenger seat. Arm in arm they entered the building, whereupon *Adler* was approached by a Captain of the Schutzstaffel. SS-Hauptsturmführer Reinhardt gently escorted the young lady away into the labyrinthine offices.

Adler couldn't help but feel a ripple of remorse trickle like ice down his spine. The pretty young woman had been very persuasive in obtaining information from the upper echelons of the Wehrmacht. There was a nice little bordello on Rue Viellejust in the 16th arrondissement of Paris that she was beginning to frequent. Being so close to the French Gestapo headquarters at 93 Rue Lauriston, it was quickly becoming a favoured haunt of French and German officers, but she was also a little too incautious.

L'Étoile de Kleber was a perfect little maison close, founded and managed by Aline Soccodato. Her first house on Rue Cardinet took as its moniker, the nickname she had been given by Grace Palmier; *Madame Billy*, having left her work as a shop assistant in the Nouvelles Galeries store in Dole to make her fortune in Paris as a prostitute. When Aline Roblot met the singer Soccodato in *L'Européen* and the *Casino de Paris*, she lived with him for two years in a wild marriage while she began working in hour hotels and making plans for a brothel of her own.

With the opening of her second house, the new establishment was to be of the highest class. Having paid 150,000 Francs for a four-storey villa with ten rooms, she furnished the apartments with armchairs in the style of Louis XVI and other selected furniture. The garden was particularly beautiful and, in the salon, filled with potted plants, she planned to host private events of the most wondrous extravagance.

Its proximity to the lion's den came with the advantage of having a ready supply of meat, caviar and champagne transferred to *L'Étoile's* kitchens, while the rest of the city would begin to suffer increasing depravations. After the Hotel Chatham had closed its doors, the Soccodatos had opened another channel for *Adler's* messages to get through to British intelligence. Aline had even managed to acquire one of the Hotel Chatham's magnificent Art Deco champagne coolers from ARGIT. The decorative ice bucket had been inexplicably discarded on the street after a raid by Gestapo. Washing out the faint smell of urine, she used it to chill the officers' bottles of grand cuvee.

However, Mademoiselle Shelly was becoming too much of a liability and was in danger of blowing the whole thing wide open. *Adler* had felt increasingly ill at ease in her presence and convinced himself that for the greater good, to ensure his communication channel remained open, she needed to disappear. Indeed, for the burgeoning French Resistance to gain any hope of a foothold, the cover at *L'Étoile de Kleber* needed to be maintained at all costs. The Soccodato Circle had agreed by a majority and so a plan was made.

The setup was simple. Having seduced a mid-ranking SS-officer in one of *L'Étoile's* rooms, the officer, impressed by Shelly's artistry, would introduce him to his commander in Germany. His own wife had recently died, and the officer needed some solace in the quiet morning hours. Sensing the opportunity of an even bigger fish to fry, Shelly could not help herself and just as *Adler* had predicted dived enthusiastically under the covers to accept her new assignment in the heartland of the Third Reich.

Such was her eagerness to please that she took no care in confirming the officer's story. This by itself alerted *Adler's* heightened sense of caution. Her devotion to the outcome of Free France was certainly admirable, and her passionate character a most desirable quality, but that she would not channel her fervour in more vigilant execution was making the whole underground operation exceedingly nervous. In a stroke, she could unwittingly expose everyone.

So it was that the newly promoted SS-officer personally escorted her to Munich, whereupon he took it upon himself to drive her directly to the Wittelsbacher Palace. She was to meet SS-Hauptsturmführer Reinhardt, who was the personal secretary to the officer's commander. From there, she would be entertained by the senior officer in question, wined, dined, then accommodated in one of the Palace's many lavish rooms. She could have anything that her heart desired.

At some future point, unknown even to *Adler*, her interrogation would commence. She had contacts, she knew names and addresses, but as yet, not enough to risk an entire network. Madame Billy had taken great care to inform her contacts and expunge any traces of resistance at the addresses well in advance of the planned subterfuge. When Shelly gave them up, as everyone knew she eventually would in time, the resulting investigation, the dawn raids, and the arrests that would follow, would only ever nibble at the fringes of the elaborate network, and thus preserve the whole.

Yet none of this did anything to salve *Adler's* conscience as he turned upon his heels and smartly marched back out to the Horch. He knew Mademoiselle Shelly would never see the sunlight again, but in handing her over to his superiors, *Adler* hoped, despite any of her denunciations of him, the revelations about their intimacy and the notes she had seen him make, High Command might see that his actions had been testing her, winkling her out and proving his own unswerving loyalty to the Reich. It might just cement himself into the inner circle of trust that he needed. For him personally it was a huge gamble, but in compromising one person directly, and risking the liberties of a handful of others, he may just preserve the channel he needed to commit an even bigger betrayal. One he hoped piece by piece would bring everything down around him. All for the good of Europe.

As his commander had once told him rather callously one afternoon, to enjoy life at the top table, a few crumbs needed to be swept onto the floor. Sitting back in the monogrammed seat of his sportscar, he recalled that night in Paris, cavorting with three princesses. An Egyptian beauty, the Italian sweetheart, and her Russian firebird. He wondered where they all were now. He knew he had been right in his assessment of the future the following morning.

He would never be happy again.

CHAPTER THIRTY-SEVEN
GERMANY, 2018

The main building of the Bundeskriminalamt in Berlin's Alt-Treptow neighbourhood was a nondescript brick-built structure completed in the 1950s. The Federal Criminal Police complex itself was a sprawling site near the River Spree a stone's throw from Treptower Park and the Soviet War Memorial.

In his office, Erwin Reinhardt was reviewing the reports on two other murders, remarkably similar to his own case. One of them occurred the previous year in the famous Petersen Museum on Wilshire Boulevard, Los Angeles. Bob Jefferson, a senior curator, and archivist had been found dead in the basement of the museum. He had been working late to prepare some of the archived exhibits for a new display to run until New Year. The world famous museum had so many historical automobiles and documentation that periodically they would devote a section to a new feature.

The gruesome find was very much the same as the scene Reinhardt had been presented with in Zwickau. A combination of strangulation and exsanguination. The wire used to strangle the victims had severed the major arteries, resulting in catastrophic blood loss. Someone was clearly intent on sending a brutal message.

It was the same with the case of André Langier in France a little over a month ago. At the revered Cité de l'Automobile located in Mulhouse, built around the fabulous collection amassed by the Swiss brothers Hans and Fritz Schlumpf, Monsieur Langier had been found dead in the Motorcar

Masterpieces Area. This section of the museum was devoted to the display of eighty of the most beautiful cars of the 1920s and 30s. The central display was reserved for the 1930 Bugatti Royale Type 41 and Napoleon Coupé that belonged to Ettore himself. In fact, the museum was world renowned for having the largest and most comprehensive collection of Bugatti motor vehicles in the world.

Graham Robertson may have been killed in Germany, but he was a well-respected historian working at the National Motor Museum in Beaulieu. The connection these three victims had to the world of classic automobiles could not be overstated. They were amongst the most knowledgeable in their field, regular attendees at concourse events all over the world. It was clear they had not been picked at random, though what their connection was to each other individually must have run much deeper than a mere professional association.

Reinhardt picked up the polythene bag with the personal effects of Graham Robertson and went through the objects one-by-one. A Moleskine notebook with handwritten scrawls, sketches, and annotations. A page of which had been torn out towards the back. He now had that missing page, abandoned by the agitated client at Erdmann & Rossi. It was a detailed hand drawn sketch of a car key. A key he was informed never existed for Horch models of that vintage. So, why did Robertson have such an image?

Surely as an automotive historian he would have known that. The sketch even had a serial number on the collar, the kinds of ridges and notches expected of the biting cuts on the blade, two profile contours and a rounded tip. The bow was embossed with the Horch logo. A capitalised H with Horch wordmark forming a stylised coronet above, surmounting the four-interlinking rings of Auto Union. It certainly looked like a genuine key.

The licence manager assured him that he had never seen such a design before, and he had cabinets full of the original designs. The coachbuilders would only be provided with a rolling chassis. Everything from there up they designed themselves, the ignition system, the interior, the bodywork, sometimes even the wheels if the standard Rudge Whitworth's were not appropriate. Coachbuilders were not just metal bashers, they had to be cabinetmakers, auto electricians and upholsterers. There was pattern making, saddlery, chrome-plating. In some ways, the chassis manufacturer had the easy part.

So, no key. Not for the Horch.

There were two sets of other keys. Separate keyrings. One looked to belong to a house. The other possibly a car. The set for the car had two keys, a leather fob and a metal keyring. Looking at the black leather torpedo fob, he turned it over and noticed the vitreous enamel badge. The badge depicted an unusual brown tortoise, surrounded by a green wreath on a yellow background. At the bottom of the badge were the words 'Gordon Keeble'. Reinhardt frowned. A relative perhaps? The second keyring was shaped like a tag, with three interlocking rings etched onto the surface. They didn't mean anything to him at all. Perhaps his colleagues in France might have some ideas.

Next was the flyer to Natalia Bielawska's lecture on photography in Dresden. It had been placed as a kind of bookmark in the notebook. Did she have anything to do with anything? There was a vague possibility that it was nothing more than a simple bookmark. He winced as he recollected his attempt to elicit some kind of confession from her at the Horch Museum. It had worked before. Taking a bank manager back to the scene of his empty vault had yielded some surprising revelations.

With a little guidance on how to use the app from his daughter at home, Reinhardt had checked Natalia's Instagram account and scrolled through the hundreds of posts she had uploaded. All landscape scenes. Some with animals, some without. The stories were divided into locations: England, Scotland, Italy, Germany, and so on. She had quite a collection of followers already. As it was a public profile, he could see who they all were. None of them appeared to be either Graham Robertson or André Langier. No connection there.

Robertson's wallet and passport were the two final things in the bag. The usual receipts, cards and a few Euros, a mixture of notes and coins. A second flap contained some pounds and pennies. Wearily he picked up the passport and flicked through it. Since the Schengen Area came into existence, tracing someone's movement through Europe was not as easy as it once was when you could simply go through a passenger's collection of entry and exit stamps.

Now, although passports were electronically scanned at points of entry, as well as hotels, it needed a formal request to Interpol in order to obtain the relevant information. Reinhardt didn't feel he was quite there just yet but knew he couldn't work on this alone. There were a few trips to America logged on the pages during the summer of the previous year. Müller had cross-referenced the dates and locations to car events on the West Coast. Monterey Car Week, Quail Lodge and Pebble Beach. The funeral of Bob Jefferson also coincided with one of the stamp sets later in the year. Coincidence? Possibly the pair knew each other well. Did they also know

IN THE DEN OF WOLVES

André Langier?

Finding the number for the Commissariat Central in Mullhouse, he picked up the phone and made a call. As he did so, Müller arrived with an excited face and a sheaf of paper. Reinhardt held up his hand.

"Bonjour Madam." He said to the woman who answered the phone. "I need some assistance." He enquired on the possibility of speaking to the detective in charge of the Mulhouse murder and was asked if he could wait. "Oui. Très bien." He placed a hand over the mouthpiece and looked up.

Both the fingerprints on the sketch and CCTV footage from Erdmann & Rossi had given them a bit of a breakthrough. The assailant had been identified as Michael Jaeger. Born in the old GDR before the wall came down, his parents had been one of the lucky ones to escape without getting shot. They hadn't seen him since, though they had tried to reach out to him once the wall came down. It seemed they were too late for any reconciliation. Jaeger had spent time in prison for a grievous assault with a steel ladle. Reinhardt had the old police file sent over from Leipzig sat on his desk. Sentenced to ten years, he served seven in Leipzig, then was transferred to Berlin but there was no record as to where.

Cross-referencing the CCTV images with anyone else fitting that description found evidence of ATM usage. There was no faked identification, no alias, everything was in his own name. Yet somehow his disappearance from the prison system hadn't been flagged up, only an expected release date. For those final three years of his sentence, he had simply disappeared. Only reappearing another two years after that with an apartment rental contract, mobile phone and bank account. Where he went or what he was doing for work was something of a mystery. Every month a payment was made from a company called OID. The name didn't appear on any known records. It wasn't registered anywhere in Germany. As far as he could find out, it didn't exist.

They had tapped his phone and requested records of any ingoing and outgoing calls over the last six months. Reinhardt put Müller onto the Prison Service of Saxony to try and work out what happened during the transfer, who authorised it, when and where. That left him with working out why he had attacked the manager of Erdmann & Rossi, and why he was looking for a key that didn't exist.

"What do you have?" he asked.

"Last sightings of Michael Jaeger." Müller explained. "He was seen boarding a train in Berlin about half an hour after the attack at Erdmann & Rossi. Heading west, it got into Mannheim Central. From there he took a second train that terminated in Paris. No trace of him getting off before the border."

"So, he could be in France even now?"

Müller nodded.

"Qui? I understand. Could you ask him to please give me a call as soon as he returns? It is most urgent…Thank you. The number is…"

Terminating the call Reinhardt looked up at Müller with a troubled expression.

"While he remains in France, there is not much we can do. I still want to know where he went for five years." Reinhardt insisted. "He could have been on our radar earlier. Why did we lose track of him? Who is this OID organisation that keeps paying him? He's doing work for somebody. We have no idea who and we have no idea what. I don't like it."

"The Major will probably want…"

"The Major can go…" Reinhardt stopped short. Sliding across media reports on the other cases, he invited Müller to sit down. "Why kill these three people specifically? Why kill them in that manner? It's the people and the method. Two elements here."

"I looked into the method."

Reinhardt cocked his head to one side.

"The SD used to kill Allied Commandos with piano wire during the war. They would hang them with it."

"He's not hanging them."

"It achieves the same ends. Its death by strangulation and massive blood loss. Whichever comes first." He pointed to the articles. "Both of these men worked in museums specialising in classic cars. Robertson worked in the archives for an automobile museum. The MO could be linked to something that happened during the war. Something to do with wartime exhibits? Perhaps that's why Jaeger chose that method."

"Robertson wasn't killed in the war section." Reinhardt recalled. "He was studying a replica of a sportscar."

"Yes, a replica of a car that disappeared during the war. Why did it disappear? Where did it go? Does the real car exist somewhere else? If the SD method of killing is being used for a reason, is someone trying to send out a message? Did the original car belong to someone that got away? Someone that the SD might have wanted to arrest at the time? Someone they would have killed with piano wire?"

"It's a morbid thought."

Müller held up his hands. "And yet…"

CHAPTER THIRTY-EIGHT
ENGLAND, 2018

"Charlie?" Deakin asked, finally returning her call.

"I'm sorry, Christopher. I didn't know who else to call." She said. Her voice quivering with emotion.

"What is it?"

"It's Gray."

"Is he okay?" Though their acquaintance at Goodwood had been brief, Deakin could already see the importance Graham Robertson played in Charlie's life. He was her mentor. Her inspiration. Her champion.

"He's dead." She said. Her voice crumbled immediately as she began to sob. Even now, several weeks later, the news was still devastating.

"Dead? How?"

Robertson may have been seventy years old, but he was as sprightly as someone three decades younger. There had been no signs of old age ravaging either his body or his mind. A heart attack? A stroke? Neither was impossible, but both seemed unlikely.

"He's been killed."

Deakin's heart sank. A car accident. Such things were indiscriminate. A drunk driver. An uninsured idiot. Some senseless lorry driver checking social media. He wondered what state the Gordon Keeble might be in. Its fibreglass body wouldn't stand up to much. Then he immediately berated himself for it. Human life was infinitely more precious than a car, however unique.

"Where?"

"He was in Germany. Doing some research." Deakin sighed and shook his head. The autobahns. Those unrestricted ribbons of tarmac through Central Europe. Was it a hire car? An exhausted Hungarian courier? Some brainless speed freak in a Brabus?

"Oh no. That's awful news, Charlie. I'm so sorry."

"The police are still looking for the suspect."

Deakin frowned. Not a car accident then. "What happened?"

"He was in a museum after hours. He had permission. Someone broke in and killed him."

"What?" This was an unexpected revelation. "He was murdered?"

Even the sound of the word was enough to cause Charlie to break down again. "I'm sorry, Christopher." She stammered between sobs. "I hate to burden you with this. I just didn't…" her voice was drowned with emotion again.

"No, no. It's quite alright." He said, trying to sound reassuring. "I'm glad you called." He really was.

They had exchanged numbers after the Revival. Texted briefly afterwards. The conversations had been casual and infrequent. Both had busy schedules. Deakin had been preparing for another deployment over Christmas and the New Year. Charlie was helping the maintenance team look after some of the more delicate exhibits over the winter period. Preparing materials for spring shows and such. He hadn't been back all that long when he had a message from Charlie.

"Can we talk?" It had said. "Please call me."

"Have the police said anything?"

"I haven't heard anything yet. They haven't contacted us. We don't know if it was a random attack or whether he was specifically targeted. It's just so awful."

"It's terrible news. Really terrible. I'll call my dad and let him know. They were close."

"Oh, how stupid, I haven't…"

"Not a bit of it, Charlie. Don't worry. I can imagine this has really taken the stuffing out of you." he paused. "How are *you* doing?"

"It's just so sad. I feel broken. He was such a lovely man. So kind and generous with everything. I don't know what we're going to do."

Deakin fell silent for a moment. Contemplating. The silence stretched on.

"Listen, I'm off for a week now. Let me come down and we can talk about it."

"No, it's okay. You don't have to. I…"

"I want to." He replied with feeling. "You need a friend right now, Charlie. There's a billet in Southampton I can use. I can head down there first thing. Perhaps we can meet up for lunch somewhere."

"Okay." She said, beginning to calm down a little. "Thank you."

"I'll text you when I'm there and we can arrange a rendezvous."

"Of course, Captain Deakin." She said, a lightness returning to her voice slightly as she picked up on his tone. Reverting to military precision. "After oh-nine-hundred would be ideal."

"Are you picking on me, Charlotte Campbell?" he asked with mock indignation.

"No, no. Just… Thank you."

"We'll speak soon. Look after yourself, Charlie."

"I will. Thanks again."

Deakin pursed his lips together and frowned as he ran back through the conversation. Robertson dead. Killed. In Germany. It was shocking news. And by an unknown assailant too. What was the motive? Where was the security? How could it have happened?

CHAPTER THIRTY-NINE

"Welcome back, Greg." Smiled Zosia, a hand poised over the pumps as a familiar face ambled into Walkers Bar. "What will it be?"

"Ah'll have a pint o' yer Tasty Blonde, Zeezee." He smiled, shaking the water off his hat as he made his way over the flagstones.

Leaning his staff up against the stone wall, he ran his fingers through his hair and settled himself down on the stool. Almost at once the black Labrador from the next table waddled over for some fuss.

"It's a wee bit wet oot there, isn't it mate?" he asked, scratching the cheerful pooch's damp head.

"Just with us the two nights?" Zosia asked, a hint of disappointment in her voice.

"Aye, ah'm trying oot the new roof tent on the Landy this week, but ah could nae come up all this way and naw drop in on ma favourite barmaid now." He winked.

Zosia placed his freshly pulled pint on the mat and leaned forwards on her elbows, frowning slightly.

"Won't it be cold?"

"It might get a wee bit nippy just before dawn," he nodded. "The sleeping bag should be up tae it though."

"I could always bring you a hot water bottle." She said, pressing the tip of her tongue to her top lip in a mischievous fashion.

Hamilton held her gaze as he brought the brimming pint glass to his lips. Sipping the top off and wondering. The arm was still a little sore where the wound was healing. Drinking pints would be good exercise. Physiotherapy.

Born Gregor Hamilton, he had grown up in Lanarkshire, leaving school at sixteen to join the Corps of Royal Marines. Earning the right to wear the green beret, he became a Mountain Leader and tried out for the Special Boat Service where he served as a Swimmer Canoeist. With eight years under his belt, after serving out his notice he took a few months out to hike the length and breadth of the Lake District. That's when he discovered the Bridge Hotel and Walkers Bar at Buttermere for the first time.

Afterwards, he took up a vacancy in the Strathclyde Police, first in uniform, then in CID. Four years on, two of those years as a Detective Constable, with a possible promotion on the horizon, he instead interviewed for the Secret Intelligence Service on the Albert Embankment to assist in the War on Terror.

Some six years later, with the so-called 'war' largely winding down, the SIS needed to downsize their corps of Operational-Officers. A new war was being increasingly waged online, and the Intelligence Service needed to be leaner, more agile, more efficient. It was a hard pill to swallow, being thought of as a cost-saving initiative, making space for hard drives and server rooms, but that was the reality of modern spy craft. Contrary to the legend, there wasn't a bottomless pit of money. No gadgets and Aston Martins.

He was given a pay out and looked to settle somewhere in Cumbria. London life wasn't for him, but any half-decent properties were a little beyond his means at the time. His brother had advised against selling the Lions Mill apartment. A shrewd observation as it turned out.

It was Doctor Harris who happened to mention that her grandparents' old holiday cabin was going begging. Located on Cornwall's Tregonhawke Cliffs, she suggested it would be ideal for his solitary nature. Though it might need a touch of modernisation. It ended up needing to be almost completely rebuilt but it had been cheap, and for the last two years it had been home, even though it was the opposite end of the country to where he had wanted to live.

His attention had then turned to another project. A 2014 Land Rover Defender 110 County Station Wagon. He had called it *Torridon*, named after the Torridon Hills in the Northwest Highlands of Scotland, although she couldn't have lived much further away from the Highlands without getting wet. Indeed, coming from Lanarkshire, Hamilton himself was a Lowlander if anything. *Torridon* was his expedition vehicle, his workhorse, and the closest thing he had to a companion.

Hamilton placed the glass back on the bar and gazed at Zosia as she served another customer. She was a pretty lady with an attractive Eastern European accent. Big blue eyes magnified by dark-rimmed spectacles. A dark ponytail streaked with blonde highlights. Along with Alisa, and some of the other girls working at the hotel, they lived comfortably in the chalets on the other side of the car park.

Situated between Cockermouth and Borrowdale, the tiny village of Buttermere was in an isolated corner of the northern lakes, just beyond Honister Pass and the old slate quarry. Near the legendary site where Jarl Buthar's band of Anglo-Scandinavian Cumbrians fought a brave last-stand against the Norman army of the Lord of Carlisle, it was the feeling of seclusion that appealed to Hamilton. The drama of the surrounding landscape and the spirit of adventure that cascaded down the hills in every beck.

"Your room is ready, Greg." Announced Alisa as she came through from the hotel reception. "We can check you in now if you like."

"Thank you. Ah'll jist finish ma pint and come on through."

"Where are your adventures taking you this time?" she asked, preparing the coffee machine for one of the residents in the lounge.

"Ah'm heading up near Hardknott tae check oot the fort."

"Is that where you're camping?" Zosia asked in alarm.

"Camping?"

"He's brought a tent with him." Zosia explained. "Says he wants to try it out."

"Couldn't we persuade you to stay here with us for the whole week instead?" Alisa enquired, a twinkle in her eye. "We have vacancies."

"Aye, yer could, but ma own wee girl needs ma attention too, ladies."

Alisa and Zosia looked at one another.

"She gets awfy jealous if I leave her parked up all the while."

Their expressions softened as they realised he was referring to the Land Rover in her usual space across the Sail Beck. Alisa turned to froth the milk.

"How do you know she's a girl?" she called over the noise of the steam nozzle.

"She's gaw a tough exterior but is a big softy at heart. She works hard, never lets me doon and responds best tae a gentle touch." He winked and took another sip of the pale ale.

"Aww. I'm sure you'll be very happy together." She teased.

Alisa and Zosia looked at each other again and laughed before Alisa went off to deliver the cappuccino.

"How's Izzy?" he asked. "Ah dinnae see her earlier."

Zosia's expression became serious for a moment. "She's not well. She's moving a lot slower now, poor thing."

Izzy was a sandy-coloured border terrier that lived at Skye Farm across the lane. To those that didn't know her, she was more often referred to simply as Little Brown Dog. Despite her diminutive stature though, she had become a big local celebrity amongst the visiting tourists. Quietly going about her doggy day, gratefully sharing any lunchtime leftovers. She was amenable to a fuss and had even been known to hold up traffic as she rolled over for a belly rub by the farm gates. The white fur around her muzzle had noticeably increased in recent years and her stout little legs hobbled along more stiffly now. Old age catching up with her.

It was catching up with Hamilton too, though on days like this, after a brisk walk in the fresh air especially, he didn't feel it so much. He was a little wiser, a little more mature, but mentally he certainly didn't feel any older than when he joined the Marines. Physically though there were a few more aches and pains, inexplicable things he would wake up with one morning for no reason at all. How could he injure himself in his sleep? Maybe those years in one service or another had artificially aged his body and his mind was still playing catch up.

His annual excursion around the lake had always been a good way of resetting himself, especially so after the winter he'd had. Looking down at his phone, he was relieved to see it still had no reception. Peace at last.

Back in the autumn he hadn't long fitted the new front winch bumper before it was called into action. The black, tubular steel structure had been equipped with a winch with an 80ft Spydura synthetic rope and a rated line pull of 12,000lbs. He had needed every inch of it. Two LED spotlights mounted to the A-bar provided needed illumination, especially when the sea spray combined with dull light of an early dusk to obscure the scene.

An unprecedented number of callouts from Her Majesty's Coastguard had required his assistance in everything from cliff falls to stranded pets. The popularity of the new Poldark TV series had drawn throngs of tourists even in the off-season, looking to recreate their own little Cornish drama.

That Christmas Day at Botallack had been particularly challenging. A party of six on a post-prandial stroll. Too much alcohol. Not enough sense. Cliff edges and derelict engine houses. High winds and angry waves. A perfect storm. Sadly, there had been no flame-haired maidens or wealthy heiresses that had needed rescuing. No out of bodice experiences. Given his windswept, rugged looks, his appearance on the local news almost resembled the brooding nobleman himself, minus the tricorn. The party all got to open their presents later that evening though, were apologetic and grateful in equal measure. A good result.

Most of the rescues had been successful that season. It was the ones that weren't which always haunted him. Two boys on a paddleboard dashed against the rocks near Pedn Vounder. Ben, the curious Jack Russell down an old mineshaft. The faces of the family left behind. They were sure he had done all he could, but there was always something in their expression, some nagging doubt.

Perhaps he was only imagining it. Reading too much into that horrifying moment of realisation. His black-roofed, dark red Land Rover with eight-point roll cage, roof rack and all-terrain tyres looked, and acted the business, but it wasn't Navy blue and yellow, there was no official crest or lettering on the side and their little boy, beloved pet, favourite aunt wasn't coming home. Maybe if a proper team had been there. Someone with a badge. Maybe...

The silly season was usually the summertime when holidaymakers would flock to the Cornish peninsula in their droves. With Coastguard, Lifeboat and Air Sea Rescue services often stretched to their limits, any assistance he could render was always gratefully received. It was all voluntary, but he was kept on a modest retainer. Not enough to live on, but it helped. A quick getaway in the middle of February would serve him well and give him the needed respite before stepping into the breach once more. Though he wasn't sure how many more times he could contend with that feeling of failure. Was he really contemplating retiring from that too?

Sensing the hot breath of the Labrador in his lap again, he looked down at the big brown eyes and happy face, wondering whether he should get a dog of his own. Having someone so unequivocally loyal to him, a best friend he could confide in without judgement. In many ways, his Cornish cliffside home was the perfect location. The beaches of Whitsand Bay stretched out beneath his cabin. Long walks right on his doorstep. An ideal vehicle to lug the beast around for longer journeys. He would never go for one of those yappy, fluffball, lap dog breeds. If anything, he would have a hound of some kind. A proper dog. Something young children could ride like a pony. A Great Dane perhaps, or an Irish Wolfhound. In temperament they would be well suited. Quietly independent, indifferent to being fussed over, tolerant around rodents and toddlers. Mostly.

When not volunteering for rescue and recovery though, his frequent travels for close protection work elsewhere could be problematic, if he still kept his hand in on the freelancing side. Although he liked the idea of a dog, the reality of shedding fur, food bills and faecal matter was decidedly less appealing. He contented himself with occasional dog-sitting duties for friends and neighbours. Just like other people's children, you could have fun with them, play with all their toys, then just when they became a handful, send them back. You were always going to be their hero and they were often on their best behaviour too. It was a perfect scenario.

"Are you okay?" Zosia asked, bringing him back to his surroundings.

"Ah think so." He murmured. It was his standard response to the question.

"You think so?" she enquired with a frown. He smiled.

"It's naw suhin' ah tend tae bother maself wi. I jist get ma head doon and get stuff done."

The admission wasn't some masculine bravado on his part, it was simply a statement of fact. Seldom did he give any consideration as to how he was actually feeling at any given moment. Perhaps it was simply being a man. Or maybe it was the Commando training. Push through difficulties. Slog it out. March on. There was never any need to look back.

He had been despatched to West Africa on the eve of the Millennium but had left the Marines before any of the deployments to Iraq and Afghanistan that came after. The infamous United Nations Security Council Resolution 1441, forcing Iraq to disarm, hadn't even been written when he cleared out his footlocker. As such he had been spared the abject horrors inflicted on his comrades by those hellish engagements that came afterwards.

Sure, he had always felt like a stranger in the places where he had been posted to, never able to truly relax. His mind had always been primed for danger. Body poised to react. He had faced the impossible, witnessed the unwatchable and missed many of life's simple pleasures, but the conflicts of the late nineties and very early noughties were not quite the same as the ones that came later. There was not the same level of attrition, the massive asymmetry, the harrowing, brutal carnage. Almost no one had ever heard of an IED outside Special Forces. Now every man and his dog knew what one was. They had entered the vocabulary of the everyday, along with their terrible aftermath. Physically and mentally.

He well understood what it was to be a Royal Marine Commando, had been privileged to serve as part of the UK Special Forces. Just not in Helmand Province. Not in Basra or Baghdad. He didn't feel he could relate to that, what those guys had seen and experienced. It didn't feel appropriate. He didn't have the same kind of emotional or physical trauma. He still had all his limbs and so did all his friends. He felt like a paratrooper dropped in after Operation Market Garden. Missed out on D-Day, missed out on that one bridge too far. Of course, in every way he was the same as them, yet also he was very, very different. It was a strange sort of survivor's guilt.

Zosia pursed her lips as her expression took on a concerned, maternal countenance.

"You should look after yourself, Greg." She whispered warmly. "Or find someone who will."

He laughed at that. "Ah'm too auld for all that now."

"Nonsense." She said with a frown, picking up a cloth to wipe down the tables. "You are never too old. You can cook, you're clean. You will make someone a fine husband someday."

"Ah doot that. There's usually a more rigorous set o' criteria."

"I don't." she said almost reproachfully.

"Yer interested then, Zeezee?" he joked. She laughed and turned to spray the tables down, hiding her flushing cheeks.

"That's the wee problem, pal." He whispered to the dog at his feet. "The one's yer sweet on never like yer back."

CHAPTER FORTY

Deakin's eyes were immediately drawn to the sound of the car that pulled up outside the café. Built to Series 4 Oscar India specification, the Aston Martin V8 Vantage Sports Saloon gleamed in a beautiful shade of Cumberland Grey. Powered by Tadek Marek's final masterpiece, his quad-cam V580X engine burbled delightfully as the car's sixteen inch Ronal wheels came to a halt. Silencing the engine, Charlie opened the door, offering a peak into the Magnolia leather, burr walnut and Wilton wool interior.

Getting up slowly from the chair, he was mesmerised by the image in grey that rested before him. Charlie came through the door and immediately saw the exact look on his face that she had been expecting. Her mouth widened into a gleaming smile that Deakin didn't notice. She hadn't smiled like that for a while. Seeing him, seeing his reaction, it just felt natural.

"That's." he stammered. "That's stunning."

"I'm fine, thank you for asking." She giggled.

"Charlie, I'm so sorry." He replied remorsefully, breaking his gaze and turning to her.

"It's okay. I wanted you to see her."

"Is she yours?"

"Yes. Why? Can't a woman drive a beautiful…"

Her words were halted as he pressed a finger to her lips to silence her.

"None of that. It was an innocent question." He softened his reaction with a smile. "I'm not here disparaging you. I think it's great. If anything, I admire you. You're the perfect woman."

"Hardly perfect."

"Why?" She paused for a moment, looking at her shoes. Suddenly feeling guilty for allowing herself to feel happiness while her mentor's body lay in a Berlin mortuary.

"You're not here for me."

"Of course I'm here for you. I know how much Gray meant to you. This is all terrible. Just terrible. How are you holding up?" he gestured for her to take the seat opposite him.

"I try not to think about it, but then I feel guilty for doing that. It's really hard to know what to do."

Deakin nodded, resisting the urge to reach across and touch her hand. They weren't there yet, and it seemed inappropriate at this time. "Do you have any details about the funeral?"

She shook her head, sniffing as she held back a sob. "His body hasn't even been repatriated yet."

Deakin could see this was becoming increasingly hard for her. She needed to cry but wasn't about to lose control in the middle of a café. "Come on." He said, standing up. "Let's take a walk."

She nodded, standing up, then paused. "Or a drive?"

"Only if you feel like it."

"Do you want to?" her dark chocolate eyes looked at him all glistening and watery. He could see sadness and heartache swirling in a sea of despair. Yet, there was also a sparkle of hope, a small glimmer of something brighter.

Deakin smiled. "Where are we going?"

IN THE DEN OF WOLVES

Britain's first supercar was still as outstanding as it had been on launch. Being a 1988 model year, many of the teething problems of previous versions had been ironed out. In addition, one of the vehicle's later owners had made the trip across Tickford Street in the early nineties to request the 6.3-litre Big Bore conversion from Works Service, as well as a Nardi wooden steering wheel and raised centre console. This factory modification increased the power to 470bhp and made Charlie's V8 Vantage arguably the definitive X-Pack model.

The grille blanking plate looked suitably imposing with twin Cibre driving lights flanking the enamelled AMOC badge mounted to the centre. Deep air-dam, power bulge and aggressive styling made the front-end appear vaguely like a first generation Shelby Mustang, but with a stylish up curl to the top lip that was distinctive to Aston Martin. Taking them out of the city, Charlie opened her up down the long stretch of Romsey Road, letting the stainless steel straight-through pipes sing out the full might of the V8 engine.

Outside of the Goodwood Revival, it was positively the loudest car Deakin had ever heard. On acceleration, the exhaust note ripped up the air like a whole paddock of 1960s Grand Prix cars. Reverberating deeply off the tunnel of trees, popping on the overrun. Delighting him immensely. Charlie's deft handling of the five-speed synchromesh accentuated the incredible machine to a superlative level. The ride was precise and poised. An immediate injection of power was available when needed. Cool wind rushing past them, sucked in by four, twin-choke 50mm Weber carburettors, air canisters and enlarged airbox trunking.

Deakin found himself laughing like a schoolboy as the landscape rushed past him. There was a tingle of excitement in his masculine regions, a wave of adrenalin pumping through him and a feeling of supreme satisfaction. The sight, the sound, the smells.

The interior was just as luxurious as the performance was ferocious. Lambswool floor rugs, burr walnut trim and buttery soft leather seats. It was oft said that no one should ever meet their heroes, but in the case of Charlie's incredible machine, he was elated and extremely grateful that he had. The reality was even better than he had imagined it.

With the exhaust popping pleasingly as she changed down, the car sedately pulled off into the car park with the grace and refinement that belied her earlier unruliness. The engine behaved superbly at low speeds and idled with a burbling promise of wonderment before she was finally silenced once more.

"Lunch?" Charlie asked, looking across with a beaming smile stretched across her face.

"That was better than sex." He uttered involuntarily. "Um… only if I pay." He added, looking over a little embarrassed by his outburst. "She is incredible."

"Do you normally pay for sex?" Charlie laughed. "Yes, she is." She added quickly, sensing his discomfiture.

Getting out slowly, Deakin needed to test his weight out on legs that had become gelatinous. He instantly regretted closing the door, longing at once to be back inside, even if not behind the wheel. Barely had he walked a half dozen paces before he was already looking back at her. Charlie looped her arm through his and guided him to the pub across the lane, lest he never leave the car park.

The Empress of Blandings was nearly as circular as it was possible for a pig to be. She resembled a captive balloon with ears and a tail. She was also the name of the pub Charlie had taken them to for lunch.

"Are you feeling a little better?" he asked once they had stepped inside.

She nodded. "A drive in the country often helps to clear my head."

"What are you drinking?"

"I'll have a ginger beer."

"You're more English than me." He smiled.

"Why wouldn't I be?"

He rubbed his eyes with his hands and shook his head.

"Why does everything I say sound so bloody racist?" he groaned. "Is this how white people always sound?"

"Um, pretty much." she acknowledged.

He lowered his head and sighed. "I'm sorry."

"Well, being a woman, I get 'babe', and 'love and 'darling' too, so…" she shrugged. "Blokes just call each other 'mate' and get on with it."

"Ah there's a few more colourful expressions in the barrack blocks, I assure you."

He took their drinks to the table by the fireplace where the wood burner was flickering away nicely.

"Still, its inciteful to know what we inadvertently say that causes offence."

"It's one of those things you learn to live with." Charlie removed her coat and the fetching baker boy flat cap she had been wearing, draping them on the arm of the club chair. "To be honest I hardly notice it, but I'm sure it was more overt in my grandad's day."

"Yes, I'm sure it was." He sighed, sipping the top off his pint. "It probably makes little difference hearing me say I'm not racist when my speech then contains any number of slurs or assumptions."

"Xiuying's opinion was that certain things had probably become so ingrained in a person's culture, that no one consciously thought about it anymore. The vast majority of people probably were not prejudiced at all. It's just that you become attuned to certain things people say when you're on the other side, so to speak."

"I get that." He nodded. "Not to the same extent of course, but when one branch of service makes a comment, you can sometimes detect the disparaging undertone, even if it's not meant that way."

"Like when Gray called you a donkey walloper." She smiled.

"You noticed too?" he grinned, feeling a little more relaxed. "That was my dad though, not me. He was cavalry."

"So, what are you in then?"

"A different regiment." He replied guardedly.

"Oh, I see." she said, bringing up the ginger beer to her lips. As she looked across at him down the length of the bottle, it was clear that she understood exactly what he meant. "Impressive."

Deakin smiled but said nothing more about it. "So, in very great danger of sounding cliché. Again," he gestured to the building they were in, "Do you come here often?"

"Every once in a while." She giggled.

"What's good to eat?"

"The honey roast ham is delicious, but anything with triple-cooked chips is a winner in my book."

"I'll place our order."

As he moved to the bar, Charlie's phone rang. She rummaged in her coat pocket and looked at the number. She frowned. It had a +49 country code, followed by -30 for Berlin.

CHAPTER FORTY-ONE
GERMANY, 2018

What a thoroughly ridiculous name, Reinhardt thought. Gordon Keeble was a car. A short-lived manufacturer but nevertheless, the keyring belonged to a car. Apparently, according to the exhaustingly enthusiastic woman on the telephone, it had come about when John Gordon from struggling manufacturer Peerless, teamed up with Jim Keeble to fit a Chevrolet Corvette V8 into a Peerless chassis for USAF pilot Rick Nielsen who was stationed in Norfolk. The woman took a short breath. Impressed with the concept, they designed a similar vehicle around the 5.4litre Chevrolet 327, using bodywork by Giorgetto Giugiaro at Bertone and eventually made of fibreglass by Williams & Pritchard.

Reinhardt intervened when the lady began to talk about supplier problems and inevitable liquidation. He just wanted to know now if Graham Robertson's Gordon Keeble had ever been picked up. As far as his colleague was aware it had not, owing to the fact that Robertson was in possession of the keys, one set of which was undoubtedly on his person, with the other secured safely at home and requiring his house keys to obtain. Keys which were also likely to be with his personal belongings, and what's more, when was his body going to be returned to the UK so that a proper burial could take place? Of course, he might have opted to take a taxi, in which case it was likely to be one of those awful TX4s built these days by a subsidiary of Chinese auto-maker Geely but were not a patch on the original Austin FX4 which…

Reinhardt terminated the call. Were all car enthusiasts so peculiar? She sounded anxious whoever she was.

From his colleagues across the border, he had discovered that André Langier preferred a Citroën DS, an iconic car in itself, but at least one with a sensible designation. Letters and numbers made sense to Reinhardt. M5, A4, E350. As soon as a car had a name it became largely meaningless. No one ever got excited about a Citroën Xsara, even when a stripping Claudia Schiffer claimed in the late nineties that it was the only thing to be seen in. Golf? Polo? He didn't play any of them.

What was also revealing, was the second keyring. An identical three-ringed metallic tag which he was told sometimes had religious significance, most often representing the Holy Trinity. Two murder victims then with strange religious keyrings. He sincerely hoped he wasn't getting involved in some kind of weird religious cult. That stuff just creeped him out, but along with their similar professions, these strange keyrings seemed to be the only link. Undoubtedly they would have known each other professionally but were clearly not rivals, having reached perhaps the pinnacle of their respective careers in their separate institutions.

A call to America might have to come next to compare findings with the murder of Bob Jefferson, but he was doubtful that the Los Angeles Police Department would be as forthcoming with information. American law enforcement agencies were notoriously difficult to deal with. At least they wouldn't be able muscle to in on his investigation over here, though no doubt they would try.

CHAPTER FORTY-TWO
ENGLAND, 2018

Due to the presence of the Royal Navy dockyard at Devonport, the whole area surrounding Plymouth Sound had been heavily fortified in accordance with the 1860 Royal Commission. The Commission had reviewed Britain's coastal defences in the wake of French re-armament and recommended a chain of forts be constructed to protect both land and sea approaches to the dockyard. Such defences would ensure Napoleon III's forces were kept beyond effective artillery range should he choose to attack.

As a result, Scraesdon Fort was built to prevent an enemy landing force approaching along the Lynher Valley. Polhawn Battery at the foot of Rame Head operated in conjunction with Tregantle Fort, the lynchpin of the Western Lines, to protect bombardment of the Tamar estuary from Whitsand Bay. Later, the Tregantle High Angle Battery and Whitsand Bay Battery were constructed to reinforce this stretch of Cornish coastline, with a military road to connect them up that wriggled along the shoulders of the Tregonhawke Cliffs.

Now a sinuous, tarmac lane, it was on this road that Hamilton's *Rockwater Cabin* was situated. Accessed down a narrow, uneven footpath about 100yards off the road, the 1930s cabin had been extended over the years as the requirements of various owners had changed. The original two-room cabin now formed the principal structure, divided between living room and master bedroom.

The porch into the living room had been blocked up decades ago after subsequent changes but keeping the alcove it created and the gable roof made for a convenient spot for a fabulous Petit Godin cast-iron stove Hamilton had reclaimed and made good. Being French it was beautifully ornamental, and the cylindrical form projected heat effectively into the living space during cooler months.

A T-shaped lean-to extension to the side and rear was split into a single guestroom and dining space, with the narrow galley kitchen forming the cross of the T and patio doors onto the decking became the new entrance. A second door in the opposite corner accessed a tiny yard squeezed between the rear of the cabin and the cliff face. The final addition Hamilton had tacked on to the other side of the kitchen became the bathroom.

Rockwater Cabin was in a spectacular spot, enjoying uninterrupted panoramic sea views from the extensive decking he had constructed around the structure, and from the two principal rooms. It was even possible to catch a glimpse of the odd porpoise or dolphin swimming out in the bay while enjoying al fresco dining from his secluded little haven. Built on a sheltered plateau of land, with the cliff rising above him towards the road and dropping away to the beach below, there was never any danger of being overlooked or having the view spoilt in any direction.

Though he loved the Lake District, after the hellish journey down motorways and A-roads to the Cornish peninsula, it was a welcome sight to see the corrugated roof of his cabin below. The Beast from the East had struck on his way down. Suddenly everyone forgot how to drive. Snow had been steadily building on the motorways and A-roads as the country was plunged into an unexpected cold spell with unusually heavy snowfall. There had even been snow settling on the Devon Expressway as it bypassed Plymouth. Almost unheard of so far south in late February.

Negotiating the lane in rapidly diminishing light, Hamilton was glad to see his usual spot open in the layby under the glare of LED headlights. Silencing *Torridon's* engine he kept the steering in full-lock, removed the walnut-rimmed three-spoke steering wheel from its quick release boss and fitted the swivel lock onto the hub. After securing the pedal pin to lock out the clutch pedal, he moved to the back and opened the tailgate to withdraw his rucksack.

Sadly, the venerable Land Rover was not immune from theft even in the most remote regions of Cornwall. An alarm, immobiliser and vehicle tracker were already installed but it did no harm to have more visible security measures fitted. The weight of the 110 made it less desirable to tow away than the lighter, shorter wheelbase 90 and the added bulk of a heavy Cummins diesel engine would have made any opportunist with a tow bar think again once they had tried to give it an initial tug.

There was a bite in the air. Already the tips of his ears were feeling it. He could hear the sea crashing like splintering glass onto the beach below. Frozen snowflakes adorned the horizontal surfaces of the Land Rover like icing on a cake. Stuck fast by the wind chill of the drive. Looking up to the roof, his tent had all been packed away neatly beneath its hard, fibreglass shell. All he needed to do was remove that from the roof rack in the morning and stow it in the small outbuilding across the yard.

With the rucksack over one shoulder and the steering wheel in his other hand, he negotiated the track down to the cabin. There were a couple of nets of split logs in the loading area too, picked up from a genial farmer on the way, but he had sufficient to get him through the night. Looe peninsula was still silhouetted by a darkening sky, but by the time he made it down once, it would be too dark to head back up again anyway without a torch. They could wait until morning. He waggled the wheel in greeting to the residents of *Homestead* halfway down the path, then took the left fork to where the blue gate entered his property.

Stepping inside the cabin, he switched on the light and dropped his rucksack under the one-man breakfast bar in the kitchen before moving into the dining room. Whitewashed throughout, the interior enjoyed a unique ambience and provided him with an overwhelming sense of calm and much needed tranquillity. In this forgotten corner of Cornwall, it was an ocean away from the tourist hotspots of St Ives, Newquay and Padstow. Lovingly restored, Hamilton had furnished it with an eclectic mix of styles; vintage campaign furniture, retro appliances and modern gadgets, supplemented by some beach finds from the surrounding sands.

Crouching down as if to unlace his boots, he instead lifted the hatch in the floorboards, pressed his thumb against the biometric scanner, and removed the Smith & Wesson R8 revolver from the sliding drawer safe. Manually cocking the hammer with his thumb indexed the cylinder round to the first of the eight loaded chambers. Turning around, he moved into the lounge, flicked on the light switch and replaced the steering wheel on the shelf above the sofa as he pointed the revolver at the bundle of blankets up against the corner. There was a small movement and a face appeared. Auburn waves and big green eyes. The messy chignon looked decidedly more rustic than it had in London and there was a bluish tinge to the lips. Hamilton couldn't help but smile.

"Whit are yer doing here, Valentina?"

"Waiting for you, of course." She replied, trying not let the shivers enter her voice.

"It's fair jeelit ootside, is it naw?" he returned, trying to keep the mirth from his. "Two things." He took a step back. "First, stand up and take off every stitch o' clothing yer gaw on."

"I'm unarmed if that's what you want to know."

"That's exactly the kind o' thing yer'd say if yer had a wee chib stashed in yer scants."

"Yes, I suppose it would be." She nodded. "You may just have to trust me."

"Ma hoose. Ma rules." He gestured with his hand. "Up yer get."

Silently she removed the blankets and stood in the middle of the room. Hamilton backed into the doorway to the dining room a little, putting distance between them and giving him a better angle of fire should he need it.

"Start wi the hairpin." He said, pointing.

"If you wanted to inspect the goods, you only needed to ask." She replied, releasing her hair onto her shoulders.

"Haud yer wheesht. Jist get it done."

Crouching down, she began to unlace her trainers, bemused by his unintelligible expressions. The Vida Viva low tops were at least a little more sensible than the Louboutin Pigalle heels she had been wearing in London. Though still ill-suited for the muddy path she had not expected to negotiate. Next came the socks. Nothing hidden in either one. The jeans were next. The belt, button-fly. The slight sway of her hips.

"Dinnae be mekin' it sexy." He scowled, trying to remain detached. It took all his concentration. Maggie Thatcher naked on a cold day. A proper mood killer to distract his thoughts.

She returned the frown and whipped them off quickly. Then she unbuttoned the blouse, almost wrenching it off and throwing it to the ground. She stood there, legs apart, hands on her hips. A face like thunder. Wonder Woman in a Wonderbra. As he had suspected, she liked to make sure everything matched.

"Ah seid everything."

"You're not serious?" she asked incredulously.

"Yer see anyone else wi' a gun aroond here?"

"Do you see any*where* for a gun?"

"Ah'll naw ask again."

Starting with her bra, Valentina unhooked the band and slid the straps off her shoulders, letting it fall to the floor as she tucked her thumbs into the waistband of her knickers and pulled them down. Stepping out of them self-consciously and shivering even more. Though he observed she made no attempt to cover her modesty. Neither balcony nor orchestra.

"Arms up and turn aroond."

As she did so, Hamilton looked her up and down. The complete nakedness was perhaps a little overkill, but he had known a fellow agent killed with thumb knives hidden in a honeytrap's lingerie. Like sharpened plectrums, the skilled assassin had buried them into her target's eyes with frightening effectiveness. There would be no surprises like that here.

"Naw fake after all then." He observed. "Impressive. Now get dressed before them paps slice suhin' open."

As he spoke, he released the hammer and crouched down to replace the handgun in the safe. With no magazine springs or chamber issues to worry about, the tactical revolver made for an effective fast-action defence weapon if he needed it.

In the tiny galley kitchen, nearest the front door, stood a 1930s enamelled cast-iron three-burner Vulcan gas stove. It had been original to the property and had come down from the foundry up in Exeter where they had once been made. Hamilton had managed to salvage it during renovations and got it working again with bottled gas piped in through the wall from outside. The original dove grey and white enamel complemented his clean interior aesthetic perfectly. He lit the small burner and reached up to the shelf to get the moka pot.

"What was the second thing?" Valentina asked, hurriedly getting dressed to generate a bit of warmth.

"D'yer want coffee?" he called, poking his head around the door.

"What?"

"That wis the second thing." He held up the bag of ground coffee beans and the scoop. "D'yer want coffee?"

"You ask me to strip, then ask if I want coffee?!" she scowled angrily, confused and outraged.

"*You* broke in." he shrugged. "Yer got tae bear the consequences o' that decision. No pun intended. Now, d'yer want coffee, or no?"

"Fine." She huffed.

Hamilton appreciated good coffee. Scooping the grounds into the infuser, he tampered it down with just the right amount of pressure, a skill honed through patience and experience, before filling the water reservoir and assembling the moka pot together. A stylish stainless steel pot with walnut handle, matching the cafetiere and spherical tea pot on the stove's shelf. The modern, cylindrical design was a departure from their usual octagonal shape made famous by Bialetti.

The concept of a stovetop coffee maker was wonderfully simple. When the pot was placed on a stove, water in the reservoir at the bottom heated up and resulted in a gradual increase in vapour pressure. This forced heated water up through the funnel-shaped filter where the compacted grounds were. Continuing up the vertical spout, coffee would then begin to collect in the top chamber.

It was important to remove the pot off the heat before it entered the strombolian phase where a mixture of super-heated steam and water passed through the grounds, causing rapid overextraction and an undesirable bitterness to the beverage. Also, the correct amount of compaction would determinate whether a good crema was produced. The more pressure, the better the crema, but too much compaction and overextraction could occur as the temperature of the water became too hot on its way through. It was a delicate science but produced great coffee and was a very cool application of Darcy's law and the general gas equation.

While the water got up to temperature, Hamilton moved into the lounge and crouched down in front of the Godin stove. A ferocious wind was whistling across the top of the stack outside. The stormfront was rolling in again. Opening the door at the front and pulling down the grate, he loaded up the grille with scrunched up newspaper, a couple of chunks of firelighters and some kindling sticks. Striking a match, he set the arrangement on fire and watched it take hold. Satisfied it was burning okay, he folded up the grate, closed the door and opened the air valve. Valentina watched him with quiet fascination as he opened the top of the stove, lifted the hotplate and loaded in seasoned split cherry logs on top of the kindling at the bottom.

"Ah'm only putting this on for yer benefit, lass." He said, dusting his hands off as he stood up. "Gie it a couple o' minutes, then get yer wee bahoochie in front o' that."

"My what?" she asked as he moved back into the kitchen to take the pot off the other stove.

"That pert wee arse yer've been sitting on for the last few hours. Sugar?"

"Pardon me?"

"D'yer take sugar?"

"No." she returned. "Thank you." she added.

Madam Sokolova had not told Valentina what to expect. Greg Hamilton was an intriguing character to say the least. After the many seedy acts she had performed in pursuit of her mistress's wishes in the past, it was odd that she felt a touch of humiliation just now, having to strip down in front of him. She had certainly done far more gratuitous things. Most of them she had even enjoyed. She observed too there had been no hint of arousal as she had disrobed in front of him. Usually, that visual spectacle alone was enough to shoot men off into the throes of carnal ecstasy. Either he was the consummate professional or he wasn't interested in women. Greg Hamilton was a curious character indeed.

Already she could begin to feel welcome heat radiate into the room. Flames devoured the wood ravenously as the stove sucked in oxygen with fierce hunger. Sliding off the sofa, she huddled in front of it, still wrapped in a rough wool blanket with its distinctive lanolin aroma like it had just been shorn from a sheep. It was the contrast that fascinated her. One moment she was being ordered to undress at gunpoint, the next she was having coffee made for her and the stove lit purely for her own comfort. She could well imagine Hamilton going straight to bed without the need to warm up the cabin first. It was exactly the kind of thing a man would do. No matter how hardened she had become though, there were still a few small comforts she appreciated. Warmth being one of them.

"Surprised a Russian lass like you is nae more used tae the cold." He said, emerging from the kitchen with a tray.

Setting it down on a driftwood stool near the stove, he pushed a demitasse towards her to indicate which cup was hers. Then, he unfolded one of the canvas and teak roorkhee chairs and set it in the opposite corner to the sofa. Sitting down on it, he could look at her face and feel the benefit from the stove as well. Reaching down, he removed the lid and selected one of the biscuits from the barrel, crunching it noisily.

"I never enjoyed the cold." She murmured quietly.

"Must have been hell growing up then. Only the freezing opposite, whitever that's called."

"Siberia." She mumbled quietly.

Hamilton gazed into the front of the stove, leaned forward and adjusted the vents to restrict the oxygen a little. "The key is tae control the oxygen for a good slow burn." He mansplained. "Once it's up tae temperature the flames should sway like lovers, naw fap away like a teenager."

"Do you really think I came here to kill you?" she asked fiercely, looking up at him.

"Ah dinnae ken whit yer came here for." He shrugged, seeing the reflected flames in those green spheres. "Yer might naw need a weapon tae kill a man anyway, but there's no way on God's green earth ah wis gonnae take that chance."

"If I did, you would be dead already."

"Aye, probably."

"Then why?"

"Ah'm sure yer've done worse."

She looked away. Her cheeks reddening. "That's not answering." she murmured.

"Yer've likely had far worse done tae yer." he added with a softer tone, almost mournful.

"I don't need your sympathy."

"Ah'm naw offering it." He took a sip of coffee. It was rich, sweet and dark. Perfect. Not unlike the woman sitting at his feet in front of the stove. Though she could do with some added sweetness right now. Perhaps in time. "Ah wid like tae ken whit you're offering though."

She looked up, studying his face for a double meaning. Finding none. Confused.

"Ah assume there wis some evil purpose in tracking me oot here."

Valentina shrugged her arms out from under the blanket and took up the coffee cup. She took a sip and closed her eyes, savouring its flavour. The velvety warmth coursing down her body, invigorating her. A slight bitterness to it. She let out a small moan of pleasure unconsciously. Her cheeks flushed again as she opened her eyes. Those green orbs flashed up to see his reaction. He was onto another biscuit, staring out to sea through the window.

"Madam Sokolova might be in danger."

"Ah daresay she is." He replied, still gazing outside. It would be clearer without the lights on. He could only see the reflection of the cabin's interior. "Still disnae explain yer presence here."

"She needs people she can trust."

"Tae protect her?"

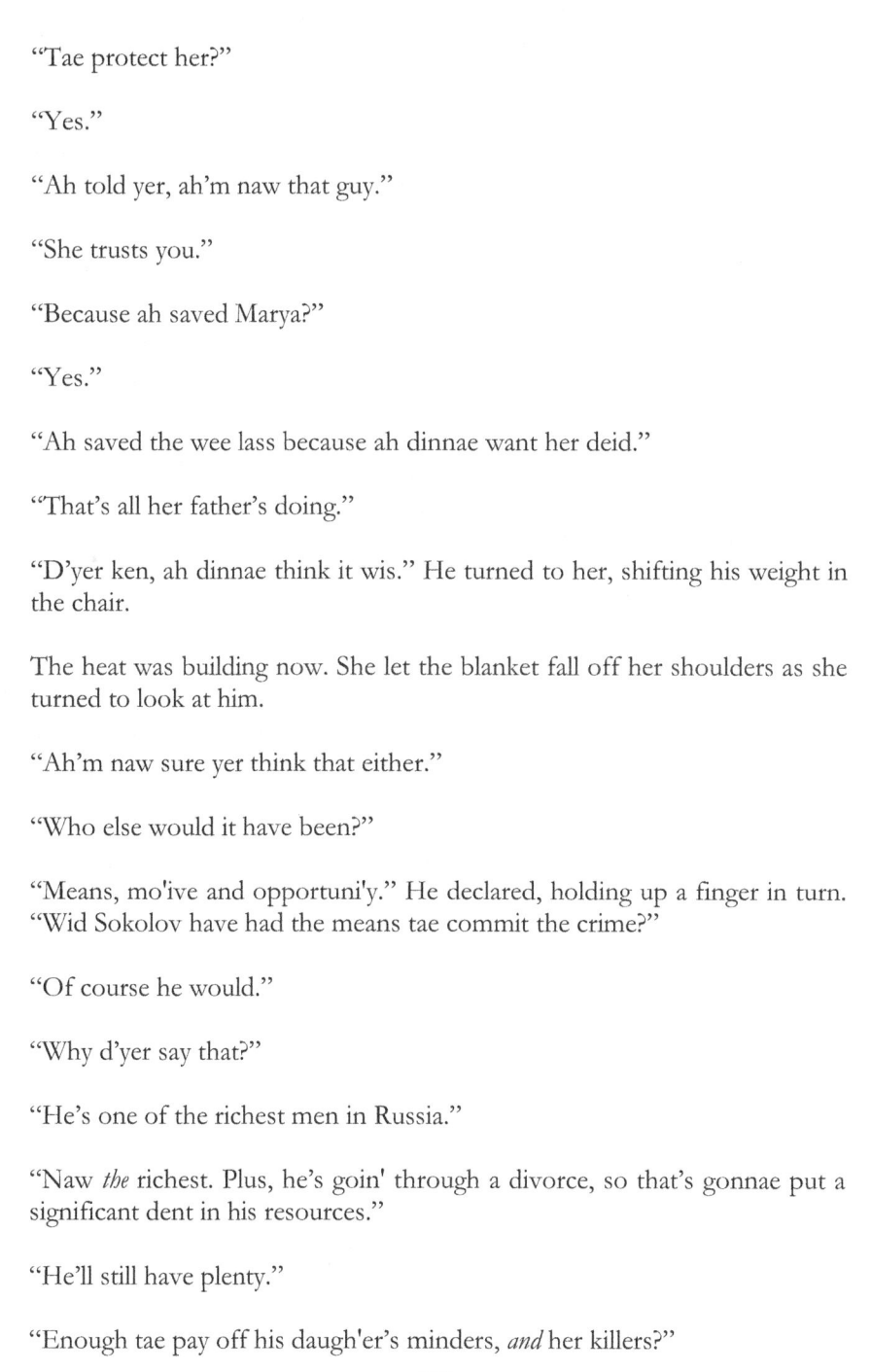

"Yes."

"Ah told yer, ah'm naw that guy."

"She trusts you."

"Because ah saved Marya?"

"Yes."

"Ah saved the wee lass because ah dinnae want her deid."

"That's all her father's doing."

"D'yer ken, ah dinnae think it wis." He turned to her, shifting his weight in the chair.

The heat was building now. She let the blanket fall off her shoulders as she turned to look at him.

"Ah'm naw sure yer think that either."

"Who else would it have been?"

"Means, mo'ive and opportuni'y." He declared, holding up a finger in turn. "Wid Sokolov have had the means tae commit the crime?"

"Of course he would."

"Why d'yer say that?"

"He's one of the richest men in Russia."

"Naw *the* richest. Plus, he's goin' through a divorce, so that's gonnae put a significant dent in his resources."

"He'll still have plenty."

"Enough tae pay off his daugh'er's minders, *and* her killers?"

"What do you mean?"

"Only one way three tooled up dobbers gaw intae that club withoot being detected or challenged by anyone." Valentina tilted her head to invite further explanation. "Marya's minders were paid tae turn a blind eye. Tae conveniently all be away from their primary at exactly the same time. More than that, they had tae have helped the squad enter the building in the first place tae bypass the club's own security.

"Tekin' that all intae consideration, no one is ever gonnae hire a bodyguard detail that wid ever make that kind of basic mistake or be turned so easily. If they're intelligent, those guys ken that too. Therefore, they wid also ken it wis gonnae be their last gig. So, if they were smart aboot it they wid have demanded a hefty pay oot. The kind that means they dinnae need tae work again. Ever. Of course, another possibility is that they've actually been working for someone else this whole time. We'll come back tae that later."

He paused as he took another sip of coffee, letting that information sink in.

"Next, they wid ken all aboot the divorce he's goin' through, and how his money is tied up in all kinds o' shady scams all over the Balkans. He might have high net worth on paper but liquidating it tae get the cash value wid take more time than he had. That's before yer factor in the hit squad he's supposed tae have hired. In summary, the dosh wis nae coming from him."

He knocked down one of the three fingers. "That's means taken care of. Now, what mo'ive would he have tae kill his own daugh'er? That's a fair savage father wid ever consider that. Killing others is one thing, but even in those circles, family is sacrosanct."

"Not always."

"Aye, true, but nine times oot o' ten." He took up another biscuit. "She's naw involved in any of the family's business interests, disnae have an unsuitable boyfriend, has nae sided with either parent in the family falloot. By all accounts he dotes on 'er. There's jist no reason tae do it." He folded a second finger down. "As for opportuni'y. There would have been far easier, less risky and certainly less public opportuni'ies than a crowded London nightclub at the weekend. The potential collateral damage wid have been an absurd and unnecessary risk. He'd be be'er off doin' it at *Fairford*." He shook his head. "If you and Madam Sokolova think Mikhail had anything tae do wi it, then the wheel's spinning but the hamster's long deid."

"Who else then?"

"Literally anyone else wi a grudge against the Sokolovs cood have done it." He took a sip. "Cood even be Madam Sokolova herself."

"What?!"

"I hear she's naw even the mother. Dinnae Daria take on Masha as a wee bairn after the first Mrs Sokolova was killed in a car accident?"

"She raised Marya as her own."

"Aye, but she's naw her own. Big maternal difference."

"She would never do that."

"If jist now yer thought her father, her actual flesh and blood might be up for it, never underestimate the cruelty of a scorned woman who disnae share that bond."

"Why would she do it?"

"Who ken that? Tae get back at the husband most probably. Hell of a parting gift after the divorce if yer think aboot it. Takes half his estate, hands over his daugh'er's ashes."

"That's horrible."

"These are naw fluffy people, Valentina."

"I mean, Madam Sokolova isn't like that?"

"Is she naw?" he asked with a tinge of sarcasm.

"No!"

"Then someone else disnae like him. Someone wants tae send a message tae the family. Perhaps a disgruntled business associate, a rival oligarch. As I said, literally anyone else."

Draining his coffee cup, he got up from the chair and disappeared into the kitchen. Valentina stared at the mesmerising flames. Thinking. Madam Sokolova was a kind and generous mistress. It was true she had a fierce temper at times, but she had only ever seen that side of her when she was in conflict with her husband. Surely the bitterness and jealousy that had precipitated the divorce proceedings wouldn't manifest itself so cruelly. It couldn't. She wasn't like that. Valentina was sure of it.

"Yer can have ma room." He said, returning to the lounge and opening the door to the adjacent bedroom. "I'll stoke up the stove tae run overnight. It will heat up the room easier than the wee back bedroom."

"No. I should go." She said, replacing the cup and unfolding her legs.

"Yer naw gonnae go anywhere the night."

She turned and looked at him. A moment of anxiety crept across her face. He nodded to the window.

"Storm's fair rashin' the day. Nowhere is gonnae be open at this time. Mobiles are pretty useless doon here, so yer cannae summon yer driver and I dinnae see any luggage wi yers." he looked around as he filled up the stove with coal and some seasoned oak for slower burning until the morning. "Probably dinnae expect tae wait for me so long and thought yer'd be back in the auld smoke by the night. Better off staying here. I can run yer back tae yer driver in the morn, wherever the hell he is."

"There's no need."

"I dinnae think yer've got much choice, lass." He smiled and turned back into the kitchen. "Goodnight!" he called back.

CHAPTER FORTY-THREE

The Kamov Ka-62 was a civilian development of the Kasatka twin-turbine military transport helicopter. With its sleek appearance it looked a lot like the Aérospatiale Dauphin produced by Airbus for executive clients. A streamlined, pointed nose, faired engine cowlings and a large Fenestron anti-torque tail rotor were amongst its most striking features. The two Ardiden 3G turboshafts had already begun to rotate its five blade main rotor as Mikhail Sokolov awaited the arrival of his most trusted lieutenant.

Appearing in the First Class Lounge of London City's Private Jet Terminal, Andrei Kazakin looked pleased with himself. His slab like face manifested this by the barely perceptible twinkle in his eye. Otherwise, his granite features remained as impassive as ever. He nodded to one of the minders as he entered. Sasha understood and moved towards the door to the tarmac and the blinking lights outside.

"It's confirmed." Kazakin murmured, taking the armchair next to Sokolov. "He is on his way back tonight."

"Cornwall?"

Kazakin nodded.

Sokolov looked at the television, showing the weather chaos hitting the west of the country. "He's driving back in this?" Kazakin shrugged. There was nothing to offer. "Where?"

"Somewhere near Plymouth."

"Let's get out of here before the airport freezes." He concluded standing up. "This is crazy. It's colder than Siberia."

Sasha emerged and gave a curt nod. The helicopter was ready. Filing out, Mikhail Sokolov and his security entourage stepped out onto the tarmac and walked the short distance to where an open door invited them inside the warm and plush interior. Once settled in, Kazakin took out his phone and made a quick call.

"Da. Kharasho." He hung up and twirled his finger in the air.

Sasha nodded and closed the doors. Taking up a headset, he gave the all-clear to the pilot and buckled himself in. Configured for eight passengers in a cabin designed to hold sixteen, the sumptuous leather seats, burr walnut consoles and thick wool carpet provided the same uncompromised luxury that Sokolov had battled for decades to obtain. His first wife, Kseniya, had supported him through all those early struggles. Their daughter Marya had been their crowning achievement. He would be damned if he was to allow Daria to take it all away from him now. Especially Masha.

"Mishkin has already set sail." Kazakin explained. "We will rendezvous with the yacht south of the Isle of Wight, then continue to Plymouth overnight."

"Good." Sokolov nodded as the Kamov took to the air. The helicopter pilots were former Russian Navy. They were used to landing a helicopter in stormy seas at night. Mishkin had been a commander of a helicopter carrier. Sokolov's private yacht was child's play for him now, and he loved it. "Do we know any more about those dogs?"

"The three at the nightclub were former members of Red Section, Estonian Special Forces. Do you remember Ragnar Lehtinen?"

"The soldier convicted of armed robbery in Tallinn?"

Kazakin nodded. "Caused the disbanding of the Special Operations Group. Seems he's the commander of this new unit. They contract their services out."

"Did Daria hire them?"

"I can't be sure yet. If she did, it wasn't done directly. In Europe they work mostly with a group called OID."

Sokolov shrugged. The initials meant nothing to him.

"Old Stasi members." Kazakin added. "They have a few individual facilitators, but when they need some extra muscle, they call for Red Section."

"Too many people trying to keep the Cold War alive." Sokolov sighed.

Kazakin fell silent for a moment, watching his master as he stared out over the frozen capital. The lights of the city like gold dust sprinkled over icing sugar.

"I don't understand, sir. Why would Daria hire someone to kill Masha, then someone else to kill them first? Why is she playing both sides?"

"This is what I'm hoping Mr Hamilton can help us with." Sokolov replied.

CHAPTER FORTY-FOUR

Greg Hamilton was beginning to trouble Valentina. She was in the habit of getting whatever she wanted. Usually this had entailed turning on her feminine charms, seducing the target. Bringing them under her spell. That was what Madam Sokolova had tasked her with. Yet so far, he had appeared indifferent to her advances.

The second concern was his theory that Mikhail Sokolov may not have orchestrated the hit on his daughter. Madam Sokolova had adamantly explained to Valentina that this was his very intention, to hurt her in the cruellest way possible. Something to take to her grave, which he hoped, perhaps even planned, might be soon.

It was why Hamilton had been hired to ensure the attempt failed in the first place. Yet the reasons Hamilton had presented as to why Sokolov might not have been behind the hit were compelling. In fact, they seemed quite obvious in retrospect. So how did Madam Sokolova know so much about the plan?

Valentina had read up on Greg Hamilton. Eight years as a Royal Marine Commando, four years with the Strathclyde Police, then six years as an SIS operative. A spook. The last two years he had spent freelancing. A wide range of skills and experience. If she couldn't persuade him to work for her mistress, might she yet persuade him to find out what was really going on?

The bedroom had absorbed warmth from the stove during the night, keeping her warm in bed. He had checked on it a few times during the night. In the morning he had stoked it up, added fresh wood and ventured outside to take a walk on the beach before the sun came up while she dozed and played these thoughts around in her head.

With the sting of sea salt in his nostrils came the distinct feeling that he had been played. Micky too. In hindsight it would have been better not to have become involved at all with the Sokolovs. It would have been better for him, better perhaps for Micky, maybe even better for Valentina. Not so much for Marya Sokolova. She would be dead on a slab in a London mortuary, or on her way back to Moscow for an Orthodox funeral.

Once he had heard the situation the young girl was about to find herself in, there was no possible way he could have refused the job. He wasn't about to have her death on his conscience, knowing he could have prevented it. He had enough deaths on his account sheet. Micky would have known that too.

Walking along the beach, leaving footprints in the firm sand, a clear blue sky began to reveal the rising sun in the southeast. Two points off Rame Head. Amidst the calming backdrop of the waves rolling up, that's when the theory struck him. Perhaps that was the whole point. The attempt on Marya Sokolova had been a ploy. What better way to compel him to come onboard? By taking out the hit squad though, he may have just placed himself in the crosshairs instead. Madam Sokolova now had a hold over him. She was using Valentina to sweeten the pill.

She was a sweet pill, but Hamilton had been wise to her tactics and refused to be manipulated. Why had he been blindsided by Madam Sokolova in the first place though? Was Daria Sokolova ruthless enough to sacrifice her stepdaughter? For what purpose? Had he known differently, would he have been prepared to call her bluff? The possibility came to him that even if he had turned down the job, she might have still had a hold over him, though of a different kind. The knowledge that he had allowed a young woman to be mercilessly gunned down in a London nightclub. He might want to make amends for that. She could give him the means.

He stood there and pulled up the collar of his button-down shirt. The rugby shirt and fleece layered over the top already had their collars upturned against the frigid breeze. It was calmer now though. There was not a cloud in the sky. Perhaps the storm had passed. The Beast from the East. Yet another overly pessimistic harbinger of destruction. The self-effacing, cynical nature of the British press had somehow gone down a dark spiral. For every silver lining there was a black cloud of disaster and depression behind it. Strange and spurious omens of doom then became self-fulfilling prophecies.

The weather was yet another target for portents of doom. Though naming storm fronts in typically British fashion was never going to have quite the same effect as it did with tropical cyclones and hurricanes. It was difficult to get excited about a storm called Emma. She was too polite. Too prim and proper to cause any real damage. Only she had been cavorting with her Nordic lover, anticyclone Hartmut, on Hamilton's way down from the Lakes to make driving conditions a little more interesting. And she wasn't quite done frolicking yet.

Right now, the sea was calm. Almost turquoise and strangely inviting under the bright morning sun. Whitsand Bay was like a mini oasis, green and pleasant, surrounded by the snowbound Cornish peninsula. It was as if the storm had never even happened. Devon & Cornwall Police were advising people not to travel on the roads that morning though. Another cold wave was predicted to be moving west. Another pessimistic prediction most likely.

In like manner, his mind considered the morbid possibility that with him in the firing line now, his secluded bolthole might be at risk. Just as he was beginning to settle into a new life. *Torridon* had a few more upgrades that he wanted to complete, but she had never been envisaged as a long-term camper. The drawer units in the loading area had been designed to contain a portable kitchen, water tanks and compressors, for living off grid, but not for months at a time. There had been no plan to install a bunk and even with a four-season sleeping bag, the roof tent wasn't suitable for all-weather camping. If he had to leave *Rockwater Cabin*, he would be starting all over again.

There was something more at work here. Some other reason why Madam Sokolova had wanted to get her claws into him. For the sake of his sanity, and his freedom, he needed to find out what it was. Looking up at the cliff, he could just make out where his little cabin was situated, setback from the edge on its isolated plateau. The balustrade around the decking, the radio aerial and the faint white smoke from the stove could just be seen wisping away on the wind. It looked like the stove needed more wood. Time to return.

The double bed had been freezing. Valentina had initially slept in her clothes. Then, as the heat increased, gradually stripped off, leaving her jeans and blouse in a pile on the floor. Now she buttoned on her blouse again as the sounds and smells of cooking could be heard wafting in. Coffee. Bacon and eggs.

"Do you have a bathroom?" she asked, padding barefoot into the kitchen.

"Other end." He replied, gesturing with his thumb without even looking up.

Without another word, she headed in the direction he had pointed. There were two doors at the far end of the kitchen, one opposite the other. Looking to the left, she could see out through the window in the door to a small courtyard and what looked like an outhouse at the far side. The cliff formed the fourth wall. She hoped the bathroom was behind the opposite door.

"Breakfast in five minutes." He called as she opened it, much relieved to see a full suite of fittings. "There's air freshener if yer need." He added with a smile to himself. Valentina was one of those women that would never admit to such ablutions, let alone engage in them in front of a complete stranger. Too refined, too dignified. Too stuck up her own posterior for anything else to come out.

The R1155B on the shelf was an old five band communication receiver sold off as surplus by the Air Ministry after the war. Doctor Harris' grandparents had been using it as a radio for years and with a little modification of the internals, could now pick up DAB stations well enough. The D&C were still strongly advising people stay indoors. Snow had reportedly fallen heavily overnight in all areas of the country again. Travel chaos was the natural order of the day. This was how the British did winter. Hamilton looked out and saw little change in the weather. It looked a little darker towards Devon, but that wasn't unusual. Out to sea everything still looked clear and bright.

Plating up as she emerged, he handed her one, dropped the knife and fork in the breast pocket of her blouse, and placed a mug of coffee in the other, this time from the cafetiere. A longer caffeine hit. Without waiting for a reply, he picked up his own plate and mug, squeezed past her to the dining room and sat in the furthest chair before digging in. She followed him, still a little bemused and sleepy. Not sure what to do. She hadn't even slipped into her jeans yet.

"Have yer even had bacon and eggs before?" he asked, looking up.

"Can't say that I remember." She replied, taking the chair opposite.

"More a seared salmon and avocado girl, are we?" He replied with a vaguely condescending tone which strangely pained her. A blob of brown sauce was added to the side of his plate. Some of it he mixed in with the baked beans.

"Do you resent me for having refined tastes?"

"No, it's none of my business."

"No, it's not, but I do understand the sentiment." She sat there in silence, considering. "I'm sorry I broke in." she murmured quietly.

"Yer gonnae eat that?" he pointed his knife at her untouched plate.

She looked down. What it lacked in presentation, it made up for with its inviting aroma. Her stomach was desperate for something and made it known that it didn't much care for the finer things at that moment. Anything would do. She removed the cutlery from her blouse and began to eat.

"I guessed yer might be an eggs over kinda lass. No mess that way."

"Do you always have this for breakfast?"

"Only when I've ran oot o' milk for cereal. Or have company." "How often is that?"

"Almost never. On both counts."

Her cheeks flushed. First the stove, then the bed, now breakfast. Yet she had broken into his residences twice and offered nothing in return but a dubious contract with a volatile mistress. His manner was interesting. It was cold and indifferent, yet the actions conveyed kindness and hospitality. Thoughtfulness. A strange compassion even.

There was a crash as she dropped the cutlery on the plate in frustration. Hamilton looked across, breaking his view of the foliage growing between the rocks in the cliff face.

"Here I am, trying to do everything I can to make you like me, and yet I'm failing at every turn."

"Then stop trying." He replied, cutting up his bacon.

"You're so different than I expected."

"Whit were yer expecting?"

"Someone…someone harder."

He looked up with a raised eyebrow. "Way tae crush a man's baws."

"I meant…" her cheeks coloured almost to the shade of her hair. Piled up again behind her. "You've treated me with respect. Even though I haven't deserved it."

"Dinnae be soft. Getting yer tae drop yer scanties in the middle o' the parlour is hardly treating yer respectfully."

"It's the job. I understand why you did it."

"We both have jobs tae do. They dinnae define us."

"Sometimes I think they do." She replied thoughtfully, her feline eyes narrowing. "Or rather, it defines me at least."

"Ah, yer wrong, lass."

"That's sweet." She breathed, looking up at him.

"Eat up."

She finished another mouthful, took a sip of coffee and looked across at him. "What are your plans for the day?"

"Unpack the car and check the frequencies." He nodded to the radio high up on the shelf, though he would actually be using the TETRA setup in the back bedroom.

"What for?"

"In case anyone needs recovery."

"Is that what you do now?"

"Amongst other things."

"So, you really won't take up Madam Sokolova's offer?"

"As ah told Micky, for what she's got coming at her, she's gonnae need a whole army. Ah'm jist one man and ah work alone. So, ah'm naw up tae it."

"What does she have coming?"

"Whoever those hitmen worked for will be oot for revenge. Three top guys killed in one night. They'll be wanting compensation at the very least." He looked up, seeing the lacy edge to her brassiere beneath the blouse again. A pleasing shade of turquoise. "Payment might be taken in bawbies, boobies or blood, if yer ken whit ah mean?" he moved his gaze higher and met her eyes. There was a bleak expression on his face. "If it transpires that it wis Madam Sokolova's plan, then Sokolov himself might decide tae escalate things. Either way, this is nae gonna end well, Valentina. It's only jist beginning. And yer right stuck in the middle of it. I'd get oot while yer can. While there's suhin' of yer soul left."

"You don't understand. I can't just walk away."

"Sure, yer can. Yer jist put one step in front o' the other. Yer need tae. Or yer could find yerself deid by the end o' the week. And I dinnae want that."

"No?"

"Course not." He shook his head, scraping his plate clean. "Everyone deserves a fair crack at life. Whitever happened in yer past, it seems tae me yer've been dealt a pretty shocking hand so far. Time tae do suhin' for yerself. Naw because someone else asked yer tae."

She stared at him silently.

"Trust me, I ken whit it's like living yer life following other people's orders. There are some things yer can never take back. When yer enter a world where you can finally say 'no', yer'll find it rather liberating."

"It's not that simple."

"Ah, it never is." He said, standing up to clear the plates. Stopping halfway, he turned. "ah'll gie yer a third option." She swivelled around on the chair, placing her arm on the back of it and looked up at him. "Heid back tae London, get yer stuff together and disappear. Start a new life. Forget about Madam Sokolova. Forget about this whole mess."

Valentina was quiet for a moment. Pondering.

"May I ask you something?" she called.

"Aye."

Hamilton had moved to the other end of the kitchen to where the Belfast sink was squeezed between the backdoor and the bathroom.

"The first night we met, I offered you something and you refused. Can I ask why?"

"Ah dinnae ken whit passes for normal in yer world, but shagging the client is nae how ah do business."

She smiled. It was a refreshingly honourable response.

"Then what is it you do?"

"Ah'm no saint, but ah wis brought up tae respect women. Ah could see whit was happening. Madam Sokolova put yer up tae it and it wis nae right."

"I…" Valentina was unsure how to respond to his observation. It was though he had seen right through her.

"Yer dinnae need tae answer that. Yer a person, naw a tool."

She was silent for a moment, leaning against the door frame, watching him wash up the breakfast things. "That statement is naïve but appreciated nonetheless."

"Well, yer've got until yer get back tae London tae decide whit tae do wi yer life."

He drained the sink, turned and tossed the tea towel over his shoulder as he leaned against the edge, folding his arms. That look. She had seen something like it before. It had made her question things then too.

CHAPTER FORTY-FIVE

The hatch in the side of the hull opened up like a clamshell. Emerging from the bowels of the superyacht, like an orca giving birth, was the sleek, streamlined form of a black 52-foot closed cockpit super catamaran. The powerboat gently edged away from the side of the vessel, waiting for the hatch to close before accelerating away. Sitting low in the water, twin Mercury Racing engines propelled the vessel beyond the breakwater and into Plymouth Sound. Heading up the Tamar, the boat came off plane and angled in towards the Mount Edgcumbe Landing at Cremyll.

The appearance of the striking vessel backing up alongside the same slipway with the Edgcumbe Belle was a marked contrast in maritime transportation. The single screw motor vessel had been launched in 1957 and could carry almost 130 foot passengers. On the opposite side of the slipway, at the other end of the spectrum, the offshore powerboat had left the MTI dockyards in Florida with a capacity of just six and served as a high-performance tender for the Baikal superyacht lying at anchor off the Devonshire coast.

A black hatch in the roof opened and Kazakin emerged from inside the catamaran, followed by Sasha. Without saying a word, they walked past the bemused crowd and headed straight for the Edgcumbe Arms. Walking up to the bar, Kazakin unzipped his black jacket and gestured for the barman.

"What can I get you, lads?" he asked cheerily. "We're serving breakfast..."

"Gregor Hamilton." Kazakin broke in. "Do you know him?"

"Sure, he lives up on the old military road."

"We need to see him. It's urgent."

"Alright. I'll give him a ring." He replied, a little perplexed but happy to oblige.

Hamilton was accustomed to doing things on his own but sometimes having a second pair of hands was useful. The rear ladder and durbar armour on the bonnet and wing top air ram scoops were not an aesthetic affectation but enabled him to climb up to the roof rack and loosen off the fixings for the tent. Having someone down below to receive the unit made it a lot easier to remove and carry back to the cabin. Valentina may as well make herself useful while she was here. Fortunately, there had been no more snow overnight, so Valentina's expensive fashion trainers didn't end up sliding her down the footpath on that shapely derriere.

With the wood supplies taken down and the camping kitchen restocked, he had pondered whether he should swap over the eighteen-inch alloys on all-terrain tyres with the fifteen-inch beadlock steel wheels he kept in storage on larger Arctic truck tyres. It would need a slight suspension adjustment to take the bigger setup, but the advantage of the beadlock was that the tyre was physically bolted to the rim, meaning pressures could be lowered even further. If he was to be called out on a rescue in the snow, the softer compound tyres at a lower pressure would be a distinct advantage.

Heading back down to the cabin, he traversed the length of the kitchen to get the wheels from the outhouse when the radio crackled into life. He had set it to scan the frequencies and lock onto a distress signal or incoming message but was surprised to hear Dave from the Edgcumbe Arms on the line. He had no landline and mobile reception was patchy to say the least. The radio was the most reliable means to get hold of him.

"Echo Alpha to Romeo Charlie One, come in please. Over." He called. "Echo Alpha to Romeo Charlie One, come in."

"Romeo Charlie One tae Echo Alpha, receiving. Over."

"Greg, there's a couple of guys asking for you down here. Say they need to see you urgently."

"Whit do they look like, Dave?" he asked. Alarm bells already going off.

"Foreign."

"Yer mean from Devon?" he joked, trying to regulate his thoughts. Looking back to the floorboards where the Vaultek Slider Safe was keeping his S&W R8 secure. In a lockable, crushproof carrying case alongside were two Glock 22 pistols. The magazines were empty to prevent strain on the springs. Cartridges were stored in pre-cut foam on the second layer. Not as easily accessible as the revolver for home defence. More useful for close protection work.

"Proper foreign." There seemed a tinge of anxiety in Dave's voice. If it was starting already, he didn't want the locals embroiled in the forthcoming. They had no share in this at all.

"Okay. Fix them up wi a couple of breakfasts and put them in a booth. I'll come doon right away. Romeo Charlie One. Over and oot."

"What's happening?" Valentina asked, listening anxiously to the radio transmission.

"Looks like ah've gaw some visitors." He remarked, stepping out of the back bedroom.

Valentina looked a little worried. Her thoughts fearing the worst too it seemed. "How would they have found you so quickly?"

"You did."

"I didn't tell anyone."

"Whit about yer driver?" he said, moving to the floorboards to pull out the case. It was no use hiding his guns from her now she knew he had them. There were not many places in a cabin this size they could be stowed.

"He just dropped me off on the road near the restaurant." She explained. "He doesn't know what cabin you're in."

"Wid nae take long tae find oot." He said, lifting out the top layer of foam where the Glocks were stored. Taking up a magazine and a box of cartridges, he set about loading it up with fifteen potent .40 Smith & Wesson rimless pistol cartridges. The kind US law enforcement favoured. Some proper stopping power.

She shook her head. "I'm sure it's not him."

"Well." He pulled on a coat, pulled back the slide and shoved the Glock into an inside pocket. "I better found oot whit they want then."

"Be careful." She said, not quite sure why she had.

He paused for a moment, frowning as he looked at her. Then loaded up the second Glock and handed it to her.

"Yer ken how tae use one?"

She gave him a disappointed frown. Of course she knew.

"Fine. Jist in case. Ah'll holler when ah'm coming back so yer dinnae pop one in ma face."

"Do you think this could be them?"

"Depends who we mean by 'them', but whatever fear yer feeling right now, remember it. If this turns oot okay, consider it a warning. Get oot of this, Valentina. While yer can. Ah mean it. There might naw be another chance."

Heading up to the Land Rover, Hamilton opened the driver's door and unlocked the hub and clutch devices, secured the steering wheel and prepared to make the short journey down to Cremyll to meet his visitors. Clambering up into the driver's seat, he looked above him where his Scottish atelier had constructed a walnut roof console to match the one running front to back down the transmission tunnel. The sides had been trimmed in the same chocolate brown mohair as its companion. Reading lights, air vents and storage compartments had been expertly crafted into sinuous cabinetry. Polished metal switches controlled interior and exterior lighting and Hamilton's mobile radio terminal was mounted in the front aperture within easy reach. A fist microphone clipped to the side.

In addition, two mohair-trimmed walnut parcel shelves above the windscreen spanned the gap between the roof console and the sides of the cabin, offering additional storage and a place for the sun visors to fold away in recessed pockets. Bolted to the top side of the driver's parcel shelf, partially concealed beneath the lip, Hamilton had installed a second Vaultek Slider Safe. As in the cabin, the unit was accessible via a backlit keypad, large biometric scanner and phone app, as well as a master key.

He reached up, pressed his thumb against the scanner to open the slide and took out a bright orange single-shot, breech loading, 12-gauge flare gun. In the space for a spare magazine was a bandolier with four aerial flares. As a back-up it wasn't a bad choice. Certainly grabbed attention. He returned the flare gun, closed the safe and zipped up the inside pocket of his coat.

From the decking down below, Valentina watched him reverse back out onto the lane, then accelerate away up the hill and out of sight. A cloud of black smoke following him. The sound of the big diesel engine and turbine whistle rattled on for some time but as she turned to see where he had gone, the clouds rolling in from Devon looked dark and threatening all of a sudden. Storm Emma was on her way.

Already the first flakes were beginning to fall by the time Hamilton parked up at the bottom of Maker Lane. The distinctive lines of the MTI-52 Black Diamond powerboat caught his eye, moored up on the other side of the landing. The ferry running between Cremyll and Admiral's Hard was usually the only vessel that made use of the concrete slipway. Looking out beyond Drake's Island, he tried to see if there was some superyacht out on the horizon. Visibility was closing in and flakes were falling fatter and faster now. The Royal William Yard just across the estuary was almost obscured by a blizzard flurrying down.

Unzipping the inside pocket but pulling the coat around him, he locked the pedal and the door before dashing across the road to dive into the pub. The wood panelling and roaring fire made for a welcoming atmosphere. It was tempting to settle into a post-breakfast pint. On seeing Hamilton walk in, Dave nodded in the direction of the bow window behind him where the two gentlemen had been positioned. Hamilton settled up their breakfast bill and turned to see them tucking into a plate of Full English. The chef at the Edgcumbe knew how to put a good portion together.

"Morning gentlemen." He greeted, stepping up into the alcove and sitting down on a stool. "Yer wanted tae see me?"

"It was me that wanted to see you?"

Looking to the front porch over his left shoulder, Hamilton saw Mikhail Sokolov wander in, followed by another minder. All four men were dressed in similar fashion. Dark waterproof jackets, thick fisherman's jumpers and pale blue open-necked shirts. That season's winter yacht casual perhaps.

"Mikhail Andreievich." Hamilton greeted standing up. It was always best to stand respectfully whenever an oligarch walked in, regardless of which side they were on. These men commanded respect. Demanded it. Common courtesies were cheap to extend but invaluable investments.

Sokolov stared at him for a moment. Weighing him up. Even without the step up into the window between them, Hamilton was a little taller, a good ten years or so younger. His stubbly beard and moustache aged him a little but gave his face a strong, masculine appearance.

Stepping up, Sokolov embraced Hamilton. The saviour of his daughter. Whatever differences they might still have, he would forever be grateful for that. A little confused, Hamilton reciprocated hesitantly, conscious of the Glock 22 pressing into his chest. No doubt Sokolov would also be aware of its presence. In any case he didn't react and gestured for him to sit back down as he took the second stool. Kazakin and Sasha were just finishing up their breakfast. The fourth man stood behind Hamilton near the wooden balustrade. Line of sight to the front door and out through the bow window.

"Tae whit do I owe this visit, Mr Sokolov?"

"Please. You of all people have earned the right to call me Misha." He placed his hands on the table, interlinking his fingers like they were at a business meeting.

"That might tek a wee bit o' getting used tae."

"You saved my Masha." He smiled. There was some warmth in it. An emotion he hadn't associated with the hardnosed Siberian before. "I am forever in your debt. She is everything to me. Especially since..." he trailed off.

Despite the years that had elapsed, Sokolov still held strong feelings for Kseniya. There were suspicions the alleged car accident had not been accidental at all. It had been a classic go-to Cold War tactic to get rid of political rivals in the Soviet Union. The same tactics had crossed over into post-Soviet capitalist Russia to achieve similar ends. It was also true that grief never diminished over time. An individual merely grew around it.

"When I wis told whit wis going doon, I cood nae just let it happen." Hamilton explained. "Whitever's going on, no way any kid deserves that."

"And just what do you think is going on?"

Hamilton pursed his lips, selecting his words carefully.

"Ma guess, Daria has gaw herself intae some pure deep shite." He decided not to risk sullying the family name by referring to her as Valentina did. Madam Sokolova. Hamilton suspected Sokolov wouldn't appreciate her term of respect for his soon-to-be ex-wife.

"Do you know who they were?"

"No."

"A man like you must have suspicions though."

"Oh, aye. There's one or two possibili'ies."

Sokolov unlocked his fingers, inviting Hamilton's conjectures.

"Either German or Estonian. Ah'm leaning towards the latter. Possibly Red Section. More likely tae be oot for hire. Might have German connections though for hardware supply unless they have someone still inside ESTSOF."

Sokolov exchanged a look with Kazakin. Indifferent as ever. Nothing. Though the very fact there was a glance at all meant something.

"They'll be coming after whoever cancelled their contract."

"Aye, ah suspected they might." Hamilton sighed. He had already envisaged watching his peaceful little existence being erased.

"Perhaps we can help each other."

Here it came. Another dubious contract. Though he suspected Sokolov might be an easier client to deal with than the ex-wife, despite the show of muscle around the table. Better to have them on his side than against.

"Yer wannae ken where yer daughter is?"

Sokolov's eyes lit up. Hamilton was hoping that might pre-empt any actual work.

"I took her back tae Cadogan Square, but she was gonnae be sent ontae *Fairford* wi a few of the lads. Given they were the same bastards prepared tae abandon her at the nightclub, if I was her Da, I'd be wanting tae get her someplace safer."

Fairford was the Sokolov's rural retreat set in the Gloucestershire countryside. The Grade II listed, Queen Anne style house was situated within beautiful, mature landscaped gardens and was particularly charming in the summer months. It was a harder property to secure though. Approached down a country lane that led to the nearby village. Wide expanses of lawn were broken up by structured yew hedging and studded with specimen trees. Boundary woodland provided ample cover for observation. The orchard near the duckpond was perhaps the only natural defence, provided the ducks hadn't moved upstream. People thought a country house was a safer alternative. In his mind, Hamilton was already planning how he might assault the property. Safer in the city.

"That will be good for her." Sokolov nodded. "She will be with the horses."

"Easier for yer tae see her too." Hamilton added. "She's nineteen now. Old enough tae choose for herself whom she lives wi." He looked out through the windows. The snowstorm was carrying on unabated.

Usually, snowflakes didn't settle all that well around Mount Edgcumbe. The proximity to the sea elevated the salt content in the atmosphere, depressing the freezing point of water. However, a substantial layer was already appearing on the road outside and thickening up quickly. Hamilton was beginning to wish he had switched to the beadlocks sooner. Climbing back up Maker Lane might be a little tricker than he had hoped.

"Wi this weather, if yer pilot can fly yer up there, now might be an ideal time tae make the extraction. Maybe say hello tae the boys. Nuhin' will be goin' in or oot of London for a wee while. Including Daria."

Sokolov looked to Kazakin. He nodded and took out his phone. The signal was stronger in the pub than back at Hamilton's cabin on the cliffs. A few short sentences were spoken. Nothing Hamilton could understand. Then the call was ended. Kazakin nodded.

"Thank you." Sokolov said, standing up. "I owe you a great deal."

"Well, if yer like, yer could start by getting Red Section off ma back." Hamilton replied, looking around. "I'm beginning tae enjoy retirement."

Sokolov looked to his lieutenant again as Kazakin and Sasha shuffled awkwardly out of the alcove. Hamilton was quietly amused as he stood up to let them out. No matter how battle-scarred, bruised and brawny anyone was, getting up from an alcove or booth seating was always an undignified affair. There was no expression on Kazakin's face at all. Nothing. It was a remarkable achievement.

"We will do what we can." Sokolov acknowledged weakly. He smiled, knowing how unpromising that sounded. "These people don't respond to the usual niceties."

"Ah'm sure yer will." Hamilton sighed. "Ah must warn yer though." He added. Kazakin reacted with a twitch of an eyebrow. A perceived threat to his master. "If they do happen tae come here and dinnae finish the job, ah will be pure raging on their bahoochies."

Sokolov chuckled. Kazakin relaxed. "Then let's hope for everyone's sake they stay away."

"Aye, let's hope." Hamilton murmured unconvincingly.

He watched the formidable foursome leave the pub and walk back past the window. Stacking the coffee cups onto the plates, he picked them up and returned them back to the bar. Heaving a heavy sigh.

"You've got some unusual friends." Dave observed.

"Yer telling me." Hamilton nodded, handing the plates over.

Making his way back outside, the blizzard was in full flow and about two inches of snow had settled on the road already. The mooring line had been wound up and the roof hatch on the catamaran was just being closed as he arrived at the side of *Torridon*. The passengers disembarking from the ferry were standing around, watching the vessel with interest as the deep burble of her engines reverberated off the concrete.

There was a slight dip of the transom as the throttles were pushed forward, propelling her out into the Tamar estuary again. Once clear of the slipway, the engine note changed and the nose pitched up a little higher, bringing the vessel on plane. Water was thrown up in its wake like a rooster tail as surface drives churned it up. The catamaran shot forward, turning around Mount Edgcumbe and disappearing behind the trees in the direction of Drake's Island. Whatever Mikhail Sokolov did now was in his own hands. Hamilton was having none of it.

He opened the door, unlocked the pedal and clambered back behind the wheel. Tapping his boots on the sidestep to remove the snow from the cleats. His phone vibrated. Number withheld. Again.

"Hello?"

"Hamilton."

"Sir?"

"How are your job prospects looking?"

"Och, yer ken." Hamilton replied casually. Of course, he wouldn't know. The Chief of the Secret Intelligence Service would have no idea, looking out across the frozen Thames from his wood-panelled office on the top floor of Vauxhall Cross.

"You're about to get a call from someone. It would be in your interests to listen to what they have to say."

"Financially or personally?" he asked, feeling a little perturbed by his old boss's cryptic statement.

"Let me put it this way, Hamilton." Came the smooth, measured response. "If you don't look into what they're asking you, I won't hear the end of it, and so neither will you."

"It's like that is it, sir?"

"Yes it is, Hamilton. Yes it is." Came the same cool reply. "By the way, *Rockwater Cabin* has some lovely views."

Hamilton never got the chance to reply. The call was terminated. Though he was too shocked to think of a suitable riposte anyway. Shocked but not surprised. If the Secret Intelligence Service wanted you, they had ways of finding you.

CHAPTER FORTY-SIX

Hamilton looked down at the ignition key in his hand. Precision milled on a CNC machine from a single piece of austenitic Grade 303 Stainless Steel. It exhibited a smooth, matte black layer of titanium aluminium carbonitride applied using physical vapour deposition. Its design form reflected the iconic alpine windows that flanked the roof. The shoulder section was colour-matched to the Montalcino Red paintwork of the body and diamond engraved on the reverse of the head was a vehicle identification box. On a black metal ring was the fob for the central locking and a keyring that doubled as a multitool. The car key was never designed to be his front door key too.

The ignition slot was just to the left of the steering column. Inserting the key into the slot, he gave it a twist to turn on the electrics, then moved to the switch next to it. Machined from aluminium billet, all the polished flick switches throughout the vehicle had been modelled on classic British sports cars. This was the kill switch for the electrics. Flicking it down, he moved across to the second switch alongside. The words START and STOP had been engraved deep onto the respective faces of the switch. Flicking it down, the big 5.9-litre 6BT diesel engine rumbled into life, rocking the cabin slightly. A 40mm turbocharger sucking in great gulps of cold air.

Since *Torridon's* completion, the intoxicating aromas of new wool, mohair and leather had always combined with the earthy notes of coco mats and wood oil to form the heady smell of adventure. It was strange to think that after a sixty-seven-year continuous production run, no more of these indomitable vehicles would ever be built again. The last time there were no Land Rovers churning out of Solihull, George VI was on the throne, Clement Attlee in

Downing Street and the independent Union of India was just a year old.

Greg Hamilton's vehicle was one of the last examples to be built. A Defender 110 County Station Wagon that had already taken some significant abuse. Though not in the manner she had been designed for. Regrettably, her previous owners had attempted to make the vehicle into some kind of stealthy urban cruiser. A blacked out status symbol for dropping the kids off to lacrosse. Something it was definitely never designed to do.

She had been sold onto him with aftermarket soundproofing, bulky body kits and oversized wheels. Unfortunately, the carpets and glued down cabin insulation just trapped dirt, odours and moisture which was already beginning to expedite corrosion.

For Hamilton, this was as cardinal a sin as boarding up fireplaces, ripping out original features and covering parquet flooring. The remedial work to strip it all out had required a complete frame-off rebuild to rectify. With *Rockwater Cabin* complete, Hamilton ploughed his energy and resources into *Torridon*, taking the opportunity to reconstruct the vehicle to his own liking.

In his view, a Land Rover was like the boot room of a country manor. It made no sense to glue down chain store fitted carpets over flagstones because the floor was too cold. Just get some high-quality sisal mats and beat the living crap out of them while sweeping out the solids.

The specialist Edinburgh atelier he went to had vision that extended far beyond just ripping out what had gone in before. They prided themselves on prioritising craftsmanship, quality and originality. Specialising in restoring and upgrading Defenders, they sought to redefine the vehicle, celebrating the essence of what it meant to be a Land Rover. Rebuilding them using high-quality, long-lasting materials which connected the vehicle to the original spirit of fun, practicality and adventure.

By using hardwood, rubber backed natural fibre and painted or powder-coated galvanised metal, there were no longer any moisture traps, no musty carpets, and no fogged up windows. Crucially for a Land Rover, no corrosion. These vehicles had a tendency to rust if someone looked at them with so much as a damp eye.

Hamilton ran his finger around the walnut rim of the three-spoke steering wheel. No airbag, just a polished billet horn in the centre boss. If it came to it, he would die like a man. Beyond the wheel, five Caerbont gauges stared back at him from the binnacle. The face of the tachometer in the centre had been colour-matched to the same dark shade of red used for the exterior. The three-in-one oil temperature, oil pressure and water temperature gauge drew the eye to the left where the dual fuel and oil level gauge was positioned on the far left of the binnacle.

The speedometer to the right of the central dial had been recalibrated to 150mph, though it was unlikely the hulking beast would ever make the ton. On the far right, enclosed by the same chrome bezels and set into the same magnolia face as the other gauges, was a warning light module with ten individual lights surrounding a central analogue clock. The binnacle was trimmed with mohair. The dials set into a thick walnut fascia. Not burred woodgrain like a Jag, just beautifully oiled and exuding natural patina. The switches, set into basket woven leather from Muirhead of Renfrewshire, in a single horizontal line across the lower edge of the dashboard, were brushed and engraved with pictograms on the surrounds. No ounce of quality was compromised.

It was as he was staring at the instruments that his phone rang once more. The ringtone throbbing through the speakers. This time the number also displayed a name on the 9-inch SatNav screen above the switches: Harrington DCB. A Dame Commander of the Most Honourable Order of the Bath. Superb. What was he getting involved in now?

"Hamilton."

"Dame Harrington. SIS. Retired. I need your assistance."

"Of course, ma'am." he replied pleasantly, the Chief's pointed words still ringing in his ears.

CHAPTER FORTY-SEVEN

Swapping out the contents of his rucksack would be the work of a few moments, but the snow was lying about four inches thick on the road by the time he returned to the cabin. It would be a day or two at least before he was going anywhere. The D&C were reiterating their earlier appeal on national radio for people to stay home if they didn't have to go anywhere. Hamilton parked up and looked out to sea as the heavy flakes landed softly on *Torridon's* bonnet.

From an inviting, tropical turquoise in the morning, the sea now possessed a brooding grey swell. It looked even colder than the temperature gauge told him it was outside. *Torridon* had just warmed up the seats for him. Now it was time to brave the elements and head down the frozen path.

Before he turned the engine off, he contemplated the phone call he had just taken from Dame Harrington. He was being asked to look for three cars. Three old cars. Harrington suggested he visit the Borromean Archives to get up to speed. Hamilton couldn't think what the connection was to the Secret Intelligence Service. He couldn't see any relevance at all. Surely the Chief wasn't intimidated by an old lady. Nevertheless, with his words still sharply in mind, it left Hamilton with little choice but to pursue this curious quest.

"It's me!" he called before entering the kitchen. Along with his steering wheel, another net of logs was in hand from the storage locker outside. "We're gonnae go nowhere for a wee while, so…"

Hamilton had supplies of food and wood and Valentina looked better in his clothes than he did. She emerged from the bedroom wearing one of his rugby shirts. A pair of cargo trousers had the hems rolled up around her ankles and there was a sooty smudge on her face.

"Yer kept the fire goin' then." He remarked, commenting on the intense warmth emanating from the stove.

"I know how to make fire." She replied. "My grandfather had a dacha in the woods."

"Yer might be useful tae have around here after all."

"Hmm. Thank you." she said. "Who was it?"

"Sokolov."

"What?! Here?" Her face immediately filled with alarm and panic.

"Chill oot. He's gone back tae his yacht." Hamilton added, lugging the wood into the living room. "Probably heading off soon anyway."

"What did he want?"

"Actually, he wanted tae thank me for saving his daugh'er's life." He removed his coat and returned it to the hook by the door, taking out the Glock from the pocket. "How's that Madam Sokolova theory holding up?"

Valentina frowned, though there was another emotion in those eyes. The sadness of betrayal. A realisation that she too may have been manipulated. That was supposed to be her forte. To manipulate. To detect and rebuff the manipulation of others.

"Coffee?" he asked.

"Hmm. Okay." She sighed, handing back the second Glock.

"Help yerself tae any of ma clothes, by the way." he called back as he proceeded to unload them. "Gaw a couple of cute jumpers somewhere."

Valentina made no reply. Instead, she slumped herself down on the sofa, up against the corner. Contemplating. Again. She drew her knees under her and pulled the blanket up around her body. More for comfort than warmth.

Hamilton meanwhile returned the handguns to the case, then set about recharging the moka pot, keeping one ear tuned into the radio scanning the frequencies. He was half-expecting to be called out at any moment given the sudden snowstorm.

CHAPTER FORTY-EIGHT
FRANCE, 1941

The Westland Lysander had initially been deployed as an Army cooperation aircraft, intended to act as an artillery spotter and liaison shuttle. However, the plane's exceptional short-field performance made it ideal for the Royal Air Force Special Duties Service. In August 1941 a new squadron had been formed to undertake covert missions for the Special Operations Executive to maintain clandestine contact with French Resistance. For this purpose, No. 138 Squadron had taken delivery of two Lysanders and promptly set about lightening them up.

The first things to go were the bomb racks and forward firing machine guns. The rear firing machine gun for the observer was also removed and range was extended by adding a 150-gallon auxiliary fuel tank underneath the fuselage. Thus, there was no defensive armament and extra inflammable liquid. Perfect. The large service radio was replaced by a much smaller, lighter one and a rearward facing bench was installed in the observer's position with a storage locker beneath. To facilitate easier access and egress, a ladder was welded to one side of the fuselage for agent drop-off and pick-ups, though if needed they could also launch themselves over the side and drop in via parachute to negate the need for a suitable landing strip.

Flying out from RAF Tangmere on the Sussex coast, the single Lysander aircraft kept low over the cold waters of the English Channel, making for an incredibly bumpy flight. As the pilot approached the French coastline he climbed to 8,000feet to clear the flak, before dropping to around 1,500feet to read the landmarks. Holding the map on his knee with one hand, he flew the Lysander with the other, checking off his waypoints with a pencil as he moved further inland.

With the final waypoint marked off, the pilot dropped down to 600feet on the approach to the landing site, still invisible even in the moonlight. A minute or so later, the pre-arranged Morse code letter was flashed up from the ground, a little to the left. Correcting his course, the pilot responded with his downward identification light, returning the designated signal. At that moment, the landing site was illuminated by five lights placed in an 'X' pattern. Sliding back the rear canopy, Grover-Williams tightened his harness straps as the pilot reduced speed to just above stalling. Then, without saying a word, he jumped over the non-ladder side and almost immediately pulled the ripcord to deploy the parachute.

At that altitude the canopy was open for just a few seconds before he hit the ground, resulting in a heavy landing. Remembering his training, Grover-Williams kept his elbows in, bent his knees and rolled to the side. Even then, the impact winded him momentarily and it took him a few seconds to gather himself up.

Releasing the harness, he kept low and made for the trees. His parachute would be collected by the men with the lights once he had made good his escape. As he approached the trees, a double flash nearby alerted him to his rendezvous. Heading in the direction of the flashing lights, Grover-Williams recognised the distinctive chrome form of the black Bugatti's horseshoe grille.

With a hand on his pistol just in case, he breathed a sigh of relief when he saw his friend and fellow operative, Robert Benoist behind the wheel. His welcoming committee had arrived.

"Am I glad to see you." he smiled as he opened the door.

"Get in. We've got a safe house to get to." Grover-Williams clambered in and closed the door. The heady smell of leather and wood a welcome aroma after the confines of the musty Lysander. The Bugatti Atlantic Type 57SC was a fabulous car.

La Voiture Noire, the Black Car, was the second of only four Atlantic models produced at the Molsheim factory in Alsace. The 3rd Baron Rothschild had bought the first Atlantic, painted a metallic grey-blue and fabricated using components from the equally beautiful Aérolithe prototype. The third

Atlantic had been delivered new to Parisian businessman and hotelier Jacques Holzschuh in December 1936. The fourth and final Atlantic, finished in a lustrous sapphire blue, had been sold to British tennis player Richard Pope.

Sitting on the passenger side, the large, four-spoke steering wheel was reminiscent of the Type 35 racing car Grover-Williams had driven to victory in the inaugural Monaco Grand Prix. A long, angled gear lever emerged from beneath the dashboard and beige leather seats accommodated the pair of them in comfort.

"How is Yvonne?" Grover-Williams asked as Benoist negotiated his way back to the main road in total darkness, not daring to turn on the headlights just yet, even though they were shrouded with blackout covers.

"She's doing fine. She will be pleased to see you."

"That makes both of us." He smiled.

Taking the revolver from the pouch on his webbing, he leaned forward and reached under the chair where a small flap in the underside of the seat had been added for stowage. Grover-Williams suspected it had been placed there for maps by Jean Bugatti. The Type 57 was designed as a Grand Tourer after all. In any case, it was a useful place of concealment and had prompted himself and Robert to make one or two other alterations.

There was no glovebox or cubby in the dashboard. The two halves of book matched wood instead contained a full suite of gauges. A legacy of their racing heritage, Bugatti had always placed the steering wheel of his cars exclusively on the right-side, to take advantage of the clockwise nature of most Grand Prix circuits, enabling the drivers to take a faster line. Thus, on his side in front of the passenger seat on the left, was a Jaeger LeCoultre A-10 Chronoflite clock with twelve hour, eight-day and elapsed time dials. He was used to seeing that dial in racing cars. The amperes and fuel gauges came next before a prominent speedometer just left of the central aluminium seamline. The rev counter, oil and water temperature gauges took up the right side before the large steering wheel emerged from the bottom of the dashboard.

The layout meant there was no dial directly in front of the driver. Grover-Williams had utilised this layout by placing a small storage box just the other side, accessible from a hatch beneath the dashboard. Here, they could store maps, plans and other documents in complete secrecy. A small keyhole meant the hatch couldn't be opened by just anyone either and the steering column passing below it made access doubly awkward, keeping the documents safe and secure.

It needed to be. Inside was a list of agents, codenames and safe houses, necessary for them to verify their network of contacts, but its discovery would destroy SOE operations completely. It was the single most valuable document of the whole French Resistance movement. To maintain its secrecy, the document itself had been written as a mirror image of English text, requiring a mirror placed alongside it for it be legible. Even so, it was a dangerous document to have lying around.

"We might need to get rid of the car." Benoist said with a heavy heart.

Grover-Williams always knew it was a possibility, but still found it difficult to comprehend the loss of such a magnificent machine.

"It's becoming too obvious."

"I know." He sighed. "Any ideas?"

"We could bury it."

"I don't want to destroy it."

Benoist nodded. He understood. It was too good a car to simply discard, but keeping it concealed would be an occupational hazard in itself. Hiding it from the Germans would be hard enough as it was, for however long the war would continue. If there was to be a second Allied invasion, hiding it from the new occupying force would be doubly challenging, seeing as they would likely seek out every last vestige of German authority in every possible hiding place. A simple solitary barn in an isolated French commune would suddenly become a very exposed location.

"I asked *Adler* for his thoughts." Benoist responded, trying to judge the reaction he would get.

"What was his suggestion." Grover-Williams asked guardedly. The last time the two had met had been on less than friendly terms.

"He suggested smuggling it out of the country."

"Of course he did." Grover-Williams groaned.

"He's a good guy." Benoist remarked. "He's taking huge risks himself."

"Is he?"

"You know he is." Benoist defended, finally able to turn on the headlights as they came to the road. "If ever the Reich Security Main Office discovered what he was doing, you know what would happen to him."

"The same thing that happened to Angelique?"

"You know he had no choice." Benoist said through gritted teeth.

Giving up Mademoiselle Shelly had been a bad day of business for all of them. In his heart he knew it had to be done. Not doing so would have risked blowing a whole network, and compromise countless others, but that fiery-haired French spirit was an admirable quality. Her courage and determination to fight was exemplary. Her caution and discretion though, decidedly less so.

"We all agreed."

"I didn't agree!" he fired back.

"There was no other way, Bill." Benoist cried, getting angry now. "You know there was no other way. *Adler* didn't like doing it any more than we did. In case you've forgotten, he's on the same side."

"Is he?"

"Don't be stupid, you know he is."

"I wonder sometimes."

Benoist sighed, shaking his head at Grover-Williams' obduracy. He was a good agent, but at times he needed to let things go. Otherwise, he would drive himself mad with the regret and the guilt. What they were doing was a dirty business either way. They were convinced they were doing it for the right reasons and for the right side, but only time would tell. History would be their ultimate judge.

"Anyway, he mentioned there was a ship sailing out of Bordeaux." Benoist began, trying again to placate his friend. "He could get the paperwork sorted."

"Sailing where?"

"America."

"Bordeaux is under German control. They're building a submarine pen to guard the Atlantic seaboard."

"And that's why it's perfect." Benoist nodded. "It would be sailing under Kriegsmarine guard until it gets to its destination."

"Why on earth would a ship be sailing to America under the protection of the German Navy?"

"In case you've been away too long, Bill, you will notice our American friends are still deciding to sit this one out."

"For now."

"So, for now might be our best opportunity." Benoist persisted. "After that," he shrugged in typical Gallic fashion. "We may have no choice but to destroy her. It's up to you, but we don't have many options and not much time to decide."

Grover-Williams shook his head, seething with the idea that he might have to concede to *Adler's* plan.

"Let me think about it." He said at last. "When was the ship leaving?"

"Two weeks."

"So, we have two weeks to sort out alternative transport."

"I can get us a Citroën 7." Benoist offered.

Grover-Williams blanched at the idea. The Citroën Traction Avant, the Reine de la Route as she was called was in comparison to La Voiture Noire, not even worthy of being a handmaiden, let alone the Queen of the Road.

"Do you know something? I think you're a snob, Bill." Benoist laughed.

"C'est la guerre."

CHAPTER FORTY-NINE
ENGLAND, 2018

"Tek one last look at the sea." Hamilton suggested, taking a deep breath as he gazed out. "It might be a wee while before we set eyes on it again."

The snow hadn't stayed around long. Just long enough to cause predictable carnage and travel disruption. He had been called out a couple of times to recover cars that had skidded off the road or been trapped in snowdrifts. There had been a couple of deaths around the country. Now, with clear blue sky above them, it was as if it had never happened.

"You love it here, don't you?" Valentina asked, looking at him thoughtfully.

"It wisnae ma first choice, if ah'm honest." He replied, turning back and opening the door for her. "Ah wid have preferred somewhere in Cumbria, a little cottage near Grasmere or Hawkshead."

She seemed taken aback by the small gesture of chivalry. Evidently, she hadn't been treated like a lady for some time. Perhaps never.

"Need a hand?"

"I'll be okay." She murmured hesitantly.

Just to be sure, he placed a hand on the top of the aperture to stop her striking her head on it as she clambered up into the cabin using the sidestep. Once inside, he closed the door and moved to the driver's side.

"So why here?" she asked, buckling up.

"Necessity. Ah cood nae afford tae buy anywhere half decent up there and this wis going begging." He explained as he removed the security devices. The wide layby had meant he could drive straight into the bay. An unspoken agreement among the other residents always reserved the first space for *Torridon*. It gave him more room to swing the rig in from whichever direction he approached. It also gave him an unbroken view of the sea from Looe to Rame Head. "It's grown on me though." He smiled, starting up the beast and reversing out onto the lane. "Whit aboot you?"

"What about me?" she asked, a tinge defensively.

"We've gaw a six-hour drive ahead of us." He selected first and coasted down the hill, the engine spinning up like a turbofan. Curiously they hadn't spoken much about themselves over the last couple of days. "Ah assume yer've read up all aboot me. Seems only fair ah ken a wee bit aboot you."

There was a noticeable huff as she bristled a little. "I realise this must be eternally fascinating for you, but I'd rather not discuss it."

"Well, that struck a nerve." He observed. "Music it is then." His hand moved down to the centre console. Below the line of switchgear, a refurbished Motorola 818 header unit had been installed in the custom fabricated dashboard. "Hope yer like Audiomachine."

As part of the extensive vehicle upgrades, Hamilton had installed a multi-speaker sound system to better enjoy his collection of symphonic, instrumental movie music. Two tweeters mounted on the top of the dashboard near the A-pillars were supplemented with two high-mid speakers on the underside of the dashboard and two mid-bass drivers at the front of the seat boxes. A co-axial speaker was positioned beneath the header unit behind a retro mesh grille, while two more sat in the rear of the loading area facing forward and a downward firing subwoofer had been located at the base of the transmission console between the second row of seats. Controlled and balanced through a five-channel amplifier beneath his seat, the result was a stirring rendition of orchestral music that seemed to suit the sweeping Cornish landscape as they wound their way back toward the Tamar Bridge.

It was to be a long journey if Valentina didn't wish to engage in conversation but at least his music collection and the immersive sound quality of the system would keep him entertained and alert on the way. He tried again once they had made the Tamar crossing, running parallel with Isambard Kingdom Brunel's impressive lenticular truss. The run up towards Exeter might at least test the waters of her willingness to chat.

"Where are we droppin' yer off?" he asked, checking his mirror as they came through the toll booth.

She turned her head towards him, her thoughts broken, almost forgetting he was even there.

"Knightsbridge." She said without thinking.

"Yer live wi Madam Sokolova?" She frowned.

"What makes you say that?"

"She has Stuart Hoose on Cadogan Square. Ah met her there when we were negotiating the particulars for *The Ministry* job."

She quietly scolded herself for forgetting. She had been otherwise engaged during that particular interview. "Would that be unusual?"

"It wid if yer were jist a personal assistant." He nodded. "Yer naw one of the hoosehold staff are yer?" he scoffed.

"Certainly not."

"So, whit else d'yer do for Madam Sokolova?"

"I make sure her day runs smoothly."

"Aye, ah bet yer do."

"Is that supposed to mean something?"

"It might explain why she has such a powerful hold over yer."

"You can infer whatever you like."

"There it is again." He remarked calmly. "A crack in the façade."

"I don't know what you're referring to."

He could sense her shutting down again. He needed to be careful if he was to try and open her up.

"D'yer ken who the hitmen were?"

She opened her mouth, immediately on the defensive. Then paused, reconsidering the question.

"No, not exactly."

Hamilton turned down the volume and looked across, inviting further discussion.

"I assumed they were Russian. Do you know something different?"

"Naw specifically." He mused. "It was jist their loadoot wisnae the usual gear for Russkies."

"What do you mean?"

"Their main armament was the Heckler & Koch MP7. That's a German SMG. In Russia, only Spetsnaz forces are equipped wi that, though more often than naw they're supplied wi any number of Kalashnikov variants or the Izhmash PP-19. Brügger & Thomet Rotax 2 sound suppressors were foond on two o' the hitmen, though strangely naw weapon equipped. Couple that wi both the MRL6 side-mounted weapon lamps and L3Harris PEQ-15 targeting lasers, yer looking at a typical loadoot for a specialist counterterrorist unit. Almost certainly naw Russian."

"You know your weaponry." She remarked with a tone of esteem. "What does that mean?"

"Jist a worrying possibility." He reflected. "Apart from the German Army, GSG9 and SEK, ESTSOF use a similar setup too." He looked across. "Ah'll strongly advise yer again tae get the hell oot o' Cadogan Square."

She frowned. A question written into the lines on her forehead.

"Ah've encountered a rogue unit of Estonian Special Operations Forces before that might use the same gear. They call themselves Red Section. It wis the name of their old unit before it was disbanded. They're mercenaries for hire. It's naw a unit yer want comin' for yer. Trust me. Ah've seen their handiwork up close. They'll kill yer, but they'll have their fun first and they'll take their time aboot it."

"You're just trying to scare me." She replied, brushing him off.

"Too bloody right ah am." he looked across at her, taking in her curves. Shaking his head at the memories. "Whit they wid do tae yer is nightmare fuel. Too horrifying tae think aboot."

"I don't believe you."

"Well, yer can take yer chances if yer like. Are yer religious?"

"Not particularly."

"Oh, they are." He groaned. "They do love a good crucifixion."

"You're not serious."

"I'm deadly serious, lass." He returned adamantly. "And so are they. Listen, ah need yer tae understand whit kind of horror show yer'll be a part of if yer dinnae get oot now."

"Why? Do you care about me all of a sudden?"

"I dinnae care who yer are, no one deserves to go oot like that." He changed down a gear angrily as he made an overtake, checking his mirror. "Poor bastards."

Valentina studied his face carefully. His hand moved the gear stick through the gate like a rifle bolt. The needle nudging over 60mph as he continued to press down on the throttle. It was clear to her that this man really did know what he was talking about. Perhaps her situation was more perilous than she had appreciated.

"I think I need to make a phone call." She called over the elevated roar of the engine.

"Private?" She paused. "Not necessarily."

Hamilton reached down and pressed the fifth button along on the radio. "Check yer phone for instructions and pair it up. Then yer can mek the call through here if yer like. Otherwise, we'll mek a stop and I'll take a wee daunder."

"Thank you. I trust you." she said. That warm honey tone to her voice again. He remained silent and brought the speed down, quietening the engine and calming his pulse at the same time. Checking the mirror again. A knitted brow.

She spent a few moments pairing up her phone to his vehicle, then dialled a number. The music faded down, replaced by a dial tone in surround sound. A moment later a crystal clear English accent came through, not unlike Valentina herself, despite her Russian heritage.

"Can I have your security number please?"

"Two-five-two-three. Three-Seven-Nine-One. Four-One-Nine."

There was a brief pause. "Thank you, Miss Volkova. How can we be of service today?"

"I would like to transfer funds to the usual account, please."

"Certainly, madam. The standard sum?"

"Yes please."

"Of course. May I take your passphrase?"

"The important thing is not what they think of me, but what I think of them."

"One moment, madam."

Valentina looked at Hamilton. He resolutely kept his eyes focussed on the road ahead but could sense her eyes upon him as her cheeks reddened slightly.

"The transfer has been confirmed, madam. Would you like any other services?"

"No, thank you."

"It's been a pleasure, madam."

The call was terminated. The volume of the music returned. Hamilton kept it low just in case she wanted to talk.

"Madam Sokolova had no idea what she was doing, trying to engage your services." She began softly. "If I can't handle you, she has no chance."

"Yer've been trying tae handle me, have yer?" he chuckled.

"Can you play something relaxing please?"

"Of course." Hamilton knew his playlist well and clicked forward a few tracks using the controls on the knurled aluminium stalk behind the steering wheel. "Try this."

The piano began a gentle, calming melody, inviting the strings to gradually join in. Violins then slowly carried the melody for the second phase, introducing the orchestra's sweeping movement through the piece. Enveloped by soothing music, Valentina's shoulders noticeably relaxed into the fabric of the seat. Tilting her head back into the headrest, she closed her eyes as music gradually swelled around her, as if carrying her away on a bed of blossoms. The clarity of the speakers seemed to bring clarity to her mind. Perhaps for the first time in a long while.

Hamilton looked across, watching her chest rise and fall. The corners of her mouth curling up into a contented, feline smile. She was back in her own clothes now, freshly laundered and ironed by Hamilton himself. He sat in silence, letting the music wash over him as he contemplated the Sokolov situation. It was a mess. Code Brown, as he would have said back in the SBS. He didn't relish the thought of having an elite unit of disgruntled and disgraced Estonian special forces on his tail. He checked the mirror again.

"Thank you." Valentina breathed as the piece faded gently into the background. "Very stirring. Perhaps not quite as chilled out as I was hoping for, but surprisingly apposite for the situation at hand. What was that piece called?"

"The Arrival of Dawn."

"Hmm." She purred warmly. "How appropriate."

"Hiding yer money from Madam Sokolova in case things go Tango Uniform? Very wise."

"That's none of your business."

"Yer sort of made it ma business by meking the call hands-free." He reasoned. "Or is it suhin' else?"

"That would also be none of your business."

"Wid yer have let Marya die?" he enquired.

"I don't see what that has to do with anything."

"Jist answer the question."

"Of course not."

"That's exactly the same answer I gave." He nodded, indicating for another overtake. "It's the answer anyone wi half a conscience would gie."

"What are you getting at?"

"That wis the bait. Getting me on the hook. Yer the honeytrap, trying tae seal the deal. Somebody wants me involved in all this, and they wannae mek sure I dinnae back oot."

"Is that right?"

"Perhaps someone wants tae make sure yer holding yer end up too."

"I'm sorry. You've lost me now."

"Ah think ah cood do wi losing them." He looked up to the mirror. "In ma experience, Audi drivers either wannae overtake everything in sight, or try and mount your bumper like a randy mongrel." Valentina looked in the side mirror. "Ah thought German indicators were an option that no one ticked, but this wee fella is being unusually cour'eous." He looked across at her. "Wis that the car that brought yer doon here?"

She turned to look at him with a fierce expression on her face. "Does that mind ever stop working overtime."

"It's whit keeps me alive, lass." He flexed his fingers around the steering wheel. "Now, if ah wis tae drop yer off on the side of the road, wid they be good enough tae pick yer up, d'yer think?"

She looked in the mirror again. "He did bring me down, yes."

"And whit's his name?"

"Why?"

"I'd like tae meet 'im."

She regarded him warily. He indicated to pull off the dual carriageway and watched as the Audi followed.

"What are you doing?"

"Ah need a pish." He returned. "They'll be a bog in Tesco up aheid."

"Vadim." She said. "His name is Vadim."

CHAPTER FIFTY

Rumbling through the village of Lee Mill, he parked up in the Tesco car park and turned to Valentina, watching the car roll in and park up nearby. Trying to be inconspicuous. Failing. Hamilton had already made it out.

"Hand over yer phone."

"What?"

"Jist do it."

Reluctantly, Valentina handed it over. Despite what she might have said to him earlier, Hamilton himself didn't fully trust her and he didn't want her calling for backup. Heading inside the supermarket, he checked his surroundings, went to the newsagent's counter and made a purchase. Doubling back, he headed for the gents, watching Vadim's indecision as he entered at the same time and found his target walking right in front of him.

Once inside the toilets, Hamilton selected a cubicle and waited. Vadim followed him inside, choosing a urinal for his business. Hamilton quickly dismantled the phone he had purchased and proceeded to enter the engineer's codes to fully unlock the handset and SIM, making it independent of any network tariffs and contracts. It was a trick he had been shown by Giles at GCHQ. There were burner phones, then there were SIS burner phones. Untraceable and totally free to use. Afterwards, he saved his number into the memory and switched it off before placing it in his pocket.

Emerging from the cubicle, he ventured over to the sinks to wash his hands. Vadim zipped himself up and joined Hamilton at the adjacent sink. That was his first mistake. Having washed his hands, Hamilton splashed a bit of water on his face, lingering a little. The man took longer washing his hands than normal. Using soap and everything. Hamilton appreciated the hygiene, but he should have dried up, left and waited outside discreetly. That was his second mistake. Cupping his hands beneath the running water, Hamilton let them fill up and flung it at the man's crotch. Pale trousers. Mistake number three.

Predictably the man looked down. A redundant action, but one that was followed up by a helping hand to the back of the head. The nose broke against the sink with a crack before Vadim was dragged backwards in a state of delirium into the cubicle Hamilton had just vacated. The Audi's fob was swiftly palmed from Vadim's pocket as he was moved. Closing the door, Hamilton locked it from the outside, flushed the fob down the next toilet and dried his hands before calmly walking out. Vadim would be out for a while and when he came back around, his trousers would still have an embarrassing watermark.

Heading out the store with a bloody nose and a wet patch would certainly get him noticed. Then he would discover the keys to the Audi were missing from his pocket and the big burgundy Land Rover had long since disappeared. An elegant solution.

"What happened?" Valentina asked as Hamilton climbed back inside with a smile on his face.

"Seems he had a wee accident." He handed over the phones. "If yer do decide tae get oot, use this. It's an untraceable phone. Ah've saved ma number. No one will be able tae track it, but yer can get in contact whenever yer want."

"Why are you doing this?"

"Ah've told yer." he said, starting *Torridon* up again and pulling away.

"What's a Code Zero?" she asked, looking at the saved number.

"It's a police code. It means Officer Under Attack. Ah've saved the corresponding number intae ma phone too. If I get a call from that number, it means yer need help. Use it wisely."

"You're making an awfully big assumption."

"Am ah?" he looked across at her. "Seems tae me yer've had reservations over whitever yer've been involved in for some time."

"I'm naturally cautious."

"Place the phone behind the cupholders. It'll charge up the battery there." He re-joined the dual carriageway and looked over. "So, where are we really droppin' yer off?"

There was a long silence before Valentina decided to provide an answer.

"Redcliffe Square."

"Walking distance tae work." He remarked, envisaging the route. Head east around The Boltons, across the Fulham Road then down Milner Street. About thirty minutes. "D'yer have somewhere else tae go? If stuff hits the fan?"

"No."

He frowned. "Well, unfortunately yer cannae hide oot at *Rockwater* now. Yer friend probably ken where ah live, so we'll have tae find yer somewhere else."

"Will they come after you?"

"Ah'm sure they'll try." Hamilton had already considered the possibility that *Rockwater Cabin* might be turned into a pile of ash when he returned. There was nothing he could do about it if they decided to do so. It was why he lingered for a moment before leaving. Just in case it was for the very last time.

"I'm sorry." She murmured quietly, lowering her head. "I didn't realise."

"Are yer malfunctioning?" he asked. "Ah thought ah jist heard yer apologise. Yer might have even meant it."

"I'm not going to argue." She sighed.

Hamilton let the silence linger for a moment. Checking the mirrors. It was a curious feeling, being a civilian operating on a slightly different plane to everyone else. All the people he was sharing the road with knew nothing of his existence, had no idea what he had just done in the Tesco toilets, or why. Yet, apart from a licence from the Security Industry Authority, allowing him to work as a Close Protection Officer, the reality was he was no different to anyone else. Not really. Not until he was on another job. Then he entered that higher plane. His heightened situational awareness became essential to his work. An asset.

In civilian life, it became something of a curse. He could never truly relax. Picking up groceries from the Co-op in Millbrook, the first thing he would do was catch the sightlines and look for an exit. Every time. Even though he had been there hundreds of times before. It was a habit. He could recite all the licence plates for the vehicles outside, and not simply because he recognised most of them from around the village. He could tell that the woman ahead of him in the queue was left-handed, the guy picking up a box of Stella weighed about fifteen stone and knew how to handle himself, and that he could run flat out all the way to the pub in Kingsand before his hands started shaking.

Meanwhile, everyone else quietly went about their day, oblivious to this information. Oblivious to the three kilograms of tar they had inhaled after smoking that same brand of cigarettes for twenty years, enough to fill in a pothole or two. Oblivious to the one-in-forty-five million chance of winning the Lotto that weekend yet choosing to play the long odds anyway. Living a normal life. Doing normal things. However irrational they actually were.

"Maybe I can help you?" Valentina asked. A hopeful tone in her voice.

"In whit way?" he replied guardedly.

"If you're right, and Madam Sokolova was behind all this, maybe I can find out who they really are."

"How wid that help me?"

"You could stop them before they came after you. Only three people know who killed the three hitmen that night. I can protect you."

"This smells a lot like blackmail."

"Well." She paused. "Perhaps it is. In a way. I need your help. You need mine."

"Ah dinnae need yer help, lass." he said firmly. "If they do come after me, then ah'll ken exactly who they are. Mek no mistake, Valentina, ah'm nae havin' some tooled up dobbers messing up ma life. Naw now. Naw ever. Ah'll fair sort 'em oot, and then ah'll be coming after yers for putting me in that position."

"They could kill you."

"If they do, ah winnae have anything tae worry about, will ah?" he looked across. "Death dis nae frighten me, lass. Neither dis the threat of violence. Ah've seen and done plenty of it and yer ken ah'm naw above doin' it again." He shook his head. "Ah dinnae need yer help at all."

"So, what are you going to do?"

"Ah'm gonnae London. Gonnae catch a plane somewhere and forget about Madam bloody Sokolova." He turned and looked at her firmly. "Unless yer've finally decided yer wannae get oot. Then ah'll maybe stick aroond a wee while and help yer get sorted." There was no response. "Well, be sure tae let me ken when we get there."

CHAPTER FIFTY-ONE
ITALY, 2018

Don Pietro Borromeo had been very accommodating of Hamilton, generously spending time with him in his private archives, patiently relaying all the same information that he had done with Natalia Bielawska. He seemed relieved that someone was actually going to take a deeper look into what was occurring. The news of three murders had shaken him up considerably and although he did not suspect that the trail would lead to him, it was nonetheless a worrying development.

Giuseppe Spinola had been similarly affable and expounded on what he knew about the Auto Club and the last known whereabouts of the vehicles themselves. It was decided that Hamilton would endeavour to track two of them down, the Horch and the Bugatti. As the Horch may still reside in Germany, he decided he would start off with the Bugatti. If he found out definitively that neither of them existed, then the whole thing could be closed and dealt with very quickly. The authorities were already on the hunt for the perpetrator of the murders. Perhaps a nudge in the right direction was all that was needed.

Unfortunately, looking in detail through the Borromeo Archives and other reference works that Don Pietro had to hand, the picture of what happened to the Lost Bugatti, La Voiture Noire, was anything but straightforward. It was known definitively that four Atlantic Coupes left the factory and who they went to. What was less clear, was how many had been made in total and what happened to all of *them*.

Examining the digital contents of the box file, the last known record of La Voiture Noire was on a list of 'Materiel Automobile' dated September 1941. The consignment was recorded as having been sent to the Bugatti factory on Boulevard Alfred Daney in Bordeaux by train. Following the outbreak of the war, Ettore Bugatti had decided to relocate the factory from the contested Alsace region on the border between France and Germany to Bordeaux in the west. It was his intention to continue producing vehicles and using the port of Bordeaux to export them all over the world. That was until Italy entered the war and his Milanese heritage called his neutrality into question.

However, there was never any record of the car being received by Monsieur Pierre Marco, who was responsible for Bugatti stock control at Bordeaux and was a very diligent employee. The Boulevard was close to the Port of Bordeaux and one hypothesis was that it was being crated up for shipping overseas. Another source suggested that while waiting in storage at the factory, the car was destroyed during the bombing of Bordeaux by the RAF.

This was inconsistent though with documented operations over Bordeaux at the time. The only recorded bombing of the port area took place one night in November 1940. Several testimonies mentioned only three bombs landing on the factory. The first burned the hangar where German officers stored their cars, destroying two of them. The second bomb fell on the office adjacent to the factory, throwing paperwork up into the air and pulverising the area where all the wooden foundry patterns had been brought down from Molsheim. The third failed to explode but still destroyed a rolling metal door that provided access to the manufacturing buildings. No additional information on subsequent bombings had been discovered by the Bordeaux City Archives and as the car was known to exist in February 1941, it couldn't possibly have been destroyed in Bordeaux during the bombing raid of the previous year.

There also appeared to be some confusion between the third Atlantic Coupe sold to Monsieur Holzschuh and the second used by Jean Bugatti. This came about because originally it was thought that only three Atlantic Coupes left the factory instead of four, The Rothschild Bugatti, the Holzschuh Bugatti and the Pope Bugatti. To add more confusion, the Holzschuh Bugatti was also known to be painted in obsidian black. Examining cross-references and sorting through contrasting testimony, it seemed that the bodywork of an Atlantic Coupe was modified by Jean Bugatti in 1939. Monsieur Jean had extended the rear fenders and substituted the louvered ventilation on the sides and top of the bonnet, making them unique to this car.

The Holzschuh Bugatti showed similar designs to the rear fenders but was only modified after the war by the subsequent owner. In addition, the car was not made available to Bugatti for modification after its sale to Monsieur Holzschuh, whereas the bodywork of the Black Car had been returned to Molshiem by Mr Embiricos and was readily available for modification at almost any time before being eventually mounted to its chassis. Thus, the pontoon style fenders seen on the still extant Holzschuh Bugatti would also have been a feature on La Voiture Noire and may even have been copied from it. This was worth noting if ever Hamilton got that far in his search.

Furthermore, there was a note that the modifications had been commissioned by Robert Benoist and Jean was only too happy to emphasise the dynamism and class of the vehicle by lengthening some of its sleek lines. The connection with Benoist was another compelling reason to believe that this was the car he was looking for.

There was speculation that after the accident which killed the occupants of the Holzschuh Bugatti in the 1950s, parts from the Belg. Coupe, also thought to be La Voiture Noire, were used in its reconstruction. All the records suggested that the Belg. Coupe, as it was named on the original build sheet, was possibly commissioned for Belgian King Leopold III to compete in under a pseudonym, or maybe even a Monsieur Gabriel Duhoux who entered the Monte Carlo Rally.

Unfortunately, that car was wrecked in 1946 by a young soldier who stole it. The bodywork was repaired but the engine was never replaced, and it was loaned to a friend to put in their showroom. Relatives had indeed recalled a blue Bugatti that belonged to Monsieur Duhoux. Though as he also owned an Atalante, which would have had a similar horseshoe grille, this might have been the car that was remembered, had been damaged and subsequently donated parts to repair the Holzschuh Bugatti of the same vintage.

Hamilton's head was beginning to hurt, and he was in need of some fresh air. Naturally Spinola was only too happy to oblige, and the Riva was called for again.

The biggest problem with delving into the histories of vintage cars was that anything and everything could change, not just ownership, which was fraught with difficulties in traceability enough as it was. Chassis, bodies, engines, everything could be altered, modified or completely swapped altogether. Even more so was this the case if the owner wanted to take the car racing or needed to repair the resulting damage.

Often the manufacturer would only provide a rolling chassis for the customers to add their own body from a wide choice of coachbuilders according to their particular desires. This too would often change as the owner's requirements altered. An open roadster might later become a fixed head coupe, a six-light sedan might end up being a landaulette. Each with their own reference numbers and some even donated from other cars. In the modern era of type approval and series homologation, such discrepancies were at least a little easier to trace. Most of the time.

He thought after delving into the archives he might have at least found a starting point for finding La Voiture Noire. What he had discovered was a miasma of misleading and spurious information, through which there may only be a very narrow channel of truth to be navigated. He still felt no closer to finding anything out than when he had been clearing snow from the deck of *Rockwater Cabin*. Although he felt more informed, he was thoroughly confused.

The breeze wafting across the waters as Spinola eased the throttles forward was wonderfully refreshing and a welcome change from the increasingly uncomfortable atmosphere of the library. Due to the delicate nature of some of the materials in storage, a specific climate had to be maintained. Discrete vents in the floor and ceiling controlled the humidity levels and temperature, producing a cool drying atmosphere that was beginning to make his eyes hurt.

The perfumed warmth of the gardens, smell of the water and cool spray running along the boat's hull made for an agreeable respite as he considered his next steps. Indeed, the fresh lake air seemed to clarify and distil his thoughts the longer they spent on the water. It all seemed to boil down to two possibilities, with multiple ramifications branching off either one.

Essentially, the Bugatti either arrived in Bordeaux or was never sent there in the first place. The consequence of the former was the difficult task of finding out which railway station it went to and how it went missing between the station and the factory. For the latter, it was further complicated by the notion that it could have been sent to anywhere but Bordeaux, which really didn't narrow the field at all. Thus, Bordeaux seemed to have settled out as a natural starting point at least.

CHAPTER FIFTY-TWO
FRANCE, 2018

Parking the hire car near the Port of Bordeaux, Hamilton set about examining the city maps on his phone. He had driven up and down the Boulevard Alfred Daney, but there was no sign of the original Bugatti factory anywhere. This was hardly surprising. Being so close to the dockyards the building would not likely have had any architectural merit and having been hit by at least three confirmed bombs, may have needed demolishing. Also, there was none of the historical or cultural value associated with the original Molsheim facility, so there would not have been any need to preserve it for posterity.

Most of the buildings along the boulevard looked to have been built in the last couple of decades, if not the last few years. There was one particularly noticeable exception. Still very much in evidence was the vast concrete structure of a World War II submarine base. One of five such immense structures constructed in French ports by Organisation Todt during World War II. The base had been the home port of the powerful Italian 11th Group and the German 12th Flotilla. The insignia of the 12th Flotilla was a capital 'U' with a half globe depicting the North Atlantic, a U-boat prow and sail in silhouette and the head of a wolf with its mouth open, ready for prey.

The Port of Bordeaux was the Den of Wolves.

The port district of Bacalan to the north of the city was first chosen for construction of the Betasom base for Italian submarines in September 1940. To begin with, around thirty-two submarines were concealed beneath camouflage nets placed along the quayside and was presumably why the port was selected for bombing in November that year. In September of 1941, work began on the construction of a larger facility. Over 6,500 labourers were used during the nineteen-month construction project, including 2,500 Spanish Republican prisoners who had fled to Bordeaux following the Civil War. Sometimes people just couldn't catch a break.

Some 2,000 reinforced concrete piles supported a roof nine metres thick covered with a fangrost superstructure, a framework of concrete beams and steel trusses to trap bombs and protect the construction below from aerial attacks. The arrival of the first German submarines from the 12th Unterseeboote Flotille began in January 1943 and marked a change in the port's status from merely a shipyard to a fully operational Kriegsmarine arsenal. During the next twenty-two months, Forty-three U-boats assigned to the Port de la Lune facility were tasked with carrying out attack missions in the Atlantic Ocean, just off the east coast of the United States.

Bringing any sort of shipment in during 1940-41 would have been a strange decision, especially if it was not related to the construction of the base. Some 60,000 cubic metres of concrete were used to create eleven submarine pens with a total length of 235metres. Even now, the structure was immense, dominating the northern quayside of the port. Despite all the new warehousing that had been erected around the docks, it was still the tallest, longest, widest building in the Bacalan area, probably even the entire city itself.

Now the Bassins des Lumière, the Pool of Lights, offered visitors an incredible audio-visual experience, making innovative use of the vast internal spaces. Stunning digital artworks came to life as they were projected onto bare concrete walls of four of the eleven alveolus, the wet docks, reflecting on the waters to add a new dimension to this unique and immersive exhibition.

Above the waterline each dock was some twelve metres high, one hundred metres long and twenty-two metres wide. The artworks were supplemented by moving images, music and lights, which took the visitor on a journey through Impressionism with Monet and Renoir, to Pointillism with Signac and Cross, Fauvism with Camoin and Marquet and finally Secessionism with the works of Gustav Klimt in the evenings.

Hamilton had to admit as he wandered around the vast spaces, it made excellent and original use of what otherwise was a rather haunting structure. German wartime brutalism at its most stark was softened by giant water lily pads floating on the surface where once the sails and dark foreboding hulls of submarines would have resided. Having seen some of the original Klimt artworks at the Belvedere Palace in Vienna, observing them enlarged and moving offered a new dimension to the pieces. Their story became more vivid.

On his route through the gallery, Hamilton clocked the security features, cameras and alarms. There was not very much to secure in the pens themselves. There was no real artwork, it was all digital. Some of the other exhibition spaces where real artwork was displayed used containment security rather than camera systems. It was cheaper but more effective, trapping the would-be art thief inside until the authorities arrived.

Towards the end of the exhibition, Hamilton quietly slipped away into a niche in one of the wet docks, tucking himself into the void as he awaited the closure of the venue at 21:00. A cursory inspection a few minutes after supposedly confirmed that all the visitors had vacated the pens. Hamilton waited another hour while the staff and security wound everything up for the day. There were no carpets to vacuum, not many pieces to dust.

The sound of giant motors starting up startled Hamilton momentarily. From his niche at the far end of the bay, he looked to where the evening sun was giving way to the illuminations of the night outside as two vast steel doors at the opening of the pen swung closed. They came together with a metallic ring of finality as a small ripple travelled down towards him. He heard it splash against the concrete at the far end and work back in the opposite direction to be consumed by another incoming wave. The artwork faded as projectors were turned off. Then the gantry lights above dimmed, finally flickering out one by one, all down the length of the pen, to be replaced by the muted glow of red lights, set low against the bare concrete walls of the pen.

Bathing the walls in ribbons of scarlet, reflected also in the black waters below, Hamilton observed how the glow from the service lights resembled the iconic vertical scarlet banners that adorned the political parades and ceremonies of the Third Reich. It was an entirely unintended spectacle. Most galleries used a red colour for night patrols as it preserved the night vision of any wandering guards.

Nevertheless, it gave him an unsettling feeling down his spine. It was as if he was stepping back into the footsteps of his predecessors. The kind of SOE saboteurs and early commandos that might have laid boobytraps and explosive charges in just this kind of place, knowing the incredible risks they were taking, the chilling cost of failure.

Looking at the depth indicator painted on the wall of the wet dock, the water was some sixteen metres deep, more than sufficient to accommodate the draft of a long-range Type IX U-boat. The more common Type VIIs would have docked here too. Some 703 had been built for the Kriegsmarine by the end of the war. Now only one example survived.

The brutalist double-skin concrete walls between the eleven pens were over two metres thick and comprised load-bearing structures that were interspersed with gaps, such that there was a continuous orthogonal interplay between connection and space. The original gangway that spanned across the width of the eleven pens, running down the length of the entire facility, had been supplemented with two more in the first four pens to provide additional viewing and walking space for the gallery's visitors, as well as extended projection surfaces and observation platforms for the artworks.

In the cavernous void, a low, mournful hum could be heard as a gentle breeze filtered through gaps in the doors. It sounded like a child blowing across the top of an empty bottle and served to give the yawning space an increasingly oppressive quality. One or two birds fluttered through the large gap between the top of the giant seaward doors and the roof, almost invisible in the low light, they were identified only by the sound of their flapping wings. Pigeon wings clumsily slapping together like chunky thighs. Gulls swooping into their own roosts on the old overhead gantry cranes. Their metallic croaks mimicking the structures they called home.

The soaring reinforced roof, usually visible as a reddish metallic network of trusses and beams beneath the concrete, now disappeared in a swell of infinite darkness. Beams of red light from below dispersing and bleeding out onto the walls long before reaching the upper extremities of the thick supporting structures.

In addition to the deepwater inlets, the building would have been a labyrinth of corridors, workshops, and various warehouses. Several smaller bunkers were built around the base to safely store ammunition, fuel and explosives. It was that part of the building Hamilton was keen to investigate. Likely, after decades of desolation and years of exhibition use, there was probably very little to be found from the time of its original incarnation. Perhaps nothing relating to the lost Bugatti had ever been here, but Hamilton had an inkling that if something existed, it may just be lingering in some dark and forgotten corner. Though it really was a shot in the dark.

CHAPTER FIFTY-THREE

Satisfied that he was now truly alone in the vast structure, he wriggled out of his hiding place and pulled on a pair of gloves. The kind manual labourers wear in factories up and down the country. Polyurethane palms and fingers gave him good grip. Woven nylon backs were breathable. A good level of dexterity was maintained for delicate operations. Looking around the site, there was nothing delicate about this place, but they would help to keep his fingerprints off the surfaces.

His eyes had adjusted now to the low light within the pens. Completely abandoned after 1944, the practically indestructible monolith had become a military ruin until rehabilitation in the 1980s. For a time, part of the structure had served as a naval museum before being abandoned again. Once again the deserted base became a place of peregrination for the city's inhabitants. Exploring the spatial spectacle of the place became almost a rite of passage for Bordelais' youth.

The concrete had become stained with age and neglect, not that it had ever been a smooth, uniform finish to begin with. The submarine base had been a functional, not an aesthetic structure. As such, variations in cementitious materials, water, calcium chlorides, sand, all had an effect in producing a blotchy, non-uniform finish. The result of rain, corrosive salts, bomb damage and mould stains had taken their toll too, adding to the chilling ambience. In the absence of art obliterating the forbidding patina, the overarching dominance of the construction itself became evident in the very texture of the material as he moved between the pens. It was strangely horrifying in its brutality and complete absence of ornament.

The gangways that connected each individual pen, one to another, pierced through vast rectangular voids in the walls. Wide concrete quaysides running down each pen would have once been crowded with crates of munitions and rations. U-boat crews lining up for rollcall before boarding their vessel. Gangplanks positioned at various intervals down their length.

Curious rusted tubes, like chimney stacks, appeared to protrude through the concrete from somewhere down below. These long, open-sided corridors were like the aisles in a strikingly stark and terrifying concrete cathedral, giving way to one water-filled nave after another. The gangway, acting as some sort of transept connecting each one.

To the rear of the building were large steel bulkhead doors that gave access to a connecting corridor that ran down the length of the base. Some were welded shut or had rusted solidly into place. Moving on into the seven dry docks, the pens were slightly narrower, drained of their water, sealed at the doors and displayed the full and tremendous depth of the concrete basin itself. When needed, these channels could be flooded too.

Ordinarily unseen below the water line, the gigantic doors at the far end were fitted with sluice gates to allow the water from the docks to rush in gradually. Steel doors between the pens and below the high watermark could be opened to allow multiple pens to be filled and the levels to be evened out before the vast doors were opened to the world, equalising the pressure and reducing load on the powerful hinge motors.

Entering Pen No. 9, this was where U-1061 often set sail from. Constructed by Germaniawerft of Kiel, one of the largest German shipbuilders, she was one of four Type VIIF submarines laid down. She successfully completed five patrols before managing to escape the base on the eve of its capture by Allied forces.

Her final commander, Oberleutnant Walter Jaeger surrendered the vessel at Bergen in Norway, from where she was transported to Scotland and scuttled. Though some of her crew eventually returned to Germany after the war, others who had been interned at Kinmel Camp near Bodelwyddan in North Wales, remained there. Settling in the neighbouring communities of Rhyl, Rhuddlan and Prestatyn was preferable to returning to Soviet-occupied areas of East Germany from where they had originated.

Between Pens No.9 and 10 was the last of the bulkhead doors. There was a simple steel handle on the plain, rusted portal. Just like all the others, he tried to pull it down from vertical to the horizontal. There was initial resistance, but he could feel there was some movement and with a bit of force it might just open. Grabbing it with both hands and hanging his weight on it, he tugged at it and felt the mechanism begin to grate and grind. Decades of rust, swelling the latches and bolts, began to be chipped off as the force of his bodyweight overloaded the deteriorating metal.

Finally, with a sudden jolt and a horribly metallic groan, the handle dropped down. Almost losing his footing, Hamilton hauled himself up using the handle and pulled the door towards him. Predictably there was an ear-splitting screech as unoiled, partially corroded hinges reluctantly yielded to his input. The door swung outwards, towards the pen, a protection against any bomb blast or sudden changes in water level. In contrast to the front of the door, the reverse side exhibited a complex of levers and slide bolts that secured it within the thick steel frame. It looked more like something from an underground bunker, but then again, this was exactly the purpose of the building.

Stepping into the corridor beyond, there was a foul smell of stagnant air emanating from the passageway. Taking out his pocket flashlight, he switched it on and looked around. The corridor continued past the final two pens to a door at the far end. The word 'Notaussgang' identified it as the emergency exit to the outside world. Hamilton spun the torch around and shone it down the length of the corridor. The darkness stretched far beyond the beam's reach, back to the main complex some two hundred metres away.

The roof was lower here. A central spine of bulkhead lights ran down the ceiling. There was no switch nearby and it was likely they were no longer connected up or operational anyway. Hoping he would get used to the smell quickly, Hamilton ventured on. Laced up into rubber-soled tactical boots that looked just like trainers to anyone else, his footsteps were dulled into soft, barely perceptible taps.

There was a small skeleton up against the back wall. A cat by the look of it. Probably died decades ago. The small bones in its stomach suggested it had found one meal at least but it hadn't processed through. He didn't know how it got in, but creatures always find a way. Finally, having walked all the way back to the main building, there was a second, narrower door on his right.

Surprisingly this was opened more easily and entered a square stairwell. Stencilled on the back wall were two signs with corresponding arrows.

IN THE DEN OF WOLVES

Familiar with the German terminology, Hamilton deduced that the one pointing up directed him to the roof and the flak cannon, one of four positioned on the corners of the building. Shining his torch up through the void, there were no ancillary doors, just one long climb to the top. Nothing of interest up there. The second sign needed no translation: *Bunker*.

Making his way down, he found himself in a lobby of sorts, a concrete corridor with doors on either side. Storage rooms. Toilets. Showers. The porcelain toilet bowls and sinks long since smashed by previous visitors over the decades. Crude swastikas had been daubed on walls of broken tiles. French graffiti proclaiming death to Fascists, de Gaulle, even Thatcher curiously.

For some reason Hamilton's mind flashed back to Valentina standing naked in the living room of *Rockwater Cabin*. Maggie Thatcher naked on a cold day. He wondered whether she was making herself comfortable in his Lions Mill apartment. For although she didn't have anywhere else to go, he had no doubt she would make use of the apartment as a safe haven while she considered her next move. Storm Emma had bought her a few days from Daria's intrigues. A few days more and she needed to be gone. Without a trace.

Returning to the lobby, one door right at the far end looked more substantial and had remained unmolested. Forcing the handle, Hamilton swung the door open and shone his torch down a flight of concrete steps. There was another level. Moving down, he followed the steps as they turned through ninety degrees and continued descending.

This looked to be part of the defensive bunker in case of enemy bombardment. Though it was unlikely that aerial assault would have afflicted the solid concrete building above significantly, due in no small part because of the cleverly designed roof. Being in range of Naval artillery though might have played on the designer's minds. After all, the Germans knew better than anyone else the capabilities of a Bofors shell to penetrate hardened concrete, even from several miles away.

The staircase ended at another door. This door led into a narrow corridor. There was a light switch but as suspected, the power was out. Perhaps an auxiliary generator needed to be fired up or the connections had been cut long ago. The musty smell of stale air was prevalent here too, though curiously it seemed a little fresher. Clearly no one had been down here for a very long time. This was merely an entrance corridor. A solitary door at the far end, on the right, was all that the corridor contained. This one appeared to be only closed to but didn't budge at all. Returning to the previous door, he had noted how the handle had been loose. Wrenching the handle around to protrude out from the profile of the door, he kicked the door closed.

The displaced handle crashed against the door jamb and flexed on its joint a little. Repeating this exercise, Hamilton exerted more force with the next kick, noticing how the handle seemed to become a little more dislodged each time. Finally, the joint gave way and the handle clattered to the floor, trapped between the door jamb and the door itself. Prising the door open again with his fingers, he grabbed the liberated handle and used it as a crude crowbar to open the door fully, making sure his only known means of escape was still available.

Returning to the second door, he placed the handle in the gap between the door and the frame and set about levering it open.

"Ah am getting too auld for this." He wheezed after several minutes of fruitless labours.

Wedging the handle into the sliding bolt mechanism, he again began to kick the handle. To no avail at first, then, little by little, with loud scraping sounds following each kick, the binding metal eventually began to move. The handle fell to the ground again, but the door was open far enough for him to get a shoulder in.

Squeezing through, he placed his feet against the frame and the wall of the corridor and pushed against the door with a rocking motion, using his leg muscles instead of his back and shoulders. The door slid open incrementally with each push, gouging track marks in the concrete. Evidently something had shifted over the years and the floor was keeping the door from moving freely.

With it open sufficiently for him to get through, he stood up, caught his breath and wiped the sweat from his forehead. It was already warmer down here without him exerting any extra efforts. Shining the torch down the corridor, he watched it disappear again down the length of the facility. This time however, the tunnel had been driven beneath the submarine pens themselves.

Water had pooled in places and there were signs of seepage through cracks and gaps in the concrete castings, yet being so far beneath the water line, the engineers had evidently done a good enough job of tanking the structure. The lower section of the Führerbunker in Berlin, situated below the city's water table, needed pumps to constantly remove groundwater. No pump had operated here for a very long time. Most likely the diesel had run out or it had been designed in such a way to negate the need of them.

He couldn't quite fathom how deep he was, but judging by the amount of water present, it had taken some time for the seepage to break through from wherever it had originated. Confident in the structural integrity of the above ground facility, the designers had clearly felt it was safe enough to build the bunker beneath the actual pens themselves. It may even have been the first construction to be completed.

Should the intricate fangrost roof fail, the water in the dock would provide cushioning for any exploding ordnance landing in the pens themselves. Still, knowing he was under the four wet docks, a quick mental calculation told him there was something like 140,000 cubic metres of water above him. Nearly 1.4million Newtons of load bearing vertically down on him from above. And there were cracks in the concrete.

He cursed and moved on, reading the signage stencilled on the walls between two more doors. *Gassschleuse*. An airlock. A way of protecting the occupants beyond from chemical or biological attack. Moving on, the words '*Gerpäckraum*', '*Küche*' and '*Kantine*' were self-explanatory. Though the atmosphere was warmer, the air felt fresher. Evidently this part of the structure still had direct access to fresh air vents rising through the building somewhere. Perhaps those rusted stacks he had seen earlier in the pens.

There were all the usual rooms expected of a bunker. Bunk rooms, living quarters, radio rooms. Most of the doors were open in readiness to receive anyone who needed to use them. There was even a library with books untouched on the shelves and covered with dust. Looking at the furniture and the dust on the bedsheets, the chairs and tables, nobody had been down here for a very long time indeed. It was like an undiscovered time capsule, sealed beneath the Port of Bordeaux. Hamilton came across a room about halfway down with the sign '*Büro 1*'. Stepping inside, the centre of the room was dominated by a desk. It was neither a big desk, nor was it a small room, but on all sides, the space was made more confined by filing cabinets.

Hamilton cursed once again at the discovery, wondering just what he had stumbled upon. Shining his torch over the drawers, he noticed they were labelled with nothing more than Roman numerals or letters of the alphabet.

Opening the first drawer, he was shocked, not only to find that the cabinet was unlocked, but that the drawer still contained dozens of files. He didn't know what he was looking for. Some of the documents appeared to be blank pro forma, others were completed and filed away, signed, countersigned and stamped with authorisation from whichever appropriate officer needed to. Most seemed to relate to the original construction of the base. Reports on material deliveries, workers, stock levels.

This would take him hours, if not days to go through in detail, if what he was looking for was even here, and he didn't even know what that was. A goods receipt? An inspection certificate? Notification of confiscation? The possibilities were endless. All catalogued and indexed on cards in separate cabinets of their own. He was lost. Completely lost.

Rallying himself, he turned to the cabinet behind him. The one marked 'B'. it was a simplistic selection, chosen only because Bugatti began with a 'B'. By the same token, the car could have been referred to as the Black Car. In French that would have been 'N', in German 'S', or even 'V' or 'A' for Voiture Noir or Schwarze Auto. It could have been listed on any number of forms identified only by their documentation number.

'B' was about as good as anywhere to start. If that didn't work, maybe he would be making use of the bunk room after all. Opening the drawer towards the latter end of the 'B's before it merged into 'C' he quickly found 'Bu's, then almost immediately stopped at one particular folder. Pulling it out, he shone the light over the cover. Then placed it on the top of the cabinet and flicked through the folder. It appeared he was looking at a special transport request for an ancient archaeological artefact. It was dated September 1941, around the time that construction of the base began.

Hamilton returned to the front and read through the covering letter. The artefact was to be stored at the base temporarily in one of the reinforced munitions stores until suitable transportation was arranged. There were two possibilities, both still being discussed by High Command. Armoured train to Berlin, or battleship to Kiel. For the latter, the convoy would need submarine escort. Unusually it would need the full security of the 12th Unterseeboote Flotille, all forty-three vessels. At the bottom was a signature. Below which was typed a decidedly non-Germanic name, but one he already recognised.

Andrew Sutherland

CHAPTER FIFTY-FOUR

Whether there was a change in air or not was uncertain, but two things happened almost at once. Firstly, he shuddered involuntarily as a chill seemed to enter the room. Secondly, the chill precipitated a movement behind him. Dropping the file on the top of the cabinet he reached up to retrieve the torch he had transferred to his mouth, just as a wire was looped over his head.

Hauling Hamilton back, instead of tearing into his throat as it had with all the previous victims, the position of his hand meant that the garotte sliced into Hamilton's wrist instead, pinning his fist around the torch between his teeth. Initially the knitted sleeve of the glove protected him, but realising the wire wasn't around the throat, his assailant began a rapid sawing action which began to tear through the fabric. Feeling the searing heat as it nicked his flesh, Hamilton realised the unseen attacker was trying to saw through his arm with a cheese wire.

Kicking back from the cabinet, Hamilton slammed up against the units on the opposite wall. The impact winded his assailant but didn't relinquish his grip on the brutal weapon. Reaching behind his back, Hamilton grabbed a handful of testicle and twisted. The effect was predictable and swift. Releasing the garotte with a horrible scream, the wooden handled wire clattered to the darkness of the floor.

Hamilton turned, his torch still between his teeth. The light revealed a big man, broad and muscular, like a dock worker. With the glare temporarily disorientating him, Hamilton drove the torch hard into the man's face.

Glancing off the bridge of his broad nose, the end of the torch found the soft orb of his eye and buried itself into the socket, shattering the bulb and blinding them both as the light went out.

With his attacker screaming wildly again, grabbing both face and crotch, Hamilton delivered blow after blow into the man's stomach. Instinctively with his right hand first, before the shock of the impact on his injured wrist made him cry out. Switching to his left, he drove as hard and as fast into the stomach as he could. Again, and again, and again. Delivering a final knee to crotch, he felt the man double over, their shoulders brushed against one another. Swinging his left fist high up above him, he brought down an elbow hard on where the man's neck might be, feeling the joint make contact and dropping the man to the ground.

Turning quickly, surrounded by the most intense darkness he had ever experienced, Hamilton felt around for the file on top of the cabinet. Finding it, he picked it up, stuffed it under his armpit and hauled on the top drawer. The old wooden cabinet shifted forward a little, then began to tip. Exerting all the strength in his right arm, fighting against the pain in his wrist, he jammed his foot against the bottom drawer and pulled back on the top, pivoting the cabinet forwards.

Feeling the weight shift inside, he withdrew his foot and let go as the cabinet toppled forward. He heard the drawers slide open as the cabinet continued its descent, before the whole thing crashed to the ground, trapping his attacker's legs underneath. Hamilton hoped it might buy him some precious few moments to grope around and find his bearings.

Not knowing whether his foe was alone or accompanied by others, he crouched down and felt around him, finding the wall, then the cold metal of the door frame and eventually the smooth concrete floor. No bulkheads to worry about. No trip hazards. The corridor outside had no door opposite, just the bare concrete wall. Keeping low he hurried out quickly, hoping that if anyone else was there, in the darkness he would crash into their legs and unbalance them. He only hoped they didn't have night vision or thermal imaging. In the infinite blackness of the bunker Hamilton certainly didn't.

His shoulder made contact with the wall opposite the office. Hamilton stayed there for a moment, still crouched low, listening. There was no movement from the office he had left. His assailant wasn't stirring from the floor, struggling with the cabinet blocking their entrance or groaning in pain. There was no movement at all. Hamilton could almost hear the dust settling, a faint hiss of static, then a quiet, high-pitched whistle in his left ear as they adjusted to the total silence. Temporary tinnitus perhaps.

A distant drip could be heard further up the corridor, sounding like a cymbal clashing as it landed in the puddle on the wet concrete. The drip was near the door he had pushed open with his legs. He listened for it again to confirm his bearings.

The wait seemed to take forever. Too long. He needed to move. With the file still tucked under his left arm, he felt the wall with his right hand, the glove filling with blood from the gash in his wrist. He was conscious of that as he proceeded down the corridor. If ever the bunker was eventually discovered, the scene would look even more horrifying. Blood smeared along the wall, heading towards the exit. He had wanted to leave no trace but that was impossible now. Perhaps if the bunker was ever found they might assume it was old. A good cop would still likely test it to make sure.

His hand reached another door frame, the canteen. Reaching across, he grabbed the frame on the other side of the aperture and carried on. A gory glove print left behind. Another doorway came up soon afterwards. The kitchen he had come across earlier. He thought momentarily about searching the room for a weapon of some kind, a knife, a pan, anything. Deciding against it, he didn't know the layout for certain from his brief glimpse in torchlight and could easily find himself trapped inside, despite the open door, thrashing around blindly for the exit while he bled out.

He remembered the skeleton of the cat above him. With no light there was nothing for the receptors in the retina to process. The cones were napping, and the rods had nothing to work with. Not down there. Conceivably it had been the same for the cat. Only its keener sense of smell and whiskers would have given it some kind of perception. The thought motivated him to move on down the corridor instead.

A little further on his hand touched something wet. The seepage from above. He was near the airlock. The fresher air from the bunker he was in began to smell a little mustier, mingling with the stagnant air of the corridor beyond, so long denied access to the air ducts from above. Finding his way to the door, he leaned against it, wincing against the pain in his wrist and shaking as the adrenalin from the fight began to subside. He could feel the blood still running from the wound. There was no way of knowing how bad it was, but he could still move his fingers and clamping his other hand around the wrist he could only feel a warm wetness there.

Shaking the blood off, he heard it spatter onto the floor of the corridor as he stumbled out. With his injured hand he tucked the folder firmly under his armpit. He didn't want to lose anything now. Then, using his left shoulder to brush against the wall, Hamilton clamped the wound with his other hand and kept the injury as high as he could. It was a clumsy shuffle to the next door, then the stairs.

Making his way back up the stairs, he was back in the entrance lobby. The toilets, showers and storage rooms. The next staircase was directly in front of him. Almost doubled over, feeling the floor with his bleeding hand to find the first step, he must have looked like some strange and frightened beggar in daylight, but it was the only way to ensure he didn't trip up the stairs and lose any of the precious paperwork stashed under his armpit.

Exiting through the main gallery entrance was out of the question. Hamilton knew they had cameras there and the exit would have been bolted shut. He hoped he had done enough but didn't want to risk another encounter with the phantom. The glimpse he had seen of him was enough. It didn't matter how long he had spent in the Royal Marines before joining the Service, a man that size was not easily overpowered.

Finding his way back to the dark corridor that ran down the length of the above ground base, he half-jogged, half stumbled down, feeling himself become a little lightheaded as the injured wrist continued to bleed. His feet clattered into the skeleton of the cat, bringing hm down to his knees. He cursed and apologised. It was an inexplicable reaction, but at that moment, his blind stumble had felt like a desecration. The two-hundred and thirty-five metres felt like a country mile. He stopped to listen again, but knew he needed to get out of there, back to the car, to the first aid kit, get a tourniquet set up and take in fluids.

Sweat was beading on his forehead as he tucked his elbow into his side to keep the precious folder under his arm. Struggling to his feet again, he carried on. Willing his legs to keep him going, knowing he still had a lot of work to do to get back to the car, practically the same distance back again to where he had parked up. Wisely choosing not to park in the gallery's own lot, a lone car at the end of the day would arouse too much suspicion, he had left it in the adjacent concrete apron behind the circus school. Even contemplating the journey made him feel weaker.

He was in trouble, and he knew it. Getting weaker by the moment. The burning fire of the laceration to the wrist became a gnawing pain in the bone as he hurried on. Fresh air at least might help revive him. Finding the door, he pushed his shoulder against the crash bar and stumbled out into the yard beyond.

There were some expensive new apartment blocks immediately opposite the submarine pen. Part of the multi-million Euro redevelopment of the Bacalan area. Using the dockyards as the focal point for a vibrant community of restaurants, galleries and luxury apartments. Glancing briefly up at the windows, there were a few lights on, but the construction containers stacked up on the side of road had helpfully concealed his abrupt exit. Taking a moment to breath the clear night air hoping it might help give him the reserves of energy he needed, he listened again for the sounds of footsteps down the corridor behind him but couldn't hear anything. Closing the door, he continued to breath in deeply, wincing as his lungs threatened to give out.

Placing the folder on the ground, he peeled the glove away to inspect the damage and immediately wished he hadn't. His whole hand was slick with blood but the wound didn't look to have reached the bone. The wire had not bitten in as deep as it had felt, but like a papercut, the wound was bleeding prodigiously. The sleeve of the glove had prevented it getting any worse. He was quietly relieved the wire hadn't cut through the watch strap.

Cursing once again, he needed to get the cut sorted. The blood had soaked the cover of the folder too as he gathered it up again. Shoving it once more under his left armpit, he tried to staunch the blood with his other hand, holding it as high as he could, and began the long stagger back to his car. If he could just get to the first aid kit. Still at the opposite end of the submarine building, another two-hundred metre slog, at least he could do it at his own pace without the imminent threat of being attacked by a stranger in the darkness.

Getting back to the car, the first thing to do was wash out the wound. Grabbing a water bottle from inside he tore off the glove and splashed water on the wrist, watching as a bloody stream trailed away beneath the car. Looking at it in the light of the vanity mirror, the cut immediately oozed blood once again. He could still move his fingers so there was no tendon damage. The knitted glove sleeve had done just enough to prevent serious injury. The wire had missed the nylon woven MoD Defence Standard watch strap by a hair's breadth. It was a cheap strap for an expensive watch, but it was original to the timepiece and meant a lot to him in its original condition.

He removed the watch, rinsing off the blood before dropping it in the passenger footwell and moving to the boot where the First Aid Kit was stowed. Sitting on the rear bumper, trying to open and apply a sterilised dressing with his teeth and his non-dominant left hand was a struggle in the darkness. Peering around, he looked towards the looming concrete of the submarine base. A gigantic black box, dropped onto the Port of Bordeaux. With no artful uplighters or nearby streetlights, and the glowing, flashing gantry cranes and yards of the dock beyond it, orange strobes and white LEDs, the base sat there in stark silhouette. Most importantly, no one was coming from that direction. There was no one around at all.

Eventually the dressing was applied. He might need to redo it again in the morning, perhaps put some butterfly stitches on to seal up the wound and get the flesh to knit, but for now it wasn't bleeding all over him and he could drive back to the motel. Disaster averted. Just. Sitting back in the driver's seat, he leaned across and inspected his watch. The blood-stained MoD DefStan 66-15 had once been strapped to the wrist of his old mentor in the Strathclyde Police. The salty detective had been a special forces diver himself in the sixties.

The Omega Seamaster 300 he had been issued still bore the MoD markings on the rear of the case. As military issue equipment it should have been handed back in when he had left the Service. Instead, it was handed onto Hamilton about a week before the wizened old seadog passed away. In the lore of military watch collecting when originality was key, his was a veritable unicorn timepiece. He wondered whether the man knew that when he handed it to him.

CHAPTER FIFTY-FIVE
FRANCE, 1941

Adler's idea was quite brilliant and suited multiple aims all in one swift stroke. The growing pseudo-archaeological movements promoted by the Nazi regime were becoming an extensive propaganda tool to search for supposed evidence of Indo-Germanic achievements. The aim was to bring research findings to the German people to reinforce the ideology of Aryan superiority. Of all the organisations involved, *Adler's* idea was perhaps particularly suited to Amt Rosenberg who saw world history shaped by the fight between the pure-blooded Nordic people of Atlantis and the Proto-Semitic peoples of the ancient Near East.

One branch of archaeology was endeavouring to find the island city of Atlantis itself, believed to be somewhere in the North Atlantic Ocean, not the Mediterranean as so often erroneously claimed. The legendary lost island was claimed to be the birthplace of the Nordic race from whom the Aryan peoples descended and who were destined to control and influence the development of mankind. A second branch was seeking to prove that the Germanic people were not destroyers of culture, as had been portrayed by the Romans, but were in fact guardians and protectors of superior Nordic values, much misunderstood by non-Aryan peoples.

In fact, a research expedition to the Middle East, funded by the Ahnenerbe thinktank was endeavouring to find evidence in support of a theory that an internal power struggle within the Roman Empire between Nordic and Semitic peoples precipitated its division into East and West. Part of the claim of legitimacy to the title of Holy Roman Emperor rested on whoever possessed the most ancient and valuable of holy relics, a clear indication of Divine favour. This, it was alleged, was part of the motivation behind the later foundation of the Hospital Order of Saint Mary of the Teutons, to protect and defend the Holy Land and the Christian territory of the Germanic-speaking peoples of northern Europe.

Predictably, the expeditions had found very little of value to support the notion of Aryan superiority, but *Adler* had managed to implant a seed that one of the expedition teams had stumbled upon the possible resting place of the Ark of the Covenant. It was a completely fanciful and fabricated claim. The last Biblical record of it was when King Josiah commanded its return to the temple in Jerusalem in 642 BCE. There was no mention of it being carried off to Babylon along with other holy utensils when the city fell in 607 BCE, suggesting it had disappeared in the interim just as the prophet Jeremiah said it would. Since its disappearance from Biblical narrative, the only other mention of the Ark was in the 14th century national epic Kebra Nagast.

Written in Ge'ez, an ancient South Semitic language of the East African branch, the text of Kebra Nagast claimed to hold the genealogical record of the Solomonic dynasty of Ethiopia. According to the account, the Queen of Sheba and King Solomon of Israel had a son together. On her return to Ethiopia, the Queen raised this son, Menelik, as a Jew according to Biblical Law, and he only returned to Israel to meet his father for the first time when he was in his twenties.

The legend claimed that Solomon begged him to remain and take over the kingdom, but Menelik wanted to return to Ethiopia. Aggrieved, Solomon despatched many Israelites to accompany Menelik and assist him in ruling according to Biblical standards. At this moment, the Ark of the Covenant was sent with them to Ethiopia and on the death of the Queen, Menelik founded the Solomonic dynasty of Ethiopia.

Not only was this theory incompatible with the Biblical record, but when the Ark itself, said to be kept in the Church of Our Lady Mary of Zion in Axum, was recently examined by a British soldier involved in the Abyssinian Campaign, they described finding just an empty wooden box of middle-to-late mediaeval construction, probably made around the time the church was destroyed by Queen Gudit. The wood was neither from acacia nor was it covered inside and out with gold. While the 225th generation of the claimed three-thousand-year-old Solomonic dynasty still ruled over the country in the form of His Imperial Majesty Haile Selassie, the Ark in Ethiopia was not the genuine article.

IN THE DEN OF WOLVES

This left the field ripe for new theories as to where the Ark disappeared to before the Babylonian conquest of Judea and *Adler* was not above stirring the pot if it served the right ends. Such was the enthusiasm within these pseudo-archaeological movements to devour anything that might promote a tentative Aryan theory, very little in the way of verification would likely be required to substantiate *Adler's* bold assertion. Though it was a high-risk gamble, it might just pay off.

The former School of Industrial Arts and Crafts at No.8 Prinz Albrecht Strasse was already an imposing building from the outside. Located next to the Prinz Albrecht Hotel at No.9 which had been commandeered as the SS-Reichsführings headquarters in 1934, the Reich Security Main Office had moved into the Gestapo headquarters at No.8 in 1939, occupying the upper floors while the Gestapo continued to use the lower storeys and the basement levels. Entering the front door, a wide staircase took *Adler* up to the Main Hall of the Gestapo where a vast vaulted corridor greeted him. To the right, between large arched windows looking down into a courtyard, were busts of Göring and Hitler, beneath vertical scarlet banners bearing the swastika.

He had seen that symbol before on a collection of Rudyard Kipling's books in his father's library in *Talisker House*. It was an ancient icon often used as a symbol of divinity and spirituality in Indian religions. The word itself came from the Sanskrit meaning 'conducive to well-being' and the symbol could be presented either right-handed, or left-handed, depending on the desired connotation. The right-handed form symbolised the sun, prosperity and good luck. The left-handed symbol represented night and the tantric aspect of Kali.

Aside from the belief that they represented the auspicious footprints of Buddha, the swastikas had been depicted in prehistoric Persian cave paintings, Balto-Slavic symbology, even in Greco-Roman mosaics. Being the right-handed form, rotated forty-five degrees on a white circle in the centre of the red banners, the swastika had been adopted as the insignia of the National Socialist German Workers' Party, the NSDAP, and had taken on a very different, and significantly more sinister suggestion to everyone who saw it now. To *Adler*, it seemed an odd choice of emblem for the ruling Nazi Party, observing that there was nothing remotely Germanic about it. He had a sense though that it would never be seen the same way again.

The impressively wide, open space of the staircase and vaulted corridor was typical of an institute of learning. *Adler* could well imagine students of the past filing through on their way to classes and lectures, bathed in the light streaming in through vast windows that overlooked the courtyard below. The sun might once have illuminated several student pieces or inspiring artworks exhibited in the hallowed hall. The grandiose proportions of the architecture suited the Third Reich very well now though and appeared both impressive and intimidating at the same time.

Adler continued onto the half-landing and took the next staircase up to the Reichssicherheitshauptamt, where his own tiny office was located. Continuing down the corridor however, he entered the office of his commander, SS-Hauptsturmführer Manfred Reinhardt, memo in his hand, newly decoded by the M4 Enigma from the outpost in Northern Syria. At least, that's what *Adler* had written down.

"Sutherland." Reinhardt said as he entered and offered the customary salute.

"Memo in from Syria, sir." He said, stepping forward and passing it across the desk, glancing at the antiquity's specialist to one side, a recent doctoral graduate in Near-East studies by all accounts. "It's been confirmed."

"They've found it?" Reinhardt stammered. "They've really found it?"

"They've found its approximate location." *Adler* remarked cautiously. "There is still much work to be done before they actually have the artefact."

"It's about time this Altheim found something." Reinhardt spat contemptuously.

Expedition leader Franz Altheim had caught wind of a second-hand rumour that his team had discovered the most likely location of the Ark of the Covenant. He didn't know who had started the rumour, but he couldn't easily rebuff the suggestion without risking embarrassment and inviting scrutiny on where the sizeable investment funds had been spent without so much as an Etruscan vase to show for it.

Perhaps his expedition might indeed find something of such historical significance as to support Aryan theory. He only hoped that whatever he did find would be of suitably high enough merit to assuage the disappointment that would follow his inevitable failure to uncover the Ark. He could say it was a prelude perhaps to a far greater discovery. Hopefully that would buy enough time to shift himself from under the weight of this ridiculous speculation. In any event, though he didn't know the source of the rumour,

Adler had now put him in a very precarious situation and on increasingly borrowed time.

Meanwhile, *Adler* was ordered to find out what material support could be offered to Altheim's team to ensure success. After a few weeks of supposed enquiry with the Syrian teams, during which time he slipped a message through to Benoist to return the Bugatti to the factory at Molshiem, Adler had returned.

"They need a box." He began. "Two metres square by five metres long."

"How big is this Ark?" Reinhardt enquired with astonishment, even the antiquities expert looked a little surprised.

"They have requested it to be lined with lead for protection. This will reduce the internal dimensions."

"Even so…" the expert chimed before *Adler* interrupted.

"Biblical records indicate the Ark was a little over half a metre square by just over a metre in length, but it may be stored with its poles which are of indeterminate length. It will need to be transported on these poles for safety."

"Safety?" Reinhardt probed.

"According to the Bible book of Chronicles, King David of Israel once arranged for the Ark of the Covenant to be brought to Jerusalem on a new wagon pulled by bulls, instead of by Levite priests using the carrying poles as commanded by God. When the bulls upset the cart, a man named Uzzah, son of Abinadab, thrust out his hand to steady the Ark but was immediately struck down by God for defying His Law. The Law stated that the Ark was only to be carried on the shoulders of Kohathite Levites and never to be touched by anyone once the sacred objects of the Israelites had been placed inside."

He glanced to the doctor who seemed to nod with understanding.

"As a precaution, the expedition leader has recommended that the box be made larger than necessary so that the artefact could be safely loaded inside without any danger of incurring the wrath of God by inadvertently touching it."

IN THE DEN OF WOLVES

Adler could see that Reinhardt was still very sceptical of such Divine power.

"Does Altheim expect us to believe such superstitions?"

Adler considered for a moment. His ploy was at a critical phase. Without Reinhardt's authority, there would be no wooden box.

"Sir," he began, attempting to acknowledge similar scepticism, but be seen to show appropriate concern and support for the team's supposed request. "With such resources already spent, it may be better to exercise due caution. After all, this is just a wooden box."

"And what do we do with this artefact once it has been retrieved?" he demanded.

"We could always send it to the Eastern Front, sir, and let the Cossacks open it. If God does indeed exercise his Divine displeasure upon them, maybe you will have your Lebensraum without need for further conflict."

Reinhardt smiled savagely at *Adler's* off-the-cuff suggestion.

"And if not?"

"Sir, even to possess such an ancient artefact would be a great triumph for the Reich." The doctor added, evidently excited at the prospect of being involved in such a wondrous discovery and perhaps even angling for an opportunity to join the expedition. "It would demonstrate that God is indeed with the German people. I don't see that any harm would come of acceding to such a modest request."

Reinhardt stared hard at the doctor. His pale blue eyes boring straight through him. Coupled with his sardonic smile, the blood in *Adler's* veins froze. Here was evil personified.

"Very well." Reinhardt nodded eventually. "I see no issue from my side. See to this box, Sutherland."

"Yes, sir." He replied, clicking his heels and taking his leave in the usual manner.

His boots resonated down the corridor as he turned and headed back to his own office, only allowing himself to smile once he was inside. It was one of the few Bible accounts *Adler* could still recall from the sermons at Dollar Academy, and only then because the Rector had related it to him most profoundly while giving him the cane. It seemed the Rector could identify a parallel between Uzzah's profane act and young Andrew Sutherland inappropriately grabbing the biology teacher's ample bosom. They had both touched a chest that didn't belong to them.

The box was duly fabricated and sent on a train from Berlin to Bordeaux with the paperwork for the Commandant at the Naval base. Once at Bordeaux, it was scheduled to be carried by battleship to Syria as part of a counterattacking fleet to wrest control of the region from Free France. On arrival, the box would be transported to the dig site ready to receive the lost treasure.

Of course, none of that was ever going to happen. The box hadn't even been lined with lead. Halfway through the European leg of the rail journey there needed to be a change of engines and some wagons too. Some of the wagons needed transporting back east and had been waiting at Strasbourg for weeks. Conveniently, just fifteen miles away from Strasbourg railway station was Molsheim, the home of Bugatti.

Simultaneously, Benoist requested that the Bugatti be transported to Bordeaux for safe-keeping, believing that *Adler* had made arrangements for it to set sail for America where it would be stored until after the war. Thus, the paperwork was drawn up declaring that La Voiture Noire, the Black Bugatti, Chassis No. 57453, whichever way she was referred to, would be sent to the Bugatti factory in Bordeaux until the ship was due to set sail.

When *Adler's* box arrived in Strasbourg, the boys at Bugatti drove the car inside it before it was transferred to a wagon heading back east. Thus, with a simple sleight of hand and a fabricated legend, *Adler* managed to spirit the Black Bugatti completely out of harm's way. The finishing touch was the seal of the Afrika Korps branded onto the side of the wooden crate. The swastika superimposed over a palm tree was a decidedly more recognisable symbol than the insignia of the Free Arabian Legion. It certainly made the desired impression on the managers of the Berlin branch of Hochtief AG who were finalising a few structures for the Führer beneath the Reich Chancellery.

The weight of the box was explained as the lead-lined inner chamber used in an effort to keep whatever mystical powers the Ark of the Covenant still possessed constrained within the crate. No additional questions were asked, and no one dared to inspect such a powerful artefact to attest to *Adler's* truthfulness. *Adler* himself was to inform the Führer of the discovery when the box was safely stowed away. In the meantime, Hochtief had its brief and the diggers got to work.

CHAPTER FIFTY-SIX
FRANCE, 2018

When Jaeger opened his right eye, he had no idea where he was. He didn't even know if his eye was open. The darkness was all-encompassing. A terrible pain boring through his left eye reminded him that it had been destroyed. The shaft of the torch was still protruding from the socket, swollen and bloody. There was no ambient light at all in the underground bunker. He was totally blind.

The dull throbbing from his abdomen registered every blow that had been inflicted upon him. One on his left side, just beneath the ribs, three more on his right side. The feeling of nausea was still there and his testicles were on fire. Something was in bad shape down there, some tearing torsional injury. The painful throbbing from his knees suggested fractures to both patella. This as a result of the solid wooden filing cabinet crashing down on his lower limbs. Paper was surprisingly heavy and with the cabinet almost overflowing, the weight had come down on him like a tree trunk.

His biggest concern was the pain in the back of his neck. He could barely move his head, the slightest rotation fired off agonising lightning bolts up into his brain and down his spine. Swelling to the muscles had stiffened it up and moving against them only increased the pain. He was in a bad way. There was no way he was getting out of there and he knew it. The bunker would be his grave. Already buried beneath tons of concrete.

This realisation at first made him angry. Why was he dealt such a bad hand in life? Why had his parents abandoned him to be brought up by an alcoholic aunt and her drug addled boyfriends? Why had Schmidt needled him so much, to the point of hurling molten steel at him and smiling as the searing liquid burnt right through his flesh?

There was a moment of remorse, of the people he had killed or maimed along the way. Not just the three members of the Auto Club, but the ones that had gone before. All in the service of the OID, the Östlicher Informationsdienst. He was a government agent. At least that's what he had been told, yet where was his government protection, his immunity? Where was the Voice? Who was this Voice?

At the end, all that was left was despair. The thought of starving down there frightened him. How long would it take? How much more pain could he endure as his body began to consume itself, trying to survive, before ultimately giving up? Reaching up to his neck with his fingers, he felt the vertebrae and located the fracture. He knew what a fractured neck felt like. He had inflicted it enough times on others.

Perhaps that was another way. So far the spinal cord hadn't been severed, only pinched by the inflamed muscles and the fractured bone. He hoped he still had the strength and the speed to do what needed to be done. There was only one way of finding out. Grabbing a tuft of hair at the back of his head, he held his breath, then tugged viciously to twist his head around. Immediately an intense fire shot into his brain and down the spine all the way to his pelvis. Then he felt nothing at all.

The last breath left Jaeger's lungs as his head fell forwards onto the concrete, rippling the surface of his congealing blood.

CHAPTER FIFTY-SEVEN

When Hamilton opened his eyes, he had no idea where he was either. The ceiling was off-white, there was a smoke alarm above his head and a ray of sickeningly bright sunlight streaming through the gap in the curtains that refused to meet in the middle. It was the curtains that reminded him. Looking down at his wrist, there hadn't been too much blood seeping through. Pleased that he had done enough, he went to the bathroom to inspect his work and see if he could make it a little tidier in full daylight after his shower.

When he emerged, he wandered over to the little desk against the wall. The lamp was shaking as the headboard in the adjacent room hammered against the wall periodically. There was no sense of urgency with it. At one point he thought his neighbours might have fallen asleep part way through. Then it started again. Shaking his head with a sigh, he picked up the folder, pulled out the chair and sat down by the window.

He looked at his redressed wound and inspected the plaster, hoping it would do the job. The angle of his arm as he had reached up to grab the torch in his mouth had presented the ulna to the wire his assailant had intended to use around his throat. Though it had still cut deep, the wound was little more than a severe papercut. Hamilton was fortunate his arm had not rotated to expose all the blood vessels and tendons to the hand. He shook the image of the attack from his mind. It was an image largely conjured up by his imagination. In the torchlight he had barely seen a thing, so his mind helpfully and horrifyingly tried to fill in the blanks.

Looking back at the folder, he thought for a moment, then gave a crooked little smile of mischief.

"La mère sacrée." He whispered.

The sacred mother. What would Ralph Lauren give to add this to his other Bugatti Type 57 Atlantic? The original black Bugatti, not Richard Pope's sapphire blue model which he had repainted to match the rest of his exotic car collection.

Hamilton's mind momentarily flashed back to the confrontation in the bunker. The wire. The stubbled face of the assailant, horrifyingly illuminated in the torchlight. Pain and anger registering on his face as that all too familiar nausea welled up from having his testicles twisted. This was quickly followed by the feeling of the torch squelching through the man's eye. He hadn't expected that, certainly wasn't aiming for it. Equally it could have been shoved down his own throat, choking him if the attacker had had the speed and presence of mind.

The thought of the incredible pain that would have induced. His merciless pummelling of the man's abdomen afterwards. The final blow to the back of the neck. Enough to break it? Had he killed the man? Paralysed him? Had his attacker somehow crawled painfully away in the middle of the night? Then there were the sounds that accompanied the attack, amplified by the darkness. The crash into the cabinets, grab, twist, the shriek of pain, the agonising cry, fist, fist, fist, fist, knee, elbow. Floor.

Hamilton took a breath and stood up straight. He had one good hand, a little dizziness, and his legs were on fire and seizing up a little after all that running. He needed coffee.

French coffee was good. Some would say better than Italian. The Italians would disagree. Hamilton had no opinion. He wasn't particularly a coffee connoisseur but he did appreciate a good cup. French motel coffee on the other hand was bad. Very bad. After stopping at one cup and helping himself to a continental version of a cooked breakfast, he ambled back to his room. His neighbour was outside smoking. Hamilton could see why the rhythm had been slow. The man was old, overweight, with a combover that had fallen to one side. The kind of catch anyone with class would have thrown back into the oily water.

"Bonjour." He greeted.

"Bonjour, Monsieur." He said with a smile full of yellow teeth. "I hope we did not disturb you too much." He added with a knowing wink.

"Ah dinnae notice anythin'." Hamilton replied, opening the door. Pausing on the threshold he added. "I dinnae think she did either."

Moving back to the desk, Hamilton rested his right arm on the surface and began to flex his fingers again. There was still movement, but the pain in his wrist burned like fire. He winced a little, then slid the folder towards him. It was a mess. The cover was stained and stiff. There was a lot of blood on it.

He had been hired to look for some lost artefacts. Old cars. It sounded very dull and very easy. Check sales records, ownership documents. It wasn't. It was much more like being an archaeologist than he realised. The reason why these cars needed to be found was that someone else was after them. Clearly the person who attacked him last night had something to do with it. He didn't know why they wanted the cars though. All he did know was that these cars had disappeared during the war.

At that point he opened the folder again and produced the covering letter he had examined previously. It was a letter addressed to the commandment of the base to request temporary storage for the artefact listed on the cover. It had been filed under 'Bu' but was not a Bugatti. The word typed on the cover was Bundeslade.

Bundesland meant Federal State. That was well known. Bund was the German word for Federation. Bundesliga, Bundesrepublik, Bundesbank. The verb 'Laden' had to do with loading. A drawer was a schublade, a lade was a chest or cabinet. The Bundeslade however, was not merely a Federal Chest. It was the chest. As if to minimise any doubt, the handwritten scrawl underneath read '*Lade des Zeugnisses*'. The Ark of the Testimony.

Hamilton was looking at a transfer order for the Ark of the Covenant.

It wouldn't be the actual Ark of the Covenant any more than the Black Bugatti was the Sacred Mother. It was the author of the letter having a little joke, but a joke that might just have been the key to hiding it for all these years. He looked down to the typed out name of the author above the signature to confirm what he had seen last night:

Andrew Sutherland.

Sutherland wanted to keep the car safe. He had done the same with his own car, *Manuela*, but this wasn't because he was a peculiar purveyor of automobiles. Even back then he recognised the importance of them as currency, especially during a time of war.

Sutherland would have known that the Bugatti was one of only four very special models built by Molsheim. Had it not been gifted to Benoist it would have been fearsomely expensive to buy. After all the Rothschild's were not known to be short of a bob or two. The car would also have been incredibly distinctive. Its most significant feature proving to be its greatest weakness once the war started. Perhaps he saw it as investment after the war.

Even if Europe was rebuilding, if the hyperinflation that brought down the Weimar Republic returned, there would still be collectors in America, willing to pay top-dollar for a rare European classic. It would be a way of starting again. A little nest egg put by for his friends. The same with *Manuela* too. The difference was that Sutherland had survived the war. Neither Grover-Williams nor Benoist did. If the Bugatti was to be found now, conservative estimates put the value at a hundred, maybe a hundred-and-twenty-million Euros. That alone would make it the most expensive car in the world.

Perhaps whoever was after the car now was after that kind of money. Being a lost car, it officially didn't belong to anyone. It wouldn't be stealing to find something that someone else had hidden which didn't belong to them in the first place. The worry for Hamilton was that he didn't know how many of 'them' there were out searching for the cars too. If they were anything like the character he met last night, things might get a little more animated.

As he examined the letter in more detail, Hamilton noticed a mistake in the typing. In it, Sutherland had described how the crate they were requested to store would be travelling West from Berlin through Strasbourg. Why they needed that superfluous information he didn't know, until he looked more closely at the typo. The 'e' in West had been corrected. Or at least, had been typed over another letter. The letter 'o'. West was spelt the same in English, but East was spelt with an 'o', as in the town names Osterburg, eastern castle, Osterfeld, eastern field, even with an Umlaut for the Eastern Kingdom. Österreich. Austria.

He went to his laptop bag, took out the computer and booted it up. A thought had occurred to him. Train lines between Bordeaux and Berlin. Using Google he typed Berlin into the search bar, then clicked Maps. Wanting directions, he then added Bordeaux. The directions automatically calculated the car journey but changing to public transport would show all the train and bus routes between the two points. The directions recalculated and displayed a couple of different routes, all converging at one point just across the French border.

Adding Molsheim between the two failed to show a route. He removed Bordeaux. Doing so showed the first half of the train journey unchanged, two routes, converging near the border, only with a small addition to Molsheim at the end using local buses. Zooming into the Molsheim area of the journey he could see it immediately. The route showed a short bus journey from the rail station in Strasbourg to the centre of Molsheim.

Next, he tried Molsheim to Bordeaux. The second half of the journey was also similarly unchanged from the complete route. He tried Berlin to Bordeaux again and the original routes returned. It seemed whichever route the train journey took through Germany from Berlin to Bordeaux, both lines would run right through Strasbourg. Presumably the route hadn't changed much in seventy years.

A wooden box travelling west from Berlin to Bordeaux. Empty. Stored at the port before travelling by ship to the dig site. Then back to Berlin with its precious cargo. That was the ruse. He pointed back to Strasbourg. Another train travelling east from Strasbourg, back to Berlin. The car was returned to Molsheim. Loaded onto a train at Strasbourg.

Now he understood it. The car had never gone to Bordeaux at all. Neither had any shipping crate. The crate had gone from Berlin to Strasbourg as scheduled. The car had been loaded inside. Then the crate returned east on a second train. To Berlin. He brought the car back to hide it right beneath the noses of the people that might have been looking for it originally. Maybe the key to the whereabouts of the Horch was in Berlin too. Perhaps the key was La Voiture Noire.

The Black Car.

CHAPTER FIFTY-EIGHT
GERMANY, 1942

1942 was a common year. In the Gregorian calendar, it started on a Thursday, the day the United States, Great Britain and twenty-four other nations signed a declaration to agree not to make any separate peace negotiations with the Axis powers. By the end of the first week, it was clear that the Führer's plan to take Moscow in four months was in ruins. The triple defensive belts established by Soviet forces had held up well, wearing down and halting the advance of Army Group Centre. Operation Typhoon was at an end and the Wehrmacht was switching from attack to defence.

Within less than a week, on the other side of the world, U-123 claimed her first kill of her seventh patrol, sinking the British cargo ship SS *Cyclops* off the southeast coast of Nova Scotia. Entering New York Harbour in the early hours of the 14th of January, Kapitänleutnant Reinhard Hardegen fired three torpedoes into the Norwegian tanker *Norness* within sight of Long Island. With an illuminated New York City skyline and thirteen USN Destroyers in the harbour, U-123 took down the SS *Coimbra* off Sandy Hook before venturing down the New Jersey coast and claiming another three vessels almost completely without interference.

Then came Tuesday 20th of January. As well as being bitterly cold in Germany it was anything but ordinary. *Adler* had received a request from the NSKK the day before to select a suitable vehicle for a conference to be held at Wannsee, a suburb in the west of Berlin. He was highly respected for his knowledge of automobiles. The NSKK had numerous vehicles to choose from, military, civilian and state.

"Who is it for?" he asked.

"That doesn't concern you." Reinhardt told him.

"Forgive me, but if I recommend the wrong kind of vehicle, we will both be shot." He said, then added with a smile. "As the junior officer, I'll just be shot twice."

"It needs to be suitable for rough ground."

"A halftrack."

"It needs to have a certain…" Reinhardt floundered for the right word.

"Qualität?"

"Precisely."

"For how many?"

"Just one driver. One passenger."

"Rough ground you say. An airfield perhaps? They want to make an entrance." *Adler* smiled. "Sounds like the kind of thing Heydrich would do."

Reinhardt fidgeted uncomfortably. *Adler* had winkled it out.

"Alright, alright, but don't tell anyone I told you."

"I am the soul of discretion." *Adler* smiled, quoting from Sense & Sensibility. Not that Reinhardt would know that. "Perhaps a Maybach then." He suggested. "There is a nice little SW38 in. Four-door Cabriolet. Beautiful bodywork from Spohn."

"I don't care where the bodywork is from!" Reinhardt snapped.

"Oh, but Captain." *Adler* said with a sly smile and a cheeky wink. "One must always take note of the bodywork."

Carosseriebau Hermann Spohn had been founded in 1920 in the city of Ravensburg, just about the same time Dr. Karl Maybach had started manufacturing automobile drivetrains and chassis in nearby Friedrichshafen. Thus, Spohn soon became Maybach's favoured coachbuilder and the vehicle he had selected would be perfect for the job. Stately, but not so much as to risk overshadowing the Führer himself.

Captain Reinhardt was satisfied and was about to leave when he stopped.

"How well does it drive?"

"Very well, so I'm told. Though I favour the transmission of the Horch 951 personally."

"Typical Auto Union man." Reinhardt replied, rolling his eyes. "It had better drive well."

"Why's that, sir?"

"Because you'll be driving it."

"Me, sir?" *Adler* asked with surprise.

"His regular driver has come down with the flu, that's why his usual Mercedes is unavailable." Reinhardt replied. "Will this be a problem?"

"Not at all, sir. It's just a rare honour."

"Well then." Reinhardt concluded, staring at hm intently "Don't mess it up."

CHAPTER FIFTY-NINE

The tiny little Storch was a liaison aircraft, very much like the Westland Lysander. Constructed by Fieseler in Kassel, plans were being finalised to expand production in the Morane-Saulnier factory in Puteaux just outside Paris. The nimble little aircraft rumbled across the sky as light flakes of snow fell from low, grey clouds. The distinctive beam cross on the wings and fuselage of the Fi-156 was supplemented by a swastika on the tail.

Specified by the State Ministry of Aviation, the aircraft's colour scheme was set out in Luftwaffe Service Regulation 521. Dispensing with the pre-war colours of 1933, the top surface was defined as RLM 75, dark grey, with a white-blue hue on the underside of the wings and belly. From above it would have blended in perfectly with the grey clouds, the underbelly camouflaged against the snow. It should have been flying upside down.

The note of the little Argus V8 engine changed as the aircraft altered course, following the gentle descent of the snow to where a dense forest yielded to the playing fields of the Wannsee Sports Club. Already on the icy road heading north along the bight of the Havel River, a steady stream of cars could be seen negotiating their way through the morning snows.

A housekeeper's footsteps resonated on parquet floor as she moved over to the decorative lamp. Gently pulling the cord, she smiled as honey-tinged light exuded its warm, decorative radiance onto the dustsheets. Moving to the large window, she pulled heavy drapes apart to allow the morning's hazy light into the room. Onto a second window, she opened these too but lingered a while as she felt the casement rattle. Opening the window, she leaned out and watched the pale blue belly of the Storch fly low overhead. Kitchen staff halted, staring redundantly up at the ceiling as the aircraft engine rattled above them.

The luxurious Persian rug could have covered half of Brandenburg and would neither have looked too flamboyant nor too immense if it had graced the very floors of the Stadtschloss. It took four servants, bent double with fine white cotton gloves to unfurl the rug onto the wooden floor of Wannsee House.

The housekeeper appeared again, this time in the vast dining room on the ground floor, decorated with exquisite stucco and painted friezes. A large sheet covered one end of a highly polished elliptical rosewood table. A senior orderly, pressed and dressed, appeared opposite her and together they folded the sheet into a neat square to be stored until later. A second sheet covered the centre, one more the far end. Watery rays of daylight trying to stream in through narrow gaps in unopened curtains cast muted shafts of light onto patterned silk wallpaper.

In the kitchens, servants were busy cleaning and polishing silverware that would be used by the many guests arriving at the palatial country residence. Parsley was chopped, sour cream and pickled herring were applied to small crackers. Cold meats and cheeses were sliced and presented on silver salvers. Pickled cabbage was piled into a silver serving dish. Soup was ladled into the tureen from a deep pot on the stove.

Elsewhere, a museum level of silence accompanied the efficient movements of staff preparing the reception. A leather guest book was placed on a side table in the atrium. The book bore the name of the house and the SS runes or lightning bolts on its black cover. Opened at the latest entries, a fountain pen was placed on top. In another corner of the house, a feminine hand meticulously wrote out the name of one of the guests onto fine cream card in her beautifully ornate Fraktur blackletters. Dipping her pointed pen into the ink well again, she continued to form intricate Gothic script, careful not to drip or smudge the table settings.

An orderly whipped the cloth from a small circular end table while a second orderly placed a vase of fresh flowers in the centre. Crystal glasses were wiped over with a fine linen duster before being replaced onto the tablecloth. A maid set about snipping the stems of fresh flowers before arranging them neatly in another tall, decorative vase. The calligrapher, finished the last card, folded it into a triangle and lined it up with the others as the supervising

IN THE DEN OF WOLVES

butler checked the settings with a ruler.

Outside, the frigid breeze had already numbed *Adler's* ears as he watched the Storch make its final approach through low mist. The sports field was ideal for the kind of short landing the aircraft excelled at and the pilot was a skilled aviator. He watched the flaps drop as final adjustments were made. Wheels touched down and bounced slightly before settling as the engine was reined in and the aircraft rolled up alongside the Maybach.

Back at the house, the Mercedes-Benz 130H was an unusual looking vehicle. One of three models produced by Daimler-Benz with a rear-mounted 1.3litre side-valve engine. Independent suspension and imbalanced mass made the car a little awkward to handle, especially in winter, and production was eventually discontinued in 1936, but a few could be seen, as on that day, transporting various State Secretaries around the capital.

The absence of the typical Mercedes front grille also made for a curious aesthetic too and the lens covers gave the vehicle a sleepy, mournful appearance as it crunched up the icy driveway. A small black triangular pennant on the front fender bore two silver lightning bolts and swayed stiffly in the frigid breeze as the car rolled up outside the house.

Meanwhile, *Adler* closed the car's sturdy door firmly and walked round to the driver's side. His Maybach sported a red pennant with black trim and infamously mis-applied ancient symbol of divinity and auspiciousness. *Adler* had been nervous before. Every time he had started up Ferdinand Porsche's supercharged V16 engine in the back of the Auto Union, a little bit of wee came out. Not enough to cause embarrassment but just enough to remind him that he was mortal. Thankfully his bladder was empty that morning, but the nerves were still there. He was driving the boss today. The Chief of the Reich Security Main Office. The man that made Manfred Reinhardt nervous.

The Maybach engine had been kept idling while he waited for the aircraft's arrival. He didn't want to risk a non-starter in the frozen morning air. His career prospects would likely be immediately curtailed. The five-speed DSG35 manual transmission was smooth and fluid, even in extreme cold, and *Adler* pulled away from the sports field effortlessly.

The streamlined Spohn body appeared to continue seamlessly into the interior. His passenger was resolutely silent but seemed impressed by the luxurious finish and clean layout. Just three beautiful chrome-ringed instruments adorned the dashboard, though the central one contained gauges for oil fuel and temperature, as well as a small clock. Leather door panels, gleaming painted surfaces and luxurious wood inlays all melded together into a single harmonious entity. Perhaps the larger 4.2lite version with Telefunken radio might have seemed too cluttered. In any event, *Adler* kept such considerations to himself as he swept off the field and onto the road.

It was a short drive to Wannsee House. No.58. Just eight minutes. It didn't matter that his passenger was the last one to arrive. That's exactly how he had planned it. *Adler* directed the car anti-clockwise around the oval turning circle in front of the house and rolled smoothly to a halt. At once, a uniformed junior officer stepped forward to open the door. *Adler's* passenger returned the salute but not the greeting, there would be a lot more of that later before the day was through and his seniority meant that he could get away with it.

Adler waited until his passenger was inside Wannsee House before rolling the Maybach around the other half of the circle and veering off towards the gardens to the south to join the other chauffeurs. There was a side road that ran down to the Greater Wannsee inlet. Cars were parked all along it. Most of the drivers were huddled around a brazier, keeping themselves warm. *Adler* pulled up and slowly drove down the line, observing the pennants displayed before reversing the Maybach alongside a Mercedes-Benz Type 320 with the four-seat, four-door Cabriolet D body style. Even amongst the chauffeurs, a certain sense of hierarchy needed to be preserved.

It was the winter of 1942 and Hitler's armies were freezing and starving in the snows of Russia. America had now entered the war, though judging by the success of U-123 in New York harbour, were more concerned with looking across the Pacific. For the first time, Hitler's dream of a German Empire to last a thousand years appeared to be in doubt. While he hired and fired Generals and the winter was growing colder, fifteen of his officials were ordered from their commands and ministries to meet at the quiet lake side residence in Berlin, far from the crisis developing on the Eastern Front. *Adler* considered the ramifications of this as he drew the fabric roof over the Maybach's interior to keep falling snow off the leather seats and thick wool carpets.

The other drivers were reluctant to approach him. This was understandable. They had just watched him deliver the boss to the conference.

SS-Obergruppenführer Reinhard Heydrich was a man to be feared and anyone associated with him tended to carry that same aura. Taking out a tin, he looked at the scene painted on the lid of a typical Turkish street. Carrying it over to them, he opened the lid and offered it around to his fellow drivers. Sulima cigarettes manufactured from Turkish tobacco in Dresden. The tin dated back to 1910 and could hold 100 cigarettes, so he kept restocking it whenever he could. It was a useful ice breaker.

They seemed reluctant at first, then graciously accepted, thinking it might be wise to acknowledge the gesture of hospitality from Heydrich's chauffeur. Finally, *Adler* took one himself, leaving the tin open on the roof of the nearest car to indicate that the men could help themselves, before preparing to light up. Like a pretty woman in a strange bar, three or four lighters came to his service at once. He picked one at random, noting which one so he could impartially choose another later on if the same service was offered, and took the first pull.

"How long do you think they will be?" he asked of the group.

"Three hours? Four?" one suggested.

"All day, I reckon." Postulated another. "They wouldn't drive out here for a five minute chat."

"Annual skat tournament?" *Adler* joked.

Skat was a popular three-player trick-taking card game of the Ace-Ten family. Devised around 1810 in the Duchy of Saxe-Gotha-Altenburg, it was still popular all over Germany. He had seen it played but had no real clue what it was all about. There was a subdued ripple of laughter at the knowing absurdity of his suggestion.

He enjoyed the cigarette, listened to the conversation, looked around him. Then, quietly withdrawing, he took a wander to the water's edge to stretch his legs. Once he was out of sight, he took out his mechanical pencil, a beautifully decorated rice paper napkin and began to write. Rice paper napkins were ideal. They came in boxes of twelve or fourteen, were wonderfully decorative and practical and then, after the transmission was made, they were easier to digest. Admiring the view, he began to list the attendees, the ones he knew by their regular chauffeurs.

Heydrich, Eichmann, Klopfer, Kritzinger, Freisler, Leibbrandt. And so it went on.

IN THE DEN OF WOLVES

CHAPTER SIXTY
ENGLAND, 1942

Nighttime was often the best time for transmission. Shortwave radio signals travelled further at night, bouncing off charged particles in the ionosphere and beyond the horizon. Station X received the transmission via the Y Stations as *Adler* was tapping it out. He had a delicate touch on the Morse key. Almost musical. Betty placed the transcript in the appropriate hut's work-tray in the Block E office where it would stay until morning. Then she returned to her billet in Hut 27. The nightshift always stayed on base.

Doris cycled in from Fenny Stratford where she had a room in the old Lock Keeper's cottage. Her journey was approximately two miles. The Grand Junction canal from London to Braunston was opened in 1805 and brought with it an economical means of transporting goods and material. As such, several wharves were constructed adjacent to Watling Street and Simpson Road. When the railway line arrived in the 1830s, the Bletchley-Bedford line provided a rail link with the London-Midland route and served as a junction for Oxford and Cambridge.

Doris used this train when she had leave to visit her parents back home in Grantchester, just outside the university city where she had graduated with a First Class Honours degree in Mathematics. She had always been good at puzzles. Each morning in Hut 3 she was presented with a new one. Configuring the enigma in accordance with the settings provided. *Adler* was using a Navy Cipher D. Doris then began to decode the messages. The Polish Biuro Szyfrów had passed the encryption machine onto *Adler* after it was taken during the Spanish Civil War, and he had been using it ever since.

Once the message was decoded, she would place the decrypted message in the out-tray and work on the next one, changing the settings or even the type of machine if necessary. Hilda or Marjorie would then pick up the messages and take them back to Block E for Maisie to transmit out.

Wireless Set No.10 at 64 Baker Street, London would then receive the message from Bletchley, which would be written out again and sent up to Harrington's desk. That morning, beneath the understated heading 'Most Urgent', she learned of the Wannsee Conference, though knew nothing of the details of the meeting itself, only the list of attendees. She frowned, wondering what the implication of such a high-profile gathering was. It was imperative to have Heydrich's movements monitored however and her boss would need to see this for the Anthropoid operation. SOE trained agents from Czechoslovakia's army-in-exile had already been dropped in less than a month beforehand and were still preparing to carry out Heydrich's assassination.

"Are you sure?" he asked her, reading the message.

"Quite sure." Harrington affirmed. "Our man drove him there himself."

"Why Klopfer and not Bormann? Or Heydrich and not Himmler?"

"Plausible deniability. Whatever was decided upon is likely to have been authorised at the very highest level, but by having deputies attend the meeting it provides an elegant cut-out if things turn out badly. Scapegoats."

"Like sending you in to tackle Broadway?" he remarked slyly. The SOE at Baker Street and SIS on Broadway had an uneasy relationship with each other.

"Precisely, sir."

"Still, I wouldn't consider Heydrich a 'cut-out' by any means." Came the shrewd observation. "Has your man ever been wrong?"

"Not so far." She replied patiently. It was always the same line of questioning. "If you remember, he warned us about the Channel Islands. His intelligence helped the RAF in the Battle of Britain. We know how many POWs the Germans have and where they're interned."

She could go on. She often did.

"Even so, its highly irregular."

"This whole war is highly irregular, sir. I wasn't aware it was supposed to follow a prescribed set of regulations."

"Don't be clever, Iris."

"Being clever is precisely what you pay me for, sir."

He looked up at her and frowned. He knew she was right. Her man had never been wrong yet either. "Alright. Carry on."

CHAPTER SIXTY-ONE
GERMANY, 1942

SS-Hauptsturmführer Manfred Reinhardt had a brother, Johannes. Most people called him Hans. When Heinrich Himmler was named Chief of German Police in 1936, after a decree to unify the police duties within the Reich, this subordinated the police services to the SS. The uniformed law enforcement agencies were thus amalgamated into the new Ordnungspolizei, the Orpo, whose main office was subsequently populated by SS officers.

The Orpo were most often referred to simply as the Grüne Polizei owing to their green uniforms. Apart from the uniformed division there was also a plain-clothed section called the Sicherheitspolizei or Security Police. This was further subdivided into the infamous secret police, the Gestapo, and the Kriminalpolizei, the Kripo.

The Kripo was a corps of professional detectives involved in actually fighting crime, not that there was much of that to do, or at least nothing that fell into the jurisdiction of merely being 'criminal'. More and more acts of basic criminality were being seen as wider subversions of the state, and as such were more often than not assigned to the offices of the Gestapo or even directly to the SS. Despite his brother's disdain for the service, Hans Reinhardt much preferred working for the Kripo. Growing up he had wanted nothing more than to be a policeman. His brother thought he was too soft, lacked ambition and was trying to abdicate his responsibilities as a true German citizen.

Conversely, Hans saw his brother as a devious, amoral, egocentric, with a disturbing lack of empathy, though he had the good sense to keep such observations to himself. It made Manfred a perfect candidate for the SS but was not the way either of the brothers had been brought up.

Their father had served in the trenches of the last war and returned a broken man from the collision of Empires on the eastern front. Like the great battles of the Napoleonic War, Eastern Prussia saw the clash of Austro-Hungarian, German and Russian Imperial armies in a bitter struggle from the Baltic to the Black Sea. Nevertheless, Friedrich and his wife Greta had raised the two boys to be kind and tolerant.

Hans could see the wisdom in that outlook on life, but Manfred saw it as the reason why Germany was crushed under the moral weight of responsibility and reparations, bearing the blame for an entire Continent's involvement in the struggle. While the division of accountability might not have been even-handed, Hans saw no benefits in the persecution of ideological opponents of the Nazi regime. In his mind, this would only serve to exacerbate any feeling of hatred and outrage among subjugated groups and repeat the mistakes made after the last war. Only this time, it would be of Germany's own making.

Hence the reason why Hans took every opportunity to distance himself from the arrests of so-called 'asocial' elements of society by burying himself in the homicide division. He could do nothing about the incarceration of ordinary criminals in concentration camps alongside Jews, gypsies and Jehovah's Witnesses, as well as anyone else seen as racially and biologically inferior. That was the decision of the wider judiciary.

It was the Nazi view that criminality was hereditary and needed to be eliminated from the German racial community. Hans saw crime as crime, and it needed to be policed either way. Though he was very well aware that some of the worst criminals in German society wore unform and held high office, there was little he could do about that. He would just do what needed to be done to solve the crimes that came across his desk.

The case of three dead officers that may have attended a recent conference in West Berlin was just one such case. The death of one might have been unfortunate, two coincidental, but three within the space of a week was clearly not right at all. Something untoward was going on. All three were NSKK officers who had been assigned chauffeuring responsibilities. It had taken Hans a great deal of effort even to secure that much information. He had reluctantly asked for his brother's assistance but could get no further than a list of the other drivers who were on duty that day. There was no record of any conference having taken place and no one had any such knowledge of it.

Having to investigate a possible homicide in the increasingly cloak and dagger existence of the Third Reich was an incredibly challenging assignment. Hans wondered how far he might get this time. It wouldn't be the first time one of his criminal investigations was closed down or taken over by the Gestapo. Hans noted that a couple of the chauffeurs were relatively new, so had decided to start his enquiry there. Perhaps they might remember something, or at least be able to help him understand why three of their colleagues now lay dead in a Berlin mortuary.

"Thank you for seeing me." He said to the SS officer behind the desk, as he was shown into his small office.

"Not at all, Kriminalkommissar." *Adler* smiled. "Whatever we can do to help."

Hans doubted the sentiment. The only thing that was universally consistent about the SS was their perpetual ability to obstruct everything he did in every conceivable way.

"Your name is Andrew Sutherland, am I correct?"

"Yes, that's right." He said, quietly impressed that Hans had mastered the English 'th' sound. Most struggled with the concept and referred to him as Sudentland, not to be confused with the annexed region of Czechoslovakia that nearly precipitated an early entry into the war.

"Not German then?"

"Scottish. So, our dislike for the English is perhaps mutual." He smiled.

Hans returned the smile weakly as he took the seat offered him.

"You recently drove to Wannsee, is that correct?"

"Did I?"

"So I believe."

"I can't recall."

"You were assigned a Maybach?"

"Oh yes, quite possibly. I'm assigned as a reserve driver from time to time."

"You were a reserve on this occasion too?"

"I'm not sure, I don't quite follow."

"Three junior officers have recently died within a few days of each other." Hans explained. "The only thing they had in common was that they were drivers for the NSKK and were on duty on the 20th of January."

"I see." *Adler* frowned. "How odd."

"In what way?"

"Just that three drivers should die." He remarked. "And officers too. Suggests they were driving someone senior. Senior types usually prefer officers. The carpool is mostly filled with NCOs."

"Is that a problem?"

"It can be." *Adler* replied with a long-suffering sigh. "Most of the NCOs are ancient. Younger men tend to have better reactions, more road sense, but are more ambitious and so get promotions quicker. This leaves me with a raft of older men. When driving in the winter, a patch of ice, a sudden snow drift, it's important to know how to handle it. I'm forever sorting out repairs because some old duffer couldn't react quickly enough to avoid an accident."

"You're a young man." Hans observed.

"Ah yes, but only a very junior officer. I may not like the English, but I'm not properly in the fold yet." He gave a knowing wink. "Wrong colour eyes."

"Any Jewish ancestry?"

"On the Isle of Skye?" he laughed. "Too bloody cold up there for that lot."

He winced inwardly, hating to put on the pretence of antisemitism. It was one thing to dislike the English, that was the birth right of every Scot, but he never considered them to be an inferior species of human. Without the English who would they have the pleasure of stomping all over at Murrayfield in the Calcutta Cup match? The connotations of antisemitic terminologies went much further than expressing just a dislike for a fellow human but considered their very existence on earth as an absolute abomination. *Adler* could never subscribe to that view and cringed whenever he heard those that did.

"Yes, I see." Hans remarked calmly. *Adler* discerned that the Kriminalkommissar appeared to be a man who also did not advocate the established opinion. "Were you there?"

"Where?"

"Wannsee."

"As I say, I can't recall."

"Isn't there some logbook?"

"One for each car, yes." He nodded. "Would you like me to have a look?"

"Could you?"

"Of course." *Adler* smiled pleasantly as he moved to the bookcase and pulled out the logbook for the Maybach. He already knew what it said for the entry of the 20th of January. He had been told what to write for all of the cars assigned that day, but it was a show of being cooperative. "Here we go." He withdrew the logbook and turned to the appropriate page. "Tuesday 20th of January. Assigned to me. Destination, West Berlin."

He showed Hans the page.

"Could that be Wannsee?"

"I think I might have remembered." *Adler* shrugged. "Sometimes a designation like that means there is more than one destination involved." He pointed to other similar references. "You see here and here."

"Yes, I see." Hans nodded. "Do you often drive out?"

"I'm always taking cars out here and there." *Adler* nodded, returning the logbook to the cabinet.

"So, no trips are particularly memorable?"

"They all blend into one another after a while." He smiled, returning to his chair. "As I say, someone like me is unlikely to get the top gig though. That would most likely go to someone of the faith."

"And what would that be?"

"Lutheran? Whatever you Germans are." He chuckled. "The Rector beat my love of religion out of me at school."

Hans smiled at that. "A godless Scot."

"Some would say we always have been."

Hans nodded and pondered for a moment. *Adler* let him have this time. No rush to get him out of the office. Any comment to that effect often only roused undue suspicion anyway. He didn't have a particularly busy morning and he suspected Hans knew that too, so it wasn't as if he could shuffle him out to get some pressing work done. He was very junior after all.

"I'm investigating a possible murder." He said quietly, looking intently into *Adler's* eyes.

"These three officers?"

Hans nodded.

"I see." It was *Adler's* turn to ponder. "Do you have their names? I could try and find out what car's they were assigned."

"Why might that be useful?"

"Perhaps those logbooks will help you find out where they went?"

"West Berlin, I suspect." Hans said meaningfully. The pair held each other's gaze for a long minute. Finally, Hans broke it and scribbled the names down on a page of his notebook, ripped it out and handed it to him. "You can reach me at the Red Castle." He said, referring to the impressive Police Headquarters Building on Alexanderplatz. "If you think of something, do let me know."

"Of course." *Adler* smiled, taking the paper as Hans stood up.

"It is still important to investigate these things you know." Hans added. "Regardless of what times we live in, murder is murder. If we stop thinking like that, then we're no better than the Nazis are we? I do hope you understand."

Not waiting for a response, Hans showed himself out. *Adler* watched him leave. A frown etched upon his face as he contemplated Hans' parting words.

CHAPTER SIXTY-TWO
FRANCE, 2018

Nothing could be clearer now. The typographical error in the transport request had been an obvious message to anyone looking for it. The car had headed east. In many ways it made sense. Even in those early years of the war, Berlin was still preparing for aerial attack. An air raid shelter had been constructed near the Reich Chancellery as early as 1936. What better way to protect such a valuable car than to have it installed in its own underground bunker? Even more so if it was disguised as the Ark of the Covenant.

The beautiful Rococo structure at No.77 Wilhelmstrasse had originally been built by Prussian King Frederick William I for his esteemed Lt Gen Count Adolph Friedrich von Schulenberg. Later the palace became the home of Polish Prince Antoni Radziwiłł, during which time he hosted the likes of Paganini, Chopin and Beethoven. Following the reorganisation of the North German Confederation and its reunification with South German States, the palace was sold by the feuding Radziwiłł heirs to the German Reich and became the Chancellery of Otto von Bismarck.

The last resident of the palace though felt that the grand building was not suitable as the headquarters for the Greater German Reich, so appointed his favourite architect, Albert Speer, to build a new, far larger structure with which to impress visiting diplomatic delegations, government officials and the people of the Reich. Organisation Todt meanwhile had contracted Hochtief to complete the first phase of a subterranean bunker complex behind the existing Reich Chancellery.

The remnants of all these structures had been completely obliterated by the Soviets after the city fell. Very likely anything of any value down there would have long been destroyed too. Unlike the submarine pen, Berlin's Den of Wolves had been systematically demolished in order to completely expunge the Nazi scourge from the city. After the atrocities meted out upon the Soviets during the invasion, who would blame them?

Hitler's plans for Moscow had been to level the city and turn it into a vast ornamental lake. In the centre an imposing statue of himself would have been erected on a plinth of red granite. That was to say nothing of the people themselves. Estimates placed the Russian death toll somewhere around thirty million. Had Hitler's plans succeeded, there would have been an even greater extermination of the peoples he had labelled subhuman. It was not surprising that total destruction of any Third Reich edifice was paramount on the minds of the eventual victors.

At the halfway point between Bordeaux and Berlin, Strasbourg was a journey of nearly ten hours away by car, right across the width of France. It would take longer than driving up from his Cornish cabin to Glasgow. Hamilton couldn't think of anything worse. The French countryside was pleasant in its own way but unremittingly boring for a driver. A similar journey would take five-and-a-half hours by train but would leave him with no transport at the other end.

He had a thought. Though he didn't know how it would play out, it was worth pursuing, so there was nothing else for it but to make the journey. The archives of Don Pietro Borromeo were extensive and very detailed but were still only copies of original documents where they had been made available to him or his father. Might there be something in the original records that he could consult?

There was evidence of the Bugatti family everywhere in the towns of Molsheim and neighbouring Dorlisheim to the south, with much of the estate and production facilities actually nearer the latter. Starting at the small, quirky little villa named Hostellerie du Pur Sang, the Thoroughbred Hostel, it had been used by Ettore in the 1920s as a private guesthouse to receive his friends and prestigious clients. The likes of Louis Chiron, Robert Benoist and Hellé Nice had been amongst the prestigious guestlist.

Moving further down the road was the Bugatti factory itself where road and race cars were designed, machined, and painstakingly assembled right up until 1956. The 1920s façade facing the road had been the assembly hall of Bugatti

Rail Cars which had been powered by the vast, 12.7litre straight-eight Royale engines. Now the whole complex of buildings had been taken over and expanded by Safran, specialising in the manufacture of landing and braking systems for aircraft.

On Rue des Peupliers, sitting opposite a carpark with a modern electricity pylon, was the once luxuriously decorated three-storey villa where the Patron himself had lived with his family. The buildings housed a works council, training centre and union premises for the new owners now, but before the war it had been the predecessor of the now hallowed grounds of Maranello. Looking around the site in its present state, it was difficult to think of the glamour and prestige entailed in a visit to the Bugatti premises back then, seeing it surrounded by depressingly ugly industrial units, car parks and a dual carriageway.

Back then it would have been surrounded by sprawling meadows that stretched between the two towns, picturesque woodlands and the meandering stream of the Bras de la Bruche. The quiet little workshop would have merrily supplied you with a grand limousine, a sporty cabriolet or even a prized race car, just so long as you came with the right kudos and the required amount of cash.

In the raised basement of the villa there had been a projection room, an early home cinema, while a large winter garden had been built on the elevated ground floor to the left, enjoying what would have been typical Alsatian pastoral scenes stretching to the eastern fringes of sleepy Dorlisheim. The Villa façade still wore the same pale ochre rendering and muted terracotta shutters typical of the region. Though still a sizeable building, it was a restrained and tasteful structure.

Looking at the complex from the outside, peering through the gates into the yard, Hamilton could imagine staff working away on early Type 13s in the shop to the right of the gates, the Hardtmühle, the original factory of 1909. Further up were the old foundry, garages, and the stables for Ettore's thoroughbred horses. He could imagine the smell of wood shavings, hot metal and rubber mingling with the sounds of hammers, hooves and saws. Castings being poured into moulds right next to where shoes were being shaped on anvils. The sawdust from body bucks being swept up along with the straw of the stables. Two different worlds melding together. A veritable grotto of activity.

The pavilion at the back of the yard had been the artist studio for Ettore's troubled brother, Rembrandt. There would have been private gardens and a dovecote, now paved over with later factory buildings encroaching.

In those heady interwar years, even the great manufacturers had started in small garages and yards just like this. The Grand Prix garagistas of the 60s and 70s, so despised by the established marques for their plucky spirit and overwhelming achievements, were merely continuing the practices initiated by the great manufacturers themselves decades before. Lionel Aston with his Coal Scuttle roadster, Ettore Bugatti and the Type 10 prototype, even Enzo Ferrari with the Tipo 815.

While some of these pioneering works exhibited a clunky, clumsy appearance which might not have suggested the same level of skill and prowess as the great masterpieces within the sacred walls of the Louvre, the craftsmanship, ingenuity and bravado of the artists themselves was no less compelling than the characters of Leonardo, Caliari or Botticelli.

Peeling beneath the skin of these early creations, the competence of the sculptor who produced the exquisite forms of Venus of Arles could be paralleled in the joining of polished brass to coiled copper, painted cast-iron and brushed aluminium. The attention to detail in the linkages, hinges and framework, in a world where such things had to be machined from scratch, not bought off the shelf, involved a deep knowledge of metallurgy, geometry and art. The finished gears, flush rivets, polished metal and oiled wood, showed the same care and attention to detail that held visitors, historians and curators in raptures before a broad canvas of Caravaggio's intricate Venetian scenes.

Arguably the most prestigious and magnificent structure of the entire Bugatti estate though was Château St Jean further south. This elegant neoclassical mansion had been built in 1857 by the Wangen-Geroldseck family on the site of a former 13th century Commandery of the Order of Knights of the Hospital of St John of Jerusalem. Descended from the Prince-Bishop of Basel, the family eventually sold the house and its deer park before the Great War. In 1928 Ettore Bugatti bought the estate from the Seltzer family with minimal heartburn. The château then became the reception venue for his clients to present them with new models and showcase the very latest in luxury cars.

Approaching from Rue Saint Jean, Hamilton rolled his borrowed car through ancient Roman stonework, forming part of the ruins of the mediaeval grange of the Knights Hospitaller. The ironwork of the gates themselves was shaped, purely coincidently, into the elemental curve at the top of the famous Bugatti trademark grille. The ruined archway was overgrown with ivy, yet its foliage dared not encroach on the niche for the statue of Saint Jean-Baptiste. A gravel driveway curved between beautifully manicured lawns towards the château's grand staircase.

Having dropped his hire car back at the airport, Hamilton had made a few calls, rekindled a few old friendships, called in a favour, and was thus rolling up the Château driveway in a two-tone blue Bugatti Chiron. It was possible to hire one for the day, but at €20,000 was considerably more than his usual operating expenses. A few bottles of Bordeaux and some choice chocolates was by far the cheaper alternative.

Expectantly awaiting his arrival was the custodian of the Bugatti estate, Pierre Legrand, immaculately dressed in pin-striped suite, polka dot tie and effortlessly tousled silver-grey hair. A sliver of a crisp white handkerchief appeared in the breast pocket, an expensive watch on one wrist and a surprising selection of beaded bracelets on the other. Not quite what Hamilton was expecting.

He had wondered on the drive over whether his choice of attire would be suitable. The alternative was to turn up in ripped jeans and a £5 t-shirt. Grunge chic seemed to be the new uniform of the ultra-wealthy. Hamilton though was never one to be shabbily dressed. Instead, he went for an open-necked white shirt and chinos, making sure they were smartly pressed before setting off. A safe choice, though ironing with his left hand had been rather more of a laborious exercise than he had hoped.

"Bonjour, Monsieur Hamilton." Legrand began.

"Bonjour, Monsieur Legrand." He replied, accepting the hand offered to him and feeling immediately inferior at the level of timepieces already. A magnificent Ulysse Nardin Diver Chronograph on the right wrist of his host. At first glance, the stained MoD strap on Hamilton's Omega gave the impression of a markedly inferior timepiece. The nylon strap was a little less than aesthetically optimum. Perhaps this would have been the place to wear it with the 1039-516 metal bracelet it had been issued with for dress wear.

"Thank you for agreeing to meet me." he continued, consciously trying to restrain his overtly Scottish tones.

"Not at all. Good of you to call us." He half-turned to the house and gestured to the sweeping stone staircase, converging towards a welcoming entrance in suitably regal fashion.

"I believe Signor Borromeo has been in contact."

"Ah, Don Pietro!" He smiled, evidently they were well acquainted. "Yes, just this morning in fact. He says you may have an interesting development in the quest for our Lost Bugatti."

"Possibly. I'm hoping you can help."

"With pleasure."

Stepping into an oval entrance hall, the grandeur of the interior space reflected the exclusivity of the marque. Two graceful staircases swept around the side of the atrium to a first floor landing, supported by two Ionic columns which framed the rear of the hallway that led through to an expansive back lawn and woodland beyond.

Subtle pastel shades of blue accentuated the mouldings, giving the space an elegant, yet restrained feel. There was almost a Wedgwood quality in the way the ornate plasterwork emerged from the walls. Château Saint Jean exuded a tasteful, timeless refinement from an age long before the gaudy display of dripping gold and acres of marble became the raison d'etre for the painfully affluent clientele that ordinarily graced the floors of Bugatti.

A gentle, floral perfume wafted through the rooms. A delicate fragrance which would have been as equally at home on either man or woman. Rich and rosy, with fruity top notes and a slight musk undertone, neither overtly feminine nor noticeably masculine. It exuded the serenity and refinement of the place with a welcoming, pleasing aroma.

Legrand led them into a sitting room where coffee and pastries had been laid out for them. To his surprise, this was not a typically Louisian château with elaborate furniture and fussy ormolu. There was restraint and subtlety even in the silk wallpaper and drapes. It was a house that bore its prestige with quiet dignity and inoffensive grandeur.

A white-coated orderly immediately plated up a selection of delicate pastries with silver tongs onto gilt-edged white porcelain with the famous red Bugatti macaron finely painted on the rim. A second orderly prepared coffee, setting the cups on saucers alongside the pastries, a jug of cream and a bowl of sugar on a butler's tray table.

Seamlessly dropping down the folding table legs as they approached, each orderly presented the individual trays on one side of each of the fine French bergère's near the window. Legrand nodded silently and the orderlies melted into the building like ethereal phantoms.

"This is a Tanzanian peaberry." Legrand explained, using the silver tongs to drop in a cube of demerara.

"Ah, from the slopes of Mount Kilimanjaro?"

"Indeed." Legrand smiled, evidently surprised that Hamilton would know that, but discreet enough not to let it show.

The Arabica beans were medium roasted and gave a complex floral aroma with hints of citrus and coconut. Hamilton could detect an almost winey hint as he poured the steaming coffee from the pot into the cup. The flavour was delicate and velvety but not as rich and deep as Tanzanian beans were known for. He was expecting a fuller, almost chocolatey quality, fading to a sweet finish. It was very good, but he was oddly disappointed. So much for not being a coffee snob, he thought.

"Is this your first time to Molsheim?" Legrand asked.

An excellent question. It would immediately decipher whether Hamilton was indeed a genuine Bugatti man, or merely someone with wealthy friends and a collection of cars.

"Aye, it is." He admitted.

There was no point hiding it. He suspected that Legrand already knew. Likely the only reason he had managed to sweep through the gates in the first place was because of Don Borromeo's reputation and persuasive personality. Legrand smiled knowingly. Hamilton felt like a peasant but was not to be intimidated. He just needed to play things well.

"I have recently stumbled upon some information that might shed some more light as to the possibility of La Voiture Noire." Hamilton began. "The original one of course." He smiled. He was well aware that Bugatti were creating a one-off tribute to the Lost Bugatti at their new factory, the Atelier, just beyond the château's southern lawns. "Hopefully there may be something in the Bugatti Library that could substantiate that, or perhaps provide some additional context to the car."

"Perhaps." Legrand nodded, sipping the coffee delicately. "What is your interest in finding the car?"

Another probing question. The hunt for La Voiture Noire had long held the promise of significant rewards. Some claimed that even in barn find condition, the Lost Bugatti would be worth a fortune. Whether that fortune was in dollars, sterling or Euros, the currency was almost immaterial, the incredible prominence that attached itself to such a discovery had often been enough of an incentive for some treasure hunters of the past: 'I was the one that found the most expensive car in the world'. Reputation sealed.

One or two had even written to Bugatti suggesting some reward, or finder's fee might be appropriate, and perhaps a suitable advance. Bugatti's refusal to offer such had always been politely robust. In the world of classic and vintage automobiles, the last resting place of La Voiture Noire had almost become the equivalent of a Grail quest. Many had tried. All had failed.

"As you will know, the car was used by Messrs. Benoist and Grover-Williams shortly before and in the early stages of the war. Both of these gentlemen were agents of the Special Operations Executive and both appeared to know the identity of a fellow spy deep within the Third Reich."

Legrand leaned forward intrigued and perhaps slightly amused. This was a new angle, but he would patiently indulge the gentleman before him, then offer him his profound regrets and apologies, best wishes in his quest, and show him the door, et cetera, et cetera.

"This spy was himself in possession of another, shall we say, automotive specialty?"

Hamilton reached into his back pocket and offered Legrand one of Spinola's reproduction photographs. Legrand took it carefully, holding it in the tips of the fingers of both hands and frowned slightly as he examined the monochrome image.

"Is this an early Audi?" Legrand asked, noticing the four miniature rings on the chrome grille.

Hamilton smiled. It was his moment to express a slight superiority in knowledge.

"It's a Horch." He said, trying not to sound too imperious. "Auto Union's luxury brand." He added with a conciliatory tone. "It was specially commissioned for their championship winning racing driver Bernd Rosemeyer. That's him in the photograph."

Legrand seemed suitably impressed and returned the photograph, leaning back indulgently.

"The car was bequeathed to a teammate by the name of Andrew Sutherland. After Rosemeyer's death in 1938, Sutherland took ownership of the car and continued to use it. Now, the prevailing view among the automotive world is that, like La Voiture Noire, this car, *Manuela*, has also been lost to the war."

At this juncture, Hamilton tapped the laptop bag he had brought with him.

"However, I have very recently discovered a covering letter from a transport request to the commandant of the Naval base in Bordeaux in 1941. In the letter Sutherland requests his help to transfer a box over to the Middle East. The train stops at Strasbourg en route."

"We have it as a matter of record that no such delivery of any cars was ever made to the Bordeaux factory..."

"I know." Hamilton cut in before the official dismissal. "Monsieur Marco's delivery records. That's because the box was never intended to carry any vehicle of any kind to Bordeaux." Hamilton nodded, silencing Legrand again. "I believe it was a cover story. The box was supposed to be used to retrieve an artefact uncovered by archaeologists in Syria. That box, travelling west from Berlin, would have passed right through Strasbourg with the train.

No doubt the Bugatti Library has the original despatch documents describing "Materiel Automobile" being transferred from here to Bordeaux, to be loaded on at Strasbourg. Perhaps the car was even crated up, but I believe it never went on any train heading west and your records may perhaps confirm that. In fact, this letter suggests that it may have boarded a different train heading in the opposite direction."

"Heading east?"

"Aye." Hamilton nodded, watching Legrand's expression change. "Possibly to Berlin. I have a theory that the car was supposedly hidden away until after the war. With nations' economies in ruins, a rare and specialist car might have been seen as an investment. Especially given the penchant for wealthy Americans to ship exotic European cars back home, even before the war. If there is nothing that corroborates that possibility in the Bugatti Library, then I can only apologise for having wasted your time, but if there is something, it may help us identify where your car could be, or at least the next step in finding it before whoever is killing people finds it first."

"Killing people?" Legrand blanched, almost offended. "Who is killing people?"

"Have you heard of the Auto Club?"

Legrand's expression told him that he had. "A group of classic car enthusiasts searching for lost cars. Yes, I have heard of them for some time now. I'm afraid it is disillusionment to a most profound degree if they expect to find her. If La Voiture Noire were indeed one of the cars this Club is searching for, then it would have been found long ago and we would certainly have heard about it, Monsieur. They are experts in their field."

Legrand smiled patiently, not wishing to formally dismiss his guest, but evidently the implication was there.

"The Auto Club were looking for three cars. Your Lost Bugatti, Rosemeyer's Horch and the lesser well known Duesenberg believed to have once belonged to Hellé Nice. Now, did you hear about the murder in Mulhouse earlier this year?"

"I did." He frowned. "Not far away from here. Very disturbing."

"The victim at Mulhouse was a particular expert on Bugatti. This came after an identical killing in Los Angeles at the Petersen Museum last year," Hamilton persisted. "Bob Jefferson had a particular penchant for Duesenberg. Then just a few weeks ago, a third killing occurred at the Horch Museum in Zwickau."

"That's awful!" Legrand remarked, clearly unaware of the other cases.

"Aye, it is." Hamilton nodded, preparing himself to deliver what might be the clincher. The coup de grâce. "The third victim had been studying the replica of this Horch in Zwickau. It was on loan from Audi and was made as a recreation of *Manuela*. These three gentlemen were the members of this Auto Club, the research group trying to find these three cars. Would that seem significant to you?"

"It would indeed." Legrand acknowledged, sitting back and grasping the arms of the chair. The conversation had taken a different direction to the one he was expecting it to.

"My interest here is not so much in the cars themselves, but who is after them and why." Hamilton said calmly, taking the liberty to pour himself a second cup. "These three killings suggest that someone somewhere believes there is something very compelling about these cars that is worth killing for. I've been asked to find the cars first."

"To what end?"

"Essentially, monsieur, to prevent any more deaths. I don't have a financial interest here at all. My expenses are being paid for by third parties." Hamilton felt it better to leave out the request from the Secret Intelligence Service.

Legrand stayed silent for a moment, considering. Hamilton sat in silence and drank his coffee. There was nothing more to be said. Either he would help, or Hamilton would have to go about it the hard way. He suspected the security at the Château Saint Jean would be considerably more sophisticated than it had been in the secret bunker beneath Bordeaux that nobody even knew about.

"Please, help yourself to some pastries." Legrand murmured at last. "I cannot permit eating in the library, and we may be some time."

Hamilton nodded his thanks. He was in. Legrand placed his coffee cup onto the tray almost silently and discreetly left to make a call. From the sitting room, Hamilton heard the tone. It was neither panicked nor insistent. Legrand was calm and measured. Either he was a very cool customer or else he really was endeavouring to help the enquiry. Hamilton picked up the plate and tucked in. Only time would tell.

"I've just telephoned our senior librarian to come over." Legrand said as he came back into the sitting room. "We can explain to her the situation and see how she can help us."

"Thank you, Monsieur." Hamilton smiled. "I'm grateful for your indulgence.

I appreciate it must seem a wee bit fanciful."

"Not at all, not at all." He waved away, resuming his seat and concealing his previous misgivings. "With such precious objects, whether it's a painting, a beautiful sculpture, a piece of exquisite jewellery, there are often many enthralling stories that might seem too fantastic and implausible, but often the realities of life are more unbelievable than any work of fiction." He took up his own plate of pastries now, clearly more relaxed and cooperative. "In my time here with Bugatti, I have found that things are no different when it comes to cars."

CHAPTER SIXTY-THREE
GERMANY, 1942

Beyond whom they had been assigned to drive that day, the names meant nothing to *Adler*. He didn't know them, and they didn't know him. It didn't matter. They hadn't gone around the carpool and introduced themselves. They had just smoked and talked.

Smoked and talked.

For some reason though, Hans was taking this case seriously. He had gone to Wannsee and taken a look around. Access to the grounds had been forbidden. It was an SS guesthouse and even though the police were subordinate to the SS, it meant they could refuse access to anyone they wanted. Fairly typical.

There was a public side road though, that ran to the water's edge where some small boats were tied up and a jetty projected out into the Greater Wannsee. It was the closest he was able to get and even then, under close supervision by the stormtroopers at the side gate.

It was bitterly cold, and a thick fog hung over the place, billowing up like wool from the water. Still, Hans had been able to see a carpet of cigarette butts near the brazier. It was impossible to tell who they belonged to, but the labyrinth of tyre tracks preserved in the ice suggested the cars had all been parked along this stretch of road while the conference took place inside.

Hans had a theory. Picking all the cigarette butts off the ground, the ones that weren't frozen fast, he had brought them back to Berlin for testing. There were three dead men. The chances of finding all three butts the men had smoked was very slight, but traces of arsenic in one of them seemed to confirm his suspicion. The deaths of three officers was not an unfortunate coincidence. It was murder. Interviews with the remaining drivers confirmed that they had smoked and exchanged cigarettes all morning. Heydrich's driver had even handed out his tin of Sulima for them to help themselves.

Heydrich's driver was Andrew Sutherland, the driver of the only confirmed delegate at the conference, and even that slipped out accidentally. Hans had paid Sutherland another visit. He confirmed that he had offered around the cigarettes, even had a couple himself. They were in a Sulima tin but were mostly whatever he could find to restock on his travels. He bought them from numerous places. If it was one of his cigarettes that had been laced with arsenic then it could just as easily have been meant for him as for any of the others.

That was the troubling factor. Sutherland had been totally unaware that his cigarettes had been tampered with. Had it been done afterwards, or had he been sold a packet of poisoned cigarettes? It was impossible to know. Was someone after him, or were they intended for someone else? Was this an SOE trick? Three cigarettes out of the dozen or so that had been distributed? Perhaps there had been more than three.

Some of the drivers helped themselves later while he took a stroll. He even invited them to. Had they chanced upon all of the poisoned ones? Had one of the other drivers poisoned them? He was merely a junior officer. Not important enough to assassinate and rarely in a position to be close enough to someone of higher value. Who had known he would be driving Reinhard Heydrich that day? Who indeed? Hans was intrigued. Sutherland deduced that he was a good detective. Perhaps too good.

Sutherland was only too happy to surrender the remainder of his cigarettes for testing. It would mean he was no longer running the gauntlet should there be any more lurking in the tin. Hans would confirm what he found in due course. Sutherland needed some time away. Some fresh air. Clear his head. He was due some leave anyway.

He took the Horch up to the Baltic. It needed a good run out and he wanted to be by the sea to get some of that air in his lungs. Lübeck was a good a place as any. The city had a long and distinguished history, becoming the Queen of the Hanseatic League and by far the most powerful member of that commercial confederation. Even seeing it from a distance it was a majestic sight.

Ambling around the island centre, in the midst of the River Trave, the architecture of the Altstadt was wonderfully quaint. It was like stepping into the pages of fairy tales. Imposing Gothic brick walls and towers. Merchant's houses along the waterfront bore the same distinctive crow-stepped gables that had become so characteristic of Scotland, whether it be humble fisherman's cottages on the East Neuk of Fife or grand and imposing stone fortresses to keep out the English.

Low, timber-framed houses all clustered together in the Mary Magdalene Quarter could have been plucked from the pages of Arthurian legend, narrow lanes and courtyards running in between hostels and inns. The smell of leather and beer from the Jakobi quarter drew him eastwards, picking up a fresh packet of cigarettes along the way. He could be confident that these at least had not been tainted.

Churches and monasteries vied with markets and shops for the peoples' attention and gold. Everywhere he turned, Sutherland found himself enveloped by the rich history and charm of the place. It brought to mind the Shambles of York, the narrow backstreets of Edinburgh's Old Town, even some of the villages on the east coast, clustered around a natural harbour, quietly getting on with life.

Though dressed in an old M37 greatcoat, the pre-war issue with bottle green collar pulled up against a frigid wind whistling through the lanes, he felt as if he was a visitor from the future, stepping back centuries into a way of life that had long disappeared everywhere else. This was not to say the people were primitive. They were happy, friendly, hospitable, despite his uniform, not because of it. In fact, he wondered whether he might have even been greeted with more welcoming arms had he not been stomping about the cobbles in his hobnail jack boots.

After a beer and a smoke, it was time to head onto the beach. Leaving the confines of a real life Camelot behind him, Travemünde was a little over half an hour away, especially the way Sutherland drove. The Horch needed to stretch her legs sometimes and Fritz Fiedler's engine was desperate to exercise itself after the confines of Berlin. Cold air suited *Manuela* and her single Solex 35 carburettor gulped in as much as it could on the journey up.

Unusually there was no passenger accompanying him. No blue-eyed, blonde-haired Fraulein. This was a solo trip. Just as his war seemed to be a solo effort. Oflag X-C was nearby, housing captured French officers from the Battle of France and more recently, British and Commonwealth officers from the North African Campaign.

He knew the war was still going on. Britain hadn't given up since Dunkirk, but still, sitting in the Reich Security Main Office on Prinz-Albrecht Street while the Third Reich seemed to go from strength to strength, he felt very alone in his pursuit of victory.

The stalemate building in Russia was a shock. Whether it would be a temporary setback or a portent of things to come still remained to be seen. Certainly, the speed with which Leningrad and Moscow had been reached had surprised everyone.

The RAF had won the Battle of Britain and thus claimed daytime air superiority, yet the Blitz that followed during the night was devastating towns and cities up and down the country. He warned them what was about to happen. He had seen the build-up on the Atlantic coast. He hoped they had been given enough time to evacuate. Even then, the bombing campaign had failed to achieve its objective. Wartime industrial output was undiminished. The British Lion was wounded and cornered but fighting on.

With help from Polish emigrants, Commonwealth and Dominion forces, as well as the first signs of American involvement, things were slowly looking like they were getting somewhere. Sutherland was well aware that Germany still had much more in the tank. This was a war not just for military dominance, racial ideology and territorial gains, it was a war for the hearts and heads of the common people. There needed to be a victory of morale too. If anything, the Blitz had galvanised civilian morale. The opposite intended effect. Would the same thing happen here?

Parking up along the promenade, Sutherland considered this as he stepped out and drew the coat around him again. It was double-breasted but still he could feel the Baltic wind cut through him. Lifting the collar up again, there was a tab he could draw around to fasten it onto a button on the other side. Feeling like some Russian Field Marshal as the collar brushed against the lobes of his ears and sideburns, he walked down to the beach.

In summer Travemünde was a popular little seaside resort. In early spring, the white sands were still covered in a layer of frost. His boots crunched through it as he ambled down towards the surf. Grey waves splashed upon the sands with a rhythmic melody. Sandpipers scurried in the surf looking for molluscs washed up on the beach. A solitary gull glided above the breakers; wings outstretched over white foaming crests of waves as they rolled lazily in. Prints in the frozen sand tracked his path from the road where he had left *Manuela*.

The sky was a watery shade of blue grey, like the glossy sheen on an oyster's body. The sea looked dark and foreboding, stretching out into Mecklenburg Bay, unbroken by distant headland or rocks. Or battleships. The beach, a silent witness to perpetual times and seasons, could have been a thousand other beaches all over the world. It could have belonged to any place or time. As he continued to amble along the shoreline, past the driftwood and the washed-up, frozen seaweed, the beach belonged to this place in history, this moment in time.

March 1942.

The pack of ten Nordlands had cost him 8½ pfennigs. At that price he wasn't sure how long he would be able to afford to sustain his habit. Fortunately, he rarely got through a pack in a single day. Even so tobacco factories were beginning to close or retool for armaments manufacture. Supplies of Crimean tobacco would probably depend on how well things went on the Eastern Front. They were only likely going to get more expensive and possibly even rationed. Even the manufacture of cigarettes now involved forced labour. He wondered how many ordinary citizens were aware of that as they puffed away.

Looking out to sea he thought about his past, contemplated his future, breathed in the salty air of the present. This war needed to be over. That was obvious to everyone. So far he had been very careful, but this situation with tainted cigarettes could very easily bring everything down on top of him. Wherever they had come from, whoever had done it, risked throwing his life into chaos. He needed the investigation to stop, the war to end, and his life to return back to some sense of normality. The tension was beginning to get to him. The ruse with the Ark of the Covenant had been a stroke of genius and so far he had managed to get away with it, but he had ridden his luck and it would only hold out so far.

The frustration for Sutherland was that he could see a potential ally in Hans. He was no Nazi. A proud German of course, no one would begrudge him that. He despised his brother's role in the war effort as much as Sutherland did. He wondered what Hans would make of what *he* was doing. Would he see it as a means to end the Nazi regime, or to bring about the downfall of Germany? The two were now virtually inseparable.

Nevertheless, he might be more tolerant if he knew Sutherland's aim was to restore Europe to peace and prosperity, and only at the expense of a cruel and amoral regime. It was important to preserve the natural pride of a country and the dignity of its people. A country with a great deal of history, culture and much more to offer the world than twisted dogma. That was the mistake of the previous war.

Germanic tribes had always been fiercely autonomous. There was little need to explain why the border of the Roman Empire ended at the Rhine. In many ways this paralleled the independent spirit of ancient Pictish tribes in Scotland. The Caledonians, Hibernians and many others. There was a reason why the walls of Hadrian and Antonine had been built too.

Letting the smoke drift from his nostrils, swirling in the cloud of his breath, it reminded him of the snorting beasts of Bugatti. Not the Type 35s that had been so dominant during the 1920s, but the thoroughbreds that Ettore had stabled alongside his famous factory. Their glossy coats gleaming over muscle and sinew like the thin metallic skin of a race car. A powerful beating heart pumping a proud bloodline through vessels of victory.

He could almost see them now, printing their proud hooves into the receding sand. Galloping full flight across the surf, manes and tails flying. Shingle and spray churned up in their wake. The ground thundering beneath their power. Unsaddled. Unbridled.

Free.

Sutherland had never visited Molsheim but had heard about Ettore's magnificent stud. During his career he had raced his own prancing horse. The rampant stallion depicted on the side of his Alfa Romeo had been taken from the coat of arms of Count Francesco Baracca, Italy's top fighter ace of the Great War. Baracca had it painted on the side of his SPAD S.XIII single-engine biplane right up until his death in June 1918. The Count's family had suggested Enzo Ferrari apply the prancing horse on his team's cars for good luck.

Sutherland imagined the two thoroughbreds galloping away up the beach. Ettore Bugatti's Percheron, Enzo Ferrari's Murgese. Snorting great clouds of breath, sweat glistening upon their flanks as white sands bespattered their hooves. Which one would claim the laurels? Curious how man endeavoured to make the mechanical mirror the power of the natural, even using them as a unit of measurement.

Gazing around, Sutherland noted a distinct absence of gun emplacements. No flak cannons, no inshore guns, not even to defend the mouth of the river, the port that adorned its banks and the yards building U-boats. A significant oversight. An opportunity too. Gulls skimming across the waves could easily have been bombers, coming in low over the water.

Turning in towards land, following the course of the river as it meandered south. He pondered the prospect for a moment. It was a terrible thought. A monstrous idea. The barmaid at Buthmann's had been very obliging. He hoped she would have time to have that glass of Sekt he bought for her at the end of the day. It was time though for *Adler* to send out another message. On this occasion though, it was time that Germany received it. Loud and clear.

The city of Lübeck was easy to find. Especially two weeks later, on the night of the 28th of March. It was a clear night and a full moon. The waters of the Trave, the Elbe-Lübeck Canal, the Wakenitz and the Bay of Lübeck all reflecting crisp moonlight. It enabled three waves of bombers to navigate their way easily down the channel. Vickers Wellingtons led the first wave, dropping blockbuster bombs to open the brick and copper roofs of the old buildings below. Short Stirlings followed with incendiaries to set them ablaze. Just like mediaeval Coventry, Lübeck went up like a firelighter. The port and submarine yards were heavily damaged and in the flames of St Mary's Church, as the bells melted, the skeletons and holy men of Notke's Gothic tapestry danced a macabre death.

234 aircraft of RAF Bomber Command dropped some 400 tons of bombs and 25,000 incendiaries with the loss of twelve aircraft. Air Officer Commanding Arthur Harris claimed it was a moderate success. *Adler* felt it was a message to the very heart of Berlin. Britain was not done yet.

CHAPTER SIXTY-FOUR
FRANCE 2018

Seeing the original drawings for La Voiture Noire was an incredible privilege. Penned by the hand of Jean Bugatti himself. The clarity of his work, some eighty years afterwards, was still exquisite to behold. Even Hamilton could appreciate his attention to detail, the quality of the sketches, skill of the draughtsman.

Handling the drafting linen with white cotton gloves, Petra carefully withdrew them from their leather tubes and unfurled them onto the drawing board. The story of La Voiture Noire had been well researched and told extensively beforehand, but it was interesting to see it afresh, direct from the vault of the Bugatti Library. He wondered what Don Pietro might have given to spend just a few minutes surrounded by such rich and fascinating resources.

The order book first noted an entry for the 10th of March 1936 from Monsieur Nico E. Embiricos. He had ordered a Bugatti Type 57S Coupé Aero. Production records for the vehicle showed that on its completion on the 24th of August, it bore chassis number 57375. All Type 57s bore the prefix 57 in their chassis numbers. This was the car that was sent to Corsica Coachworks for its unusual lobster tail body. The engine, number 3S, was retained for the vehicle but her original body was returned to Molsheim.

This Coupé Aero body was later married to chassis 57453. Ordinarily, most Type 57s were built to the lowered S 'Surbaisse' specification, direct from the factory. This was because the build process was significantly involved. The rear axle for the lowered specification passed through the rear frame rather than riding under it and a dry-sump lubrication system was needed to fit the engine beneath its lowered bonnet. However, most of the 57S owners later wanted the increased power of the C specification too, the 'Compresseur', or supercharger, so were more often shipped back to have the supercharger installed. This resulted in a Type 57SC vehicle, or more accurately, a 57S (+C).

In the case of La Voiture Noire however, Jean Bugatti configured the car with both S and C specifications from the outset. Thus, when engine 2SC was mounted to the car, La Voiture Noire became the first and, as it transpired, the only Bugatti Type 57 Atlantic Coupé to have the supercharger installed straight out of the factory. When the car was completed on the 3rd of October 1936, she was already unique. In addition, the colour of the bodywork was noted as 'Noir Obsidienne' and was thus the first such car to be painted completely in this colour. While black was often used, it had only ever been in conjunction with a second colour, usually French Aircraft Blue, sometimes red or even Ettore's favourite colour, yellow.

"These are the first documented appearances." Petra explained, showing Hamilton some original photographs.

Since their acquisition by the Volkswagen Group, Bugatti had hired a German archivist to care for their impressive and valuable history. She was very meticulous, very organised, it was an ideal match. The company's 1937 promotional brochure showed the sleek machine at the start of the year. Later photographs showed displays at both the Nice and Lyon Motor Shows in the spring. Some of these Hamilton had seen in the Borromeo Archives too.

"The car was called the Atlantic as a tribute to Jean Mermoz," she added. "At the time he was a celebrated Air France pilot, but his plane was lost in the south Atlantic during a routine mail flight from Dakar in French West Africa to Natal in Brazil. Monsieur Mermoz had been a close, personal friend of the car's designer Jean Bugatti."

After the shows were completed, Petra introduced him to a set of new drawings, dated June 1937. This showed the elongated modifications to the rear fenders. Compared to the slightly pert rear end of the original, beautifully executed but somehow an abrupt finish to the elegant lines, these new fenders accentuated the design just that little bit more and improved her overall harmony.

On completion, the car was presented to Robert Benoist as a gift. Together with fellow Frenchman Jean-Pierre Wimille, they had recently won the 14th Grand Prix of Endurance at the famous Circuit de la Sarthe near Le Mans. The dark brown leather and beige cloth of the interior was retained, and the modified bodywork was finished in the same obsidian black as before. There were no photographs of it after the alterations and even though Jean Bugatti, Benoist and the Grover-Williams couple used the car frequently, the car was never registered to an owner.

The car officially therefore still belonged to the original company, Automobiles Ettore Bugatti, though this original incarnation had ceased operations by 1952. The question of ownership then would likely be an interesting legal quagmire if it was ever found. Had it unconsciously passed onto Bugatti Automobili S.p.A. when Italian entrepreneur Romano Artioli acquired the brand in 1987? Or had it now passed onto the French subsidiary of the Volkswagen Group? Based on recent research into such things, Hamilton doubted the answer would be quite so straightforward.

"The registration is misleading too." Petra continued, picking up a sheaf of papers. "You see, this is the famous list, the Bordeaux List some might call it, of all the items sent to the factory there." She pointed to one of the entries on the list. "We have Chassis 57454 with registration: 1244 W5. This is the closest we have to La Voiture Noire being sent to Bordeaux." She continued, returning to the papers. "The problem with this is that there is no record of Chassis 57454 being used for a complete vehicle until 1951 when it was used for this Type 101."

She presented Hamilton with a series of photographs, both black and white and colour, showing a much more modern looking vehicle, finished in blue.

"This looks like it's in a museum."

"It is." she nodded. "The car is now part of the Schlumpf Collection in Mulhouse."

Hamilton exchanged a glance with Legrand.

"To restart production after the war, three original Type 57 chassis were used for the new sportscar. Four new ones were made afterwards with the 101 prefix. Four different coachbuilders were eventually used for the bodywork of the seven examples. This one is a Gangloff example."

IN THE DEN OF WOLVES

"So, not La Voiture Noire."

Petra shook her head. "Not even close. Also, the registration is not helpful." She continued, placing more photos in front of him. "Notice anything familiar?"

Hamilton examined each of the photographs in turn. One showed a Type 57 in profile with a very different style of bodywork from the Aero Coupés, another looked to be a cabriolet with a very pronounced boot and double spare wheels, the third was of a coupé with three headlights, one at the bottom of the grille but without the pronounced seam that made the Type 57s standout, and the fourth picture was a racing car with streamlined open bodywork. Four completely different cars. Yet, apart from the car in profile, on close inspection, they all bore the same registration number: 1244 W5

"Well, this makes no sense at all." He remarked "What are all these?

Petra smiled and pointed to the first photograph. "This is a Type 57 Coupé with a Graber body from Switzerland. The photograph was taken just outside here." She pointed to the gravel roads beyond the glass gable end of the library. "This second one is a Type 50T Tourer. The 'T' stands for 'tuned'." she pointed to the cabriolet. "Then we have a Type 64, and finally the Le Mans winning Type 57C Tank which Jean Bugatti was killed in."

"This car?" he pointed to the black and white image of the car with the No.1 in a white roundel on the side.

"This one." She nodded. "Pierre Veyron and Jean-Pierre Wimille claimed Bugatti's second victory in 1939 and a few weeks later, Monsieur Jean was taking it out for a test drive on the road between here and Strasbourg."

"Why do they all have the same registration plate?"

"For this we have to go to another set of records." she smiled, moving to the compiled papers she had prepared. "For testing purposes and trial runs, Bugatti registered a number of provisional licence plates. After World War I the Alsace-Lorraine region reverted to France and came under the Strasbourg département. Before the FNI system was used in France, the département code for Strasbourg was 'J', but the letter 'W' was reserved for provisional licence plates."

She showed him a list of the plates registered to the company Automobiles

IN THE DEN OF WOLVES

Ettore Bugatti. There it was: 1244 W5.

"So, this was like a trade plate?" Hamilton mused.

"A temporary plate yes." Petra nodded. "This allowed a racing car to be driven on public roads to the race circuit. Also, for a car that had been sold but not yet registered to the owner in their own country, it could be driven there with this plate, for example."

"So, in the manifest, shipping 'Materiel automobile', an unused chassis and provisional licence plate was basically just stock clearance."

"Whatever it was." Legrand remarked. "It certainly doesn't add up to a car."

"No, but this might." Petra said, with a glint in her eyes. "This has been in the library for some time but did not really fit with these other records." She produced a piece of paper, handwritten and addressed to a Monsieur Deville. "Monsieur Deville was in charge of the inventory here in Molsheim, just as Monsieur Marco was in Bordeaux. He received this letter from Robert Benoist in September 1941."

"I'm afraid I struggle with French." Hamilton admitted.

"It reads:

Dear Jacques,

Sadly, things are getting more difficult for all of us and I feel that driving Monique is becoming too dangerous. Not only for me, but for the magnificence of Jean's legacy. For this reason, I kindly ask that she be packed up for ready for shipping.

I have a friend who is arranging for her to be picked up at Strasbourg and assures her safe return to me when this horrible time is over. I know I can entrust Monique into your careful hands and would never choose to leave such a wonderful car were there not any other way.

Jacques, you have been a most excellent friend and I hope we can meet up again for food and perhaps a little wine. Kisses to Marie. Au revoir for now.

Yours

Robert

Hamilton looked at the letter. The date it was written. There was a stamp indicating when it was received by the offices in Bugatti.

"Is he referring to the car as *Monique*?"

"It's possible." Petra nodded. "As you see, the letter was posted from here, while Robert was visiting. Perhaps to drop the car off itself. He wanted it be made very clear what to do with the car."

"Benoist was not leaving anything to chance." Hamilton remarked. "Do you know if it was packed up?"

Petra shrugged. "Sadly, the only records we have of any shipments from that time are the ones, as you say, generic to Bordeaux."

"If they were all being loaded on at Strasbourg though."

Hamilton placed his laptop bag on the table. It seemed better than entering with a blood soaked Nazi folder. Carefully he retrieved the folder and showed it to Petra. The sight of blood, though dried now, was still something of a concern to both Legrand and Petra.

"Don't worry about that." Hamilton said. "It's mine."

Legrand looked horrified, then noticed the plaster under the sleeve of his shirt and looked to Petra.

"Paper cuts are real bleeders." He smiled. "This is a file I retrieved from an office in Bordeaux. I'm entrusting it to you and would appreciate your discretion." He looked at both Legrand and Petra seriously. "So that you know that this is genuine. I will tell you where I found it, but apart from myself, you two will be the only people that know of its existence and where it came from."

"I am a little nervous, Monsieur." Legrand remarked.

"I understand that." Hamilton nodded. "When the time is right, and when we can get the right people involved, we can verify the authenticity of this, as well as everything else in the office where I found it. For now, as long as I can have copies, I would ask for your patience, confidence and trust. It is a lot to ask, I know. Is that okay?"

Legrand looked to Petra, looking back at him for some form of reassurance.

"We have come this far." Legrand shrugged. "Let us see what you have."

Hamilton nodded and slid the folder closer to him, placing a hand on top of the stained buff cover.

"In Bordeaux, there is a large submarine base, built by the Nazis during the war."

"I know of it." Legrand nodded.

"It's now been turned into a digital art gallery. Quite a place actually, well worth a visit. Anyway, underneath the old submarine pen is a bunker. Based on what I saw when I went down there, no one else has been there since the war. It's exactly as it might have been left. I don't think it's a fake. All the doors were well sealed up and the amount of dust down there suggests it hasn't been disturbed."

"You broke in?" Legrand flinched.

"I was a paying guest of the art gallery. I still have my ticket. I merely continued to explore the premises after hours." Hamilton could see that Legrand was not pacified by this revelation. "One of the offices down there was filled with filing cabinets. Most of them still full of paperwork. I don't know what they all are. I didn't stay long enough to go through them all in detail. That's a job for specialist historians really. But this I did find of interest." He left the part out about despatching a murderous assailant in the same office.

"You stole it?" Petra stammered.

He rolled his eyes. "Who did I steal it from, Petra?" he asked, pointing to the insignia of the Kriegsmarine on the cover. "These guys? They've been out of business for over seventy years. I don't think they'll miss it."

Opening the folder, he showed the documents to his hosts, briefly explaining the history of Andrew Sutherland, his role as a spy within the SS and the elaborate cover story of the box for the Ark of the Covenant being transported by rail to Bordeaux. He pointed out the typographical anomaly. Petra was impressed with his command of German. The switch of boxes would not have been hard to imagine but would be impossible to verify. Yet, it did suggest another avenue for the possible whereabouts of La Voiture Noire. *Monique.*

"Now," he said, after they had absorbed the information. "You have documentation confirming transfer of various materials to Bordeaux. You also have documentation that Benoist entrusted his car, *Monique*, to a friend who promised to keep the car safe."

"He said it was to be shipped." Petra pointed out.

"Look at the letter." Hamilton pointed to Benoist's note. "Didn't you say to be packed ready for shipping? How would that be done?"

"In a wooden crate."

"And then what was his friend going to arrange to do with it?"

"Pick it up at Strasbourg."

"You see?" he nodded. "Of course, we don't know exactly what Sutherland may have told Benoist he was going to do with the car, but Benoist trusted someone to keep it safe. The reality is, as we all know, the car never left here to go to Bordeaux, but that doesn't mean it didn't leave here to go somewhere else."

"Back to Berlin." Legrand added, remembering his earlier conversation in the château.

"Where Sutherland was primarily operating from." Hamilton nodded, pointing to the dates. "And during this time, late 1941, Berlin was having one or two air-raid shelters constructed." He tapped the documents. "If this agent had the audacity to create the idea that archaeologists might have found the Ark of the Covenant in the Middle East, it's also quite possible that he arranged for its supposed safekeeping in the heart of the Fatherland."

"*Monique* masquerading as the Ark of the Covenant."

"Wouldn't anyone have checked?" Petra surmised.

"Have you seen the film?"

She frowned. "The film?"

"Indiana Jones?"

"Yes, but that's a fiction."

"Maybe, but the power of the Ark to kill people is a matter of Biblical record. Whatever the truthfulness of those accounts is, it's pretty unlikely that superstitious Nazis would have wanted to risk finding out for themselves. Just to be in possession of something so powerful though may have been enough for them."

"What do you mean?"

"Imagine you steal the Mona Lisa. What are you going to do with it? You can't hang it up on the wall in your own house because immediately everybody will know that you stole it. So, you keep it locked away in a vault. Somewhere no one can ever find it. Perhaps you visit it from time-to-time, perhaps you don't, either way you have the satisfaction of knowing that you own perhaps one of the most valuable and famous paintings of all time."

"What is the point?" Petra asked.

"The point is that you own a masterpiece." Legrand replied. He understood the principle. "To own something so precious, so valuable. Merely to be in possession of it. That is worth more to the collector, the thief, than the value of the object itself."

"Spoken like a true Thomas Crown." Hamilton winked.

"So, they believed they had the Ark of the Covenant, when in reality they had La Voiture Noire?" Petra asked.

Hamilton nodded. "*Monique*. It's a possibility, is it not?"

"But why?"

"I suspect Sutherland wanted to help his friends and fellow agents out. They needed to get rid of the car. He could facilitate that. Doing so in such a way that the car was not destroyed. As I explained to Monsieur Legrand earlier, with most national economies in ruins after the war, something like that might have been seen as a sound investment. Cash could be lost, stolen or devalued. A property portfolio in a time of war would clearly be no good afterwards. Art was either being looted or destroyed. Nazi gold?" he gestured to the drawing board. "This may have represented a sounder investment, providing they all survived the war."

"It is possible." Legrand shrugged. "Americans were often shipping rare European classics back to the States after the war. So, when Benoist and Williams are killed, there is no one to claim the 'inheritance'."

"Why not Sutherland?" Petra asked. "He knew where it was."

"Because he had likely been too deep inside the SS to just wander back home again after the hostilities." Hamilton explained. "To do that he would risk being hung as a war criminal before any of his story was checked out. Likely, no one would be able to anyway because he was working solo. Neither his superiors nor colleagues within the SS would have known what he had been up to and any agency files that might corroborate things would have been sealed up for decades."

"Where do we go from here?" Legrand asked.

Hamilton closed the file and slid it across to Petra.

"We go to Berlin."

CHAPTER SIXTY-FIVE
SCOTLAND 2018

A fear of spiders is fairly rational. It probably has something to do with their eight legs. Arthropods with their six legs generally don't inspire the same level of fear. Aversion, certainly. Perhaps even revulsion at times. Rarely fear. An ant has hardly ever caused anyone to run out of a bathroom in fear. A beetle will quietly go about its business while being observed by a curious child crouched over it. Bees will buzz around, dusting up the fluffy jumper mum made for them with pollen.

Wasps get the most hostile reaction. Yet were it not for wasps, the natural yeast found in ripe fruits that kickstarts the fermentation process, enabling the production of wine, just simply wouldn't be there. They have a sweet tooth. That really is the only reason why they're after a person's jam sandwiches in summer picnics.

Arachnids though are almost universally scary, irrelevant of size or potency. That extra pair of legs, their carnivorous nature, those eyes. Observing the manufacture of a web, whatever a person's particular view of spiders, is still an incredibly educational experience. There is a rare skill employed to direct that strand of silk, emerging from the abdomen, across the radial threads to form another viscid span. A knowledge of structural engineering is required too, knowing where to place the anchor points, frame threads, bridging threads, all to support the capture spirals.

The little cave spider was barely a centimetre long, but it liked the corner of the Coach House. It was a quiet space, cool and dark, exactly like the kind of cave they would normally prefer. The rattle of the diesel engine outside didn't trouble it too much. The noise soon stopped anyway. Two doors closed and the sounds of footsteps followed, crunching on the gravel.

When the garage doors were opened, the little spider paused momentarily, sensing movement. And light. Two figures appeared in the doorway. They were vaguely human shaped. Not useful. Not unless they brought some bugs in with them. The spider carried on its business for a moment until the doors were opened fully and the light became too much. Then the harmless little arachnid removed itself deeper into the corner where the light couldn't reach.

Sun filtering through the aperture illuminated a shapeless form under covers. Tarpaulin was breathable to protect the paintwork. Old bed sheets and decorating rags got damp and held moisture against the body. This could cause micro-blisters that would turn milky white and need careful attention. They needed to preserve what there was. Starting from the front, the human shapes began to remove the protective cover from the thing underneath.

Light from the open doors fell on the front bumpers, pitted and chipped from stones and gravel, with a little rust and blistered chrome, but surprisingly intact. Two small Bosch driving lamps were mounted on steel brackets bolted to the bottom of the sweeping fenders. One of the lenses was broken and the light was angled down in a melancholy pose. The fixing nut on the bracket was loose and rusty.

When the cover was rolled further up, sunlight revealed two horns, curved light bar, large, monogrammed headlamps fixed to it and an impressive, swept back waterfall grille. The four interlocking rings of Auto Union were mounted to the central spar of the grille that divided the radiator in two halves, just above the light bar stretching between the front fenders. A capitalised letter 'H' crowned with the word Horch was fixed to the front of the grille surround at the top while an Art Deco style globe and wings surmounted a knurled circular radiator cap.

As the two men continued to carefully peel the shroud back, more details of the car enrobed beneath were revealed. Chrome seam lines running over the top of silver fenders. A long, louvred, gull wing bonnet. Raked back, split windscreen. Semaphore indicators. Fabric sunroof. Turning the handle, the door swung open on its rear mounted hinge. The usual mix of volatile organic compounds usually confronted in a new car were distinctly absent in the cockpit of the old relic. Less alkanes, benzenes and ketones, more old leather, musty wool and a vague whiff of unburnt petroleum wafting through from the other side of the bulkhead.

The two men looked around inside the old car, opened the bonnet, kicked the tyres, spoke in low, muted tones to one another. The spider didn't see what happened next. It had tucked himself deep into the corner of the roof space, waiting until darkness returned. Then it could carry on spinning its web in peace.

CHAPTER SIXTY-SIX
BERLIN, 2018

The Berlin Underworlds Association had been documenting the subterranean development of the city since 1997. Its membership varied from academics, architects and historians, to teachers, policemen and pensioners, all bringing their unique stories and contributions to the organisation, focussing on unearthing secrets beneath the sprawling metropolis.

Located in an air-raid shelter within the Gesundbrunnen subway station, the association endeavoured to explore, document and preserve the many caverns, shelters, disused railway tunnels and derelict brewery vaults that the general public ordinarily had no access to. If Hamilton was to find the location of Sutherland's Ark of the Covenant, they would be just about the best people to consult.

In contrast with Paris, London and Moscow, the subterranean development of Berlin was comparatively modern. Much of this was due to ancient deposits of the Warsaw-Berlin glacial valley which left the centre of the city in a marshy lowland swamp, just a few metres above the ground water table. Unpredictable layers of peat, moor soils and alluvial sandstones made all construction projects until the second half of the 19th century a notably challenging enterprise.

Deep storage cellars for the fermentation and cooling of beer in Prenzlauer Berg and Kreuzberg became the first underground structures to be completed. Then came the urban water supply, sewage and pneumatic postal service before electrification and the telephone network moved underground. Piles driven through marshland to stabilise the subsoil enabled the Reichstag and other larger construction projects to be completed.

A subway followed by the beginning of the twentieth century and many deep cellars and blind tunnels were excavated, endeavouring to expand the rail network and utilise properties even more economically before the financial crisis following the Great War brought such projects to a dead end.

Later developments largely consisted of constructing air-raid shelters, underground bunkers and communications tunnels while the city braced itself for attack. Some of the labyrinthine remains had been deliberately destroyed by the occupying forces of the Soviet Union. Almost no trace of the Führerbunker remained beneath the Chancellery. Indeed, both the old and new Reich Chancellery buildings had been completely levelled with new buildings constructed in their place.

Even whole streets had been destroyed or changed names to try and erase painful memories of the past. The street formerly named after Prince Albrecht of Prussia and the nearby Palace, which had later become the infamous address for the Reich Security Main Office, Gestapo and the SD, had been retitled Niederkirchhner Strasse.

The buildings themselves had already been razed to the ground by the RAF and their remains had been completely swept away by the mid-fifties. Though formerly attractive and historical buildings, these were some of the few within Germany not to have been reconstructed as they once were. Their latter usage, perhaps for little more than a decade, completely eradicating the preceding two-hundred years of history from the public appetite for any idea of rebuilding them as they once were.

The Chairman of the Association had agreed to meet Hamilton at the Berlin Gesundbrunnen railway station. The station served the northern area of the city with regional and intercity trains as well as U-Bahn links. On arrival, the Chairman introduced himself to Hamilton as Dieter and led him down into the U-Bahn ticket hall.

Next to a concrete staircase, surrounded by acres of pale green and turquoise tiles was an ordinary looking door. Though securely padlocked, the door bore no other markings or clues as to its eventual destination and only bore a quote from Spanish philosopher George Santayana above it in German which read:

IN THE DEN OF WOLVES

Those who cannot remember the past are condemned to repeat it.

Hamilton thought the quote was sadly less a philosophical observation and more a straightforward statement of fact. He often baulked at people who would quote the 'Lest we Forget' mantra around Remembrance Sunday whilst neglecting what it was they were supposed to remember in the first place. In any event, bringing himself back to the present, Hamilton watched as Dieter unlocked the doors and showed him inside.

Once beyond the green door, the familiarisation of being inside a German World War Two era bunker quickly returned. Though this one was experienced with a modicum of light. Katya, a local guide entered a few minutes later and introduced herself. The trio then began to wander through this eerie, subterranean world as they awaited the arrival of others.

The brief tour Katya provided to Hamilton was more than just a walk through cold, concrete tunnels while she recited a memorised script or various anecdotes from the people that had actually experienced living in the shelters. There were specific exhibits in various rooms, as well as authentic artefacts that demonstrated what a room was really like or how it was used. This all resonated very keenly with Hamilton as he followed in their footsteps, observing how closely these recreations resembled the bunker in Bordeaux.

When Dieter turned off the lights outside the Command Post, the walkways glowed with bright illumination from luminescent stripes and markings. Hamilton would have been grateful for such provisions in Bordeaux and wondered why the same paint hadn't been given to the builders. In a couple of the rooms were bunks that folded up against the walls and low benches where residents would sit.

An occupant's allowance was just one small suitcase per person, and it had to be small enough to fit beneath the narrow benches. Typically, most of the older generation chose to remain above ground, taking their chances with the bombs and leaving space for younger citizens in the shelters below. It was sobering to think that the bunkers had not been a brief requirement during the great unpleasantness of the Second World War. They had an extended life during Cold War tensions too, when the prospect of total annihilation was only too real for the citizens of Berlin, regardless of what side of the Wall they inhabited.

After the tour, they brought Hamilton into a side room which had once been an old office and communications centre with the world above ground. This now served as the hub of the organisation's activity. And was filled with cabinets and maps, pieces of exploded ordnance and old luggage. Coffee and biscuits were supplied, and a small team of the organisation's researchers had gathered while the tour was being given. A historian, an architect, and a town planner.

"Thank you for meeting with me." Hamilton began, addressing his audience in German.

"With pleasure." Dieter smiled. "When you told me of your unusual request I thought it best to assemble a few of us together."

He then introduced each member in turn. Jurgen, the planner, Michael the historian and Inge the architect. A variety of ages from late-twenties to mid-sixties. A diverse but enthusiastic mix.

"Now, you already mentioned to me on the phone, but perhaps you could explain to us what it is that you are looking for." Dieter said, gesturing for him to sit as he served the coffee.

"Of course." Hamilton took a deep breath, preparing to relay what he knew.

First, he needed to provide a little background on Andrew Sutherland once more, at least the snippets he had been able to discover so far. No doubt there was more in the Archives, but whether they would be held in Germany or under the offices of the National Archives in Kew, Hamilton hadn't yet discerned. Afterwards, he related Sutherland's brief activity with the Resistance and his contact with Benoist and Grover-Williams. Fragments prised from Dame Harrington's labyrinthine memory banks. This brought in the Bugatti.

With the knowledge he had gleaned from Molsheim, he could now provide a little more context to the car before revealing Sutherland's role in hiding it. This then led to the discovery of the transport request in Bordeaux and the letter from Benoist to Bugatti. The revelation of an undiscovered bunker beneath the submarine pen in Bordeaux didn't cause nearly as much consternation as he expected, though the potential treasure trove of documents that may still have been entombed within sparked a lively conversation.

"We have to leave all that to the French authorities." Dieter called, bringing the meeting to order. "I'm sure they will reach out for experts if they see fit. What we are concerned about is the possible whereabouts of this artefact."

"So, the car is inside a wooden crate, disguised as an ancient artefact, is this correct?" Katya asked.

"I believe so." Hamilton agreed.

"Fascinating."

"Fanciful." Jurgen proclaimed. "It wouldn't be very easy to hide something that big without someone knowing about it, even underground."

"So, who might have known about it?" Dieter asked.

"Apart from the Führer himself?" Jurgen returned.

"Possibly he might." Dieter acknowledged. "I think he would have wanted it close to him, but maybe not near the Chancellery, just in case anything did happen with it."

"Are you saying this English spy managed to convince the entire Nazi hierarchy that they were in possession of the Ark of the Covenant, when in fact they had nothing but an old car?" Michael enquired doubtfully.

"Scottish." Hamilton replied.

"What?"

"Sutherland was Scottish, and that's exactly what I'm saying."

"It's a little bit far-fetched."

"No more far-fetched than Germany losing the war." Jurgen frowned as the room fell silent.

"Let me explain what I mean by that." Hamilton continued quickly. "On paper strategically, tactically, militarily, Nazi Germany had Europe by the balls in 1941." He stopped and looked at the ladies. "Apologies, but as far as Europe, even the rest of the world was concerned, the war was practically over by the summer. Britain might have pledged to fight on, but realistically wasn't in any position to do so. Churchill famously claimed that the

Commonwealth Nations and Empire would come to the rescue of the old world, but I honestly doubt they would have done so, especially as most of them were busy fending off the Japanese and wanted to be independent from Britain anyway.

"So, to even imagine a German defeat at the time this car went missing would have been inconceivable, and if the Soviet defence hadn't managed to hold things up during the winter, with Moscow and Leningrad captured, there's very little chance America would have actively intervened on the European front. They'd happily smack the Japs about the Pacific, sure, but would have totally written off any engagement in Continental Europe. Maybe they would have signed up to the defence of Britain, but then…"

His words trailed off as he held out his hands.

"Germany did have the belief that they could do anything." Dieter agreed. "It may sound unbelievable, but it may not be all that implausible. The only way to find out is to try and find it."

"What would we be looking for?" Jurgen asked.

"A vault, or a blind tunnel, or cellar of some kind, large enough to accommodate the box."

"That doesn't narrow it down." Inge smiled.

"It takes out many of the civilian shelters." Dieter replied. "They simply wouldn't have had the access."

"Beer cellars too, sadly." Jurgen smiled. "Though they're always worth a look, just in case." He winked.

"You said it would have come into Berlin by train?" Katya asked, looking at Hamilton with interest.

"Most likely."

"How would it then go underground?"

"A disused railway tunnel would be the easiest way." Jurgen remarked. "Back the wagon in there, disconnect it and seal off the end. Perhaps a tunnel with alternative access routes."

"That gives us something to work with, then." Dieter smiled. "Are you with us, Michael?"

The team looked at the historian as he struggled with the improbableness of it all. To him it seemed highly unlikely that a junior SS officer, a foreign one at that, would have had the gumption, let alone the authority to have pulled something like this off without being discovered.

"Wouldn't anyone have inspected this crate?"

"It's the Ark of the Covenant." Katya said. "According to the Bible, people who touch it die. Perhaps that was exactly the legend that Sutherland was banking on people believing still."

Michael frowned, still struggling with the notion. "Go through the facts again."

Hamilton patiently presented the evidence he had retrieved, hoping to show the logical conclusion he had come to. He could understand Michael's reticence. There were literally hundreds of miles of subterranean tunnels and storehouses. The organisation was only scratching the surface, and those were only the ones they knew about. How many more still remained a secret? Potentially this was exactly what he was asking of them, to find a secret tunnel they didn't yet know existed.

After Hamilton's explanation, Michael still looked a little troubled.

"Coming in from Strasbourg the train would have taken two different routes in." he began. "First stop after Hannover would have been Wolfsburg, then Spandau, before terminating at Berlin Central. The second route would have come direct through from Frankfurt, but it might have diverted off to Tempelhof on its way around."

"Tempelhof was the largest building in the world at the time." Jurgen exclaimed. "That alone has over four kilometres of walk-in supply ducts."

"And an underground railway connection." Michael added. "It was originally prepared for the Olympic Games but was believed to have been re-purposed for the Führer's private use afterwards."

"Using U6?" Dieter asked.

Michael nodded. "It's believed there was a branch off U6 near Stadtmitte which curved northwest to the old Chancellery."

"That would make sense." Jurgen agreed. "The Wilhelmsplatz Subway entrance is not too far away. Where are the city plans?"

Michael moved to the rolls in the cabinets and fumbled through them.

"Once he has convinced himself of the factual evidence." Dieter whispered to Hamilton, "Michael is a real treasure hunter. He will be very useful for you."

CHAPTER SIXTY-SEVEN
BERLIN, 1942

In mediaeval Berlin the field originally belonged to the Knights of the Order of the Temple of Solomon. After the dissolution of the Templar Knights, the land to the south of the city became a parade ground for Prussian forces from the eighteenth century until the Great War. In later years, both Armand Zipfel and Orville Wright made brief demonstrations of flight before the Tempelhof Airport was formerly founded by Deutsche Luft Hansa in 1926, taking its name from the defunct Order of Knights. At the time of the terminal's original construction, it was the world's first airport to be served by an underground railway.

As part of Albert Speer's ambitious plans for the city, the new terminal building was to become the gateway to Europe and a symbol of the world's capital, Germania. Designed to resemble an eagle in flight with semi-circular hangars forming the bird's outstretched wings, the façade of shell limestone formed a vastly imposing three-quarter-of-a-mile quadrant around the northwest of the airfield.

Although it was possible to take the U6 U-Bahn line up to Stadtmitte, and then walk the remaining few blocks to Wilhelmsplatz, SS-Hauptsturmführer Reinhardt wanted to feel the full and impressive impact of the glorious Third Reich and all its trappings. He had requested Sutherland to arrange a car, the Horch 780 B Sport Cabriolet from the NSKK waiting for him outside the reception hall. Emerging into bright May sunshine after having inspected the underground hiding place for himself, the bumptious officer settled into a monogrammed leather seat alongside the chauffeur and nodded for him to drive on.

Approaching from Wilhelmsplatz, the Borsig Palace on the corner of Voss Strasse was the first building that came into view and was still one of the grandest Italianate villas in the capital. The villa had been completed for industrialist Albert Borsig who died before he could move in. The palace then served as a bank until becoming the official residence and offices of Vice-Chancellor Franz von Papen.

It was here, during the Night of the Long Knives, that Papen's office was ransacked by the SS, while Herbert von Bose, the Vice-Chancellery Press Secretary and outspoken political opponent of the National Socialist Party was conducted into a conference room and shot in the back almost a dozen times. Speer retained the building, completely gutting its interior, and incorporated it into his design for the New Reich Chancellery, with an extension adjoining the Palace to the old Reich Chancellery in the nearby Radziwiłł Palace.

Driving through great panelled gates that pierced through this extension, Reinhardt was conveyed into the Court of Honour. His Horch rolled up to the foot of the external staircase of the carriage entrance to the New Reich Chancellery, offloaded its obsequious burden, then took its place alongside the other vehicles assembled along the side of the courtyard.

Flanked by two vast bronze statues, they each stood twice the height of a man, one holding a torch, the other a sword, representing the Party and the Armed Forces respectively. Sculpted by Arno Breker, they were seen as the perfect antithesis of degenerate art and had been selected by Speer himself for the headquarters of the Greater German Reich.

Two soldiers from the 1st Panzer Division stood guard at the top of the steps. Two more were positioned at almost every doorway inside. Acting as the private bodyguard of the Führer, the soldiers were absolved from offering the customary salute as Reinhardt approached. He stepped beyond them, beneath the bronze gaze of the Reichsadler above, to enter a medium-sized reception room.

Carrying on straight ahead, Reinhardt walked through immense double doors, some seventeen feet high, and proceeded into the Mosaic Hall. A soaring cavern of red marble some 52feet high, 65feet wide and 150feet long. Nine vast mosaic wall panels depicting a pair of eagles holding torches were illuminated by the sun shining through a glass roof above, casting an ethereal, diffused light into the vast space below.

To enter the New Reich Chancellery was to feel that one was in in the presence of the Lords of the World. That was the objective Hitler had given to Speer, and nowhere was this felt more keenly than in the Mosaic Hall that Reinhardt traversed. His boots resonating on polished marble floor. At the far end, ascending several more steps, Reinhardt entered a round hall with a domed roof. A mini-Pantheon of sorts. An anteroom whose sole functional purpose was to realign the visitor from the curious bend at the end of Voss Strasse.

Passing through, Reinhardt then entered the incredible Marble Hall beyond, stretching theatrically away before him. At twice the length of Versailles' Hall of Mirrors, Hitler was especially impressed by this gallery. Halfway down the Marble Hall, flanked by two more guards, was the private study of Adolf Hitler himself. Larger even than the Cabinet Office, the vast space was the inner sanctum of the Third Reich, the seat of power, yet once again, a four-and-a-half-thousand square foot office that was almost never used by the Führer. He never had the patience for desk work.

Nineteen windows all along one side overlooked Voss Strasse. Some 20feet high and recessed a little over six-feet from the gallery, the architraves were carved from a deep red, distinctly veined Deutschrot marble, complementing the finely detailed structure of red Saalburg marble on the floor, polished to a high sheen. The other side of the gallery was adorned with large tapestries depicting tales from Germanic history, beneath which were groupings of sofas and armchairs for the ministers and officers as they waited for an audience with the Führer.

Reinhardt inwardly groaned, hoping he wouldn't be kept waiting long. He had important news to convey about the Bundeslade and its new resting place beneath the streets of the capital. It would form a fitting addition to the vision of Berlin that Hitler had commissioned Speer with realising. Perhaps even a centrepiece.

In any event, the hurried footsteps coming down from the opposite end of the hallway would only delay Reinhardt's eventual audience. Reaching the doors before him, the officer showed the message to the guards, and was hurried inside, much to the chagrin of those patiently waiting.

"News from Prague, my Führer!" the officer was heard calling out as soon as he entered, by way of justifying his sudden entrance. "Heydrich has been…"

the doors closed before Reinhardt heard anymore.

There was a general murmuring among the gathered officers, discernible consternation on the faces of the ministers, just grasping the words lost as the doors were closed. Something significant had happened. Something terrible. Almost at once Reinhardt suddenly wished he was anywhere else in the world. Being just a few hundred feet away from the Führer when he was told bad news, despite all the marble and granite in this foreboding structure, would not be sufficient to shield anyone from the invective that would inevitably follow.

CHAPTER SIXTY-EIGHT
BERLIN 2018

"Here is our first obstacle." Michael murmured. "Between 1940 and 1944, Weser were assembling aircraft in the unfinished hangars of the new terminal. They were supplied by a railway and trucks via a connecting tunnel here." He pointed to the map of the old airport plans.

"That leads to the U6 line." Jurgen observed.

"It's possible they were connected and there was another spur off. Perhaps a ghost station somewhere. Let's hope so." Michael sighed.

"Why do you say that?" Hamilton asked.

"Whatever was under the airport may have already been destroyed." Michael explained. "When Soviet forces took Tempelhof, they scoured the terminal buildings searching for treasures, hiding places and documents. You've heard all the stories about troves of Nazi gold and precious art. Anyway, during their search they blew up the fortified entrance to a three-level bomb shelter in the north office wing, just here." He pointed to the building extending out along one side of the forecourt. "It was being used by Hansa Luftbild as storage for their aerial photographic records. The explosion ignited all the celluloid film stock, turning the shelter into a furnace for several weeks."

"Sounds typically Soviet." Jurgen rolled his eyes. "They were always very good at blowing things up."

IN THE DEN OF WOLVES

"What happened?" Katya asked.

"No one could go in, so the inferno prompted the Soviet commander to order that the lower levels be flooded."

"The city had no water supply." Jurgen remarked.

"No, but the airport had its own electricity and groundwater supply from reservoirs under the forecourt." He pointed to the location on the map. "Fortunately, this was close to the film shelter, but…"

"If anything else was down there it would either have been torched or flooded out." Inge concluded.

Michael nodded. "Unless they got it out using this rail line here."

"Packed up with surplus aircraft parts?" Hamilton postulated.

"Possible."

"Where else is a likely location?" Dieter probed. "We can put together separate teams if needed to look at different areas."

"There is always the mystery of the Nord-Süd Tunnel." Michael suggested.

Hamilton's expression invited further explanation.

"It's a section of tunnel that crosses the city centre from here at Gesundbrunnen to Yorckstrasse on the other side of the river." Jurgen commented as Michael searched through the series of maps. "It needed to cross the other U-Bahn lines as well as pass under all the city's rivers and streams. Because of that there are tighter corners and steeper inclines than normal."

"Here." Michael cried finding the appropriate map. At once Jurgen leapt up to examine the details. "Again, shortly before the end of the war, there was an explosion beneath the Landwehr Kanal which runs parallel to the Spree. The entire tunnel, as well as part of the S-Bahn was flooded. To this day no one knows who detonated it, or why, or how many were killed, but whoever did must have had a good knowledge of the tunnel network."

"Isn't there a theory that the explosion was undertaken by members of the

SS?" Dieter asked.

"That's one theory." Michael nodded. "Another is that the tunnel was already partially flooded because of the fractured water mains and sewage pipes from the bombing. We may never know the truth."

"If it had been the SS, what would have been the purpose?" Hamilton enquired. "Why flood the tunnel?"

"Unless…" Jurgen murmured, looking over the map. "They were not actually looking to flood the tunnel. It was just a consequence of another idea altogether."

"Another self-destruction operation?"

"Possible." He pointed to the map. "So, we have the Chancellery on Voss Strasse," he moved his finger down. "The Landwehr Kanal." Next, he drew a line with his finger north to south. "And the U6 Line to Tempelhof."

"And this was the area of the S-Bahn that was flooded at the same time." Michael observed, pointing to the former railway yards at Gleisdreieck, almost due south of the Chancellery and separated by the canal.

"The assumption has often been that this was the spur to the Chancellery, branching off from U6 at Stadtmitte and passing beneath U2 to a tunnel leading down from the Führerbunker, but what if the spur was from the U2 line instead?" Jurgen asked, looking at Michael.

"From a planning perspective it would make more sense."

"It's what I would do." Jurgen nodded. "U2 already passes so close to the Chancellery it would be the work of a moment to add a short spur to the bunker."

"It would need a longer loop to junction with the U6 line to Tempelhof though." Michael observed, studying the map.

"No." Jurgen shook his head and pulled over a newer map, drawn up in 1944. "Look."

Jurgen traced his finger along a line running down from the railway lines at Gleisdreieck, looping to the southeast until it joined up with the combined

Tempelhof S- and U-Bahn lines located on the western end of the old airport's south runway.

"This was a private underground line. It was planned in 1944, but supposedly never built. If it had been, it would have taken the Führer directly to the airport where an aircraft would have been on permanent standby."

"Ja, but if it had been built, would he not have used it?" Michael asked.

"Almost certainly," Jurgen nodded. "Unless it had already been blown up beforehand. In that case, he knew he would have been effectively trapped inside the Führerbunker and would have had to see out the end of the war from there."

"Which is exactly what happened."

"Who would have done that?" Katya asked. "A saboteur citizen, or a defector from within the SS?"

The team thought for a moment, then individually they each began to look towards Hamilton, until five pairs of eyes were staring at him meaningfully. The implication was clear.

"It sounds exactly like the kind of thing Sutherland might have done." Hamilton admitted.

"Don't you know what this means?" Dieter asked.

"Potentially he sealed off the tunnel that could still contain the box that we're looking for." He leaned over the map. "Either between the bunker and the canal, or the canal and the airport."

"It means more than that." Dieter said gravely. "It means that this Sutherland knew exactly where the Führer was. His action almost certainly prevented his escape and shortened the war."

"This challenges much of what we thought about the closing stages of his downfall." Michael cried. "Had there been a means of escape, he would most likely have taken it, regardless of the risk to the Luftwaffe pilots escorting him. He would have been determined to fight on until captured or killed. The fact that he committed suicide in the bunker has always been seen as a last resort, because he knew there was no way out. The last means of escape available to him..."

"Had already been destroyed." Jurgen blurted out.

Dieter nodded. "Let's get some expedition teams together, contact BVG, see if they can loan us some engineers and enlist our caving teams. It looks like we have at least two locations to start with."

"Where do we start?" Inge asked.

"Tempelhof." Jurgen suggested. "There may be a phantom platform somewhere, or a sperate tunnel adjacent to the main branch. The rail engineers should know." He turned to Hamilton with an apologetic look. "This may take us some time to investigate. Many of us are volunteers and we will need agreements from the planning departments and railways before we can begin any excavation works."

"Aye, it's no bother." Hamilton shrugged. "You've got my contact details?"

Dieter nodded.

"I've got two other cars to try and find now anyway." He said, getting up and offering his hand to the team around him.

CHAPTER SIXTY-NINE
BERLIN, 1942

Hans Reinhardt was shown into Sutherland's office again and greeted amicably enough. Sutherland didn't have anything to hide, inasmuch as there was nothing very much he could add to the deaths of the Wannsee chauffeurs. As for anything else, Sutherland himself had a great deal of other things to hide.

"Kriminalkommissar." He greeted, gesturing to the visitor's chair. "Please, take a seat."

"Thank you."

"Brandy?" Sutherland offered, moving to the tantalus on the credenza behind his desk.

"I won't, thank you."

"Well, I shan't offer you a cigarette." He added with a sideways smile as he resumed his own seat.

Hans returned the smile. He looked tired, withdrawn. Life was taking its toll. He was the younger brother but had aged more than Manfred.

"It's about those that I came to see you." he shifted in his seat and removed the cigarette tin from the pocket of his overcoat. "Nothing was found in any of them. You're in the clear."

IN THE DEN OF WOLVES

Hans leaned forward and placed the old Sulima cigarette tin on the desk.

"I always was." Sutherland said calmly. "I had nothing to do with the death of those officers. Even if they were my cigarettes, as I told you, I buy them from lots of places so knew nothing about any of them being tainted."

"The laboratory confirmed it anyway now." He sighed.

"So, who is next on the suspect list?"

"I don't know." Hans shrugged, clearly resigned to the situation. "No longer my case." It was a familiar story. "The SS are handling it personally. To be honest, I'm surprised I was able to run with it for so long."

"Perhaps because your brother sits next door?"

"It's because he sits next door that I was expecting the rug to be pulled much sooner."

"I see." Sutherland paused. "So, what are you working on now?"

"Domestic abuse. Inge Ley."

"Oh?"

"Wife of Robert Ley? Reich Commissioner of Social Housing Construction?"

"Can't say I know either of them." Sutherland admitted.

"No, well. His wife is very beautiful. A regular at balls in the NRK. He's a womanising alcoholic, but still a senior figure. Another investigation to tread very carefully over."

"NRK?"

"Die Neue Reichkanzlei." Hans explained. The New Reich Chancellery.

"You Germans do love your acronyms. NRK. NSKK. NSDAP."

"RAF?" Hans uttered with a hooked eyebrow.

"Well. Okay then." Sutherland chuckled.

"You went to Lübeck recently, didn't you?"

"Back in early March." Sutherland replied, instantly seeing the connection Hans was trying to make. "Hardly recent."

"You heard about the bombing?"

Sutherland nodded. "I was fortunate to see it beforehand. It was a pretty little place."

"Fortunate is one way of looking at it." Hans observed.

"And what would another be?" Sutherland asked pointedly, careful not to sound too irritated or defensive. There was nothing to link him to anything.

Hans leaned forward, opened up the tin and helped himself to one of the remaining cigarettes. He tapped the end on the arm of the chair from habit, placed it between his lips and took out his lighter. Sutherland watched him calmly light the end, replace the lighter and blow the first puff of smoke towards the ceiling.

"Just an observation."

"Well, here's another." He said, pointing to the SS Eagle on the left arm of his field grey jacket. "You get shot for wearing this on Princess Street, so I've no intention of going back home."

Hans held up his hands as if in apology.

"I'm not even working homicides now. Who am I to judge?" he took another puff. "I'm sure if you would have seen anything or anyone suspicious though, you would have reported it in."

"Of course. It's my civic duty."

"What's more compelling? Civic duty, or patriotic duty?"

Something in the way Hans asked the question made it seem rhetorical. Sutherland remained silent.

Hans nodded slowly and smoked in silence for a moment. Sutherland watched him briefly, then carried on with his work, organising the carpool for the guests attending Heydrich's funeral. There were cars to be serviced, washed and fuelled up. Nothing was to be left to chance. Though the coffin would be conveyed into the NRKs Court of Honour upon a gun carriage with a grand foot procession escorting it, at the conclusion of the state ceremony, for a moment at least, the cars would arrive and be the centre stage. It was imperative that they were in full working order and polished to within an inch of their paintwork.

The Mercedes-Benz 770K of the Führer himself was due an oil change. This car at least was beyond Sutherland's jurisdiction, entombed as it was in the West Wing garage of the NRK under the direct supervision and care of SS Division Leibstandarte. Hitler's personal bodyguards. At least if they got the level wrong, or used the wrong grade, it wouldn't be him facing the bullet.

Looking up again, he folded his hands on the blotter and frowned slightly.

"Are you sure I can't offer you anything?" he asked.

"We both want this war to end, don't we?" Hans asked after another puff.

"I'm sure everyone does." He replied flatly. "Then the great rebuilding work can begin."

"Have you seen plans for this new capital, 'Germania'?"

"I have."

"What do you think of it?"

"It looks to be suitably grand for the Greater German Reich." Sutherland replied carefully, unsure whether Hans was on another fishing expedition.

"I wonder if there will be anything left to rebuild."

"I'm sure there will."

Hans stared at Sutherland for a long moment. Deciding.

"What's it like being a racing driver?" he asked.

IN THE DEN OF WOLVES

"Those days are long gone now."

"What *was* it like?"

"Dicing with death on a daily basis?" he chuckled. "At times extremely exhilarating."

"And at other times?"

"Bloody scary." He said.

There was no point denying it. Sometimes it just was, sitting in a bathtub of fuel with a fire-breathing engine trying to shake itself to pieces right behind his head. He recalled the moments he had become airborne at the Nürburgring, at Donington. The fearsome sound of those V16s, the whine of the superchargers, squealing brakes.

"You cope well with fear?"

It was an odd question. Sutherland wrinkled his brow a little, but he sensed there was a deeper meaning behind Hans's enquiry, behind his whole line of questions. Was he scared? Was it his brother? The far-reaching talons of the German Reich, encroaching even to his own livelihood? Taking away his profession and replacing it with, what? How was justice being preserved? What real difference was he making anymore?

"If you need to find a way through this," he said finally as he stood up. "Let me know."

Sutherland didn't quite understand his meaning and decided not to react. Though as Hans left his office, Sutherland was left with the distinct impression that he had seen right through him. Pierced through to his very soul. Sutherland was left with the disquieting impression that Hans Reinhardt knew he was a double agent. He looked to the tin. Open. Inviting him to take one. Had they really been tested? Was he now playing Russian roulette with his own cigarettes?

Bringing the tin closer to him, he took one out and inspected it, not sure what he was even looking for, what the signs would be that it had been tampered with. Perhaps the factory itself had been infiltrated, adding poisoned tobacco to certain batches of cigarettes. That way there would be no evidence of any tampering at all. He always suspected the medicinal benefits of smoking were over-emphasised. Maybe it was time to give it up.

CHAPTER SEVENTY
ENGLAND, 2018

Opening the Land Rover's front passenger door, the two sensuous curves of the transmission console could be seen cascading down from the storage cubby like a mountain stream. Splashing back continuously through to the bulkhead behind the second row, the sweeping form was repeated and gave the two rear passengers a touchscreen multimedia display, additional storage space and recharging docks. Constructed from one-inch-thick walnut and trimmed in chocolate brown mohair, the use of wood and hard-wearing fabric provided a functional yet beautiful aesthetic.

After sweeping out and hosing down the interior, Hamilton replaced the coco mats in the front footwells and climbed up to reach the parcel shelf above the passenger seat. Gathering up his Cornish compendium of OS maps, he exchanged them with a newly acquired Scottish selection before heading back down the path to bring up the rest of his gear.

Autumn had come to Cornwall and the waves crashing onto the sands of Whitsand Bay looked grey and threatening. Gorse bushes on the cliffside surrounding *Rockwater Cabin*, usually a riot of delicate, coconut-scented yellow flowers during summer, had died back to reveal their evergreen needle-like foliage. Anorak rippers. Grasses were turning yellow and autumnal leaf litter was collecting in the small yard between the back of the cabin and the hillside above.

A leaden sky hung low over the horizon and the sound of Ralph Vaughan Williams' Tallis Fantasia playing loud on his Bose embodied the age of sail and the perils of those at sea. He could almost smell the creaking ship's timbers, musty sail cloths and salted beef as he prepared his gear for the next voyage. Woodsmoke and sea sulphides wafting throughout the cabin already formed an evocatively nautical bouquet.

In Germany, the Berlin Underworlds Association had made significant progress in their expedition beneath the city's streets. A few probing holes had been made and with the assistance of robotic cameras, miniature drones and expert knowledge of the railways, they had discovered a few viable potentials worthy of further exploration, both beneath the old Tempelhof airport and nearer the demolished Reich Chancellery. There was now just the small matter of raising adequate funds for the endeavour.

Being a non-governmental organisation, they relied on the money raised through educational tours and seminars to defray the costs of upkeep and maintenance, as well as surveys of new areas. There was still the mountainous task of clearing up, preserving and protecting the remains of Flak Tower III in Humboldthain Park, one of the biggest bunkers in the city and now ideal accommodation for endangered bats.

Hamilton had managed to secure a small allowance from the SIS which he hoped might be able to defray some of their costs. The ramifications for Vauxhall Cross of not providing him with the money would have been a phone call to Dame Harrington. Though she had officially retired long before the Berlin Wall came crumbling down, the measure of influence she still wielded in certain circles was quite phenomenal.

His quest for the Duesenberg of French racing driver and dancer, Mariette Hélène Delangle, had stalled very quickly after it had begun. There was scant little documentation about her more famous car, a Hispano-Suiza H6. Almost nothing about her lost Duesenberg, even in the Borromeo Archives, other than a vague suggestion that it might have been Chassis No.2150. Duesenberg's own registry had no detailed information on the car, other than a Model J with that chassis number was built at some point between 1930 and 1936. Apart from the photograph of her villa in Nice dated around 1944, there was quite simply nothing else to go on.

Sadly, the preeminent Duesenberg specialist had been the first murdered member of the Auto Club, and with his death sending shockwaves through the tight-knit classic car community in America, flying over there to ask specific questions about a very particular car less than a year after his death might have aroused rather too much suspicion at the present time.

As regards the third car of this sacred trinity, there was more information on *Manuela* but almost all trails universally ended abruptly after Rosemeyer's death. Some speculative reports that it was returned to Zwickau and was subsequently destroyed in the bombing were never verified. Other sources claimed that the car disappeared after falling into the Russian sector of Germany and may have ended up in Ukraine.

Researching a different angle, the extensive Motoring Archives at Beaulieu were a treasure trove of information on Sutherland's Grand Prix racing career, both his early seasons as a private entrant in a second-hand Delage, and his three years for Ferrari's Alfa Romeo outfit. There was surprisingly less information following his switch to Auto Union when he was becoming more successful and approaching the pinnacle of his career. Again, at the present, with the loss of Graham Robertson weighing heavily on their hearts, and with his death at the Horch Museum, Hamilton trod very carefully around the subject of what he was working on specifically.

Without the clout an official investigation gave him, complete with suitable identification and investigative credentials, there were limits as to how far a private citizen could enquire. This was part of the exciting challenge with his new life. Part of the frustration of freelancing too.

That was until Hamilton received another direct call from the old fruit herself, Dame Iris Harrington DCB. It appeared there had been a very recent discovery some miles north of Hadrian's old garden fence. An old car had been found dumped at the bottom of a Highland Loch. Could it be *Manuela*? Had Sutherland somehow smuggled it back? Hamilton was quickly discovering that impossibilities were not in Sutherland's vocabulary.

The irony of his homeland journey was not lost on Hamilton as he opened the tailgate and loaded up the Land Rover. Especially as Harrington lived on the south coast herself, over in East Sussex. However, she had arranged to meet him at Glasgow Airport and had given him her flight details and instructions on what to do when he got there. Already he felt somewhat intimidated by the idea of finally meeting up with the venerable peer, yet there was little choice but to hightail it up the length of the country to make the agreed rendezvous. A journey of over five-hundred miles.

Returning to the vehicle with two pairs of sandboards, he looked down at the walnut treadplate running down the length of black powder coated, galvanised steel side step. As part of the atelier's trademark, the name of each build was routed into the wood of the steps and the central slat of the loading area. From front to back, the letters spelt out the word:

TORRIDON

At least the Land Rover would finally be heading up to her natural habitat now.

Not sure what to expect, Hamilton imagined camping would be out of the question, so had dispensed with the idea of taking up the roof tent. Still, depending on how accessible the loch was, or where else the peer would wish to pursue the project, he opted to take the hi-lift jack and secured it to the roof rack. Should he pick up a puncture, it would be of profound embarrassment to be left stranded without the ability to change it over himself. A canvas storage bag, fastened over the spare wheel on the tailgate carrier, contained all necessary tools and accessories should he need them. He hoped not. All-Terrain BFGoodrich was expensive rubber to replace.

In case they really did venture off the beaten track, he secured the sandboards to the cage-mounted picnic table on one side to get them out of any sticky situations. Two yellow jerry cans containing spare diesel fuel were secured in carriers to the other to ensure he would never be caught short. He wasn't about to wear a suit and tie, so his luggage comprised of walking boots and hiking gear, with one notable addition.

Swapping out the flare gun in the Vaultek Slider safe with a Glock 22, the modified coyote brown frame and 15round standard magazine, was a lighter carry than the Glock 17 he had been issued with in the Royal Marines. He inserted the pistol, already loaded with one magazine, along with one spare magazine into the universal foam holster before securing the three-point sliding drawer in place.

Having already been ambushed once during the hunt for these old relics, he wasn't about to be taken by surprise a second time, though even being in possession of it was a risky strategy to employ. The original Peelian principles governing UK policing outlined the forces primary policy was public protection, rather than public order. As such their duty was to protect the public from crime, rather than enforcing law imposed by the state. While specially trained firearms units would be called upon if necessary, British police were essentially unarmed. After the Dunblane massacre, private gun ownership and transportation in Great Britain was strictly controlled and licenced. This significantly reduced any threat to the public and police from gun crime.

Simply put, it meant unlike the United States, there were no open or concealed carry laws in Great Britain. Even though he had valid shotgun and firearms certificates, the mere presence of the gun in the vehicle without membership of a gun club or justification for transport was now a criminal offence. Although the concealed nature of the gun safe made it very unlikely that he would ever be caught out, it increased the probability from certain, to very certain, that he would be prosecuted should it ever be found. Feeling the tightness of the skin around the scar on his wrist however, if he found himself up against someone else like the phantom in Bordeaux, he was willing to take the risk.

With his clothes and gear packed into a rucksack and loaded, the moka pot washed out and replaced on the shelf, he was good to go. Taking a deep breath as he locked up the cabin, he looked out to sea and contemplated the rigours of the long-distance journey. Thankfully his choice of Recaro sports seats would make the motorway miles more comfortable and supportive. Enrobed in hard-wearing mohair and inset with nickel ventilation grommets on the seat and backrest, reminiscent of old-fashioned Scheel racing buckets, basket woven leather fluting provided textural complexity to the interior, and heated cushions and lumbar support took the autumnal chill off as he pulled out of the layby.

Almost immediately, Jayden from Millbrook nearby pulled into the spot with his van and began to offload surfboards. Hamilton rolled his eyes as he watched his local window cleaner in the rear-view mirror. He had probably been waiting for Hamilton's space from the early hours.

When Hamilton had picked up the Land Rover, the original, factory fitted 2.2litre diesel engine had already been replaced with a much coveted 6.2litre Corvette LS3 V8 petrol unit. This was the direction a lot of Defender conversions went in, and the noise and performance were incredibly impressive. However, despite the remarkable power and raw, muscle car sound, he had wanted more low-end torque for towing and the fuel economy of the small-block Chevy engine was shocking. He could get the torque with some tuning, but the economy would plummet off the cliff completely. Hamilton might have been given a reasonable pay out when he left the Service, however his frugal nature still flowed strong and unlike her original owners, he wasn't after a showy cruise down the High Street in a blacked out urban wagon. He needed a powerful and dependable workhorse.

Swapping out and reselling the LS3 to his Edinburgh atelier for another project enabled him to invest in a brand new, practically indestructible six-cylinder Cummins diesel unit, complete with striking red engine block, valve covers and silicon hoses. The vibrant colour made for a pleasing visual treat through rear-facing louvres of the vented Puma bonnet while he was driving. Usually installed in Royal Mail delivery trucks and coupled with a beefy Holset turbocharger, the motorway miles were easily devoured while still giving him reasonable fuel economy and much improved levels of performance.

Though the agricultural diesel rattle was much deeper, a billet manifold produced a more raucous exhaust note, and on acceleration *Torridon* sounded like a jet engine winding up. The HX40 turbo whistle surprising several tailgating German cars with a quick downshift through the six-speed manual transmission, a ready burst of speed and most often, a billowing black cloud from bellowing stainless steel exhausts. With the aerodynamics of a brick outhouse however, Hamilton's Land Rover was never going to be a high-speed cruiser, especially with sun visor attached to the leading edge of the roof, the roof rack and roll cage, but at least it got up to a moderate motorway speed a lot quicker now.

Setting off a day earlier, Hamilton stopped overnight at the Bridge Hotel, in Buttermere once more. Rolling slowly into the village from Honister Pass, he noticed that Izzy was definitely moving slower now as she crossed the lane to the farmyard, looking a lot greyer around the muzzle than he remembered too.

Hamilton felt exactly like she appeared; grizzled, weary, yet still endearing in his own way, even if he didn't quite get the head scratches and belly rubs. Alisa welcomed him back with a smile, gave him the key to his usual room and pulled a pint of ale in the bar ready for when he came back down. It would be an early start to meet the flight from Southampton that came into Glasgow midmorning. No cheeky hike around the lake this time.

CHAPTER SEVENTY-ONE
GERMANY, 2018

The QinetiQ Talon V was a multi-mission Explosive Ordnance Disposal Robot usually employed by military, law enforcement and first responders for dealing with Improvised Explosive Devices. With many unexploded bombs still to be discovered beneath the streets of Berlin, it was the ideal robot for exploring uncharted subterranean labyrinths. Capable of negotiating stairs, steep slopes and rubble, with four hours of battery life and multiple camera systems, the exploration team could safely navigate the robot through the depths of even the most damaged and inaccessible locations.

Just before the Berlin Tempelhof U-Bahn station there was a deep alcove in the tunnel wall. After an ultrasonic examination and an exploratory hole, it was shown to be an old tunnel entrance long since blocked up. On the earliest plans there appeared to be no tunnel originally. Yet, by 1944, a new tunnel had been pushed through, veering off to the north and west. Jurgen interrogated the town planning archives and found a bill of materials for the construction of a wall to block up this tunnel dating back to the mid-fifties. This was a time when the desire to defect from east to west was increasing exponentially and some of the old U-Bahn stations had been providing the means to do so undetected.

From inside a worker's tent, pinned down and secured well inside the leeward end of the alcove as U-Bahn carriages buffeted past, the explorers huddled around the monitor as the robot operator guided the vehicle down the slope. Any residual tracks had been removed from around the tunnel entrance, before reappearing a few hundred yards further down. Some tunnels had exhibited lost shoes, items of clothing, even a children's toy here and there, either as a result of being used as an air-raid shelter, or to defect to the west. There didn't appear to be anything of the sort down here, just a lot of dust and rubble.

At about 2,500 feet into the tunnel, nearing the extremity of the robot's operating range, there was a fork in the tunnel and two huge rubble piles sealing both entrances. In the torchlight it looked like both tunnels had collapsed completely. After months of searching the depths of the airport basements, those still accessible, and the tunnels beneath the converted rail yards near Gleisdreieck, this was the last hope of finding something.

The extent of the rubble though seemed to suggest that the whole structure might have been compromised, much as it had beneath Gleisdreieck when the canal flooded in. There could have been tons of water dammed up beyond, trapped for decades and harbouring all manner of microbiology.

It was the end of the road.

"I'm sorry. We can't go any further." The robot operator said, turning the robot round.

"Wait!" Michael cried, just as a train passed by.

Pointing at the screen, he directed the operator to focus on a part of the tunnel wall near the right-hand entrance. Turning the robot around, its camera focussed on an area he indicated and began to zoom in. On a white rectangle, shaped to a point at one end was a single stencilled word, evidently for the engineers to signpost their way around. Clarifying the image, the operator stabilised the robot and stared at the screen as the word became clear.

FÜHRERBUNKER

"This is it." Michael explained, turning to Jurgen alongside. "This is the escape tunnel."

"The underground train to the airport." He nodded. "So, it was built."

"And then destroyed." Michael gestured to the screen.

"It would have needed a second explosion." Jurgen assumed. "Perhaps after the one that flooded Gleisdreieck."

"No. Before." Michael replied. "Think about it. The explosion at Gleisdreieck was designed to bring the water in the canal down to flood the tunnel." He pointed to the wall of rubble barring any further exploration. "This explosion would have been to hold back that water, trapping it inside. It would have completely prevented any chance of escape from the bunker. Behind there is probably the original canal water, running all the way back to the old bunker itself. The robot is much deeper there, so the water would have run down to that point, like a sink."

"If that's the case, then that might explain the big puddle here." The operator remarked, turning the robot and shining a torch onto the base of the rubble. Sure enough, a large pool of water, as still as a millpond, perfectly reflected the crumbled concrete above it.

"How deep is it?"

"Perhaps five or six feet, judging by the wall."

"What's this tunnel?" Jurgen asked. "It doesn't appear on any plans."

"It's a different mix of concrete." The operator remarked. "You can see the join in the material. This tunnel was built at a different time."

"Before or after?"

"It's difficult to say. The design is similar, so within a year or two either way."

"Not likely to have been after 1945." Michael pondered.

"Perhaps the original then." Jurgen suggested, waiting for another train to go by. "Before the link to the bunker was completed."

"The first phase of the Führerbunker was completed in 1936, the second phase in 1944."

"So, if this happened before the second phase, maybe in 42 or 43…"

"That might fit our timeframe." Michael nodded. "Is there any way of finding out how deep that tunnel is, or where it goes?"

"If it's not on any plans or anything, there's only one way I know." The operator said. "We would have to dig it out."

CHAPTER SEVENTY-TWO
SCOTLAND, 2018

Leaving the Lake District long before the sun got up, the weather was predictably miserable. The switches on the roof console operated various lights, internal and external, including LED spotlights on the roof and the winch bumper's A-bar. Navigating Newlands Pass with the additional lights and the rain lashing down made for an easier run to Keswick and the road back to the motorway. As part of the modifications, Hamilton had set up a triple wiper arrangement using some CAD magic to calculate the optimum sweep and balanced positioning for three 13inch blades. In the dark, pouring with rain, it no longer felt like he was driving underwater.

Though technically a civilian, because of his volunteer rescue work he had been given a special permit to fit blue strobes and a wigwag device for alternately flashing the headlights, though no siren. This was an addition normally only reserved for law enforcement agencies, security, and emergency services. Inverting the mesh grille in the Aircon grille panel brought Lazer light units into the top corners, making them visible above the winch bumper, while a blue strobe light bar was mounted to the lower cross-member of the roll cage beneath the windscreen. He was desperate to try them out but running up to the airport to chauffeur someone's nan wasn't adequate justification.

Approaching Larkhall, Hamilton looked at the SatNav unit for the journey up ahead. Harrington had told him to drive them to Loch Etive after picking her up from the airport. To his shame Hamilton was nowhere near as familiar with the Highlands as he should have been, both as a proud Scot and a former

Royal Marine Commando.

Having come from Coulter in South Lanarkshire, there had seldom been need to venture much beyond Glasgow. Family holidays were often taken on the Ayrshire coast and nights out in the big city. Commando Training at Lympstone had involved yomping over Dartmoor and Woodbury Common. The ML2 course to become a Mountain Leader had taken place in Cornwall, California and Norway while the training for the Special Boat Service had taken him to the Brecon Beacons, Brunei and back to the South of England.

As he had never enrolled in officer training, he neither made it to Britannia College nor the West Coast of Scotland, being content to remain at OR-4. Even his stint with Strathclyde Police between the Senior Service and the Intelligence Service had largely been confined to Glasgow city centre. He suspected today was going to be another long and arduous day of travelling.

Since the failed car bomb attack on Glasgow Airport, it was no longer possible to simply roll up to the front of the terminal building and pick up his passenger. He understood the security implications, but it gave unscrupulous car park companies another means to extort ridiculous amounts of hard-earned cash from the pockets of unsuspecting visitors. Hamilton glanced down at the far right of the binnacle gauges to the clock. He was making good time and would be there with nearly an hour to spare. More money for the car park meter.

At this point, making his final approach to the airport, Hamilton was both anxious and uncertain what to expect. Harrington had sounded commanding and authoritative over the phone, yet to have been so significantly active in the spy game during the Second World War, she must be approaching the ton now.

Would she be physically doddering about while her sharp and frustrated mind barked orders? Or would she be striding out confidently and with purposeful alacrity, betraying none of her advanced years? What did she even look like? Old woman was rather too generic a description. Should he have made up one of those naff cardboard signs that everyone else was holding up? He always thought they looked rather ridiculous but as he stood in the Arrivals Hall, he wished he'd had the forethought to put something together.

From somewhere out of sight came the sound of a rather piercing and unnecessary beep. The kind of thing attached to lorries when they were in the process of reversing. He was about to walk away and let the horrid noise move past, whatever it was, when the airport buggy came into view, conveying an elderly passenger into the hall. A bony finger quickly pointed in his direction and Hamilton suddenly felt very exposed. Being singled out from the crowd by an arthritic digit, extending from the sleeve of a boucle jacket, felt like being identified in a police line-up. Not that he had ever experienced the process from the other side of the glass.

"Hamilton isn't it?" she said as the driver brought the buggy to a halt, mercifully silencing the beeping.

"Aye, it is, ma'am." He stammered hesitantly.

"Good." She nodded curtly as the driver helped her alight. "Finally, someone who doesn't need a silly little sign." She added slightly too loudly, clearly oblivious to those nearby. There seemed to be a collective lowering of clipboards, cardboard box flaps and anything else used to scrawl a surname over. "Thank you, my dear." She smiled pleasantly to her chauffeur, instantly changing tone to one considerably more agreeable.

"Is this all yer luggage?" Hamilton asked as he took up her overnight bag. It weighed next to nothing, and he wasn't even sure it was full.

"How much do you think I need?" she asked indignantly.

Hamilton exchanged a glance with the buggy driver. She smiled knowingly and pulled away, leaving him with his formidable charge. He offered an arm but was refused with robust fashion as Harrington produced something from her handbag.

"I can walk." She said resolutely as she thrust out a collapsible cane. Unfolding itself as it flew through the air, the cane narrowly avoided striking Hamilton in the leg as he stepped briskly aside. "Lead on."

He decided to make the rest of the journey as painless as possible and escorted her to *Torridon* in silence, wondering what she would think of scrambling into his elevated beast as opposed to being cosseted in some government limousine. Strangely, she didn't comment at all but silently accepted his offer of assistance to clamber inside. Hamilton was quietly relieved that his choice of Recaro seat had come with lower side bolsters for easier access. Heaven knows how she might have struggled otherwise. No sooner had he climbed into his own seat than a package was deposited in his lap.

"Whit's this?" he asked, looking down at it suspiciously.

"The person who invented envelopes made them open as well as close." She remarked with ill-disguised acerbity.

Taking a calming breath, Hamilton lifted the flap and saw a wad of cash as well as a black leather ID wallet and lanyard. Taking out the wallet he opened it up saw the lanyard was attached to a second card holder tucked inside. Both the card holder and the wallet bore an all too familiar cast metal UK coat of arms crest on one side, while his old SIS Operational-Officer identification card was inserted behind the clear plastic windows of both. He noted the details were exactly as he remembered them, only the photograph had been changed, matching the one on his driving licence and passport which had both been updated since he had left the Albert Embankment.

"I've had your old credentials reinstated." She said. "For the time being at least. Should get you out of a hole if the rozzers find that gun safe."

Hamilton looked across at her, but she was staring impassively straight ahead. Somehow, despite her diminutive stature, shrivelled no doubt by age and infirmity, she had managed to see and recognise exactly what was located above his head.

"And the money?"

"Sufficient to at least get us out of the car park, wouldn't you say?"

Taking the hint, Hamilton kept the IDs on his person and placed the envelope in the central cubby before rolling the rig towards the barriers. He had already settled up at the meter and inserting the flimsy paper ticket brought up the barrier, allowing him to make good his escape.

CHAPTER SEVENTY-THREE

The Loch Etive Monster meanwhile was never going to sell any postcards. For one thing, the loch in question was at the end of a very rugged, single-track lane. Nevertheless, there was something stirring beneath the inky black waters on Argyll's northern border. Whatever it was though, the Police Scotland Inspector would just have to wait a little longer.

He looked at his watch impatiently. His counterpart from Edinburgh glared at him meaningfully. He didn't know what her problem was. A blob of water landed on the dial of his watch. He pulled up the collar of his coat and sighed as police divers sitting on the back of the barge flapped their flippers idly in the water, ready to submerge again whenever they were called upon. It was already becoming a frustrating day of waiting around.

By chance, a shard of bone had been discovered on the estate road that ran along the loch. The local ghillie knew immediately that it didn't belong to any sheep or deer. It looked like a piece of human bone, most likely originating from the sternum. Police were called and sent in the divers to search near the shore where the bone had washed up. There was nothing to see so the search was extended. In the end, it was decided to try and use a sonar device.

That's when they found the car. In the darkness of the loch, it was impossible to tell what it was, only that it was old. One of the divers claimed it was very old. Sensing an opportunity to palm off what might turn out to be a complicated and fruitless investigation, the cold case team were called in from Edinburgh and a dive barge was summoned.

Hearing about it on the news feeds, the Chief of the Secret Intelligence Service thought it best to inform the old dear personally before she informed him. In his limited experience with her, he had already found it advantageous to try and be one step ahead. Though, despite her age and operational isolation, he was finding it a surprisingly difficult thing to achieve. She seemed to have spies everywhere.

This hunt for old cars seemed to mean something significant to her and he was quietly questioning his decision to pull Natalia off it. At least he could control Natalia. Harrington was something of a wildcard now, and with Hamilton now at her disposal…

CHAPTER SEVENTY-FOUR

His charge collected, Hamilton resumed the journey north as the sky darkened and clouds rolled in. From habit he checked the mirror for a tail as they approached the Tarbert Bay Hotel on the A82. One of those curious TOTSO junctions that seemed to proliferate the British road network. Turn-off-to-stay-on. The car immediately behind carried straight on up towards Inveraray, while a few others followed him on the main arterial route to the north.

Hamilton looked across at his passenger as they skirted along the dramatic north-western shoreline of Loch Lomond, past the Loch Sloy Hydroelectric Plant with its enviable vista and on towards Ardlui. He didn't know how she fitted into all this, but Dame Harrington's frail form had looked listless and disinterested since they had left the airport. Her ancient, bony hands were resting on the handbag in her lap. The cane folded up and poised for action. Was this really the same person that had sent him on a treasure hunt all over Europe?

Rounding the corner near the impressive Victorian built viaduct, he thought she might even have dozed off. It would have been an early start for her after all. Then at Pulpit Rock she seemed to come alive. A new nine-million-pound road viaduct widened the carriageway from a narrow single-track series of bends, controlled by temporary traffic lights for thirty-years, into a five-pile, six-span cantilevered bridge hanging five metres out over the water, providing a first class S2 standard road.

"Hmm, they've improved this immeasurably." She purred quietly.

Even given the subdued clatter of *Torridon's* cab, her thin yet worryingly ominous voice startled him momentarily.

"Aye, they have ma'am." He nodded, choosing to agree with her rather than admit that he had never had cause to travel on this particular stretch of Scottish road before.

She looked across at her chauffeur carefully, narrowing her eyes like a cat considering whether to pounce or go back to sleep.

"When we do get there, I shall be remaining in the car, on dry land. I'm far too old to be bobbing about the place."

"As yer wish, ma'am." He nodded.

"Drop the ma'am, please." She said crisply. "It makes me feel old." She looked across at him. "Of course, I am old, but that's not the point. Iris will do perfectly well."

"Of course, ma'am." He nodded again, knowing full well he could never bring himself to address this dignified, intimidating old lady so informally.

"Just park me up near the bothy. There is a layby on the left after you pass it. I would still like to observe proceedings." She added, rummaging through her handbag.

"Yes, ma'am."

"And ring this number when they've dragged it out, would you? In case you didn't already add me to your contacts." She passed over a card with a mobile number on it. "Should just get enough signal there."

"Of course."

"Lovely isn't it?" she said, staring out of the windscreen with renewed enthusiasm as they left the loch behind and followed the River Falloch, coming across the Drover's Inn on the right-hand side. "The landscape up here."

"Aye, it is." He said, gazing out at the autumnal colours, blazing in all their vibrant glory as watery sun sneaking through dappled the *Torridon's* dark red bodywork with light. Rouge and russets, flames dancing from the boughs of the trees as wind rustled through. Sleepy mountains on the far shore, a preview of much grander peaks ahead, shimmering with a tinge of heather on their whitened summits. Darker and more foreboding clouds in the direction they were heading. Rain had cleared the further north he had travelled but it was on its way back again now.

For the remaining forty miles she regaled him with the last time she came up to the Scottish Highlands. Over fifty years ago now. Though the purpose of her journey was never divulged, she enthused about her impressions on the scenery at the time, having laid eyes on the untamed ruggedness of Glencoe, the barren beauty of Rannoch Moor and the expansive entrance to Glen Etive at the foot of the Buachaille. It was totally different to the South Downs, thoroughly enrapturing. She felt it even now.

Threading past Crianlarich, the road took them through Tyndrum and the vast and barren moorland either side of the Bridge of Orchy before making the ascent up past the Loch Tulla viewpoint and onto the dramatically bleak Rannoch Moor. Hamilton himself had to admit, having not had cause to venture much further north than Helensburgh in his time with Strathclyde, the landscape was astonishingly impressive. It was exactly the kind of terrain he had built his expedition vehicle for. The wilds of Cornwall, though beautiful in their own way, suddenly looked decidedly tame in comparison. If he could move the cabin here…

Traffic began to thin out the further north they pressed; crazy local drivers choosing to overtake on the long, clear straights, hurtling past at ridiculous speeds, a few brave holidaymakers seemed to take their cue and followed the atrocious example. Hamilton passed a few sedate motorhomes but with his precious cargo onboard, was reluctant to push it beyond what he deemed a comfortable, yet effective pace.

An upgraded suspension made for a poised but comfortable ride and the vehicle could pitch over on uneven terrain at some quite frightening angles. Nevertheless, he didn't want to experience that sensation at speed with soft moorland on the verges of broken tarmac and unforgiving granite boulders looming up from blanket bog.

Indicating early, he slowed, changed down through the box and made the left turn after the Glencoe Mountain Resort. The golf ball size walnut and maple gear knob fitted in the palm of his hand perfectly, and the short CrispShift mechanism made for a satisfying, rifle-bolt movement through the gates of the milled shifter plate. It was these details that Hamilton appreciated when driving, and with the surrounding scenery made the long journey north suddenly worthwhile.

The seldom travelled single-track lane had a faint veneer of ice on the junction and the long first stretch towards Dalness, but soon, as the mountains either side began to enclose the road, the sheltered track became a little more treacherous over the twists and turns. Thick early frost lay on the ground all around, before miraculously disappearing again after Invercharnan where the temperature was milder, the road surface less broken up and the grip more assured.

The River Etive appeared little more than a wide stream as it followed the undulating course of the road to the left, then widening out progressively as they ventured further on, cascading over rocks and into pools hollowed out through the centuries. Low streaming rays of sun struggling to peak through the rapidly closing gaps in heavy clouds temporarily ignited the south face of Buachaille Etive Mòr, standing guard at the head of the glen, while the clouds shrouded the north side of Beinn Mhic Chasgaig with deep and ominous shadow. It was as if two seasons were being expressed in one view, with the river forming a dividing line between them.

Near the Allt a' Chaorainn tributary, where a small bridge traversed the river, the landscape opened out, affording a spectacular view across the glen towards Meall Carbh. This was where M and 007 had stood on the side of the road in front of his Silver Birch Aston Martin DB5 in the Skyfall movie, gazing through the mist at bleak moorland rising from the valley floor to scree clad shoulders.

Some four miles in and the first dwelling appeared, sitting on the far side of the river as the road followed the bends around rocky outcrops piercing though machair and heather, offering stunning views of the cascades below. Glenceitlein Cottage was part of the Dalness Estate, with Dalness House itself, built in 1884 as a typical Highland hunting lodge, situated further on. The shoulders of the hills squeezed in from either side as the river flowed closer to the road, taking a sinuous line between Stob na Bròige at the southwestern edge of the Buachaille ridge and the Beinn Ceitlein massif.

The road then snaked past the rear of Dalness House, now a luxurious holiday home, screened from the road by a plantation of trees, before emerging once more into the glen, ascending slightly above the valley floor and running through forestry and moorland fields. It was here, emerging through a glade of rhododendrons, that Hamilton encountered a stag in the middle of the road.

The C1094 was by no means a fast route and so Hamilton brought *Torridon* to a stop easily enough and a good distance away from the magnificent beast. The stag turned his head imperiously to stare at the vehicle that had so rudely interrupted his ruminations. Hamilton counted about seven or eight spurs on his antlers and, looking to the moorland round about, between the road and the trees, there appeared as many as a dozen hinds, some more curious than others, and a few juvenile stags nearer the trees, keeping themselves to the periphery of the harem.

"Just move on slowly." Harrington murmured. "They'll shift themselves eventually."

The noise of the engine dispersed some of the younger ones. An old deer turned nonchalantly in the direction of the rattling stranger. The stag turned his rear end to face them and began to walk away slowly. Rolling carefully forwards, Hamilton negotiated his way through the herd, making sure not to startle them or set them off in a panic. Some were a little more stubborn, others a little more curious, but eventually they made way for him, and he was able to carry on to Invercharnan and eventually the Gualachulain bothy at the end of the twelve mile stretch of one of the finest roads in all the Highlands.

Gualachulain, which meant Holly on the Bank in Gaelic, was a six-berth bothy, situated just below Hollybank House itself. Both provided holiday accommodation but had now been commandeered by Police Scotland and their crime scene examiners. Carrying on beyond, at Harrington's direction, Hamilton pushed on down to the very end of the road, where a gravel car park was indeed etched out on the northern tip of Loch Etive, just past the bothy exactly as she had said.

A metal farm gate up ahead ordinarily closed off the road to all but estate traffic, though unusually a veritable hive of activity was gathered just beyond on their arrival. The gate was guarded by a white Volvo marked up in a half-Battenberg style, blue lights on the roof and strobes on the grille. Vans and other 4x4s were scattered haphazardly further down the road.

"This will be it then." He remarked, pulling off just short of the car park, to where Iris directed him down an anonymous track.

Some twenty yards or so to the shore of the loch, the layby was clear of the trees on the near shoreline, providing an uninterrupted view of the proceedings taking place on the black waters. Hamilton turned *Torridon* around, so the vehicle faced down the length of the loch, giving Harrington a clear line of sight without having to twist her elderly frame.

Clambering out, Hamilton popped up the collar of his fleece, pulled his coat about him tighter and looped the lanyard over his neck as he made his way down the road to where a police cordon was stretched across the farm gate opening. Though it was still autumn, the bite in the air held promise of a bitter winter to come, perhaps even a heavy covering of early snow. Good news for the adjacent ski resort down the road. Not so much for the tips of Hamilton's unprotected ears.

Two Police Scotland constables in hi-vis jackets and tartan banded hats approached him as he reached the gate. The female officer asked with a pleasant, disarming smile whether they could assist him. He presented his SIS identification wallet and was promptly shown beneath the blue and white police tape as the gate was swung open.

The male officer remained at his post and stared suspiciously at the Land Rover. The dark, glossy finish of Montalcino Red was not an official colour of any agency that he was familiar with. His companion, the senior constable, led Hamilton towards a small huddle by the shore a little further along the track. He was introduced to a weary looking Detective Chief Inspector, happy enough to welcome him to Loch Etive at long last, but suspicious as to what Hamilton's intentions were.

Hamilton didn't recognise him from his time with the Strathclyde force. though that wasn't unusual. With amalgamations had come inevitable downsizing, relocations and reshuffles. It was just coming up to ten years since his own service now too.

"Thank you for waiting for us." Hamilton began, firmly taking the hand offered him.

"Aye, no bother." He said a little abruptly, clearly irritated. The police had been told to put a hold on all activities at the site until they could arrange for Hamilton and Harrington to be in attendance. If he was somewhat irritated now, Hamilton suspected that might only peak further before the day was out. "I'm naw really sure why the Intelligence Services would be interested in an abandoned car though." He shrugged.

"There's a wee possibility it might belong tae one of our auld boys."

"Yours?" the DCI began, but Hamilton was off.

Tucking his credentials into an outside pocket to stop them from swinging around he struck out purposefully to the shoreline where a black Humber Destroyer was tied up. Hamilton wasn't here for the conversation. Without asking permission, he clambered into the RIB and waited for the Glasgow DCI, the Inspector from Edinburgh and their respective assistants to join him. No one did.

"Drive that can yer?" the DCI cried mockingly.

Without missing a beat, Hamilton moved to the helm and fired up the engines. Quickly realising their mistake, the police hurried over to him, climbing aboard as he cast the lines off.

"Five years, Special Boat Service." Hamilton said simply, a scowl wrinkling his forehead as he guided the craft through the water.

The fetid smell of rubber brought back memories for Hamilton as the 'V' hull efficiently cut through the water to where a dive barge was anchored about a mile out from the head of the loch. The large Multi-Purpose Offshore Vessel had to be drafted in by Harmony Marine from the Kishorn Wind Farm project for the purposes of the relic's retrieval. Every day it was delayed on Loch Etive was another anxious day for the Scottish Government and its renewable energy investors. Given the signal from the DCI, there was a splash as divers plunged back into the murky depths to guide the retrieval operation from below.

"D'yer know whit we're actually doin' here?" the DCI began, by way of making conversation, "Other than recovering your property?"

"Judging by the size of that thing, it may as well be a missing U-boat." Hamilton replied, nodding at the immensely capable cranes and casting his mind back to the gantries of Bordeaux.

The DCI smiled for the first time. "Aye, it's always the Nazis whenever there's a sea loch is it naw?" He looked to his subordinate and rolled his eyes with a chuckle. "It's naw like they became the Lord o' the Isles or suhin'. Bobbing aroond in their wee boats looking for an Irish trawler tae point them in the right direction now."

Hamilton remained silent. The Inspector was clearly in a disagreeable mood. He let the man have his little rant.

The DCI gestured to the Edinburgh Inspector. "Bloody cold case unit came all the way over from Auld Reekie." He looked to Hamilton with a curious grin.

"Inspector Morag McCormack." The Inspector introduced herself, holding out her hand cordially to the visitor, who had barely acknowledged her presence up till now. "Cold Case Review Unit."

Hamilton shook her hand and acknowledged her with a curt nod of his head. She had a face like a slab of granite and eyes to match. The name Morag sometimes referred to the loch monster of Lochaber. Her name seemed curiously apposite.

"Strange that she got here before you."

Not strange at all, Hamilton thought, He might sound like a local from central Scotland, but he had driven nearly six hundred miles to get there. He chose not to bite, and the rest of the journey proceeded with an uneasy silence. Then the motor was cut, and the boat drifted to rest, steered expertly into place. The DCI called over the radio to the deck crane operator, signalling that they could begin. Hamilton turned back to look towards the shoreline. His burgundy Land Rover a mere speck on the horizon now. He imagined a pair of binoculars trained on him, studying the scene, he could almost feel Iris Harrington's intense stare, even from down range.

As the police divers emerged, the aft crane slowly rumbled into action. Being a hugely powerful knuckle and telescopic boom deck crane from HS Marine in Italy, the unit was massively over-engineered for the task it was assigned to do. Yet the crew whirred into action very carefully, deliberately slow, taking no risks with the prized artefact beneath the inky black waters. Weighing just over a ton-and-a-half, the object, even waterlogged, was no match for the 33ton capacity of the immensely formidable marine engineering.

Staring at the crane in amazement, Hamilton was a little startled when an air bubble, trapped in the submerged treasure, escaped with a ripple that rocked the RIB. From the hoisting winch, four lines attached to the four corners of the object as it sedately emerged from the loch.

In the wake of the air bubble, the rusty roofline of a car began to be visible above the waters. As the window line broke through the surface, a torrent of water gushed out through the shut lines from the interior, revealing the grinning, fleshless faces of two human skulls, gazing through a murky windscreen from their places in the front seats.

Hamilton frowned as he stared at the rusted form of a Mk II Rover P5 3-Litre Saloon. This wasn't the car he was expecting. This wasn't *Manuela* at all. Nothing like. He doubted Harrington had expected this either. She had neglected to mention anything about any possible occupants too.

It took another few moments to swing the car slowly onto the deck of the barge, where a forensic team were already suited up and ready to set to work. Once he had manoeuvred the RIB into position at the rear of the service vessel to allow the occupants to disembark onto its main deck, Hamilton took the opportunity to call the old fruit on the shore.

"Can yer see everythin', ma'am?" he asked.

"As well as can be expected." She sighed, sounding frustrated by her detachment from the scene. "Can you see the number plate?"

Hamilton turned back to where the old, rusted white on black licence plate hung on gamely to the rear of the boot. He read out the number.

"That's my car." She sighed.

"Are yer sure?"

"Yes." She said tersely, clearly as irritated by the surprise as Hamilton was surprised by the discovery.

"And the occupants?" he asked, referring to the skeletons in the front. "Two bodies in the front seats. Who are they?"

"Open the boot."

"The police are treating the car as a crime scene, ma'am." He explained.

"Hamilton, I arranged the reactivation of your credentials for a reason. Just get it done." She snapped abruptly, terminating the call.

Feeling thoroughly reprimanded he took the arm of the deckhand as he was helped onto the barge. Without another word, taking a deep breath, he moved to the rear of the vehicle, depressed the boot lock barrel, and grabbed the handle before anyone realised what he was doing.

"Whit d'yer think yer doin'?" the DCI demanded hotly.

Finally, the boot yielded to his efforts and slimy, icy water poured out onto Hamilton's trousers. He cursed and stepped back as the forensic team gathered angrily around him, staring as menacingly as it was possible to do from inside a hooded paper suit.

The interior of the boot was caked with silt on the carpet, battery box and wheel arch covers. A slimy residue covering what used to be an exceptionally fine Norfolk hide briefcase with a brass plaque engraved in beautifully flowing Copperplate script, still clear after all this time. Wiping away the slime with his thumb, Hamilton revealed the name:

CAMERON.

"Well," the DCI said caustically. "I wonder which one that wis."

"Gone a bit heavy on the keto diet, sir." His sergeant joked.

Hamilton, McCormack and the DCI just stared at him. No one was amused by the attempt at humour.

CHAPTER SEVENTY-FIVE
GERMANY, 1942

The flag prepared for the fender of the metallic blue Mercedes-Benz 540K Spezial Roadster was unique to the illustrious passenger. Its design consisted of pale blue material upon which was placed a golden Reichsadler holding a wreath of laurel leaves with crossed Field Marshal batons and a golden swastika in the centre. On the reverse, the black Grand Cross of the Iron Cross was placed in the centre, surrounded by a wreath of laurel leaves with a golden Luftwaffe eagle and crossed batons set in each of the four corners.

The perimeter of the whole was then surrounded by a golden border of laurel leaves with the straight-armed Balkenkreuz in each extremity. It was a grandiose flag for a grandiose individual, designed personally by the ever humble Reich Minister for Aviation and Commander-in-Chief of the German Air Force himself, Hermann Göring.

Following behind in a Horch with a mere Generaloberst of the Luftwaffe and some fellow officers, Sutherland's suspension was given less of a trying time by the lean figures of senior staff. His fender bore a significantly simpler triangular pennant with the Luftwaffe eagle on a pale blue field surrounded by a golden braided edge. Once the staff were all aboard, they set off on the long journey north.

The Peenemünde Army Research Centre had been founded back in 1937 when the Ministry of Aviation paid the town of Wolgast for the whole of the northern peninsula of the Baltic Sea Island of Usedom in Pomerania. While Werk Ost and Werk Süd sites were used by the Army, the Werk West site was exclusively set aside as the Luftwaffe testing facility. Having flown into the main headquarters facility at Rechlin Airfield for an inspection, the onward journey would take a little over two-and-a-half hours.

As expected, the Horch was a supremely comfortable car and with the cabriolet roof drawn over the top, was reasonably quiet too. The General didn't see the need to be seen, unlike the Reichsmarschall who wanted to be seen by everybody.

There was a comment made about the purpose of bulletproof glass and armoured bodywork on an open-topped roadster with a canvas roof and a few chuckles from the other officers, but largely the journey passed in relative silence. Sutherland, in his capacity as NSKK driver for the day, was an SS officer after all and therefore not one of them. Like the high-end, large displacement Maybach, the Horch had been equipped with a Telefunken radio and the General was content to listen to classical music for most of the journey which suited Sutherland very well too.

Retribution Weapon No.2 had been developed by Wernher von Braun and Walter Riedel as a Vengeance Weapon in retaliation for Allied bombing of German cities and infrastructure. Using the basic design of the A4 rocket, a modified, liquid-fuel engine and the data from successful test-firings of scale models, the weapon was finally ready for launch from Test Stand VII at the Peenemünde Airfield. The final checks and refuelling had already been completed by the time the entourage arrived and while not attached to the tour itself, Sutherland could see what they were all here to witness.

Supported by a tower of braced steel was an object nearly fifty-feet high, bulging to about five-feet in diameter across the middle with four large fins at the base. It was painted in a distinctive chequered pattern of alternating black and white panels and was just about the most horrific thing Sutherland had ever seen. All personnel were required to come inside during the test-firing in case of any anomalies in the guidance system. The first three rockets had shown limited success with the furthest distance travelled being a measly five-and-a-half miles. With Göring personally in attendance, there was evidently an expectation of much greater success.

Excusing himself to visit the bathroom, Sutherland's extended toilet break allowed him time to locate the design offices. There was a wealth of material around with many prototype sketches, chalkboard calculations and scale models scattered about the place. He didn't have long and couldn't go through anything in detail but managed to swipe a cut-away of a complete rocket. Entitled 'Aggregat 4' the drawing showed dimensional information for a rocket with a 1ton payload. Sutherland dreaded to think what carnage that would cause on the streets of London.

Folding it up, he stuffed it into a pocket of his tunic and returned to the observation site just as the countdown was being concluded. An explosion announced the ignition of the B-Stoff ethanol/water fuel mixture with liquid oxygen in the combustion chamber. Initiated by concentrated hydrogen peroxide and sodium permanganate driving a steam-turbine, the fuel and oxidiser pumps pressurised the mixture, increasing the thrust from 8tons during this preliminary stage, until a second large explosion announced the ignition of the main rocket engine.

With thrust building to 25ton, the 13.5ton rocket began to lift on a white-hot column of flame as the roar ripped the air asunder. While the billowing dust and smoke dissipated, the slender form of the rocket continued to ascend skywards, heading out into the Baltic. The tremendous roar slowly diminished as the rocket picked up speed. It's flame becoming a bright speck in the clear blue sky before disappearing altogether. An engineer was monitoring the altitude from instruments on the rocket itself, sending signals back down to the test site.

"Eighty kilometres, ninety, ninety-five."

"That's it!" Braun cried, delighted with the achievement. "That's the edge of space."

"Horizontal distance?" Riedel asked.

There was a moment as the data was still being recorded.

"One-hundred-and-fifty…seventy… one-hundred-and-ninety-kilometres. Splash down."

"We could reach London from the coast of France." The Generaloberst observed.

"That's terrific!" Göring exclaimed beaming with happiness. "We must have this at the first Party Rally after the war!"

"It's still early stages." Braun added cautiously. "But we are already seeing much greater potential with this design."

"New York?" Göring asked.

Braun looked at Riedel and Dr Thiel, his deputy director.

"Almost certainly." Braun nodded. "Perhaps even as far as Chicago."

"Well then, I was right to convince the Führer to allow the project to continue." Göring smiled with his usual modesty. "I will report back on this success directly."

Sutherland had mastered the art of appearing detached and disinterested while his intestines were churning up inside. He had started that practice during his Grand Prix days. Right before the start of the race the drivers posed for photographs on the grid. It was a small thing, but soon became a tradition, almost a superstition. Sometimes it was the last photo ever taken of one driver or another, smiling in the camera, belying the fact that they were absurdly terrified yet exhilarated all at the same time.

Here, Sutherland was quite simply appalled and alarmed. He was watching the dawn of a new age of warfare. A frightening phase where adversaries didn't even need to be on the same continent to bring about total destruction of one another. The world couldn't survive this level of escalation. It was time for *Adler* to trim the eagle's feathers.

CHAPTER SEVENTY-SIX

Hans Reinhardt had begun to frequent Sutherland's office more often as autumn progressed. The visits were less business related, more personal, friendly chats. Sutherland recalled the life of a Grand Prix driver, Hans described the work of a policeman, mostly during the closing stages of the Weimar Republic when he was starting out. Things were different then.

After the crisis years and hyperinflation, the Golden Twenties was a renewed time of optimism. The Great Depression of the early thirties flipped that all on its head again and social unrest had increased. A growing number of suicides made for an opportune time to commit murder and it was often a challenge to work out which was which.

They smoked and even drank a little at the end of the day. Sutherland usually had a nice little obstler in the decanter. The apple brandy was not top shelf stuff, but it was passable and made for a pleasant relaxant at the end of another stress-filled day.

On one particular visit, though Hans rarely discussed what he was investigating, he happened to mention that the Gestapo were taking an interest in a Roman Catholic priest. An Austrian who had apparently alerted the authorities and they suspected him of working for some Resistance movement. Hans asked if Sutherland knew anything about him. He didn't but wondered if this might just present a chance. It was a significant risk, most certainly to Sutherland, perhaps even more so for Reinhardt. If he agreed.

Opening the drawer of his desk, he reached deep inside and dropped down the false back that he had fabricated early on. Taking out the piece of paper, he regarded Reinhardt carefully for a moment. Then, with the policeman's curiosity aroused, Sutherland withdrew the paper and handed it over to him.

Hans took it and began to unfold it. He stared at the schematic of the A4 rocket, then at Sutherland. There was a flicker of realisation in his eyes, yet not of surprise, more restrained unease, as if it confirmed what he had suspected. Nevertheless the realisation was still deeply distressing.

"Why do you have this?" he asked quietly.

"It happened to fall off a desk somewhere." Sutherland answered vaguely.

"And you happened to be walking by?"

"Indeed."

Hans looked down again at the rocket, taking in the magnitude of what it was he held in his hand. The depiction of a man had been drawn near the base for scale reference. The figure was barely visible.

"Why are you showing me?"

"It might help you."

"How?" Hans enquired, feeling suddenly fearful.

"You could use it to test this priest."

"Test him?"

"If he passes it on, then you will know for sure that he is a member of the Resistance. If not, then you don't need to worry about him. Hopefully he will denounce whoever passes it onto him and you have your answer one way or another."

"This is not something I can just pass on." Hans replied.

"Why not?" Sutherland asked. It was a straightforward question, but one where the answers involved incalculable risks.

"What you're asking me to do is simply impossible. If anyone finds me with this…" Hans replied, placing the paper back on the desk again. "I won't do it."

"Take a look at it." Sutherland spoke slowly.

"I've seen it." Hans shuddered.

"Look at it." Sutherland said, keeping his voice low and his tone measured, but there was fire in his eyes. "This isn't war." He added. "This isn't about restoring German pride. This is about all-out vengeance. This is total annihilation. You're a man of honour, a man of principle. You can't possibly condone this."

"This country was on its knees after the last war." Hans re-joined. "Crushed under the heel of reparation. We had people dying on the streets for want of bread. It was as if the accident of being born German was a very stain upon world society."

"I understand that." Sutherland returned quickly. "My father fought in the last war and it bloody near destroyed him. Yours too probably. He told me once he wondered why you were fighting each other. Thought it would have been better to join forces and fight the French instead. What came afterwards was too severe and cut too deep, but as a civilised man, you can't see this as the way for the world to respect the achievements of the German nation again.

He tapped the paper. "This won't instil awe. This will simply entrench fear and hatred and bitterness into generations of humanity. With the destruction this weapon will rain down on mankind, every man, woman and child throughout the world, not just Europe, will call for Germany to be expunged from the map forever. You'll be the new Edomites, the Babylonians. You'll cease to exist. The victims of this weapon will only want a bigger and more permanent reckoning.

"On the other hand, think what would happen should Germany win with this thing, and Berlin does indeed become the world capital. Every moment of every day, any citizen anywhere in the world will live under the perpetual dread of being carted off in the middle of the night because they dared to hold a different opinion, they possessed the wrong colour eyes or, heaven forbid, might even have a speech impediment."

He stared hard at Hans, remembering the time he had mentioned the stutter his youngest boy had whenever he got nervous. Hans could see it too. There was a frightening sense of realisation that such a statement wasn't mere hyperbole.

"To save Germany, Hans, we have to destroy what it has now become."

Hans paused, deep in thought, pondering where the war was going, what it was doing to his country, his people. It wasn't merely the destruction, the death, the immediate effects of battle. There were other things too, more disturbing things. Indoctrination of the young, teaching them the supposed corrupting influence of the Jew. The apparent degeneration of art. Book burnings. Principled people turning a blind eye to the forced labour camps, the expulsion of whole swathes of the population, friends and neighbours, an acceptance of it, resignation to it. Sometimes even approbation.

Corruption at every level of government, the criminality of high office. How could he police the general populous when those in authority were carrying out far worse atrocities and remaining immune from prosecution, justifying actions for the greater good of the German Reich? How long would it take before the very fabric of civilised society would be frayed beyond all recognition, nothing more than a useless bundle of threads?

If Papa could kill a thousand people because they disagreed with government doctrine and because he wore a uniform, why couldn't little Joachim kill Stefan at school because they didn't agree who would captain the next scouting expedition? He too had a uniform. How could you punish the son and not the father?

What would happen to the German people if this madness continued? What would happen to the honest, moral, civilised masses who begrudged what was happening all around them, who hated looking the other way but were powerless to do anything else? What happened when their scruples, their principles, their morals became the object of persecution itself?

Hans looked at the paper again, examined the dimensions. The weapon was huge. He knew if it had already got to the final testing stage, the Air Ministry would stop at nothing to bring this project into full production. When that happened, how would the world respond? Would they capitulate, and allow the dark shadow of Nazism to take over Europe, or would they retaliate with overwhelming force and fury? What form would that reply take? Either eventuality was too frightening to contemplate.

Hans slowly picked up the drawing and folded it back up again. Placing it inside the jacket of his suit, he took up his brandy and drained the glass. Sutherland refilled them both immediately, replacing the stopper before holding his glass up.

"For Germany?" He toasted.

Hans saw the look of comradeship in Sutherland's eyes. Even relief. He had an ally at last. Hans knew the risks Sutherland had already taken. Now it was up to him to do his part. Not for him, nor even for his wife and children, but for the future of Germany, and by extension the very continent of Europe itself.

"For Germany." He nodded.

CHAPTER SEVENTY-SEVEN
SCOTLAND, 2018

The venerable old fruit had installed herself in a folding canvas chair in a marquee that had been erected on the shore of the loch. While Azimuth Stern Drives brought the Dive Support Vessel closer to the shore to offload the Rover, allowing it to return to the north, the RIB sped back ahead of it to deliver the briefcase for her inspection. Now, on a robust Peli Case in front of her was the slimy, swollen, and distorted form of the Norfolk hide case. It was not quite how she remembered it but narrowing her eyes she could see it as it had once been, a burnished rich conker brown, solid and robust with a soft leather lining.

The DCI and his sergeant, along with McCormack and a forensic scientist gathered around the case, eager to determine its contents. They all wanted to see inside but had somehow fallen under the matriarchal spell of the frail but formidable old lady in the chair.

"Okay, Hamilton." She said at last. "Let's take a look."

Hamilton crouched down and sprung open the latches, a slimy trail of water seeping out, ran down the front of the case. A technician, white paper suit and forceps stood ready to receive. In his excitement he snapped them together subconsciously, like a teenager revving a car. Harrington wasn't impressed and the man meekly took half a step back.

Despite the age of the case and its distortion, the two halves were well sealed together, and Hamilton spent a few moments trying to gain some purchase between the leather to lever it apart. Eventually though, but with less care than he had hoped, the two halves parted ways and the case sprung open.

Expecting to see a mush of rotten contents, Hamilton was surprised to see a layer of tightly packed clothes, almost in the shape of the case itself, sitting on top of the lower half. The remnants of a Tweed jacket were prominent on top, Harris cloth, judging by the weight. What remained of the paisley lining bore a label, George Jamieson. Fort William. It meant nothing to Hamilton, and he offered it up to the technician.

"Look at this." They remarked, pointing to the breast pocket. "There's a bullet hole here. Doesn't seem to have gone through. Must have been stopped by something in the pocket."

"Lucky." Hamilton replied.

"Hip flask." Harrington said frankly. "Where Cameron was concerned, luck had nothing to do with it."

Hamilton exchanged a look with the technician, then returned to the case. Next there was a dissolved mess of a once fabulous dark blue silk dress.

"An odd choice for our Mr. Cameron." Hamilton remarked as he carefully conveyed that up to the second technician.

"It's a Drecoll." Iris said, remembering when she had shuffled her own younger, slender frame into it. Back then her breasts didn't hang down limp and useless like rocks in a sock. They had been pert, well formed, admired. She had fitted into it well. "Or at least it was. Terribly expensive. Premiered by Jacqueline Janet in the 1937 Bagatalle Concours d'Elegance."

"Soonds like a car thing." Hamilton replied. He was getting used to the lingo of such things.

"It was," Iris nodded. "Mademoiselle Janet had her boyfriend repaint his Bugatti in the same colour as that dress before she entered his car."

"That's a wee bit extravagant." Hamilton commented.

"When you're the reigning Miss France and your boyfriend is the wealthy heir to a vast pharmaceutical fortune, you can make happen whatever you desire." Iris responded in that classic unvarnished manner characteristic of her age and service. No one beat about the bush back then. You said what had to be said and dealt with the aftermath. "That's not what we're here for though, Hamilton." She added, gesturing for him to continue in his search.

Thus chastened, he crouched back down again and removed what at first appeared to be an old, waxed coat. As he picked it up, he realised the remaining contents had been wrapped up inside. Digging his hands down the sides of the case to feel for the bottom, feeling the slime ooze through his fingers, he cradled the bundle in his arms and set about carefully transferring it to the nearest trestle table. Certainly glad he wasn't wearing a suit as a mildly putrid smell emanated from somewhere within the bundle.

"I wondered how he was going to do it." Iris murmured, almost to herself. "This was locked away long before your plastic Bags for Life came in." she said to Hamilton. "People actually had to think about things then."

Getting up from the chair stiffly, she walked with as much dignity as her frame could muster to where the gathering had now shifted its focus.

"Be careful with this." She said sternly. "We don't want to lose everything now."

"Yes, ma'am." Hamilton nodded, before receiving a withering look.

At this prompting, the two forensic technicians on hand stepped forward and began to carefully unwrap the fabric parcel. Turning the jacket over onto it's back, they noticed it had been bound together with string, much of which had rotted away, but where it had looped beneath the arms, some of the fibres remained.

"It's an early Barbour." One remarked as they discovered the yellow label stitched to cotton plaid lining. "A waxed stockman's coat. In good condition considering. Whatever is inside may still be reasonably well preserved."

"That's what I'm hoping for, young man." Iris nodded, somehow sounding disapproving of his assessment, as though he should not have expected anything less.

They carefully removed the remaining string that had kept it bound up so tightly, then unfolded the flaps, arms, and collar until it approximately resembled an actual garment, with a noticeable bulge about the abdomen. Carefully they began to unfasten the press studs down the front placket, then slowly unzipped the coat itself, peeling back the flaps to reveal a leather case.

Secured by a leather strap and a brass stud, the flap of the case opened to reveal a glass spirit flask with silver bayonet fitting and a hinged sandwich tin. On the top of the flask, the initials ADC had been professionally engraved into the cap.

"Aide de camp?" Hamilton guessed.

"Alexander Donald Cameron." Harrington corrected.

"Which one is he?" he gestured in the direction of the car outside.

"Neither. He was the father of the gentleman who put that case in there." Harrington remarked.

"And the liquid?"

"Probably whisky, but not the good stuff. James would never waste the good stuff."

"We can test it back at the lab." The technician remarked, receiving a nod of approval from the matriarch.

Hamilton was willing to test it there and then, but procedures and such. He had already incurred the wrath of McCormack and the DCI from Glasgow who had not even introduced himself. Probably quite deliberate, Hamilton presumed.

The sandwich case was tightly sealed, its tarnished silver leaves binding together over time.

"We can open this back at the lab too." The technician reassured.

"No, you will open it now." Harrington demanded, pointing a bony finger at the object. The technicians looked to the DCI for permission nervously. "Don't look at him. I'm telling you what to do." She said firmly.

The DCI nodded wearily and gave a visual sigh as he placed his hands in his pockets, feeling more and more like a spectator in his own investigation.

Carefully, nervously, the technicians worked a scalpel between the two halves of the tin, slowly scraping the blade down the length of the join to break up the oxide, acting like a weld between the halves. With a little WD40 sprayed onto the hinges the technician slowly worked away at the tin until the two halves came apart.

"The maker is Swaine & Adeney." The technician remarked, reading the marking stamped onto the hinge plate. "London, England. Good set of hallmarks too."

"Quite likely." Harrington nodded "His father liked the finer things."

"The other half has been stuffed with a handkerchief." The technician observed with some bewilderment.

"Packing material." Harrington remarked. "To keep whatever is inside protected."

Duly informed, the technician carefully worked through the handkerchief with forceps. "Monogrammed 'JC'." He murmured.

"That's our man." Harrington nodded.

"James Cameron?" Hamilton suggested, picking up on her use of the first name a little earlier.

Harrington remained tight lipped and continued to stare at the back of the technician as they carefully pulled out the cotton handkerchief, not sure what to find.

"Here's something."

Carefully he picked up the container with his gloved fingers, holding it up for a closer look. It was an old aluminium film canister, a shade under two-inches tall. Made in Germany and dated 1944. The remains of the adhesive label on the top bore the Agfa logo followed by *Röntgen-Fluorapid-Film Patrone 1,60m Film*. On the side of the canister was embossed *I.G. Farbenindustrie A.G. AGFA Berlin SO 36*, with the Agfa logo on the reverse.

"Whit is it?" Hamilton asked, watching a smile play across Iris's thin lips.

"Just what I thought it would be." She said. "He never disappointed."

She was speaking in riddles. Hamilton frowned and pointed to the canister. "It has a handwritten label on the lid."

Iris leaned closer and squinted, her old eyes barely able to discern the scrawled handwriting.

"It's an address." She said, then turning to one of the technicians. "Can you clean that up first and preserve it for me? I want the label to remain legible, but the canister is only to be opened in a dark room. The film may still be unprocessed. Understood?"

They both nodded meekly. Carrying the canister carefully over to the table like it was an unexploded grenade with the pin removed, before setting to work on cleaning and preserving the ancient label. Finally, after applying some clear lacquer to the top surface and a plastic protective film, they brought it to her for inspection.

"*Villa des Pins.*" She said with a flourish. "Avenue Jean de la Fontaine, Nice." Not all the address was still legible, or indeed had even been thus inscribed, just the name of the house, but it was enough.

"Whit is that?" Hamilton asked.

"What it is now, I have no idea." She shrugged. "Back then it was the most fabulous villa." She explained, almost becoming misty-eyed at the recollection.

CHAPTER SEVENTY-EIGHT
FRANCE, 1943

Villa des Pins was a luxurious sixteen-room manor house across three-storeys set in three acres of parkland with simply sublime views over the city below. A long cork-screw driveway beyond ornate gates wound through a mature garden shaded by cedars, sequoias, and Cypresses. There were two-Drawing Rooms, a Dining Room, a lavishly equipped and well-stocked kitchen, eight bedrooms, four bathrooms and an office.

Newly constructed in 1943, the architectural style had been lifted directly from the pages of the latest design portfolios, complete with pale cream stucco, cool marble floors and wonderfully geometric forms. The terrace of the main bedroom provided a spectacular view of the elegant spit of Cap Ferat, and a sneaking glimpse of *Villa Tunis* just below, belonging to her patron Ettore Bugatti.

She was enjoying her morning coffee as usual, sitting in a bathrobe and taking in the sumptuous view. Placing the cup back onto its saucer, she seemed oblivious to the fact that living in such a decadent haven, even in southern France, was highly unusual. Her bathrobe slipped and exposed a knee to the warming sun. Her injured knee. The one that brought her dancing career to a premature end. She leaned forward and rubbed it to soothe the throbbing. It always hurt in the morning.

Had she not jumped across the chasm the avalanche might have killed her. In the end, her awkward landing killed off her means to fulfil an intense desire for high-speed thrills. Having been refused permission to compete at

Brooklands because she was a woman, she had sought satisfaction elsewhere and the slopes of the Pyrenees had welcomed her with open arms and beautifully powdery snow.

As it happened, in the same year of her skiing accident, the first Women's Grand Prix was to be staged at Montlhery. Though she had been but three years old at the time, the memory of seeing Charles Rolls, Vincenzo Lancia and the Renault brothers thundering through her village in their fearsome machines was still vivid. Now, finally, on the second day of June 1929, she had been given a chance to prove her mettle. It was her first victory. There came many more. Racing for Bugatti, winning the crowds, if not the races. Setting the world alight with her blonde hair, winning smile and fearless driving.

Of course, racing was suspended for the foreseeable future now. She hoped to make a comeback after the war ended, but the crash in Sao Paulo had unfairly tarnished her reputation. The horror of the accident came back to her frequently. She had no memory of it but the newspaper image of her lain out on the ground amongst the dead had been shockingly graphic.

It was her mechanic, her lover, that had exonerated her after the accident. There had been a photographer present at the scene. Just moments before the fateful collision he caught the moment when an enthusiastic crowd, cheering on their local hero, inadvertently dislodged a hay bale right into her path. Coming up fast on de Teffé's Alfa Romeo, she moved to the outside as they both rounded the corner and there it was. She had no chance of avoiding it. No chance at all. Binelli had tracked the photographer down and the photograph was produced. It took several years but Hellé was in the clear.

Following three days in a coma, her recovery was nothing short of miraculous. Apart from an intense feeling of guilt, she had come out surprisingly unscathed. The helmet that had fatally fractured the skull of an unfortunate spectator had saved her own life. She often thought about that poor man.

Years before, she had raced supercharged Miller cars around American dirt tracks without a helmet because the crowds liked to see her flowing locks. She wondered whether that might have been the more prudent course. Of course, she would have certainly been killed, but perhaps that would have been easier than living with the consequences of the aftermath.

Even after she was cleared of causing the accident, manufacturers had stayed away. Bugatti had humiliatingly refused to take her back. She suspected their golden boy, Louis Chiron, might have had something to do with it. He had never liked the fact a woman had taken some of the gilding away from his own rising star. Even after the Yacco endurance trials enabled her to break ten world records, sponsors had stayed away too.

It was fortunate therefore that her exoneration for Sao Paulo had provided her with substantial compensation. Though only in terms of a financial settlement. The ongoing damage to her career was as yet undetermined. Still, there were other ways of making money. Selling names to the Gestapo. Names of Jewish immigrants, people who had escaped the German onslaught elsewhere and who had come to Nice to escape. It had been Binelli's idea. It was a sure thing.

The window of opportunity had presented itself rather unexpectedly and may only last so long. Things had been relatively peaceful under Italian occupation the previous year, and people had still been able to go about their lives as normal, but having left Paris, Mariette Hélène Delangle and her lover Arnaldo Binelli, settled comfortably into the villa while the Hotel Excelsior nearby became the regional SS Headquarters.

When the Nazi regime took over from Mussolini's men, they were keen to purge the coast of Jewish refugees. Some 2,000 had already been arrested in their beachwear and hustled away. That was before she had arrived, but there were still enclaves to be found if you knew where to look. Hellé Nice knew exactly where to look. Crucially though, she also knew who to talk to so they could get out first.

CHAPTER SEVENTY-NINE

The air was warm. A beautiful azure sky stretched out clear to the horizon. The fabulous Louis XIII style of Nice-Ville station greeted him with the promise of a wonderful summer on the Côte d'Azur, yet its glorious façade belied the horrors that it was witnessing each day. Forced migrations of persecuted people.

A strange, sombre atmosphere cast a pall over the scene. Even amidst the summer sun, Sutherland had detected it immediately on arrival. Sadly, he well knew the source of the foreboding, oppressive air. It was the reason why Reinhardt had dispatched Sutherland to the south of France.

The Italians had done nothing to solve the increasing problem of Jewish immigration into the region. When the Allies had invaded North Africa, Nice had fallen under Mussolini's rule. However, Il Duce had no intention of collaborating with the Vichy regime. He refused to implement the obligation for all Jews to wear the yellow star as he considered it to be inconsistent with the dignity of the Italian army. Thus, the French Riviera had quickly become something of an asylum for Jewish refugees from all over the Continent.

That all changed following Italy's surrender. The Germans moved in and SS-Hauptsturmführer Alois Brunner setup his headquarters at the Hotel Excelsior on Avenue Durante, just a stone's throw away from the railway station. His teams of SS officers routinely patrolled the city's streets, rounding up anyone who might look remotely Jewish. Once registered in the hotel's visitors books they were being sent by rail to the Drancy internment camp outside Paris, then onwards to the infamous death camps where the eradication of humanity had been grotesquely industrialised.

Now there was talk of possible invasion, Sutherland expected the exterminations to accelerate. He suspected this was why Brunner had been made the commandant at Drancy, to effect the transfers more quickly. He had taken the train north just a few weeks before Sutherland's arrival. Reinhardt's own supply problem though was not in the numbers being deported north. His own camps further south, in Equatorial Africa, were running short on labour after nearly twelve months with no new arrivals and incredibly inhospitable working conditions taking their toll on diminishing survivors.

Sutherland watched *Manuela* being unloaded from the box cart safely, shuddering as he well knew how many people he was expected to cram inside the same wagon. Then, he drove the short distance to the hotel to report in with the local Gestapo. Stepping out onto the pavement, he took in the charming Belle Époque façade of the luxury hotel, now stained with a scarlet banner. He suspected the stench of blood would remain long after that hateful pennant was rolled up and put away.

"Untersturmführer Sudentland." He was greeted in the lobby by a non-commissioned officer. A Chief squad leader, judging by the pips on his collar. "We have been expecting you. I am Hauptscharführer Hoeschl, at your service."

"Hauptsturmführer Reinhardt told you why I am here?"

"Yes, he explained that we are to give you our full cooperation."

"Good, then let's get started." He smiled, feeling distinctly like a sheep dressed in a wolf's clothes.

"We have prepared a cell for someone you might want to talk to before we deport them."

"Oh?"

"A Monsieur Jean Chaigneau. He was the Prefect of the Alpes-Maritimes department. He has been accommodating many Jewish families in the Prefecture apartments and may know where a great deal more could be sheltering."

"Are you holding him here?"

"In the wine cellar."

"Take me to him."

"This way, sir."

The brick vaulted cellar still retained an enviable selection of wines, though most of the better ones had already been consumed shortly after occupation. The remaining space had been turned into holding cells where hundreds of people had already been interned while they awaited the arrival of another train. Perhaps the very train Sutherland had just arrived on.

Crammed between brick pillars, sitting on old wine crates, straw, and whatever meagre luggage they had been able to gather up, the wretched faces of infirm men, elderly widows, young women, and children barely old enough to walk looked back at him as they moved down the central corridor.

Behind the iron grates that had once kept the most expensive wines safe and secure, sat a man who looked considerably older than his forty-nine years. An empty crate of Bellet turned onto its end had become a makeshift seat for him, yet still he looked decidedly uncomfortable and cramped.

Sutherland looked around the space, the dim lighting, the coolness of the air and the haunting faces looking back at him. Knowing his face might be one of the last any of these people saw was a poignant reminder of just exactly how important it was that he was here, and what he was trying to do.

"I cannot talk to him here." Sutherland gestured around, indicating the lack of privacy in the cellar arrangement. "Is there an office somewhere?"

"Of course." Hoeschl said, a little taken aback.

"Can you arrange for some coffee and that we are not disturbed?"

"Sir, this is a little unusual."

"Will it be a problem?" he asked, fixing the young sergeant with a fierce scowl.

"No, not at all." Hoeschl stammered nervously. "Right this way, sir."

Returning to the lobby, Sutherland watched as half a dozen SS soldiers dragged in three or four families through the front door. A young girl dropped her teddy and started screaming, trying to reach back and grab it before she was kicked to the floor.

"Soldier!" Sutherland cried, silencing the barked orders.

The soldiers halted and turned, saluting him as the families looked at him with total fear in their eyes. Sutherland looked at them intently, keeping a firm scowl upon his face, the anger for these atrocities fuelling his evil look while his conscience supplied tears he needed to keep restrained. This was the front line of the holocaust. A word derived from ancient Greek for 'whole burnt offering'. It was an abomination.

Stepping forward, he bent down and picked up the teddy bear, a ragged looking thing stuffed with sawdust and wearing a kaftan. The eyes were dull black beads and the remains of a pink tongue protruded from an open mouth. Walking towards the girl, he held it out to her, not trusting his voice to say anything as he looked down into those frightened little eyes. She took the teddy bear and clutched it tightly to her tiny body.

"Dyakuyu." She croaked in quiet Ukrainian.

Looking up at her parents, he could see it in their eyes. They had experienced much suffering already. Escaping the horrors of *Barbarossa*, the German invasion of their homeland. Trekking across a war torn, ever expanding, increasingly hostile Third Reich, hiding out for months at a time, constantly in fear of death or discovery, finally reaching sanctuary in Nice. Now that too was being cruelly ripped away from them. There was despair. Utter hopelessness. They had no fight left. Nothing.

He looked sternly at the soldiers. A reprimand would do no good, either for him or the families. It would only single them out for extra brutality and raise a question or two about his own loyalty. Turning away, he headed for the stairs and began to climb, allowing the unfolding tragedy in the lobby to continue.

Hoeschl showed him into one of the old guest rooms. The bed had been shoved to one side and a walnut, Empire Line dressing table had been repurposed as a desk in the centre of the space. He positioned the chair behind the desk, with its back to the balcony, before sitting down and facing the door. Monsieur Chaigneau was promptly brought up and made to sit down on the bed to the side. A tray of coffee was then brought in, and Hoeschl stood by the door.

"This is a private interrogation." Sutherland remarked. "Best you don't see what takes place."

Hoeschl nodded his understanding and departed the room, leaving Sutherland alone with the haggard prefect. He noticed the man's eyes were focussed on the new Union Flag patch on his left sleeve. The Legion of Saint George.

"I don't have much time here and you have even less." Sutherland began in perfect French as he poured coffee into the single cup. "I need names and addresses." He pushed the cup forwards, offering it to Chaigneau. "Drink. It might be the last time."

Chaigneau leaned forward and took the cup, bringing it tentatively up to his lips.

"You've been busy sheltering persecuted families. I've been sent from Berlin to ship them out." He continued. "Unfortunately, there is nothing I can do for you personally. You're already dead, but I might be able to help all the families you've sheltered."

Chaigneau frowned as he swallowed the coffee, unsure that he understood was his interrogator was saying.

"What do you mean?" he asked. His voice was quiet and reedy. No strength left.

"You're affiliated with a Resistance network."

"Am I?" he replied evasively.

"I know you are."

"You're a traitor." Chaigneau murmured angrily, staring at the Union patch.

"Well, better not shout it." Sutherland smiled getting up and walking around the desk. "My bosses might want to do something about that." He perched on the edge in front of Chaigneau, folding his arms across his chest and crossing one boot over the other.

Chaigneau narrowed his eyes again, trying to decipher what Sutherland was driving at.

"Help me continue the work you've started." He continued quietly. "All my superiors want is a list of names. Three-thousand names. I don't care if they're real or not, but if they are, help me to get them out before I hand over the list."

"Why should I?"

"Because I'm their only chance now." He looked meaningfully into Chaigneau's eyes. "There will be no more evacuations possible once I go back to Berlin. If the Allies invade they may even start shooting Jews on sight and save the trains for soldiers."

Chaigneau thought carefully for a moment. "Do you know a man called Jean-Pierre Wimille?"

"Know him? I raced against him." Sutherland smiled. Chaigneau seemed surprised by this. "His Bugatti beat my Auto Union at Pau in '37."

"He can get them out."

"How do I find him?"

"*You* don't." Chaigneau said bitterly. "I already have someone who can do that."

"Then I can stall for time while JP gets it done." Sutherland replied, thinking through the plan. "But I will need the lists soon. I have a couple of days at most."

Chaigneau paused again. He knew he didn't have any time left but was not totally convinced he could trust this man. It seemed a very clever plot to try and get him to divulge more information, compromise the network and put even more people at risk. It was exactly the kind of the thing the SS were known for.

"Three thousand, you said?" Sutherland nodded. "You won't find that many around here now. Maybe a few hundred at most."

"Where?"

Chaigneau shook his head. "There are many vineyards around here. Not many have grapes now."

"This is why I found you sitting on a box of Bellet?"

"You're observant."

"My survival depends on being observant."

That word seemed to strike a chord with Chaigneau. Survival. An interrogator wouldn't ordinarily use that word. They had no need to. Even someone who had been turned to the Nazi cause would not likely express themselves that way. Maybe this man could help. If there was a chance…

"You will need to visit the *Villa des Pins*. Avenue Jean de la Fontaine. Hellé will give you what you need but you must promise me that you will help her too. Brunner's men have been onto her for months. They know she has been giving me information."

Sutherland nodded.

"Why has she not been arrested?" he asked quietly, then thumped the table loudly for the benefit of Hoeschl outside.

"I heard Brunner was planning to, but he was called to Paris first."

"I'll do what I can." Another question was on his lips. "Why are there supply problems in Africa?"

"Africa?"

"My superior wants me to find new labourers to send to Equatorial Africa."

"My God. It's true then." Chaigneau wheezed.

"What's true?"

Again, Chaigneau considered how to reply. "I heard a rumour that the Nazis were sending workers to French Chad."

"Chad?" Sutherland frowned. "But they're fighting for Free France."

"This is true." He nodded. "The Governor-General is doing great work rousing soldiers for the cause." Chaigneau took the opportunity to have another sip of coffee. "Some of the junior administrators though are sent there from France as a punishment posting. They get what they can and leave. Bribes. Corruption. They do what they have to." He paused again. "There was a deal. Before the war, before Éboué became governor, to supply America with some kind of resource from Chad."

"What resource?"

"I don't know anymore. I don't. Chad doesn't produce anything." Chaigneau replied, holding up his hands. "It was all just a rumour."

"But prisoners are still being sent there?"

Chaigneau shrugged. "It's possible. The indigenous population is too busy fighting for France."

"Who would know more?"

"All I heard was that the deal was struck in Paris before the war."

Sutherland frowned as he contemplated the news Chaigneau had given him. He vividly remembered a party at *Le Boeuf sur le Toit* in Paris. It was an intoxicating evening all round. There was a moment at the bar. While a Lieutenant of the gendarmerie waited to hear from the Opera, there had been two men talking nearby. An American and a German. He met the German later in Berlin. He was now Sutherland's boss, Manfred Reinhardt. He never did find out who the American was. Had that been the deal that was struck?

"I will do what I can." Sutherland murmured quietly again. "Do you have any loose teeth?"

Chaigneau nodded pressing the side of his face. "I've been here a while. The food they serve…" he trailed off.

"They'll give you hell later." Sutherland nodded. "Forgive me, Jean."

Suddenly Sutherland swiped the back of his hand hard against Chaigneau's face, knocking him sideways off the bed. "Give me those names!" he cried.

Chaigneau looked up, momentarily startled and shaking his head.

"I said now!" Sutherland cried, grabbing Chaigneau's shirt with one hand and striking him with his fist in the same place. He felt the teeth come loose and Chaigneau nodded, mouthing something groggily.

"The vineyards." He croaked. "They have no grapes, but plenty of goats."

"Hoeschl!" Sutherland cried as he slapped Chaigneau on the back of the head. This prompted the prefect to spit out the dislodged teeth and mouthful of blood exactly on cue as Hoeschl came back into the room. "Take him away. I have what I need."

Chaigneau surreptitiously made the sign of the cross, as if blessing Sutherland, while Hoeschl dragged him back out into the corridor. Sutherland stood there for a moment, lowering his head as he plunged his hands into the pockets of his trousers. He breathed a deep sigh and considered Chaigneau's parting words.

They have no grapes, but plenty of goats.

What was he trying to say? Shaking his head, Sutherland looked at where the coffee cup had been dashed to the floor in the struggle, then to the small puddle of blood where three yellowish teeth protruding from the pool of liquid. This was a messy business indeed.

CHAPTER EIGHTY

Avenue Jean de la Fontaine reminded Sutherland of an alpine road as it wound its way tightly up through the fashionable Cimiez neighbourhood. Any significant speed was impossible. The road was narrow, hairpin corners tight and the plunge treacherous if he got it wrong. The views though, peering through the foliage, were magnificent. The old city of Nice down below, a turquoise sea framed by the boughs of trees in full bloom, their scent filling the sultry air.

Thankfully *Manuela* was a competent hillclimber. Approaching the pinnacle of the ascent, Sutherland passed by the high garden walls of the Villa Tunis where it was rumoured Signor Bugatti was seeing out the war with his ailing wife Barbara in quiet seclusion. Since the death of his son Jean, the fortunes of the company had nosedived. The Molsheim factory was in ruins, there were no cars being built. It was a sad demise for one of the greatest names in the business.

Finally, Sutherland rolled through the open metal gates of *Villa des Pins*. Framed by stuccoed pillars with marble capitals engraved with the name of the residence. The driveway curved through sumptuous mature trees; majestic stone pines, from which the villa obtained its name, soaring sequoias, scented cedars and stately Cypresses. At the entrance to the house, a grand Hispano-Suiza H6C Boulogne was parked, the striking stork mascot pointing back down the hill.

Clambering out of *Manuela*, he ambled past the imposing machine, admiring its coachwork and the extraordinary length of its bonnet. Negotiating the steep, twisting mountain roads in such a vast and unwieldy vehicle must have required rare skill and confidence. Turning back to the house, a raised patio leading to the entrance was shaded by pergolas covered in bougainvillea and wisteria, providing a welcoming display of pink and lilac garlands.

Stepping up onto the courtyard, defined by squared-off stone pillars, Sutherland took in the scene around him. Made from a series of connected boxes, the exterior managed to seem graceful even in its severity. Pale beige stucco provided a canvas for dangling boughs of flowers. The soft scent of Fer à Cheval hand soap emanated from inside. Charles Trenet was singing "Boum!" on a phonograph. It was hard to believe that *Villa des Pins* resided in the same city where thousands of families were being dragged off the sands and hurled into box carts to be taken to their place of execution. All occurring beneath the same, pristine, cloudless sky.

On entering the villa, Sutherland encountered a floating three-tiered open staircase dominating the rear of the spacious hallway. A masterful mix of dusty pink Candoglia marble, walnut handrail and Bohemian glass balusters, bolted to the stairs with bronze studs set the material tone that was felt throughout the astonishing residence. Geometric patterns and square coffering were applied to the underside of the staircase and plaster ceilings. Copper light fittings were suspended from a ceiling rose soaring far out of sight. The effect was transparent and ethereal, a modernist cathedral.

"Bonjour, Monsieur." A warm, sultry voice echoed in the impressive void.

Turning to face the direction of the sound, Sutherland beheld the sumptuous form of Hellé Nice. In possession of an exotic caramel complexion, inherited from her white postmaster father and black housewife mother, she retained the poise and grace of the dancer she once was. Indeed, in the way she held herself as Sutherland looked on, he half-expected her to spring into a flurry as Charles Trenet sang out the whimsical chorus once more.

"Chaigneau sent me." He said flatly.

There was no flicker of recognition or alarm on her face. Her serene, hospitable appearance remained intact.

"Would you like to come through into the garden? We're just having some lunch."

Sutherland turned and followed her as she descended three Brazilian onyx steps into a sunken lounge where simple white walls allowed two-tone parquet floor to take centre stage. Despite her knee injury, she still moved with lithe fluidity of the cabaret, her bare feet hardly making a sound as she glided across the floor. Three soaring Crittall-style doors opened out onto a rear terrace where a swarthy, well-proportioned young man was sunbathing on a lounger and a tray of bread, cheese and olives resided on the wicker table nearby.

"Did you get the wine?"

"Arnaldo, we have a visitor." She announced breezily as she sauntered over to him.

Turning his head, Arnaldo looked up at Sutherland from behind the darkened lenses of his glasses. "So I see." he said with a cheery air. "What brings the SS all the way up to our humble little abode.

With an enviable view over the bay of Villefranche-sur-Mer and the Cap Ferat beyond, *Villa Tunis* below and the luxury of an outdoor swimming pool, Sutherland would have hardly called the sixteen-room villa a mere abode, let alone humble. That was precisely Arnaldo's point, of course.

"I don't have much time, so I'll be direct." Sutherland began, removing his hat and tucking it under his arm casually. "I've been summoned from Berlin to round up Jewish immigrants and send them down to Africa. You know where they're some still sheltering in the mountains. I want their names and addresses."

"For what price?" Arnaldo asked coolly. "There's always a price."

"Your freedom." He said bluntly. "Chaigneau told me you can get in contact with JP."

"How do you know Jean-Pierre?" Hellé asked.

"We used to race against one another."

"Auto Union?"

"How did you know?"

"You don't look German." Hellé laughed. "Tazio was a dwarf and poor

Dickie was killed at Spa, so that only leaves Andrew Sutherland as the last non-German driver for the Silver Arrows."

"You remember me." He replied, quietly gratified.

"Oh yes, you were very good." She smiled. "I think you might have had a chance at Donington in '39 if, you know…" she trailed off and shrugged.

"You've been keeping yourself busy in the meantime, by the looks of it." Arnaldo remarked, sitting up on the lounger and appraising the uniform.

"I fight my own way."

"So, what do you need?" Hellé asked.

"I need you to get me these names."

"I'll not send people to their deaths."

"Neither will I," Sutherland returned quickly. "But you should know, the Excelsior have only allowed you to live like this while they're supplied with Jews. The trouble is they're now drying up. Not all the people on your lists have been found, so you're both on borrowed time."

"How many names do you need?" Hellé enquired.

"My boss sent me down here to find another three thousand."

"There is nothing like that number still here. Most have been deported already."

"Chaigneau told me." Sutherland nodded. "I don't care if the names are genuine or not. I just need a list to send up the chain and full box carts going to Marseille."

"Filled with what?" Arnaldo asked.

Sutherland finally understood what Chaigneau was trying to tell him. Hellé tilted her head to one side, seeking further explanation. He decided to keep it to himself for now.

"Bring me a list. Send the names of the genuine refugees to JP. It will be their last chance to escape. After that I hand the list to my superiors, and they take their chances with the Gestapo. I can only hold them off for so long, but it should just give you time to get out."

"Why would we want to leave?" Hellé asked, gesturing to her luxurious surroundings.

"You might not want to, but you don't have much choice." Sutherland replied. "Brunner is onto you. He knows you've been feeding the Resistance with information. Chaigneau told me he even had plans to arrest you before he was called away. How long do you think you have before there's a knock at the door anyway?"

"And what do you get from all of this subterfuge?" Hellé asked with a flirtatious smile.

"A salve for the conscience."

"And something more?" she asked, stepping forward and placing a hand on his chest. She looked up at him with liquid blue eyes, like the bodywork of the Bugatti she had raced.

Sutherland looked from her to Arnaldo and saw his mouth twist into a crafty smile as he gave him a wink.

"I'll get the wine." He said, standing up. "Take your jacket off. Relax. We're all friends here." He nodded to his muse. "Why don't you make a start on lunch. I'll join you shortly."

IN THE DEN OF WOLVES

CHAPTER EIGHTY-ONE
SCOTLAND, 2018

Her magnificently opulent Hispano-Suiza with its Marc Birkigt designed 8litre engine and custom fabricated coachwork by Kellner Carrosserie of Paris had often swept up Avenue de la Fontaine without a care in the world. The impressive flying stork mascot crowned a unique sloping grille as the former Bugatti racing driver glided through to her private paradise. Yet what price had Hellé Nice paid for her liberty? Iris suspected, as she had all along, that the answers may be contained within the canister.

"Is this it?" Hamilton asked as the silver sandwich tin was catalogued and added to the film canister and spirit flask taken from inside the old, waxed cotton stockman's coat.

"It?" the old lady asked.

Hamilton gestured to the table with the items all artfully arranged. "An auld tin, some film and a hip flask."

Dame Iris Harrington smiled slowly as she turned away from the objects. "Oh, by no means, young man." She said, unravelling her cane and holding out her arm for some support. "Show me the car."

Hamilton took her arm and supported her as they made their way slowly out to the old Rover. She had promised the police a full and frank statement and the DCI was placated with that. McCormack still had a face like a dropped pie, but it wasn't her case yet. Not until the DCI officially handed it over.

They emerged from the marquee as the first body was being carried away in its black rubber shroud. Dark clouds were rolling overhead and a light smirr had begun to fall, preceding the heavy, freezing rain that was blowing in from the Hebrides. Hamilton was anxious not to keep her out, but she was insistent and peered into the driver's seat. Squinting through the window, she gazed at the skeleton, shaking her head sadly before moving round to the boot.

She instructed Hamilton to open the boot again and peered inside as the acrid smell of decay struck her. She pointed a bony finger to a loop of leather on the rear bulkhead. Hamilton reached in and tugged at it, but the decayed leather came off in his fingers.

"Perhaps you would like to try again?" she said with a mildly scathing tone.

With a deep sigh Hamilton reached in further, almost clambering completely inside, his one knee on the floor of the boot, soaking up foul-smelling water from saturated carpet. Prising his fingers around the edge of the bulkhead, he struggled to get reasonable purchase on it, having to resort to the small penknife on his multitool keyring to make a suitable gap. With a final tug it gave way. He cursed as a gush of water poured out, soaking him from the waist down as the deluge brought another body rattling into the boot with it.

"I did wonder." She said to herself quietly, stepping forward, touching the boot almost reverently. As one might the coffin of a deceased loved one. She turned around as a clap of distant thunder, almost on cue, rumbled overhead. "You see, young Hamilton." She smiled. "The story of Sutherland and Cameron is only just beginning."

CHAPTER EIGHTY-TWO
FRENCH CHAD, 1943

Dust. Heat and dust.

The wind howled, churning the dried-up lakebed into a choking hell. Fine grains filling the nose and mouth, suffocatingly, scouring away at uncovered eyes and picking bones clean. No one would hear your cries for help. No one cared anyway. Not out here. He pulled the scarf wrapped around his head up over his nose and down lower over his eyes. The sting of sweat was more bearable than the scourge of the sands.

The arrival of a Citroën Traction Avant was confirmation of everyone's worst fears. The little governor was here. A self-proclaimed, pompous little junior administrator who had the lives of hundreds in his hands. Sent over from Paris years ago in disgrace. Taking out his malice on others. It meant there was no fresh meat, no one to pick up the slack, no new labourers to shovel dry dust into tightly woven sacks. Seeing this, Esther collapsed. She knew what it meant. She was too exhausted to continue. Knowing she couldn't double the quota. She could barely do what she was asked as it was. Stepping out of the car, goggles pulled down over his eyes, Christoph Patrice cast his eyes over the desperate scene.

Three-hundred-and-seventy-two labourers. A tenth of the required number. A third of the original shipment. Whittling down day-by-day. Exhaustion, starvation, heat, disease. Pick one. Yet still they wanted more. It was impossible. Simply impossible, but he was being paid on results. He stretched out his arm, pointing to where Esther's prone body lay on the ground.

Zechariah knew it was best to leave her. He didn't want to. Had promised her he never would, but he had seen it before. A wife stumbled and fell, the husband ran over to catch her. Both were shot.

As expected, a soldier marched over to her, removed the Luger from his holster and shot her in the back of the head. He looked at Zechariah meaningfully. Eyes full of malice. Challenging him. Do you want some of this too? He continued to dig. Dig and fill. Dig and fill. Until all the sacks were done. That's all they had left.

Long ago he had stopped asking why. Governor-General Éboué was proudly and eagerly sending troops to fight the Nazis. French Equatorial Africa chanted the cause of Free France louder than the mother country herself. The consequences of losing the war were too terrible to contemplate for the African colonies and nowhere in Equatorial Africa was there a stronger bastion of anti-Fascist rhetoric. So why were there labour camps in the desert? Why were they shovelling dust into sacks? Why were French administrators taking German money right under the noses of their compatriots?

If he survived, then he would ask why. Now he just needed to dig. Dig and fill, amidst the heat and dust.

CHAPTER EIGHTY-THREE
SCOTLAND, 2018

The Minox Riga sub miniature camera had been made in the VEF factory in Latvia according to the design of German inventor Walter Zapp. It was intended as an easy-to-use alternative to more complicated cameras from Karl Zeiss and Leica. Using 8x11mm Minox Riga film, at a time when 35mm was considered miniature stock, the camera was used simply by pulling it open to reveal the fixed 15mm f/3.5 lens and depressing a tiny shutter release button on top. Film was then advanced by closing and reopening the camera, in a similar manner to a pump-action shotgun, but for quite a different kind of shooting.

Having left the scene later in the afternoon, Hamilton had driven the old fruit to the Ballachulish Hotel on the shores of Loch Linnhe, at the northern end of Glencoe. She wanted to be nearby as the forensics continued to pore over their findings. The hotel itself was a venerable old building in an enviable location just past the Ballachulish Bridge where Loch Leven flowed out into Linnhe. With a view across the water to the settlement of North Ballachulish, the hotel had been welcoming travellers through its doors since John Honeyman and his apprentice, a certain Charles Rennie Mackintosh, had constructed it in 1877.

Once she was installed in a comfortable armchair by the fire, Hamilton went off to order a cream tea at her request while Diego, the resident cat, jumped on her lap for some fuss and an afternoon snooze. Then he checked them both into their rooms for the night and carried up the luggage. He returned to see the glossy black moggy curled up with his head twisted at a curious angle while his chin was given a welcome scratch.

"Is it whit yer expected?" he asked as he took the sofa opposite.

Dame Iris Harrington paused for a moment as she considered her response. "In some ways." She nodded. "Though I was surprised by how little they had left behind."

"There you are." The waitress smiled pleasantly as she brought the tea tray and set it out on the coffee table between them. "Ooh, I see someone's comfy." she added, glancing at Diego as he stretched out on Iris's lap, spreading his little black toes with contentment. "You'll have to watch him. He'll be after the cream."

"I shall keep him under close supervision." Iris said with a rare smile of her own.

"The sandwiches and cakes will be out shortly."

"Thank you, my dear." Iris nodded, looking every inch an amiable grandmother, instead of the indomitable battle-axe Hamilton had so far experienced.

"Sugar?" "Just one lump please. I'm supposed to be cutting down."

"So, whit d'yer think is on the film?" he asked, dropping a sugar cube into each teacup with the tongs. "And who are Cameron and Sutherland?"

"I couldn't even begin to guess what the film contains, but it was definitely linked to one of them. Sutherland most likely." She looked across as Hamilton sat back in the seat, letting the tea brew for a little while longer.

"Ah'm naw familiar with Cameron."

"You won't be." She smiled. "His file will be somewhere in the basement archive of Vauxhall Cross." She added, referring to No.85 Albert Embankment, the home of the Secret Intelligence Service. "There is where it will likely remain too."

"Whit aboot the Freedom of Information Act?"

"Absolute exemption." She said rather stiffly.

"So, they were involved in some awfy high-level stuff."

"The highest." She nodded.

"Am ah ever likely tae ken?" he sighed, feeling rather deflated. Why had he even been brought in if he wasn't allowed to know any of the particulars of the individuals involved? It all seemed rather too much of the old school cloak and dagger stuff.

"Certainly not." She frowned, then softened a little as the cakes arrived. "Well, not here anyway."

"Dis this discovery bring us any closer tae finding any o' these relics?"

Harrington considered the question for a moment. "It might do." She nodded. "At least to one of them."

"Which one?" Hamilton asked, leaning forward to give the tea a stir before pouring.

"Hellé Nice, I would suggest. The Bugatti is more of a distraction. Strategically it's less useful."

Hamilton nearly dropped the teapot on hearing this. The Lost Bugatti was about the best chance he had of finding any of the three, and even then the chances depended on whatever might have been left under the streets of a bombed, burnt and broken Berlin.

"Why wid yer say that?" he asked, trying not to sound alarmed.

"It was squirrelled away fairly early on." she explained. "Things were only just getting started in '41. The really interesting stuff didn't start happening until the end of '42." She paused and looked at the ceiling wistfully. "So many things happened it sometimes feels as if the war lasted longer than it did. Everything was so compressed."

"So, why are we even bothering with the Bugatti?"

"Historically, it's still important to those who put great stock in such things." She explained leaning forward. "I'll add the cream."

Diego shifted a little on her lap, then resumed his position as she brought the cup and saucer back with her from the tray. Hamilton had made a start on the sandwiches, giving Harrington further opportunity to explain what she meant.

"Apparently there was a box under the dashboard. A sort of secret safe for hidden documents. It would be interesting to find out if it was there or if that was all just a myth. There might be a useful list of names inside. In the early days we needed to be sure who was on our side and who wasn't. Individuals would be given codenames. Some of these would be friendly, others not. It was a shorthand way of communicating what was happening, where and who told us, so it was useful to know if the information came from friendly channels or those rather less agreeable to the cause." She took a sip and placed the cup gently back on the saucer. "A quick cross-reference with the list of known codenames and their allegiances would ensure the message was forwarded to the right channels and handled in the appropriate manner."

She dipped her finger in the cream jug and offered it to Diego. He hooked her hand with a paw and brought the digit gratefully to his lips, still sprawled across her lap. Were he to be fanned with ostrich feathers and fed on grapes he would have resembled a veritable Pharoah puss.

"Legitimate intelligence or deliberate misdirection." Hamilton muttered after finishing the first sandwich. They were only small, and he was ravenous.

"Exactly." She nodded. "Information from a subversive type could be just as valuable in its own way. Trying too hard to convince someone of something, for example, or cover something up. We needed to see the lay of the board, set out our pieces as it were. It was all an elaborate game of chess in the beginning."

"If the list wis still in the Bugatti, whit would that prove?"

"Call it professional curiosity." She smiled. "It might be interesting to discover who actually had been our allies and who managed to slip away. It would have been dash handy at Nuremberg."

"So, it cood still be a Nazi hunters wish list?"

"Possibly."

Hamilton took a sip of tea to wash down the sandwich and selected another.

"Whit d'yer ken aboot the Auto Club?"

"I know that they were a loose association of enthusiasts looking for lost cars. That's all they were. No hidden secrets there."

"So, the fact that they happened tae be looking for cars driven by auld spooks is jist a coincidence then?"

"Cars of that vintage would have likely been driven by one or the other."

"Whit aboot pacifists?"

"In my experience, pacifists rarely drive cars." She smiled.

"Ah thought all the focus seemed tae be on the Horch." Hamilton commented. "The three murders. Okay, so they were specialists in their own way wi the Bugatti and Duesenberg, but this seems tae be all aboot Sutherland's car. Graham Robertson, Zwickau, and the Borromean Archives."

"That's because Sutherland's car is the only one really worth finding." She saw the consternation in Hamilton's face. "From an intelligence point of view."

"So, there is something in these relics containing secret documents then?"

"Perhaps not all of them, but Sutherland's Horch, definitely." She nodded. "If anything, I suspect he went to great efforts to keep his car away from me."

Hamilton nearly dropped his plate, looking across at her with a frown and a mouthful of coronation chicken.

"All I know is that together, Cameron and Sutherland discovered something that went all the way to the top." Harrington explained. "I asked them to look into it and that's the last I heard from either of them." She paused for a moment. Reflecting. "Until seeing the car this morning."

Hamilton's scowl intensified, trying to weigh up whether he was on the right side or not given Harrington's revelations.

"Whatever it was, it probably has more to do with his car than most people realise."

"Why keep the car away from you?"

"I hope to find out before I leave this world, Hamilton." she sighed, stroking Diego's belly as he purred loudly. "That's why I asked you along."

"If *they* dinnae trust yer, why can I?" he asked, observing the curious similarity between Harrington and the black moggy Diego with Blofeld and his white Persian pussy.

"Oh, don't be silly." She said scathingly. "I'm an old woman. I can't do anything now. I can barely walk."

Hamilton looked at her carefully, doubting the statement profoundly. She had already managed to winkle him out of his enforced retirement. Then, by applying sufficient pressure on the new Chief of the Intelligence Service, had reactivated his official status. It was anyone's guess as to how far reaching her influence still extended.

"From whit Don Pietro told me, the Auto Club wis still trying tae find the cars."

"Perhaps they were." Harrington replied. "Or at least one of the cars. I suspect Graham Robertson knew exactly where Sutherland's Horch was and very likely told the other two. That's probably what got them all killed."

"Who else wid be after Sutherland's car? Someone who is nae after the money. The Bugatti is head and shoulders more valuable."

"No indeed, though no doubt a little extra cash would be useful to them." She placed her teacup back on the table and helped herself to a cake. "Who would be after them? I suppose that rather depends on whatever it was the boys discovered. Makes you wonder, doesn't it?"

CHAPTER EIGHTY-FOUR

It didn't always rain on the Isle of Skye. Though in mid-October one might be forgiven for thinking otherwise, especially standing on the wild west coast.

Iain and Craig Sutherland stood on the black and white sands of Talisker Bay, watching the tide roll back. Burns flowing down from the hills created complex patterns in the sand as they stretched out like tendrils to meet the Sea of the Hebrides. To the south, two impressive sea stacks rose from a common rocky platform, braving the worst of the waves. The sun, appearing just beneath a thick, swaddling band of storm clouds, was slowly approaching the horizon in the space between the sea stacks and the cliff. Its reflection in the surf resembled a solitary tongue of fire, flickering with each new wave washing up.

"What do we do now?" Craig asked.

"It's been months." Iain commented, tilting his head down to let the water run off the wide brim of his waxed hat. "The trail has probably cooled off."

"Or they're biding their time."

"For what?" Craig pondered for a moment.

"To see what we will do?"

"And what would they be looking for?"

"I dinnae know." he said defensively. "See how determined we are to get this relic working again. Find someone else to have a look at her, maybe."

"I think to do that we're going to need to go over to Germany now." Craig shuddered at the prospect.

"What?"

"That's where it happened."

"Aye, and in France, and Los Angeles too." Iain pointed out. "These people will travel around a bit, if they feel the need."

"Maybe we should just give them what they want."

"Without finding out what that is?"

"Listen, you've got a wife and wee bairns. You dinnae want these people after you." Craig reasoned. "Cut our losses. Get shot of it. Why not?"

"Because there's a reason Granda dragged it all the way up here. It's got to be more than just a clapped-out old wreck."

"Aye? So, why did he get the Aston?"

"Why not, eh?" he laughed. "Better daily runner I imagine." Iain surmised. "Man like him was never gonnae have a sensible set of wheels. His Da already had the Landy for that and you can't exactly go collect the paper in that silver missile in the barn."

"That looks a bloody death trap, that does." Craig shook his head.

"You should hear it." Iain chuckled.

"You've started that thing up?"

"Oh aye." Iain smiled. "Had to be done. Bloody near blew me head off mind, and I now know why the back wheels are chocked up in the air." Craig looked at him inquisitively "Start that thing up and they're already spinning away as soon as you put it in gear. Would have shot it right out the shed into the front garden."

"Do you think he ever raced it?" Iain shrugged.

"I don't know, but if he ever did, he would have needed bloody big baws."

"This is Seanair we're talking about." Craig reminded him. "He did have bloody big baws."

"So, there's got to be another way." Iain pondered. "I just don't know what it is yet."

The pair fell silent for a moment, watching the sun sink lower, the dark grey clouds turning anthracite as the sea stacks rose up from the waters like black phantoms in silhouette.

"We're not pushed for time." Iain spoke up, raising his voice over the wind. "No one else knows where she is."

"Just us." Craig sighed. "That's what's scaring the shite outta me to be honest. If they do find us…"

"They won't."

"If they do find us, do you think they'll just let us be after they've got what they want?"

"Why not?"

"Because we'll know they've killed three people to get to us."

"Not necessarily."

"I'm not sure I want to take that risk."

"Listen, right now, she's still safe and no one knows anymore about her than before." Iain continued, becoming a little irritated by his brother's nervousness. "If they did, if Gray had told them where to find her all those months ago, they'd have been here by now."

"I don't know how you can stay so chilled out. You've got more to lose." Craig turned, finally having enough of the weather and heading back up to the rocks. "We didn't find anything anyway."

Heading back to the house, Craig whistled, and the two Collies came bounding over from where they had been playing together on the beach. Following obediently, the bedraggled foursome made their way back to the lane. Smoke rising from the kitchen chimney held the promise of another one of Emma's wonderful suppers. Craig needed something to cheer him up and his stomach was a good place to start.

"Nothing obvious." Iain replied following him. "If Granda wanted to hide something, he would nae have made it obvious."

"We can't strip it down."

"No." Iain shook his head. "We would have needed Gray to do that for us. It's got be done sympathetically. Something that old." He sighed and shook his head, "Let's just leave it be for now. There's no good worrying about it."

"Alright." Craig replied sceptically.

CHAPTER EIGHTY-FIVE

Hamilton assisted Dame Harrington into the Land Rover once more, guiding her onto the sidestep that ran down the length of *Torridon*. While the adjustable Bilstein shock absorbers and Eibach springs greatly enhanced ride quality, the one-inch lift kit did nothing to help little old ladies get themselves safely inside. He was tempted to get a mounting block made up. Once securely installed he moved to the rear and opened the tailgate to load up the luggage.

Rich aromas of oiled walnut, woven wool and tanned leather were even more pronounced in the load area. Carloway Mill, the oldest Harris tweed mill in the world, had supplied the fabric for the roof lining and door cards. Waterproof mohair and Muirhead's distressed mahogany hide had been selected to trim the boxed in storage units and the interplay between light and darker grains made the walnut decking an aesthetically pleasing as well as hard-wearing functional element.

The floor itself was much higher than normal, owing to the customised Thewlis & Gregson drawer units that Hamilton had installed for when he went off-grid. Fortunately, Harrington's overnight bag was as light as a feather anyway, especially when compared with his own lumbering rucksack.

Returning to the driver's seat, he buckled up and started the engine. *Torridon* coughed into life with a distinctly agricultural growl and a puff of black smoke. Hamilton rested his hand on the gear knob, ready to shift it through the gate. Despite the increased power of the engine and upgraded transmission, there was no stick waggle. No vibrations at all, not even that ticklish buzz that sometimes accompanied light industrial vehicles. It was this attention to detail that made *Torridon* a pleasure to drive.

"Back tae the crime scene, ma'am?" he asked.

"No." she said huffily. "What did I tell you about that?"

"Aboot whit, ma'am?"

"That!" she said fiercely, pointing a scolding digit in his direction.

Hamilton looked confused for a moment, then sighed.

"Iris will do." She said firmly.

"Ah'm gonnae struggle wi that, ma'am, if ah'm honest wi yers."

"Well don't" she uttered fervently.

"Ah'll see whit ah can do..." He immediately cursed under his breath as he almost slipped up again. "Iris." He dared to look across the cabin and saw her expression soften a little as finally used her name. "So, where are we off tae?"

"Would you indulge an old spinster, Hamilton?" she asked. Her tone took on a surprisingly warm quality he hadn't expected. Within just one sentence she had transformed from battle axe to favourite grandmother again.

"Spinster? Yer surprise me, Iris."

She grunted at that. "Would you take me to Glenmore House?"

"Aye, we can do that. Where is it?"

"On the road to Newtonmore. I'll direct you. It'll be quicker to head through Fort William from here."

"D'yer have a postcode?" he asked, setting up the SatNav to receive the address.

Harrington looked across at him with a sympathetic expression. "My dear boy, Scotland didn't have any postcodes the last time I came up here. We used things called maps."

"Right, ah see." he said, reaching up to the shelf above her head.

Bringing down a sheaf of Landrangers and Explorers, he fanned them out like a deck of cards. She frowned and looked at the covers.

"That one should do it."

She pointed to OL56, the Badenoch & Strathspey Explorer. "Glenmore House is there." She pointed again on the area covered, to a point between the Rivers Spey and Tromie, just south of Newtonmore.

Replacing the other maps, Hamilton unfolded it and examined the area she had indicated.

"Just to the left of the Cairngorms." She added helpfully.

Hamilton followed the roads south of Newtonmore. The A86 branched off southwest, the A9 due south. Then he found it, just off the A9 on an unclassified minor road in the Spey Valley.

"Right. Let's see whit we can find." He muttered, inputting the route he needed to take.

"For a Scot, you're surprisingly ill-informed about your own country."

"Aye, that ah am." He nodded.

"Pity. It is rather agreeable up here." she gazed out through the windscreen as a moody sky shrouded the peak of the Pap.

"Ah think ah've gaw it." He said at last, comparing the destination on the SatNav with the OS map. Folding it up he placed it back on the shelf above him. "Permission tae use the strobes?" he asked, moving his hand over to the roof console to turn on the headlights.

"Denied." She said. "I would like to get there in comfort, without feeling seasick at the end."

"Ah thought ah wis pretty smooth on the way up."

"You don't have the balance of a centenarian." She remarked quietly.

"Duly noted." He sighed, shifting the steel gear stick crisply into first and releasing the handbrake. Negotiating his way out of the car park, a small orange lamp in the binnacle reflected the turn indication as he checked for traffic coming from Oban. "So, whit's at Glenmore?" he asked, pulling out and heading towards the Ballachulish Bridge.

"It's the home of our man. James Alexander Cameron." She said. "Or at least it was. Not sure what it is now. That's why I want to see it."

"The Cameron from the briefcase?"

"The very same."

"How is he involved?"

"Now that is a very long story indeed." Hamilton looked across at the screen again. "Looks like we've gaw an hour-and-a-half tae fill."

"Not long enough."

"Well, how aboot yers pretend it's the war again, Iris. Condense it."

"Now then young man." She said flatly. "You're just supposed to drive me around and do a bit of thinking from time to time. You're not supposed to start sounding like me as well."

Hamilton looked across and their eyes briefly met. If he wasn't mistaken there almost appeared to be a curve of a smile playing across her thin lips.

CHAPTER EIGHTY-SIX
GERMANY, 2018

It had taken days to drain out. Water had continually seeped back through the rubble to refill the puddle but eventually the level seemed to have settled out to a lower, manageable level. No doubt it had once sat in the original Landwehr Canal. Once that operation had been completed it had taken a few days more to assess the rubble pile blocking the left-hand tunnel and make a hole sufficient to push through a borescope. To dig the tunnel out completely, they would need to brace the roof so it was necessary to find out if there was anything worth salvaging first.

Michael, Jurgen and Inge were nervously watching the progress of the borescope through the tube that had been pushed through near the top of the pile. Dieter and Katya were huddled around the monitor. There was a low, haunting whistle as U-bahn trains pulled into Tempelhof down at the other end. The whole atmosphere was melancholy. They were stood in the very centre of history. No one had been down here since at least the mid-fifties. That realisation was both exciting and deeply sobering.

What they first saw on the monitor was horrifying.

The scope had penetrated through to the other side. Light shining through the optic fibre was bright but couldn't quite project all the way in. Yet, what they were seeing immediately painted a terrifying picture.

In the midst of the tunnel, the outline of a large wooden box could just be made out. It looked like an ordinary shipping crate until the torch illuminated the insignia of the Arika Korps. It was the bodies around the bottom of the box that made Katya yelp. Michael clambered down from the rubble to take a look. He glanced at the screen and gasped.

"Scheisse!" he looked to Dieter. "What have we found?"

Dieter continued to look at the screen as the borescope relayed the images back to them.

"A tomb." He said quietly. "And the last resting place of the Ark of the Covenant."

The railway engineers looked at one another uneasily.

"Are you serious?" they asked. "Is that what killed them?"

"No." Dieter shook his head. "I suspect what killed them was being trapped behind a wall of impenetrable rubble." He gestured around the macabre discovery. "Unlike us, they would have no light, no food, and very likely sometime later, no oxygen."

"It's a terrible way to die." Katya remarked.

"They had guns." Michael noted, pointing to the body of the nearest soldier. Clasped still in the fingers of the mummified skeleton was an MP-40 submachine gun. "That's probably the way I would have gone." He added grimly.

"Looks like he did too." Dieter nodded.

The ragged hole at the top of the helmet indicated the point where a bullet exited the top of the soldier's head, tearing through steel.

"This needs to be fully excavated." He continued, turning to the engineers. "The bodies need to be retrieved and laid to rest. This is now an archaeological site. How long will it take to brace the roof?"

"Several more weeks, maybe longer." He shrugged. It depends how much weight is directly above us. We don't want a building collapsing on us."

"Or a whole street." Suggested another.

Dieter looked to the walls and ceiling of the tunnel they were in.

"Where's the nearest access point?"

"Tempelhof."

"Are you sure? There's not one closer?"

"There's nothing listed on the plans." He gestured to the rubble wall. "This tunnel isn't on any plans."

"Then we need an accurate schematic of this whole section and overlay that on everything we have. Sewage, gas, electricity, everything above ground and below. It's the only way we will know how to tackle this."

The engineer shrugged. "You're talking months."

Dieter looked to Michael. Jurgen and Inge had joined him at the monitor, looking at the entombed bodies of the soldiers. Men of the 1st SS Panzer Division Leibstandarte. The Führer's personal bodyguards. He nodded. It needed to be done. Now they had been rediscovered, these men needed to be laid to rest with respect and dignity at least.

"Well then," Dieter smiled. "Let's get started."

CHAPTER EIGHTY-SEVEN
SCOTLAND, 2018

Cruban Beag was a craggy cornerstone between Glenmore and the uppermost Spey. It's rough, complex, north-eastern ridge looked down towards the sprawling Glenmore Estate below. Nestled in the confluence of the Rivers Spey and Truim, three miles south of the village of Newtonmore, the estate was surrounded by enchanting woodland with unparalleled views over the Spey Valley and the Monadhliath and Cairngorm mountains.

Diverting off what was once the original A9 route and onto one of General Wade's military roads, Hamilton was struck by how open everything was. After the confines of the Spean Valley and its meandering course from the bridge that crossed it, the views around Glenmore and the River Spey were much more expansive.

A single-track road traversed undulating moorland, crossed through extensive woods and passed the Clan Macpherson Memorial Cairn before approaching the Mains of Glenmore. Somewhere in the centre of the estate stood a stone marking the point in the Highlands furthest from the sea in every direction, the geographical heart of Scotland. Against this rugged backdrop, Glenmore House was set amongst lawned gardens and extensive grounds that had long been acknowledged as some of the most beautiful in the central Highlands.

Passing Glenmore Farm, Hamilton approached the house through Gate Lodge, doubling back from the lane to pass through the handsome wrought iron portal. Taking the private driveway beyond, the house slowly began to emerge from the trees as they approached it from the south gable.

Built as a family home between 1835-40 by Major Ewan Macpherson on land purchased from the Duke of Gordon, Glenmore House still retained its traditional character and charm. Major Macpherson had made his money in India before returning to his ancestral lands in the District of Badenoch. Dying in 1847 he was laid to rest in a small walled burial ground with a commanding vista of the Spey Valley.

From any angle, Glenmore House was an unmistakably handsome dwelling. Originally late Georgian, very early Victorian, with 1870 additions, then again in 1901, it was a long asymmetrical 2-storey gabled house over a raised basement on an east facing sloping site with west entrance front. The building was built in all tooled grey granite ashlar with some pinning and ashlar granite dressings. In form it had an irregular 7-bay gabled west front with a crenelated porch from a projecting hall gable. To the left of the hallway was a 2-bay Dining Room addition, with an original single bay Library to the right, both projecting from the main. To the rear was a similar irregular east facing garden front with late 19th century tower addition.

Emerging from the three-storey square tower in the near centre of the east front arose a small square cap topped with a flagpole. Distinctive crowstepped gables, some with tall, corbelled octagonal coped stacks, adorned the roofline while the roof itself was of slate from the Foudland quarries at Ballachulish. There was a new service court to the north with decorative wrought iron gates built onto the single-storey three-bay, shallow pyramid-roofed extension added during more recent renovations and an extensive orangery on the south side built at the same time.

"This is new." Harrington said, pointing to the orangery that greeted them first. "This used to be a little lean-to conservatory."

"Yer've been here before?" Hamilton asked as he rounded a raised stone circle in the middle of the gravel driveway.

"Oh yes." She nodded. "Back in the day. This wasn't here then, either. Couldn't have got the van round if it had been."

"Whit van?"

"Another time, my boy, another time."

Hamilton completed the circle and drew up outside the impressive stone porch as a Labrador came bounding out to greet the new visitors.

"Are we stopping?"

"Just for a moment." She nodded, looking almost mournful as she gazed up at the grey stonework.

Hamilton silenced the engine and stepped out, receiving a warm muzzle in his crotch as he did so. Giving the amiable beast a good fuss, he moved round to open the door for Harrington as a young woman emerged from inside.

"Good morning." She greeted. "Are you staying with us?"

"No, no." Harrington said, as Hamilton helped her down. "I just wanted to see the old place again."

"Have you been here before?"

"Oh yes, many years ago." She nodded, looking more wistful as she took in the place. "When the family was still here."

"The Camerons?"

Iris nodded sadly.

"Has much changed?"

"Quite a bit. You have a new orangery." She pointed to the grand, yet sympathetically designed Georgian style conservatory.

"Yes, we host wedding receptions in there. It's a beautiful space. Would you like to come and see?"

"Oh no, it's quite alright." She replied hastily, wanting to preserve her own memories of the house and worried what horrors the new owners might have subjected it to.

Harrington remembered the place for what it was the last time she had visited, and who had been there. It was very often the people that made a place, and she was anxious that seeing the extent of any changes done to the inside would, in some way erase the memories of the people she had known before. There were fewer enough of them around as it was.

Looking to the north gable, beyond the dining room, it was evident that a new kitchen block had been built, enclosing the old courtyard and probably greatly extending the old kitchen. She wondered what the housekeeper might have made of it. Dear Isla Buchanan. She had been a marvel, there was not a thing she couldn't cook. Other than those few exterior modifications, the house looked exactly as she remembered it. Even the colour of the front door hadn't changed.

Then of course there was the owner himself, Lt Col James Alexander Cameron. Detective Chief Superintendent. The Lord Dalwhinnie. Was it really his body in the old Rover they had just dredged up from Loch Etive? It was possible. If that was the case, then the other one would almost certainly have been Sutherland. Those two were joined at the hip. And the third body?

"Iris?"

Hamilton's voice broke her reverie and she turned to look at him, misty eyed with a faraway expression on her face.

"Are yer okay?" There was genuine concern on his face. She looked to have aged terribly whilst she had been standing there.

"Yes, yes. Quite alright, thank you." she sniffed. "Time to go I think, Hamilton." She then turned to the young woman and smiled. "It's been lovely seeing the old place again. One last time."

With Hamilton's help she returned inside. Looking back at the windows, she half expected to see a face she recognised up there. Of course, there was no one. She was the last of her generation. She had been for some time. It was a terrible burden to bear.

Hamilton started up *Torridon* and pulled away, leaving the chocolate Labrador to return to its owner and sit there obediently, unsure whether they were happy to have met someone new or sad that they were going away again so soon. The owner looked equally confused. Hamilton watched them recede in the side mirror before taking the turn past the orangery and back down to Gate Lodge. He didn't know where he was going and didn't want to break into the silence just yet. He sensed Iris wanted to be at peace for the moment.

Looking to the binnacle gauges, he noticed they were getting low on fuel.

There was likely to be a petrol station in Newtonmore just up the road. He would head up there. Perhaps by then the moment would have passed and Harrington would be giving out her orders again. There was too much locked up inside that head of hers. If he was to make any progress on all this though, at some point some of it would need to start spilling out.

CHAPTER EIGHTY-EIGHT

Harrington had remained silent ever since leaving Glenmore House. Hamilton was struggling to know what more could be done in this quest. There was no word from Berlin, no leads on any of the other two, and now a new mystery had just emerged from the waters of Loch Etive. All of it seemingly intertwined in the mind of the woman sitting next to him, looking even more tiny and fragile in the watery sunlight, bursting through gaps in the clouds with angelic rays. A light smirr had started again and the wet road was dazzling him, facilitating the need for sunglass in a middle of a generally dreich day.

"Ah'm missin' suhin'." Hamilton murmured as they approached the turreted gatehouse to Ardverikie House across the river.

"You're missing quite a lot." She said, finally breaking her silence.

"Then tell me what ah'm missing."

He looked across, but nothing was forthcoming. Suddenly, veering across the road, Hamilton swerved into the forecourt of the old filling station and jammed on the brakes, pulling on the handbrake for good measure to bring *Torridon* skidding abruptly to a halt.

"Listen. Ah cannae help yer if yer dinnae talk tae me!" he began angrily. "You dragged me up here. Yer dinnae want jist a driver; yer wanted ma assistance on this. Someone has already tried tae kill me, and ah can do wi'oot that kind o' hassle. So, for goodness' sake, Iris, drop the cloak and dagger bollocks and tell me whit yer know, or ah'll make ma way back home today and forget all aboot this!"

"Is that your usual interrogation technique?" she asked coldly, turning calmly towards him.

"Ah'm naw in the habit of interrogating auld biddies."

"Glad to hear it."

"Tell me! Whit d'yer know?"

"I know Cameron and Sutherland had made a discovery. Whatever it was implicated some very senior people, including my old boss. Not knowing who they could trust is probably the reason why they decided to keep me out of the loop. I know I haven't seen or heard from either of them since and I know we have three dead bodies in a car that I bought for them."

"How dis any o' this relate tae these other three cars?"

"It doesn't." She shook her head. "Not all three of them. Just the Horch. It's possible that whatever Sutherland stashed in his car will tell us. I just don't know where his car is. What troubles me is that whatever it was they discovered all those years ago, may still have relevance today. That might be the real reason why Mr Robertson was murdered. The others are just collateral damage."

"And the Chief?"

"I don't know how much he will know about any of this. Either he's just as deeply involved as his predecessor, or he has absolutely no knowledge of it whatsoever."

"Whit exactly is this thing these lads discovered?"

"This is precisely the point, Hamilton!" she spat fiercely, enunciating every word. "I do not know. But I do intend to find out, if it's the last thing I do, which judging by my age it bloody well will be. Now are you going to help me or are you just going to sulk?"

"Can ah naw do both?" He replied firmly with a scowl, curious as to how she had turned things around to make it suddenly his fault.

"Well, if you must." She nodded. "Seems you're the right man for the job after all. I need someone who can multitask."

Hamilton glared at her but said nothing.

"Find somewhere for lunch. We can talk more then."

Still not amused, Hamilton at least felt there may be some scant progress. Selecting first gear, he checked for traffic and re-joined the carriageway. The road took them along the northern shore of Loch Laggan, the grand edifice of Ardverikie just peeking occasionally through the trees, before following the River Spean to Laggan Dam near Roughburn.

The route was twisty in places and undulated along the shoulders of Glen Spean and the Aberarder Forest. Hamilton used the gears to brake the engine, dabbing the pedal only when a bend tightened unexpectedly, or he was carrying just a little too much speed into an apex. Otherwise, it was a smooth and exhilarating drive and one of the many reasons why he preferred a manual transmission. This, he discovered, was the real home for *Torridon*. She was wasted on the Cornish peninsula. She belonged here. The more he guided her through the landscape, the more he felt drawn to it himself.

For someone that enjoyed the journey as much as the destination, Highland roads in the autumn took some beating. Even as shafts of golden sun became extinguished by rolling vapours as drizzle became heavier and harder, subdued colours reflected the vastness of the sky above the mountains. Burnt oranges, dusky browns and soft, floral purples made for a wild and dramatic palette. Splashes of pink from late-flowering heather, white from early snow on the highest peaks and foaming waterfalls cascading along the road from the hills above. Glaucous grey scree and black, rain-slicked rocks all blended to evoke a strangely calming sensation, soothing his earlier outburst.

Reaching up to switch on the lights again, Hamilton then flicked on the wipers from the stalk on the steering column. The knurled steel felt cool to the touch. Temperature had dropped and there was earthiness in the air. Petrichor released by the fine rain carrying geosmin into the cabin, the scent of the earth. Moving to the central dash, he flicked two switches, one at each side, adjusted the air flow quadrants above the Motorola and shifted down the box to set *Torridon* up for another tight bend.

After a few moments there was a warm glow emanating from the seat beneath him, spreading down the back of his thighs and up the small of his back to the shoulders. Iris would be feeling it too.

"What's that?" she asked.

"Whit?"

"That warmth?"

"Where?"

"In the seat?"

"Yer ha' nae pished yerself have yer?"

"Certainly not!" she replied with predictable outrage. "I may be ancient, but I haven't lost all bodily functions just yet."

"Must be the heated seat then." He said with a crafty grin.

"You might have warned me."

"And spare yer that wee moment o' panic?" he shook his head. "Naw a chance."

"I suppose I better make a start." She huffed, staring at the evergreen plantations on the other side of the loch. Forestry tracks weaved up between them. Higher up, the mountains were barren and brooding beneath a brow of low cloud and mist. It reflected her mood.

"James Cameron." She began. "He came back from the Far East in 1958 to look after his dying father. Old Alexander was going senile by the end and only lived for another year afterwards. With his death, James inherited the Glenmore Estate, including the house we just visited, and his father's title. He also gamely agreed to take up the vacant position of Detective Chief Superintendent for the Lochaber Division of the Inverness-shire Constabulary."

"Quite the task."

"Policing the Highlands wasn't as stressful back then. Petty poaching and illegal stills were about the extent of crime."

"Ah dinnae imagine it's anything like the Gorbals even now." He remarked, remembering his time with the old Strathclyde force. "Fred West used tae be the ice cream man."

"It was only supposed to be a temporary arrangement until they found a more permanent replacement. He never really wanted the job, but somehow felt obliged to take on the responsibility."

"Ah'm guessing they never did."

"No. Though partly that was Cameron's own fault. He was too bloody good at his job."

"Ah cannae say ah've ever been accused o' that." Hamilton joked. "So, how dis he come intae all this?"

"James's mother died when he was nine years old. While she was alive she refused to send him away to school, so he used to go up to Newtonmore. After her death, Alexander didn't quite know what to do with him, so packed him off to Dollar, his old alma mater. It was there that a young James Cameron boarded together with Andrew Sutherland. They were in the same quint together. Indeed, the very same one as their fathers were before them. Once they finished school, they kept in touch but went separate ways. Sutherland became a racing driver, as you know. Cameron ended up an engineer."

"So, whit happened?"

"Invergloy happened. At least that's where it all started."

CHAPTER EIGHTY-NINE

The Rover was strapped down to the back of the low-loader, ready to be carted back to Glasgow for further analysis. A tarpaulin had been secured over the top of it and police tape at the gate was being rolled up. Surveying the scene, the Detective Chief Inspector gave out a heavy sigh as he turned to his sergeant coming down from Holly Bank House.

"Any word from the old bat?" he asked.

"Nuhin', sir. I dinnae think she's coming."

The DCI nodded. That was something perhaps. He turned to DCI McCormack. "All yours then."

"Three dead bodies in an old government car?" she said grimly. "I don't like it at all."

"We dinnae get to pick and choose our triumphs, Morag." He smiled darkly. "This could have a promotion for yer at the end of it."

"We're all done, sir." Called the lead forensic inspector, now attired in something less papery, less all-inclusive.

Seeing him dressed in normal clothes was like looking at someone without spectacles for the first time. They were the same person, but also different. It was weird.

"Do we have a dark room to get that microfilm processed?" he asked. Everything was digital these days.

"Ah'll gie it tae Jenn. She's intae all that dark room stuff."

"She's a Goth, Jaime, it's naw the same thing."

"She also happens tae be a keen amateur photographer." Jaime replied. "Gaw one setup in her flat. She likes the 'analogue' style." He added, using his fingers to denote the inverted commas.

"Just make sure she dinnae baws it up."

"Ah'll send her yer best wishes, sir." Jaime smiled.

He shook his head and turned back to the loch. He never liked these rural cases. They were notoriously grim. Too much history, too many unspoken secrets. Nothing would be said for a generation or more, then suddenly someone would flip a switch and go mental with a shotgun or an axe or something. It was always grisly. Always. At least the violence had been done long before he arrived on the scene this time.

Still, it left him with an unsettling feeling. He would wander back to Glasgow, make his report and email it off to McCormack and her team. It wasn't his case anymore and he was glad to be shot of it. He was one of those strange types that hated nature. It was too quiet, too remote, too devoid of human interaction. Not that humans were great company either. He was a misanthrope that preferred city life to the rural. A paradox within a mystery.

"Right then." He said, turning back to his sergeant. "Let's be off."

The low-loader had pulled through the gates and off into the layby, orange lights flashing from the cab. It would be the slowest vehicle and would only hold everybody up down the single-track lane. The police marquee had been packed up inside the van and would head back with the truck. With the estate lands cleared of vehicles, McCormack closed the gate behind them and released the scene back to the local ghillie. Then she clambered into one car, the DCI into another and led the convoy back along the C1094, the Skyfall road. Back to civilisation. It was raining again. It always seemed to rain up here.

CHAPTER NINETY

"Whit started the fire?" Hamilton asked, pulling into the carpark of the Stronlossit Inn at Roybridge.

"I don't know the details." She said quietly then frowned as a thought occurred to her. "It might be useful if we did though."

Hamilton pondered what she meant as he parked up and went round to help her out. Opening the door, he found her on the phone to someone.

"Can we still get into the old police archives?" she asked. "Really? That's annoying... Do you think you could? It might have something to do with what we're working on... I know you'll do your best, my dear." She terminated the call and turned to him with a smile. "We'll see what Natalia can come up with."

"Who's Natalia?"

"A friend I have in the Service."

"Reactivated or..."

"No, she's a genuine agent."

"Ah'm a genuine agent." Hamilton protested.

"Well, for the moment." She nodded in acknowledgement. "I doubt once this is over that badge will get you into the car park of the Ziggurat." She said, referring to one of the many nicknames for the Vauxhall Cross headquarters.

"Yer soond almost disappointed." He smiled, dodging her unfolding stick.

"I am." She said curtly. "Too many bloody good agents have been let go already. Do you think spotty little boys in beanies are the future?"

"It seems tae be the way terrorism is going." He sighed, offering an arm. "If it's naw crude, but effective bombing campaigns on civilian populations, it's cyber-attacks on infrastructure and financial services."

"Both have their questionable headwear." She groaned, taking his arm.

"Whit's Natalia gonnae be looking at for us? The old police files?"

"If she can." Harrington nodded. "It's possible with the correct authorisation. So many procedures these days though." She rolled her eyes.

"Whit are we looking for? Ah might know a few people still in the force."

"I'm not sure, but something at Invergloy kicked this all off. There was a Royal Marine involved, so clearly it was something dodgy." She said with a twinkle in her eye. Hamilton chose not to bite. "I can't quite remember how or why though. The curse of old age, Hamilton. Don't under any circumstances do it. Hopefully the case file will bring it back."

"We cood always ask 'em directly." Hamilton proposed. "We passed the Fort William Police Station on the way here. We'll pass it on the way back."

"No, without a formal request they're unlikely to be so forthcoming these days. It's all data protection rubbish."

"There's the Freedom of Information Act." He said, forgetting he had already punted that particular proposition forward before.

"Two turds flying in opposite directions." Harrington said robustly. Hamilton was a little taken aback by her bluntness. Evidently she wasn't impressed. "Neither of them is helpful. One tends to make secret things public and the other keeps public things secret. It was so much easier in my day."

Hamilton held the door open for her and found them a table inside near the fire. On the cornice above the wood panelling was a collection of whisky tubes and boxes. Mostly standard fare, a few specials, nothing too expensive. Still, they caught her eye as she shook herself out of her coat and sat down.

"All they would do, if anything, is tell us whether there had or had not been an arson investigation in 1959 at the property formerly known as Invergloy House. We may as well make candles out of earwax for what use that is."

"Ah see that." He nodded meekly.

"How are things going with the other cars?"

"Dead end with the Duesenberg." Hamilton sighed. "A little more promising with the Bugatti."

"Oh?"

"There's a possibility it might have been buried in a disused U-Bahn tunnel in Berlin. Ah have some people looking intae it."

"I wonder if Sutherland even knew about Hellé's other car."

"*Marie?*"

"Who?"

"The name given to Hellé's car, the missing Duesenberg." He explained. "'Kisses to *Marie*'." Hamilton murmured, quoting Benoist's letter to Deville. Perhaps there was something in it. Perhaps it was just a happy coincidence. "*Manuela*, *Monique*, and *Marie*." Harrington frowned. "The Horch, the Bugatti, the Duesenberg. All girl's names."

"All beginning with 'M'." she smiled. "Elegant."

"Is that significant?"

"It might have been. A little in-joke amongst themselves. That was their nickname for me."

"Yer name's Iris."

"The 'M' was for Mother, because they used to think I bossed them around like one."

"Imagine that." Hamilton murmured.

Harrington frowned as the waitress came with their drinks. Hamilton's phone buzzed with an incoming WhatsApp message. Taking it out of the pocket of his fleece, he checked the ID.

"This cood be interesting."

Unlocking the phone, he read the message from Dieter. It was supplemented with pictures taken from a borescope camera.

It looks like we've found something. We might have it out by New Year. Unfortunately, it will be slow and expensive. I don't like to ask, but you know how things are. We will do what we can to secure funding on our side too. There is a local connection now. Call me when you can.

Hamilton couldn't help but feel excitement at the prospect of discovering a lost treasure. His excitement was tempered by the images Dieter had sent through. The outline of the box was just visible in the gloom, the torchlight reflecting off the wood and picking out a palm tree stencil.

The remains of the soldier on the reverse glacis with a fist-sized hole in the top of his helmet though told another story. Looking closer, he could see there were more bodies scattered around the space too. It looked as if someone might just have opened the Ark of the Covenant after all.

"Is it?" Harrington asked.

Hamilton hesitated, unsure whether to show her or not. He considered asking if she was squeamish, then deemed that might be a redundant question. Only the day before she had seen three skeletons up close and not even flinched. He handed her the phone and waited.

"Some kind of mass suicide perhaps." She observed. "Seems about the best thing to do under the circumstances.

"Is it?"

"Consider the alternatives. The roof collapses and you're sealed behind impenetrable rubble in a completely blacked out tunnel that no one even knows exists. The Soviets are surrounding the city, you have no food, no water, limited oxygen and you're there with what looks like a dozen of your comrades. Digging your way out isn't going to work and at some point someone is going to get hungry. So, either you kill yourself or you all scrabble around in the dark eating each other while hoping someone notices you're missing and sends down a search party. Which of course they won't because everyone else is either dead or captured."

Hamilton blanched a little at Harrington's frank but fair assessment of the horrid reality the guards would have found themselves in.

"Or yer kill yerself and yer mates decide tae chomp on yer anyway."

"Better that way. At least you wouldn't know about it." She shrugged.

"Are you ready to order?" the waitress asked?

"I'll have the beef and ale pie, please." Harrington spoke up with shocking enthusiasm given their previous subject matter.

"Certainly, and for you, sir?"

Hamilton hesitated. No doubt about it. Harrington was *not* the squeamish kind.

"Ah'll jist have the fish and chips, thanks."

CHAPTER NINETY-ONE
FRANCE, 2018

Svetlana Dobrovolskaya had been a young, high-flying Lieutenant Colonel in Ukrainian Criminal Police before being put in charge of the European Section of Interpol. She had reviewed the evidence provided by the respective forces to the Command & Coordination Centre, and after a call from the BKA and months of wrangling, had finally managed to get them all together in one room.

Despite all being member states of the International Criminal Police Organisation, the sovereign independence of the individual police forces was always maintained and invariably became something of a battleground. Contrary to popular belief, Interpol had no agents with arresting powers themselves.

Instead, the organisation functioned more as an administrative liaison between various international law enforcement agencies. Thus, when it came down to actually making an arrest, that would all be down to the respective police forces of the member states themselves. That's when the war of urination began with regard to jurisdiction, especially when American agencies were involved.

Looking around the busy conference room on the fourth floor of the Interpol headquarters in Lyon, it looked likely that one of those wars was about to take place. Officers from the Departmental Gendarmerie were joined by colleagues from the BKA in Germany and detectives from the Los Angeles Police Department. Hampshire Police had sent their detectives over to observe, but although the third victim was a British national, as the crime had taken place in Germany, they were happy for their German colleagues to take the collar. So polite. So very English.

Independently, the police services had only be able to get so far before reaching something of a dead-end, yet with the similarities between the victims in Mulhouse, Zwickau and LA becoming increasingly apparent, their combined resources needed to be brought together to find this killer. Following a minor breakthrough with the security camera footage, now even the LAPD were able to confirm that Jaeger was their man.

"We got Jaeger coming into LAX on the 22nd of November last year." Detective Losario began. "He books out a hire car for three days, the tracker then has him go to Wilshire Boulevard where he waits it out. Next time we see him is on airport security that same night, parking up the car before flying out."

"A whistle-stop tour." Svetlana remarked as she reviewed the information.

"Looks like he knew exactly what he wanted and who to get it from."

"Can you put him in the Petersen Museum?"

Losario shook his head. "That's the thing. We know Jaeger was around there at the time, but the basement level doesn't have cameras and he didn't show up on any others."

"The DA would throw it out even before it went to arraignment." His partner added.

"The same in Mulhouse." Depailler nodded. "We see glimpses around the town but nothing in the museum specifically. Unfortunately, where Monsieur Langier was at the time is not covered too well either."

"And in Zwickau?" Svetlana asked.

"Here, we have a little more luck." Müller began. "The camera in the museum was high up and we only see the back of him, but we see the whole murder take place." He looked to the ladies in the room. "I warn you; it is not pleasant viewing."

Svetlana nodded and Müller played the footage. The clarity was excellent.

IN THE DEN OF WOLVES

Clearly the museum hadn't skimped on security for their precious exhibits. Located in the ceiling of the two-storey dealership exhibition, the camera easily covered all four of the exhibits. Robertson could be seen examining the car, taking photographs and measurements. Then he crouched down by the wheel. It was then that a dark figure emerged from the bottom corner of the shot.

The angle of the camera looked down on Jaeger from above and behind, no facial recognition was possible, and the assailant didn't turn round. There was an exchange of conversation, the wire was produced, then a longer conversation with Robertson on his knees. He flicked through his notebook, ripped out a page and gave it to Jaeger who looked at it and put it in his pocket. The conversation continued, then Robertson got to his feet and tried to escape. That's when Jaeger pounced.

After looping the wire about Robertson's neck, Jaeger pushed his victim to the ground, placed a foot in between the shoulder blades and hauled back on the wire, crossing it over and using his incredible strength to finish the deed. The effect, witnessed from above, was horrifyingly effective. Even the seasoned LA detectives winced at the footage.

Keeping his victim almost at arm's length seemed to prevent the worst of the arterial spray from staining the attacker's clothing, though it certainly went everywhere else. Once Robertson's body had collapsed, Jaeger backed away out of camera shot and left. From the other cameras around the site, it wasn't clear how he got in or out. It was as if he had just melted back into the shadows.

Svetlana sighed. Dealing with authoritarian regimes had many pitfalls but the one thing they generally all had in abundance was surveillance cameras. Britain too, one of the most highly surveyed countries in Europe had an abundance of CCTV. Some of it of dubious quality, but nevertheless if one camera missed something, another was likely to pick it up from a different angle. Here, the assailant had clearly studied the weaknesses of the target buildings and exploited them effectively. Either he had done his research well or had a good team behind him.

"Jaeger arrives for only a day," Svetlana began, "Goes to where he knows his victim will be, talks with them for a few minutes, then kills them."

"All three men were automotive historians and worked in national museums and archives. That's all they have in common." Losario murmured.

"Not quite." Reinhardt put in. "They all have the same keyring."

"Why is that relevant?" Svetlana asked.

It's not." Losario scoffed.

"It could be." Reinhardt countered. "It's a keyring with an unusual three-ringed symbol." He looked at the information on his pad. "It's not for a car. Mr Robertson drove a Gordon Keeble, Monsieur Langier a Citroën."

"Bob Jefferson drove a '67 Firebird 400." Losario interjected.

"It's not even a recognised car badge." Reinhardt continued, showing Svetlana the photographs of the keys from Robertson and Langier.

"They could have been part of a religious group." Depailler suggested, looking at the symbol. "I've seen this before. Sometimes it represents the Holy Trinity."

"A secret religious society?" Svetlana enquired, arching an eyebrow. "It doesn't seem likely. Monsieur Langier was Catholic."

"Robertson was a non-practicing Presbyterian." Added the detective from Hampshire CID.

"What does that even mean? Non-practicing?" Losario chuckled. "Jefferson liked barbecues with the family."

"Anyone can have a keyring." Reinhardt shrugged. "It doesn't prove much by itself, but the fact they've all got the same one is a little strange. I looked for it on the internet. For sure, you can get one custom made, but it's not an off-the-shelf design."

"So, it does represent something." Depailler added.

Reinhardt nodded his agreement with that theory. "Maybe something else they were involved in."

"Three rings. Three victims." Losario suggested.

"Let's get back to what we know." Svetlana suggested. "Based on the

Zwickau footage, Jaeger was extracting information from Robertson. After he got the information he wanted, he killed his victim. So, it's likely that Jaeger did that with the other two. The information then leads him to Berlin where it appeared he was looking for a key to an old car."

"A key that never existed." Reinhardt added.

"The information was bogus." Svetlana picked up. "It looks like it was never meant to lead him anywhere. If anything, the whole purpose of the information these three men had was to lead whoever was after it to a dead-end."

"Information on what?" Losario asked.

"The origins of this Horch perhaps." Reinhardt passed around the postcard of the replica in the museum. "That's a reproduction. The original was made by the people he visited in Berlin, looking for the key, or at least the designs for it. Apparently the car was lost during the war."

"So, why bother looking for it?"

"Because maybe it wasn't lost." Müller put in, producing some internet magazine articles. "These three men also have a reputation for finding old relics. Some of them eventually sell for millions. Perhaps they knew where the original Horch was."

"Why go to Bordeaux if he is looking for this car?" Svetlana asked.

"To find another lost relic." Depailler added gloomily. All eyes swivelled in his direction. "Our Monsieur Langier was a historian specialising in Bugatti. This was why he worked so closely with the Schlumpf Collection. For those that look into such things, and Monsieur Langier was one such, Bordeaux was the last known destination of a famous Lost Bugatti."

"Our killer is after more than one car then?"

"Perhaps." Depailler shrugged. "It is a theory only."

"And there have been no further sightings?"

"Not since he arrived in Bordeaux."

"He can't have just disappeared." Svetlana frowned. "We have issued a Red Notice for him, but we need to know where he's slept, where he's eaten. Everything."

"We've checked all that." Depailler nodded. "It ends suddenly on this date." He showed the last transaction, almost two months ago.

"He's gone to ground somewhere." Reinhardt pondered.

"What about this OID organisation?" Svetlana probed.

"We have nothing new. There was an outgoing phone call from the number used to contact Jaeger. The call was made about two days after his arrival in Bordeaux. Barely ten seconds long. We haven't been able to trace it back. Nothing since."

"How can someone just disappear for a couple of months?" Svetlana asked, becoming increasingly irritated and confused.

"Maybe he didn't." Reinhardt replied after a brief silence. "Maybe someone got to him instead."

"You think he's already dead?"

"He was clearly agitated about something when he left Erdmann & Rossi. He made a phone call shortly afterwards, then goes to Bordeaux and no one sees him again. There's no more calls, no transactions, no withdrawals. Nothing. He's not eating anything; he's not sleeping anywhere. He's gone. So, maybe someone made him go away."

"Who, and why?"

"Perhaps whoever he was working for. This OID, whatever it is."

"They lure him to Bordeaux and then kill him?"

"It's just a thought, but it explains why we have nothing more on him since."

"Where might he have gone in Bordeaux? Where was his last known appearance?"

"That we do know." Depailler said with a rare smile. "He was captured on the cameras of the Bassins des Lumière. He slid across some photographs captured from the footage. "It's an art gallery in the old submarine base."

"Was he on another job?" Losario asked, "Staking out an art gallery?"

"There is not much actual art in there." Depailler explained. "It's more an art experience. It's a visual art gallery."

"I didn't think there was any other kind." Losario joked.

"They project the art on the walls." Depailler explained patiently. "There are no actual paintings. Some sculptures, yes, but it's more of an exhibition space."

"He had a reason to go there though." Svetlana concluded.

Depailler nodded in a non-committal fashion. It was a possibility, but he had no clue why.

"Do we know the reason?"

"No."

"Maybe we should find out then. Call the gallery. Schedule a meeting. Then we should look around the place."

Depailler looked at Reinhardt and Losario. It seemed a reasonable suggestion, embarrassingly simple. Why hadn't he thought of it? Because he was a Lieutenant in Mulhouse, not Bordeaux, that's why. At least that's how he reconciled it to himself. He would need their permission of course. Maybe the Bordeaux police would like to look around too. That way no one would be stepping on anybody's toes. French police were notoriously territorial.

"I make the call." He conceded with a sigh.

CHAPTER NINETY-TWO
SCOTLAND, 2018

"So," Hamilton began, returning from the bar after settling the lunch bill. "Where do we go from here?"

Harrington was expecting the question, though it didn't make her feel any less anxious about it. In truth, she had no idea. In all her years of intelligence service, she had been seldom lost for direction. The sight of the old Rover again after all these years had completely thrown her off track. And the bodies…

Hamilton gazed down at her on the edge of the booth near the fireplace, looking small and fragile. Almost sensing her disquiet, he stood with his hands in his pockets and muttered quietly.

"Let's jist go for a wee drive oot, shall we? See where it teks us."

Quietly relieved, yet feeling foolish and helpless, she acquiesced to his suggestion with a slight nod. The stick was extended with a little less vigour, though she got to her feet with an assured movement, determined not to let the side down just yet.

"This is not a normal Land Rover, is it?" she asked when Hamilton joined her back in the cabin, rubbing the back of her fingers over the mohair, leather and tweed door card.

"No, it's naw." he smiled, running his fingers around the wooden steering wheel with a certain sense of pride.

"You've put a lot of effort into it." She moved to the dashboard in front of her.

Above the stereo were three brushed metal heater control quadrants, adjusting left and right temperature and airflow direction. The metal switchgear stretched in a continuous horizontal line on a fascia of basket woven leather. The unique design of the dashboard conjured up the layout of *Torridon's* utilitarian predecessors.

Although Hamilton's Land Rover was a late-model Puma variant with bulbous bonnet and modern comforts, the Edinburgh specialist had completely redesigned the plasticky factory interior to be more in harmony with the vehicle's function and Hamilton's vision for the project. His concept had not merely been an attempt at some retro pastiche or shoehorning an older design into a newer model. Instead, it had been about reimagining a timeless classic that was still recognisable as part of the Defender lineage while adding a touch of high-end, modern luxury.

"That mind is working on suhin'." Hamilton remarked. He was quietly gratified that Harrington seemed to approve of his adjustments but was wise enough now to know her thoughts were converging towards another object.

"How much did it cost?"

"Naw sure ah've to'alled it all up." He replied, trying to anticipate where her thoughts might be leading them. "Yer dinnae think Sutherland jist abandoned the Horch in Germany, d'yer?"

Harrington was silent for a moment. Her silence didn't trouble Hamilton this time. He was sure he might just have hit upon her train of thought.

"No." she said at last, feeling the texture of the fabrics with her fingertips, almost caressing it. "No. I know for a fact that he didn't." She twisted in her seat to face him.

This new disclosure came as a surprise to Hamilton, though he chose to keep silent, sensing there was something more she wanted to say first.

"They requested I obtain a car for them." She recalled, speaking quietly, barely above a whisper, as though anything louder and the memory might be shattered and lost forever. Like waking up and trying to recall a dream. "Actually, it was Cameron that requested it." She added, going back over the arrangement.

CHAPTER NINETY-THREE
SCOTLAND, 1963

"You may be the Lord Dalwhinnie," Harrington muttered irritably, "But that doesn't make me your personal maidservant, to be summoned at your beck and call."

The Johnson Collection had been a small, private gallery in Ainslie Place, part of Edinburgh's Regency New Town suburb. Cameron had only made the arrangement a couple of days beforehand and getting permission to galivant up on the train from London had not been without its difficulties.

She had been admiring works on the other side of the room as he made his way in. He had an air of quiet competence about him. Neither arrogant, nor aloof. There was no swagger, but Cameron was a man becoming increasingly confident in his own skin again. After the pummelling he had taken during the War, it had been a long and arduous road.

"And yet, here you are." He replied casually.

"What are we doing here?" she asked, still somewhat vexed.

"Adelaide Johnson was quite a lady in her day, by all accounts. Sadly, she passed in '42, well into her nineties, but she bequeathed this gallery and its contents to the British people." Cameron began, imparting his limited knowledge from the leaflet he had picked up at the front desk.

"A remarkable gift." Harrington replied cheerlessly.

"Isn't it?" he agreed with a little more colour. "Take these for example." He said moving to the coloured sketches framed in a cluster to one side. "The work of Giovanni Nanni has exceptional clarity and texture, though beyond its aesthetic appeal, might otherwise have been consigned to history had it not been for Mrs Johnson's foresight."

"Is this going somewhere?" she asked impatiently.

"How might you steal one of these?"

"Why would you want to?"

"Not your thing, then." he flicked through the leaflet. "Apparently Mrs Johnson managed to assemble a complete collection of all his original postcards. The curator has assured me that they're all here, but he's checking the basement anyway. I suspect there may be at least one of them missing."

"And you think our man might have it?"

"Oh no, I suspect it's the one in Councillor Beattie's office. Gifted to her by our local provost who was recently bludgeoned over the head. It did get me thinking though. What other kinds of things get mislaid, lost, even stolen, and nobody notices."

"What are you talking about, Cameron?"

"Let's say we were to ask someone who used to work in the old Lagonda drawing offices whether they had a complete set of drawings for everything they ever made before the war. They will most likely say one of two things. Either they've all been destroyed, or that they're safely archived in one of their plan chests." He held up a finger to pre-empt his question. "Are they really all there though?"

He turned as the gallery's curator appeared, looking a little perturbed.

"One of them is missing." He muttered quietly. "Number twenty-seven."

"A young woman with a large straw hat, polka dot scarf and a bay horse." Cameron said calmly.

"Yes." The curator replied with surprise. "Your knowledge of the subject is…"

"Not a bit of it." He shook his head. "I think I know where it might be." He turned to Harrington. "You see, just as in London during the war, this whole collection was put into storage to protect it in case Edinburgh was ever bombed. The collection was transported to a disused railway tunnel just south of Fort Augustus, so Mr Chamberlain informed me." He indicated the curator. "The line had long been abandoned before the first war and a landslide had blocked off one end completely. The other had been shuttered up for decades but inside it was still dry and cool, unusual for a railway tunnel in fact, but there was just enough moisture to prevent the wood from drying out and cracking." He ran his hand over the glossy surface of a console they were standing in front of. "Yet not enough for the artwork to moulder. Perfect for storing this entire collection."

"Why are you telling me this?" Harrington frowned.

"It just so happened that the movement was coordinated by a detachment of Royal Army Service Corps, to which our local provost was enlisted." He looked across at the agitated Chamberlain. "I'll come and see you presently."

Chamberlain moved away nervously, leaving the two of them alone again.

"Technical drawings completed in 1939 by Charles Kingsbury at Lagonda Motors were sent off with an American for patent registration in New York. The drawings never arrived at the Patent Office, but they did turn up a few years later at a Soviet Design Bureau responsible for aircraft engine development. Now, who do you think that American was?"

"Are you sure?" Harrington asked after a moment's silence.

"Not definitively, but we would like to find out."

"'We?'"

"Sutherland and I have a little theory, but we need your assistance to prove it."

"Sutherland is with you?" Harrington exclaimed, keeping her voice down but her displeasure up. "He was supposed to report to us when he got back to Southampton."

"I think he's done quite enough of that over the years, don't you?"

Harrington frowned and let out a sigh. "What kind of assistance?"

"We need a car."

"You have a car."

"Everyone knows I have a car, and everyone knows exactly what it looks like. If you want us to finish what we've started, we're going to need something a little less conspicuous."

"What do you have in mind?"

"Nothing too fancy. Something nobody would look twice at. A Rover should do it, but not the latest model."

"Are you expecting me to buy you a car?"

"Do you want definitive information or just hearsay and speculation?"

"I don't understand why you need a car."

"I would have thought in your line of work the less you knew the better, especially as this is probably all very unofficial."

"Do I have a choice?"

"Of course, you do, but then in a few days' time when our man returns home, our moment will have gone. There's no guarantee he will ever come back to the UK, and we know how forthcoming our Trans-Atlantic cousins can be when it's one of their own we would like to talk to."

Harrington huffed again, taking a decided disliking to the position Cameron had forced her into. "When will you need it?"

"Freya and I will be returning home this afternoon. It would be good if we didn't have to take the train."

"That's impossible."

"Ah that word again." He smiled as he began to walk away. "It's entirely up to you, of course. Now if you'll excuse me. I need to have a word with our Mr Chamberlain."

Harrington was left standing before Icarus, staring at the mythological figure feeling annoyed and frustrated. If the wings of the sculpture had been made from the wax of legend, they might have melted under her very gaze. She had a decision to make and precious little time to make it. She knew trying to get anything out of the American was always going to be a challenge but was hoping Cameron might have had at least something to give her. Either he did have something, and wasn't telling her, or else he was up to something not altogether legal. Not altogether ideal for a Detective Chief Superintendent.

She wasn't sure whether to be disappointed or angry, but in the end, there was nothing else for it. Crossing the parquet floor briskly, she came up to his elbow, just as Cameron had reached Chamberlain's office door. "Two o'clock. Tell me where to meet you."

"Jamaica Street." He whispered. "You'll find it behind Heriot Row. It's rundown and derelict so should be fairly quiet."

"Don't be late." She said, fixing him with an irritated scowl before taking her leave.

CHAPTER NINETY-FOUR
SCOTLAND, 2018

"Why did they need yer tae get 'em a car?" Hamilton asked, back on the road again, heading for Spean Bridge.

"Cameron's car was too distinctive. Everyone around here knew it by sight." Harrington explained. "He was the DCS for the whole of the county, remember, so he drove everywhere in it."

"Whit wis it?"

"Some big red thing." She waved dismissively. "I didn't pay much attention, but it was old, and it was rare around these parts. Probably the only one in Scotland at the time."

"The car needed tae be fairly anonymous then."

"Correct." She nodded. "I did the best I could and managed to supply them with the Rover. After I left it at Jamaica Street I never saw it again."

"Until two days ago."

She nodded, stiffening her upper lip, feeling strangely emotional.

"It meks sense then." Hamilton nodded. "Even if Sutherland had managed tae bring his auld car back home, provided it wis still in working order, the Horch wid have been too distinctive as well. Impossible tae carry oot any kind o' covert work wi it."

Harrington nodded in silent agreement, her mind wandering again as they approached Spean Bridge. A decision needed to be made.

"So, which way?" he asked.

Which way? North or south. Which way indeed?

CHAPTER NINETY-FIVE
GERMANY, 1943

The British Empire Trophy held at Donington Park in 1939 had been a glorious affair. Along with the Nuffield Trophy in June, the event endeavoured to consolidate the racetrack's position as the country's only permanent road circuit. With rising uncertainty in Europe, what the racing calendar itself may have lacked in quantity, it made up for in variety, with events for the University Clubs, VSCC, MCC and SS Car Clubs, not to mention the fifth International Donington Grand Prix all pencilled on the calendar.

Racing for English Racing Automobiles, a twenty-year old Anthony Roylance Rolt entered a B-Type machine similar to the *Remus* model he had bought from fellow Old Etonian Prince Bira Birabongse the year before. Leading the field from A B Hyde's Maserati, Reg Parnell's Bugatti-Hassan-Wilkins Special and a host of other cars in a surprisingly large field, Tony Rolt completed the race's 200-mile stretch of 64-laps in 2 hours and 35 minutes.

Though Sutherland never had opportunity to meet Rolt in open competition, he knew the aspiring young man by reputation. Had the war not intervened, the pair of them would very likely have competed against one another at the Donington Grand Prix that never was. In a race where Auto-Union would have been looking to secure their third consecutive victory at the Leicestershire circuit, it would have been fascinating to see what the plucky little Brit could have achieved.

Events though conspired to take another turn as Rolt found himself a year later with a field commission in the Rifle Brigade, defending Calais from the 10th Panzer Division with a Bren gun. Having held up the German advance for three days, delaying the attack on Dunkirk, and helping a wounded comrade in the process, Rolt was eventually captured and transferred to Oflag VII-C in Laufen. Rolt subsequently escaped seven times from various prisoner of war camps throughout southern Germany and Poland, and was eventually transferred to the maximum-security prison Oflag IV-C.

It was here, in the Renaissance style Colditz Castle, that *Manuela* swept in through the gates. *Adler* had persuaded the new commandant that an interview with the audacious young officer might bear fruit in preventing a further escape attempt. Having been confined for so long, he may even be ripe to the idea of something a little more conducive to the Nazi cause, as so many others had who were making up the ranks of the British Free Corps.

In an attic room there ensued a brief, but significant scuffle, raised voices were heard and Rolt was described by *Adler* as the Cock of Colditz, before being led back to his cell and labelled as irredeemably patriotic in *Adler's* report to Oberst Prawitt. Yet, what had really transpired between them, would set in motion one of the most daring escape attempts from the impregnable castle ever conceived.

There, along with two RAF and one Naval officer that *Adler* brought to his attention after reading their files, they would construct a workshop amidst a castle teeming with highly suspicious Germans. Then, using only the materials that they had available, they would fabricate a glider using bed slats, floorboards and sleeping bags and launch it from the roof.

The materials, the design, the engineering behind it was all Rolt, *Adler* had merely implanted the very seed of an idea, and only if the war began to turn against the Germans decisively. *Adler* was very aware that should the tide turn in favour of a German defeat, the SS may well take it upon themselves to slaughter their prisoners en-masse. He had seen the carnage they were prepared to exact.

Rolt had taken some convincing. Only natural, given that the idea was mentioned to him by a Scot in a Nazi uniform. After the deliberately feisty encounter in the attic, Rolt could eventually see in *Adler* a man who regarded it as his duty to defend Europe from Nazi oppression.

"I fought for my country!" he had cried after hurling a chair at *Adler's* head.

Unlike the films, furniture doesn't break as easily in real life, and the blow really hurt *Adler*, but for the sake of credibility he didn't let that phase him.

"Where did that get yer, eh?" *Adler* had replied acerbically. Then launching himself across the room, he pinned Rolt to the floor and whispered, almost tenderly in his ear.

"I could nae do what you do." He began. "They're giving yer the Military Cross for Calais. Yer deserve it. No doubt yer'll get a Bar for this." He nodded to the rafters, indicating the escape attempt *Adler* was about to propose. "You fight on the ootside. I'm fighting on the inside." He gave Rolt a stern look as if to say, 'Don't believe the uniform, believe the man.' Then he delivered a savage blow to Rolt's stomach, partly payback for the bruising that he could already feel across his shoulder and back from the chair, partly a way of keeping the charade alive.

"You think yer just gonnae fly outta here, do yer?" he bawled meaningfully with his Hebridean brogue, getting to his feet. "Swoop away like some bird?" he nodded again. "You're a bloody cock if you think that. The Cock of Colditz they'll call yer."

And so it was that the glider got its name. The Colditz Cock.

CHAPTER NINETY-SIX
FRANCE, 2018

Management of the Bassins des Lumière had arranged for the gallery to be closed early to allow the police to make a thorough search of the place. It didn't take too long as much of the structure basically comprised of vast concrete spaces. Svetlana had gone with Reinhardt and Depailler to review the CCTV footage again in the offices with local Bordeaux police. Müller and Collard had been accompanied by the gallery's security to inspect each of the pens in turn. The British and American detectives had returned home. There was no need for their involvement at this stage, but each force would be kept in the loop.

Only the first four pens were used by the museum for the gallery, but Svetlana insisted that the whole site be inspected. Eventually access into the service corridor behind the pens was gained by forcing open one of the bulkhead doors. A torchlight inspection initially revealed nothing of any value. There were the scattered remains of a feline skeleton, a musty smell of stale air, but nothing else. At the far end, the corridor led back into the sculpture gallery. The other end led outside to the new apartments across the street.

It was as they were making their way through this fire exit that they noticed a trace of something on the crash bar. A cleaner might have missed it. If they even ventured to this end of the structure. Security may only check whether the door was unlocked and operable, though being at the end of a disused and unlit corridor, probably not even then. This was technically not even part of the gallery complex. The trained detective's eye however observed a dried blood stain on the corner of the hinge. As they shone the torch around the corridor, they noticed another couple of spots on the concrete floor.

"I'll check to see if there are any more." Collard volunteered.

"No," Müller replied, nodding to the two officers accompanying them. "Let's both see where it leads. Get the locals to put their forensics team on it."

Collard nodded in agreement and explained to her compatriots. They got on the radio to call it in and one of them remained in position at the fire exit while Collard and Müller resumed their search down the corridor.

Heading back towards the main administration building, the trail seemed to stop just short. Shining their torches around, Collard found another door on the opposite side, almost completely concealed in the shadows. Shining the torch inside, she instantly recoiled. Müller looked at her, then shone his own torch in and saw the reason for her reaction. A bloody smear was found on the walls of the stairwell, coming from down below. It was as if someone had been trying to escape. Müller looked to Collard. They both looked pale. What horror were they about to find down in the bowels of the submarine base.

"Better get backup." He suggested.

As Collard got onto the radio again, Müller unholstered his sidearm, bracing it on the fist of his left hand that held the torch.

"Ready?" he asked.

"Ready." She replied nervously.

Slowly they stepped inside the stairwell and made for the banister, shining their torches down the void. As a precaution, Müller also looked up and watched as the beam of light disappeared towards the top of the structure. There didn't appear to be anything of interest going on up there. He read the sign and concluded that the staircase only gave access to the roof itself. No other rooms or corridors above. Just the crumbling remnants of a platform for an old flak cannon. Certainly, no blood trails. Leading the way, Müller cautiously proceeded down the steps, following the trail down to the bunker.

On the level below they found themselves in a concrete corridor with doors on either side. The blood trail hadn't deviated into any of them but seemed to emerge from the open doorway at the far end. Carrying on, Müller and Collard briefly scanned the walls, noting the graffiti, the lewd cartoons, all standard vandalism. Stepping through the open doorway they found another staircase. This one only descended deeper below ground. The smear on the walls returned.

Whoever it belonged to, it seemed clear they didn't have the benefit of a torch. Moving down, they followed the steps as they turned through ninety degrees and continued descending. The staircase ended at another open door leading led into a narrow corridor. Collard tried the light switch but as she suspected, this part of the building had been disconnected years ago.

"What's that smell?" she asked.

Müller didn't answer. He knew only too well the source of the putrid atmosphere. It was the smell of death.

"Brace yourself." He said. "This might not be pretty."

Moving towards the solitary door at the far end, they entered the airlock and through the second door. Blood was smeared along the left hand wall. There was the shape of fingers, a hand. For someone escaping, it suggested an injury to the right hand, they were using it to feel their way back out. The smell was becoming stifling. Müller heard Collard gag and fought back the reaction to retch himself.

Carrying on, he shone the torch into the luggage room. Empty racks and coat hooks. Then came the kitchen. He recognised some of the gadgets from his grandmother's house. It was strange seeing them down here too. The canteen was next. Tables and chairs still neatly arranged. Not hurled about or broken. No one had been down here before. Not the people responsible for the graffiti upstairs. Only the one who had bled.

And the one who was dead.

The unoccupied bunk rooms looked eerie. Living quarters were lifeless. The smell was intensifying. They were getting close. Old radio sets looked like museum props. Müller half-expected a mannequin in uniform to be sat at the desk with a headset on and a notepad. A pencil balanced in pale, unresponsive fingers.

Swinging the beam of light back to the other side of the corridor, the stencilled sign next to the door read '*Büro 1*'. The scene within was worse than Müller had expected.

As torchlights came towards them, Collard's feet could be heard sprinting down the corridor.

"Merd!" she screamed. "Merd!"

The uniformed officers looked at one another uneasily. Then directed their beams towards the screams. Her face looked wild and pale. One of the officers caught her mid-flight, stopping her retreat.

"My God! What is it?" he asked. The bloody trail had already unsettled his comrades. Seeing Collard emerge alone did little to pacify their disquiet.

Collard managed to wriggle free of him just in time as vomit gurgled up into her throat and exploded onto the floor at his feet. The officers looked to him with apprehension etched onto their faces.

"Get down there now. We still have someone inside." she spluttered.

"Ma'am?"

"Now, damn it!"

Drawing their weapons, the three officers crossed the corridor and began the descent to the next level. Already the smell of death was bubbling up towards them.

"Police!"

"Down here!" Müller cried, still rooted to the spot outside Büro 1.

The sounds of footstep preceded them. Then torchlight bounced along the walls and floor as the officers ran down the corridor.

"It's okay." He cried. "Don't panic. We need some more light down here."

The three policemen came up to Müller, covering their mouth and nose as best as they could. One of them was heard retching down the corridor, followed by a splatter of something liquid

"God dammit, Pierre!"

IN THE DEN OF WOLVES

As the two others came up to Müller, they could already see it in his face. They poked their heads around the door and shone their own torches inside. A desk, a room full of filing cabinets. Paper and files all strewn around. One of the heavy wooden units had toppled over and beneath it, trapped by its considerable weight, a decomposing body.

CHAPTER NINETY-SEVEN
ENGLAND, 2018

There had been nothing more for Hamilton and Harrington to do up in Scotland. Nothing tangible. Harrington had expressed a vague notion that *Manuela* might just be right under their noses somewhere, perhaps on the Isle of Skye where Sutherland had come from. Though without a clear indication of that, merely turning up in the hopes of finding it wasn't likely to be effective.

Hamilton enquired how she knew for a fact that *Manuela* had left Germany with Sutherland. She didn't reply to that but promised him that she would tell him everything in good time. He needed to know. She was just finding it hard to confide in someone. It was something she had never done before. Never had to. Never could. All part of the job. They could do nothing more but to head back home and wait to see what the laboratories of Police Scotland could come up with from the old Rover.

Hamilton drove her back to East Dean, then headed back up to London. There was something he wanted to check up on. The caretaker was out, so Hamilton let himself in with his own key, made his way up to the apartment and unlocked the front door. It had that familiar stillness to it that came with an unoccupied dwelling. The guest bedroom was empty, exactly as he had left it. In fact, everything was. It was as if no one had set foot in the place at all. Perhaps no one had. His heart sank as he let out a deep, regretful sigh.

"Ah told yer tae get oot, lass." He murmured.

After the anti-climax in Scotland, Hamilton dragged himself sullenly up the stairs to bed. Unless he heard anything back from Harrington, he would head back to Cornwall in the morning and see who needed any recovery work. So far nothing had any closure. Everything seemed to be on pause. It was only when he got to the top of the stairs that he noticed something was different.

They were a little dry and crispy now, going brown at the edges, but as he looked down he discovered the bedsheets were covered in hundreds of rose petals. A note was left in the middle of them. He picked it up and immediately recognised her fragrance. It was what had tipped him off when he had set foot in Rockwater Cabin. He had sensed it before when she had come here the first time, wafting past him to take her place on the sofa next to him.

He sat down on the bed, unfolded the note and read it.

Thank you for everything. Call me. V.

There was a phone number inscribed neatly underneath. Different to the emergency number he had given her outside Tesco. Different to the mobile she had used to communicate with Madam Sokolova. This one was a landline. It had a country code of +679.

"Respect." He remarked, nodding with approval. It was difficult to get any further away than Fiji.

As he moved, the petals beneath him crunched. He brought the note up to his nose again and savoured her seductive perfume, placing his lips where she had left a lipstick imprint of hers, then looked down at the bed.

"Spare room ah think the night." He chuckled. There was no way he was going to clear all that lot up. Something for the caretaker to do. She liked to be kept busy.

CHAPTER NINETY-EIGHT
GERMANY, 1943

If Hans Reinhardt needed anymore reassurance that he was doing the right thing, the desperate case of Boris Lüdke confirmed it. Even basic police procedure was no longer being followed. Officers had not even paid lip service to the dictates of professional investigation. Lüdke was intellectually disabled. He was known by local police as a petty thief and a peeping tom. Yet somehow they had connected him with over fifty murders spanning fifteen years. There had been no similarities in modus operandi, no signature or motive. No fingerprints had ever been found or even recorded at the scenes and no evidence was ever presented.

Having looked over the reports, Hans found them to be inconclusive, incoherent and vague. His son could have done a better job. It was inconceivable to him that a semi-illiterate who had once got caught stealing a chicken, had managed to evade the authorities for so long, let alone commit murder. Hans had complained to his boss but had been given short shrift and effectively suspended from the Berlin police force. The Reichkriminalpolizeiamt had no patience for people with intellectual disabilities. For the good of the nation, this couldn't go on for another year, let alone a thousand.

With Goebbels speech the following month, declaring total war on Allied powers, it was clear to Hans that Nazi Germany was facing the very serious risk of total defeat. Japan had lost the Guadalcanal. The tide was turning. Better he be on the right side of history.

Information he had managed to obtain from colleagues suggested something terrible had been discovered by the Wehrmacht near Smolensk. He passed on what he knew, and Sutherland transmitted it back to his handler in London. Less than a week later, Radio Berlin announced the discovery of Polish graves. Military officers and intelligentsia massacred by the Soviets in the Katyn Forest.

"The world is going mad." He exhaled as they sat and enjoyed a brandy together. "Just mad."

Sutherland nodded as he lit up a cigarette. There was desperation on all sides. He doubted Western Allies would resort to such savage brutality, but in a time of war almost anything could be excused. No doubt a team of Ivy League lawyers would be scrabbling away to ensure that whatever atrocities were being carried out in the Far East had a legal framework to legitimise them. The collapse of civilised society seemed imminent at every corner.

"How is your new legion?" he asked, gesturing to the Union Flag stitched to the shoulder of his uniform.

"Barely a dozen dissolute youths." Sutherland replied, rolling his eyes. "There are one or two making a fair go of it though."

"Be careful, Andreas." Hans said, using the German equivalent to Andrew. "They will be the ruthless ones."

"And I'm not?" he replied darkly. "Ironic that you're telling me to be careful."

"We both need to be careful."

"You have more to lose."

Hans shrugged. It was true. Joachim and Julia were bright kids. Carina had done so well with them. At least his temporary suspension meant he could spend more time with them. Though if it went on for too long Carina might have to find more work. Factory work was being taken up by forced labourers and there was hardly anything in the shops to sell. Housekeeping might help keep their heads above water. Hans had to keep his below the parapet.

While he was thinking thus, a small bundle was pushed across the desk.

"What's this?" he asked suspiciously.

"Some salami and speck."

"We're not that hard up yet."

"Take it anyway." Sutherland shrugged. "We draw rations for twenty people, so it's a shame to let it go to waste."

"I can't. What will I tell Carina?"

"Tell her the truth."

"The truth?!" he leaned forward, almost spilling his brandy in the act. "Are you crazy?"

"You love her, am I right."

"With every fibre of my being. You know that."

"And she loves you?"

"Of course, we would do anything for each other."

"Then trust that love." Sutherland said. "What you have is a rare and precious thing. Don't risk destroying it, destroying her trust. If the time comes, she may be your greatest ally."

Hans regarded Sutherland for a moment. On the one hand he knew he was right, extolling a wisdom beyond his experience. If things really did start to go bad, his world would very rapidly start closing in around him. The more people he had with him, perhaps the greater chance of survival. Though who could tell in this era of industrialised slaughter?

On the other hand, risking her life as well as his own was simply inconceivable. If ever he was discovered, he alone would take the blame. And the bullet. Carina and the children could carry on. If the Third Reich allowed them too. He was inclined to think they might just exterminate his whole family anyway. In which case, having an ally at the bitter end would be a better way to go.

He looked at the package again. The meat would make Carina's life a little easier, reduce the stress on the household budget. She would work wonders with it. That alone would have been enough to convince him to take it. In Sutherland though, he genuinely felt that he had a friend. Someone who might actually care if he lived or died.

"So, what next?" he asked, swiping the package off the desk and depositing it inside the pocket of his coat.

"Have you ever been to the Ruhr Valley? I've heard its nice there."

"It might have been. Before the life was bombed out of it."

"Isn't it supposed to be good for birdwatching? Lake Möhne is particularly favoured by waterfowl."

Hans smiled, sensing what Sutherland was driving at. There had long been a suggestion that the dams along the North-Rhine area might be vulnerable to attack. Perhaps this was a reconnaissance mission. No doubt there would be loss of life. He had resigned himself to that now. Of greater importance now was the loss of industrial output.

"I'll put together a little family outing." He smiled, staring at the brandy in the glass as he swirled it around. "It's not that I have anything else to do."

CHAPTER NINETY-NINE
ENGLAND, 2018

As it turned out, Hamilton didn't quite make it back to Cornwall. He got a call that kept him in London instead. Jennifer MacGregor had taken great care in developing the old film. The canister retrieved from the bottom of Loch Etive had contained several undeveloped spools of the Minox Riga film. She had taken them back to her homemade photographic laboratory in the boxroom of her apartment and spent several evenings on it to ensure she didn't make a mistake.

The importance of forensic investigation could never be overstated. Very often she would only have a single sample to work with. Even then it might consist of a single strand of fibre, a solitary drop of fluid, a few micrograms of substance. With the fates of a case often hanging on the results, there was no margin for error.

Once developed, Jenn began to make enlargements before digitally scanning them into the central police database, tagging them and sending them across to Edinburgh. The originals were carefully packaged up and sent Special Delivery to London. New Scotland Yard passed them to the Home Office who viewed the coverslip and forwarded them onto the old International Nickel headquarters in Thames House. The Director General of MI5 contacted his opposite number in the SIS across the river. He was asked to invite the venerable peer and her new sidekick to view the images first-hand. Only then would he take a view on their potential value.

The photographs had undoubtedly been taken by the resident of *Villa des*

Pins herself, Mariette Hélène Delangle, sometime between 1943 and 1944, when she had been living in the villa with Arnaldo Binelli. The first fifty-exposure film opened with a few pictures of the mansion itself, an exquisite up-to-the-minute-style villa high up in the hills above the Côte d'Azur. There were a few external shots showing the pool, the house itself and the gardens overlooking the sea below. Even one of both of her beloved cars. The Hispano Suiza for once was sharing the limelight with the Duesenberg Model SSJ in the background.

A few internal images of the reception rooms inside captured the wondrous splendour of the Villa. A significant architectural resource of the period. Yet all of these were merely test shots, designed to distract and dissuade anyone from looking more closely at what followed. The next spool started with an image of her lover in deep conversation with an SS officer, paying them a visit from the Hotel Excelsior in Nice.

As the image was displayed on the screen in a conference room of Thames House, Harrington's breath caught in her lungs. The Director General looked across as her eyes moistened. He was coming up to retirement but remembered her when he had been a young intelligence officer. He had never witnessed the vaguest emotion from her before. Hamilton glanced over too, unaccustomed to seeing his esteemed benefactor so disturbed.

"*Adler!*" she breathed at last, recognising the man in SS uniform.

The next frames were of the lists themselves, names and addresses of those known to be Jewish, or suspected of having Jewish ancestry. As the spool ended, the third one began on the same page, ensuring nothing was missed. The names ran into their hundreds, then a thousand, two thousand. At the top of the opening page of the respective lists were three lines of German text:

ACTION-TIGER

Für den sofortigen Transport

ZIEL

The destination was handwritten next to the word Ziel. For some, it was the infamous Drancy internment camp just outside Paris. A holding area before their ultimate destination. One of the Third Reich's six extermination camps. For others however, there was a new and unfamiliar destination:

TSCHAD

"Who is *Adler*?" Hamilton asked, returning to the image of Sutherland and Binelli. It was clear she was referring to one of the two men.

The Director General looked across the table and shared a glance with the venerable Dame. "I can make the call." He offered.

She nodded, then turned to her protégé. "It's about time you found out." She said.

CHAPTER ONE HUNDRED
FRANCE, 2018

Collard and Müller's discovery was disagreeable to say the least. The quiet, low-key inspection of the gallery had now become a full-on crime scene. Police cordons and forensics teams were called in to analyse every inch of the vast spaces. Even the chief of Bordeaux police had arrived to personally take charge of the investigation.

Industrial work lights were brought in to illuminate subterranean corridors and rooms and the gallery's gantry lights were switched on to guide the police in the pens. A small corps of journalists had gathered, tipped off about a significant discovery in the dockyards but no information was coming out of the Bassins des Lumière.

"What is the approximate time of death?" Chief Reynard asked his medical examiner.

"Hard to say exactly." He shrugged. "Based on the amount of decomposition, I would say several months. Three at least."

"That ties in with when this suspect disappeared." Svetlana added, careful not to use any possessive pronouns. It tended to antagonise any typically territorial police forces.

"We need to confirm who this person is first." Reynard remarked cautiously.

"We'll send over the medical records for the suspect." Svetlana replied, looking to Reinhardt for his agreement.

He nodded, unsure whether to feel relieved or aggrieved that Reynard appeared to be taking over the reins.

"There are blood smears on the walls." the medical examiner added. "And droplets that seem to make up a broken trail out through the bunker and the service corridor to the rear of the pens."

"Someone else was here with him." Reynard concluded. "His killer, most likely."

"We also found this." One of the forensic technicians handed the ME a sealed plastic bag containing the brutal looking garotte. "Dried blood on the wire. Could be a match for the smears we've found."

"Could be the murder weapon." Reinhardt commented, looking to Svetlana.

"Yes but let's be sure. Can we send over the blood samples from Zwickau and Mulhouse for comparison? There may be some trace still left."

Reinhardt and Depailler both agreed, and Reynard seemed content that Interpol were not trying to muscle in on his case, though he wanted to be reassured.

"What will Interpol do if we find out that this is the man you are also looking for?" he enquired curiously.

"First, we will need to take down the Red Notice." Svetlana asked. "After that, unless you would like our assistance in finding his attacker, there's nothing more for us here. This is in French jurisdiction."

He smiled slightly with apparent satisfaction.

"Very well." He moved to the stairs, taking a packet of cigarettes from his pocket as he did so. "We thank you for your assistance."

Svetlana and Reinhardt watched him disappear back up onto the ground floor, then shared a look.

"He was attacking someone else." Reinhardt suggested. "I would like to find out who."

"And why." Svetlana added.

"What happens to all the records?" Depailler enquired.

"I think it would be best if we leave that to the appropriate experts." The medical examiner remarked. "We can clean up the scene, but it really needs some proper historians and archaeologists to go through everything in detail. There is so much paperwork down here."

"We should let our American friends know." Depailler suggested.

"Once we have a confirmed ID." Svetlana added. "At the moment there is nothing to say." She frowned. There was much more to this, though it seemed doors were already beginning to close on whatever it might be. It would be interesting to see this through to the end if she was allowed to. "I'm going up to get some fresh air."

CHAPTER ONE-HUNDRED-AND-ONE
ENGLAND, 2018

The National Archives in Kew contained over a thousand years of history, stretching from the Domesday Book to the present, with records on parchment and digitised formats. Its parent division, the rather grandly titled Department for Digital, Culture, Media and Sport, had its headquarters in the ornate Edwardian Baroque Revival edifice of 100 Parliament Street, in the windowless fourth floor of the Government Offices Great George Street.

Yet due to the sensitivity of the records, neither location contained any files on a British spy codenamed *Adler*. For this reason, Dame Harrington and Hamilton were chauffeured across the Thames to No.85 Albert Embankment where the driver swept them into the underground car park of Vauxhall Cross, the Babylon-on-Thames ziggurat that housed the Secret Intelligence Service.

"Here we are, Iris." The driver said as he pulled up by a set of non-descript steel doors.

"Thank you, James." She said, then turned to Hamilton, muttering quietly. "I'm afraid I might need your arm."

"Of course." He said, before alighting the vehicle and hurrying round to assist her. Holding out his arm she struggled out of the vehicle, letting the stick unfold and feeling her age every moment, but refusing to resign herself to a motorised scooter, despite Claudia's insistence.

The doors opened and a trim young lady with a bright open face and the most wonderful hair emerged.

"Good morning, Natalia." Iris greeted with grandmotherly warmth.

"Morning, Miss Harrington." She said with a sweet, open smile as she stepped forward and took her other arm.

"Now, you see?" Iris said, turning to Hamilton. "This is a young lady who knows how to address me properly. None of this 'ma'am' nonsense." She said sharply.

Natalia passed an embarrassed smile in Hamilton's direction and brushed a lock of hair away from her face as she pressed her card against the reader in the elevator's control panel.

"This is Hamilton." Iris continued, making the necessary introductions. "He's helping me with some work."

Hamilton nodded pleasantly, struck by the archivist's astonishing beauty. Certainly not the typical librarian kind he had been used to.

"Ah used tae work here, maself." Hamilton said. "Never quite made it tae the Archives though."

"Well, no, you wouldn't have." Iris replied, almost scathingly. "A missed opportunity."

"Aye, ah'm beginning tae think that." He said as he looked across at Natalia.

She was professionally dressed, white blouse, smart trouser suit, black patent brogues with a mid-height block heel. It was her face though, that captivated Hamilton's attention. She was astonishingly pretty. Dark, well-defined eyebrows, long sweeping lashes, and the most amazing pair of expressive, glittering eyes.

It was those eyes that particularly intrigued him. Her right eye gleamed with a beautiful hazel lustre, while the left was a striking ice blue with a warm tan segment splashed near the pupil, like liquid gold dropped into a pool of crystal clear water. Set into her delicate face, cheekbones moulded from finest porcelain, framed by cascading layers of rich chocolate brown hair, he silently cursed himself for not being at least a decade younger than he was. Though that didn't stop him surreptitiously glancing at her hands to look for signs of a ring.

Iris must have detected his intentions because almost at once she turned to Natalia and asked.

"How is your boyfriend, Natalia?"

She looked at her with a thoughtful expression, turned the corners of her mouth down and shrugged. "He's okay."

"Agreeable to you spending long nights away from home?" she continued. Hamilton could have sworn. "The project I have in mind for you two might keep you down here for some time."

"It's okay." She replied with a smile.

"She's one of my Polish girls." Iris said, though Natalia's English was perfection itself. "I knew her grandfather. Dashing chap. Bloody good pilot too. 302 Squadron."

"My grandfather was evacuated from France during the German invasion." She added, indicating that was the extent of her continental origins without contradicting the venerable and intimidating peer, however warmly she regarded young Natalia.

"Ah'm from Scotland maself." He replied, though his accent somewhat rendered the statement redundant. Like some teenager trying to impress a girl and ending up making some cringeworthy admission, he immediately felt foolish for even opening his mouth.

"No one's perfect, Hamilton." Harrington said as the lift came to a halt.

The doors finally opened and revealed a vast document repository crammed with Bruynzeel's Compactus Double Decker mobile shelving units. Providing four-times the capacity of ordinary static storage, touch-sensitive electronic panels allowed the shelves to slide open safely, without vibration and at a constant speed, regardless of load. Clear sight lines were maintained between the two levels by the addition of a steel mesh mezzanine. Fitted with LED lighting which gleamed off a polished concrete floor, auto air circulation and fire alarm integration ensured the precious and sensitive materials were safeguarded against any eventuality.

Natalia and Hamilton assisted Iris to a chair that had been placed nearby, before Natalia moved over to an unusual contraption at the foot of the mezzanine steps. Wheeling it over, the M-Desk was a practical and very sleek piece of furniture. Comprising a base unit on robust rubber wheels, a tambour door could be opened to gain entry into the cupboard, while a drawer above pivoted out from a corner hinge around a LINAK column which supported an extendable worktop presently laden with files and a laptop.

"When I got the call, I managed to gather some of the archives together." She said, lowering the worktop down to a level that Iris could easily reach.

"You are a treasure." She cooed softly.

Iris definitely seemed to prefer female company to their male counterparts, Hamilton observed. Though it very likely had much to do with her time with SOE during the war, training female operatives for wartime espionage deep behind enemy lines in a very male-oriented service would have required both determination and a certain empathy for the girls themselves. The risks they were taking were huge, the costs of failure or discovery, catastrophic. Robertson's demise came to him sharply. That would have been the merciful ending for one of Harrington's girls. It didn't bear thinking about.

"I'm afraid I didn't manage to find them all. They're spread out a little." She explained apologetically, handing Iris the box file on top of the pile, tucking her hair behind her ear as she did so. "This is probably the one you need."

Iris looked at the cover and nodded.

"You're absolutely right." She said, reading the spine and opening the cover. "SOE files are closed during the lifetime of the individual." Iris explained, looking up at Hamilton. "Or until their 100th birthday, when it is assumed that they have died."

Hamilton immediately had a question at the tip of his tongue. He could sense that Iris knew it, but he could also sense prudence in silence at this point as there was more explanation to come.

"Good." She nodded, satisfied that he wasn't going to speak. "Some files, however, will never be opened. You'll not find this one going to Kew." She then gestured to the selection on the desk before her. "Or any of the others, for that matter." She turned to Natalia. "What do we have on Cameron?"

"I'll have to contact Hanslope for his war service, but his other work will be here."

"That's fine." she said. "We'll need everything, but first." She opened the file and took out an old magazine, offering it up to Hamilton. "This is probably one of the few references that you might actually find in the National Archives. Page 13."

Hamilton took it gingerly, unsure whether he should have white cotton gloves on at this point.

"It's not the Magna Carta." Iris sighed, noticing his evident delicacy. "There are copies of this at Beaulieu and goodness knows where else. Probably every grandfather's attic." She smiled at Natalia. "There's no value in it."

Hamilton was looking down at a copy of The Motor Sport magazine, dated November 1935. Obediently turning to page 13 the article was entitled 'Shuttleworth wins the Donington Grand Prix'.

"You see the photograph in the bottom right corner?" Iris said.

Hamilton nodded. It was a shaky monochrome image of an Alfa Romeo P3 hurtling across the start line towards Redgate Corner to begin another lap. The caption read 'A promising start for young Scottish driver Andrew Sutherland as his Scuderia Ferrari Alfa Romeo displayed amazing acceleration during the first part of the race'.

"Well, that's *Adler*."

"*Adler* is Andrew Sutherland?"

Iris nodded.

"Now, I would like you two to start piecing together everything you can on Sutherland and Cameron." She said, handing the box file back to Natalia before getting to her feet. Hamilton closed the magazine and came to her aid. "Just see me to the lift, Hamilton." She said. "You have work to do here with Natalia. I'm off to give C an ear bashing. Whatever happened to them at Loch Etive is now directly linked to this institution."

"The bodies in the car?" Hamilton remarked quietly.

Iris looked at him. He couldn't be sure, but there appeared a little moistening in those old eyes, recalling something from the distant past. It was evident she had known Sutherland personally. Seeing human remains in the front of the old Rover must have been a shock to her after all these years. Sometimes closure wasn't all it was cracked up to be.

CHAPTER ONE-HUNDRED-AND-TWO

Having assisted her ladyship to the lift, Hamilton returned to the archive room and saw Natalia smiling at him.

"Ah tell yer it feels like the first day all over again." He muttered.

She held out her hand for the ID card he had about his neck. Relinquishing it, he stepped back and looked around the vast repository. In the eight years he had worked out of this building, he would never have suspected that there was so much paperwork below ground. What stories were contained within. It would have been a conspiracy theorist's dream.

"Seems Iris trusts you." She said, turning the card over. "Even arranged reinstatement of your old SC clearance."

In the Secret Intelligence Service there were four levels of personnel security controls; Baseline Personnel Security Standard, or BPSS, was the entry level clearance obtained during the recruitment phase. Counter Terrorist Check, CTC, was required for individuals whose posts involved proximity to public figures, access to information or material useful for terrorists and allowed unescorted access to certain military, civil or industrial establishments. The Security Check clearance was the base level held by all serving Operational-

Officers. It allowed uncontrolled access to SECRET and supervised access to TOP SECRET assets. There was an enhanced level of clearance, eSC, before the highest levels; Developed Vetting, DV, and eDV, which Hamilton always thought sounded like an advanced course at the Royal Veterinary College.

"Dis that even get me tae the canteen?" he joked, remembering how he had once held eDV security clearance when he had been a fully active operative for Her Majesty's SIS.

She smiled and handed the card back. "It won't get you down here into the Archives." She replied. "For that, you will have to come with me." She winked. "Okay." She began in a tone suggesting business, returning to the M-desk. "SIS files are given an HD reference, SOE, HS, GCHQ, HW and MI5, KV." She said, placing her hand on each box file in turn.

"He has all of them?"

She nodded, turning to him with puckered lips. "He was quite a guy, it seems."

"Have yer read all of these?"

"Only some of the SOE files so far. Iris suggested I start there."

"How long have yer been working on this?"

"Not long. Miss Harrington briefed me back in February. AA pulled me off the investigation, but it seems she's off to wage war with C to get us back on. It's taken some time to collate the records. Then it was a case of re-ordering everything." She turned to him with a weary look. "It wasn't always so neatly segregated."

"Yer've done a grand job." He said, looking at the identical box files, each with a reference number and subject. It reminded him of the Borromeo Archives. Then he remembered she had been there too.

"Well, we'll see." She said self-effacingly. "As I'm sure you appreciate, an individual never has just one file with everything all neatly arranged like they do in the films."

"Aye, more's the pity." He nodded, remembering grimly having to wade through all manner of documents to find the information he needed. Security Service work was very rarely about the gadgets and the fast cars.

Natalia took up the SOE box file and opened it up to show the index page as an example. "It's especially challenging when they're not collated in the National Archives. At least they have some semblance of order. For instance, Andrew Sutherland has files in HS4 for Eastern Europe, HS6 for Western, 7 and 9, and 11 through to 14. So, it's very possible I might have missed something."

"Ah s'pose that depends on whit we're looking for." He mused. "If yer have, it might naw even be relevant." He turned to the file and frowned. "So, whit is all this exactly?" he held up the copy of Motor Sport again. "And how dis it relate tae this?"

"Well," she smiled, evidently relishing her work. "This section here wasn't in any official files." She explained, picking up a sheaf of documents all neatly bound in a separate folder. "Some of it was obtained from archival research, others from the National Motor Museum Collections. It documents his motor racing history, covering the period 1935-40. Fascinating if you're into that sort of thing."

"Are yer?" he asked, trying to gauge her interest.

"Not particularly, but it provides the context for his later operations."

"A summary then?"

She paused, taking a breath to help set all the elements in order. "He was known to be racing earlier than 1934, but in junior races here and there, probably only listed in programmes of the day. So, as Iris said, only archived in someone's old attic storage if they happened to be there, but of no intelligence value to us. In '34, however, he made his big break with Alfa Romeo, even winning a few non-championship Grand Prix. That eventually brought him to the attention of Auto-Union who were looking for a rollcall of accomplished drivers. Basically, that's how he entered the SS."

"As a racing driver?"

"The Waffen-SS began to recruit members of the National Socialist Motor Corps in 1938. When Aryan ancestry was relaxed, Sutherland used that opportunity to his advantage. He became a member of the Legion of St

George in '43 and was tasked with recruiting members into what would eventually become the British Free Corps."

"Don Borromeo told me a wee bit aboot the NSKK." he nodded. "I dinnae realise Sutherland wis one of them."

"You went there too?" She tilted her head to the side.

"Miss Harrington's suggestion."

"Well, it's thanks to him that the unit never really got off the ground."

"How wis he instrumental in that?"

"It was his responsibility to visit the internment and interrogation camps where he was to try and recruit any POWs sympathetic to anti-Bolshevik sentiments. That was the angle they were using."

"Better tae be against the commies than a card-carrying Nazi, I suppose."

"That was his cover." She smiled. "But it gave him unfettered access to interned sailors, soldiers and airmen all over the Third Reich." She turned to the box file and pulled out the HS4 and HS6 references, covering Eastern and Western Europe. "Through encoded messages back to Station X he was able to inform SOE of the layout of camps and prisons, numbers of men, machinegun posts and guards etc. They then relayed escape plans back and he passed them onto the POWs themselves during so-called recruitment drives."

"Right under the guards' noses?" he asked in disbelief.

She nodded.

"Pretty bawsy stuff." He whistled.

"That's all detailed in there." She said, handing him the files. "We have a reading room." She said as she pushed the M-Desk along the floor to the back of the Archive Hall. A row of glass-fronted offices was squeezed between two large server rooms. "Coffee?" she asked. "I'm just going up to the restaurant." She added with an arch smile.

CHAPTER ONE-HUNDRED-AND-THREE
FRANCE, 2018

"I thought you would both like to know." Depailler said in conference with Svetlana and Reinhardt, now back at their respective agencies.

The decomposing remains of the man had been lying there for several months, according to the medical examiner. That tied in with when Michael Jaeger had last been seen on the Gare de Bordeaux cameras. Decomposition made it difficult to identify the body visually, though with Michael Jaeger's police file and medical records, it should be possible to confirm everyone's suspicions.

The body had taken a substantial beating, so clearly, he hadn't been alone in the bunker. Work lights that were brought down revealed bloody smears on the walls outside the office. As Collard and Müller had suspected, they seemed to be leading back towards the stairs. A broken trail of drops led back to the service corridor and out through the door at the far end. After that the trail ended as the rain had washed away any possible traces since they had been left. Swabs were taken from inside the museum at various places, so it was hoped they might provide the identity of the injured. If they were lucky, perhaps they would match up with someone on some database somewhere.

"It's good of Reynard to keep you in the loop." Svetlana observed.

"Hmm." He replied, unconvinced. "It gives him an easy way out if things go badly." Depailler sighed. "Better to blame the provincial gendarmerie."

"Sounds familiar." Reinhardt sighed.

"What else do you have?"

"The blood on the wall is not old. By that I mean, it's not contemporary with the age of the bunker. In fact, we may know who the blood came from." He explained. "Nothing definitive but going back through the security footage from the gallery, there is one individual we see going in that we don't see coming back out again. And it's not Michael Jaeger."

"Oh?"

There was a match for the bloody smears on the garotte that was discovered alongside the body. Beneath this were traces of three more blood samples, two of them belonged to Robertson and Langier. It was suspected that the third might have been from Bob Jefferson, though Svetlana was still waiting for the lab results to be released by the LAPD before sending them onto Reynard.

If that was the case, then they had found the murder weapon for all three victims, and a potential fourth victim that had managed to escape. In the body sprawled beneath the filing cabinet, they may just have found the murderer too.

In some ways, this would be a relief to them all. The transatlantic serial killer was no more. Yet that did leave the rather chilling question still unanswered. Who killed the killer?

At this point Depailler directed them to the email attachment he had sent through ahead of time. "This is him entering the building in the morning, leaving again the same afternoon. He then returns for the evening exhibition of Klimt."

"Quite the art enthusiast." Reinhardt remarked.

"There are not many other cameras around, but we see him around the place throughout the day. Only after the evening exhibition, he is not one of those we see leaving again."

"So, he stayed behind after hours." Svetlana concluded.

"Possibly."

"Who is he?"

"This is where it becomes... delicate." Depailler replied, choosing his words carefully. "Facial recognition gave us his name as Gregor Hamilton. Forty-years old, from Lanarkshire in Scotland." The images were compared with those scanned from the biometric passport scanners at the border.

"A British national."

"More than that." Depailler said, pausing as he waited for them to open up the final attachment.

"An Operational Officer." Reinhardt said, calling up the images of his identification.

"A spy." Svetlana added, simplifying the terminology. "What does British intelligence want with Michael Jaeger?"

"Evidently, they didn't." Depailler observed. "That's why he's dead."

"What was the cause of death?" Svetlana asked.

"A fractured neck." Depailler replied. He didn't divulge anymore.

Curiously, the victim's hand was grasped around a tuft of his own hair. It almost suggested that he had wrenched his own head to sever the spinal cord where some original blunt force trauma had merely broken the vertebrae. A very bizarre and disturbing discovery. It suggested a strange kind of self-determination and strength. A certain level of desperation.

Apart from severe abdominal bruising and fractured lower ribs, the testicular torsion, two shattered knees and the mini torch protruding from the left eye indicated that he was in a considerably bad way and would have had an impossible job to drag himself out of there in the darkness. It had taken three men to lift the filing cabinet back up again, while a fourth carefully ensured none of the contents spilled out as the drawers slid open. Maybe all that had led the man to finish the job somebody had already started.

The body's location, deep within a previously undiscovered bunker was another disagreeable facet. Historians, researchers and archaeologists seemed to be descending from every corner of Europe, wanting to be the first to set foot inside a silent time capsule, capturing and chronicling everything they found.

"Jaeger attacked this Hamilton character?" Reinhardt suggested.

"It's possible." Depailler returned. "So maybe there was something in that office that related to this mysterious Horch, or maybe the lost Bugatti."

"Jaeger was stumped after his failure here in Berlin." Reinhardt picked up. "So he goes off in search of something else in Bordeaux."

"I've done a little bit of digging." Depailler added. "Something Reynard doesn't seem to appreciate yet."

"Go on." Svetlana encouraged. "This supposed lost Bugatti. If it ever existed. Apparently, it once belonged to Robert Benoist. He was a war hero here in France. According to legend, he and another gentleman, A Monsieur Grover-Williams used to run several Resistance cells. They were both trained by the British."

"We assumed Jaeger and this OID organisation might have wanted these cars for their monetary value. Are you suggesting there is another angle here?"

"It's not my place to suggest anything." Depailler chuckled. "This is not my case. It just seems interesting that a British intelligence officer would be looking into this some seventy years later, non?"

CHAPTER ONE-HUNDRED-AND-FOUR
ENGLAND, 2018

"D'yer ever get bored doon here?" Hamilton asked, gazing around the shelving units.

The reading room was glass on all four sides, the roof was the metal mezzanine floor of the level above. There were two desks, a map table and computers. The back wall was one long server enclosure with lights blinking like a Christmas tree.

"Bored?" Natalia replied. "How can anyone get bored? The stories these files contain is incredible."

"Spending all day down here though."

"I come down here out of choice."

"Yer dinnae like the offices upstairs?" he chuckled.

Natalia smiled but said nothing.

"Yer naw an Archivist are yer?"

She opened her mouth to answer, then looked through the glass wall as the lift doors opened. Dame Iris Harrington was helped along the floor to the chair by the Chief of the Secret Intelligence Service himself. C.

Natalia got up and walked around her desk to join them. Hamilton followed. It was strange seeing his old boss again, like seeing a teacher outside of school. They were the same person, but different somehow.

"Miss Harrington has convinced me of the merits of pursuing this investigation." He began with evident reluctance. "I'll reinstate your eDV clearance and reactivate your old double-O number." He said to Hamilton. "Then you can come and go down here as much as you need. Let me make this clear though, Hamilton. You and officer Bielawska are only to work this case and this case alone. You're not to deviate into anything else. The leash will be short, and you will report directly to me at all times. Am I understood?"

"It's pure joy tae be back, sir." Hamilton remarked casually.

C looked him at him sternly, then seemed satisfied and turned to Harrington. "Don't let me regret this, Iris."

"Now, now dear boy." She patted his hand before letting him leave.

Turning back to face them once he had stepped into the lift, it was clear that C was still very sceptical over the whole thing, but he wasn't about to reconsider and expose himself to another tongue lashing from the old battle axe.

"Now then." Iris began once the lift doors had closed. "What do you have?"

"Ah've had a message from ma contacts in Berlin." Hamilton began.

"When?" "While yer were bending the Chief's ear, we went tae get coffee and it popped up. Between this wee bunker and Thames House I've naw had signal all day."

"What did they say?"

"They're ready tae pull oot the Ark o' the Covenant."

"How are you going to verify the contents?"

"Ah've gaw some friends doon in Munich. We've arranged tae have it transported there. They have an x-ray machine that can look intae the crate wi'oot even opening it jist in case it actually is an ancient Hebrew relic."

"Better to be safe than dead." Harrington mused. "Well, you two should probably get to it then."

"What about all this?" Natalia asked, gesturing to the records she had uncovered.

"They'll still be here when you get back."

"Jist one question." Hamilton spoke up. "Whit d'yer have on Red Section?"

IN THE DEN OF WOLVES

CHAPTER ONE-HUNDRED-AND-FIVE
BELGIUM, 1944

Iris Harrington had made the drop herself. She had lost too many girls. She didn't want to lose anymore. Her superiors would have been furious had they known. Fortunately, the Lysander pilot had been amenable to the change in payload. She had requested a few days leave and the arrogance of her Section Leader was such that he was more than happy to grant it, just to be rid of her for a moment.

During the flight she went through the cover story Sutherland had supplied her. Checking the details, memorising the facts, adjusting her Luftwaffe uniform and flight jacket. The landing in occupied France in the early hours of the morning had been hairy, but no less than expected. She had descended the ladder and immediately transferred to the Storch aircraft in German colours on the opposite side of the makeshift airstrip.

This particular aircraft had rolled out of the Morane-Saulnier factory at Puteaux, built under contract from Fieseler in Kassel. The French it seemed were content to build arms for the Reich while waiting for the Allies to liberate them. It made Harrington's hackles rise.

Hopping across the border, she was initially alarmed at the sight of the Horch on the Belgian landing strip but seeing no accompanying three-axle Mercedes-Benz staff car, assumed that the area was safe. There was nothing else to be done now anyway. She had risked everything on this mission already, flying into the dragon's lair.

IN THE DEN OF WOLVES

The driver of the Horch gallantly held the door open for her before moving round to the driver's seat. She was quietly impressed by the mode of transport offered, but there was a spike of panic pricking the back of her neck as she contemplated the prospect that she had just been betrayed. As if to keep the tension on her, the driver said nothing as he drove calmly away.

An hour later, still not having uttered a single word, the Horch pulled off the road, through some wrought iron gates and up a rough drive to an abandoned farmhouse. It was at this point that Iris began to seriously have some doubts over her mysterious chauffeur. She could feel her heart rate increasing as her breathing became more urgent, almost hyperventilating. The silence as the car rolled to a stop became ominous and altogether unsettling. The driver quietly clambered out, moved around to the passenger side, and held the door open for her.

She alighted gracefully, belying the rising apprehension she could feel bubbling up inside her, even managing a smile at the admittedly handsome officer. He gestured for her to go on inside and immediately her thoughts ran to Elise and Eloise and Elodie and the other girls she had despatched across the Channel. Codenames all of them, and only she would know their true identities. Some from good families, discontent with sitting at home, wanting to do their bit for the war effort. Wanting to be useful. She wondered what their last, horrifying moments had been like.

Beyond the hallway the room opened into a sitting room where there was a piano next to the fireplace. She shuddered as she walked past it, wondering gruesomely how many notes still played.

It was then that another man entered the room. He stood in the doorway at the far end, transfixed. Staring at her like he had seen a ghost. It couldn't be her. She was in Iran, trapped in a loveless marriage, with a womanising husband in a tempestuous household. If the reports were true, she was even now being treated for depression while yearning to return to her native Egypt.

Queen Fawzia.

A Princess when they had first met, a teenager. She had given him her headscarf before the Tripoli Grand Prix. Then that night in Paris, a lifetime ago, he had whisked her away to the Opera. And yet, the woman standing opposite him bore a striking resemblance to her, both in form and facial features. Luxurious dark hair, a sensuous oval face, piercing expressive eyes.

It couldn't be her.

He moved forward slowly, fixed on her eyes, shimmering orbs of sapphire, glistening in the dim light of the shuttered room. Reaching inside his uniform jacket slowly he withdrew a packet of Eckstein No.5 cigarettes, removed one from the pack and asked in a surprisingly Scottish lilt.

"Got a light, hen?"

She shook her head. She knew she hadn't. Luftwaffenhelferin would not be expected to light their own cigarettes, female pilots even less so. Yet, as she patted herself down out of habit, she felt a little bulge in one of the pockets of her tunic. Inspecting the pocket, she retrieved the matchbox and looked up at him with an expression of annoyance and surprise.

"What yer got there, then?" he asked with a smile.

She tossed it over to him without properly looking at it, simply happy to be free of whatever it was. He caught it, turned it over and raised an eyebrow.

"Yer gotta be kiddin' me." He laughed. "England's Glory?" he said, showing her the front of the slipcase.

Her eyes widened as her expression changed to one of panic.

"Och, dinnae fesh yerself." He winked. "It's a wee little trick we played on yer."

"We?" she spat, the first word she had spoken since landing.

"Yer pilot for the crossing." He nodded. "I asked him tae plant them on yers before yer left him."

"You did what?" she cried. "That's bloody madness. What if I'd been caught?"

"Well, I guess that wee cyanide pill yer got stashed in yer back tooth would sort it oot, now would it not?" He replied flatly. "Anyway. I knew yer'd make it, and I've ran oot of matches." He smiled. "How's your German?"

"Excellent." She said, still utterly stunned by the bravado of the man in front of him.

"Good." He nodded upstairs. "There's a wee little something I'd like yer tae try on upstairs, if it's not too much bother."

"Do you know who I am?" she asked a little surprised.

"Aye, and yer know who I am. That's why yer here, lass. Now get yer kit off and get yer glad rags on. We got a wee knees-up to head to and yer my dark-haired Prussian girl."

"A party?" she asked, rather confused.

"Aye." He nodded, striking a match to light the cigarette. "Yer wannae know how genuine the information is? I'm about to show yer."

She stood there for a moment, utterly bewildered, affronted and outraged by the shear audacity of the man. She was tempted to head back to the airfield and fly straight back across the Channel, but the reality was she already knew she was in too deep, and a man who had infiltrated the inner circles of some of the most tightly knit chambers of the regime couldn't be anything but audacious.

With a huff she stomped up the dusty stairs and found the room at the back of the house. It was surprisingly clean, well-kept with open shutters looking out over the garden and a gorgeous dark blue silk dress on a hangar on the back of the door.

"It's a Drecoll." He said from the landing. "Extremely expensive."

She whipped round with a start. She hadn't even heard him come up behind her.

"As worn by Miss France 1937 herself." He said, tilting his head to the side to admire her curves. "Yer a little fuller figured, but with all the right curves in all the right places, yer'll look even better in it." He winked. "Miss Janet was a little less..." He made a cupping gesture over his chest. "Blessed, shall we say." He smiled. "Angelique will help yer get ready," he nodded to the young woman who suddenly appeared silently from the next room. "I'll wait downstairs."

To her surprise, he did exactly that, almost as quickly as he had appeared, leaving Iris Harrington even more perplexed about the kind of man she was dealing with. The dress was an absolute masterpiece though, matched with a perfect pair of shoes. She slipped out of the uniform and looked rather shamefully at her undergarments. They were functional but couldn't be worn with the dress at all. The cut of the dress would reveal them in the worst possible manner. The result would be an awful display. There was nothing else for it, they had to be dispensed with. It was thoroughly irregular.

Angelique was a wonder. Expertly applying the makeup from her little case, she perfectly complemented Harrington's natural complexion, making the most of her fulsome lips and accentuated her naturally long lashes. Restyling her hair, she allowed it to cascade onto her shoulders with a slight wave to it while pinning back the sides with two diamante combs.

As Harrington glided down the stairs, feeling very self-conscious, yet also incredibly glamorous, Sutherland just stared at her, mouth almost as wide as his eyes. She hadn't looked her best, the headphones and side cap ruffling up her hair and a face devoid of make-up, but after Angelique's glamorous makeover, it was secretly gratifying to her that she could still elicit such a reaction after so long in dowdy civilian attire, heavy tweeds and unflattering blouses, trying to be as inconspicuous as possible.

"Aye, yer'll do." He gasped, barely able to formulate the words.

"Everything seems to have been arranged rather well." She confessed. "Though the place could do with a tidy up."

"I dinnae live here." He nodded in the direction of the town. "I've got rooms elsewhere. In a hotel run by the Resistance." He could see the wheels in her mind turning. "Forget about it." He shook his head. "The Belgian resistance is hopelessly fragmented. They'll never be sufficiently unified to mount a significant threat. Yer've got Commies, Fascists, Monarchists, even groups with absolutely no political affiliations whatsoever. All disagreeing on what they should do, so they each do their own thing." He shrugged. "It's kind of effective, but best left alone. They've done a lot of good though, especially for the Jewish population."

"They know you're…"

"Of course." He smiled. "The irony is, tonight, the Major we're having dinner with is staying in the same boarding house. Totally unaware. It's brilliant."

"How have you managed to survive this long?" She asked. "Why are you doing this?"

He smiled grimly, his face losing its natural joviality for the first time. "Let's get yers in the car." He said. Holding out his hand, she gently looped her arm in his.

"Who was the man that drove me here?" she said as they made their way through the building.

"Postmaster's son." He said. "He intercepts letters of denunciation, warning different families to flee. Only time I've ever let anyone else drive her." *Adler* explained, gesturing to the car as he walked Iris round and opened the door for her. "Yer asked why I do this." He said as he joined her inside the Horch. "It's just another way to fight, that's all." He started up the Horch and smiled. "And I've always been pretty shocking with a shotgun. So, I'd be shite with a Lee-Enfield." He laughed. "Now, where are you from?" he asked, slipping effortlessly into German.

"Königsberg." She replied.

"And…"

"My father served on the Eastern Front during the Great War," she began, reciting her cover story in pitch perfect German as *Adler* swept out of the corroding gates.

"And then I became a test pilot." She concluded as Sturmbannführer Manfred Reinhardt stood with his own muse, listening with rapt attention to her story.

"Andreas tells me you're just back from Paris." He replied with a smile, using Sutherland's Germanified name. "Though he wouldn't tell me why."

She looked at him with a sideways glance and a lover's smile.

"That's because I didn't tell him." She said, touching his face.

"Ah, you're a good German girl." Reinhardt smiled. "Even lovers must have their secrets. Come Andreas, I have something for us to discuss."

Sutherland winked at Iris before following Reinhardt while his squeeze for the night took Iris by the arm and walked her towards the bar for a drink and a girly chat.

CHAPTER ONE-HUNDRED-AND-SIX
GERMANY, 2018

The soldiers' bodies had been carefully removed and quietly buried several weeks before. Fifteen in all. A Captain, two Lieutenant's and nine men. Then the rubble had been cleared and extensive steel bracing erected to support the roof of the tunnel. During the rubble clearance another three more bodies had been found at the very bottom of the pile. Massive crushing injuries were evident on the skeletal remains. Not surprising given the weight of material that had landed on them.

It was finally time to bring the artefact out from its underground resting place. There was an air of reverence as the team prepared to roll the flatbed truck out for the first time. Many of the Berlin Underworlds Association were in attendance. They had been hugely instrumental in getting to this moment. A few local government officials, representatives from the BVG public transport company, as well as the engineers responsible for the steel structure that was shoring up thousands of tons of earth above them.

This was a very big deal.

Markings on the flatbed rail truck suggested that it had originally belonged to the *Compagnie des chemins de fer de l'Est*. This was one of the early French railway companies that merged in 1938 to form the nationalised SNCF. At the time of the merger, they had operated the Paris to Strasbourg route, thus terminating not twenty miles away from the Bugatti factory. It was a surprising discovery but provided compelling evidence for what Hamilton suspected might be inside.

From the tunnel where it had been entombed for nearly eighty years, the shipping crate would be transported down to the Tempelhof station where it could be brought above ground on the S-Bahn line to Treptower. From there it would be stored in the BKA barracks while arrangements were made for its safe transportation to Munich for further analysis. Before it was brought above ground, arrangements had been made to paint over the Afrika Corps insignia. Parading that through the streets of Berlin would have caused even more of a disturbance.

Overseeing the transfer from the tunnel somewhere beneath Yorckstrasse to the BKA headquarters was Hauptkommissar Erwin Reinhardt. He stood alongside Müller with his arms folded, observing the proceedings wearily. There were plenty more things he could have been getting on with than watching an old box being dragged out from a tunnel. His superiors had insisted however and after his failure to capture Michael Jaeger alive, he was not in their good books.

Looking around the anonymous faces gathered in the illuminated tunnel entrance, he was surprised to recognise one of the guests at the unveiling. Her face was impossible to forget, though as she had assured him that her subject matter was landscapes and nature, her appearance here was something of a mystery.

He nudged Müller and nodded in Natalia's direction. She was standing next to another man, talking quietly and just happened to catch his eye. There was a flush to her cheeks and a shy wave, before she murmured something to the man she was with. He didn't seem to react, he just stared ahead impassively. Who was he? And what was she doing there?

"My friend from the BKA is standing over there." She murmured. "The one who thought I might have killed Robertson in the Horch Museum."

"Hmm." Hamilton hummed. "Local colour perhaps?" he added quietly, barely moving his lips.

"I don't know." She frowned. "Seems odd."

At that moment a loud squeak announced the first movement of the flatbed wheels. A small, diesel-powered maintenance tug connected to the old wagon began to move slowly back into the main spur. Moving in painfully small increments, the flatbed finally emerged from the blind tunnel.

Even though Dieter had shown him the pictures of the crate once the rubble had been cleared, the sight of the palm tree and swastika still gave Hamilton pause as the box finally emerged. There was a collective gasp, as though they were genuinely witnessing the discovery of an ancient artefact emerging from its tomb.

The story of Sutherland's subterfuge had been wisely kept away from the media. Even the prospect that the contents might contain the Lost Bugatti had been kept out of press briefings. The public story was that an old blocked up tunnel was yielding an unknown treasure hidden away during the war. For many of the esteemed bystanders assembled, the emergence of the wooden box fired off all sorts of imaginative ideas as to its contents.

There had been speculation that it might contain looted works of art. Already descendants and relatives of holocaust victims were stepping forward, hoping the crate might contain their ancestor's long-lost treasures. There was talk that perhaps the panels of amber taken from the Catherine Palace outside St Petersburg might have been stowed in the box, gold bullion, the bronze statue of Hitler intended for the centre of Moscow. Other fanciful suggestions had been postulated while the Berlin Underworlds Association kept a discrete silence.

Pierre Legrand had been contacted as soon as the discovery was confirmed. He chose not to make the journey himself as he was the public face of Bugatti Automobiles. His presence would immediately raise questions and fuel the Lost Bugatti speculation unnecessarily. Instead, he sent over their archivist, Petra Lindt. Like most librarians, she was an anonymous figure, but would be able to observe the extraction and report back directly to Château Saint Jean.

Once the flatbed was clear of the tunnel entrance, spontaneous applause echoed around the passage. Recognition for the extraordinary engineering feat required to extract the wooden box safely. The flatbed then slowly rumbled its way back to the main subway line where a new set of rails had been laid down and connected to the track through a series of temporary points. It was vital to engage them at the right moment to prevent the U-Bahn service making an unscheduled detour. A tight schedule had been drawn up to ensure regular services were not disrupted.

With the main extraction having been completed, many of the visiting dignitaries began to disperse. There was nothing more to see and the crate needed to have its insignia defaced before it was brought above ground anyway. The spray painters were getting suited up.

Reinhardt took the opportunity to make his way over to Natalia and reintroduce himself.

"Miss Bielawska. I am surprised to see you here." He remarked, choosing not to conceal his curiosity.

"Captain Reinhardt." Natalia replied with a smile. "Lieutenant Müller."

"What is your interest in this little discovery?"

"The interest is mine." Hamilton interceded. "When Tali told me aboot her wee run in on her last visit, ah wondered whether this might have suhin' tae do with whit Graham was working on when he wis killed."

"You knew Mr Robertson?" Reinhardt frowned, struggling a little with the accent, but recognising the face at once. The man that never left the Bassins des Lumière, the Pool of Lights. The man whose blood might indeed have been daubed all over the walls. Gregor Hamilton.

"Aye, a wee bit." He lied.

"And what was he working on?" Reinhardt enquired innocently.

"Him and a team o' colleagues used tae search for lost classic cars." Hamilton explained. There was no need to hide anything. The BKA might come in useful if anyone else decided to lay claim to the discovery. He would sooner take his chances with Captain Reinhardt than with the likes of his attacker in Bordeaux any day of the week. "He wis in Zwickau tae check oot a Horch replica, so I wondered if he thought that's whit wis in the wee box."

"Interesting theory." Reinhardt nodded, considering the possibility. It was certainly an angle he hadn't contemplated. Robertson making measurements of the replica to see how it compared to the original hidden away underground. "And the Afrika Corps?"

Hamilton frowned, feigning confusion.

"The insignia on the box." Reinhardt expanded. "It was used by the Afrika Corps. Would that have any relevance?"

Hamilton puffed as he gave out a sigh and shrugged. "Ah cood nae say. Tae be honest wi yer, I was surprised jist now tae see it. Meks me think it might naw be a car at all."

"What do you think could be inside?" he probed.

"Who knows?" he gave a half smile. "Could be the Ark of the Covenant."

Reinhardt gave a short laugh at the statement. "Ha! And I thought you Scottish didn't have a sense of humour."

"Ah thought the same about you."

"Ah. This is true." Reinhardt nodded as they seemed to collectively turn to leave the tunnel.

Further explorations had uncovered a narrow service staircase for maintenance workers leading down from Yorckstrasse into the Nord-Süd Tunnel they were in. This was the entrance everyone had used to gain entry into the passage. It was safer than jumping down from the platforms at Tempelhof and walking against the flow of the U-Bahn to where the spur had burrowed off the main line for a couple of kilometres.

"So, tell me Natalia. Are you here to take some more photos, or is this a tourist visit?"

"I always take the opportunity to bring my camera." She smiled. "Even if I'm not officially working, you never know when a good opportunity might present itself."

"Indeed." He smiled, looking at her more closely. "So, where is it?"

"I wasn't going to bring it down here." She replied, thinking quickly. "I wasn't sure how dusty it would be."

"Ah, of course. So, you left it at your hotel?"

"That's right."

"And where are you staying?"

"The Holiday Inn, near Tegel."

He frowned. "Really? This is quite a change from your suite in Dresden, yes?"

"When I'm paying for the hotel myself, all I need is a bed for the night." She chuckled.

"Ah yes, of course. You were lecturing before, so the university must have paid." He smiled as they emerged into the autumn sunshine. "Well, it is good to see you again. And to meet you, Mr…" He concluded, holding out his hand to them both.

"Hamilton. Greg Hamilton."

"Mr Hamilton."

"And to you." Natalia smiled.

Reinhardt and Müller turned and walked away in the direction of the S-Bahn stop that would take them down to meet the train at Tempelhof. From there, they would escort the crate to Alt-Treptower and watch it being conveyed into their barracks. Reinhardt turned to Müller and frowned.

"Put a tail on them."

"Yes, sir."

"Do you think they suspect anything?" Natalia asked as she and Hamilton ventured in the opposite direction.

"Oh aye, absolutely." Hamilton nodded. "He clocked yer in a heartbeat."

"I need to get myself a camera then."

"Dinnae bother. They'll be putting a tail on us soon enough. The moment they spot us go in tae a camera shop, they'll know we were being economical wi the truth."

"So, what do you suggest?"

"We leave the night."

"Tonight? We only arrived this morning."

"They'll be checking the hotels this afternoon and will find oot we've naw booked anywhere. The moment we do try and check in, they'll be half a dozen cars sealing off every exit." He shook his head. "It's naw worth the hassle. We'll fly doon tae Vienna the night and drive back across the border once the crate is in Munich. Gives us a couple o' days. At least then if anything kicks off, being in Austria will give us a buffer between us and them."

Sometimes the territorial jurisdiction of the police could prove useful, especially if the extradition process depended on convincing local judiciary of the immediate need to hand over a person of interest. What could Germany possibly want with law-abiding British tourists in Austria? There were international reputations to uphold, and one couldn't be too rough with visitors without solid justification.

CHAPTER ONE-HUNDRED-AND-SEVEN

Standard ISO shipping containers were 2.4-metres wide by 2.6-metres high and came in two basic lengths, six metres and twelve metres, though usually referred to by their Imperial units. Smaller lengths were available, but for the purposes of transporting the crate down to Munich, the standard 20-footer would suffice.

Reinhardt was wary about the prospect of interference from this mysterious OID outfit, the organisation that had hired Jaeger to be their personal assassin. If the contents of the box were what they had sent Jaeger to seek out, he felt they were unlikely to quietly watch it be transported down the length of the country now its existence was public knowledge.

Natalia's friend had made an interesting point. The mysterious Horch could well be inside. It many ways it made sense. The car had disappeared after Rosemeyer's death. He was a Nazi hero. What better place to keep a relic safe than in an underground tunnel? Jaeger had come to Berlin believing he would find it. Perhaps the car had been stored away, intended to form some centrepiece of Aryan supremacy in the new world capital of Germania. He could almost imagine it, an exhibition space in an annex of the Great Hall. Displayed there might have been Heinkel's aircraft, Henschel's tanks and Rosemeyer's cars.

Reinhardt considered the possibility that the OID wanted the Horch as some potent symbol of the regime. Ever since the Brexit vote, there had been a worrying trend of far-right, political rumblings throughout Continental Europe. Other countries were quietly considering the possibility of re-establishing their own nationalist pride, wresting control back from the bureaucratic brume of Brussels.

Though such thoughts were generally hushed in the hallowed halls of the Reichstag, perhaps by way of preserving the decontamination of history from the last time the country wanted to exercise national pride, it was clear that some circles believed Germany should consider the possibility of going it alone too. Reinhardt himself was also too well acquainted with Neo-Nazi organisations which had long been the bane of German law enforcement and sought to achieve the same result. Any band wagon to jump on seemed to be the consensus.

With all this in mind, Reinhardt had devised a plan to ensure the box was conveyed to the railhead safely. From there, it would be loaded onto a goods train and shunted overnight to the Bavarian capital. In order to preserve the element of surprise, contrary to the established belief, the crate wasn't going to remain for several days in the BKA barracks at all. It was leaving that night. The sooner, the better.

"They've just checked in for a flight down to Vienna." Müller reported, calling Reinhardt over the radio as his men updated him on Natalia and her Scottish companion. "There never was a hotel reservation for them."

"Okay. Leave them for now." He called back, looking at his right-hand man from the adjacent vehicle. "If they come back, we'll pick them up then."

"Okay."

"You clear on the route?"

"Yes, sir."

"Let's go then."

Unusually Müller himself wasn't driving. Instead, he turned to his driver across the cab and nodded as four black BMW 5-Series put on their blue strobes. Müller was sat alongside the lorry driver in the cab of a plain white MAN TGX tractor unit. Reinhardt was in a second identical lorry as they were led out by two of the BMWs. With the traffic controlled by police as they emerged onto Elsenstrasse, two of the BMWs lead each truck toward Puschkinallee before they would eventually peel off and go their separate ways.

The last two BMWs brought up the rear of each convoy and as quickly as the traffic had been stopped, the police waved it on as if nothing had happened. Both lorries carried anonymous shipping crates on their articulated load beds. Only one contained the actual wooden crate from the Nord-Süd Tunnel. The other was a decoy, in case the OID was watching the transfer and wanted to create an ambush.

Reinhardt had a wanted a third convoy to increase their odds and a helicopter overwatch just in case but had been overruled. This was costing enough as it was. Despite the public interest surrounding the contents of the mysterious box, no one further up the chain considered any possible OID intervention to be a credible threat. The OID didn't exist. Jaeger had been a wildcard, a lone wolf, plain and simple. Reinhardt wasn't so sure. Jaeger had disappeared from the prison system, and no one batted an eyelid. He had been well funded and well connected. All that resource had to originate from somewhere.

Orange strobes on the front and rear of the lorries made the wet tarmac gleam like amber as slushy rain fell steadily over the city. While Müller's convoy would eventually take a route out of Berlin to the southeast, towards the cargo terminal at Königs Wusterhausen, Reinhardt's route would take him further into and across the city, traversing the Landwehr Canal and eventually over the Spree itself to the nearer terminal at Westhafen. Both containers would be loaded onto trains heading down to Munich on separate rail lines.

While one would be offloaded at Dachau, to the north, the second would be taken off at the vast container base near Dornach to the east. Then a BKA convoy out from the Munich field office would repeat the escort, all the way to the BMW Group Forschungs und Innovationszentrum. Reinhardt was assured that gaining access to the inner sanctum of the auto manufacturer's Innovation and Development centre would be harder than the Wiesbaden headquarters of the BKA. He didn't doubt that assurance. Once there, the actual wooden box would be submitted for analysis in their giant x-ray machine.

Reinhardt contemplated whether he should have taken the decoy truck down to Königs Wusterhausen. It was a longer route and some of it would be out in a more rural setting. The actual box was being loaded on at Westhafen though and he felt he need to be there to supervise its safety. Müller was more than capable of the task, but it was his responsibility. If anything was to go wrong, it should be him to take the blame.

The convoy rolled into the container terminal as the advance team were just finishing up their vetting process. With the area cleared, the two BMWs hung back at the entrance to stop anything coming in or out while the lorry positioned itself beneath the gantry crane. Unless someone piled in with a truck, Reinhardt hoped there was little chance of anything going awry now. Still, he checked in with Müller.

"We're clear of the city." Müller reassured him. "On Federal Highway B1 heading east."

"Good. Keep your eyes open. Check for tails or anything suspicious. We're unloading now."

"Yes, sir."

Reinhardt sat anxiously in the cabin as the container was lifted off and transferred to the train. He would be happier when Müller made it to the autobahn. There were still traffic lights and road junctions to negotiate before he reached it.

Watching the container being lowered, Reinhardt breathed a sigh of relief as the crane relinquished its load. Once the lifting gear was clear of the trucks, the train was given the signal to pull out and a blast from its horn acknowledged its departure. Watching the train roll out, he waited until the last truck disappeared out of sight before calling Müller again.

CHAPTER ONE-HUNDRED-AND-EIGHT

Müller's driver knew his route, knew the roads, which bridges to avoid and which ones he could safely pass beneath. For a container lorry he needed a bridge with more than 4.5-metres clearance between the road and the bottom of the deck. This meant he had to take an extended route out of the city to avoid the lower bridges that carried the S-Bahn out of the Treptow borough. A long, looping line up to the north before joining the federal highway due east. It was inconceivable that such precious cargo would be exposed for so long on a more convoluted route, which meant it could just be the actual container they were after. A double bluff.

At that time of night, the only traffic tended to be other goods vehicles, vans and trucks, carrying all manner of cargo across the breadth of Germany. The highway they were on stretched like a tarmac ribbon from the Dutch border all the way across to Poland. Given the short timeframe, the journey had been as carefully planned as possible. The second advance team had arrived at the container terminal and were holding station, checking everything that came in and out, there was no roadworks on the route, traffic was steady. Everything was going to plan.

On the approach to the autobahn, the crossroads just before was controlled by traffic lights where the road from Vogelsdorf crossed the highway to the shopping complex on the other side. The blue strobes behind the grille of the BMW should have alerted the other traffic that the convoy was going straight through the red lights, but a dark grey delivery van had already made its way across most of the intersection when the lead BMW hit the siren.

The van stopped suddenly, directly in front of the path of the convoy. As the BMW driver punched the horn, both of the van's side doors slid open. Müller barely had time to acknowledge what was going on before the rocket propelled grenade struck the BMW. With the explosion looming large in the lorry's windscreen, the driver stamped the brake pedal to bring the truck to a halt.

"No! Keep going, keep going!" Müller yelled.

The lorry would easily clear the road ahead with its weight and momentum, pushing the flaming wreckage into the obstructing van, but the driver's natural instincts had already kicked in and the advanced ABS brought the lorry to a shuddering halt. A second RPG took out the trailing BMW as it manoeuvred to overtake the lorry while a masked-up gang surrounded the cab with automatic weapons.

Müller's door was wrenched open, and he came face-to-face with blinding illumination from a side-mounted tactical weapon lamp.

"Drop your weapons!" the voice cried through the Kevlar SRU helmet.

Müller removed his Sig Sauer P229 from the shoulder holster beneath his jacket and dropped it out over the side.

"The driver is unarmed." He cried clearly.

"Get out!"

In case there was any hesitation, while two more MP7 submachine guns were trained on him, the man giving him the order reached up and pulled him down from the cab. Looking to the rear, Müller watched as the flame engulfed wreckage of the trailing BMW was raked with gunfire to make the sure the burning occupants were dead. With his hands clamped to the top of his head, Müller and the lorry driver were led separately to the back of the truck to unlock the container.

"Open it up!"

Müller looked up at the driver, his eyes wide with terror. He nodded. There was nothing else for them to do. Resistance wasn't an option and backup wouldn't arrive. Retrieving the keys, they separately disengaged the locks that had secured the locking bars on each door. Once done, they were hauled out of the way as two of the armed gang grabbed a handle each, rotated the cams and pulled open the doors.

The MRL6 weapon lamps that were shone inside didn't need all 350 lumens to show that the container was empty. Whatever expressions were concealed behind the tactical full-face helmets, without showing any signs of a reaction, the men turned round and pushed Müller and the lorry driver face down on the ground. Then, Brügger & Thomet Rotax 2 sound suppressors hissed quietly as a short, sharp volley of bullets was fired into each man.

CHAPTER ONE-HUNDRED-AND-NINE

There had been huge controversy over Berlin's airports for decades. With the closure of Tempelhof, international air travel was handled jointly by Tegel and Schönefeld, neither of which were considered adequate for the job. The plans for a new airport for the capital had been proposed almost immediately after reunification, when Berlin once again became the federal capital. Tempelhof, Tegel and Schönefeld would be closed as soon as the new airport was completed, and the shiny new construction would be a fitting symbol of the city's rejuvenated importance.

Fast forward almost thirty years and the new Brandenburg airport was only just nearing completion, though no one knew exactly when it would actually open. The whole thing had become something of a national embarrassment. Hamilton was coming back with some coffee when he found Natalia staring at the television screen at Tegel's departure gate. They both preferred their coffee black; she took one sugar while Hamilton usually spooned in two. Though with the tediously small packets offered at the stand, he had emptied about half a dozen into the discouragingly feeble offering.

"Whit's occurring?" he asked as the news showed camera footage from a helicopter hovering over two smouldering cars on a highway outside Berlin.

"Seems like there's a major incident unfolding out towards Vogelsdorf." She replied. "My German isn't great."

"Two burning cars." Hamilton read the strapline that was running across the bottom of the screen. "Eyewitnesses saw a gang o' masked gunmen tryin' tae hijack a lorry."

"What was it carrying?"

Hamilton shrugged, taking a sip of the coffee and instantly regretting it. The watery beverage was bitter, sickly sweet and scalding hot. The worst kind of coffee.

"Looks like suhin' tae keep yer friend occupied though." He threw the coffee in the bin as the announcer's tannoy crackled into life. "That's our call."

CHAPTER ONE-HUNDRED-AND-TEN

Scheisse.

It was the first word Reinhardt had uttered as he arrived on the scene. Local fire crew were still damping down the wreckage. Two unmarked BKA vehicles destroyed. A crack team of MEK, Mobile Mission Commandos in each. Two dead bodies in the middle of a federal highway. Either this was a random, yet highly organised attack, or his suspicions over the OID had just been proven to be horrifyingly correct. He looked down at the corpse of Lieutenant Müller. A trail of bullets stitched into his back and a dark pool beneath his prone figure.

"Scheisse!" he cursed again.

"Sir."

"What is it?" he cried angrily, turning from the body to where an officer was holding out a phone.

"It's the Chief."

"Fat bastard." He muttered quietly, stepping up to take the phone. "Kriminaloberrat…"

"Reinhardt! What the hell is going on?"

"We're still investigating, sir."

"Masked gunmen! Car bombs! An attempted hijack! You need to get to the bottom of this quickly. The President is already asking questions."

"I will, sir."

"How long?"

"Before what, sir?" he already knew the answer.

"Before you know what this is all about."

Reinhardt suspected he already knew what it was all about. He didn't think it was a coincidence that the decoy lorry had been targeted. This wasn't a random attack. Whoever had masterminded it knew the lorry would have escorts and had made sure they were taken care off first. Quickly and effectively.

"I'm operating a man light, sir."

"I need answers, Reinhardt."

"Let's start with Kriminalkommissar Müller."

"What about him?"

"You tell his wife she's now a widow. I'll find out why he was killed." Reinhardt terminated the call and tossed the phone back. Middle-management and their need for immediate answers. He wanted answers too. Gerhard Müller had been a first class detective. Did the bastards think of that? "Don't answer calls from that number again."

"Yes, sir."

Scheisse.

CHAPTER ONE-HUNDRED-AND-ELEVEN
GERMANY, 1944

The advantage of being good friends with a police officer was that they knew all kinds of nefarious characters. Of all the abominable criminals Hans had come across, Franz was something of an artist. A con artist perhaps, but an artist nevertheless. Franz's specialism had been recognised by the Third Reich early on and although he had been imprisoned for forgery in 1938, by 1940 he was employed directly by the SS as part of *Operation Andreas*.

"Did you know Heydrich named the operation after you?" Hans remarked one evening as they sat together enjoying a brandy.

"Me?" Sutherland replied, looking slightly alarmed.

"Apparently he felt naming the operation after you was somewhat apposite."

"Why would he think that?"

Despite Heydrich's death, his name still prompted a feeling of uneasiness in Sutherland. Hans's brother Manfred, already promoted and hoping for even greater things, appeared to be modelling himself on the fearfully revered saint of the Schutzstaffel.

"Perhaps he suspected you too might be counterfeit." Hans teased.

Operation Andreas was an exercise begun in 1940 to forge British banknotes. The aim was to drop them over Britain to bring about the collapse of the economy and the loss of its world currency status. Before being wound up in 1942, the operation had successfully duplicated the rag paper used for the white fivers and Franz Berger had been drafted in to produce engraving blocks. Reproducing the vignette of Britannia had given him the greatest trouble because of its complexity and size.

"He never mentioned it."

"Would that be while you were driving him to Wannsee?" Hans winked. He was enjoying this.

"You'd think he would have let me know." Sutherland continued, ignoring Hans's jibe. "He only sat a little further down the corridor."

"I doubt he would have suspected you that early." Hans murmured. "You were still racing cars back then. Maybe that was the reason."

"I was a good driver." Sutherland defended.

"A counterfeit Rosemeyer." Hans chuckled to himself. "Driving around in his car but with none of his wit or charm."

"You're a bloody bastard, Hans, you know that?" Sutherland smiled as he shook his head. It was good to see him making jokes again.

The last twelve months had been hard on him. Finally, he had been reinstated back into the police, but demoted down to petty crime and told to get himself a uniform. He would, just as soon as he could afford one. In the meantime, his new unit had taken him in, looking to him as their de facto chief. They too had been given the brush off by the hierarchy. Too good at actually solving real crime. Too much of a nuisance to the upper echelons because of it.

It was ironic then that the plan to issue forged British, and now American banknotes, had originated from the head of the central criminal investigation department, Hans's ultimate superior. Though it well illustrated how deeply woven felonious conduct had already been within the higher reaches of the regime. A further irony was how select Jewish prisoners had been corralled together in Sachsenhausen's Block 19 for the sole purpose of reinstating the project. Under a new name, *Operation Bernhard* was busy printing pound notes and US dollars. This time to finance German intelligence operations.

IN THE DEN OF WOLVES

Special paper from the Hahnemühle mills was brought in, complete with minute silk threads running through it like the original. Berger was enrolled to head up the forging department, engraving the plates for US currency. The artwork was more complex than British notes and the intaglio printing technique produced distinctive ridges in the paper. It was a painstaking process and the prisoners realised that the quicker they completed the task, the less likely their lives would be safeguarded.

As *Manuela* rolled up to Guard Tower A, presided over by an old Maxim machine gun, this provided Sutherland with a double opportunity. Removing his papers, he handed them over to the guards who approached him. Without a word, they examined them closely, stared at him, then headed inside. While Sutherland waited, his gaze turned to the gates in front of him, beneath the main entrance tower. Iron letters had been welded to the structure to produce the slogan 'ARBEIT MACHT FREI' in the centre of the two leaves.

Sutherland knew that was a great hypocrisy. No one was ever set free after working in one of these camps. People were being worked to death. Heinkel, AEG and Siemens were making use of the labour force. Albert Speer had contracted some of them in the brickworks for his Welthaupstadt Germania vision of Berlin. Sutherland was here for another work assignment though and hoped he might be granted an audience with Bernhard Krüger, the SS officer in charge of the resurgent currency counterfeiting operation.

Sutherland was surprised when Standartenführer Kaindl himself appeared from the administration building. Anton Kaindl was the camp commandant and a hateful little man. Beady eyes, a balding head and a grey, emotionless demeanour.

"Your request is unusual." He began, his voice like a rifle crack. Harsh, high-pitched and clipped. "We cannot allow you to see the prisoner you have requested."

"My orders come from the SS Main Office." Sutherland lied.

"Even so."

"Then, perhaps I can make a telephone call, sir?"

"May I ask why?"

"So, I can speak to someone more senior, less obstructive."

Kaindl's eyes narrowed as his anger was triggered. His cheeks seemed to glow red with fury as he looked at Sutherland, almost disbelieving the impudence of this junior officer. Sutherland had to tread carefully.

"Perhaps Obergruppenführer Berger can explain."

"You cannot pull rank here." Kaindl cried. "This is Sachsenhausen."

"Very well." Sutherland replied, snatching back his papers and turning to leave.

"What is the nature of your visit?" Kaindl asked once Sutherland had opened the door to *Manuela*. "So, I can report this impudence to High Command."

"I am not at liberty to discuss that, sir." Sutherland replied. "It was High Command that assured me their authorisation would be sufficient. Obergruppenführer Berger gave the Führer his personal assurance that it would be handled. I shall inform them that they were quite mistaken." He smiled pleasantly, though his heart was racing inside his chest. His plan foiled, the sooner he got away, the better.

"One moment." Kaindl called sharply, holding up a hand to reinforce the command.

Sutherland took a deep breath, wondering whether he had overstretched himself this time. The Maxim seemed poised and hungry. His luck would only hold out so long and sometimes his bravado outweighed his judgement. A counterfeit Rosemeyer, Hans had joked. He was probably right. Bernd knew exactly when to execute a pass on track, when to hold off and wait for a more favourable opportunity. By contrast, Sutherland had often piled in a little recklessly and muscled his way through, his boldness perhaps covering for his deficiencies in skill.

Having conferenced briefly with his senior guards, Kaindl waved Sutherland over. Sutherland closed the door and stepped forward.

"You can have five minutes with the prisoner. No more."

"Not enough time, sir." Sutherland shook his head. "What I have been asked to ascertain from him is not the work of moments. He is an intractable individual, as I'm sure your men are very well aware."

"How long do you think you will need?"

"Half an hour, at least." Sutherland replied, sensing a possible opening after all.

"You can have fifteen minutes."

Sutherland frowned and gave out a suitably dissatisfied sigh. In reality he hadn't expected to be given such a window.

"Very well." He conceded. "Thank you, sir."

"He will be under close supervision at all times."

"I understand."

"One more thing." Sutherland smiled patiently. "Is it necessary to interview him in Block 19?"

"It is essential to the objective I have been sent here to achieve." he stressed.

Kaindl paused for a moment, then nodded and turned away. Interview concluded. Sutherland had his audience. He breathed a sigh of relief and followed the guards inside.

Major Bernhard Krüger's office was surprisingly roomy, given the limitations on space within the camp. The guards had escorted him inside, then left him to talk with the Major while they ventured to the Zellenbau isolation cells to the north to fetch the prisoner.

Sutherland was about to lay all his cards on the table. It was the biggest gamble of his life. If he failed, one way or another he would be dead. At this juncture, there was nothing to lose. Given the destruction of the Sixth Army at Stalingrad, followed by the Italian surrender and the Normandy invasion, Germany was facing inevitable defeat anyway. The only question that remained unanswered was how stiff the resolve of the defence would prove to be. Sutherland was rapidly heading towards the final roll of the dice. Depending on how things ended here, he may not get another shake.

"You and I both know that you're on borrowed time, Major." He began swiftly. "Once this operation has achieved its objectives, you'll be sent to face the Soviets on the Eastern front. We both know how that will end. Keep this racquet going for as long as you can, you might just live to see the end of this war instead. At that point, you'll need my help."

"Your help?" he asked incredulously. "Why do I need the help of a Junior Lieutenant?"

"Because I'm a very senior spy in British Intelligence and will have the power of life and death over the likes of people like you."

Krüger was stunned, staring up at the face of this man like he had seen a ghost.

"Counterfeiting Allied currency in a time of war? They'll hang you on the spot. Unless I give you a way out."

"What would that be?" he asked sceptically.

"When the Allies get closer, as many prisoners as possible will be killed. They will try and remove all traces of what's been going on here. Your lot will be sent to Mauthausen in Austria for extermination." At this juncture, Sutherland produced a piece of paper from his document folder. "With this signed order, you will issue a transport request for all your workers to be taken there by truck."

"I have 140 prisoners running this operation. They won't all fit in one truck."

"I know." Sutherland nodded. "That's precisely the point. It will take three trips at least. This order specifies that the prisoners must only be executed once the last truckload has arrived. Not before. Only that way can the SS be sure they have hidden every last trace of this counterfeiting operation." He presented the unsigned order on Krüger's desk. "However, the final truck will be delayed. By then the first two groups will have already been released into the general prison population. Impossible for them to be killed now. With their lives saved, if I do my job well enough, you might just be spared the hangman's noose too."

"And if I refuse?"

"Then we're both dead, but I'll just shoot you now." He replied, retrieving a pistol from the document wallet.

Krüger took a few seconds to decide. "This order is unsigned."

"It needs an appropriate signature. Kaindl's will do. You have a specialist forger by the name of Berger in your workforce. Put him onto it. That will slow down his work on the plates too. While he is doing that he will make two sets of forged identity papers."

"Two?"

"One set for me, and one set for the prisoner who is being brought here. You will arrange to have this prisoner smuggled into your workforce and shipped out with the rest to Mauthausen."

"How do I do that?"

"That's for you to work out, but if he is executed first, I will make sure you die too." Sutherland fixed him with a stern gaze, flicking the safety catch off the Luger to show he was serious. "Do we understand each other?"

"Yes." He nodded. "Yes, I think so." He licked his lips, suddenly dried up. "How do I get the papers to you?"

"Post them directly to Andrew Sutherland at the Reich Security Main Office on Prinz Albrecht Strasse, Berlin. Mark the package 'URGENT: KATEGORIE C'."

Krüger nodded again.

Hearing footsteps on the tiles outside, Sutherland replaced the Luger and turned to the door. In fifteen minutes, he needed to convince the prisoner that he was there to get him out. Fifteen minutes to convince his compatriot that he wasn't the man he was looking at in the uniform. All under the watchful gaze of the guards of the SS-Totenkopfverbände. As William Grover-Williams was shown into Krüger's office, the look on the Englishman's face told him fifteen minutes was not nearly enough time.

IN THE DEN OF WOLVES

CHAPTER ONE-HUNDRED-AND-TWELVE
GERMANY, 2018

No chances were being taken at Dachau the following morning. A team of fully-kitted out Mobile Mission Commandos had been flown down overnight from BKA Headquarters. Tactical units from the Bavarian State Police had joined them from Munich and Dachau itself to oversee the escort from the train to BMW FIZ. A helicopter was equipped with more armed units and would provide overwatch from above. Police and army vehicles surrounded the lorry, and a rolling exclusion zone was setup around the convoy as it made its way down the highway.

The attack on Reinhardt's decoy had grabbed the nation's attention and Reinhardt wasn't about to give them a second bite of the cherry. Now though, he had the backing of his superiors. Whatever that box contained, the rogue organisation had suddenly been willing to break cover and engage in a full-blown shootout on German streets. The contents needed to be secured and they needed to be investigated with all haste.

Picking up the hire car on their arrival, Hamilton and Natalia had driven back through Austria and across the border again to re-enter Germany. En route Hamilton had placed an apologetic early morning phone call to Pierre Legrand in Molsheim and asked how quickly he could get to Munich. GCHQ had picked up the two trucks leaving the BKA barracks on satellite. It was inconceivable that one of them didn't contain *Adler's* artefact. Thus, it looked like their timeline had been contracted in an attempt to make the identification sooner and safer. The attack on the truck near Vogelsdorf suggested that someone was already ahead of the game.

"This man that attacked you, then." Natalia asked as they passed beneath the impressive and illuminated Benedictine abbey, dominating the hillside above Melk. "What did he look like?"

"He wis a big guy." Hamilton replied. "Taller and broader than me. Beard and moustache. Cannae say much else, it wis fair dark doon there."

"He attacked you with a wire?"

"Aye. Looped it over ma heid. Pro'ly tryin' tae do me like he did Robertson and the others."

"Why didn't he?"

"As it happened, ah had jist reached up tae take the torch oot of ma gob." He rubbed his wrist where he bore the scar. "Nicked ma arm, instead."

"You were lucky."

"Bloody right ah wis." He nodded. He had tried not to think of the alternative but knew the reality would have been very different half a second either way. Even with his background, given the amount of brute force and determination, he wouldn't have stood a chance.

"Judging by what they've just discovered in the basement there, it's quite fortuitous that you're now back in the fold."

"Ah recced the area before ah went in. There were no cameras overlooking the car park where I left the hire car, and naw many around the perimeter of the base."

"No, but they've probably examined the footage from the entrance and seen you legitimately enter the evening exhibition but not leave the building later. With your picture and a call to the hire car company, it wouldn't take them long to surmise you're the one that bled out all over the walls."

"Aye, probably." He sighed. "Naw much ah cood do aboot that though. Cannae make a decent bandage in the dark."

Natalia remained silent on that point. She doubted given the same situation she would have fared any better.

"So, what do you think is in this crate?"

"Ah'm beyond speculation now." He shook his head. "This Sutherland guy wis unbelievable. Knowing him, it cood actually be the bloody Ark of the Covenant. Or it cood jist be the Führer's dirty magazine collection. Who knows?"

"Did they have dirty magazines back then?"

"Ah'm sure they wid have been pretty rank after he finished wi them."

Natalia grimaced and changed gear to overtake.

"What did Monsieur Legrand say?"

"He's getting on the corporate jet now. Said he wid meet us there."

"Champagne breakfast no doubt. How the other half live." She sighed, rubbing her empty stomach. "How did you manage to arrange this analysis?"

"Ah know a guy." Hamilton smiled, offering no further explanation.

"At BMW?"

Hamilton retained his smile but said nothing.

At the border, they swapped over driving duties, and Natalia reclined the seat a little to get some rest. Hamilton looked across as they approached Passau. Her eyes were closed in the serene throes of slumber. Loose strands of hair fell across her face and her chest rose and fell gently as she breathed. She was a pretty sleeper, though he expected no less. Natalia was a pretty lady all round.

The armed convoy made quite the impression as it arrived with lights flashing and surrounded by vehicles, many of them belonging to BMW's own product portfolio. The container lorry was driven right into the heart of BMW Group's Pilot Plant deep inside the vast and secretive FIZ complex where its contents would be unloaded amidst the tightest security the site had ever witnessed.

Not even a new vehicle launch had caused so much of a stir. The seriousness and realities of what had transpired in Berlin to transport the artefact down had become all too horrifyingly apparent. An explosive and brutal act of terrorism had suddenly and very clearly announced that someone wanted to get their hands on the crate and was prepared to go to extreme lengths.

"He looks tired." Natalia remarked sympathetically as they watched the rolling news on the widescreen monitor in the entrance to the FIZ Project House.

Reinhardt was making a press conference, revealing the details as they knew it, making public for the first time the existence of an underground organisation known as the OID. He didn't elaborate on the attack, nor explain the supposed reason behind it. Details were still emerging. It was a sensitive and fast-moving case. More updates would follow.

"He's been up all night." Hamilton replied.

"Andrew." Came a voice he recognised.

Hamilton looked up to see a smartly dressed man crossing the airy atrium towards them.

"Wolfgang." He smiled. "This is ma colleague, Natalia."

"Welcome, welcome." Wolfgang smiled shaking their hands. "Monsieur Legrand and his assistant are already here."

"His assistant?"

"A woman named Petra?"

"Petra Lindt." Hamilton nodded "She's their senior researcher."

"Ah, that makes sense." Wolfgang passed them each a plastic credit card-sized security pass for the glass speed gates to allow them to enter the facility. "Come this way, the crate is just being unloaded and prepared now."

Relinquishing their mobile phones at the security post, they arrived as the wooden crate was being rolled carefully through external doors and positioned precisely inside the shielded chamber. Greeting the guests from Bugatti, the little huddle watched as engineers programmed the robots' coordinate system to allow for a complete scan of the box.

Although the shape was significantly simpler than an entire prototype vehicle assembly, the size of the crate meant space for the robot arms themselves was considerably tighter than normal. Travelling on rails either side of the crate, bright orange robot arms would move around, over and under the article. Even inside the largest 3DCT machine in the world, it was still a squeeze.

When the lead engineer was happy, a test run was carried out to check for clearance and access. Satisfied, he gave the go ahead for the program to run. The team of four, coordinated robots moved methodically around the crate, working in pairs to send X-rays through the object to its counterpart on the other side. The data was collected and then put through a specially developed computer program that reconstructed the object as a multi-layered, three-dimensional image.

Just like a hospital CT scan, this would enable the engineers to rotate the crate around, moving through the structure of it to see inside and any detailed internal configurations of its contents without ever having to open it up. A safe way of determining whether this was indeed a holy Hebrew relic or something rather more earthly.

Ordinarily the degree of detail achieved enabled the engineers to check welds and punch screw connections, verify body condition before and after painting, where extreme temperatures could affect adhesive bonds. The detail was sufficient to find tiny anomalies in wiring looms and connections, even down to a hundred micrometres.

Findings from the scan of a complete prototype vehicle could then be used as a basis for making targeted modifications for series production tooling, optimise process controls in machining procedures, and ensure zero-defect manufacturing processes across their worldwide production network. This was the first time the advanced technology had ever been used for an archaeological project.

Very quickly, as the images began to form on the screens, it became clear that more energy was required to penetrate through the wood. The initial images had revealed only the Afrika Korps insignia beneath the fresh paint. The engineers looked a little concerned. Wolfgang looked at Hamilton.

"Problem?" he asked.

"Where did you say you found this?"

"In a disused tunnel beneath Berlin." He replied. "On the escape line from the Führerbunker." he added intentionally.

"And you are sure this is not dangerous?"

"Did yer see all the palaver ootside jist tae bring this in?"

Wolfgang said something to the engineers and the x-rays were intensified. Once through the wood, the beams easily passed through the air gap before encountering an object inside. It soon became clear the entity was no religious artefact. There was no cherub-crowned box suspended by poles. No stone tablets, jar of manna or Aaronic rod. Though this wasn't entirely a surprise, it still came as blessed relief.

Starting from the front, the curved outline of a pontoon fender began to become visible, building up slowly as the scans were digitally rendered by the software. Different views showed the object inside from all three axes: side-on profile, top down, and a view from the front. A three-dimensional rendering of the scans was then produced from the resulting imagery. As the scans continued, the outline of the headlights began to form, the pressed alloy wheels with a thick outer rim of chrome and two-eared knock-off wheel nuts, then, unmistakeably, the characteristic, swept back oval grille.

Focussing on the top of the grille surround, one of the engineers wanted to examine the calibration of the software for fine details as the images continued to be rendered in the background. The material composition and thickness of the enamel even enabled the details on the hand-painted badge at the top of the radiator to be clearly discerned. The distinctive macaron, folded back from the centre where it followed the contour of the grille, was surrounded by a border of tiny dots.

On the oval field itself, at the top, were the distinctive initials EB, with the E written backwards and adjoining the upright of the B. On the left side of the central fold, three letters 'BUG' could be made out, followed by the letters 'ATTI' on the right side.

Could this be *Monique*?

The Lost Bugatti.

La Voiture Noire?

CHAPTER ONE-HUNDRED-AND-THIRTEEN

While Petra and Monsieur Legrand stayed behind to watch the images unfold, Wolfgang took Hamilton and Natalia for breakfast.

"The scans will take several hours to completely process. There is a lot of data with a complete vehicle." He explained as they found themselves a table.

"I can imagine." Natalia agreed, pouring her yoghurt over the bowl of chopped up fresh fruit.

"Is it related to what happened in Berlin last night?" Wolfgang whispered leaning forward.

Hamilton filled his mouth with bacon and sausage and gave a vague sort of shrug.

Wolfgang leaned back. There was nothing more to be gained from that enquiry. "This would be quite a find if it can be verified."

"Ah'm sure." Hamilton mumbled around a mouthful of food.

"I suppose it would explain the interest."

Hamilton swallowed and took a sip of coffee. "How will yer announce it?"

"We were asked by the Berlin Underworlds Association to see if we could use our equipment for an exciting archaeological discovery."

"Sounds plausible."

"It is." Wolfgang laughed. "Mr Kaufmann phoned me this morning to check the crate had arrived safely."

"Dieter Kaufmann?"

"The Chairman, yes."

Hamilton looked across at Natalia. "How did he know it was coming down this morning?"

"Well…" Wolfgang didn't exactly know. "Wasn't it supposed to?"

"When the crate wis pulled oot of the tunnel yesterday, we were told it wid be staying in Berlin for at least the next couple o' days while arrangements were made for its analysis here. Ah assumed it wis because the x-ray machine wis in use."

"Really?" Wolfgang looked surprised. "That's interesting." Natalia looked at him with an enquiring look. "No, we got a call last night from a Captain Reinhardt, asking if we could make the x-ray available today. He wanted to bring it down as early as possible."

"How did he know it wis coming here?"

"Mr Kaufmann told him the arrangements had been made to analyse the crate here." Wolfgang looked a little confused. "Isn't that what was decided?"

"Sure, ah asked if yer cood work on it, but ah left the 'when' tae you guys tae figure oot. You know when the machines are needed and everything. It's naw for us tae expect yer tae disrupt development. Yer doing us a favour."

"I see." Wolfgang mused. "It's fortunate that we were able to make it available today then."

"Aye." Hamilton nodded, giving Natalia a meaningful look. "Fortunate."

CHAPTER ONE-HUNDRED-AND-FOURTEEN

Looking from the front, on the right side of the firewall, against the engine turned bulkhead were two brass plaques. The larger one was headed BREVETS ETTORE BUGATTI and consisted of three columns with a list of the patent numbers filed in nine different countries against the design. Covering everywhere from France to Russia, the numbers were debossed onto its surface before the plate was riveted to the bulkhead.

The smaller plaque though was of significantly more interest. Located just to the side, it was noticeably simple in form, yet crucially more valuable. Embossed into the metal were the words:

ETTORE BUGATTI
MOLSHEIM ALSACE

CHASSIS   MOTEUR   POIDS
No. 57453   19 CV

This indicated that it was the correct chassis, but there were further identifications to be made to be absolutely sure of the vehicle's authenticity. Legrand whispered to Petra, who then translated it into German and directed the engineers. Moving around to the engine, the engineers focussed in on the upper crankcase and scanned slowly across the cast metal surface.

"There!" Legrand cried, pointing to the screen.

Scrolling back to where he had pointed, the engineers, centralised the view and zoomed in closer. On the surface of the casting were two small letters 'SC' with a larger number '2' beneath. The engine number: 2SC. Then, crucially, below this a five digit number could just be made out. These figures were smooth and raised from the surface of the casting, not sharply engraved into it and thus easier to fake. This meant they had to have been stamped into the surface of the individual mould cavity itself at the time of the pour, making the crankcase casting utterly unique. Adjusting the resolution, the image sharpened up and the number became clear:

57453

The evidence was unmistakeable. The numbers matched. This was a crucial detail. A numbers matching vehicle meant total originality. It meant that Jean Bugatti's streamlined body had never been separated from the chassis, or the engine, since it had left the Molsheim workshop on the 3rd of October 1936. There were other details that needed to be confirmed to authenticate what they were looking at, but already Legrand could feel the unfamiliar buzz of excitement in the pit of his stomach.

"The material." Petra explained. "On this brass plaque. Can we obtain a chemical composition?"

"For sure." The engineers nodded. "But why?"

"The brass that was used for the plaques was very specific." Petra explained. "These early plaques were made from old French shell casings from the First World War. There were many lying around Alsace at the time, so…" her words trailed off, deciding not to venture further. The implication was clear.

"Do you have a comparative analysis, or reference samples?"

"Yes, I brought some with me." Gesturing to the doors they had entered through. "They're in my handbag."

"Then we can make a comparison with the original materials and produce a certificate."

"And fuel samples?"

"Possible. We might be able to determine the age of it based on its oxidisation, if there is some still left in the system."

"What about the enamelling?" Pierre asked.

"Yes, of course." Petra replied.

"This too. If there are any identifying methods to distinguish between a reproduction or a fake and the original materials, we can test for these."

"Leather testing." One of his colleagues mentioned. "We can ask the labs. Different methods would have been used back then to dye and process the leather. We could detect if there are any newer chemicals present in the treatment or pigments."

"Paint thickness and composition. We can do that non-destructively. Basically, anything you think off to check the age and authenticity."

"How much will this cost?" Petra enquired.

"A drive in a Chiron would do it." One of the engineers joked. "We'll check with our managers."

"How is it going?" Hamilton asked as they returned to the analysis centre.

"It's astonishing. I believe you've found her. You've actually found her." Legrand said, his eyes beaming with excitement. Beckoning them both over, he pointed to the rear fenders as they were just being rendered. "You can even see the welds beneath the paintwork here. These are the new extensions that Jean added for Benoist when the body came back from England." He brushed his hand in a short curve over the image. "Originally you see where they would have ended. This new look is very much like the Holzschuh Bugatti, but you can see it's been executed with a little more grace. Jean's design looks more refined and finished."

Hamilton nodded, seeing where the lines of the technical drawings he had examined in Molsheim were now mirrored in the metal itself. Yet, his eyes were drawn to something else entirely.

"Whit's this?" he asked, pointing to the dashboard.

"Where?"

"Jist above the steering column, behind the fascia."

The engineer frowned and rotated the images around, then proceeded to zoom in and section away the car like it was going through a virtual slicing machine.

"It looks like a wee box."

"Like a safe?"

"Aye." Hamilton looked to Legrand. "That wisnae on the drawings. Wis that an optional extra?"

"No." he said, frowning with evident interest. "This is something I have not seen before. The Atlantic models did not have gloveboxes or even space for a cubby hole."

"There is something inside." The engineer observed, enlarging the image. "This…this looks like a pistol. And something else. I can't make it out. Could be the x-ray was too powerful and gone right through, but you see an edge of something here. Looks like a spring."

"Could it be the coil from a notepad?" Hamilton asked, tapping the manual for the 3DCT on the top of the desk.

"It could be. Without adjusting the intensity, the beams would go straight through paper."

"That's where *our* interest lies." Hamilton said to Legrand. "If we can just take that box away wi us, the rest of the car is yours."

Legrand nodded, a sombre expression on his face, remembering their conversation in the château about spies and clandestine operations.

CHAPTER ONE-HUNDRED-AND-FIFTEEN

Though St Mary's had originally been constructed as a Roman Catholic church in the thirteenth century, following the Reformation in 1539, it had converted to the Lutheran Protestant faith. Standing towards the back of the congregation, looking up the full height of white stone columns to a ribbed, vaulted ceiling above, Hamilton was reminded of his own mortality. He wondered how he would be perceived at the end among friends and family. In contrast with dark wooden pews, the bright, cavernous interior almost foreshadowed a vision of heaven itself.

Lieutenant Gerhard Müller had been a well-liked member of the congregation. The death of a policeman had also shocked the city, as well as much of the nation, swelling the mourners still further. Everyone wanted to pay their respects, support his widow and their two small boys. It was an incredibly sad day.

Erwin Reinhardt and his wife were also in attendance. Marina was standing next to Frau Müller throughout, helping her get through the emotional service. Hamilton and Natalia maintained a respectful distance as the mourners began to file out. There would be a burial in a private cemetery elsewhere, but the BKA had requested the use of the church for the service and the bishop was never going to refuse for a devout member of his parish.

Being amongst the last to file out, Reinhardt looked up and saw them in the corner. He carried on out into the grey dismal day. There was a bite in the air. It wouldn't be too long before the first snows would start to fall. Losing their father a few months before Christmas would be hard on the boys. They would have them over, at least for a few days over the festive period. Marina was an excellent cook.

He turned back and saw Hamilton and Natalia leave quietly and head towards the Neptune Fountain.

"I'll just be a moment." He whispered to Marina.

Finding them near the female allegory of the Rhine, Reinhardt could not help but let his consternation show. Their presence here, at the funeral of his assistant, was not a coincidence, neither was he pleased to see them.

"We were sorry to hear about Lieutenant Müller." Natalia began soothingly.

Reinhardt acknowledged the platitude but wasn't feeling the love.

"What are you doing here?"

"We came tae pay our respects." Hamilton offered.

"And?"

"And tell yer whit we know. It might help."

"I'm listening." He said, though his expression hardened.

"The man who wis found in the submarine base in Bordeaux." Hamilton began, looking at Natalia. "We believe he may have worked for this OID organisation that yer mentioned on the news."

"I know he did." Reinhardt replied acidly. "I've known for a long time. Who exactly are you?"

Rummaging in the pockets of their coats, together they showed them their identification. Opening the wallet up to display the coat of arms, then holding it sideways so he could read the details on the card.

"You're both British intelligence." He said with a scowl. "So, you're not a photographer after all."

"I'm both." Natalia explained. "It helps me get around places."

"I'm sure it does. Why do you think this helps me?"

"Will you be at the barracks later?"

"No. My superiors have given me the day off. I'm going to be spending it with my wife and family. We're having Julia and the boys over." He nodded to where Marina was looking over anxiously.

"What about tomorrow?"

"Tomorrow I'll be investigating who killed my partner."

"Then, what we have might help you with that."

Reinhardt looked at them sternly for a moment. On another day he might have arrested them. He didn't know what for but would find something. Today was not that day. He looked back at Marina.

"Tomorrow then." He turned to go, then paused and turned back. "By the way, where are you staying?"

Without waiting for an answer, he briskly headed back to his family. Putting a hand on his daughter's shoulder, he wrapped an arm around his wife as they escorted Julia and the boys to the cars.

"What do you think?" Natalia asked, watching them go. "Can we trust him?"

"We'll find oot tomorrow."

CHAPTER ONE-HUNDRED-AND-SIXTEEN

Hamilton was already showered and dressed when the phone rang. He listened to what the concierge had to say, thanked him, then hung up. He could already hear the telephone in the adjacent room ringing. Two cars were waiting to take them to the BKA barracks. He knew how this would play out. Likely he would be the one placed in a holding cell while Natalia was taken up to a comfortable office. Then the questioning would start.

"You take the safe." he said as they both emerged from their rooms. "It'll be taken off me anyway. Yer might have a better chance of getting it open."

She nodded. "Good luck."

"Aye, you too."

Just as he had predicted, the plain clothed BKA officers escorted them to separate cars. As soon as he was inside, the officer next to him produced a pair of handcuffs. Hamilton shrugged and held out his hands. He was already expecting it. The cuffs were clamped down painfully tight. He winced but was expecting that too. They had just lost one of their own. Courtesy was not high on their agenda that morning.

Conversation was not really an option. No one felt like talking on the journey. The time for that would come. Both cars travelled in silent convoy to the Treptow district and entered the barracks through different entrances. Natalia stayed above ground and rolled to a halt outside the main office building. Hamilton was taken underground into the central complex. From there he was hustled through blockwork corridors and deposited in a cell. As the door was closed he sat down on the bunk calmly. His fate no longer in his hands. It felt strange, a little unnerving. He was at the mercy of others.

"Please, sit down." Reinhardt greeted with no warmth as Natalia was shown into his office. "You lied to me."

Natalia remained silent.

"When you told me you're a photographer. It was a lie."

"No. No, it wasn't." she shook her head. "I'm professionally accredited and internationally recognised. My credentials are genuine."

"I've seen your social media. Very convincing, but it's a lie."

"And yet when you gave me that DSLR in Zwickau, I knew exactly how to handle it, where all the controls were and why the images were all substandard."

"Including mine?"

She shuddered at the memory. "Especially yours."

"And what was wrong with it?"

"You had left the IS switched off the lens; the edges were fuzzy. Image Stabilisation would have accounted for your unsteady hand and sharpened the image. I shoot Nikon where VR does the same thing."

"You could have learned that reading magazines."

"So could you." she replied. "The difference is, I actually know what it all means."

"So, you're a genuine photographer then?"

"Yes."

"Giving a lecture in Dresden."

"At the university."

"And you know nothing about Graham Robertson?"

"No more than I did when you dragged me over there the first time."

"And yet now you claim you can help."

"We might be able to."

"In what way?"

"The box your boys took from me at the hotel…"

"It's being examined."

"Good." She nodded. "I would expect no less. A couple of days after losing a man, I wouldn't have expected to be allowed to bring it all the way up into the offices. Presumably it will be x-rayed?"

"Among other things." He replied, intrigued. "What is in this box?"

"An old pistol and a notepad. The pistol dates from before the war. We don't know what's on the notepad yet."

"So, how do you think it will help me?"

"It's who wants them that's important." "This OID organisation…" "And who are they?"

"Do you know?"

"You would need to ask my colleague for that information." Natalia returned pointedly.

Reinhardt frowned. He wasn't in the mood for games. He could have had Hamilton interrogated at great length and very uncomfortably for as long as he wanted, but his superiors needed answers and he had little time to provide them. Angrily he picked up the phone. "Lang. Bring Hamilton up here." Slamming the receiver down he invited her to take a seat. "So, is there anything that *you* can tell me?"

"I contacted my boss." Natalia explained. "He's heard of the OID before.

We opened a file on them when they started out. He's agreed to send you a copy."

"You've heard about them?" he asked incredulously. "How have you heard about them?"

"We're an intelligence service." She replied. The implication was clear. The SIS knew about everything. Or at least, it wanted to let people think that. Sometimes while scrabbling around trying to actually find out.

"As we're going to start being civilised, we may as well get some coffee." He sighed, stepping towards the room to make the arrangements.

"OID stands for Östlicher Informationsdienst." Hamilton picked up when they were all seated back in Reinhardt's office.

"Eastern Information Service?" Reinhardt repeated.

"After reunification, some senior members of the Stasi setup the OID in '91. Its basic mission objective wis tae sell on information from the West tae Russia tae sort of keep the wee back channels open. A way of continuing the Cold War. By the late nineties they changed tae selling information from anyone tae anyone, whichever wis more lucrative, but wi most o' the auld guard dying off it had mostly fizzled oot by the turn of the millennium."

"So, why now?" Reinhardt asked. "What's triggered this latest surge of activity."

"*Manuela*."

"Who is she?"

"Naw who. Whit. *Manuela* is the name Bernd Rosemeyer gave tae his personal car."

"The Horch 853 Streamliner." He said, looking at Natalia meaningfully.

"Yes." She nodded. "It was passed onto his teammate, Andrew Sutherland. Now, without going into too much history, while serving in the Waffen-SS during the war, Sutherland was also spying for Britain. After the war the car disappeared."

"So why are they interested in it now?"

"Sir, its clean." Came a voice from the door. A BKA officer brought in the lockbox from the Bugatti, presenting it to him.

"Because of that." Hamilton added.

"What is that?"

"It's a lockbox found inside an auld car. That auld car wis whit wis dragged oot from Berlin a couple o' days ago and that auld car belonged tae two spies."

"Different car. Different spies." Reinhardt returned.

"Same handler. Same mission." Hamilton countered. He held Reinhardt's gaze for a moment, then looked at the box. "May I?"

"For sure."

Taking the box, Hamilton felt the weight of it. Nothing had been removed. Neither had the lock been tampered with. Producing his multitool, he quickly set about picking the lock. After a few seconds the door opened.

"I'll jist tek the pistol oot first." He said, making sure Reinhardt wouldn't be alarmed.

It was a Webley Mk IV revolver. The classic Boer War model. Almost ubiquitous among officers and NCOs, even after the First World War. It was chambered for .455 calibre rounds and still had a full cylinder. He placed it on the desk. Next was a well-worn notepad, spiral bound and written in some kind of coded language. Hamilton remembered his earlier conversation with Dame Harrington about some kind of list. Names. Good, bad and indifferent.

"Whit wis the loadoot on the terrorists that attacked the lorry?" Hamilton asked, stalling for time as he looked at the confusing jumble of letters, trying to figure out a meaning.

"What do you mean?"

"Whit kit did they have?"

"I don't know. I wasn't there."

"Okay, let me ask yer this." Hamilton tried again "Whit bullets was Müller killed wi?"

Natalia balked at the question, thinking it a little insensitive but trying to play along.

"Lieutenant Müller was gunned down by …"

"Heckler & Koch." Hamilton remarked.

"Possibly."

"And no one heard the bullets."

"Not in the usual sense, no." Hamilton frowned. "I mean, there were no loud bullet noises."

"Soond suppressors. Any IDs?"

"They were all wearing face masks. No one could see them."

"Lucky."

"What?!"

"It's lucky they were masked up. No witnesses. If someone had seen their faces yer wid have had a whole lot more bodies."

"What are you suggesting?"

"Ah'm suggesting this OID hired oot an external contractor for the hit on yer lorry." Hamilton looked to Natalia.

"Red Section?" she surmised.

He nodded. "Whit's the Gaelic word for eagle?"

"You're asking me?"

"Ah'm from Lanarkshire. We barely speak English."

He looked to Reinhardt and his computer. "You guys gaw Leo or suhin' on there? Check oot Scots Gaelic word for eagle."

Reinhardt frowned but acquiesced.

"Iolair."

Hamilton looked across at Natalia again. "Gaw a wee mirror?"

Natalia looked a little confused but produced her compact and handed it over. Flicking it open, Hamilton held the mirror up against the notebook. His frown melted into a smile. A look of realisation dawning on his face.

"Iolair, the Gaelic word for eagle. Translates as *Adler* in German. *Adler* wis the codename the SOE gave tae our man Andrew Sutherland who drove aroond in Rosemeyer's Horch." He held up the book. "And guess whit? He's on Santa's good list."

"What do you mean?"

"Everything in here looks tae be written in Scots Gaelic. No way any one wis ever gonnae break that code. Tae make it even more difficult, its written all joined up as a mirror image." He handed the book across to Natalia. "Look at it. It's absolute gibberish." He handed her back the compact. "Yer hawd that mirror up against it though."

"I see it."

"What is it?" Reinhardt asked, peering over.

"A list of contacts used by SOE. People they trusted, people they didn't and everyone in between. It lists them by codename and tabulates them according to status and value." He looked up and locked eyes with Reinhardt. "Could be some interesting old names in here. Probably still worth killing for."

"You mentioned something about Red Section?" Reinhardt picked up.

"Assassins for hire." Hamilton replied. "Comprised mostly of ex-Estonian special forces. They were issued wi German hardware so probably still use it. Check tae see if there are any backdoor deals going on, or missing stocks in any o' yer armed response units, army and police. Look for H&K MP7s, MRL6 weapons lamps and Brügger & Thomet Rotax sound suppressors. Chuck in a couple o' PEQ-15 targe'ing lasers too." He looked first at Natalia, then Reinhardt. "Ah reckon they're the ones who comple'ed the hit." He held up the book. "And ah reckon they want whitever is in this list, and probably whitever *Adler* stashed away in the auld Horch too."

CHAPTER ONE-HUNDRED-AND-SEVENTEEN
GERMANY, 1945

The situation was becoming increasingly desperate, and Sutherland knew it. He had a very narrow window to work in, even then it was touch and go as to whether it would all work. Months ago, negotiating his way down the Nord-Süd Tunnel, he had set the first charge to the roof above the entrance to the dead end where he had stowed the 'Ark of the Covenant'. Still in its wooden shipping crate on the back of the French flatbed rail truck, the artefact would remain there until it could be retrieved at the end of the war, depending on who controlled Berlin after the dust had settled.

The second charge had been placed in the roof of the adjacent tunnel, leading to the Führerbunker. The poor lighting down there had kept them concealed until now and a long wire had been rolled down the railway line. The third charge had been positioned further up the line, right beneath the Landwehr Canal. He had rigged up the first two charges to the third and set up a tripwire to run across the track near the bunker's escape hatch.

When the Führer's train was summoned into the station, as he suspected it would near the end, the trip wire would set off the charge, bringing down the roof of the tunnel and draining the canal into the subterranean cavern. The connected charges would then seal off the tunnels at the far end, simultaneously holding back the water, and blocking the entrance to the ancient treasure. He just hoped he hadn't calculated too much explosive and would end up bringing down half of Berlin instead.

The plan, he hoped, would end any prospect of the Führer escaping the city and preserve *Monique* for the future. Sadly, Robert Benoist had already been captured and executed at Buchenwald. Grover-Williams had been arrested even earlier and had suffered extended interrogation at Sachsenhausen.

However, Sutherland's plan to have him smuggled into the *Operation Bernhard* circle had come off. When two truckloads of prisoners from Block 19 had arrived at Mauthausen, they had originally been segregated, pending execution. An unscheduled delay in bringing the third and final truck had meant that the prison governors had no choice but to release the first two loads into the general population. By the time the final load arrived, it was too late to do anything about it and the camp was liberated a matter of days later.

A company of stormtroopers from the 1st Panzer Division were still on rotating guard duty in the tunnel leading to *Adler's* 'Ark of the Covenant'. They had been placed there by the orders of Hitler himself when the Soviet invasion became even more critical. A Captain, his Lieutenant, two sergeants and a dozen men stood ready to deploy the artefact if needed. It was a fanciful idea, yet should the Führer find himself trapped beneath the New Reich Chancellery, this might be his last chance to unleash the wrath of God upon his enemies.

"The enemy has broken through along a wide front." Explained Generalleutnant Hans Krebs, Chief of the Army General Staff as he pointed out the features on the map in front of Hitler. "They have taken Zossen to the south and are advancing towards Stahnsdorf. They're at the northern city border, between Frohnau and Pankow. In the east, they've reached Lichtenberg, Mahlsdorf and Karlshorst."

"If Steiner attacks, everything will be brought under control." Hitler replied confidently, waving away the concerns of the German High Command gathered around his desk in the bunker.

Burgdorf looked uneasily at Krebs.

"My Führer." Krebs began uneasily, afraid to deliver the bad news. Steiner had not long informed him over the phone that neither he, nor General Wenck had the forces and weaponry required to break the Soviet grip on the city. "Steiner…" Krebs couldn't quite bring himself to finish.

"Steiner couldn't mobilise enough men." Jodl picked up. "He wasn't able to carry out the assault."

IN THE DEN OF WOLVES

There was a pause as the words sank in. Jodl, as Chief of Operations Staff for the Armed Forces High Command, was nominally responsible for the defence of the country. His words were tacit acknowledgement that he no longer had the means to do so.

Hitler's hand began to shake as he reached up to remove his spectacles.

"These men will stay here." he murmured quietly with unsettling calm. "Keitel, Jodl, Krebs, and Burgdorf."

The room began to empty quickly as officers rushed to remove themselves from the impending vitriol that would be launched forth at the top Generals left behind. Despite the clear order, Goebbels and Bormann chose to remain standing in the corner behind Hitler's desk. Goebbels' Ministry was still churning out propaganda, trying to convince the defenders that some wonder weapon would soon be deployed to assist them.

Keitel looked anxiously across at Krebs and Jodl, standing side-by-side in front of the Führer's desk as the door closed behind the departing party.

"That was an order!" Hitler burst out, jabbing the map angrily. "Steiner's assault was an order! Who do you think you are to disobey an order that I give?"

There was silence. Silence in Hitler's private office. Silence outside in the corridor.

"So, this is what it has come to!" his voice was heard screaming. "The army have been lying to me! Everybody has been lying to me. Even the SS!"

Amidst the gathering of army officers and civilian workers, Hitler's private secretary comforted her weeping comrade standing alongside her.

"Our generals are just a bunch of contemptible, disloyal cowards!" he continued, rising stiffly to his feet, pacing from one side of his desk to the other.

"My Führer, I cannot permit you to insult our soldiers." Burgdorf cried out in defence of the brave, but hopelessly outnumbered remnants of the Wehrmacht, desperate souls dying on the streets above with every passing second.

"They are cowards, traitors and failures!"

"My Führer, this is outrageous!" he countered hotly.

"For years, the military have hindered my plans!" Hitler continued raging.

Outside in the corridor, Eva Braun made her way through the assembled audience, a look of concern on her face as Hitler's shrill voice echoed from the confines of his office.

"They've put every kind of obstacle in my way! What I should have done is liquidate all the high-ranking officers, as Stalin did!" he paused, slumping back into the chair, facing Goebbels and Bormann in the corner. "Traitors." He hissed. "I've been betrayed and deceived from the very beginning! What a monstrous betrayal of the German people. But all those traitors will pay. With their own blood they will pay. They shall drown in their own blood!"

He stopped, looking down at the concrete floor beneath his shoes.

"Gentleman," he began quietly, yet with determination crackling hoarsely in his voice. "If you believe I am going to leave Berlin now, you are seriously mistaken." He turned and looked up to Goebbels. "We still have the Bundeslade?"

Goebbels nodded, though he had long been sceptical of what the mysterious wooden crate might contain.

"Take it to Tempelhof." He murmured. "Make it ready."

Keitel turned to Burgdorf. They had heard what the plan entailed. In the act of saving the Führer, unleashing the Bundeslade would destroy everyone else. The plan was egotistical madness, and the Army High Command knew it. Krebs too looked to Burgdorf for confirmation as Goebbels made for the door. Opening the portal, Goebbels found SS-Generalleutnant Fegelein nearest the door in the packed corridor outside.

"Make it ready." He said simply.

Fegelein nodded and turned back to the corridor. "Reinhardt!" he cried.

In the event the order to deploy the Bundeslade was ever given, Burgdorf had drawn up a contingency plan to ensure it never happened. In one sense, the Führer had been correct. The army had indeed been lying to him for months. In the face of total defeat though, no matter how loyal to the Party, it was every man for himself.

Reinhardt entered the tunnel, not expecting it to be quite as dark as it was. In his hasty exuberance, he had foolishly only brought along a small handheld torch. The meagre beam was just about enough but he was surprised that there were no lights on. The power must have been cut down there already. He stepped forward cautiously at first, one step placed carefully in front of the other. Finding the floor even and unbroken, he picked up the pace.

As the door from the bunker opened behind him, he began to panic. Had the evacuation started already? He needed to get to the train, to get everything prepared. It was the sound of gunfire that told him all was not well. A searing pain stabbed into his back as bullets tore into him, sending him sprawling to the ground.

As he fell, a wire caught around his ankles and triggered the explosive charges. With blood beginning to seep from his mouth, Manfred Reinhardt looked up as a breeze billowed down the tunnel towards him. Broiling flames gave way to an intense cloud of thick dust and steam before a tidal wave of water began to barrel down towards him.

He struggled in vain to get to his feet, his lungs were filling with fluid and his strength was giving out with each painful breath. Then a lump of concrete, liberated from the roof and pushed by the wall of water, pulverised his body against the rails as it hurtled towards the escape hatch of the Führerbunker.

Meanwhile, a figure emerged from the bowels of the subterranean labyrinth beneath Tempelhof airport. Dressed in a grey wool M41 greatcoat and a bolt-action Mosin-Nagant rifle slung over his shoulder, he moved slowly, but with purpose, to Weser's abandoned aircraft production hall. Tying two red banners to the quarterlights, he climbed in behind the steering wheel and went through the familiar starting procedure, adjusting the knobs, flicking on the magnetos, depressing the accelerator.

Manuela started first time. She had never let him down. Not since the day Elly Rosemeyer had handed her over to him. With the banners catching the breeze, Sutherland drove out of the production hall and onto the vast concrete apron outside the terminal building. In the time it would take him to cross the airfield, he would say goodbye to *Adler* forever and, with his forged Soviet papers in his tunic, become Major Andrei Mikhailovich Zagorienkov.

END

ABOUT THE AUTHOR

Eden James lives in Staffordshire, where he works as a laboratory specialist for an automotive manufacturer. Graduating as a mechanical engineer he has always had a love of history, engineering and cars, especially the old classics. Not just as mechanical devices but as compelling design motifs and silent commentators on the world in which they were born and the lives of people that they shared. As such, a connection to cars is present in most works that he has written, not merely as props, but as a way of expressing an individual's unique character.

BOOKS IN THIS SERIES
CHASING SHADOWS

The hunt for three lost cars, the lives of the people that drove them and a deadly game of cat and mouse unfolds as secrets from the past refuse to remain buried.

BOOK ONE: In the Den of Wolves

A scrap of paper found in a pocket. The writing was clear and precise and consisted of nothing more than half a dozen figures. Only one man knows exactly what they mean, but when he is found murdered in a museum the quest to rediscover a car thought lost to history takes a sinister turn.

Dame Iris Harrington remembers the car from her youth. She had been a passenger in Belgium during the Second World War. The driver had been an undercover agent posing as a chauffeur for the Nazi regime. What secrets it could reveal. It would seem someone is keen to find out.

Delving into her own history, Harrington needs to enlist help to find out why someone would kill to find just another old car. As Gregor Hamilton and Natalia Bielawska begin to dig deeper into the mystery, it becomes apparent that the hunt for secrets doesn't just end with the discovery they were looking for...

BOOK TWO: Where the Red Deer Roam

Coming Soon...

Boots and bones. The only remains of a political commissar who mysteriously disappeared from the Moscow Kremlin. Being so close to the Trans-Siberian line, the investigating officer has to determine whether he jumped from a passing train or was pushed to his death. By whom, and why?

A fire at a Scottish Highland estate becomes the first major case for James Cameron, the new Detective Chief Superintendent of the Inverness-shire Constabulary's Lochaber Division. Arson is suspected. Then a body turns up in the basement and a manhunt for a missing soldier begins to unravel murky secrets as Cameron is forced to confront a Nemesis from his past.

Hamilton and Natalia are still on the hunt for hidden secrets as their journey takes them back through Cameron's old case files in a bid to discover the link between himself and a long-lost school friend turned Cold War spy. Time is running out to find answers. Their elderly patron isn't getting any younger and without her staunch backing, they may never be able to discover the truth behind the legend…

BOOK THREE: From an Eagle's Nest

Coming Soon…

Relics from the past keep resurfacing as Hamilton and Natalia have a race on their hands to find out just what Andrew Sutherland had stashed away all those years ago.

Cameron's quiet existence as a provincial policeman is turned upside down once again. First by a prisoner's recant on the eve of his judicial hanging, then by the discovery of a mutilated corpse out on an exposed glen. With one conviction to reinvestigate and another to prosecute, things don't get any easier when the victim is identified as the daughter of a former Chief Constable.

Meanwhile Sutherland's misadventures continue after his defection from the Soviet Union. Acting as chauffeur to the Chairman of the Chinese Communist Party, his information begins to bring attention to a formidable, sleeping dragon. Yet, with a murder hanging over his head and a determined investigator from Moscow, has his luck finally run out?

BOOK FOUR: A Ptarmigan's Fate

Coming Soon…

In the chaos that followed the Japanese invasion of Burma, Cameron lost all contact with friends and colleagues in the Rangoon Police. Above all, the disappearance of the woman he loved the most still haunts him decades later. With his Nemesis determined to end Cameron's meddling once and for all, his quest for her whereabouts may never finally be resolved.

Just how did three bodies find themselves in the bottom of a Scottish loch inside a car owned by the British Secret Intelligence Service? Who were they and what happened to them? Hamilton and Natalia finally discover what Cameron and Sutherland were working on all those years ago when the deadly consequences of keeping the back channels open confront them head-on. Yet how far up the chain does this treachery go and who can be trusted now?

See more at:

www.edenjames.net

IN THE DEN OF WOLVES

Made in the USA
Las Vegas, NV
29 January 2025